THE
REAGAN
PRESIDENCY

THE

REAGAN

PRESIDENCY

An Actor's Finest Performance

Wilbur Edel

HIPPOCRENE BOOKS
New York

For information, contact:
HIPPOCRENE BOOKS, INC.
171 Madison Avenue
New York, NY 10016

ISBN 0-7818-0026-9

Printed in the United States of America.

To Marie

Whose love and understanding
provided the inspiration for
all that I ever accomplished.

Acknowledgments

My gratitude, as always, goes to the Ellen Clark Bertrand Library at Bucknell University for the courtesy shown me in permitting access to the library's excellent collection of documentary materials. Special thanks are due the reference staff, in particular for the ever-ready assistance of Tom Mattern, whose expertise in government source documents has been invaluable to me.

All responsibility for the contents of this work is mine, but I am indebted to Cindy Whitmoyer for aiding with the research, to David Freeman Hawke for his advice on preparation of the manuscript, and to Muriel Nellis for the help and encouragement she provided when I needed it most. I also owe thanks to Betty Koons and Gloria Mincemoyer for their meticulous typing and editorial assistance.

Permission to use material published by the following journals and organizations is gratefully acknowledged.

Academy of Political Science
Bulletin of the Atomic Scientists
CBS News, "60 Minutes"
Current Digest of the Soviet Press
Current History
Index on Censorship
King Features Syndicate
New York Times
Newspaper Enterprise Association
Time Inc. Magazine Company
U.S. News & World Report
Washington Post
WETA-TV 26, "Ben Wattenberg at Large"

CONTENTS

INTRODUCTION

The autobiography Ronald Reagan wrote with Richard G. Hubler in 1965 was entitled *Where's the Rest of Me?* In the opening chapter Reagan explained that he loved three things: drama, politics, and sports. Chronologically, his love of sports was the first to surface, enlivening his high school and college years with the joy of personal participation, particularly in football, and continuing in his postgraduate employment as a sports announcer for radio station WOC in Davenport, Iowa. Drama came next, with amateur performances at Eureka College, followed by twenty years as a professional actor in Hollywood.

During the last years of his Hollywood experience, Reagan said he "began to feel like a shut-in invalid, nursed by publicity." Worse still, he wrote, "I had become a semi-automaton 'creating' a character another had written, doing what still another person told me to do on the set." At that point, he said, "I decided to find the rest of me."

From this opening explanation, the autobiography goes on to recount Reagan's youthful experiences with family and sports, his years in Hollywood followed by employment with General Electric, and his emerging political consciousness. Then, without any mention of his early involvement in political campaigning, or how his association with politicians or party leaders led him to the decision to devote the rest of his life to politics, he abruptly ended his personal history with the declaration, "I have found the rest of me."

Biographical works about political leaders are generally considered incomplete if they do not establish a framework—part historical, part Freudian—based on parental and/or environmental influences, beginning with the subject's birth and working through his or her formative years to maturity. Other writers have treated the life of Ronald Reagan in this fashion, and to the extent that their work is relevant, it is recognized here. However, this book has a more limited purpose, which is to evaluate the Reagan presidency in terms of those specific aspects of his performance that illustrate his qualifications—or lack thereof—for the highest office in the land.

Begun midway in Reagan's second term as president, the present study was influenced by the writer's background of knowledge and experience, accumulated over a lifetime that began only a decade after Ronald Reagan's birth. As a political scientist, a registered Democrat, and a professional observer of the activities of public figures in and out of office, I had by 1980 concluded that however personable and politically successful Reagan had been to that point, his world was still the world of Hollywood-like illusion. This belief was based largely on his own writings, speeches and public appearances, all of which indicated that his approach to politics reflected an abysmal ignorance of history, a habit of confusing fact and fiction, and an inability to examine introspectively his own reasoning and conclusions.

That preliminary judgment—bias, if you will—was subjected to the same test as any project I had undertaken previously: the collection and examination of as much information as could be gathered concerning all of Reagan's activities that had a bearing on his political career. With this information I conducted a detailed study of every public and private statement, opinion, and action by Ronald Reagan that I could find in official records and in the commentaries and written works of his associates in government, his friends in private life, and independent observers of the political scene. In evaluating his concept of government in what he called the "creative society," I considered the origins of his ideas, the assumptions on which they were based, and the means by which he attempted to put them into practice. As often as possible I have used Reagan's own words to explain his actions, beliefs, and intentions, taking care to present each quotation in its proper context.

Evidence of Reagan's presidential policies in particular areas I have gleaned from documents and publications issued by the various executive departments and agencies of the federal government. Congressional attitudes, both for and against his policies, are found in the debates, hearings and committee reports of the House and Senate, many of which are cited in this study. None of the records used is classified, although some originally carried classifications ranging from confidential to top secret. I have not attempted to uncover still-secret documents or to explore private sources of information. On the contrary, one of my basic assumptions is that the character of the Reagan presidency is clear from the public record, and that the conclusions reached here are fully justified by that record. Others may interpret the facts differently, but the reader who wishes to check the accuracy of the material presented here, and fully documented in the notes, will have little difficulty doing so. Readers who are interested in background beyond what is provided in the text will find that many of the notes contain additional detail as well as source references. All documents and publications cited in the text or in the notes are included in the bibliography.

The end result of this study is not one President Reagan would appreciate if he were to read it, but I believe the picture I have drawn accurately portrays the character of his administration. As time goes on and more information becomes available, others may judge his performance differently. But I am convinced that the documentary evidence offered in this volume justifies the interpretation placed upon each aspect of his White House operation and upon the final overall evaluation of his performance as chief executive.

CHAPTER 1

Preacher

*"The Bible contains an answer to just about
everything and every problem that confronts
us."*[1]

THE MOST STRIKING ASPECT OF RONALD REAGAN'S POLITICAL CAREER IS HIS
fundamentalist religious approach to public service. No hint of this appears
in the autobiography he composed during the year in which he entered the
national arena in support of Barry Goldwater's presidential campaign. Nor
does that volume introduce any significant religious element into the description of Reagan's boyhood, or in the many chapters devoted to his battles with
communist elements in Hollywood. Yet, considering the importance of
religion to his Protestant mother and Roman Catholic father, plus Reagan's
own choice of a college affiliated with his mother's church, Disciples of
Christ, the absence of any but passing references to religion in his memoirs is
quite remarkable.

The turn of mind that was to lead to Reagan's association of godliness with
his political beliefs was suggested by a paragraph in a 1961 speech that was
subsequently selected by the chairman of Americans for Reagan as the first
important expression of the actor-turned-politician's political philosophy.
Addressing the annual meeting of the Chamber of Commerce, Reagan
focused on the danger of expanding the government's social programs and
business controls. This trend, fostered by "those of liberal persuasion," he
saw as part of a global war between communist tyranny and capitalist
democracy, a war he was convinced would end in total victory for one side or
the other by 1970. Evidence of socialist encroachment in the United States,
he said, could be seen in legislation providing for government-paid medicine, social security, the National Education Act of 1958 and, most important of all, the progressive income tax. This last form of subversion, Reagan
asserted, came "directly from Karl Marx." It was at this point that he offered
the Bible as a guide to government decision-making. The tax system, he
insisted, should be based on the biblical instruction regarding tithing: "We

1

are told we should give the Lord one-tenth, and if the Lord prosper us ten times as much, we should give ten times as much."[2] That single reference to the Bible as the source of inspiration for public policy was a forerunner of a later campaign in which Reagan would ultimately offer biblical injunctions in support of almost every aspect of his political program, from military preparedness to prayer in public schools.

In the early stages of his political career, Reagan's perorations on the Marxist threat to the American way of life contained few of the charges of godlessness that became a hallmark of his later speeches. His famous address on behalf of Barry Goldwater's presidential candidacy, televised nationwide on October 27, 1964, included only two oblique references to the religious influence. One was the grossly inaccurate statement—repeated time and again throughout his career—that the courts consider "a child's prayer in a school cafeteria endangers religious freedom." His concluding blast at liberal appeasement in the face of the communist threat repeated his auto-biographical appeal for Americans to emulate the courage of Moses in leading the Israelites out of Egypt and of Christ in accepting crucifixion to save mankind.[3]

*　　*　　*　　*

Election to public office seemed to arouse in Reagan a sense of mission that was more than political. Urged to run for the governorship of California by affluent Republicans who recognized his effectiveness in the art of public speaking, Reagan responded with a campaign that won him a resounding victory over Democratic Governor Edmund G. ("Pat") Brown. Biblical references were not a feature of his pre-election speeches, which Reagan's most informed biographer found "as simple and unspecific as the one which had emerged from the GE [General Electric] days and excited the followers of Barry Goldwater."[4] However, Reagan's inauguration as governor opened a new chapter in his colorful career. The concluding flourish in his autobiography, "I have found the rest of me," announced his arrival at a decision to pursue the most rewarding of the three loves he had identified at the outset of that narrative as "drama, politics and sports."[5]

Reagan's final choice of vocation was quickly revealed as more than that of politician. On the political stage he blended the talents of actor with those of fundamentalist preacher. Taking office as governor January 2, 1967, he introduced his plan for what he called a Creative Society with these words:

It is inconceivable to me that anyone could accept this delegated authority without asking God's help. I pray that we who legislate and administer will be granted wisdom and strength beyond our own limited power; that with Divine guidance we can avoid easy expedients, as we work to build a state where liberty under law and justice can triumph, where compassion can govern, and wherein the people can participate and prosper because of their government and not in spite of it.[6]

Developing this theme in major speeches delivered over the following weeks, Reagan proposed private initiative as a substitute for government action in social matters, suggesting that the churches take over the welfare function,[7] and that freedom is best defined in religious, not political, terms.[8] He continued along this line later in the year, but in a way that revealed a philosophical dilemma he himself failed to recognize. Speaking to the students and faculty of his alma mater, Eureka College, he questioned the attempt to "solve human problems with material means." He reminded his audience that "the world's truly great thinkers have not pointed us toward materialism; they have dealt with the great truths and with the high questions of right and wrong, of morality and integrity."[9] To a more political audience the governor boasted that "our materialism has made our children the biggest, tallest, most handsome, and intelligent generation of Americans yet."[10]

Reagan's concept of America as a country chosen by God to save mankind was expressed more frequently as time went on. During his second term as governor—and in the course of a countrywide tour that suggested higher ambitions—he quoted the World War II remark of Pope Pius XII that "the American people have a genius for splendid and unselfish action, and into their hands, the hands of America, God has placed the destinies of an afflicted mankind."[11] The association of the Deity with political morality was continued, with variations, as Reagan openly entered the contest for nomination to the presidency. In an address on the need to restore basic values, televised nationwide, candidate Reagan ran an inventory of government meddling with problems of morality that he declared were best left to parents. Two objects of his attention were to recur endlessly over the remaining years of his public life: abortion and prayer in public schools. He concluded this speech with the same quotation from Pope Pius XII that he had used in Atlanta three years earlier, adding his own inevitable benediction, "God bless America."[12]

Reagan's practice of concluding every speech or public appearance with a religious reference or appeal had by this time become his standard procedure. Addressing the American Conservative Union in 1977, he closed his remarks with this definition of a political party: "A political party is a mechanical structure created to further a cause. The cause, not the mechanism, brings and holds the members together." The cause of his party, he said, "must be to rediscover, reassert, and reapply America's spiritual heritage to our national affairs." If we can accomplish this, he concluded, "then with God's help we shall indeed be as a city upon a hill, with the eyes of all people upon us."[13]

This reference to the most famous sermon of pilgrim preacher John Winthrop, repeated in many subsequent speeches, reveals the depth and direction of Reagan's fundamentalism. Winthrop arrived in America in 1630, leading a fleet of seven ships and a thousand pilgrims to reinforce a settlement that had been established only a decade earlier. A successful attorney and member of the company whose 1629 charter set forth the boundaries of the Massachusetts Bay Colony, Winthrop was appointed governor of Massachusetts Bay and became one of its most influential leaders.[14] A staunch Puritan, Winthrop saw Massachusetts as a "holy commonwealth" in which he and other Puritan leaders would establish "a society so faithful to the rules of God that other men would see and imitate them." It was in this sense that he offered his vision of "a city upon a hill."[15]

For a time, it appeared that Winthrop's goal would be realized. New England towns were organized and governed by Puritan leaders whose religous purity earned them the title of "saint." This theocratic society was well-established some years before the growing strength of Puritanism in the English Parliament brought a confrontation with King Charles I which ended in civil war and the establishment of a Puritan commonwealth under Lord Protector Oliver Cromwell. Thus, by the middle of the seventeenth century, Puritans in both the mother country and Massachusetts Bay Colony controlled the government and, through the government, imposed their standards of behavior upon society as a whole.

Interestingly enough, although control in England was maintained by an army faithful to Cromwell, that dictator was more tolerant of other Protestant sects than were the Puritan "saints" in New England, whose control was exercised through their dual role as religious and political leaders. The intensity of Puritan intolerance in America was illustrated time and again, as laws imposing punishment ranging from public flogging to death were applied to members of other sects. And Puritan dissidents like Anne Hutchinson and Roger Williams were tried and convicted of heresy—*by the colonial legislature,* not the church—for contesting the right of government officials to dictate matters of conscience. This was the character of the "city upon a hill" that Reagan idealized in his frequent references to the country's spiritual origins.

The implications of his glorification of John Winthrop's goal escaped Reagan for the same reason that led him to misconstrue other aspects of American history: his tendency to focus on a few widely publicized quotations of famous people without having any knowledge or understanding of the context in which their remarks were made. Thus, to support his repeated appeals for legalizing prayer in public schools he would offer remarks or acts of early American heroes that are either apocryphal or irrelevant. A sample of the former is his reporting as fact the scene in a famous painting of George

Washington that shows the general kneeling to pray in the snow at Valley Forge, an act that the very private Washington was never known to perform outside his church or home.[16] Similarly, Reagan quoted Thomas Jefferson in such a way as to suggest that the country's foremost opponent of church-state ties was actuated by the same principles as John Winthrop. This kind of sleight-of-tongue is evident in Reagan's salute to Senator Jesse Helms, in which he coupled Helms' effort to "welcome the Lord back to the classroom" with the biblical instruction to pray for God's forgiveness of sin and, in the same paragraph, Jefferson's warning, "I tremble for my country when I reflect that God is just."[17]

Most ridiculous of all are his quotations from Thomas Paine, whose writings reflect a social and political philosophy almost as remote from Reagan's as that of Karl Marx. The revolutionary radical whose deism, as well as his "crude, ignorant" notions of government, were scorned by John Adams, is pictured by Reagan as another "city-on-a-hill" visionary because of his ringing declaration that "we have it within our power to begin the world over again."[18]

The notion that America is God's chosen land, and "the American dream is that every man must be free to become whatever God intends he should become," is another Reagan theme. This did not appear with any regularity until after he discovered that "the rest of me" was to flower in a political setting.[19] In this sense, the governorship of California was a training period for his entry into national politics. By 1976, recognition of Reagan's kinship with religious fundamentalists was clearly evident. Challenging Gerald Ford for the Republican nomination in that year, Reagan drew support from fundamentalists of all faiths who were attracted by the "traditional biblical moral values" of the "New Right."[20] This was not a purely Protestant movement. Leadership of the New Right included the Catholic publisher of *Conservative Digest*, Richard Viguerie, and the Jewish organizer of the Conservative Caucus, Howard Phillips, as well as Baptist fundamentalists like Jerry Falwell and Pat Robertson. When, after losing to Ford in 1976, Reagan rebounded to defeat Carter in 1980, the non-clerical New Rightists were as quick as their religious brothers to associate themselves with the prayer politics that Reagan made part of his campaign. Richard Viguerie's place in the Reagan camp earned him joint billing with Edward McAteer, of the Religious Roundtable, on a MacNeil-Lehrer program on school prayer. Introduced as "one of the leading apostles of the New Right," Viguerie acknowledged that although he had not considered himself in that light, he did like the title "apostle," and he proceeded to defend Reagan's school prayer drive as an appropriate response to what he called the religious feelings of most Americans.[21]

The contribution of religious fundamentalists to the Republican victory in

1980 was not as substantial as some analysts believed at the time, but there is no doubt that among born-again Protestants—not necessarily fundamentalists—Reagan won a majority of the votes that had gone to born-again Jimmy Carter four years earlier.[22] Reagan's appeal to these groups was clearly expressed, both before and after the election. Drawing on the invariably successful formula of blending religion and patriotism, he interspersed these sentiments in his 1980 acceptance speech:

> It is impossible to capture in words the splendor of this vast continent which God has granted as our portion of His creation. There are no words to express the extraordinary strength and character of this breed of people we call Americans. . . . Can we doubt that only a Divine Providence placed this land, this island of freedom, here as a refuge for all those people in the world who yearn to breathe free? . . . Can we begin our crusade joined together in a moment of silent prayer? God bless America.[23]

In the same spirit, his inaugural address included a proposal that "on each inaugural day in future years it should be declared a day of prayer." This was followed by a litany of American heroes and heroics from revolutionary days to the war in Vietnam. Assuring the American people in this nationally televised address that the crisis the country faced when he took office did not require the kind of sacrifice made by earlier heroes, Reagan concluded:

> It does require, however, our best effort and our willingness to believe in ourselves and to believe that together with God's help we can and will resolve the problems which now confront us. And after all, why shouldn't we believe that? We are Americans. God bless you, and thank you.[24]

Secure in the belief that his election demonstrated the American people's faith in his kind of leadership, President Reagan told the group that attended his first annual national prayer breakfast that he would be guided by a faith like that of Abraham Lincoln, whom he quoted as having said, "I would be the most foolish person on this footstool earth if I believed for one moment that I perform the duties assigned to me without the help of one who is wiser than all." Assuming a far more personal association with the Deity than was ever claimed by Lincoln, Reagan likened himself to an anonymous storyteller who impressed him with a tale of walking with God. Reagan said he, too, expected to walk with God on his journey through the presidency and, in times of great difficulty he expected to be carried by God.[25]

A month later the president proclaimed a national day of prayer. Citing the "spiritual foundation" established by the rigidly intolerant pilgrim fathers as one "that has served us ever since," he defined "the essence of liberty" as the "freedom to choose a Godly path," presumably the path prescribed by the followers of John Winthrop. Continuing the Chosen People theme, he issued the following call for observing May 7 as the National Day of Prayer:

> On that day I ask all who believe to join with me in giving thanks to Almighty God for the blessings He has bestowed on this land and the protection He affords us as a people. Let us as a Nation join together before God, fully aware of the trials that lie ahead and the need, yes, the necessity, for divine guidance. With unshakeable faith in God and the liberty which is our heritage, we as a free Nation will surely survive and prosper.[26]

The appeal to "all who believe" may have been simply an acknowledgment that Reagan did not expect nonbelievers to join in this ceremony. It may also have reflected an assumption that only true believers—in the Reagan sense—could be relied upon to keep the nation on course, and that any overture to secular humanists and other nonbelievers would be fruitless. Certainly, Reagan's subsequent calls for moral regeneration were most frequently directed to those conservative Protestant, Catholic and Jewish organizations most likely to support his fundamentalist views. Among Protestant groups, his sermon to the largely evangelical National Religious Broadcasters became an annual affair.[27]

More interesting is the special attention Reagan gave Mormon leaders. His periodic tributes to the solidly Mormon Utah delegation in Congress, led by Senators Orrin G. Hatch and Edwin J. ("Jake") Garn, are understandable expressions of appreciation for the unflagging support which that congressional faction gave to every aspect of the Reagan program, from prayer in public schools to tax reforms that would not only reduce personal and corporate income taxes but would include substantial benefits to church schools.[28] Some meetings were reported with "religious leaders" otherwise unidentified,[29] but nowhere does the record report meetings with the more traditional Protestant groups who frequently were opposed, or were indifferent, to Reagan policies on prayer, abortion and taxes. On the other hand, Reagan never missed an opportunity to chat with groups of "Christian women" or residents in heavily Catholic Hispanic or Irish communities.[30] And to Catholic Cardinal J. Terence Cooke, who visited the president when he was recovering from the bullet wound he received during the 1981 assassination attempt, Reagan declared, "I have decided that whatever time I have left is left for Him."[31]

The Jewish people also received a full share of attention as Reagan regularly extolled "our Judeo-Christian heritage" and annually proclaimed the importance of Passover and Rosh Hashanah. Until 1985 he constantly warned of the danger of forgetting the horrors of the Nazi effort to exterminate the Jewish people. Claiming to have participated in the collection of combat film that included scenes from the Nazi death camps, Reagan in 1981 asserted that those scenes should be constant reminders of the need to "rekindle these memories, because we need always to guard against that kind of tyranny and inhumanity." He assured the U.S. Holocaust Memorial Council that the presidential "bully pulpit should be used on every occasion where it is appropriate to point the finger of shame" at any evidence of religious persecution.[32] In October of that year he signed a bill extending honorary U.S. citizenship to Raoul Wallenberg in recognition of the "biblical proportions" of that "Swedish savior of almost 100,000 Jewish men, women and children" in Nazi-occupied central and southeastern Europe.[33]

In the ensuing years Reagan continued to pay tribute to "the richness and strength of our Judeo-Christian heritage," annually proclaiming Jewish Heritage Week in April and sending "special greetings to the Jewish people" during Rosh Hashanah, Yom Kippur, Chanukah and Passover. Although presidential messages to the Jewish community during the high holy days had been traditional in every post-World War II administration, Reagan's attentions were far more lavish. No fewer than six of his published papers of 1983 were directed to Jewish audiences.[34] On each occasion the message was clear: "It's incumbent upon us all, Jews and Gentiles alike, to remember the tragedy of Nazi Germany."[35]

Reagan's shocking abandonment of his earlier pledges, demonstrated when he joined West German Chancellor Helmut Kohl in a memorial to German soldiers—including SS troops—buried at Bitburg, was not as inexplicable as it seemed at the time. As far back as June 1983, Reagan's concern for world Jewry had shifted from remembrance of the Holocaust to the evils of Soviet designs on both its Jewish citizens and the state of Israel.[36] The election year of 1984, which brought even more frequent appeals to Jewish audiences, brought repeated denunciations of communist oppression of Jews, Nicaragua occasionally sharing the spotlight with the Soviet Union.[37]

Following his reelection to the presidency, Reagan accepted an invitation from Chancellor Kohl to participate in a "ceremony of reconciliation" on the 40th anniversary of V-E Day. In subsequent months, the president's itinerary underwent a number of changes. A ceremony commemorating the Allied victory over Nazi armies was scheduled and then cancelled. A proposed visit to a Nazi concentration camp was rejected by Reagan as "reawakening the memories and the passions" of World War II.[38] Instead of these events, the White House said, the president would stress reconciliation by laying a wreath at a German military cemetery.[39]

Although in this sequence of events Reagan never resorted to his favorite explanation, "realism," of his decisions, it is clear that his fear of embarrassing a valued partner in the anti-Soviet coalition overrode all other considerations. Only widespread criticism of his plan led him to backtrack on one count, agreeing to visit the notorious Bergen-Belsen concentration camp. But he would not withdraw from the ceremony at Bitburg, characterizing the German soldiers buried there as "victims of Nazism . . . just as surely as the victims in the concentration camps."[40] Attempting the following day to repair the damage incurred by this incredible equating of oppressors and oppressed, Reagan resumed deploring "the genocidal undertaking of the Nazis" in his proclamation of Jewish Heritage Week. At the same time he paid tribute to Elie Wiesel, presenting that intense but soft-spoken campaigner against anti-Semitism with the Congressional Gold Medal. Accepting the award on behalf of "all those who remember what SS killers have done to their victims," Wiesel used Reagan's own words in an attempt to shame the president into abandoning his plan to join in the wreath-laying at Bitburg. "The issue here," he said, "is not politics but good and evil."[41] As often as Reagan had painted the picture of an America that, under his leadership, would lead the world in the battle of good against evil, he remained unmoved by Wiesel's plea that he continue to uphold that standard. Visions of the death-camp films so vividly described in Reagan's 1981 commemoration of the Holocaust faded before the more immediate reality of his alliance with Chancellor Kohl.

* * * * *

If Reagan lost the respect of many Americans by his performance at Bitburg, he could take comfort in having gained wide support in another area by a perfectly timed diplomatic coup: establishment of formal diplomatic relations with the Vatican.

The part of America's Judeo-Christian heritage represented by the Catholic church received much of Reagan's attention during his first four years in the White House. As he told the National Catholic Education Association in 1982, "I'm grateful for your help in shaping American policy to reflect God's will."[42] Major policies on which the president and the church interpreted God's will in like fashion were anti-communism, abortion, and government aid to parochial schools. In these matters Reagan did not restrict himself to seeking support from the Catholic community in the U.S. Going directly to the top of the church hierarchy, he grasped every opportunity to demonstrate the closeness of his objectives with those of Pope John Paul II. Opening personal communication with the pope after the attempted assassination of the pontiff in 1981, Reagan renewed the association at regular intervals, ultimately bringing John Paul into his discussions of U.S. policy in international affairs.[43]

Throughout this period, Reagan made a point of incorporating in his public statements and announcements frequent references to his friendship with Pope John Paul II and his liaison with the Catholic church in support of domestic legislation and foreign aid for the oppressed people of Poland, the pope's native land.[44] What he did not reveal was the more ambitious plan to formalize the relationship between the U.S. government and the Catholic church by exchanging ambassadors with the papal state.

Exactly how the move to open diplomatic relations was initiated may not be known for some time. Ultimately, we can expect that Mr. Reagan will include a discussion of this matter in his memoirs, although we cannot anticipate any acknowledgment of behind-the-scenes negotiations to induce members of Congress to take the first steps toward this end. A more likely source for that information would be the reminiscences of those members of Congress with whom Reagan undoubtedly conferred in order to have the process started by the legislature, rather than the White House. For, in fact, it was a legislative act that eliminated the ban against diplomatic relations with the Vatican that had existed since 1867. Equally significant, the change was accomplished by means of this single sentence, inserted into a 47-page bill originally intended simply to authorize appropriations for the Department of State and related agencies:

Sec. 134. In order to provide for the establishment of United States diplomatic relations with the Vatican, the Act entitled "An Act making Appropriations for the Consular and Diplomatic Expenses of the Government for the year ending thirtieth June, eighteen hundred and sixty-eight, and for other purposes," approved February 28, 1867, is amended by repealing the following sentence (14 Stat. 413): "And no money hereby or otherwise appropriated shall be paid for the support of an American legation at Rome, from and after the thirtieth day of June, eighteen hundred and sixty-seven."[45]

Considering the fundamental implications of this act for the traditional American policy of political noninvolvement with the Vatican, it is reasonable to ask what unpublished negotiations or discussions led Republicans and Democrats to join in reversing a century-old tradition, and why the Senate Foreign Relations Committee neglected to hold a public hearing on the proposed amendment before acting on it. These questions were raised in letters addressed to the originator of the amendment, Senator Richard C. Lugar, cosponsor Senator Daniel P. Moynihan (Foreign Relations Committee chairman Charles Percy having left the Senate after losing the election of 1986), Stephen J. Solarz, a senior member of the House Foreign Affairs Committee (chairman Clement J. Zablocki having died), and Dante B. Fascell, House representative on the House-Senate conference committee that approved the bill as revised by Senator Lugar. Only Representative Fascell deigned to reply to the inquiry, merely saying that because then-chairman

Zablocki had introduced a similar measure in the House, "it was therefore a relatively simple matter for the House to recede to the Senate and the conference report."[46]

The plain, unvarnished facts are that repeal of the 1867 law was not included in the original bill that was passed by the House June 9, 1983; that Representative Zablocki subsequently suggested an amendment that the House never acted upon; that the bill was amended in the Senate at the suggestion of Senator Lugar; that the amendment was not subjected to either a hearing or open debate; and that the only explanation for the amendment offered in the conference report was that it was intended to give the president "the flexibility to establish formal relations with the Vatican if he determines that to be in the national interest."[47] At no point was there the slightest hint of White House interest—much less influence—in opening the door to diplomatic relations with a religious agency. Yet, after the bill had been passed, President Reagan lost no time in announcing his intention of appointing an ambassador—not to the Vatican, which Senator Lugar argued was a "sovereign state . . . analogous to religious states such as Israel, Saudi Arabia, and others"—but to the Holy See, world headquarters of the Roman Catholic church.[48]

Aiding in the passage of the repeal amendment was the lack of attention by the media. For despite the extraordinary character of the proposed policy change, more immediate and violent events dominated the headlines. When the State Department appropriations bill was first considered in the Senate in September, the country had not recovered from the September 1 shooting down of a South Korean airliner by a Soviet fighter pilot. The tension surrounding American troops in Lebanon was continuous, and Senate passage of the amended bill was followed quickly by an attack on the U.S. military barracks in Beirut that killed 241 U.S. Marines and sailors. In their preoccupation with problems of national security, news agencies gave scant space to the few published protests that appeared in the *Christian Science Monitor* and *Church and State*.[49] Not until William W. Wilson was nominated as ambassador to the Holy See did a Senate hearing elicit substantial public comment, including a rehash of the brief diplomatic tie with the Vatican from 1848 to 1867 and the informal relations established by President Roosevelt in 1939, which were continued by Presidents Truman, Nixon, Ford, Carter and Reagan, though not by Eisenhower, Kennedy or Johnson.[50] But by then diplomatic recognition was a fait accompli, and Wilson's appointment was approved by the same extraordinary coalition of Senate Republicans and Democrats that had supported repeal of the 1867 law. Not even Democratic sponsors chose to recall the bitter opposition to John F. Kennedy's presidential bid by Reagan's fundamentalist Protestant supporters who had accused Kennedy of being a tool of the Vatican. And no legislator was courageous enough to compare Reagan's insistence on a political tie with the Holy See and Catholic John Kennedy's unequivocal statement, "I am flatly opposed to appointment of an ambassador to the Vatican."[51] Only a few members of Congress—including Senator Jesse Helms—withdrew their support for the already-enacted law in response to protests by such organizations as the Southern Baptist Convention, Seventh-Day Adventists, Church of Christ, National Association of Evangelicals, National Council of the Churches of Christ, Americans United for Separation of Church and State, American Civil Liberties Union, United Methodist Church, and Christian Civil Liberties Union.[52] The overwhelming majority of the bill's original sponsors remained silent but held their ground and voted 81 to 13 in favor of Wilson's appointment.[53]

*   *   *   *   *

Some observers attributed Reagan's opening of diplomatic relations with the Holy See as an effort to attract Catholic support for his 1984 re-election campaign.[54] Certainly the coincidence of the president's and the church's views on abortion and tax credits for students in parochial schools suggested a connection between the election and the timing of Reagan's appointment of an ambassador to Rome. However, the move was also consistent with Reagan's broader goal of convincing Christians of all denominations that he was following in the footsteps of Jesus and would lead the nation in the path of righteousness to that great destiny which God had placed in America's hands.

Reagan's elevation of the Holy See to the status of a national state irritated many religious and non-religious organizations, including the largest Protestant congregation in the U.S., the conservative Southern Baptist Convention. But the protests of these groups were more than offset by the unfaltering support he continued to receive from fundamentalist leaders whose radio and television programs were followed by millions of people nationwide. Even if only the major religious programs are considered—Jerry Falwell's "Old Time Gospel Hour," Jimmy Swaggart's "Crusade," Jim Bakker's "PTL Club," Oral Roberts' "Sunday Night Live," and Pat Robertson's "700 Club"—their combined audiences could be measured not only in tens of millions of viewers but in hundreds of millions of dollars cheerfully donated to ensure their continuation.[55]

The appeal of Reagan for these religious showmen was evident in 1980 when he—alone among all presidential aspirants—attended a meeting sponsored by the Religious Roundtable, a fundamentalist organization promoted by some of the best known television personalities, including Jerry Falwell,

Pat Robertson and James Robison. Reagan delighted this gathering with a "shining city on a hill" sermon that concluded with this profession of faith:

> I can only add to that, my friends, that I continue to look to the Scriptures today for fulfillment and for guidance. Indeed, it is an incontrovertible fact that all the complex and horrendous questions confronting us at home and worldwide have their answers in that single book.[56]

One of Reagan's most enthusiastic rooters at the time was Pat Robertson, who subsequently disassociated himself from the Religious Roundtable. However, his withdrawal from that particular group did not signal a change in his view of Reagan as a leader chosen by God to carry out His will. Recalling a personal discussion with God—a frequent occurrence, according to Robertson—he announced in January 1981 that "God told me that Ronald Reagan was going to win the election." Robertson also reported the Deity as saying that he was going to bless Reagan and "we were not to criticize him."[57]

Initially, Reagan's gratitude to his religious supporters was not expressed directly. Rather, he gave thanks to the National Conservative Political Action Committee (NCPAC) in terms that fundamentalist preachers would readily understand and applaud. Denying that he had separate agendas for social, economic and foreign affairs, Reagan told his March 20, 1981 audience:

> We have one agenda. Just as surely as we seek to put our financial house in order and rebuild our nation's defenses, so too we seek to protect the unborn, to end the manipulation of school children by utopian planners, and permit the acknowledgment of a Supreme Being in our classrooms just as we allow such acknowledgments in other public institutions.[58]

Setting the stage for the crusade in which he would find all the world's problems turning about the conflict between Godless communism and Christian faith, he declared, "This is the real task before us: to reassert our commitment as a nation to a law higher than our own, to renew our spiritual strength." He concluded by associating "personal initiative and risk-taking in the marketplace" with "our own spiritual affirmation in the face of those who deny man has a place before God."[59]

If evidence of fundamentalist influence was minimal in the 1980 election, by 1984 it had grown to significant proportions. After sending the Senate his nomination of William A. Wilson to the post of ambassador to the Vatican, the president renewed his assurances to New Right Protestants of his faith in their concept of the good society. Accepting Pat Robertson's notion that peace, plenty and freedom are based on "the principles of the invisible world" of Christian faith, Reagan told a convention of National Religious Broadcast-ers that "the spectacular growth of CBN [Christian Broadcasting Network], PTL [Jim Bakker's Praise the Lord ministry] and Trinity" was evidence of a "hunger for your product—God's good news."[60] Two months later, in an overtly political pitch for support of his foreign and domestic policies, he thanked members of the National Association of Evangelicals for their efforts "in promoting fundamental American values of hard work, family, freedom, and faith."[61]

The effectiveness of Reagan's appeal to religious conservatives was apparent in the Republican nominating convention, which Connecticut delegate Julie Belaga characterized as dominated by "the New Right or fundamentalists." This faction, she said, controlled the platform committee and, through that committee, the definition of Republican party philosophy as it applied to every question of policy. The attitude of the women on the platform commit-tee reflected the new trend, Louisiana delegate Marilyn Thayer boasting of the increase in female convention delegates from 27 percent in 1980 to 47 percent in 1984, with the majority of those in the 1984 convention favoring Phyllis Schlafly's anti-Equal Rights Amendment (ERA), anti-abortion, pro-prayer position. In every vote on matters such as these, Schlafly forces joined with those of Jesse Helms to defeat—by a substantial margin—efforts of Republican moderates to alter either the position or the rhetoric of the platform.[62]

The ultimate victory of the New Right was forecast by fundamentalist preacher James Robison, who opened the convention with a prayer for God's guidance; the finished product was given divine sanction in a closing bene-diction by W. A. Criswell, best known for his fundamentalist, overtly anti-Catholic attacks on John Kennedy in the 1960 presidential campaign.

Reagan's satisfaction with the platform was evident even before that document was presented to the body of the convention. Following the committee's rejection of a proposal to soften its anti-ERA stance by indicat-ing respect for those who favored an equal rights amendment, the White House representative at the convention assured reporters that the president would be "very comfortable" with the platform designed by his ultraconser-vative supporters.[63] This modest description of the president's position fell far short of the enthusiastic approval Reagan gave the Helms-Schlafly plat-form in his speech accepting the party's nomination.

Although he did not acknowledge the religious influence in the Re-publican program, the implications of Reagan's moralistic approach to cam-paign issues was not lost on the media. The New York Times called editorially for an end to Reagan's "holier than thou" attitude.[64] Oblivious of such criticism, the president brought religion directly into the campaign when he announced to his listeners at a prayer breakfast in Dallas that the country's history demonstrated how "politics and morality are inseparable," and that "our government needs the church, because only those humble enough to admit they're sinners can bring to democracy the tolerance it requires in order to survive."[65] When, a short time later, a reporter asked, "What about the religious issue that's come up? Are you all overplaying it?", the president's answer was, "No, but I think some people in your profession here are."[66] On the campaign trail, the architect of Reagan's reelection philosophy, Jesse Helms, appealed for acceptance of the kind of Christian doctrine that is "higher than religion . . . the meaning of America."[67]

Notwithstanding the landslide victory Reagan won in 1984, and the significant contribution made by New Right religionists in swelling the Reagan vote, post-election analysis of why people voted for Reagan revealed that the overwhelming majority did so because they approved his economic policies in particular, and his overall performance in general. There was no evidence that his religious appeals had played a significant part in the balloting.[68] Nevertheless, when Reagan addressed the National Religious Broadcasters early in 1985, he cited "recent Gallup surveys" to prove that the majority of Americans agreed with his view that "religion can answer all or most of today's problems."[69] In fact, what the Gallup poll revealed in the only "recent" canvass of religious belief (released December 20, 1984) was that church membership and church attendance had changed very little from 1937 to 1984. It did not deal at all with opinion on the role of religion in the solution of everyday problems.[70]

This penchant for quoting nonexistent statistics went hand-in-hand with the recounting of apocryphal—or, at least, unprovable—events. In his remarks at the January 1985 national prayer breakfast, Reagan outlined the history of what he said was a movement to establish the prayer breakfast on an international scale, with political leaders from all over the world participating in this "fellowship" of Christians and non-Christians. Explaining the origin of the movement in the Congress, and its extension to the White House by President Eisenhower, Reagan quoted the late Kansas Senator Frank Carlson as saying that Ike had confessed to having "felt the hand of God guiding him" during the World War II campaign in Europe. Reagan referred to Carlson as "Ike's Paul Laxalt," suggesting that Carlson's association with Eisenhower was as close as that between Reagan and his friend and campaign manager of that name.[71] If there was such an association, it is not evident either in the two-volume biography of Eisenhower so carefully detailed and documented by Stephen E. Ambrose, or in the Eisenhower diaries. As to Eisenhower's religious beliefs, Ambrose recounts the general's reaction to Harold Stassen's suggestion that Ike put "a bit more faith" in his first inaugural address. "I don't want to deliver a sermon," was Eisenhower's reply, adding in equally unReagan-like fashion, "It is not my place."

Eisenhower did acknowledge that the American government "is deeply embedded in a religious faith," and he decided for appearance's sake to break a lifetime habit of nonattendance at church by joining and attending regularly the National Presbyterian Church in Washington. His thinking on this subject was summed up by Ambrose as follows:

> He felt it important for the President to set an example. He did not think the denomination important. Theology was a subject about which he knew nothing and cared nothing; *he never discussed his idea of God with anyone;* he did talk, sincerely and earnestly, about the need for a spiritual force in American life, but the specific form that the religious content should take did not concern him [italics added].[72]

Reagan's acceptance of Carlson's anecdote about Eisenhower's religious beliefs squares with his friend Mike Deaver's assertion that "Ronald Reagan is nuts for religious phenomena. He reads whatever he gets his hands on, watches any movie or television show that deals with the subject."[73] It also illustrates Reagan's preference for fictional accounts over documentary records of the sort contained in carefully researched historical works.

Speaking of the spread of the international religious fellowship movement, President Reagan said that its prayer meetings "are not widely known to the public." Then, in a rare departure from his normally critical attitude toward the media, he gave reporters credit for "great understanding and dignity" in keeping quiet about the meetings. Having said that, he went on—in remarks he knew would be published in the official *Weekly Compilation of Presidential Documents*—to talk about the "wonderful things [that] have come out of this fellowship," reporting that the movement had spread from the U.S. "throughout the capitals of the world, to parliaments and congresses far away." Tantalizing his listeners with the assertion that "a number of public figures have changed as human beings" through their association with the fellowship, he then closed the door by saying that he'd like to talk about these transformations, "but it might reveal too much about the membership." Nevertheless, he insisted that "in some of the most troubled parts of the world, political figures who are old enemies are meeting with each other in a spirit of peace and brotherhood."[74]

This revelation, coming in January 1985, could lead one to conjecture that Reagan was referring to meetings between American and Iranian officials, subsequently explained as efforts to establish relations with Iranian moderates. Certainly there was no evidence of budding brotherhood among old enemies anywhere else in the world. An inquiry to the White House requesting such additional information about this movement as could be revealed "without impairing its effectiveness" went unanswered.[75]

In the same talk, Reagan repeated a story he had told previously about how the ancient Roman practice of gladiators fighting to the death had been terminated abruptly in the fourth century by an Asian monk who, with his dying breath, pleaded with the gladiators, "In the name of Christ, stop."[76] Miraculous as this account appears to be, it is no more startling than for historians to overlook—as they have—the miracle suggested by this appeal: that administrators and spectators of the legendary Colosseum battles suddenly lost their taste for combat entertainment. What historians do report is that the persecution of Christians—including their forced participation as gladiators—came to an end following the conversion of Emperor Constantine to Christianity in 324 A.D. But battles between professional gladiators continued to delight Roman audiences into the fifth century.

There is no doubt that many Christians met death in sporting arenas throughout the Roman Empire, but their numbers were few compared to those killed in the deliberate persecution campaigns of Emperors Decius, Diocletian and Galerius. The Greek bishop Eusebius, one of the earliest church historians, made no reference whatever to killings in Roman arenas in his detailed chronicle of the persecutions that preceded the reign of Constantine.[77] Nevertheless, U.S. news reporters continued to demonstrate great understanding and dignity by not asking questions about either Reagan's description of the international prayer fellowship or his account of Roman history.

Throughout his second term, Reagan continued to preach the godliness of his program. In the process he told and retold tales that had become his stock-in-trade, even repeating the highly confidential international fellowship story, with few changes in wording, at his 1986 prayer breakfast.[78] Other favorites involved incidents or conditions bearing on the subjects of abortion and prayer in public schools. Comparing abortion with infanticide[79] he campaigned to overturn the Supreme Court decision in the 1973 case of Roe v. Wade. From his reelection in November 1984 through 1987 he included this topic in 17 of his public addresses.[80] In the process, he abandoned his earlier position that there was no need for a constitutional amendment because "the Constitution already protects the right to human life."[81] Criticizing the Supreme Court for striking down "efforts by states and localities to control the circumstances under which abortion may be performed," he began in 1983 to call upon Congress "to restore legal protections for the unborn, whether by statute or constitutional amendment."[82]

Equally persistent was Reagan's plea to "return God to the classroom." Invoking the names of such disparate heroes as Thomas Jefferson and Jesse Helms, he insisted that "the right to pray in school is a fundamental American liberty,"[83] invariably giving the false impression that children are forbidden that privilege when, in fact, what the courts have forbidden is a prayer period arranged by public agencies and supervised by public employees. On several occasions he attempted to bolster his prayer program by a wholly inaccurate report of the origin of daily prayers in the national legislature, repeatedly citing Benjamin Franklin's suggestion that the Constitutional Convention of 1787 open each session with a prayer. Ignoring Franklin's principal purpose, which was to cool the rising tempers of the delegates, Reagan either gave the impression that Franklin's proposal was approved, or stated flatly and incorrectly, "From that day on they opened all of the constitutional meetings with a prayer."[84] In fact, the convention refused to adopt Franklin's motion, just as the first Continental Congress had rejected a similar proposal in 1774, approving only an opening-day prayer.

Having concluded in 1982 that, notwithstanding a contrary opinion by the U.S. Supreme Court, New York State's "nonsectarian prayer . . . would meet all the [constitutional] needs," Reagan continued his campaign to legalize organized prayer in public schools. Only in his 1984 debate with Walter Mondale did he sing a different tune, telling a nationwide television audience, "I, too, want that wall that is in the Constitution of separation of church and state to remain there."[85] Reverting to type after his reelection, Reagan incorporated a plea for public support for a prayer amendment in more than a dozen of his 1984–1987 addresses.[86]

Like self-acknowledged fundamentalist ministers, Reagan dismissed criticism of his moralistic approach to legislation as based on "modern-day secularism," which he contended had discarded "the tried and time-tested values upon which our very civilization is based."[87] Yet he has never been known to comment on the values that characterize both the life-styles and the fund-raising methods of fundamentalist clerics. Indeed, if he reacted in any way to Oral Roberts' outrageous televised appeal to the public to buy a reprieve from God's threat to take his life, or to Pat Robertson's repeated claims to discuss current problems directly with God, or to Jim Bakker's display of opulent living and disregard for at least one of the Ten Commandments, his opinions were never made public. Yet the ordinary people he claimed to represent showed considerable despair over the essentially anti-Christian aspects of fundamentalist leadership. This was evident from the drastic drop in contributions from supporters of the major television evangelists, most of whom reported after the Bakker debacle that they had to cut staffs and programs.[88]

Nowhere was public disillusionment more evident than in opinions that appealed to rural communities like Lewisburg, Pennsylvania, a town of 5,600 people situated in the middle of a solidly Republican farming area. One columnist featured in a local paper recalled that in the 1950s and 1960s she willingly took part in daily school prayers until the prayer leaders extended their activity to rallies in which students were terrified by threats of everlasting damnation into requesting to be saved. Even as she made this request, little Sarah's most fervent wish was to be free of the fear instilled by the preacher's threats.[89] Another writer recalled asking evangelist Rex Humbard if he couldn't be as happy in a $75,000 home as in the three properties he had purchased, at a cost of $600,000, with funds solicited from his viewers. Humbard's answer was that "it is an asset for me to have a nice house and an asset for my organization, because I entertain outstanding people." His further explanation was that "his evangelist father was almost penniless and his poverty 'turned people off'." The writer's concern for this approach to Christian living was obvious from his comparison of the Humbard-Roberts life-style with that of a Jesuit priest whose advice was "Don't get too attached to material things, to promotions, to power, to bank accounts."[90]

Among the many letters President Reagan reported receiving from supporters of his high moral ground, none reflected the doubts or the disillusionment expressed by these two Pennsylvanians. In all probability such letters and articles were never brought to his attention by a staff that was fully aware of Reagan's aversion to evidence or anecdotes that would challenge the philosophical basis of his view of the good society.

CHAPTER 2

Philosopher

*"The liberal believes in the philosophy that
control is better than freedom . . . conservatives
believe the collective responsibility of qualified
men in a community should decide its course."*[1]

RONALD REAGAN NEVER PRETENDED TO BE A PHILOSOPHER, YET HE SPOKE
often of his philosophy of government and the "Creative Society." On the
other hand, he always presented himself as an ordinary individual with
ordinary tastes, likes and dislikes. In one respect this was an accurate self-
portrait. His preoccupation with sports, his preference for light reading of
the Horatio Alger type, his penchant for treating the make-believe world as
real, and his inability to deal with complex problems that were not annotated
and capsulized in *Reader's Digest* form, substantiate his claim to ordinariness.

Like most religious fundamentalists, Reagan had no capacity for intro-
spection. He was incapable of examining and weighing philosophical alternatives. When he pretended such an analysis, the result was the kind of
sophomoric summary quoted at the head of this chapter. Even—perhaps
especially—in the field of religion, he showed no ability to consider the
possibility that belief in God as the creator of all things need not require
belief in the Bible's account of how and when all things were created.
Similarly, he evidenced no understanding—nor even an inclination to wonder about—the reasonableness of the world's other great religions, some of
which, like Islam and Buddhism, attract millions of followers whose faith is
at least as firm as that of most Christians.

The shallowness of Reagan's thinking in shaping what he conceived to be
the good society is evident in his attempt to build a political philosophy on a
Puritan base. Time and again he referred to John Winthrop's "city on a hill"
concept as though the principles of that Puritan saint needed only minor
modifications to provide the foundation for an ideal socio-political organization. In modern terms, Reagan saw the struggle for political purity as one of

good versus evil, the good represented by religious-based free-enterprise democracy, the evil, by godless communism. The threat to the United States, according to Reagan, lay in the tendency of American liberals to adopt policies that drew them ever closer to acceptance of the communist view of total control over individual activity. Having considered himself a liberal in the Franklin Roosevelt-Harry Truman years, Reagan lost sympathy for the policies of the Democratic party as he climbed the economic ladder to affluence. In the process, he was particularly influenced by two experiences: the post-World War II red scare in Hollywood and the delights of high-paid employment by General Electric. Communist infiltration of the entertainment industry he dealt with in such detail in his autobiography that there is little doubt that his disenchantment with what he termed "the seamy side of liberalism" began with his 1945–46 battle with left-wingers in the Hollywood Independent Citizens Committee of Arts, Sciences, and Professions (HICCASP).[2] Brief as his membership in that organization was, it served to focus his attention on the evils of communism and led directly to his mental image of a biblical-type confrontation between the American good and Soviet evil. So seriously did he view this situation that in one of his earliest speeches on the danger of expanding government control he concluded with his apocalyptic prediction:

> There can only be one end to the war we are in. It won't go away if we simply try to outwait it. Wars end in victory or defeat. One of the foremost authorities on Communism in the world today has said we have ten years. Not ten years to make up our minds, but ten years to win or lose—by 1970 the world will be all slave or all free.[3]

*   *   *   *   *

Reagan's political metamorphosis from a follower of what he called "naive liberalism" to a vigorous crusader for conservatism paralleled his emergence as a religious fundamentalist. For as long as he remained under the influence of his father's attachment to the Democratic party, his liberalism was expressed in terms of policies consistently supported by Democratic leaders from World War II to the present day. Reagan himself summed up the Democratic view when he campaigned for Hubert Humphrey in the latter's 1948 effort to replace conservative Republican Joe Ball as U.S. Senator from Minnesota. "While Ball is the banner carrier for Wall Street," Reagan told voters in a radio address, "Humphrey is fighting for all the principles advocated by President Truman, for adequate low-cost housing, for civil rights, for prices people can afford to pay and for a labor movement free of the Taft-Hartley law."[4] Like the International Ladies Garment Workers Union, which sponsored his broadcast, Reagan combined his pitch for Humphrey with a plug for the reelection of President Truman.

By the close of Truman's second administration, Reagan was ready to join in the move by a number of Democratic leaders to entice General Eisenhower to run for president on the Democratic party ticket. For most professionals in the Democratic National Committee, the objective was to take advantage of the general's widespread popularity as the man most responsible for leading the Allied forces to victory over the Axis nations. They also knew that if the Republicans ran Eisenhower for president, he would easily defeat any candidate the Democrats could put up. Whether or not Reagan was more interested in Eisenhower's known conservative views on domestic policy he does not make clear in his autobiography. Nevertheless, despite Eisenhower's refusal to call himself a Republican while both major parties were courting him, it was obvious, as an October 25, 1951 editorial in the *New York Herald Tribune* pointed out, that the general was "a Republican by temper and disposition . . . by every avowal of faith and solemn declaration."[5]

The absence of any discussion of the politics of the 1950s and early 1960s in Reagan's autobiography is one of the most remarkable aspects of that work. The omission is particularly noticeable in a volume that is so obviously pointed toward the conclusion that the author's ultimate and most important role in life would be as a crusader dedicated to redirecting the nation's political orientation. When *Where's the Rest of Me?* first appeared in 1965, it followed a tumultuous period marked by such notable events as the Army-McCarthy hearings, war and revolution that involved the United States in Vietnam and the Middle East, the revolutionary Supreme Court decision in Brown v. Board of Education, and the passage of the landmark Civil Rights Act of 1964. If the political impact of those events had any bearing on Reagan's transformation from liberal Democrat to conservative Republican— as his later conduct indicates they did—there is no evidence of it in his autobiography. Indeed, the names Truman, Humphrey, Eisenhower, Nixon, McCarthy, the Soviet Union, Vietnam, Iran and Israel do not even appear in the index of that work. Nor is there any discussion of the influence these people and countries had on Reagan's political education—with the single exception of the Soviet Union and the threat that country posed by way of what Reagan saw as its "plan to conquer the world."[6]

Equally significant is the absence of any reference to Reagan's change of mind about the character and leadership quality of particular individuals. Two years after campaigning on behalf of Truman and Humphrey, he supported a 1950 Democratic ticket that included Helen Gahagan Douglas, who was running against Richard Nixon for one of the two California seats in the U.S. Senate. By 1952 Reagan had become a Democrat for Eisenhower, and the general's subsequent choice of Richard Nixon as his running mate gave Reagan no second thoughts. On the contrary, as he explained to Lou Cannon thirty years later, even as he supported Helen Gahagan Douglas in 1950 he thought her "awfully naive about the subject of communists."[7] Whether or not this indicates his acceptance of Nixon's utterly scurrilous charges of communist influence in the Douglas camp, Reagan recalls no feeling of disgust at the character of the Nixon campaign. On the contrary, Nixon's subsequent reputation as an anti-communist crusader in Congress must have endeared him to Reagan, whose Hollywood experience and high regard for the Un-American Activities Committee were critically important in the development of his syllogistic philosophy: communism is the essence of evil; modern-day liberalism will lead to communism; therefore, liberalism is evil.

Following a decade of posing as a Democrat while voting and campaigning for Republican candidates, Reagan converted formally to Republicanism by joining the party in 1962. Shortly thereafter, he designed the following definition of the difference between modern liberals and the conservatives he now professed to represent:

> The classic liberal used to be the man who believed the individual was, and should be forever, the master of his destiny. That is now the conservative position. The liberal used to believe in freedom under law. He now takes the ancient feudal position that power is everything. He believes in a stronger and stronger central government, in the philosophy that control is better than freedom.[8]

Based on this sophomoric analysis of liberal and conservative philosophies, Reagan goes on to point to the "degeneracy" of society under the guidance of liberals like scientist J. Robert Oppenheimer, journalist John Crosby, and the English commentator Kenneth Tynan, whom he credits with coining the phrase "better red than dead." The conservative spirit, on the other hand, he felt was represented by some of the greatest revolutionaries of all time: Moses, Christ, and "those men at Concord Bridge."[9]

If Reagan's writings reveal anything of his capacity for analytical thinking, they surely demonstrate that, of all the ordinariness he claimed for himself, his ability in this area was most ordinary of all. That conclusion is supported not only by the way in which he attempted to define opposing political forces in the U.S., but by the contradictions between what he advanced as theory and what he put into practice. In Reagan's theory, the objects of democratic government were: winning the war against international communism; maintenance of free enterprise; a government conducted "with honesty, openness, diligence and special integrity" but limited to those few functions that "people can't do for themselves"; and a system that will foster fundamentalist belief in God and "protect individual freedom, family life, communities and neighborhood."[10]

Few aspirants to political office would openly contest any of Reagan's stated objectives. However, the politics Reagan adopted to achieve these goals during his presidency shed new light on his philosophical generalities as it became clear that his practical purposes were: to brand as communist-oriented (tainted by socialism, liberalism or merely "uninformed") all opposition to his particular method of combatting communism; to give government sanction to religious fundamentalism by way of laws or constitutional amendments supporting religious activity in both public and private schools; and to cloak government operations with a greater degree of secrecy than practiced by any of the Democratic administrations he so frequently castigated for keeping the public in the dark. In a 1977 defense of "the new conservative majority we represent," he offered this picture of the liberal elitism that he saw shaping America:

> Let us lay to rest, once and for all, the myth of a small group of ideological purists trying to capture a majority. Replace it with the reality of a majority trying to assert its rights against the tyranny of powerful academics, fashionable left-revolutionaries, some economic illiterates who happen to hold elective office, and the social engineers who dominate the dialogue and set the format in political and social affairs.[11]

To counter the influence of the dominant left-revolutionaries he offered the Republican platform of 1976, which he called unique in that "it answers not only programmatic questions for the immediate future of the party, but also provides a clear outline of the underlying principles upon which those programs are based."[12]

The charge that the Democratic party had fallen into the hands of leaders who believed "only a chosen elite in the nation's Capitol can make the decisions and find the answers" Reagan offered as a major reason for having left that party.[13] This attempt to turn the face of elitism away from the Republican party and pin it on the Democratic leadership became a recurring theme as Reagan's interest in national political office sharpened. Running for the Republican presidential nomination in 1976, he asserted that the Democratic party had been "taken over by elitists who believed only they could plan properly the lives of the people."[14] This, he said, accounted for the "arrogant officialdom" of successive Democratic administrations. Little more than four years later, in his inaugural address as president of the U.S., Reagan promised an administration that would reject the notion that "government by an elite group is superior to government for, by, and of the people."[15] This assurance was given even as he was in the process of installing a government led by department and agency heads whose claimed expertise made their decisions unchallengeable. The observant public quickly learned that those who disagreed with administration policy were regarded as either Democratic malcontents or misinformed individuals who could not be expected to understand the complexities of the situation facing Reagan's experts. Opponents of Reagan's confrontational policy toward the Soviet Union were denounced as dupes of the communists who were either purposely or misguidedly "carrying the propaganda ball for the Soviet Union."[16] Those who were merely ignorant of the facts he urged to give him "their trust and confidence" to "allow us to take the actions that we think are necessary to lessen this [Soviet] threat."[17] Conveniently forgotten was his earlier indignant indictment of the Johnson and Carter administrations for what Reagan had termed a "trust me" approach to government policy-making.[18]

* * * * *

The Reagan elite brought its own brand of ethics to Washington. Convinced of the superiority of their own judgment, Reagan and his administrators established a pattern of operation that contradicted the president's publicly stated princples. As governor of California, he had challenged the value of material gain when he put this question to the students of Eureka College: "Aren't liberty and morality and integrity and high principles and a sense of responsibility more important?"[19] As a Goldwater supporter, he had stressed "the people's right to know" what government is doing, repeating an earlier pledge to California voters to make available "all the facts concerning the people's business."[20]

As a later chapter will demonstrate, the most damning evidence of Reagan's violation of his own principles can be found in his conduct of foreign affairs. However, signs of what the new morality really meant appeared long before Reagan reached the White House. In December 1973, after President Nixon's personal attorneys had become convinced of his involvement in illegalities, lying, cover-up and obstruction of justice, Reagan publicly deplored the "cloud of doubt, mistrust and cynicism generated by something called Watergate."[21] Professing great indignation at the "illegal and immoral acts of a few individuals," he made it clear that no wrongdoing attached to President Nixon. Equating Watergate with the fraudulent activities of Democrats Bobby Baker and Billie Sol Estes, Reagan called upon "some politicians"—obviously those pursuing the Watergate investigation—to "put Watergate on one side of the scale and weigh it against the free world leadership that is ours whether we like it or not."[22] President Nixon, he said, had demonstrated the effectiveness of American leadership by keeping the Soviet Union out of the Middle East and bringing "an easing of tensions worldwide such as we haven't known since World War II." Subsequent revelations of Nixon's perfidy brought no change in Reagan's attitude. He continued to regard the entire episode as no more than routine party peccadillos, though by August 1974 he concluded that Nixon would have to resign. However, on the key question of whether the president is above the law, Reagan gave advance notice of his own approach to the office by supporting Nixon's view that the president may take illegal actions to protect national security, saying: "When the Commander-in-Chief of a nation finds it necessary to order employees of the government or agencies of the government to do things that would technically break the law, he has to be able to declare it legal for them to do that."[23]

* * * * *

"Reaganethics" never became a slogan like "Reaganomics," but it deserves an equal place in the history of the Reagan administration. Enamored of the businessman's way of "getting things done," Reagan looked to people who had made it big in business to run the government. What he overlooked—or never knew from personal experience, having had no managerial duties in any business organization—was that business ethics rarely preclude the use of bribery, kickbacks, fraudulent advertising, stock manipulation, tax evasion, and a host of other illicit practices. After only twelve months in the White House, the largely supportive editors of *U.S. News and World Report* felt obliged to question the president about what they politely called "errors in judgment" by his senior administrators. A portion of the interview went like this:

Q. Some of your aides have caused you embarrassment lately, and some critics have said that you've been too slow to crack the whip. When should a president fire somebody who has embarrassed him?
A. When it is very definite that the individual is guilty of wrongdoing and of not fulfilling his responsibilities. . . . I don't think that just because the immediate furor is embarrassing, you should punish or separate an individual before it has been proved whether he is guilty of what has been charged.
Q. Even if an aide admits an error in judgment?
A. It depends on the error in judgment. Everyone makes mistakes, including when you sit on this side of the desk. But if it's an error in judgment that lessens public trust in public institutions, then separation has to take place.[24]

After six years in which not a single person was fired by Reagan, despite widespread recognition of many so-called judgmental errors as malfeasance, misfeasance or nonfeasance, the variety and extent of corruption among officials of his administration led *Time* magazine to ask in its May 25, 1987 cover story, "What ever happened to ethics?" Comparing Reagan's entourage with those of Harding and Nixon, the writer found the "sleaze" of the Reagan administration less flagrant than that of the Teapot Dome scandal and less pernicious than the maneuvering behind Watergate. But the pattern of misconduct observed in more than 100 of Reagan's top administrators was found to be "without precedent" in any former administration.[25] Some historians would consider the corruption of Grant's administration more pervasive than Reagan's, but even rating the latter next-to-worst is hardly a compliment.

A thorough study of this aspect of the Reagan presidency would require a volume of its own. However, a review of eight years' press reports, congressional investigations and court cases brings out not only the flavor of Reaganethics but the pervasive nature of the immorality that infected almost every department and agency in the executive branch. The following are only a few of the many examples.

Central Intelligence Agency

CIA director William J. Casey will be remembered best for his devious maneuvering in the Iran-Contra affair, which will be treated in a later chapter. Long before "Irangate," however, Casey's habit of withholding non-security information from Congress raised questions, beginning with his promotion from Reagan's campaign manager to director of the CIA. Pretending a level of morality that would automatically preclude any action on his part that could be influenced by private interest, Casey long resisted the standard requirement that a federal official in a policy-making position place in a blind trust stock holdings in companies with which his agency might do business. This despite documentary proof, discovered later, that a number of the companies in which Casey owned stock did have contracts with the CIA.[26] When, finally, under pressure from Congress (not from President Reagan), he agreed to establish a blind trust, he did not include his $7.5 million-worth of stock in Capital Cities Communications, a media conglomerate he had helped organize.[27]

Casey's interest in control of the news was evident in 1984 when he demanded that the Federal Communications Commission apply sanctions against the American Broadcasting System for its report of CIA involvement in a conspiracy involving the death of a U.S. citizen.[28] And all the president's assurances of his friend's honesty, decency and integrity did not prevent Casey's CIA from resisting for seven years a suit to reimburse a man who had been reduced to near-vegetable existence by an earlier CIA hospital experiment in brainwashing that was conducted without informing or getting the consent of the patient.[29]

Casey's indifference to normal reporting procedures was also displayed by his failure to disclose, at the time of his appointment, many of his recent legal clients—including the governments of South Korea and Indonesia.[30]

When it was recalled that in 1976 he had lobbied the Treasury Department on behalf of the Indonesian government without registering as a foreign agent, Reagan's attorney general William French Smith came to Casey's aid, declaring that the CIA director's actions had been legal because the law permitted an attorney to represent a client "in the course of established agency procedures" without registering as a foreign agent.[31] In the face of "accidental" omissions and obvious evasions, but without courtroom evidence of criminal action, the best the Republican-dominated Senate Intelligence Committee could do in approving Casey's appointment as CIA director was to say that "no basis has been found for concluding that Mr. Casey is unfit" to hold that office.[32]

Commerce Department

Deputy Secretary Guy Fiske resigned in the face of charges of conflict of interest in the negotiation of contracts with private firms. Assistant Secretary Carlos Campbell resigned when it was revealed that he had made grants to companies headed by his friends under conditions that a professional evaluating panel would not have approved.[33] Assistant Secretary D. Bruce Merrifield, on the other hand, suffered no penalty for having acted as a lobbyist for the Industrial Research Institute which he had formerly headed, pressuring the department into awarding a $970,000 contract to the institute, even though the responsible review panel rated that organization below most of the other bidders. Pretending a greater degree of expertise than panel members—"people who have a limited understanding of technology and management"—Merrifield ignored a warning about conflict of interest, claiming he wasn't the one who made the award decision "except for identifying very positively that this is what I want."[34]

Defense Department

Second only to Caspar Weinberger in the management of the country's defense establishment, Deputy Secretary Paul Thayer resigned his post when the news broke of his involvement in illegally passing to friends confidential information that netted them profits of over $1.5 million in stock trading. Calling the charges "entirely without merit," this captain of industry later pleaded guilty not only to breaking the law against insider-trading, but also to lying about it under oath. Sentenced to four years in prison, he served nineteen months of that term.[35]

On a lower, but still influential level, Deputy Under Secretary Mary Ann Gilleece, who was responsible for overseeing military procurement, resisted congressional efforts to examine procurement records and defended even the most inefficient contractors. She was forced to resign after press reports of her attempt, while still on the public payroll, to establish a private consulting firm and to solicit business for that firm from 29 of the country's largest defense contractors, promising services that would insure "good working relationships" with government contract officers and inspectors.[36]

Evidence of widespread disregard for the department's own directive on standards of conduct appeared in a 1983 audit. This internal investigation revealed not only that many Pentagon employees were buying stock in companies with which they were doing business, but that failure to file the required financial disclosure statements was ignored by responsible officers, and exceptions were made even for some employees engaged in contract negotiations.[37]

Subsequently, as evidence of both fraud and incompetence among military contractors mounted, Assistant Inspector Brian M. Bruh resigned in protest over the department's failure to press investigations. Soon afterwards, all five of his assistants in the contract fraud division were removed, one resigning, the rest being transferred to other duties.[38] Thus, only three years after the Defense Department had announced a joint effort with the Justice Department to combat contract fraud, the sincerity of this venture was questioned by DOD's own inspection staff.[39]

Environmental Protection Agency

From the very first year of Reagan's White House tenure, the operation of this agency gave warning of the varieties of corruption that were later to appear in other offices as well: conflict of interest, conniving with private industry to evade the law, cover-up of questionable activities, and lying to support the cover-up. After more than a year of reports of maladministration by the assistant administrator for research and the enforcement counsel, and evidence that executives from companies regulated by EPA were enlisted to look for ways of cutting agency costs and increasing efficiency, a congressional committee demanded to see the records of the $1.6 billion "superfund" that Congress had authorized to clean up toxic waste sites.[40] President Reagan's immediate reaction was to claim executive privilege. Accepting EPA's explanation that some of the requested documents were in "open enforcement files," he wrote to EPA administrator Anne Gorsuch, "I instruct you and your agency not to furnish copies of this category of documents to the subcommittees in response to their subpoenas."[41] The Justice Department, under Attorney General William French Smith, supported the cover-up by instructing EPA to give it all existing copies of the requested documents, even though EPA counsel Robert M. Perry later acknowledged that those documents were not involved in any civil or criminal case.[42]

As evidence mounted of non-enforcement of the law and of private company participation in drafting EPA reports, Reagan replaced Anne Gorsuch with William Ruckelhaus.[43] Calling the attacks on EPA "unwarranted," the president later protested that only one person in that organization had been criminally indicted. But as Representative John D. Dingell, chairman of the House Committee on Energy and Commerce pointed out, the president "conveniently overlooks more than 20 resignations."[44] Both before and after the conviction of Anne Gorsuch's assistant, Rita Lavelle, for perjury and impending congressional investigations, resignations were tendered by counsel William A. Sullivan, records officer Louis J. Cordia, deputy administrator John W. Hernandez, Jr., assistant administrator John Horton, inspector general Mathew N. Novick, consulting lawyer James Sanderson, and general counsel Robert M. Perry, among others.[45]

Health and Human Services Department

The department secretary's chief of staff, C. McLain Haddow, resigned before being indicted on seven counts of fraud and receiving kickbacks.[46]

Housing and Urban Development Department

While Reagan still occupied the White House, only the relatively minor peccadillos of regional administrator Bill J. Sloan and his deputy, Wayne W. Tangye, reached the public through press reports of their persistent misuse of travel funds. Only after Reagan's retirement from office did the media discover a pattern of "widespread waste, influence peddling, fraud and theft" apparently unknown to the president but perpetrated with the knowledge and participation of his department secretary, Samuel R. Pierce, Jr. Thought initially to be guilty only of Reaganesque hands-off management, Pierce was later found to have been personally involved in the favors-for-friends approach taken by his aides in the funding of housing projects, more than half of which were found by one report to have been infected with "fraud, mismanagement and favoritism." Pierce flatly denied all charges, but his response to a House committee's demand for his testimony was to take the Fifth Amendment.[47]

Interior Department

Nowhere was the arrogance of power—so vigorously condemned by Reagan over the years—more blatantly demonstrated than in the Department of Interior under the leadership of Secretary James Watt. Within months of his appointment, this former president of the anti-environmental Mountain States Legal Foundation threatened to hold up completion of a congressionally approved Arizona water project if that state's representative, Morris K. Udall, didn't control the "hostile" questioning of Watt in his committee. Boasting of his power to determine the fate of such projects, Watt told reporters, "There are parts of this job I enjoy."[48]

In these early months Watt also undertook to carry out a policy of opening public lands to private developers, a cause he had long championed as head of the Mountain States Legal Foundation. Among the earliest beneficiaries of this largesse were three major oil companies that had been contributors to Watt's legal organization.[49] Watt's concept of the national interest was revealed in his cozy relationship with oil and coal companies, lending departmental assistance to the American Petroleum Institute in the conduct of a survey that was intended to prove that oil drilling is no threat to wildlife, authorizing a coal leasing program that the General Accounting Office found to have cost the federal government $100 million in lost revenue; and a federal judge was led to declare that Watt had exceeded his constitutional authority when he issued coal leases in North Dakota despite a House Interior Committee order to postpone that action.[50]

When this authoritarian secretary defended his policy of serving special interest groups by disparaging his opponents for seeking the same "centralized planning and control of society" as the Nazis in Germany and communists in Russia, calls for his resignation came from many quarters.[51] Watt's subsequent "truth campaign," undertaken to prove his dedication to conservation, was highlighted by such falsifications as a claim that "the governors of the West fully support everything we're doing," a statement that was contradicted by a nine-governor criticism of his land-sale policy and written complaints from Governors Richard D. Lamm of Colorado and Toney Anaya of New Mexico.[52] His further assertion that he had the "full support of Congress on all issues" was followed a few months later by a formal resolution, introduced in the Senate by West Virginia Senator Robert C. Byrd, stating that "the President should, without delay, request the resignation of Secretary James Watt."[53]

Ultimately, Watt's basic approach to government was revealed to be that of a religious fundamentalist. In May 1983 he warned the students at Jerry Falwell's Liberty Baptist College that the government was threatened by "the enemies of liberty and freedom here in America, God's chosen place," and declared that "we who have committed our lives to Christ want to revolutionize the world for Him."[54] This was the same committed Christian who later defended his selection of an advisory panel by remarking that he had given the group balance by including "a black, a woman, two Jews and a cripple."[55] His subsequent—and only known—apology was expressed in a letter sent to President Reagan, rather than to those he had slurred. This final display of Watt's concept of the Christian ethic was more than the administration could endure, although his resignation—like those of most disgraced Reagan appointees—was received by the president with praise for "an outstanding job" and for Watt's "dedication to public service." In an ironically accurate judgment, the president concluded his letter with the prediction that "his accomplishments as Secretary of Interior will long be remembered."[56]

Justice Department

For a law-and-order administration, the number of lawbreakers in the Department of Justice was particularly disturbing, although no evidence of distress at this situation was ever evinced by President Reagan. Nevertheless, the deputy chief of the department's Public Integrity Section acknowledged concern about the unusual number of cases in which both prosecutors and FBI agents were found guilty of what he characterized as "casual betrayal, with no great agonizing."[57] This comment was unrelated to the performance of Attorney General Edwin Meese during the Iran-Contra affair, or the troubles he had experienced before being moved to the Justice Department from his earlier post in the White House.

Labor Department

The head of the Occupational Safety and Health Administration, Robert A. Rowland, was charged with participating in the application of regulations affecting companies in which he held more than $1 million in stock. Rowland resigned his post even though the Office of Government Ethics, in characteristic fashion, found no conflict of interest. He received Secretary of Labor Brock's blessing "for his unflagging commitment and tireless effort on behalf of the president," an assessment that said as much about the president's indifference to the ethical behavior of his officers as it did about the Labor Department's own standards.[58]

Until late in Reagan's second term, OSHA was little feared by industry, having shown no enthusiasm for enforcement of regulations to protect the health and safety of workers. Complaints from Congress fell on deaf ears until the president nominated Robert E. Rader, Jr. to the Occupational Safety and Health Review Commission, which hears appeals against OSHA citations. A Texas lawyer, Rader had made a career of advising industrial clients to block OSHA inspections, even when backed by warrants. On one occasion he was fined by a federal court for misrepresenting the facts in defense of a client. Appointment of so dedicated an opponent of OSHA offended even Republican members of the Senate committee that reviewed his qualifications.

As a result, Rader's nomination was rejected by a committee controlled by a Republican majority.[59]

State Department

Some of Reagan's diplomatic appointees showed no greater regard for ethics than their counterparts in administrative agencies. The well-known activities of Reagan's first ambassador to the Vatican, William W. Wilson, will be discussed elsewhere. In a less critical area, this former financial advisor of the president refused to relinquish his position on the boards of directors of two major corporations, as required of all federally appointed officials. Because of his long and close friendship with the president, the State Department granted him an exemption that had not been accorded even to Secretary Shultz. When Wilson resigned as ambassador to the Vatican, he left behind charges of attempted intervention in two international criminal investigations and a record of having failed to submit—before, during and after his ambassadorship—the financial disclosure statements required by law.[60]

Reagan's ambassador to Switzerland, Faith Ryan Whittlesey, felt equally free of department regulations. Some $80,000 of the funds intended for entertaining officials of the country to which she was assigned were spent, instead, on parties for the president's friends and cabinet members. In staffing her office, she appointed to a $62,400-job that called for the skills of a trained foreign service officer the completely unqualified son of one of her "contributors." Administration acceptance of this approach to diplomatic practice was demonstrated by Attorney General Meese—one of Whittlesey's occasional guests—who "found no evidence" of wrongdoing by the ambassador, and who rejected the demands of both Democratic and Republican members of the House Foreign Affairs Committee to appoint an independent counsel to investigate her performance.[61]

U.S. Information Agency

In the free-wheeling, luxurious style so beloved of his millionaire friends, Reagan's California buddy Charles Z. Wick asserted in 1981 that the high-living, party-going routine of the new administration provided enjoyable entertainment for the country's economically deprived, comparing the Washington extravaganza with the performances of Hollywood stars who gave so much pleasure to the unemployed during the depression of the 1930s.[62] Not content with the rich living he could personally afford, once he was appointed director of the International Communications Agency (later the USIA), Wick did not hesitate to tap the public till for extraordinary expenses, some merely indiscreet, others completely illegal.

Where questions of legality overlapped those of ethics, Wick was equally unconcerned. Secretly taping telephone conversations to and from a variety of locations—including Florida, one of thirteen states in which taping without permission of the other party is a felony—Wick initially denied recording conversations with government officials and later acknowledged that he had done so only for part of 1983. Given the lie on both counts by records that revealed secret taping through 1982, as well as calls to White House Chief of Staff James A. Baker III in 1983, Wick offered no apology for having ignored the written warning about this practice sent to him by his general counsel in 1981. Rather, he could take comfort in President Reagan's dismissal of Wick's actions as mere forgetfulness, and his assurance that Wick was to stay on the job regardless.[63]

Following the president's example, Wick staffed his agency with so many friends that the professional staff of USIA protested, in an open letter, the director's appointment of "more than four times" the number of political appointees ever hired previously. In such an atmosphere it is not surprising that the agency's radio service, Voice of America, was subsequently found to have been used for private business dealings by a number of employees, including a gold-trading operation by two producers of its programs.[64]

U.S. Postal Service

Historically a haven for patronage, the public might have expected something better from the Postal Service under a president so devoted to professional integrity and political morality. But neither the president nor his Office of Government Ethics found any cause for action against members of the Postal Service Board of Governors, whose vice-chairman was convicted of contract swindling and whose chairman was found to have intervened in the service's management to have a lucrative contract awarded to a client of his private accounting firm.[65] Not until prison gates had closed behind the vice-chairman, Peter E. Voss, did the Postal Service board adopt a code of ethics that expressed the novel notion that moral principles take precedence over loyalty to friends and political parties.[66]

*   *   *   *   *

Most significant in the pattern of what came to be known as sleaze in government operations is the plethora of evidence that the ethical level of the White House staff was no higher than that of lesser members of the administration.[67] Reagan's longtime friend and associate Edwin Meese offers a case in point.

Through most of his first four years in office, President Reagan relied upon Meese as his man-in-charge in the White House. In a three-page listing of presidential assistants, Meese's name led all the rest.[68] During that four-year period Meese sought loans ranging from $15,000 to $60,000 from people who were subsequently appointed to positions in the federal government. When, in 1984, Meese was nominated to the position of attorney general of the United States, questions regarding the propriety of his actions in connection with these and other matters were raised in the nomination hearings held by the Senate Judiciary Committee.[69] Shortly thereafter an independent counsel was appointed to determine "whether a federal criminal law had been violated" by Meese in any of the incidents considered by the judiciary committee. In each of the eleven inquiries, Counsel Jacob A. Stein found no evidence of criminal activity or intent.[70] Stein emphasized, however, that his assignment did not call for him to comment on "the propriety or the ethics" of Meese's conduct, nor to evaluate his "fitness for public office." At almost the same time, but not revealed until months later, the staff of the Office of Government Ethics found that Meese had violated federal ethics regulations on at least two occasions, an opinion that was reversed by the director of that office, David H. Martin.[71]

Prior to this revelation, a considerable segment of the American press had concluded that although Meese's activities may have been legal, many were ethically indefensible. Thirty-seven newspapers, representing every geographical area of the country and every shade of opinion except the far right, advised editorially against the appointment of Meese to the nation's highest law-enforcement post, describing the nominee in such terms as "Crony-General," and though "not a crook," guilty of "ethical blindness."[72]

Undeterred by widespread criticism of Meese's performance, President Reagan resubmitted his nomination on January 3, 1985,[73] ultimately winning Senate approval of his choice. Meese's appointment was followed by further revelations of ethical blindness, including a belated acknowledgment by the Office of Government Ethics that he had failed to abide by government regulations in setting up a limited blind partnership in 1985.[74] Meese also neglected to include in his 1985 statement of investments one that he had placed with a consultant closely tied to the infamous Wedtech Corporation.[75] Claiming never to have discussed Wedtech with his financial advisor, Meese was nevertheless tied to the rise of that company through friends like E. Robert Wallach and Lyn Nofziger, who were instrumental in securing for the company a series of lucrative, no-bid military contracts.[76] Finally, Meese's refusal to permit an independent counsel investigation of two former Justice Department officials on charges of false testimony in an EPA case led even administration stalwart Representative Henry J. Hyde to observe that the attorney general didn't seem to understand that an independent counsel should be independent of the attorney general in determining when an investigation is necessary.[77]

As allegations of impropriety continued to plague the administration,

Meese requested that a special prosecutor be appointed to investigate the charges against him. But no sooner had a federal judge authorized special prosecutor James C. McKay to extend his investigation of Lyn Nofziger to include Edwin Meese, than the latter challenged as unconstitutional the law that provides for special prosecutors.[78]

Meese was not the only White House aide infected by the sleaze virus. Special presidential assistant Thomas C. Reed resigned his post in 1983, facing accusations of insider-trading in securities. Acquitted of criminal charges for lack of positive proof that inside knowledge of his father's company permitted him to turn a $3,000 investment into a $427,000 profit in two days, Reed nevertheless acknowledged backdating documents, signing others' names to stock-option transfer instruments, and giving false information to SEC investigators of his investment coup. Never losing the confidence of President Reagan, who was "thoroughly familiar" with the problem, according to White House spokesman Larry Speakes, Reed finally placated the SEC by giving up the profit.[79]

Unlike Reed's sleight-of-hand maneuvering, which occurred entirely in the private sector, the unethical practices of Reagan's political adviser, Franklyn ("Lyn") C. Nofziger ran afoul of the Ethics in Government Act for lobbying his former government associates on behalf of private clients less than a year after leaving federal service. His attempts to use his influence in executive offices were directed principally toward improving his clients' chances of gaining lucrative government contracts. Letters like those in which he sought assistance for Wedtech from White House counselors Edwin Meese and James E. Jenkins provided evidence of such illegal activities for which Nofziger was indicted in 1987 and found guilty by a federal district court in 1988.[80] After Reagan retired from the presidential office, two of his appointed judges, in a 2 to 1 appellate court decision, voided Nofziger's sentence on the grounds that the statute under which he had been prosecuted was "ambiguous" as to whether proof of "criminal intent" was required for conviction. In effect, the court said that anyone who insisted that he really didn't intend to break the law—as Nofziger had repeatedly stated—could not be prosecuted under the Ethics in Government Act. The charges of illegal lobbying that had induced the district court to impose a 90-day jail sentence and a $30,000 fine lost Nofziger no respect at the presidential office. Long after he had come under investigation, the White House was taking telephone calls for Nofziger and forwarding messages to his unlisted private number.[81]

Richard V. Allen's improprieties seem almost insignificant compared to those of other members of Reagan's White House staff. Designated by Reagan as his first national security adviser, Allen was attacked, even before the 1980 election, for his earlier lobbying on behalf of Japanese and Portuguese clients, reputedly using as leverage his employment as a White House adviser to President Nixon.[82] Withdrawing temporarily to avoid becoming an election issue, Allen returned to be appointed assistant to the president for national security affairs in January 1981. In that post he was careless enough to accept a $1,000 "gift" from Japanese journalists for arranging an interview with Nancy Reagan. When the money was discovered in a White House safe, where Allen said he put it and forgot all about it, the seeming "safe of influence" created a scandal that prompted Allen to resign. Accepting Allen's resignation "with deep regret," President Reagan assured his friend that he was leaving "with my confidence, trust and admiration for your personal integrity and your exemplary service to the nation."[83]

Far more serious were the depredations of one of Reagan's most intimate associates, Michael K. Deaver, deputy chief of staff and assistant to the president. Deaver's credentials as a Madison Avenue ethicist were established early in his association with Reagan. As Deaver's partner, Peter Hannaford, says in his admiring portrait of Ronald and Nancy Reagan, "Deaver and Hannaford, Inc., opened for business Monday, January 6, 1975, and, along with it, private citizen Ronald Reagan's new office," which was part of the suite rented by D & H in Los Angeles' Tishman Building.[84] Private citizen Reagan was then ex-governor of California and prospective candidate for president of the United States.

Hannaford describes in detail the services his firm provided its principal client, including merchandising Reagan's lectures and newspaper column and arranging his travel program. With the assistance of Richard Allen, Deaver and Hannaford laid out a round-the-world trip for Reagan in 1978. An important stop was Taiwan, whose government was then paying D & H $5,000 a month to represent its interests in Washington, a fact Hannaford neglected to mention in his book.[85] Two years later, newly elected President Reagan appointed Deaver as one of his top three assistants. Only presidential counselor Meese and Chief of Staff James A. Baker, III outranked Deputy Chief of Staff Deaver.

At the White House Deaver continued to provide the services he had made available to private citizen Reagan, planning and overseeing his tours, contacts, summit meetings, etc. That he was not above profiting personally from his high position, even on a small scale, was revealed when, in the course of scheduling the president's trip to the Bonn economic summit in the spring of 1985, he also arranged to purchase for himself an expensive German BMW at a 20 percent discount from the price paid by other American tourists. Some time later a reporter asked the president about the propriety of a White House aide using his official position to negotiate such favored treatment. Reagan's response might have come from any party hack accustomed to using public office as a means of self-enrichment. This was the exchange:

> Q. Mr. President, do you think it's appropriate for Mr. Deaver and the others to have taken a discount on those cars?
> A. Now that's another question that doesn't have to deal with the farm problem {the main subject of the press conference}.
> Q. Well, would you nod or shake your head?
> A. But you're talking about something that has gone on for a great many years, that exists in our embassies in all other countries. It's a standard practice that's been used for many, many years.
> Q. So, you see nothing wrong with what he did, sir?
> A. No.[86]

With Reagan's blessing, Deaver left government service in the spring of 1985 to set up a new consulting firm, Michael K. Deaver and Associates, whose principal asset was its owner's influence in federal offices. Major government contractors and foreign governments rushed to secure the advantages of what was referred to simply as "access" to policy-making individuals in the Reagan administration. Admitting later to having been "kind of stupid" in flaunting his close personal association with the president and other high officials in the executive branch, Deaver nevertheless professed innocence of any breach of ethics, or of the law that says former federal officers may not, for a year after leaving the government, act as lobbyists before the very agencies they worked with.[87] Others looked at the list of Deaver's clients, which included the governments of Canada, Saudi Arabia and South Korea, and giant federal contractors like Boeing and Rockwell, and asked why these organizations should pay Deaver hundreds of thousands of dollars annually if not for his ability to walk into any federal office— including the Oval Office of the White House—to present their case in a way unavailable to the average citizen. Criticism ranged from demands by members of Congress for appointment of an independent counsel to investigate possible breaches of the Ethics in Government Act, to an acknowledgment by Norman Ornstein, resident scholar at the strongly pro-Reagan American Enterprise Institute, that Deaver had "at least abused the spirit if not the letter of the law."[88]

Down to his indictment in May 1986, Deaver relied on the support of a president who told reporters when the story broke a month earlier, "I have the utmost faith in the integrity of Mike Deaver." As to the charges of illegal influence-peddling, Reagan said, "I think maybe the criticism is just because he's being darned successful, and deservedly so."[89] Nevertheless, Republican members of a House committee joined their Democratic colleagues in approving unanimously a request that the independent counsel extend his examination of Deaver's activities to include the question of "perjury, false statements and obstruction" of that committee's investigation.[90]

By this time, President Reagan had grown more cautious in responding to questions about Deaver's use of White House influence, saying, "It's a little difficult for me to speak to this right now because this is now before the Justice Department and under investigation." He added, however, "I think it is well for us to note that he was the one who asked for an investigation and a special investigator, which I think shows his confidence in his innocence."[91] Deaver had, indeed, demanded that an independent counsel be appointed to investigate the allegations against him. And like Meese, when the investigation assumed threatening proportions, Deaver challenged the constitutionality of the prosecutor's appointment.[92] Rebuffed by the courts, Deaver was forced to stand trial for violation of the Ethics in Government Act. Convicted of perjury on December 16, 1987 for lying about his lobbying, Deaver ultimately withdrew his appeal of the sentence that ordered him to pay a fine of $100,000 and perform 1,500 hours of community service.[93]

A less lucrative traffic in access to the White House was carried on by David C. Fischer, one of the many special assistants to the president. Unable to command the six- and seven-figure contracts enjoyed by Deaver, Fisher used his White House connection to negotiate payments of $20,000 a month for arranging meetings between the president and wealthy contributors to the Nicaraguan Contras. This was revealed in the course of the Iran-Contra hearings when committee documents showed that Fischer left the White House for a job as consultant to Contra fund-raising organizations but continued to work hand-in-hand with David L. Chew, staff secretary and deputy assistant to the president.[94]

*   *   *   *   *

If President Reagan was serious about maintaining a high moral level in all areas of his administration, it might be expected that he would have insisted on rigid enforcement of the Ethics in Government Act, both by his own office and by the Office of Government Ethics. As the record of his immediate associates indicates, those worthies had as little regard for ethical standards as their colleagues in the executive departments and agencies. Nor did the Office of Government Ethics exhibit any of the characteristics of a watchdog after Reagan installed his own director, although its responsibilities under the law were clearly defined to include monitoring and investigating compliance with the Ethics in Government Act and ordering "corrective action on the part of agencies and employees which the Director of the Office of Government Ethics deems necessary."[95]

The director Reagan inherited from the Carter administration, J. Jackson Walter, resigned in disgust after tangling with presidential assistant Richard V. Allen, Attorney General William French Smith, and CIA director William J. Casey over their reluctance to submit acceptable financial statements. Although he won one battle when he refused to give the agency's O.K. to Attorney General Smith's financial disclosure statement until that cabinet officer had returned a $50,000 fee he had received from a private company, Walter found that, in general, "it's hard to make a big decision stick in this town, because someone is always trying to tarnish the decision-maker." By August 1982 he was ready to call it quits, and President Reagan was free to appoint a successor whose attitude would reflect that of the administration.[96] His success in picking the "right" candidate was pointed up by Representative Gerald E. Sikorski (D, Minn.) who in 1986 charged Reagan appointee David H. Martin with having failed to bring a single federal employee to book for ethical violations in the three years that he had been director of the Office of Government Ethics.[97] Pleading inability to take action against a presidential appointee, even when the record showed that a deputy budget director had attempted to influence an Energy Department enforcement case against his family's oil company, Martin finally—after charges of financial impropriety against Attorney General Edwin Meese had been publicly aired for months—dared to report that Meese had failed to comply with the Ethics in Government Act by not reporting the securities held by his limited blind partnership.[98] Chastised by the attorney general's public relations officer for having supported "a cheap shot" by the congressman who had revealed Martin's evaluation, the ethics director did not again challenge the action of any high-level Reagan official.

President Reagan's own contribution to the rules of ethical behavior was, if anything, a negative one. His administration began with an effort to water down the 1977 Foreign Corrupt Practices Act;[99] it celebrated the Constitutional bicentennial by "selling" to the American Broadcasting Company the exclusive right to televise every presidential action during the July 4 Liberty Weekend activities;[100] and the president himself permitted his laudatory remarks to William Buckley's *National Review* staff to be used in the commercial solicitation of subscriptions to that journal.[101]

Observing this Madison Avenue approach to the presidency, one can't help wondering what happened to Reagan's purported aim of achieving the highest ethical level in government. It would seem, rather, that he came to accept Irving Kristol's view that the post-Watergate clamor for morality in public service is incompatible with the realities of political life.[102] Yet, when NBC's Andrea Mitchell asked the president about the ethics of Republican staffers who stole Carter's briefing book to prepare Reagan for the 1980 debate, Reagan evaded the question twice, and then said that he deplored the commonly accepted double standard in politics and that politics "should be above reproach . . . there shouldn't be unethical things done [even] in campaigns."[103]

The demand that those in politics "should be above reproach" is seen to be rhetoric when compared with Reagan's reaction to charges of unethical conduct leveled at his own appointees. Convinced that anyone he selected for federal employment was a person of impeccable moral character, he stoutly defended every appointee charged with misconduct, no matter what the evidence to the contrary. He dismissed out of hand the "wild charges and accusations" against William J. Casey, asserting that they had "no substantiation behind them."[104] He avoided any comment about Rita Lavelle's conviction in a federal court, but insisted that "not one single allegation" had been proven against Lavelle's boss, Anne Gorsuch Burford.[105] When the independent counsel reported "no evidence of criminal activity" by Edwin Meese, Reagan ignored the further comment that counsel was offering no opinion as to Meese's ethics or fitness for office and hailed the report as complete vindication of the "honor of a just man."[106] Of his friend of 25 years, Reagan turned a blind eye to Deaver's dealings with other members of the White House, saying, "I've known him probably longer than anyone else in the administration . . . and Mike has never put the arm on me or sought anything or any influence from me since he's been out of government."[107]

In some cases Reagan offered no comment about charges of unethical conduct by his friends and associates. But he expressed his appreciation for their loyal support of his administration in other ways. Thomas C. Reed's resignation as special assistant to the president was followed by his appointment as vice-chairman of the president's Commission on Strategic Forces.[108] Faith Ryan Whittlesey gave up her post as ambassador to Switzerland to take the position of assistant to the president for public liaison.[109]

Reagan's see-no-evil-hear-no-evil-speak-no-evil policy with respect to his associates was discarded only when one of them disloyally revealed the weakness of one of his most cherished programs or ideals. David Stockman's post-employment recollection of the failure of Reagan's economic policy was dismissed as worthless by the president, who admitted he had not read the book and had no intention of reading it because, he said, "I don't have too much time for fiction."[110]

Reagan's final effort to support the claim that his administration had "a very high moral limit" came in the waning days of his presidency. Faced with a bill that would have strictly curbed influence-peddling by lobbyists who traded on the contacts they made when they worked for the federal government, he pocket-vetoed the act. He rejected this reform measure even though it contained—at his own insistence—a provision that would apply the new ethical standards to members of Congress as well as officials in the executive branch.[111]

CHAPTER 3

Economist

"I cannot believe that we should open the door to government interference with regard to the individual's right to the disposition of his own personal property. Because once that door is opened, government has been granted a right that endangers the very basis of individual freedom, the right to own and the right to possess." [1]

THERE WAS A TIME WHEN RONALD REAGAN MADE A POINT OF SLIPPING into his public speeches a reference to his bachelor's degree in economics. During the 1980 campaign for the Republican nomination for president, George Bush put something of a damper on that boast with his derisive characterization of Reagan's theories as "voodoo economics." This was dismissed as campaign rhetoric after Reagan won the nomination and took Bush to his bosom as his vice-presidential running mate.

After ascending to the presidency, Reagan tended to avoid allusions to his training in economics, except when addressing non-critical audiences like those at the 1984 London Economic Summit conference or at the dedication of a new General Motors plant. [2] He was well advised to play down his expertise in this area, as even the most cursory examination of his credentials reveals that Reagan devoted no more time to his college studies—including his major subject—than was necessary to get the C grade required for "eligibility for outside activities," principally football. Indeed, his professor of economics and sociology later observed that he had been forced to give Reagan a passing grade simply because the young man's photographic memory permitted him to regurgitate textbook material on demand. [3]

Given his belief that property rights are the most basic of all human freedoms, Reagan's view of the most desirable economic pattern for the

43

American people—or any other people—comes as no surprise. His ideas in this area were strengthened by his conviction that the welfare of the U.S. is the key to freedom and security the world over. In his first major political speech (in support of Barry Goldwater's presidential candidacy) Reagan said: "There can be no security anywhere in the free world if there is not fiscal and economic stability within the United States."[4] He did not change this position in all the years that followed.

The economic hash that ultimately came to be known as Reaganomics was an attempt to combine such diverse views as those of Milton Friedman, Arthur Laffer, Martin Feldstein and supply-side congressman Jack Kemp. Milton Friedman's concept of the good society Reagan could accept wholeheartedly, stressing as it does the belief that uninhibited freedom in economic activity is basic to all other freedoms and permits each individual to reach the highest level of achievement of which he or she is capable. Equally appealing to Reagan was the simplistic truism of the so-called Laffer Curve: the supply-side rule that declares the ideal income tax rate to be somewhere between zero, which produces the government no income, and a 100 percent tax which destroys initiative and produces little or no revenue.

Accepting as a compliment the popular designation of his program as Reaganomics, the president frequently harked back to the Friedman bible, Adam Smith's eighteenth-century treatise on *The Wealth of Nations*. Basic to the Smith-Friedman analysis is a system of "voluntary exchange" of goods and services in which "no external force, no coercion, no violation of freedom is necessary to produce cooperation among individuals, all of whom can benefit."[5] The external coercive force to which Friedman refers is, of course, government.

The liberal use of quotations from Adam Smith is most persuasive to the 99.44 percent of American readers whose knowledge of *The Wealth of Nations* is limited to the selective bits and pieces offered in Friedman's book *Free to Choose*. What Friedman omits in his explanation of Smith's thesis are the severe limits of the so-called voluntarism or free-exchange system that Smith himself pointed out 200 years ago. In the absence of government restraint, Smith said, as between employees and employers, "it is not difficult to foresee which of the two parties must, upon all ordinary occasions, have the advantage in the dispute, and force the other into compliance with their terms." He goes on to say that as a result of their disadvantage, the workers "are desperate men, who must either starve, or frighten their masters into immediate compliance with their demands."[6] In a later discussion of the opposing aims of different elements of society, Smith makes the following observations:

> The interest of the dealers, however, in any particular branch of trade or manufacture, is always in some respects different from, and even opposite to,

that of the public. To widen the market and to narrow the competition, is always the interest of the dealers. To widen the market may frequently be agreeable enough to the interest of the public; but to narrow the competition must always be against it, and can serve only to enable the dealers, by raising their profits above what they would naturally be, to levy, for their own benefit, an absurd tax upon the rest of their fellow-citizens.[7]

Aware of the repeated efforts of the manufacturers and traders to have their practices legitimized by being enacted into law, Smith issued the following warning:

The proposal of any new law or regulation of commerce which comes from this order, ought always to be listened to with great precaution, and ought never to be adopted till after having been long and carefully examined, not only with the most scrupulous, but with the most suspicious attention. It comes from an order of men, whose interest is never exactly the same with that of the public, who have generally an interest to deceive and even to oppress the public, and who accordingly have, upon many occasions, both deceived and oppressed it.[8]

Notwithstanding these warnings about the dangers of uninhibited economic freedom by his favorite philosopher, Friedman insists that this is the path to follow in order to achieve the highest level of freedom in the political as well as the economic sphere. Ironically, he cites Hong Kong as "perhaps the best example" of an unimpeded free-enterprise society, having "no tariffs or other restraints on international trade . . . no government direction of economic activity, no minimum wage laws, no fixing of prices. The residents are free to buy from whom they want, to sell to whom they want, to work for whom they want."[9] The irony is that, far from leading to the ultimate in political freedom, Hong Kong's "progress" has been achieved as a Crown Colony of Great Britain. As such, it is ruled by a crown-appointed governor, without the inconvenience of elections that would permit the citizens of this Garden of Eden to be "free to choose" their own legislative and executive policy-makers. Beyond that, the Friedman measure of the good society takes no account of such simple things as living conditions. Hong Kong may indeed boast the highest per capita income of any country in Asia, but that statistical average has little meaning to "a million homeless in huts on the hills, without water or sanitation, and others on rooftops where space costs a little money to rent, [nor to] thousands of pavement-dwellers for whom it costs money even for a space to lie on."[10] Add such other quality-of-life factors as "a voluntary but not free" educational system, inadequate health and hospital services except for those who can afford expensive private clinics, and "a wide-open laissez-faire outlook in which to get away with as much money as possible is so evidently the credo of the successful that old [Chinese] virtues like honesty quickly fall victim."[11] And, finally, as if to anticipate the 1997 transfer of the colony back to China, a law passed in 1987 by the Legislative Council of this eastern paradise proposed both fines and imprisonment for publishing "false news which is likely to alarm public opinion or disturb public order."[12]

Arthur Laffer joined in the praise of Hong Kong for its "low taxes and rapid economic growth," adding as a clincher, "and it has fiscal solvency." As this comment suggests, Laffer's first consideration is tax policy, which should be based on the Laffer Curve. But as Leonard Silk has pointed out, neither Laffer's evidence nor his assumptions about how to apply his formula to specific situations were accepted by other economists in Reagan's own camp—including Alan Greenspan, George Shultz, Arthur Burns and (did Reagan notice?) Milton Friedman.[13]

*   *   *   *   *

In accepting the basic, if somewhat conflicting, principles of Milton Friedman, Arthur Laffer and Jack Kemp, Reagan embraced a doctrine that one commentator likened to the notion that the world is flat.[14] He wished to free the individual from the shackles of big government, with its high taxes, unnecessary spending, and bureaucratic intrusion into the activities of business and personal life, and he insisted that all this could be accomplished by removing government from almost every aspect of economic life and permitting the "magic of the marketplace" to control the destinies of us all. What Reagan failed to recognize was that neither the American people nor the people of other countries are willing to return to the days when the world was flat; that the well-being of tens of millions of people cannot be left to the tender mercies of the marketplace; and that government is the only means by which effective protection can be provided for the less affluent and less powerful. However, these were not the issues that were put to the electorate in 1980.

Against the prospect of a continuation of President Carter's policies, which were associated with rising inflation, mounting budget deficits and a feeling of helplessness in dealing with the hostage situation in Iran, Reagan offered a program of lower taxes, reduced government controls and spending, a balanced budget, and a revitalized defense establishment that would take no nonsense from either Iran or the Soviet Union.

Reagan's sweeping election victory convinced him that the country at large supported all aspects of his program. In fact, like most recent American presidents whose election has depended on support from a minority of an electorate that now rarely exceeds 60 percent of those eligible to vote, Reagan was put into office by less than 28 percent of all qualified voters.[15] Public opinion polls taken both before and after the election indicate that Reagan was supported in his proposals to cut taxes, increase defense, balance the budget, and reduce welfare expenditures. On the other hand, a majority favored a return to wage and price control—the very opposite of Reagan's concept of government non-interference in the marketplace. Moreover, given a choice between a balanced budget and large tax cuts, the majority indicated they preferred the former. Finally, more than 60 percent opposed cuts in federal funds for education and health care, while over 70 percent favored reducing the amount Reagan would spend on foreign economic and military aid.[16]

Never one to consider evidence that his mandate was not all-encompassing, Reagan sent Congress a budget message that assumed public approval of every aspect of his economic program.[17] Implementation of the grand plan was left to the director of the Office of Management and Budget, David Stockman, who embraced supply-side economics enthusiastically and whose "anti-spending ideology meant that the tax cuts could be paid for under any economic forecast."[18] It was this assumption that marked the plan for failure from the start, for as many observers—including Stockman—warned, success of the supply-side element of the "Reagan Revolution" depended on massive cuts in spending to match the deep cuts in income taxes.

The program so carefully crafted by David Stockman, Jack Kemp, Jude Wanniski and Arthur Laffer began with Reagan's promised tax cut. As Stockman pointed out later, this was "the side of the doctrine that had to do with giving to the electorate, not taking from it." The "taking" imperative of the revolution neither Reagan nor the Congress was willing to support. For, in Stockman's words, "it meant complete elimination of subsidies to farmers and businesses . . . no right to draw more from the Social Security fund than retirees had actually contributed."[19]

Vigorous as Reagan had been in his early diatribes against farm subsidies and the entire Social Security concept, he was forced to recognize that he was incapable of making these institutions disappear. Equivocating on the farm issue, his election platform called Social Security "one of the nation's most vital commitments to our senior citizens" and pledged "to oppose any attempts to tax these benefits."[20]

Despite the obvious inability of the administration to make good on both revolutionary fronts, when Congress approved most of Reagan's first budget, which featured a sharp income-tax reduction along with cuts in some domestic (non-military) programs, the president assumed that his economic philosophy had been accepted in its entirety. As he signed the 1981 tax bill, he told the assembled reporters: "This represents $130 billion in savings over the next three years and . . . $750 billion in tax cuts over the next five years."[21]

The question raised immediately was how this would affect government receipts. Although the administration's projected income was based on the

Laffer theory that reduced tax rates would bring higher revenues, one reporter noted that the *Wall Street Journal* had forecast much lower government income and greater economic hardship. Reagan evaded the journalist's question about this and said simply that he expected a "sagging economy for the next few months," but that things would pick up when his program really got under way. Two months later he was still insisting that his case for increasing revenues by reducing taxes had been proved by President Kennedy who, he said, had "cut those tax rates and the government ended up getting more revenues because of the almost instant stimulus to the economy."[22] This comparison with a period in which interest rates, unemployment and budget deficits were at only a fraction of their 1981 levels indicates the simplistic approach Reagan took to economics, the subject in which he majored in college. Or perhaps it illustrates his habit of parroting whatever statistics or examples his aides could dig up without knowing whether or not they were appropriate.

Shortly after his triumphant announcement of the Reagan Revolution's opening victory, the president was embarrassed by an article in the *Atlantic Monthly* that revealed the first signs of administrative doubt about the success of Reagan's economic program.[23] Based on a series of interviews conducted by William Greider with David Stockman, the budget director's admission of basic weaknesses in the plan struck the White House like a bolt out of the blue. Asked about the damaging article by reporter Sam Donaldson, Reagan initially said only that he intended to discuss the matter with Stockman. Subsequent reports from the obviously enraged White House staff charged that Stockman had been misquoted, and that although he had been forgiven his indiscretion, he had been "taken to the woodshed" by the president. Reagan later reinforced the distortion-of-the-facts charge, but denied that Stockman had lost credibility over the incident, insisting that "in that *Atlantic Monthly* story he was the victim, not the villain."[24] Five years later, freed from the shackles of White House employment, Stockman wrote: "If I had to pinpoint the moment when I ceased to believe that the Reagan Revolution was possible, September 11, 1981, the day Cap Weinberger sat Sphinx-like in the Oval Office [resisting all defense budget cuts] would be it."[25]

If Reagan was blind to the probable impact of tax cuts on federal revenues, he was equally naive in thinking that he could vastly increase military expenditures and, by savings in other programs, reduce the budget deficit. For years he had denounced successive Democratic administrations for their uncontrolled spending. In 1967 he had charged President Lyndon Johnson with accumulating deficits that "total $50 billion," adding, "the credibility gap is almost as big."[26] Challenging Jimmy Carter in 1980, Reagan's televised acceptance speech to the Republican convention included this criticism:

The head [Carter] of a government which has utterly refused to live within its means and which has, in the last few days, told us that this year's deficit will be $60 billion, dares to point the finger of blame at business and labor.[27]

His further campaign promise of a balanced budget by 1983, reinforced by a pledge to support "a constitutional amendment to limit federal spending and balance the budget except in time of national emergency as determined by a two-thirds vote of Congress" had substantial public support. What Reagan overlooked was evidence that the public was willing to forgo large cuts in taxes for the sake of a balanced budget.[28]

Holding firmly to his tax-cut plan, Reagan retreated from his balanced-budget position in his very first budget message to Congress. The retreat was carefully camouflaged by the letter that accompanied a 159-page document, but although the covering message stressed only budget cuts and expected increases in economic growth, an examination of the detailed report revealed these annual projections: 1982 deficit $45 billion; 1983 deficit $22.9 billion; 1984 surplus $0.5 billion; 1985 surplus $5.9 billion; 1986 surplus $28.2 billion.[29]

By December of 1981, following the uproar over the *Atlantic Monthly* article, Reagan had withdrawn to the point of refusing to answer a direct question as to the probability of a $100 billion deficit in fiscal 1982, saying—at great length—that no one could properly estimate what the deficit would be, and that the goal should not be to arrive at a particular figure but to eliminate "every bit of unnecessary spending."[30]

Early the following year, Reagan acknowledged in his 1982 State of the Union message the fact of decreasing revenues, as well as increasing government costs, but he blamed both on the recession that he said he had inherited from the previous administration.[31] After a sharp drop in fiscal 1983, revenues began to rise, but not nearly enough to balance expenditures or to offer the faintest hope of eliminating the annual deficit.

By the time budget proposals were due for the final year of Reagan's first term, the deficit projected by the administration for fiscal year 1983 (exclusive of "off-budget Federal entities") was $207 billion; for 1984 it was $188 billion, and for 1985 $147 billion.[32] Blaming Congress for its refusal to cut the heart out of most domestic programs, Reagan would not acknowledge that, as a Congressional Research Service study so succinctly put it, the federal deficit was "a product of the 1981 tax cuts, the 1981–82 recession, and big boosts in defense spending." Nor would he face the fact that "most economists believe that these budget deficits are a principal cause of the nation's huge international trade deficit and that, over the course of time, unless substantially reduced, they will undermine the rise in U.S. standards by limiting domestic investment and saddling future Americans with payments on a large foreign debt."[33]

As he approached the end of his second term in 1987, Reagan was obliged to report that the losses anticipated for 1985 and 1986 had been underestimated and had to be corrected to $221 billion and $237 billion, respectively. After that, he promised to reduce the deficit to $147 billion in 1988 and $144 billion in 1989. Two years later, the final budget he submitted on January 9, 1989 omitted one significant item from his recap of the aims set forth in 1980. Recalling that his goals had included reducing taxes, inflation, federal spending and regulation of industry, he neglected to mention his promise to balance the budget. In the same document he showed a deficit of $155 billion for 1988 and an estimated shortfall of $161 billion for 1989.[34]

The extraordinary budgeting imbalance produced under an administration devoted to the principle that government expenditures should never exceed revenues is partly explained by the reluctance of Congress to decimate the many social programs so long and so frequently attacked by Reagan. However, more than one analyst concluded that the administration's continued presentation of deficit budgets was a deliberate attempt to force Congress to cut domestic programs to the bone. Even the idol of the supply-siders, Friedrich von Hayek, was quoted in an Austrian journal as saying he had been told by a Reagan confidant that the only way to pressure Congress into accepting the cuts the president insisted on was to "create deficits so large that absolutely everyone becomes convinced that no more money can be spent."[35] Prior to the publication of Stockman's book, Senator Daniel Patrick Moynihan reported that as early as 1981 the then budget director had admitted to him that the purpose of the ever-increasing deficits was to force Congress to accept severe spending cuts. Stockman denied that this was his intent, but admitted that "they let it happen just the same."[36] However, in the spring of 1985 a New York investment consultant, in an analysis of the 1985 *Economic Report of the President,* came to the same conclusion as Hayek and Moynihan.[37]

This flirting with fiscal disaster may have been less the president's doing than the work of David Stockman and his supply-side budgeters. Stockman revealed after his resignation as budget director that he had been personally responsible for designing the first Reagan budget, "browbeating" cabinet members into accepting cuts that appalled Reagan's department heads. He acknowledged, also, that this first budget set the stage for all that followed, and that President Reagan "was unable to learn anything of the substantive content of his radical new program, or about why individual cuts were so important." Explaining that "the fruits of the Budget Working Group's labors were presented to him [Reagan] in several hour-long blizzards of paper, with justification for each cut boiled down to a half-page explanation," Stockman concluded that when the president "was later called on to justify the cuts, he would remember only that he was making the cut, not why."[38] Nevertheless, both during and after Stockman's reign as budget director, Reagan approved a succession of budgets that added $1.7 trillion to the public debt of $907 billion which had existed when the president took office.[39] Thus, in eight short years, the Reagan Revolution accumulated a debt amounting to more than 2.5 times the total of all deficits experienced by the nation during the previous 200 years—including the enormous deficits incurred in the two world wars, the wars in Korea and Vietnam, and the great depression of the 1930s. Assuming that the federal government must pay an average interest rate of 8 percent on Reagan's portion of the public debt, today's American taxpayers (and very likely their children) will be forced to bear an extra burden of $120 billion annually for the rest of their lives—even after the budget has been balanced![40]

Running for reelection in 1984, Reagan could boast of having made good on two major promises: cuts in personal and corporate income taxes and reduction in the rate of interest and inflation. This introduction to the Reagan Revolution, he said, would ensure attainment of all the goals targeted in his five basic principles by producing more jobs and greater national output, which in turn would increase tax revenues and thereby eliminate budget deficits. He studiously avoided pointing out that a 10 percent reduction in the income tax paid by a $20,000-a-year wage earner with a spouse and two children would provide minuscule relief to that family, whereas a 10 percent reduction in the obligation of an individual whose tax alone would normally be as much as the wage earner's total income would be a substantial amount.[41]

Nor did Reagan take pains to mention in his tax lectures to the public the vastly different impact that Social Security and the various federal excise taxes have on different income groups. The 7.51 percent withheld from a wage-earner's $20,000 income—regardless of the number of his or her dependents—depletes that individual's take-home pay by $1,502 per year, a significant sum for a family at this income level. By comparison, the $75,000 to $100,000 earner suffers little from the loss of the maximum deduction of $2,838.[42]

The same principle applies in the case of taxes on gasoline, tobacco, liquor, telephone service, etc., the very items Reagan agreed to increase in 1983 when it became clear that even by "cooking the books" Stockman could not avoid showing sharply increased deficits for the indefinite future. The burden of indirect taxation was further increased by the 1984 budget which called for "a tax increase of $50 billion per year, on top of the large tax increase he had approved a few months earlier."[43] Yet during this period, in his frequent public speeches on administrative tax policy, Reagan mentioned only the gasoline tax increase which, he said, was necessitated by the deteriorated condition of the nation's highways and bridges.[44] Even the formal budget document avoided any reference to a boost in taxes, explaining the plan in this murky, meaningless language: "The act increases receipts primarily by eliminating unintended benefits and obsolete incentives, and providing mechanisms to increase taxpayer compliance and improve collection techniques."[45] Subsequently, when given an opportunity to renege on his many pre- and post-election promises not to touch the Social Security system that he had previously sought to destroy, Reagan embraced enthusiastically a bill that levied a tax on half of the Social Security benefits of families whose total annual income exceeded $32,000 and single taxpayers having more than a $25,000 income.

As late as July 1984, in an address to the Texas Bar Association, Reagan had said, "no plan will be allowed to reduce the payments to the present recipients of Social Security. This has been my pledge from the very beginning."[46] The tax on Social Security benefits that he approved two years later could readily be justified, but only using a concept which Reagan had consistently and vigorously rejected: ability to pay. Passage of this law was marked by the White House with great fanfare and distribution of handfuls of pens used by President Reagan to sign the various sections of the new statute.[47]

The full impact of indirect taxes was noted in a report of the Federal Reserve Bank of Philadelphia which declared the "significant" tax reductions claimed by the administration to be "illusory," in large part due to offsetting Social Security and indirect taxes.[48] Subsequent reports by both Treasury and congressional economists revealed that under the Reagan tax program the heaviest burden fell on people near the poverty level. Until an adjustment was made in 1986, even those below the poverty level were brought into federal income tax brackets by the 1981 legislation, according to the administration's own Treasury economist, Eugene Steurele.[49] In short, Reagan's notion of equal treatment in the tax area took no account of either ability to pay or responsibility for supporting the established system based on the rewards each individual or organization realized under that system.

Chief beneficiaries of Reagan's tax plan were corporations that were indirectly subsidized. The extent of the giveaway under this system is indicated by a comment made by the American Mining Congress which, as it studied the administration's first tax package in 1981, "pointed out to the Treasury that the administration's business depreciation proposals were so generous that mining firms would not be able to make full use of their percentage depletion reductions."[50] A study of the effect of corporate taxes made four years later listed 40 major companies that not only had paid no federal income taxes from 1982 to 1985, but had collected tax refunds during that period. The Tax Reform Act of 1986 did not alter corporate tax rates, but the effect of the subsequent economic slowdown was to reduce the corporate share of the total tax burden and increase, by the same amount, the share paid by individuals. Both the Treasury Department and the Congressional Budget Office acknowledged that this occurred in the years 1986 to 1989, and both predicted a similar trend through 1992.[51]

A far more impressive accomplishment of the administration was a reduction in the annual rate of inflation from over 10 percent to less than 5 percent. This was accompanied by a drop in the prime rate of interest from a 1981 high of 18.87 percent to a 1986 low of 7.5 percent.[52] Reagan took credit for both achievements, although as he acknowledged when complaining that interest was not coming down fast enough, Paul Volker's Federal Reserve Board was principally responsible for this aspect of the country's fiscal control.

When nervousness about renewed inflation caused both the Fed and the country's major banks to move their interest rates back up in 1987, the prime rate rising from 7.5 to 8.75 percent in less than six months, the president took no notice. In the eight talks on the national economy that he gave during this period he never once referred to the reversal in interest rates.[53] His silence on that subject persisted through the balance of his second term when, by December 1988, the prime rate had risen to 10.5 percent.

Reagan's success in the battle against inflation was not matched by equivalent progress in solving the unemployment problem. "Putting America back to work means putting all Americans back to work," Reagan said in his inaugural address.[54] Already on the rise from its 1979 level of 6.1 million, the number of unemployed reached 8.2 million the year Reagan took office. As that number crept past the 9 million mark, he assured the country that "in the next several years we can create 13 million jobs."[55]

All through this period Reagan addressed the problem not in terms of unemployment, but by referring to the number of people still working. In most years this number did increase, for the simple reason that a growing population creates more customers whose demands require more employees to produce the needed goods and services. However, at times Reagan used figures that were plainly wrong, as when he stated in 1982 that "there are a million people more working than there were in 1980."[56] Only when the tally of people out of work began to recede from its peak of 10.7 million did he start talking about the administration's success in reducing unemployment. Further reductions brought the percentage of unemployed down until, by December 1988, it reached a low of 5 percent. Given the growth in population during that interval, however, a 5 percent rate meant that there were still 6.6 million unemployed, approximately one-half million more than in 1979.[57]

Unrevealed by gross employment statistics are several significant facts that newspapers rarely bother to report. One is that "discouraged workers"—those who have not looked for work during the four weeks prior to a Bureau of Labor Statistics canvass—are not counted as part of the labor force and therefore are not included in the tally of the unemployed. Nor do the totals indicate how many of the employed have only part-time jobs, or the number who have lost good-paying positions and are making do with employment that pays considerably less than necessary to meet home mortgage payments and the spiraling cost of education and medical services. Many of the re-hired were among the 5.75 million workers who in July 1987 sought full-time work but could find only part-time employment. Jobs of this kind rarely offer such fringe benefits as paid vacation and sick leave, medical insurance, or pension rights. Although the BLS regularly reports the number of people in this part-time category, it does not explain the extent of the financial sacrifices that part-time employees incur through loss of fringe benefits. Nor does it always report the number of discouraged workers, who are not counted among the unemployed. However, the January 1989 issue of *Employment and Earnings* reveals that in 1988 there were 5.4 million people who wanted jobs but had given up looking for them.[58]

If one ignores the omission of discouraged workers from official unemployment figures, and if one accepts the implication that a job is a job even if it offers as little as one paid hour a week (the BLS definition of part-time employment is work of from 1 to 35 hours per week) then the gross figures compiled during Reagan's second term would appear to support his claim that Reaganomics had produced, as its namesake had forecast, more than 13 million new jobs. But the implication—again rarely discussed in news reports—that "new" meant "additional" was false. The number of additional jobs created was little more than enough to accommodate the growth in population and the resulting expansion of the labor force. The balance constituted those new jobs that offered employment to the millions who had previously been let go by their employers, particularly during the deep recession of 1982. It was the nature of this new employment that demonstrated the changing character of the American economy. Although the decline in the value of the dollar helped to restore some of the losses in manufacturing brought on by foreign competition, economists considered at least 2 million of the manufacturing jobs lost from 1979 to 1986 as permanent.[59]

Even more significant were studies based on Census Bureau data that showed the extent to which the distribution of low, middle, and high-paying positions had changed from previous years. During the high-tech era from 1963 to 1973, more than 40 percent of all new jobs paid better than $29,600, while those paying less than $7,400 a year accounted for only 20 percent of the total. Jobs in the middle range were the big gainers from 1973 to 1979. But from 1979 to 1985 low-paying positions leaped to more than 40 percent of the total, only slightly below those in the middle range, while high-paying posts accounted for little more than 10 percent.[60]

The president's "safety net" for those unable to reap the benefits of Reaganomics was the Job Training Partnership Act of 1982, which he termed "the centerpiece of federal policy to alleviate long-term unemployment."[61] Even here, the administration's insistence on curtailing expenditures for any program conceived to be "social" in nature made a mockery of the job training program. As early as August 1983, it took a federal court order to force the Department of Labor to release funds for retraining workers who had lost their jobs as a result of foreign competition in the automotive industry—funds that the administration had impounded to prevent their being spent in accordance with the law.[62] A 1986 study of this aspect of the retraining program by the Office of Technology Assessment concluded that "no more than 5 percent of displaced workers," which were estimated to number 3 million, were being served in the first two years of the law's operation. Although the president proudly announced in October 1986 that administration of the job training act had "helped millions of youth and adults," he offered no evidence to support that claim. In all probability, neither he nor his speech-writers had any relevant data on the subject, for as the OTA study observed, "JTPA reporting is minimal."[63]

One result of the massive unemployment of the early 1980s was a sharp increase in the number of people at or below the poverty level. Poverty is not new to this country. Even in periods of widespread prosperity, thousands of families have been unable—certainly not unwilling—to share in the benefits of the affluent society. During his 1928 campaign for the presidency, Herbert Hoover claimed that the U.S. was "nearer to the final triumph over poverty than ever before in the history of any land," and he looked for the day when "poverty will be banished from this nation."[64]

In most respects Reagan's recollection of the depression of the 1930s was a nostalgic one in which he recalled the joys of childhood in the midst of the poverty his family had experienced in pre-depression years. Interestingly enough, that condition did not prevent the family from maintaining an automobile—albeit a secondhand model most of the time—throughout a period in which not one American family in five could boast ownership of a car.[65] Nor was the family's financial condition so serious as to require young Ronnie to share the burden of support with his teenage summer earnings, all of which went into his "college fund." Reagan's four years at Eureka College, paid for in part by a scholarship and in part from his own fund plus earnings from a job he later delighted in describing as "washing dishes in a girls' dormitory," marked him as among only 7 percent of the 18-to-24-year-old group who could afford such an education.[66]

Upon graduation from college in 1932, Reagan was given "the family Oldsmobile" to go job-hunting, and before the year was out he had found employment at a time when 25 percent of the nation's workers were unemployed.[67] But in recounting his depression experience years later, he gave the impression of great personal suffering in statements like this one, made when he was governor of California: "We did not have to make a field trip to the ghetto or the sharecropper's farm to see poverty. We lived it in a great depression."[68] The fact is that Reagan was one of the very lucky young men who not only obtained employment (as a radio sports announcer) within months of his graduation from college, but also, while the depression was still very much in evidence, made good on his college boast that within five years of graduation he would be earning $5,000 per year. When Reagan reached that level of affluence in 1937, the average annual income of working Americans was $1,258.[69]

The first serious attack on indigence was President Lyndon Johnson's "war on poverty," which made limited progress before being dismantled by President Richard Nixon. In 1983 a "perplexed" President Reagan learned from a Census Bureau report that the number of Americans living in poverty had risen to a level equal to that of the years prior to the Johnson program.[70] Though lower relative to the total population than the 17.3 percent reached in 1965, the 14 percent-of-population poor in 1982 totalled 34.4 million, more than 5 million above the peak of the 1960s and 2.5 million above the 1981 figure. Reagan's immediate reaction was to revive the distribution of government-stored cheese—which had been discontinued when dairy interests complained of falling sales—and to appoint a Task Force on Food Assistance to study the problem.

Before the task force could complete its work, an administration view of the situation was offered by the president's chief counselor, Edwin Meese, who declared he knew of no "authoritative figures that there are hungry children." Casting an inadvertent slur on Reagan's favorite method of documentation, Meese scorned the evidence of hunger as "a lot of anecdotal stuff," adding, "I know we've had considerable information that people go to soup kitchens because the food is free, and that's easier than paying for it." Like his boss, he did not identify the source of his information, which was contrary to every report from soup-kitchen operators that flooded into press rooms in the weeks following Meese's remarks. Shortly thereafter, an inkling of one task force member's approach to the problem came with the comment by Dr. George Graham that "blacks are the best-nourished group in the country." Released January 18, 1984, the task force report avoided any such idiocy as that offered by Graham, but it agreed with the president's and Meese's view that "allegations of rampant hunger cannot be documented." The report was immediately challenged by 42 national organizations intimately concerned with the problems of hunger and poverty.[71]

Administrative indifference to the plight of those least able to cope with the problem of economic survival persisted through Reagan's second term. As late as October 1987, and without any public announcement, the associate commissioner for Social Security decreed that the value of any food, shelter or clothing donated by private charities to elderly, blind or otherwise disabled people was to be deducted from their benefits under the Supplementary Security Income program. Only the storm of criticism that erupted when the confidential order was revealed brought cancellation of a directive whose effect would have been to ensure that, as one Catholic charity officer put it, "the more we help people . . . the poorer they will be."[72]

In large part, the change in employment conditions reflected the shift in emphasis from manufacturing to service industries. This trend, which had been observed in the mid-1970s, continued during the Reagan administration when the number of people employed in service industries rose from 17.96 million to 24.27 million, accounting for almost half of the new jobs for which Reagan claimed credit.[73] Employment in some industries, such as advertising, data processing, law, engineering and architecture paid handsomely. A survey of lawyers' salaries made in 1987, for example, revealed that the amount paid beginning lawyers—new law school graduates with no experience whatever—by 250 of the country's largest law firms, ranged from a low of $40,000 to a high of $65,000 a year.[74] But the number of people involved in these high-paying professions was small compared with those engaged in personal service, hotels and motels, recreation centers, nursing and retirement homes, etc. Employees in these latter pursuits were paid on a scale similar to that of clerks in retail trade, who accounted for another 3 million of the 13.5 million job increase from 1980 to 1987 and who, in September 1987 were earning less than $10,000 per year.[75]

As American manufactures declined in the face of foreign competition, more and more American companies moved their manufacturing facilities to countries where labor costs were only a fraction of those at home. A Brookings Institution study explains the rationale for this "international reorganization of production":

The traditional industries have generally been associated with fairly labor-intensive technologies and, because of low wage rates in the third world and the relatively low development cost of establishing a production capability in these older products, these industries have been the leading edge of the burgeoning exports of manufactures produced in developing countries.[76]

American investment in plants abroad has a long history. However, as the Brookings study pointed out, "volume manufacture in foreign locations for re-export to the home market or other export markets is a qualitatively new feature of foreign manufacturing operations that emerged in the late 1960s."

The total value of products assembled abroad for export back to the U.S. rocketed from $1.465 billion in 1969 to $19.534 billion in 1983.[77] Countries like Mexico, which by 1983 had 600 plants employing 150,867 workers in this endeavor, were delighted to assist American companies by allowing "duty-free import of machinery, equipment, and components for processing or assembly within a twenty-kilometer strip along the border, provided that all the imported products were re-exported."[78]

Reagan's response to the economic effects of increasing foreign competition and the flight of American industry to other countries reflects the confusion—and frustration—he felt. A firm believer in free trade, he would have preferred to follow Milton Friedman and consider the subsidies and trade barriers used by other nations as burdens placed upon their own people which amount to "gifts" of lower prices for American consumers. However, he was faced not only with demands for protection of American industries and jobs, but also with a set of facts which challenged Friedman's assumption that if foreign competition caused havoc in the U.S. steel industry, "there need be no net loss of employment and there would be a gain in output because workers no longer needed to produce steel would be available to produce something else."[79] In an aging society, increasingly service-oriented, the "something else" that was being produced was more nursing homes, entertainment, speculative investment and fast-food eating places, none of which registered a "gain in output" that strengthened the nation's economy or improved the quality of employment.

Intent on resisting the protectionist measures demanded by some industries, labor unions, and members of Congress, President Reagan conducted a marathon negotiation with Japan, half-threatening, half-cajoling its ministers into curtailing their exports of cars and television sets. Simultaneously, he attempted to raise domestic farm prices and exports by a series of subsidies that violated every principle he had expressed over the previous three decades. In doing so, he established a subsidy system under which almost 70 percent of government payments went to the country's largest corporate farms, which were already enjoying a profit, while less than 10 percent was given to small operators who represented 72 percent of all farm owners and who, as a group, were earning little money but many news headlines for the number of bankruptcies, foreclosures and suicides.[80]

After a decade of rising prices and, by 1980, the highest level of agricultural exports ever achieved, Reagan felt confident that he could begin to dismantle the system of price supports that had been in existence since the depression of the 1930s. However, the two huge harvests of 1981 and 1982, coming at a time when other countries, as well as the U.S., were heading into a recession, resulted in accumulations of grain that tripled federal expenditures for the price support programs that Congress had insisted on retaining. The administration's response, which Reagan credited to Agriculture Secretary Block and "his team" was a program under which farmers who "divert additional acreage into a soil-conservation use . . . would then be paid in kind from our bulging government surpluses." Facing a major farm disaster, Reagan approved a plan that would not only take millions of acres out of production but would pay the cooperating farmers "in bushels of the same surplus commodity they might otherwise have grown." Always stressing the new and different character of his "initiative," Reagan announced this payment-in-kind (PIK) giveaway as a "good, imaginative program" and "a highly innovative approach that will enhance long-term prospects for recovery in the farm community."[81] Forgotten was his earlier, biting criticism of "the farm mess" created by a policy that, in his usual pseudo-factual fashion, Reagan had described as enabling a farmer to "rent state-owned land in New Mexico for twenty-five cents an acre and immediately apply for and receive $9 an acre from the federal government for not planting the land."[82] The reality of Reagan's agricultural initiative was to remove from production acreage ranging from 78 million acres in 1983 down to 45 million in 1985 and back up to 69 million in 1987, with further raises predicted for the future.[83] The net cost, as measured solely by the president's budget for the Commodity Credit Corporation, rose from $15 billion to over $23 billion in fiscal 1986, and just under that in 1988.[84]

President Reagan's preoccupation with reducing income taxes, slashing social programs, and building the military did indeed alter the character of American life. His pursuit of these three major goals left little but rhetoric to indicate concern for the inequalities of economic opportunity reflected in reports of growing poverty and hunger that persisted throughout his second term.[85] Nor did he acknowledge the growing threat to the country's ecology that was fostered by his insistence that damage to the environment from industrial waste could best be prevented by controls voluntarily exercised by the industries which generate the smoke, toxic chemicals, radiation, etc., that pollute the air we breathe, the water we drink, and the land we build on.

*   *   *   *   *

Reagan's view of controls in general was expressed in a speech to the National Alliance of Business when he said, "Voluntarism is an essential part of our plan to give the government back to the people."[86] Ignoring reports from the congressionally mandated Council on Environmental Quality, he created his own Task Force on Private Sector Initiatives "to promote private sector leadership and responsibility for solving public needs." This action was heralded by a formal executive order.[87] Losing no time appointing members of the task force, and entertaining them in the state dining room at the White House, the president touted the work of this body to reporters, youth groups, civic and religious organizations on 19 occasions in the first year of its operation.[88] And although the president lauded the task force for eliciting a response from the private sector and local governments which he found both "wonderful" and "amazing," he never mentioned receiving a report on its work. Perhaps for that reason, the task force was suddenly replaced by a President's Advisory Council on Private Sector Initiatives, which was to report to the previously established White House Office of Private Sector Initiatives.[89] Appointed for a two-year period, the council met for the last time on June 14, 1985 to receive "C" Flag awards from the president for their "enormous commitment, dedication and patriotism" which he credited with such developments as Bank America's financing of 27 rehabilitation projects in distressed areas, and the South Shore Chamber of Commerce finding jobs for over 1,000 juvenile offenders. This without benefit of any formal reports from the council or other documentation.[90]

While private individuals and organizations were being extolled for their voluntary contributions to the welfare of the nation, the federal departments and agencies responsible for protecting the public interest were doing all in their power to turn that function over to private industry. Deregulation of industry, the public was assured, would reduce production costs which, in turn, would lower consumer prices. However, the measure of success in deregulation, Reagan said, would not be demonstrably lower prices, but "a reduction in the number of pages in the Federal Register"! This inane assertion accompanied the president's announcement that he was establishing a Task Force on Regulatory Relief.[91] Two and one-half years later, task force chairman, Vice-President George Bush, issued his final report, which predicted savings of "up to $150 billion" for producers and—ultimately—consumers.[92]

Evidence has yet to appear that retail price reductions have resulted from such deregulation as was effected by the Reagan administration. On the other hand, volumes of testimony illustrate the way in which deregulation was accomplished either by non-enforcement or by making enforcement a "voluntary" function of industry. As early as April 1982, the EPA's enforcement counsel was relieved of his authority to take any action without prior approval from director Burford's counsel.[93] A year later, when an Interior Department attorney wrote a report that questioned the legality of Secretary Watt's relaxation of protections for wilderness areas, his memorandum was ordered destroyed.[94] After EPA administrator Anne Burford had been forced out of office, Reagan reinstated her as an advisor. When newsmen attempted to question him about this during a talk on environmental problems, their queries were interrupted by White House Deputy Press Secretary Larry Speakes and television lights were turned off—actions not mentioned in the official government report of the event.[95]

Other agencies of the executive branch worked in similar fashion to protect business interests at the expense of the general community. The first emergency rule ever issued by the Reagan administration for the protection of people against corporate interests did not appear until late 1983, when the Labor Department reduced the level of permissible exposure to asbestos in manufacturing and construction operations.[96] This action of the Occupational Safety and Health Administration (OSHA) was an exception to its normal do-nothing policy and was prompted by public outcry at the discovery of thousands of schools and factories with deteriorating asbestos insulation whose fibers were known to cause cancer when inhaled. In the spring of 1985 the congressional Office of Technology Assessment completed a study that charged OSHA with failure to keep abreast of the changing needs in health and safety standards and of ineffectiveness demonstrated by infrequent factory inspections and "fines of less than $200" even for serious violations.[97] This analysis came nine months after Reagan's own administrator of information and regulatory affairs in the Office of Management and Budget has admitted that, after three years in office, "we have not advanced a single detailed proposal of our own for reform of any of the major health, safety or environmental statutes."[98]

Not until the last two years of Reagan's eight-year presidency, when he and his staff began to think about a successor and the kind of record Reagan would leave behind, did EPA evidence a will to enforce the laws under which it functioned.[99] In this apparent turnabout, the president urged Congress in 1986 to renew the "superfund" cleanup legislation that he had opposed up to and including the last previous extension of the act in 1984.[100] In a message to Congress, Reagan boasted of his "enormous national commitment" to environmental quality, and made the patently false claim that "the largest sources of environmental pollution have been controlled, and critical lands protected." He also reiterated his belief that "free markets rather than centralized controls will work to promote environmental health."[101]

Like other administrative agencies, OSHA's "reform" took shape in 1986–87 while congressional elections put Democrats in majority control of the Senate as well as the House. As campaigning for the 1988 presidential election began, OSHA made headlines in 1987 when penalties amounting to hundreds of thousands of dollars (in three cases over $1 million) were imposed on major manufacturers for violations of health and safety regulations and fraudulent record-keeping.[102]

No reduction in the rhetoric of voluntarism and deregulation accompanied these concessions to public anger at the indifference to general welfare shown by Reagan's administrators. The president continued to act and talk as though everything was going according to his master plan. Quoting the annual report of his Council on Environmental Quality, he told Congress:

"Time has tested our policies and programs and our resource managers, both public and private. They appear to have served Americans well." Ignoring the implications of the council's cautious use of the word "appear," Reagan drew his own conclusion: "We can be proud of our environmental achievements."[103]

Had some miraculous turn of events brought Reagan's proposed economic reforms into being in time to affect the budget for his last year in office (fiscal year 1989), the country would have witnessed a presentation of presidential priorities—clearly defined in his 1988 budget—in a new budget of $976.2 billion, with allocations of $312.2 billion for defense, $230 billion for Social Security, and $141.5 billion for interest on the public debt, leaving $292.5 billion for all the programs and functions that in 1988 were budgeted $416.2 billion.[104]

Using the formula of "programmatic changes" proposed in Reagan's 1988 budget as a means of reducing the deficit, the $123.7 billion cut of 1989 would have had to have been divided among these programs, as defined in the 1988 budget:[105]

	1988 Budget	% of Total Cut*	Amount of Cut	1989 Budget
Major Medical	$112.3	23	$28.5	$83.8
Other Mandatory	114.5	24	29.7	84.8
Economic Subsidies & Development	80.9	31	38.3	42.6
Social Programs	44.4	22	27.2	17.2
General Government	34.1	—	—	34.1

*Calculated from 1989 column of "programmatic changes," sec. 2, p. 53 of the 1988 budget.

What Congress would have done with this imaginary 1989 balanced budget is immaterial, as the document actually submitted for fiscal 1989 was similar to that designed for 1988, albeit with a projected addition to the existing debt of only $129.5 billion, compared with the $146.7 billion deficit of the previous year.[106] In fact, despite some 24 years of ranting about the need to mandate a balanced federal budget, Reagan never once offered such a document, even as an alternative plan for Congress and the country to consider.

*   *   *   *   *

Every president tries to maintain a degree of consistency throughout his political career, but few have pursued the image of uncompromising adherence to principle that was the mark of Reagan's term in Washington.

However, notwithstanding his repeated pleas to Congress and the general public to "stay the course" in all aspects of his program, he changed his tune on a number of occasions, although he rarely admitted it. Where once he advocated voluntary assistance among neighbors as a means of solving the unemployment problem, in seeking nationwide support for election to the presidency he acknowledged that a government "safety net" might be required to sustain "the truly needy."[107] His early tirades against the Social Security system and in favor of private pension funds (see his 1964 Goldwater speech, cited earlier) were dropped in 1980 to be replaced by the bold assertion that "Social Security is one of the nation's most vital commitments to our senior citizens {which} we commit the Republican party to first save and then strengthen."[108] His pre-election pledge to "oppose any attempt" to tax Social Security benefits was conveniently forgotten by 1983, when he supported such a tax as part of a package of cutbacks, the most serious of which Congress deleted before amending the Social Security law.[109]

Equally important, but more revealing of Reagan's inability to focus on the true significance of specific fiscal measures, was his double switch on withholding taxes on dividend and interest income. His pre-election stand was unequivocal: "We oppose Carter proposals to impose withholding on dividend and interest income. They would serve as a disincentive to save and invest and create needless paperwork burdens for government, business, industry, and the private citizen. They would literally rob automatic dividend reinvestment programs."[110] After assuming office Reagan became converted to the idea (no longer Carter's) that, in all fairness, dividend and interest "cheaters" should not be permitted to evade taxation as so many had done in the past. He flatly denied that the costs of administration would outweigh the multi-billion-dollar benefit that would accrue to the Treasury by closing this tax loophole, asserting that noncompliance in this area "is costing the government $9 billion a year."[111]

In 1982 Congress passed, and Reagan signed, a law requiring withholding of taxes on dividends and interest. This was followed by a massive savings bank campaign in which millions of depositors were led to believe that they were being subjected to a new tax that would cost them untold amounts of compounded interest. Both White House and congressional courage wilted under the barrage of mail that this campaign produced and Reagan signed the repeal legislation, not only without protest, but without any comment whatever.[112] Significantly, in his scattered references to tax loopholes Reagan did not reveal his own Internal Revenue Service commissioner's view that non-farm businesses were the worst offenders in the realm of tax cheating, which the commissioner estimated cost the federal government $300 billion annually.[113]

Even the sacred realm of tax reduction did not escape revision—often by interpretation. In the face of mounting budget deficits, Reagan urged Congress and the nation to "stay the course" on income tax cuts even as he was considering the various excise taxes mentioned earlier. His 1984 budget revealed the extent of the increases in indirect taxes he either proposed or accepted, including a 125 percent rise in the federal gasoline tax, a "temporary" doubling of the tax on cigarettes, and a tripling of the telephone excise tax.[114] The gasoline tax, which Democrats originally proposed as a source of revenue to create jobs for highway construction and repair workers, Reagan referred to as a "user fee." He approved this levy less than two months after declaring that such a tax would not pass "unless there's a palace coup and I'm overthrown."[115] Not until the 1986 Tax Reform Act was there a move to offset the effect of these regressive taxes on those hovering near the poverty level. This was accomplished by raising the personal exemption and standard deduction to levels which by 1989 would exclude the first $5,000 of income from any tax.

In this area Reagan went a long way toward the goal he had set many years before: a uniform rate for all taxpayers. In the relatively short space of seven years, he convinced Congress to abandon the long-established system of graduated tax rates, and to contract the scale that had a maximum rate of 70 percent for the highest bracket down to a two-level schedule with a minimum tax of 15 percent—ultimately to be phased out—and a maximum of 28 percent, plus a 5 percent levy on a third bracket that varied with the taxpayer's filing status but was never to be applied to income above $149,250.[116] Had Reagan been able to accomplish this without adding to the ever-burgeoning public debt, he would have earned a place in history as an economic miracle worker. However, the impossibility of reaching both goals was foreseen by most economists, including his own onetime chairman of the Council of Economic Advisers, Martin S. Feldstein. And when Feldstein was indiscreet enough to suggest that greater effort be made to reduce the deficit, even if that meant a cut in military spending and/or increased taxes, he was subjected to such public abuse by White House spokesman Larry Speakes that he felt obliged to modify his stand. That retreat only postponed by five months his departure from the council.[117]

Overall, Reagan's approach to the nation's economic problems reflected his poor understanding of the economic world of the 1980s and the changes that had occurred in public attitudes toward the responsibilities of government. In large part this lack of understanding stemmed from the distorted picture of history—of this country and others as well—that he had built up in his mind and to which he clung relentlessly.

CHAPTER 4

Historian

"If you want to know which way to go in the future, you have to know which path you took in the past and where you stepped in a gopher hole along the way."[1]

IT WOULD BE DIFFICULT TO DEMONSTRATE, ON THE PART OF ANY OTHER American president, an ignorance of history equal to that Ronald Reagan exhibited throughout his political career. The least educated presidents of the mid-nineteenth century—Zachary Taylor, Andrew Jackson, and Reagan's "favorite president," Abraham Lincoln—never presumed so much or revealed so little understanding of the country's past and the forces that had shaped its development.

In part, Reagan's ignorance stemmed from a provincialism that transcended politics, having its roots in personal experience which seemed to weigh more heavily in his thinking and his decision-making than the combined wisdom of the rest of the world. That experience, however, provided little guidance in understanding the origins of American politics or the politics of other nations—or, for that matter, the evolution of American institutions and attitudes.

Reagan's irrepressible optimism and acceptance of fantasy in place of fact followed logically from his early reading and his adoration of Horatio Alger-like heroes. That combination gave rise to an outlook he acknowledged at the age of 66 when, shortly before his election as president of the United States, he reminisced: "All in all, as I look back, I realize that my reading left an abiding faith in the triumph of good over evil." As biographer Lou Cannon put it, Reagan's fascination with heroic fiction led him to believe that "the myths which Hollywood promulgated as history became actual explanations of the past." Even Reagan's jokes, which were so important a part of his public presence, reflected the same make-believe approach to life. After being coaxed into running for the governorship of California, when he was asked what kind of governor he expected to be, Reagan quipped, "I don't know, I've never played a governor."[2]

In addition to his long association with the Hollywood world of fiction, Reagan's adult reading habits also help explain his historical illiteracy. By his own admission, he rarely "cracked a book" during his four years in college, except to prepare for an examination. There is little evidence that he found more time for the study of history in later years. Thus, it is hard to imagine anyone dropping in on him at the governor's office in Sacramento, California and finding him immersed in volume three of Douglas Southall Freeman's biography of Robert E. Lee, an experience reported by a journalist who once visited with Senator—later President—Harry Truman.[3] Given his extraordinary isolation from the real world, it is difficult to take seriously Reagan's pontifical admonition to a group of Canadian officials: "Let us always remain realists but never blind to history."[4]

Few of Reagan's critics will fault him for his pride in the progress this country has made, or for his obviously sincere desire to see others benefit from American experience. But rarely has an American president shown the degree of carelessness in the handling of historical facts, that has been such an outstanding feature of Reagan's political life. This is as apparent in his description of American development as it is in his narration of world events.

*   *   *   *

American colonial and revolutionary times Reagan saw through a haze of religious moralism. His pride in the pilgrims' hardiness in attempting to establish a shining "city on a hill" made him oblivious to the intolerance of their leadership, which extended beyond religious belief into the very fabric of political and social life. Americans whose grasp of history is based on more than a casual acquaintance with the facts will blush at Reagan's shallow account of the long and difficult road that the U.S. has traveled to put freedom and equal rights within reach of the majority of its people. His ringing declaration that the founding fathers "brought to all mankind for the first time the concept that man was born free; that each of us has inalienable rights," ignores the fact that the freedom and inalienable rights propounded by the founding fathers were borrowed from the earlier writings of the English philosopher John Locke.[5] His simplistic characterization of revolutionary America glosses over the further fact that "each of us" did not include women, slaves, or indentured servants who, taken together, comprised the great majority of the population down to 1860. Only in passing did he acknowledge the many decades of struggle required—even after slavery had been abolished—for blacks, women, and organized labor to achieve the kind of freedom that had long been regarded as a basic right of the more influential members of society. And despite his claim of lifelong support for equal treatment of these groups, his opposition to constitutional or legislative reforms that would put them on a par with white males and business organizations is a matter of record.

Reagan's concept of states' rights is similarly flawed. His repeated pronouncement that "the federal government did not create the states; the states created the federal government" reveals his superficial knowledge of America's beginnings.[6] The political structure designed by the country's founders was the product of a national convention called by the Continental Congress, not by the states. The Constitution produced by that convention was the product of leaders like James Madison, Edmund Randolph and James Wilson, who believed in and pressed for a strong central government. Adoption of the Constitution was opposed—often bitterly—by the states-rights advocates of that period, including Virginia's Patrick Henry, New York's Governor George Clinton, and Maryland's Luther Martin.[7] When ratification was achieved, it was not by the established state governments which, as Madison pointed out, would have taken the decision out of the hands of "the supreme authority of the people." Rather, approval came from conventions chosen by the voters in each state for this specific purpose.[8]

The revolutionary heroes Reagan delighted in quoting time after time were as far removed from him intellectually and philosophically as one can imagine. Three of his favorites—Benjamin Franklin, Thomas Jefferson and Thomas Paine—he cited frequently in his appeals to "return God to the classroom" and to accept the Bible as a source that would provide "an answer to just about everything and every problem that confronts us." Had he ever read their works, or even a brief biography of each, he would have recognized that all were deists who did not ally themselves with any established church and would never have accepted Reagan's judgment regarding the Bible. Franklin, for all his talk about morality, had little to say about the Bible. Jefferson took pains to give his nephew the following advice on the subject of religion:

> Question with boldness even the existence of a god; because if there is one, he must more approve of the homage of reason than that of blindfold fear. . . . Read the Bible then, as you would read Roman historians Livy or Tacitus. The facts which are within the ordinary course of nature you will believe on the authority of the writer, as you do those of the same kind in Livy and Tacitus. . . . But those facts in the Bible which contradict the laws of nature must be examined with more care. . . . Do not be frightened from this inquiry by any fear of its consequences. If it ends in a belief that there is no god, you will find incitements to virtue in the comfort & pleasantness you feel in its exercise, and the love of others which it will procure you. If you find reason to believe there is a god, a consciousness that you are acting under his eye, and that he approves you, will be a vast additional incitement.[9]

As for Tom Paine, Reagan's repeated suggestion that his own version of the future was akin to that of the fiery Paine is simply ludicrous. Not only did Paine ridicule Old Testament accounts of Adam and Eve and God talking to Moses, he challenged New Testament stories of the immaculate conception, of Christ as the son of God, of the resurrection, and the Trinity. More than that, Paine advocated a socio-political system that would have obligated the government to introduce a progressive tax system, undertake direct support of the poor, and drastically reduce the army and navy. Any one of these proposals would have horrified Reagan, if only he had been aware of it. [10] Being unaware, he did not hestiate to quote the Revolution's most radical spokesman to the National Association of Evangelicals, of all people, in a speech that concluded with a combination of the words of Isaiah and Paine's declaration, "We have it in our power to begin the world over again." [11]

A clearer perception of his own country's past might also have prevented Reagan from indulging in such global generalities as, "History shows that democratic nations are naturally peaceful and nonaggressive." [12] Unless he went back on himself and denied that the U.S. was a democratic nation in its early years, he would have had difficulty explaining such events as the pervasive influence of the "War Hawks" of 1812; the 1844 election of President James K. Polk, whose campaign featured militaristic challenges to England over territory in western Canada ("54'40" or fight!") and to Mexico over lands from Texas to California; as well as the war hysteria incited by the Hearst press ("Remember the Maine!") that was instrumental in bringing on the Spanish-American War. [13]

One could understand—even forgive—Reagan's superficial view of early American history, although it raises serious questions about the failure of his professional staff to correct his faulty impressions after the more obvious errors had been pointed out by others. But both understanding and for-giveness were harder to come by when Reagan managed to misread the events of his own lifetime and subsequently to build a philosophy of government on a foundation flawed by his distorted vision. This occurred despite his auto-biographical claim that, as a result of the postwar experience of fascism-versus-communism debates, "I determined to do my own research, find out my own facts." He was of the same mind in the late 1950s and early 1960s when he offered his General Electric audiences evidence of the "quickening tempo in our government's race toward the controlled society." At that time, he said, "I learned very early to document those examples." [14] In that period, and through all the years that followed, the documentation produced by his "research" invariably turned out to be his own unsupported assertions as to what a government official or agency had done, or what the Supreme Court had said in a case that usually was unidentified. During his governorship and presidency the quotations culled from histories and biographies by his staff were more likely to be accurate, but even in official documents they were only rarely accompanied by source references.

Observing the Reagan version of American political development from the 1930s to the present is like looking into a mirror in a carnival fun house and seeing the twisted limbs and features of a once-familiar figure. In his 1965 autobiography Reagan recalled "vividly" the depression of the 1930s, when life was hard for the great majority of people, and when he, along with millions of others, looked to Franklin D. Roosevelt to restore the country's health and flagging spirits.[15] Yet he later referred to the country's worst depression as "the days of Franklin Roosevelt," rather than as the product of Republican policies designed by Warren G. Harding, Calvin Coolidge and Herbert Hoover.[16] A Democrat by family tradition, Reagan's recollections of the politics of the 1930s focused almost exclusively on his father's experience as a government employee "handing out the foodstuffs the government bought and shipped in" for distribution to the unemployed, and the "almost permanent anger and frustration" his father developed over the mushrooming bureaucracy which he felt tempted his friends and neighbors to remain on welfare instead of seeking or accepting temporary work.[17]

This period was also marked by the hard times that his family experienced and the fact that he had to work to get through college. But despite the economic insecurity that he and his parents shared with millions of other Americans, Reagan's self-confidence and his ability to sell himself carried him up the economic ladder at a relatively rapid pace.[18] When he signed his first Hollywood contract in 1937—still a depression year—his income rose to the fabulous level of $200 a week.[19]

This continuing success had less to do with his abandonment of the Democratic party than his Hollywood encounter with communist and other left-wing politics. The association he began to form in his mind between communism and liberalism gave him a new view of the depression, as well as of the years that followed. Forgotten was the simple fact that the economic remedies undertaken by the Roosevelt administration were intended to shore up the free-enterprise system, not tear it down. Even before his formal conversion to Republicanism in 1962, Reagan took to picturing the offspring of New Deal liberalism as a belief in a system of government controls that was, in his words, "the very essence of totalitarianism."[20] As time went on, his recollection of the totalitarian trend of the New Deal hardened, although he seemed confused about the nature of New Deal philosophy. At one point he called it fascism, at another, communism. "Fascism was really the basis for the New Deal," he said in 1976, explaining that "it was Mussolini's success in Italy, with his government-directed economy, that led the early New Dealers to say, 'But Mussolini keeps the trains running on time'."[21] Like so many of Reagan's recollections, this one was a complete reversal of the facts.

Not only had Mussolini's charm begun to fade before Roosevelt took office, in historian John Diggins' words, "With few exceptions, the dominant voices of business responded to Fascism with hearty enthusiasm . . . the list of outspoken business admirers reads like a Wall Street *Who's Who.*"[22] As the editor of *Nation's Business* explained in 1927, businessmen admired Mussolini because his methods were "essentially those of successful business. Executive actions, not conferences and talk. . . . Accomplishment! Not fine-spoken theories; not plans; not speeches he is going to make. Things done! And this is your successful American executive."[23]

Never one to depart from a firmly fixed concept, Reagan continued to voice the opinion that fascism in the U.S. was supported principally by New Deal leaders. If this charge had been made once and then dropped, or acknowledged as a slip made in the heat of a political campaign, it might be discounted or attributed to an inept speech-writer. But Reagan repeated this idiocy time and again, from as far back as his first race for the presidential nomination in 1976 down to his occupancy of the White House. Almost a year after his election as president, he reaffirmed as "my own analysis" his 1976 assertion that "fascism was really the basis for the New Deal." As he explained to his interviewer, "many of the New Dealers actually espoused what today has become an epithet—fascism—in that they spoke admiringly of how Mussolini had made the trains run on time. In other words, they saw in what he was doing, a planned economy. Private ownership, but government management of that ownership and that economy." Hardly drawing a breath, he went on to cite Roosevelt's secretary of the interior, Harold Ickes, as having said that the goal of FDR's New Deal administrators was "a kind of modified form of communism."[24] Typically, he refrained from any mention of the source for this quotation, and his interviewer did not challenge its accuracy. In fact, Harold Ickes' writings convey not the slightest hint of the attitude attributed to him and his colleagues by Reagan. On the contrary, Ickes' entire career, including his view of communism, indicates uncompromising support for the free-enterprise system.[25]

Had Reagan's so-called research taken him beyond the realm of reminiscence, he might reasonably have concluded that it was FDR—the one New Dealer he exempted from charges of fascist inclinations—who showed remarkable tolerance of the Italian dictator during his first term in the White House. In 1933 Roosevelt wrote to one correspondent, "I am keeping in fairly close touch with that admirable Italian gentleman"; to another, "I am much interested and deeply impressed by what he has accomplished and by his evidenced honest purpose of restoring Italy and seeking to prevent general European trouble."[26] Prevention of general European trouble was Roosevelt's major overseas concern in 1933. However, when visions of empire led Mussolini to invade Ethiopia and, later, to join Hitler in an unannounced invasion of southern France, Roosevelt did not hesitate to criticize both attacks and publicly to denounce Italy's attack on France as a "stab in the back." This latter pronouncement, which produced banner headlines in newspapers across the U.S., was only one of many events of outstanding importance that Reagan totally ignored in his autobiographical report of the 1930s and 1940s.

The seeds of Reagan's conversion from a supporter of FDR's policies to a believer in the Calvin Coolidge-Herbert Hoover approach to political and economic problems may have been planted during his early years in a conservative, small-town, Midwest environment. However, during and after college he had ample opportunity to observe and explore the contests of ideas that brought people and nations to boiling point in one part of the globe after another. Yet his approach to foreign affairs was as flawed as his evaluation of the domestic scene, ignorance playing an even larger role where other nations were concerned. By 1965, when the first volume of his memoirs was written, Reagan's recollection of the years prior to World War II indicated little concern for international problems—political, military or economic. Witness, for example, this confession of his mood on receiving his first acting contract: "In 1937 there was a Spanish Civil War going on, the Japanese were again fighting in China, and Hitler repudiated the Versailles Treaty—but I wasn't mad at anyone."[27] His elation at being accepted in Hollywood may well have driven international politics out of mind at the time, but his 1965 summary of the major events of 1937 should have recognized that the Spanish Civil War was going into its second year, Mussolini's armies had completed the conquest of Ethiopia, Hitler's denunciation of the Versailles Treaty had occurred two years earlier, and the Japanese army had been ravaging North China for six years.

Four decades later, despite endless opportunities to improve the knowledge and wisdom of his earlier years, Reagan's understanding of United States foreign policy during the 1930s had not improved. In one of his earliest presidential interviews he described President Roosevelt's famous 1937 "quarantine" speech as a call "on a free world to quarantine Nazi Germany." As is plainly apparent, that speech was aimed at Japan, not Germany, and was intended to counter widespread isolationist sentiments in the United States.[28]

On another occasion he labeled as "a communist brigade" the American volunteers in the Abraham Lincoln Brigade who fought for the loyalist government against the overtly fascist forces of Francisco Franco in the Spanish Civil War. "The individuals that went there," he went on, were "in the opinion of most Americans, fighting on the wrong side." Reagan's tendency to associate the general public's attitude with his own makes it reasonable to infer that he would have preferred to see volunteers from the

U.S. fight on the side that, with the aid of Nazi German tanks and Fascist Italian armies, installed Franco as the dictator-for-life over the Spanish people.[29]

Not only was his blanket representation of the volunteers inaccurate, his report of the American public's opinion of the Spanish Civil War was simply false. The earliest poll of public opinion about that conflict was taken in January 1937, only months after the revolt led by General Franco began. Follow-up polls were taken in February and December 1938. In each case respondents were asked whether their sympathies were with the loyalist government or the opposition, which was referred to initially as "rebels," later, "insurgents," and finally, as "Franco forces." Initially, only one-third of those questioned expressed an opinion, but of those, almost twice as many sided with the freely elected republican government as with the rebels. A year later, when it had become clear that Franco was receiving substantial military aid from both Hitler and Mussolini, the preponderance of loyalist sympathizers rose to three to one. As 1938 came to a close with the establishment of Franco's fascist dictatorship a foregone conclusion, American sympathy for the loyalist cause—notwithstanding the support it had received from Soviet Russia—stood at 76 percent, against 24 percent favoring Franco.[30]

If subsequent events in Europe and Asia made any impression on Reagan, there is no evidence in his memoirs, even though he recalls that in 1941 "I loved three things: drama, politics, and sports."[31] The politics he discussed in his story of the twenty-odd years that followed the opening of World War II was limited almost entirely to leadership and policy struggles among the several unions that dominated organized labor in the theatrical world. The labor-management and inter-union battles of that era he associated with the international scene only when some union members became targets of the Un-American Activities Committee.[32]

* * * * *

World War II saw Reagan in uniform as a lieutenant in an air force unit organized to "turn out training films and documentaries and," according to Reagan, to "conduct a training school for combat camera units."[33] His recollections of that momentous period, in which the very existence of the western democracies was at stake, are full of humorous incidents that occur in everyday soldiering, but they are notably lacking in references to the significance of the war itself. In all probability this was due to the fact that his military duties consisted largely of participating in the production of films aimed at entertaining or bolstering morale at home and among the armed forces.

The most operationally useful projects that Reagan claimed to have been involved in were to prepare films for bomber crews to plan their attacks on Tokyo and the German rocket research center at Peenemunde.[34] Curiously enough, this aspect of Reagan's service was not discovered by any of the biographers who have researched his background in some detail, even though their works were published long after the volume in which Reagan related his military experience.

Reagan's description of these assignments, which he characterized as "ranking up with the atom bomb project," can be taken as the kind of exaggeration common in people's accounts of their own wartime achievements. But even these personal experiences were narrated with scant regard for accuracy. Reagan's reference to Peenemunde as a base for "Nazi missile launching sites" that were destroyed by the American Eighth Air Force "in time to postpone the V-2 launchings long enough for D-Day to take place on schedule" is incorrect on almost every count.[35] Peenemunde was an experimental station for rocket research and development located on the Baltic Sea in eastern Germany; the V-2 launching sites were in the occupied countries far to the west; and the bombing of Peenemunde was undertaken by the RAF, was only partly successful, and had no significant impact on the Allies' ability to mount the D-Day invasion of the French coast.[36] In his wartime memoirs, General Eisenhower remarked that British and American bombing of the testing, manufacturing and launching sites "undoubtedly greatly delayed" the development and employment of V-2 rockets, but his only suggestion as to their impact on Allied plans for D-Day was a conjecture that "if the German had succeeded in perfecting and using these new weapons six months earlier than he did, our invasion of Europe would have proved exceedingly difficult, perhaps impossible."[37] Reagan's sadly inaccurate account of this phase of the war is all the more remarkable in light of his later claim that the unit he was in "was directly under Air Corps Intelligence, and we had access to all the intelligence information."[38]

Reagan's later references to World War II actions in which he did not participate are even wider of the mark. Explaining his Central American policy to Congress in 1983, he stressed the need for defending against the threat of Soviet intrusion into that area. Calling the Caribbean "our lifeline to the outside world," he raised the specter of Soviet submarine attacks on American ships supplying its allies, saying, "It is well to remember that in early 1942 a handful of Hitler's submarines sank more tonnage there in the Caribbean than in all of the Atlantic Ocean."[39] To characterize the Caribbean as America's lifeline to the rest of the world is simply silly. That generalization apart, it is impossible to determine the source of his figures on the volume of shipping sunk in this sector. However, he could have learned from any World War II history that of the total losses in the first six months of 1942, "90 percent was in the Atlantic and Arctic," on the main supply routes to England and Russia.[40]

Fantasy played as great a part in Reagan's picture of race relations during World War II as it did in his memory of military contests. Lou Cannon, who followed Reagan's political career more closely than any other reporter, offered this particularly revealing paragraph:

> In 1975, campaigning for president, Reagan gave a cinematic version of how segregation had ended in the armed services: "When the first bombs were dropped on Pearl Harbor, there was great segregation in the military forces. In World War II, this was corrected. It was corrected largely under the leadership of generals like MacArthur and Eisenhower. . . . One great story that I think of at the time that reveals a change was occurring, was when the Japanese dropped the bomb on Pearl Harbor there was a Negro sailor whose total duties involved kitchen-type duties. . . . He cradled a machine gun in his arms, which is not an easy thing to do, and stood at the end of a pier blazing away at Japanese airplanes that were coming down and strafing him and that segregation was all changed." When a reporter pointed out that segregation in the armed services actually had ended when President Truman signed an executive order in 1948 three years after the war, Reagan stood his ground. "I remember the scene," Reagan told me on the campaign plane later. "It was very powerful."

It was this incident that Cannon used to point up Reagan's habit of accepting Hollywood myths as historical facts.[41]

Subsequent international conflicts involving the U.S. Reagan portrayed in the same fictional fashion. That is, if he dwelt on them at all. He seldom mentioned Korea, where the war against the communist armies of Kim il-Sung was led by a Democratic president, with almost uncontested support from the American public, and was ended, without victory, by a Republican president. However, he commented frequently about the course of history in Vietnam, bitterly criticizing the American decision to withdraw, even though the war was brought to a close by a Republican president as a result of rising public opposition to American participation.

Many Americans would agree with Reagan's view that the U.S. cause in the Vietnam War was "a noble one."[42] But few would attempt to make their case, as Reagan did, with so little regard for the facts.

Reagan's fanciful view of Vietnamese history demonstrates the empty rhetoric of such advice as he offered to Canadian political leaders: "We must never stop trying to reach a better world, but we'll never make it if we don't see our world as it truly is."[43] Reagan's notion of reality in southeast Asia begins with this 1979 observation to a radio audience regarding the history of North and South Vietnam: "They have been separate nations for centuries."[44] He held firmly to this non-fact throughout his presidency, repeating it in 1982 and again in 1984 when, as president, he had complete access to government records and advisers.[45] On the second of these occasions he reminded reporters that, even before he became president he had advocated a formal declaration of war against North Vietnam which, he said, had been created a separate nation by the Geneva Conference of 1954 and had been a separate nation "back through history." Had he bothered to make use of the resources available to him at the White House, he would have learned that during the centuries between its domination by China (from 111 B.C. to 939 A.D.) and later by France (1858 to 1954), despite periodic internal struggles for power Vietnam was ruled as one country by a single emperor. The American army's own history of the origins of U.S. involvement in Vietnam attests to the unity of the country in its continued battle against predatory neighbors.[46]

Referring to French occupation of "the Two Vietnams," Reagan told a 1968 radio audience that both countries "were freed a few years after World War II."[47] Fourteen years later, in a White House news conference, he repeated both the myth of the two Vietnams and the fiction that prior to the 1954 Geneva Convention "France gave up Indochina as a colony."[48]

The facts are very different. Almost immediately after the defeat of the Japanese in World War II, their erstwhile puppet, Vietnamese Emperor Bao Dai sent messages to General Charles de Gaulle and President Harry Truman warning that if the French attempted to reestablish their sovereignty over Vietnam they would be resisted by Vietnamese in every quarter of the country.[49] His pleas for independence were ignored by both leaders.

On the American side, Truman abandoned President Franklin Roosevelt's anti-colonial stance and his notion of trusteeship for most former colonies. Roosevelt had stated that "Indo-China should not go back to France but . . . should be administered by an international trusteeship." He insisted that "the case of Indo-China is perfectly clear. France has milked it for one hundred years [and] the people of Indo-China are entitled to something better than that."[50] President Truman, on the other hand, ignoring not only his predecessor but also personal appeals sent by both Bao Dai and Ho Chi Minh, as well as warnings from Far East specialists in his own State Department, acceded to the wishes of French Foreign Minister Georges Bidault and accepted the restoration of French sovereignty over Indo-China.[51] France promptly brought its military forces into Vietnam and, in the words of a U.S. Air Force historian, the French "ruthlessly suppressed Vietnamese aspirations for independence," with the result that they "regained their former colonial status by the end of the year [1945]."[52]

As the only recognized leader of the independence movement who was untainted by collaboration with the Japanese, Ho Chi Minh attempted to negotiate with the French "for recognition of his new government and ultimate independence." That effort ended in November 1946 when, after a skirmish between a French patrol boat and Ho's guerrillas, "the French responded by brutally bombarding the city [Haiphong] and killing an estimated 6,000 civilians."[53] Only after five years of all-out war, and in response to rising discontent at home, did the French take the token step of establishing Vietnam, Laos and Cambodia as "autonomous states within the French union." The "independence" granted ex-Japanese, now French, puppet Bao Dai left all political and economic authority in French hands.[54] Four years later, as French authority came to a practical end with the fall of Dien Bien Phu, an ongoing conference in Geneva, Switzerland concluded its discussion of the Korean problem and took up the matter of Indochina.

Attended by delegates from England, France, the U.S., U.S.S.R., China, the French-controlled State of Vietnam, Ho Chi Minh's Democratic Republic of Vietnam, Cambodia and Laos, the conference reached three major decisions affecting Vietnam: contending forces would agree to a cease-fire, would temporarily be separated by a line between north and south drawn at the 17th parallel, and would agree to hold nationwide elections on the reunification of the country in 1956.[55] Only the U.S. refused to associate itself with the final program. President Eisenhower announced at his July 21, 1954 news conference that this country would not be bound by the decisions of the conference, but he offered the hope "that it will lead to the establishment of peace consistent with the rights and needs of the countries concerned."[56]

Eisenhower's reason for this stand is clear from the State Department's record of American preparations for the conference. In a February 24, 1954 memorandum, Edmund A. Gullion of the State Department Policy Planning Staff wrote: "Most Vietnamese would prefer free elections or some accommodation with Ho Chi Minh to a partition of the country." In view of this, he concluded: "Obviously, our side would strive for an arrangement which would defer elections until we had been able to make effective propaganda and until arms and troops were disposed in the best possible positions."[57] Although elections were not scheduled until 1956, South Vietnam President Ngo Dinh Diem indicated as early as July 1955 that "he was not going to hold them."[58] Instead, Diem said, he would hold a national referendum "at which voters would choose between Bao Dai's monarchy or a republic which he [Diem] would head."[59]

Notwithstanding the abundance of evidence in official U.S. documents that elections were blocked by Diem, Reagan always insisted that unification of the country was prevented because "Ho Chi Minh refused to participate in such an election."[60] On another occasion he compounded his error by stating that the Geneva accord "created two nations—South Vietnam and North Vietnam," a completely inaccurate account of the conference agreement.[61]

Reagan was equally careless in his account of America's first move to upgrade the corps of military advisers which it had sent to Diem by introducing a Marine combat contingent. Characterizing the thousands of military trainers, air force maintenance crews and special forces as advisers "in civilian clothes," Reagan reported that when attacks on these noncombatants became too great, "John F. Kennedy authorized the sending in of a division of Marines."[62] Wrong again. President Kennedy sent no Marines to Vietnam. Thirteen months after Kennedy's assassination, President Lyndon Johnson authorized a program of continuous bombing of North Vietnam troop concentrations by American air force planes (known as Rolling Thunder), and followed that a month later, in March 1965, with assignment of the first American ground combat force: two battalions of Marines.[63]

In 1971 Reagan had an opportunity to learn something of Vietnam firsthand when he went there as an emissary of Richard Nixon, the president who initiated the withdrawal of American armed forces from that country. Reagan arrived in Saigon after Diem's ultimate successor, General Nguyen Van Thieu, had won the presidency of South Vietnam in an election in which no other candidates were allowed on the ballot. When reporters asked him what he thought of such an election, Reagan professed puzzlement at their questions. "I am unable to understand," he said, "why so many people in our country, especially the communications media, are so charged up by this one-man election." He went on to explain how similar Thieu's unopposed election by 94 percent of the vote was to early American experience when George Washington was unopposed for the presidency of the United States.[64] The published report of this incident did not indicate whether the newsmen present groaned, guffawed, or turned away in despair. In any case, Nixon's plan for Vietnamization of the war—which meant turning the defense over to presumably well-trained South Vietnamese forces—was already marked for failure.[65]

During and after the war, Reagan insisted that it could have been won if only "the politicians" had had the will to win and the courage to give the military what they needed to do the job. Of America's enormous investment of men and material in the Vietnam conflict, Reagan's final, bitter, and blindly ignorant evaluation was that "no one had any intention of allowing victory."[66]

* * * * *

More recent history in areas closer to home was as hazy to Reagan as the years past. His 1982 appeal to the Organization of American States for unity in the western hemisphere was understandable as a political maneuver. But he fooled no one—least of all the assembled representatives of the Latin American dictatorships that made up a majority of OAS members in 1982—with his reference to the common character of all American revolutions, and the "common principles and institutions that provided the basis for mutual protection."[67] Many in the U.S. may have been as uninformed as Reagan about Latin American history, but his OAS audience knew full well that, unlike the experience of the North American colonies in their revolt against Great Britain, the first 100 years of revolution in Central and South America produced nothing but a series of dictatorships. Nevertheless, listeners in the U.S. were led to believe that all those Latin American nations Reagan called friends were as democratic as their own country, or were being guided toward democracy by leaders whose common goal was to adopt the same principles and institutions as those of the United States. Such distortions of facts also offered false hopes to Americans outside the U.S., while giving aid and comfort to the dictators who held them in subjection. The later progress in the direction of democratic government made in some Central and South American countries led Reagan to declare in a 1985 news conference that "the only two totalitarian powers in our hemisphere are Nicaragua and Cuba." No member of the media asked the president why he failed to mention Chile, Paraguay, Panama or Surinam.[68]

Even personal contact with officials in countries south of the border did not improve Reagan's understanding of their problems and attitudes. Some months after the OAS meeting he made a tour of Latin America. On his return he reported that, having gone "to find out . . . their views," he had "learned a lot." To demonstrate the extent of his learning, he offered this observation: "You'd be surprised. They're all individual countries." In an immediate "clarification" the State Department explained that the president meant other people would be surprised to find differences from one nation to another, but Reagan's own words made it clear that this was a discovery he had made for himself.[69] Equally clear was the impression that while Reagan had been enlightened as to the different attitudes toward domestic and international questions taken by both elected and power-by-force leaders in Latin America, he had learned little, if anything, about their countries' basic internal problems, the sources of domestic upheaval, or the rivalries that had kept the neighbor nations of that region at odds with one another for well over a century.

* * * * *

Any accounting of the sources of Reagan's incredible record of misinformation must put ignorance and self-delusion at the head of the list. A contributing factor would be his habit of accepting as solid truth what a more cautious observer would regard as rumor. Even pure gossip had its appeal, particularly when the tale matched Reagan's own attitude toward a particular subject. On one occasion a Reagan aide acknowledged that his boss had passed on as fact a comment about the mismanagement of school lunch funds that he had "heard at a dinner party."[70]

Not infrequently, a critic would accuse Reagan of having resorted to an outright lie, which the dictionary characterizes as "a deliberate falsehood." But once Reagan accepted as true an opinion, statistic or supposed event, it could not be a lie to him. And once he had publicly declared a thing to be a fact, it was recorded as such in his computer-like memory, which was programmed to reject all evidence to the contrary. When triggered by a new reference to the same subject, his computer repeatedly recalled the misinformation stored in his memory bank. The pity of it was that most of Reagan's errors were contested feebly, if at all, and challenges that appeared at a later date carried little of the impact of the presumably authoritative presidential statement. Not until the Iran-Contra hearings did the general public become aware of the frailty of Reagan's claim to honesty in all things.

The White House staff did little to wean Reagan away from his cavalier indifference to facts, despite the frequency with which they were called upon to issue corrections, often euphemistically referred to as clarifications. Worse still, some of his assistants felt free to adopt Reagan's method of playing with history. Examples ranged from the innocently ignorant representation of the table used for the signing of the INF treaty as "the table on which they signed the treaty ending the Civil War," to the unremitting stream of false, distorted, or misleading statements made by participants in the Iran-Contra affair.[71] After leaving the president's employ, White House spokesman Larry Speakes acknowledged having graduated from defending Reagan's use of fabricated incidents ("He made his point, didn't he?") to giving the press presidential quotations of his own manufacture, without the president's knowledge or approval. When this confession appeared in Speakes' book, the news headlines reflected only the "outrage" expressed by his successor, Marlin Fitzwater. "I guarantee you," Fitzwater told reporters, "that he [Reagan] does not approve of making up statements or misleading in any way." The president could not be reached for his reaction until three days later when, accosted on the way to his helicopter about Speakes' forced resignation from his vice-presidency at Merrill Lynch, his only response was, "No comment." However, when addressing the American Society of Newspaper Editors, he passed the matter off in typical fashion by remarking, "That's the nice thing about this job: you get to quote yourself shamelessly, and if you don't, Larry Speakes will."[72]

Little media attention was directed to the most important aspect of Speakes' revelation: the extent to which casual falsification of the historical record had come to be an accepted tactic of an administration whose leader endorsed that neo-Orwellian tradition, who defended every such action by a subordinate as long as he remained loyal, and who dismissed as "fiction" the testimony of anyone whose kiss-and-tell memoirs revealed the true character of Reagan's addiction to disinformation.

Reagan's secretary of education, William J. Bennett, once warned an audience of teachers that "to be ignorant of history is to be, in a very fundamental way, intellectually defenseless, unable to understand the workings of either our own society or other societies."[73] Obviously, his warning never reached the White House.

CHAPTER 5

Champion of Civil Rights

"Wherever in this land any individual's constitutional rights are being unjustly denied, it is the obligation of the federal government—at point of bayonet, if necessary—to restore that individual's constitutional rights."[1]

THE PLATFORM REAGAN OFFERED THE PUBLIC IN 1980 CONTAINED NO civil rights plan. In a three-page preamble that focused on the domestic economy and the Soviet threat, a single sentence was devoted to "our deep commitment to the fulfillment of the hopes and aspirations of all Americans—blacks and whites, women and men, the young and old, rural and urban." This was followed by a section entitled "Free Individuals in a Free Society" that reflected Reagan's concept of freedom as basically economic in nature. Minorities, it said, could best achieve their freedom through employment and new business opportunities. Equating equal rights with equal opportunity, the platform denounced "quotas, ratios, and numerical requirements to exclude some individuals in favor of others," and promised "laws to assure equal treatment in job recruitment, hiring, promotion, pay, credit, mortgage access, and housing."[2]

Only in its treatment of women's rights did the platform go beyond economics. That section abandoned the party's earlier boast of having been "the first national party to back this ERA amendment" and its 40-year-old pledge—repeated for the last time in 1976—to "work towards ratification of the Equal Rights Amendment."[3]

Acknowledging "the legitimate efforts of those who support or oppose ratification of the Equal Rights Amendment," the 1980 platform went on to say that "the states have a constitutional right to accept or reject a constitutional amendment without federal interference or pressure."[4] Confident that Republicans in state legislatures would oppose ERA, conservative convention forces under the leadership of Senator Jesse Helms of North Carolina defeated every effort to secure platform support for the amendment, voting 90 to 9 in favor of the equivocal statement quoted above. This so disturbed the party's co-chairman, Mary Crisp, that she resigned from the national committee and threw her support to John Anderson, declaring that the Republican party was "suffering from serious internal sickness."[5]

Crisp and her liberal Republican allies were also defeated in their attempt to secure a moderate statement on abortion. Again they were routed, in a 75 to 18 vote, by conservatives who insisted on a pledge to fight for a constitutional amendment that would prohibit abortion under any circumstances. Coupled with that policy statement was a protest against "the Supreme Court's intrusion into the family structure through its denial of the parents' obligation and right to guide their minor children."[6]

Having turned from his earlier support for ERA—an about-face that one biographer ascribes to Nancy Reagan's influence—candidate Reagan looked for other ways to attract the feminine vote. One was a promise to select a woman for one of the first Supreme Court vacancies he would have an opportunity to fill.[7] When, subsequent to his election, he made good on this promise by appointing Sandra Day O'Connor to replace the retiring Potter Stewart, Reagan insisted that his choice had been based on the extraordinary qualifications and high standards required of Supreme Court justices and not on O'Connor's gender.[8] Nevertheless, the appointmnt was a clear departure from his practice as governor of California, when he filled three vacancies on that state's supreme court with male appointees.[9]

Throughout his presidency, Reagan insisted that he was, and always had been, in favor of equal rights for women, and that the only difference between his view and that of ERA supporters was his belief that equality could best be achieved by changing state and federal laws that were found to be biased against women. Repeatedly, he referred to the "14 statutes in California" that he first said he had passed to eliminate discrimination, and later explained that he had "wiped off the books" to accomplish this.[10] When asked if he would continue the existence of the President's Advisory Commission for Women, his hesitant and equivocal response that he "assumed" he would "probably" do so, suggested that he had no idea he had inherited such a group from the Carter administration.[11] However, in characteristic fashion, he let the advisory commission die on the vine and established his own Fifty States Project to help the states ferret out and correct all laws discriminating against women.[12] Subsequently he issued Executive Order 12336 establishing a Task Force on Legal Equality for Women.[13] Although his announcement of this action implied that it was one of his own initiatives, reporter Sarah McClendon corrected him on this and brought an acknowledgment that the task force had originally been brought into existence by President Ford, and funded by President Carter. In that same exchange, McClendon asked President Reagan what he was going to do about a report that had been submitted to him showing "the discriminations that actually exist on the books in Federal agencies and departments against women." Reagan denied having received the document, but McClendon knew better, citing the day, place, and government official who had delivered the report. Reagan parried the question with a joke about not seeing any such R-rated document, and when pressed, brought the news conference to a close. [14]

Mary Crisp was not the only Republican who refused to accept the administration approach to women's rights. Kathy Wilson, who chaired the National Women's Political Caucus in 1983, called Reagan "a dangerous man," joining more than one-third of Republican women voters in the opinion that Reagan should not be reelected. Of the caucus members attending a July 9 convention, only Betty Heitman, Crisp's replacement as co-chair of the Republican National Committee, defended the president publicly. [15]

A month later, when a scheduled tour of the White House by members of the prestigious International Federation of Business and Professional Women's Clubs was cancelled without notice, Reagan's apology included a reference to "women's place" that further enraged the group. [16] But when asked by Ann Devroy of Gannet News Service, "Why are you so misunderstood on this issue?" the president could offer no reason other than that "part of it is very deliberate and political," suggesting that this was demonstrated by the character of support given Democratic candidates in the 1982 congressional elections. [17]

During this same period the Justice Department appealed to the Supreme Court on behalf of Grove City College, which had refused to submit an assurance of compliance with the federal law barring sex discrimination. Claiming that federal funds constituted only indirect assistance to the financial aid office of the institution, Justice Department lawyers argued that the college as a whole should not be made subject to the anti-discrimination law. Criticism of this interpretation came not only from Reagan's attorneys and his Commission on Civil Rights, but from Republican Senator Bob Dole and 49 other members of Congress who filed a brief with the court contesting the view of Attorney General William French Smith. [18]

When the case was finally decided by the Supreme Court six months later, all of the justices agreed that the federal Department of Education was required by law to withhold student aid money if an institution refused to execute an assurance of compliance with the anti-discrimination provisions of the statute. However, on the more important question of whether the law should be applied college-wide or only to the financial aid office, the majority upheld the narrower view advanced by the Justice Department. Three justices—Stevens, Brennan and Marshall—disputed the majority's interpretation of the word "program," insisting, as Senator Dole had done, that "when financial assistance is clearly intended to serve as federal aid for the entire institution, the institution as a whole should be covered by the statute's prohibition on sex discrimination." Citing the history of the law, to which the majority referred only in passing, the minority concluded that "any other interpretation clearly disregards the intent of Congress and severely weakens the anti-discrimination provisions included in Title IX."[19]

The Civil Rights Act of 1984 was written in such a way as to reverse the court's decision by making institutions receiving federal funds responsible for applying the nondiscrimination rule across the board. Asked if he would approve such a change, President Reagan said he would support a law preventing discrimination against women in educational institutions receiving federal funds, but he felt the broader aspects of the proposed act "would open the door to federal intrusion in local and state governments and in any manner of ways beyond anything that has ever been intended by the Civil Rights Act."[20] This same position was taken by the Senate Republican leadership which blocked action on the bill in October 1984, when they still retained majority control of the Senate.[21]

As the 1984 election approached, with little likelihood that the Equal Rights Amendment would receive the necessary 34 state petitions, Reagan's platform no longer argued that case, but claimed that "Republicans pioneered the right of women to vote," an assertion that is plainly denied by the record.[22]

Shortly before election day in 1984, and three years after the Task Force on Legal Equality for Women was formed, that group presented the president with a report of its accomplishments. Considered less significant than other campaign materials, the report did not merit a hearing by the president until after the election was over. A clue to the relative importance of task force activity overall is seen in Reagan's praise of the members for their diligence in performing "a very nitpicking job." He did not recall that the group had picked so few nits in its first year and one-half that the Justice Department attorney assigned to ramrod the operation resigned in disgust because of its lackadaisical approach.[23]

The lack of enthusiasm shown by the task force was less significant than the attitudes expressed by some of Reagan's more influential appointees. Two days after the task force report was released, U.S. Civil Rights Commission chair Clarence M. Pendleton, Jr., prejudged his own agency's position on women's rights and attempted to dilute the effect of the evenly divided opinion among sixteen reports on "comparable worth" by publicly blasting that concept as "probably the looniest idea since Looney Tunes came on the screen."[24] Advancing the administration view that applying the concept of comparable worth would interfere with the marketplace determination of pay rates for male and female employees, Pendleton said it was not the government's prerogative to end discrimination created by the law of supply and demand, even in public service positions. This was the same chair whose "inflammatory rhetoric" and "fulminations" against those holding opposing views ultimately led John H. Bunzel, another member of the commission appointed by Reagan, to call for Pendleton's resignation. Pendleton, however, was not the type to resign, and the president was not likely to relieve one so closely attuned to his own ideas, particularly a person who had the political advantage of being black.

Reagan's choice for general counsel to the Equal Employment Opportunity Commission reflected an attitude similar to Pendleton's. Despite multiple federal court decisions that women must be paid the same wage or salary as men for doing an identical job, Jeffrey Zuckerman denied that this rule need apply unless the two were doing the same work at the same time.[25] On-the-job equality was of even less concern to rural electrification administrator Harold V. Hunter, who believed women's place was in the home, not supervising in the government. And Agriculture Department undersecretary Richard W. Goldberg announced that women should not be made judges—or even admitted to law school—an opinion offered five years after Sandra Day O'Connor had been appointed associate justice of the U.S. Supreme Court.[26]

In the president's own office, White House Chief of Staff Donald Regan showed his disdain for feminine ability to cope with such complex problems as those which his technically untalented boss would deal with at the Reykjavik meeting with Soviet leader Mikhail Gorbachev.[27] Unfazed by Regan's assumption that women "would rather read human interest stuff" and would not understand "throw weights, or what is happening in Afghanistan or what is happening in human rights," the president assured reporters that Regan meant only that women "also had an interest in children and a human touch."[28]

* * * * *

Reagan's record on broader civil rights questions was equally dubious. Assertions that "this administration is dedicated and devoted to the principle of civil rights" punctuated many of his speeches and news conferences.[29] But the evidence Reagan offered in support of his dedication failed to convince those most in need of protection: blacks, Hispanics and other minorities, and the powerless poor of all races and nationalities. Doubters among these groups, seeking action on current problems of discrimination in employment, housing, education, criminal prosecution or voting rights, frequently were frustrated by Reagan's habit of harking back to events in his early life to demonstrate his dedication to antidiscrimination. On one occasion he told members of the National Council of Negro Women, "As a radio sports announcer almost 50 years ago, I used to speak out on the air against the then ban on blacks in organized baseball."[30] There is no recollection in his autobiography of so bold an action, which in the 1930s probably would not have been tolerated either by his Midwest radio-station employer or the then lily-white Chicago Cubs and White Sox whose games he was broadcasting. Nor is there any support for his claim, made on another occasion, that as a sports announcer he was battling what he said was the *Official Baseball Guide's* assertion that "baseball is a game for Caucasian gentlemen." A St. Louis sports editor who examined issues of the guide published in the 1930s could find no such statement.[31]

When someone attempted to bring Reagan back from the 1930s to current reality, he seldom responded directly to a specific query or demand for action, asserting only that his administration was committed to protect the constitutional rights of all people, or that, in the area of civil rights for women and minorities, "no administration has done more than we have done."[32] To reporters who challenged such claims in 1984 he suggested that they get their information "from the horse's mouth, our administration, and not from the political rhetoric that has been so prevalent in the last year."

When he did offer concrete evidence of his administration's success in the defense of civil rights—usually in the form of statistics—his figures frequently were either incorrect or misleading. For example, when he claimed to have initiated more school desegregation suits than the Carter administration, it turned out that he was comparing his Justice Department's *authorizations* for filing suit with *actual* filings made by Carter officials. Questioned about this three months later, Assistant Attorney General William Bradford Reynolds acknowledged that the suits which the president took credit for were still in the authorization stage, with no indication of when, if ever, they would be filed in a federal court.[33]

On the question of public housing, Reagan strove to eliminate all federal support for what his deputy housing commissioner called "new semi-luxury buildings for poor people." Cutting subsidized housing and rent supports in his first year, he eliminated the entire construction and rehabilitation program from his 1983 budget.[34] Private owners of apartments in buildings subsidized by the federal government were permitted to forego the subsidy after five years, raise rents, and evict those tenants who could not pay the new rates.[35] Until 1987, when Congress forced through a new federal housing program, the public housing burden fell largely on the states and local communities.

In the area of civil rights enforcement generally, Reagan seemed to make a good case when he told the American Bar Association that from January 1981 to June 1983 his attorneys had filed "more than a hundred new cases charging criminal violations of civil rights laws," and that this was "substantially more than any prior administration during a comparable period." But as *Readers Digest* writer James Nathan Miller pointed out in an *Atlantic Monthly* article, the difference between Reagan and Carter criminal prosecutions was unsubstantial (114 to 101), while in the equally important area of civil suits—which Reagan did not mention at all—the number of cases dropped from 124 under Carter to 42 under Reagan.[36]

No matter what type of audience Reagan addressed, his listeners were never able to challenge, on the spot, the statistics he put forth to prove the effectiveness of his administration. And few who heard him bothered to check after the fact. This was especially true of audiences made up of nonprofessional people. Thus, Reagan was perfectly safe in telling a student group, "Don't let me get away with it, if you have any question as to whether any of my answers were not based on fact, check me out."[37]

Disinformation on civil rights was not solely a product of the White House and Justice Department. Other offices were responsible for monitoring civil rights violations, especially as they affected the disbursement of federal funds. The Department of Housing and Urban Development was cited by a federal judge for following a deliberate policy of discrimination against minorities throughout eastern Texas by dividing many of its public housing projects into separate black and white communities.[38] In the Department of Agriculture, where the civil rights staff had been cut to the bone, the Office of Equal Opportunity had by 1984 stopped investigating complaints of discrimination, had all but discontinued compliance reviews as well as reports on minority participation in department programs, and had prepared none of the regulations called for by amendments to the Civil Rights Act of 1964.[39]

A congressional committee found that the Department of Education had falsified, by backdating, records of compliance with a court order that had set specific time limits for processing complaints regarding segregation in state colleges and universities. The committee also discovered that the Education Department managed to avoid its own enforcement responsibilities by referring cases to the Department of Justice, which took no action.[40]

An article in the *National Journal* reported in 1982 that the Department of Health and Human Services had a file of 30 violations that should have been sent to the Justice Department for action but were "put on hold" for an indefinite period. And over in the Justice Department, the groundwork was being laid for its campaign to support private colleges like Grove City, regardless of their discriminatory practices, by exempting from civil rights laws some 300 schools that were receiving federal funds only through student loans.[41]

Where executive agencies were found to be operating on a different wavelength, the White House stepped in to show them the error of their ways. The most shocking reversal of policy came early in 1982 when the administration decided to ignore a 1970 federal court decision that had barred the Internal Revenue Service from granting tax-exempt status to private schools that practiced racial discrimination, a judgment that had been upheld by the Supreme Court.[42] At that point the IRS had formally adopted a rule which stated that "all charitable trusts, educational or otherwise, are subject to the requirement that the purpose of the trust may not be illegal or contrary to public policy."[43] Based on the "national policy to discourage racial discrimination in education," the IRS concluded that "a private school not having a racially nondiscriminatory policy as to students is not 'charitable' within the common concepts reflected in the [tax] code."

On October 30, 1981, Republican Representative Trent Lott wrote President Reagan to inform him of pending court cases brought by Bob Jones University and Goldsboro Christian Schools, both of which had been denied tax exemption because of their discriminatory treatment of black students. To Lott's suggestion that the IRS administration take steps to reverse the rule, Reagan wrote in the margin of the letter, "I think we should." Following the president's lead, and after a strategy session with presidential counsel Edwin Meese, the Treasury Department overrode the objections of the commissioner of Internal Revenue and announced on January 8, 1982 that the policy had been reversed and that the IRS had been instructed not to deny exemption to segregated private schools.[44] Four days later, President Reagan issued a formal statement which endorsed the Treasury decision to reverse the rule which IRS had adopted in accordance with the 1971 Supreme Court decision. Insisting that he "would not knowingly contribute to any organization that supports racial discrimination," Reagan ignored the Supreme Court's warning that "when the Government grants exemptions or allows deductions, all taxpayers are affected; the very fact of the exemption or deduction for the donor means that other taxpayers can be said to be indirect and vicarious 'donors'." Instead, he opened the door to public support of racially discriminatory schools, on the grounds that the IRS had exercised "powers that the Constitution assigns to the Congress."[45]

Because the IRS was not permitted to appear before the court in opposition to the Justice Department, the court took the unusual step of appointing an independent counsel to present the IRS case. Significantly, the brief filed on behalf of IRS by Republican attorney William T. Coleman, Jr., formerly President Ford's secretary of transportation, was supported by another brief filed by the National Association of Independent Schools.[46]

In an 8 to 1 decision, with Associate Justice William H. Rehnquist the only dissenter, the Supreme Court upheld the IRS position that Bob Jones University and Goldsboro Christian Schools did not qualify as tax-exempt organizations because of their racially discriminatory policies. Countering

Rehnquist's argument that despite the existence of "a strong national policy in this country opposed to racial discrimination" Congress had failed to incorporate this sentiment into the tax law, the majority pointed to specific evidence in both the law and congressional resistance to efforts made to legislate a change in the IRS rule.

Months before the case was argued before the Supreme Court, Reagan explained the situation to a group of Chicago high school students in this way: "I didn't know there were any court cases pending—but I was under the impression that the problem of desegregated schools had been settled, that we have desegregation." At his next news conference a reporter pointed out that when the president made his decision about tax exemption for segregated schools he had already received, read, and commented upon a letter from Congressman Trent Lott in which the court cases were discussed. Reagan's convoluted reply, that his original instruction to the Treasury secretary to investigate IRS harassment of schools that were desegregated was given much earlier, "and then sometime later this order was issued. . . . And the minute that I heard about how it was interpreted, that this was going to change the whole situation with regard to segregated schools and tax exemption, I said, 'Well, then the answer lies it should be by law, not by bureaucratic regulation'." Having juggled the sequence of events in such a way as to make it appear that his January 12, 1982 decision really was made long before he read about the court cases, the president concluded his exchange with reporters by saying, "I'm glad you asked me, because now, just like the children, I've told you the truth"—which was a lie. [47]

Coming on top of an administration-wide slowdown in the general enforcement of civil rights laws, the decision to back segregated schools in the tax exemption fight brought a letter of protest from 200 lawyers in the Justice Department. This was the second mass protest from Justice Department employees in the first year of William Bradford Reynolds' tenure as assistant attorney general for civil rights. The Reaganistic approach to enforcement taken by Reynolds was to "work things out voluntarily instead of asking a court to determine guilt or innocence and, if guilty, an appropriate penalty." Reynolds always cited as justification for his policy the few cases in which this procedure had worked successfully. However, his method left many violations untreated or, at best, resolved with few concessions made by the perpetrators. [48] It was this which later led even Republican members of the black community to see the Reynolds tactic as a way of appealing to white voters. Opinion of Reynolds' actions among leaders in this group ranged from "negative" by Clarence Thomas, chairman of Reagan's Equal Employment Opportunity Commission, to "despicable" by William T. Coleman, Jr., President Ford's secretary of transportation. [49]

Criticism of the Reynolds type of justice did not deter other departments

from embracing the spirit of voluntarism in civil rights enforcement. Well
into the second Reagan administration the director of the Education Department's enforcement section challenged his boss' procedure of attempting to
"cut a deal" with individuals filing complaints, before undertaking any
investigation. Even the Justice Department had warned against this practice,
but four years after its warning was issued Assistant Secretary of Education for
civil rights Harry M. Singleton claimed to be unaware of the existence of the
cautionary memo.[50]

Enforcement was at its lowest ebb in matters involving affirmative action
laws and agreements. More often than not, the Justice Department would
take the employer's side, challenging the constitutionality of affirmative
action programs and criticizing the Supreme Court whenever it upheld one of
those programs. Two members of Reagan's Commission on Civil Rights went
so far as to declare that civil rights laws were not intended to protect all
Americans, but had been passed for the special benefit of "blacks, Hispanics,
and women of all races . . . because they belonged to disfavored groups."[51]
Another minority commission opinion, supported by chairman Clarence M.
Pendleton, Jr., attacked a Supreme Court ruling that upheld an affirmative
action plan which favored employment of women and minorities to adjust "a
conspicuous imbalance" in staffing.[52]

As attorney general, Edwin Meese insisted that affirmative action hiring
goals meant establishing a system of quotas, which he characterized as "a new
version of the separate-but-equal doctrine" and a return to the pre-Civil War
attitude that "slavery was not only good for the slaves but for society."[53] Both
he and Assistant Attorney General William B. Reynolds consistently criticized what they termed the quota basis of affirmative action, even though
quotas were banned by law and the explicit purpose of affirmative action was
not to establish a quota system but to provide a means for remedying what
the Supreme Court called a "manifest imbalance" resulting from
discriminatory personnel practices.[54]

*   *   *   *   *

Abortion and busing were major targets of the administration throughout
the eight years of Reagan's presidency. Because busing was almost exclusively
a school-related problem, it will be treated in the later discussion of educational policy. Abortion was peripherally related to schooling through the
debate on sex education, but the problem was argued principally as an issue
of right to life versus right to privacy and personal decision-making.

Anti-abortion sentiment, as expressed in state laws prohibiting such
procedures, ruled for most of the country's history. Reagan first faced this
problem as governor of California when, in response to a growing demand for
freedom of choice in the matter of childbearing, a bill was introduced in the

state legislature to ease the restrictions on abortion. The one earlier exception to absolute prohibition, permitting abortion if the mother's life was endangered, was broadened to include rape, incest and danger to the mother's mental health. Reagan's problem was that his own staff, as well as Republican legislators, were divided on the issue. Accustomed to having such difficulties ironed out and a staff consensus presented to him in an easily digestible form, Reagan suddenly found himself without solid support for the negative response he preferred. As biographer Lou Cannon observed, "left to his own devices, he didn't know where to turn." But having successfully fought to eliminate other "loopholes" in the bill, he accepted what he considered a compromise measure. Even as he signed the law, however, he anticipated the rapid increase in abortions that actually occurred, saying, "The prognosis of mental health would be easier to exaggerate than the diagnosis of physical health."[55] Years later he explained the California situation rather differently, saying, "I once approved the law in California that allowed that [abortion] as a justification in the line of self-defense. . . . I have found out since, that that was used as a gigantic loophole in the law, and it literally led to abortion on demand on the plea of rape."[56] According to his foremost biographer, "Cardinal McIntyre warned Reagan exactly of what would happen" *before* he signed the bill, and the major loophole Reagan acknowledged at the time was not the plea of rape but "mental health deterioration."[57]

After leaving the governor's office, Reagan frequently expressed his regret over signing the California abortion law, but he never admitted that it had been an error in judgment. His anti-abortion position was always stated clearly, although his tone grew more strident after he reached the White House. During his first campaign for the presidency, he put it this way: "I personally believe that interrupting a pregnancy is the taking of a human life and can only be justified in self-defense—that is, if the mother's own life is in danger."[58]

Oddly enough, in his first presidential discussion of this issue, Reagan said that once the existence of human life [in the mother's womb] is determined, "then there isn't really any need for an amendment, because . . . the Constitution already protects the right to human life."[59] A year later he still seemed to equivocate when asked if he supported Senator Orrin Hatch's proposal for a constitutional amendment "to ban abortions for all women, rich or poor." Addressing a Knights of Columbus convention in August 1982, he said, "The Senate now has three proposals on this matter from Senators Hatch, Helms, and Hatfield." Without identifying any as a constitutional amendment (only one was), he added, "I'm urging the Senate to give these proposals the speedy consideration they deserve."[60]

This marked the beginning of his direct attack on the Supreme Court's 1973 decision in Roe v. Wade, which held that during the first three months of pregnancy "the attending physician, in consultation with his patient, is free to determine, without regulation by the State, that in his medical judgment the patient's pregnancy should be terminated."[61] Arguing that once life has begun, aborting that life amounts to murder, Reagan introduced this topic into speech after speech, at universities; Republican rallies; gatherings of business groups, veterans, religious leaders; and fund-raisers for supporters like Jesse Helms and Strom Thurmond.[62]

In support of his position Reagan sometimes offered "facts" that defied all available evidence. Speaking to a group of editors of religious publications he said, "I think the fact that children have been prematurely born, even down to the 3-month stage, and have lived—the record shows—to grow up and be normal human beings, that ought to be enough for all of us." Three days later the *Washington Post* reported that when one of the president's assistants tried to verify this with the president of the National Right to Life Committee, that official had to admit that he knew of no occasion on which a 3-month-old fetus had survived.[63] On other occasions, Reagan stated that "adoption is a readily available alternative" to abortion, ignoring the persistent pleas of orphanages and adoption agencies unable to place tens of thousands of children left without parents.[64]

In many of his discussions of abortion, Reagan acknowledged a difference of opinion between those who held the right-to-life position and others who stressed the rights of privacy and free choice. However, his attacks on the latter, like many of his other challenges, sometimes began with an overtly false presentation of the opposing point of view. On one occasion he described the philosophy of the pro-choice group in this way: "Too frequently I heard the argument that 'imperfect life is too expensive to maintain and prolong'."[65] The attitude that imperfect babies should be allowed to die can be found only in societies like those of Nazi Germany or ancient Greece which, each in its own way, worshipped physical perfection. No pro-choice group in the U.S. was ever known to express such an opinion. Nor has anyone used the high cost of medical service as the reason for terminating life support when that was all that was keeping a child alive.

More emotional than any other appeal was one based on a film of the abortion of a 12-week-old fetus. Titled *The Silent Scream,* it purported to show that even at an early stage a fetus reacts with pain and fear to "the violence of abortion." President Reagan suggested that "if every member of the Congress could see this film . . . Congress would move quickly to end the tragedy of abortion." In making this judgment he took no account of the views of five physician members of the American College of Obstetricians and Gynecologists who reviewed the film and came to a different conclusion. Asserting that a fetus allowed to develop normally would go through the same motions as the one in the film, the group's spokesman denied that a 12-week-old fetus could perceive and react in a knowing way to pain, or experience "the most mortal danger imaginable." He charged the film producer with having manipulated the pictures by changing from slow motion during the pre-abortion period to normal speed as the abortion procedure began.[66] However many Washington legislators may have seen the film, they were not induced to reverse their decision made in 1983, to reject a constitutional amendment that would have denied abortion any constitutional protection and thereby negate the Supreme Court's decision in Roe v. Wade.[67]

Shortly after the Senate had reported the 1983 Human Life Amendment, Reagan repeated his earlier warning, recalling his prediction that "the philosophical premises used to justify abortion on demand would ultimately be used to justify other attacks on the sacredness of human life—infanticide and mercy killing." As evidence that this forecast had come true, he asserted that "only last year a court permitted the death by starvation of a handicapped infant."[68] This was an area in which the courts acknowledged having great difficulty, but their decisions invariably were based on the care given a child, taking into consideration both medical evaluations and parental decisions made in light of medical opinion. The likelihood that a child would be "imperfect" or go through life with a serious handicap was never accepted as a reason for failure to provide adequate medical treatment. Yet this was the impression Reagan conveyed when discussing the series of "Baby Doe" cases that had come to the courts. He would compare a case in which medical treatment or life support had been withheld because of body or brain damage so severe as to indicate little or no prospect of life beyond the vegetable stage to one in which a child with similar but much less extensive damage had been treated and was able to live for years with its handicap.[69]

The government's position, as expressed by the Departments of Justice, and Health and Human Welfare, and of Surgeon General C. Everett Koop, was that federal authorities were entitled to intervene to enforce medical treatment for any child classified as handicapped when non-treatment could be construed as discrimination based on the child's handicapped condition. To make intervention possible, federal authorities insisted on the right to examine the hospital records of any handicapped child suspected of being mistreated by way of withholding medical treatment. The attempt to put this policy into practice under the provisions of the Rehabilitation Act of 1973 was rejected by federal district and appeals courts in 1984, a decision that was later confirmed by the Supreme Court in a ruling in 1986.[70]

A majority of five of the eight participating justices found that the report "makes irresistible the inference that the Department regards its mission as one principally concerned with the *quality* of medical care for handicapped infants" rather than with implementation of the law relating to discriminatory treatment. In support of this view, it cited the lower court's finding that the department's regulation "provides for an intrusive on-premises enforcement mechanism that can be triggered by a simple anonymous call" to the Baby Doe hot line.[71]

*　*　*　*　*

Perhaps the most remarkable aspect of the Baby Doe controversy was the way in which it demonstrated a complete reversal of the old Reagan philosophy that family matters should be decided without interference by government. As early as 1961 Reagan had accused "those of liberal persuasion" of rejecting "the notion that the least government is the best government." By using a "foot in the door" technique, he said, liberals work to expand government activity, "always aiming at the ultimate goal—government that will someday be a Big Brother to us all." Apparently, nothing accomplished in the eight years of the conservative Eisenhower administration altered Reagan's 1961 opinion that "we now have a permanent structure of government beyond the reach of Congress and actually capable of dictating policy. This power, under whatever name you choose, is the very essence of totalitarianism."[72] Three years later, in his famous Goldwater speech, Reagan declared: "Either we [as individuals] accept responsibility for our own destiny, or we abandon the American Revolution and confess that an intellectual belief in a far-distant capitol can plan our lives for us better than we can plan them ourselves."[73]

Running for the presidential nomination in 1976, Reagan stressed the importance of the family and the freedom of parents to decide what is best for the family. The threat of intervention from Washington, he warned, came in such legislation as a pending proposal "which in the name of child care would insert the government into the family's decisions with regard to children, decisions which properly are the right of the parent."[74] Applying this principle to family problems in general, and women's rights in particular, the platform on which he ran for president in 1980 stated: "We oppose any move which would give the federal government more power over families."[75]

The theme of the independent family persisted throughout Reagan's presidency. A 1983 address included this question in a wide-ranging attack on "modern-day secularism": "How far are they willing to go in giving to government their prerogatives as parents?" Reagan's answer was that "the rights of parents and the rights of family take precedence over those of Washington-based bureaucrats and social engineers."[76] In 1984 he repeated his attack on liberals for "paying parents for expenses they used to handle themselves," warning that the result would be "big government becoming Big Brother, pushing parents aside, interfering with one parental responsibility after another."[77] He continued to sound the Big Brother warning[78] even in the face of his own Department of Health and Human Services' practice of investigating every hot-line complaint of alleged parental mis-

treatment of ailing children, and its attempts to enforce its superior judgment upon parents, doctors and hospitals whenever it deemed this necessary.
When, a few days after rejecting the government's Baby Doe arguments, the
court reaffirmed its Roe v. Wade decision in a new abortion case, Reagan
issued a statement calling for elimination of that right, "whether by statute
or constitutional amendment."[79]

Reagan's preoccupation with abortion as an inhuman act was not accompanied by an equal show of concern for the inhumanity of physical attacks on
clinics and consulting offices maintained by pro-abortion personnel, or for
the ill-fed, ill-clad, and ill-housed babies born into a level of poverty that all
but guaranteed the kind of life that seventeenth-century philosopher Thomas
Hobbes described as "nasty, brutish and short." As one Catholic, pro-life
member of Congress remarked, "Reagan himself is anti-life once the kid is
born. He is opposed to any program that would help a poor child and the
child's family."[80]

The immediate problem of violence perpetrated by anti-abortionists Reagan never discussed with the media. But after picketing, intimidation and
invasions of clinics and family planning centers escalated to bombings and
arson, he issued a one-paragraph statement in which he said, "I condemn, in
the strongest terms, those individuals who perpetrate these and all such
violent, anarchist activities. As President of the United States, I will do all in
my power to assure that the guilty are brought to justice."[81] On most other
occasions he deplored only "the violence of abortion," which he compared
with pro-life leader Nellie Gray's "nonviolent commitment to life."[82]

Congress took the arson and acts of violence more seriously, despite the
assertion of Pro-Life Action League executive director Joseph M. Scheidler
that "I don't know if I'm in a position to condemn them; I'm not sure [the
charges of violence] are true."[83] Scheidler went on to say he would not
condemn such actions "until they [pro-abortionists] are willing to condemn
the greater violence" of abortion. He compared the laws permitting abortion
to those of Nazi Germany that said "you could kill people."

The effectiveness of the campaign of violence by some anti-abortionists
was evidenced by the number of such incidents, which rose to 224 in 1985
and included 32 bombings documented by representatives of the FBI and the
Treasury Department's Bureau of Alcohol, Tobacco and Firearms.[84] When
insurance companies began cancelling their coverage of community health
centers that had been subjected to violent attack, anti-abortionists were
encouraged to further violence as a means of forcing centers to close or risk
operating without insurance protection.[85]

*   *   *   *   *

"The crown jewel of American liberty," President Reagan told his Saturday
radio audience in 1983, is "every American's right to vote."[86] This statement

came little more than six months after Congress had ignored the president's plea to let the Voting Rights Act of 1965 stand as originally written and had revised the act to permit discrimination to be demonstrated by election results rather than solely by the proven intent of those running state or local elections.

The difficulty of proving intent had surfaced on many occasions. Where the evidence was direct, as in attempts to rig elections by buying votes, stuffing ballot boxes, gerrymandering based on race, or denial of some citizens' right to vote by the use of poll taxes and literacy tests, challenges had been successful.[87] However, until 1962 the federal courts had refused to pass judgment on the reasonableness of a state's arrangement of electoral districts except when there was clear evidence of an intent to discriminate against a particular class or race of voter.

A dramatic change in the Supreme Court's attitude was heralded by the declaration in 1962 that federal courts do have jurisdiction over a challenge to a state's district system based on a violation of some citizens' equal protection rights "by virtue of the debasement of their votes."[88] This opened the door to suits charging debasement or "dilution" of voting power resulting from an arrangement of electoral districts whereby some had much larger populations than others, or providing for election of legislators at large instead of one per district, a system that allows the majority party or faction to win all the seats and leaves even large minorities with no representation.

Two years after the Supreme Court accepted jurisdiction in such matters, the principle of equal voting power for all was established when the court declared that Article 1, Section 2 of the Constitution meant that "as nearly as practicable one man's vote in a congressional election is to be worth as much as another's."[89] This was followed by an equally important decision which held that the Fourteenth Amendment's guarantee of equal protection of the laws "requires that a State make an honest and good faith effort to construct districts, in both houses of its legislature, as nearly of equal population as is practicable." As Chief Justice Earl Warren put it, the effectiveness of some voters' choices is "diluted" when an apportionment system gives citizens in one part of a state "two times, or five times, or ten times the weight of citizens in another part of the State." Equal representation, he said means that each person's vote will be "weighted equally with those of all other citizens."[90]

The following year this principle was recognized by Congress when it passed the Voting Rights Act of 1965. Still, the act left intact the necessity of proving "intent" to discriminate, although any *change* in voting procedure had to be tested by the Justice Department to insure that it "does not have the purpose and will not have the effect of denying or abridging the right to vote on account of race or color."[91] Relying on the intent requirement, the courts continued to reject charges of discrimination in existing arrangements of electoral districts unless the departure from the principle of equal-population districts was such that at least one could be shown to be over 25 percent bigger—or smaller—than the average.[92]

In 1981 Congress set out to remedy this situation by amending the Voting Rights Act to permit challenges to existing apportionment systems based on the discriminatory effects they produced. President Reagan met this test of his devotion to the crown jewel of American liberty by objecting to any such change. Even before any revision had been drafted, he expressed his doubts about the original Voting Rights Act. In a request to Attorney General William French Smith for an assessment of the act, Reagan indicated that the major question was not "whether the rights which the Act seeks to protect are worthy of protection, but whether the Act continues to be the most appropriate means of guaranteeing those rights."[93] On the day the attorney general's report was due (October 1) a reporter asked the president about his attitude toward an extension of the Voting Rights Act. Reagan replied that he had not yet received Smith's report but, resorting to the equivocal language of diplomacy, said, "I am wholeheartedly in favor, let's say, in principle of the Voting Rights Act."[94]

The attorney general's report was not made public, but in mid-October the confidence that some of Reagan's supporters had in his approach to the problem was expressed by the editor of an unidentified Virginia newspaper. Complaining that the Voting Rights Act had "deprived the citizens of the City of Richmond of the right to run their own government," he assured the president that "the prevailing mood of the people in Virginia is to hope that you will continue to oppose extension of the Voting Rights Act in anything like its present form." Again Reagan hedged, but he concluded his answer by saying, "I agree with you that the perpetuating of punishment for sins that are no longer being committed is pretty extreme."[95] The following month, in his third "crown jewel" announcement, the president stated in a press release that he would approve extension of the Voting Rights Act—which by then had been passed by the House of Representatives—but that the law "should retain the 'intent' test rather than changing to a new and untested 'effects' standard." Asked later in the day how he had reached this decision, he said simply, "I made it."[96]

Refusing to support White House and Justice Department objections to a change from proof of intent to proof of the effects of discrimination, the Republican-controlled Senate approved several 1982 amendments to the Voting Rights Act, including a provision which stated:

No voting qualification or prerequisite to voting or standard, practice, or procedure shall be imposed or applied by any State or political subdivision in a manner *which results in* a denial or abridgement of the right of any citizen of the United States to vote on account of race or color. [Emphasis added.][97]

In the face of strong bipartisan support for this change in the law, President Reagan bowed to the inevitable, announcing that he was "pleased" to sign an extension of the Voting Rights Act which "says to every individual, 'your vote is equal' [and] no vote counts more than another." Acknowledging differences of opinion as to how equality should be attained, he said the legislation proved his "unbending commitment to voting rights."[98]

Reagan's attempt to associate himself with the accomplishment of new guarantees of voting equality in no way altered the attitude of those Justice Department officials most responsible for implementing the law. Assistant Attorney General William Bradford Reynolds, in charge of the department's civil rights division, continued to oppose the "results" test with the same arguments he had used before the extension bill was passed: that the new measure went beyond the Fifteenth Amendment's guarantee of the right to vote by establishing a right to get a particular person elected—in effect making proportional representation the new standard.[99] When North Carolina adopted a redistricting plan for the state Senate and House of Representatives in 1982, which was challenged by a group of black voters, the U. S. Justice Department's assistant secretary for civil rights and its solicitor general filed a brief in support of North Carolina, contending that a decision in favor of the black voters would be contrary to the intent of the law by guaranteeing minorities representation in the legislature "based on their percentage of the population." An outraged group of ten senators—including Republican Majority Leader Robert Dole and four other Republican sponsors of the 1982 Voting Rights amendments—took the extraordinary step of filing a counter brief, charging the Justice Department with "blatantly misrepresenting" the law they had helped to draft.[100]

This first test of the revised Voting Rights Act produced a variety of opinions on the eight questions posed by the case, but all nine of the Supreme Court justices agreed that North Carolina's use of multi-member districts in parts of the state violated the 1982 statute. In doing so, they accepted the decision of Congress to alter the standards by which discrimination is determined.

Acceptance by the Justice Department was another matter. Even as the North Carolina case was being tried, the department promulgated a new set of regulations in which it proposed shifting the burden of proof from the state to those alleging violation of the law, raising the standard of proof, and giving the attorney general the right to determine when a state's districting system was "unreasonable," "unnecessary" or "unfair."[101] After examining the department's proposed revision of its regulations, a House committee effectively blocked its adoption by stating that "if adopted, the proposed regulations would undermine effective enforcement of the Voting Rights Act."[102]

William Bradford Reynolds' contribution to the Reagan administration's record on civil rights, long criticized by minority and women's organizations, came under the scrutiny of the Senate Judiciary Committee in June 1985 after he had been nominated by the president for promotion from assistant to associate attorney general of the United States.[103] Many of the questions raised at that time concerned Reynolds' approval of state redistricting plans, especially those which his own staff objected to, and some that federal courts subsequently struck down as racially discriminatory.

Sensing the seriousness of the opposition from the first two days of testimony, President Reagan devoted almost the whole of one Saturday radio program to Reynolds' defense, charging that his critics "tell us that the government should enforce discrimination in favor of some groups through hiring quotas" and that "some bluntly assert that our civil rights laws apply only to special groups and were never intended to protect every American."[104] The latter statement, as indicated earlier, had been made not by administration critics, but by a member of the president's own Civil Rights Commission.

When the Judiciary Committee reconvened for a third day of hearings, Democratic Senator Metzenbaum denounced the president's attempt to confuse the issue. "It is not a matter, Mr. President, of busing and quotas" the senator said. "It is a matter of Mr. Reynolds' dedication to the laws of this land, and their enforcement."[105]

In the end, it was the manner in which Reynolds undertook to interpret and enforce civil rights laws, often in a fashion that most senators regarded as contrary to the law's intent, that led to rejection of his nomination by a Senate that was still dominated by a Republican majority.

CHAPTER 6

Apostle of Justice, Law and Order

"Justice can be good, bad, or indifferent, depending on the judge and on the man who appoints the judge. He, in effect, controls the administration of justice through the men he chooses."[1]

RONALD REAGAN'S CONCEPT OF JUSTICE CHANGED RADICALLY OVER THE years. Where once he believed in the Hubert Humphrey-Harry Truman approach to solving social and economic problems through low-cost housing for the poor, civil rights legislation, and "a labor movement free of the Taft-Hartley law," he entered the political arena as an opponent of almost every legislative program aimed at achieving this kind of justice.[2]

The problem of union organization did not become a personal one for Reagan until he was well into adulthood. For the first 27 years of his life he gave little thought to what a union meant to the otherwise unprotected American worker. It may have been true, as he recalled in his autobiography, that for a small-town teenager looking for summer employment in 1925, "unions were something you only read about." But even in 1938, having landed a movie contract, he seemed unaware of organized labor's struggle for the basic legal rights that had finally been won through the Norris-LaGuardia Act of 1932 and the National Labor Relations Act of 1935. Indeed, if he had ever heard of this history-making legislation, there is no evidence of it in the four chapters of his autobiography that were devoted largely to the internal politics of the Hollywood unions. By his own account, his temporary awakening came from "an hour's lecture on the facts of life" from a member of the Screen Actors Guild. His conversion, he wrote in 1965, was immediate, and at that point he said, "I have considered myself a rabid union man ever since."[3] His subsequent record reveals that he remained a firm supporter of the Screen Actors Guild, but his enthusiasm for other unions depended on their attitude toward his newly adopted conservative Republican philosophy.

Reagan's first major political speech was a slashing attack on all government activity that would place limits on the freedom of private industry to operate entirely by its own rules. Included among a long list of anecdotes intended as demonstrations of the idiocy of government harassment of business was an unidentifiable and untraceable charge of interference in company management by the National Labor Relations Board. Little more than two years later, taking the oath of office as governor of California, Reagan followed an assurance of support for the union shop with the assertion that "government must accept a responsibility for safeguarding each union member's democratic rights" by instituting laws that would "guarantee each union member a secret ballot in his union on policy matters and the use of union dues." In plain English, his goal was to prevent unions from supporting Democratic candidates in a way that would offset the enormous financial backing he and his Republican colleagues could count on, year in and year out, from their unregulated friends in industry.[4]

No such intervention in business management would be tolerated, as the governor made clear when he told a convention of industrialists, "My administration makes no bones about being business-oriented." His discussion of labor problems in subsequent speeches was always made in terms of the jobs that would be supplied by a prosperous business community. In a rare reference to union leadership, he paid tribute to Samuel Gompers, president of the American Federation of Labor from 1886 to 1924 and admired by Reagan for his refusal to engage in any political activity or labor bargaining beyond questions of wages and hours.[5]

Failing to win the Republican nomination for president in 1976, Reagan nevertheless fully endorsed the party platform adopted for that election. In a February 1977 speech to the American Conservative Union he quoted, word for word, more than a dozen paragraphs of the platform. The one portion of that document he ignored completely was an unusually lengthy section, devoted exclusively to labor unions, which supported collective bargaining as well as the restrictive Taft-Hartley Act that Reagan had so abhorred when he was a Democrat.[6]

When Reagan became the Republican candidate in 1980, he no longer spoke directly to union leaders, with one outstanding exception. His alliance with Teamsters union officials brought a disavowal of one of his basic principles. Soliciting Teamster support during the presidential campaign he wrote, "Although I have long been opposed to increased and unnecessary government regulations, the current policy of the Carter administration on deregulation of the trucking industry is ill-conceived and not in the best interests of the country." The Teamsters' magazine was quick to reprint that letter for the benefit of its more than two million members. As a post-election follow-up, Reagan paid his respects at the union's Washington headquarters, a visit headlined in the Teamster magazine under the slogan, "First Our House, Then The White House."[7]

Other references to labor, both in the Republican platform and in Reagan's speeches, were made in terms of jobs and the need to make more work available through reduced business taxes and economic expansion. Both promised a "safety net" of unemployment compensation benefits and retrain-ing of displaced workers—appying a new catch-phrase to legislation already in existence—and proposed a "youth differential" below the minimum wage to open more jobs to the millions of unemployed young people. Reagan had long advocated this lower wage scale despite the charge from organized labor that it would only lead to the firing of mature employees and their replace-ment with cheaper young workers.[8]

As president, Reagan's attitude toward labor problems was indicated by his appointment of Labor Secretary Raymond J. Donovan, a New Jersey building contractor whose only experience was as an employer of union workers in the shady construction industry. Donovan's reputed association with leaders of organized crime made no more impression on the president than did the knowledge that the only union to support his presidential candidacy was the racket-ridden International Brotherhood of Teamsters, whose officers were subsequently rewarded by being given regular access to the White House throughout Reagan's entire term of office. Donovan's history of indifference to either government or union regulations dismayed both Republicans and Democrats and, when revealed by a congressional committee after his appointment, led Reagan's own White House Chief of Staff James Baker, III to call for the labor secretary's resignation.[9]

Undeterred either by Baker's recommendation or by Donovan's indictment on charges of fraud and grand larceny, Reagan could say "I told you so" when his labor secretary was acquitted in 1987. But by that time Donovan had resigned in the face of continuing criticism, arising partly out of a charge by a Republican-led Senate committee that the FBI had withheld information bearing on his fitness for office and had instead supplied information that was "inaccurate, unclear and too late."[10] Meanwhile, Donovan did the job he was hired for, enacting Reagan's concept of workers' rights to occupational health and safety by applying the principle that, beyond "certain minimal stan-dards," government should have no control over business management of the workplace.

A similar bias was demonstrated in other areas of labor law. As a House subcommittee on labor-management relations disclosed early in 1984, unions were forced to submit endless documents that employers could use against them, while employers were permitted to virtually ignore their legal obligation to provide similar reports. In effect, the committee chairman said, "the administration is enforcing the law only as it applies to unions" and was encouraging employers not to comply with the law.[11] Tolerating deliberate evasion of the law by employers, Reagan was quick to fire some 13,000 air traffic controllers 48 hours after they had gone on strike August 3, 1981 to protest the government's refusal to go beyond its initial offer of increased pay and improved working conditions. Taking the position that "there is no strike" because the law doesn't permit it, he said that "in effect, what they did was terminate their own employment by quitting." In this respect he had come a long way from the position he took in 1965 when, as a confirmed conservative, he could still say, "I think we have the right as free men to refuse to work for just grievances: the right to strike is an inalienable weapon of any citizen."[12] At that point he made no distinction between strikes against private employers and those against public agencies.

As to the promised safety net for the unemployed, Reagan failed to honor his pledge to provide more than token training and other assistance for workers who had been laid off or could not find jobs. Part of his spending reduction program involved elimination of the Comprehensive Employment and Training Act (CETA) program, which was supporting state and local employment of over 300,000 people when Reagan took office. Within a year these people were out of work, along with more than 500,000 others who were stripped of aid they had received "because they had lost their jobs in part or wholly because of import competition."[13] As indicated earlier, Reagan's substitute Job Training Partnership Act of 1982 did little to resolve the problem of displaced workers.[14]

Shortly before the 1984 Republican convention, Reagan's labor liaison officers warned union leaders against opposition to the president's reelection, "to avoid bad feelings in a second Reagan administration." The message to all employees—union and nonunion—was clear: play by Reagan's rules or face four years of even rougher treatment than he and his subordinates had meted out thus far.

Under Labor Secretary Donovan's successors, William E. Brock, III and Ann Dore McLaughlin, the threats and harsh rhetoric disappeared, but there was no basic change in policy or attitude. Except for the corrupt but pro-administration Jackie Presser and his fellow-officers of the Teamsters Union, organized labor was still associated with the enemy.[15]

*   *   *   *

In broad terms, Reagan spelled out his view of law and order while he was governor of California. Concerned, at that point, principally with conditions within that state, he built a case for crime control based on his earlier assertion that states' rights "are a built-in guarantee of freedom."[16] Acknowledging the need for cooperation among local, state and federal authorities, he warned National Institute on Crime and Delinquency (NICD) members against allowing the federal government to take on the primary role of law enforcement. "When this happens," he said, "we will have, in effect, a national police force. And we will have taken steps to abolish crime only at the risk of our freedom." Ignoring the fact that a national police force had been in existence since the establishment of the FBI more than forty years earlier, he pressed the incontestable argument that strong law enforcement is essential at the state and local levels.

Carrying the local autonomy principle further, Reagan told his 1968 audience that the first weapon needed was "an effective law to restore to the cities and counties the ability to enact local laws designed to meet local problems."[17] This open invitation to local groups to design rules governing crime and punishment based on their particular preferences and prejudices was in accord with Reagan's conception of the community as the next most important societal unit after the family. Even if this evaluation is accepted, his suggestion would have destroyed the illusion that states rights are a guarantee of freedom and would have produced a disastrous mishmash of local laws and an unprecedented logjam of civil rights cases.

Addressing the law-and-order problem as a national issue two years later, Reagan explained the terms "equality" and "born equal" to a 1970 gathering of Republican women in this fashion:

> We are equal before God and the law, and our society guarantees that no acquisition of property during our lifetime, no achievement, no matter how exemplary, should give us more protection than those of less prestige, nor should it exempt us from any of the restrictions and punishments imposed by the law.[18]

This speech, as much as any other, reveals the nature of Reagan's notions of justice and of the good society. The association of law and order with the Deity was vintage Reagan. After reaching the presidency, Reagan offered an amendment which would justify overruling man-made law if it did not measure up to his more righteous view of the Lord's intent: "It's not good enough to have equal access to our law; we must also have equal access to the higher law—the law of God."[19]

In the first of these pronouncements, the reference to acquisition of property as a major standard of achievement reflected Reagan's belief in the right to accumulate wealth as "the very basis of individual freedom."[20] Yet those with little wealth, according to his explanation, are entitled to the same protection as those with great wealth, and the latter must suffer the same punishment as the former for breaking the law.

Critics of the Reagan philosophy are tempted to label these premises mere rhetoric, if only because they ignore the enormous advantage wealth affords in securing the protection of government officials, in access to the courts of law, and in buying the services of legal talent capable of keeping punishment, if any, to a minimum. Beyond rhetoric, however, they would point out that both as governor and as president Reagan did his best to dismantle the legislatures' programs to guarantee government-funded legal aid to those too poor to pay for legal representation in court.

In another context, Reagan's praise of Martin Luther King, Jr. was effusive after congressional action and knowledge of the growing force of the black vote had forced him to accept the designation of King's birthday as a federal holiday in 1986.[21] In this case, we have no assurance that he had changed his mind about civil disobedience, which King encouraged and Reagan deplored. We know only that he recognized the political force of the movement to pay tribute to King's influence in the battle to change laws that had long upheld racial discrimination. However, in the 1960s, when King was breaking the law by leading "freedom marchers" without a local permit, and when a black woman was arrested for refusing a lawful order to move to the back of the bus, Reagan never challenged the application of local justice to these transgressors. Indeed, under the leadership of avowed segregationist Governor George Wallace, the state of Alabama and the cities and towns in that part of the country were following the Reagan formula of "enacting local laws designed to meet local problems." As an unannounced candidate for the Republican presidential nomination in 1968, Reagan offered no criticism of candidate Wallace's discriminatory policy. On the contrary, he characterized as "attractive" his opponent's emphasis on "law and order, patriotism, and so forth." His only complaint against Wallace was that "he showed no opposition particularly to get programs of federal aid and spending programs and so forth."[22] And as he had told a California audience in 1967, when oppression becomes unbearable, everyone is free to "vote with his feet" by quitting his or her job, uprooting the family, and draining the family resources to travel to another part of the country without knowing anything of the possibilities of finding work or shelter there.

* * * * *

"The fellas," as Reagan affectionately referred to his kitchen cabinet of California boosters, performed many services beyond fund-raising and electioneering. They handpicked the overwhelming majority of the senior administrators who were to run the executive branch in Sacramento. When

Reagan won the presidency, they performed the same function by selecting top officials for the federal departments that were responsible for administering the law of the land. The approach that most of these administrators took toward implementing federal statutes has already been covered in some detail. However, the office of the nation's chief law enforcement officer—the attorney general of the United States—deserves special attention.

Reagan did not have to look far to find an attorney general to his liking. William French Smith was not only one of "the fellas," he was Reagan's personal attorney and financial adviser who had been instrumental in arranging the investments and real estate deals that made Reagan a millionaire within months of assuming the governor's office in California.[23] Smith was also a member of President-elect Reagan's executive search team, a circumstance which suggests that the search for an individual with outstanding talent in the field of public law enforcement was both brief and limited in scope.

A corporate lawyer in private practice, Smith had no experience in either criminal law or those areas of civil law with which government is most concerned: civil rights, national security, economic controls and the administration of social programs. On the other hand, he was wholeheartedly in agreement with Reagan's view of what constitutes the good society, and he was fully as business-oriented as Reagan. In fact, much of his private practice had involved representing major industrial clients in their disputes with labor unions.

Smith did not remain in the cabinet through Reagan's second term, but he set the tone for the administration by announcing that the judiciary had intruded into executive policy-making and that his department would "attempt to reverse this unhealthy flow of power from state and local governments to the federal level." Asserting, like Reagan, that the 1980 election reflected "a groundswell of conservatism" that would support any and all administrative views, he felt it "an especially appropriate time to urge upon the courts more principled bases that would diminish judicial activism." The phrase "judicial activism" was to become an administrative slogan that even the *American Bar Association Journal* recognized as indicating an effort to "politicize the federal judiciary and constitutional law."[24]

Smith's desire to return to private practice opened the way for Reagan to reward his longtime friend and associate in government Edwin Meese, III with the nation's highest law-enforcement post. Meese's reputation as a hardnosed law-and-order advocate had been earned in California, where he was employed successively as deputy district attorney, legal affairs secretary to Governor Reagan, and then his executive assistant. His attitude toward law enforcement was demonstrated on a number of occasions during that period, including planning the strategy for controlling student uprisings by force of arms, rather than by patient dialogue, as had been successfull elsewhere.[25] When a civilian was killed by a sheriff's deputy during a battle between students and so-called street people over the use of People's Park in Berkeley, California, Meese's prosecutor-judge-and-jury conclusion was, "James Rector deserved to die."[26] But when it came to facilities for the defense of people who could not pay lawyers' fees, Meese led Governor Reagan's drive to subvert the California law authorizing the use of state and federal funds to support legal services for the poor.[27] As for the one private organization best known for its defense of poor and otherwise unpopular clients against what it considers the overwhelming advantage of government over the individual, the American Civil Liberties Union was characterized by Meese as a "criminals' lobby." This was on a par with his assertion that individuals are not arrested if they are innocent, implying he assumed every arrested person to be guilty before being brought to trial.[28]

This sequence of events and opinions was important to the Senate committee that considered Meese's nomination to the post of attorney general of the United States, not only for what it said about Meese's approach to law enforcement, but because it clearly represented the views of President Reagan as well. White House reporters found the minds of Reagan and Meese so closely attuned that in the very first year of Reagan's presidency Meese came to be known as "keeper of the philosophical flame," and was frequently referred to as "President Meese."[29]

In the committee hearings, Meese assured members of the Senate Judiciary Committee that he would do everything in his power to uphold the Justice Department's "tradition of integrity, professionalism and independence."[30] He made no mention of ethics in his pledge, yet time and again that issue came up in the committee's discussion of his qualifications. In every case, the affable candidate's answer to queries about the ethics of a particular problem was either, "It depends on the situation" or, "I have no recollection," or a flat denial that his recommendations for appointments to federal offices had anything to do with the nominees' loans of money or aid to him in financial transactions.[31]

Opposition to Meese's appointment to the highest law-enforcement position in the land delayed Senate approval for almost ten months. The objections and suspicions voiced at his nomination hearings by Senators Joseph R. Biden, Edward M. Kennedy and Howard M. Metzenbaum, supported by a number of civil rights organizations, were reinforced shortly after Meese's assumption of office in the Justice Department. In the first of a series of public addresses beginning July 9, 1985, Attorney General Meese opened a campaign for what he called a "Jurisprudence of Original Intention." The effect was to formalize the Reagan administration's conception of how the Constitution should be interpreted in three areas: federal-state relations, criminal law, and religion. His analysis of First Amendment protections against "an establishment of religion, or prohibiting the free exercise thereof" was particularly enlightening, as it paved the way for the renewal of Reagan's long campaign to reintroduce prayer into the classroom and extend government support to schools operated by religious institutions.

Meese began his attempt to "make sense of the religious cases" that had been reviewed by the Supreme Court in its 1984–85 term by recalling that "it was not until 1925, in *Gitlow v. New York* that *any* provision of the Bill of Rights was applied to the states," and not until 1947 "that the Establishment Clause was made applicable to the states through the Fourteenth Amendment."[32] Denouncing these and subsequent court decisions which invalidated state laws permitting public employees to teach in church-operated schools, or authorizing organized but voluntary prayer in public schools, he cited as the most authoritative source in this field his own choice for chief justice of the Supreme Court, William H. Rehnquist. As an associate justice, Rehnquist had joined then-Chief Justice Warren Burger in dissenting from the majority opinion of the court in all of the cases which Meese now used to argue that the majority view rested upon an "intellectually shaky foundation."[33]

The slipshod character of Meese's review of constitutional history is seen first in his initial assumption that in 1787, "since each state had a bill of rights," anti-Federalist opponents of the Constitution considered it appropriate that the federal document have one as well. In fact, what in 1787 was commonly referred to as a "declaration of rights" was included in only eight of the first thirteen state constitutions.[34]

A serious demand for a federal bill of rights arose *after* the convention had completed its work and released the proposed constitution for publication. Pleaders for this cause were not, as Meese suggested, limited to anti-Federalists. Moreover, of all the protections sought, freedom of religion was mentioned only occasionally, largely because religious prejudice was still widespread. As historian Jackson Turner Main notes, "most opinion voiced in New England was animated by a desire to exclude non-Protestants from public office—not by toleration but by intolerance."[35] New Jersey and North Carolina also retained a Protestant-only rule for public officials. In other states, the requirement of Christian belief ensured Catholics protection of their civil rights and the right to hold office. Massachusetts, New Hampshire and North Carolina laws sanctioned religious bias, either by permitting public support of Protestant churches and ministers or by making Protestantism a requisite for public office. Only Virginia and Rhode Island had eliminated all religious preferences by 1787.

In his reconstruction of America's early history, Meese assumed that because the First Amendment was intended to apply only to the national government, its sponsors were unanimous in the belief that the states should be free to deal with civil rights—including religious liberty—in any way they saw fit. This was not true even among critics of the Constitution, much less among those who pressed for a strong central government. Thomas Jefferson, for example, expressed serious doubts about the plan designed in Philadelphia, but he had no doubt whatever about the need for a "wall of separation" between church and state, at the local level as well as in national affairs. Prior to the Philadelphia convention he had demonstrated his devotion to separation of church and state by winning a long and bitter struggle with members of Virginia's established Anglican church, convincing the state legislature that "Almighty God hath created the mind free, and . . . all attempts to influence it by temporal punishments, or . . . civil incapacitations, are a departure from the plan of the holy author of our religion."[36]

Given this background, the Supreme Court had every reason to insist that the originators of the Bill of Rights intended these limits to apply only to the national government. On this point Meese was correct. However, what neither Meese nor the court ever pointed out is that the originators were not the men who designed the Constitution; they were the delegates in the state ratifying conventions who petitioned for precisely those restrictions on the national government that the founding fathers refused to include in the Constitution drafted in Philadelphia.

If Mr. Meese's reconstruction of the 1780s was something less than accurate, his interpretation of the Civil War amendments was equally flawed. It is true that for decades after the Fourteenth Amendment was ratified, most Supreme Court justices could find no reason to believe that Congress intended it to extend Bill of Rights limitations to the states. Yet the record of that intent is clear from statements in and out of Congress by Representative John A. Bingham of Ohio, who authored the key first section of the amendment, and by Senator Jacob M. Howard of Michigan. Bingham told the House that his specific purpose was "to arm the Congress of the United States . . . with the power to enforce the Bill of Rights as it stands in the Constitution today." In the Senate, Howard argued that to force states to respect the federal Bill of Rights required an amendment that would "forever disable every one of them [the states] from passing laws trenching upon those fundamental rights and privileges."[37] Although some aspects of the Fourteenth Amendment were bitterly debated, the broad purpose of the amendment as defined by Bingham and Howard was not challenged in either House or Senate.

As political power in the South was recaptured by advocates of white supremacy and the North rushed to industrialize, the goal of providing the newly freed slaves with the same civil rights as the white population was forgotten. Most of the civil rights cases that came before the Supreme Court in the next half-century were brought by corporations in defense of property rights, rather than by individuals seeking personal protection. And it was in a dispute over property rights that the court first suggested a connection between the Fourteenth Amendment and the federal Bill of Rights. This break occurred in 1903, not 1925 as asserted by Attorney General Meese. In that earlier case the court observed that the Fourteenth Amendment extends "the same protection against arbitrary state legislation affecting life, liberty and property, as is offered by the Fifth Amendment."[38] Although the same logic would clearly apply to First Amendment protections, it was not until 1925 that the court concluded that "freedom of speech and of the press— which are protected from abridgement by Congress by the First Amendment—are among the fundamental personal rights and liberties protected by the due process clause of the Fourteenth Amendment from impairment by the states." Another fifteen years passed before the court would acknowledge that the same protection should be accorded the religious clause of the First Amendment.[39]

In his chronology of Supreme Court civil rights cases, Meese jumped from 1925 to 1947, when the court admitted that the First Amendment ban against "an establishment of religion" was made applicable to the states through the Fourteenth Amendment.[40] He felt that this case, and those 1984–85 decisions that failed to meet his test of original intent proved his principal point: that because "the Bill of Rights, as debated, created and ratified was designed to apply *only* to the national government," nothing can be permitted to alter that immutable law.

In his robot-like reiteration of this theme, Meese not only overlooked the intent of the framers of the Fourteenth Amendment, he implied that no change in circumstances, national opinion, or concepts of right and wrong can justify any departure from the formula devised by the founding fathers. The implications of this stand are startling, to say the least. If adopted by the Supreme Court, the result would be a return to a nineteenth-century philosophy that permitted each state, if it wished, to support an established church, and each community to force school children of all faiths to participate in religious exercises dictated by adherents to the faith of the political majority. This danger was recognized in 1845 when the Supreme Court considered an appeal requesting it to declare unconstitutional a New Orleans ordinance aimed specifically, purposefully, and solely at the Catholic church. Even as it castigated some states for the continued religious discrimination evident in their statutes, the court acknowledged that the First Amendment did not give it authority to overturn those laws.[41] For almost a century after that 1845 decision, Catholics, Jews, minority Protestant sects and conscientious objectors continued to suffer discriminatory treatment because the federal courts played it Meese's way.[42]

Fortunately, even the conservative members of the Supreme Court appointed by President Reagan are not as ignorant of Constitutional history as Attorney General Meese. And although some have professed to follow the concept of original intent, they are unlikely to return federal jurisprudence to its nineteenth-century status. Should they do so, it will be in spite of, not because of, the efforts of James Madison, Thomas Jefferson, and their many supporters in the battle for religious and other First Amendment freedoms.

*   *   *   *   *

President Reagan made no secret of his desire to completely reshape the character and philosophy of the federal courts. In his selection of judges he had much in common with previous presidents, all of whom weighed judicial candidates largely in terms of their political, social and economic outlook. When George Washington became president, he never considered anyone to be eligible for judicial appointment who was not a firm supporter of the new constitution and what it meant in terms of a strong central government. His choice for chief justice of the Supreme Court was John Jay, who had coauthored the Federalist papers with Alexander Hamilton and James Madison. His five associate justice appointees (the court began with only six members) had been either members of the Constitutional Convention or leading proponents of ratification in their respective states.[43] All of his subsequent appointees were Federalists who were equally strong in their support of the Constitution.

Washington's successors were similarly influenced in their choices, although most also took into account the need to see that various parts of the country were represented. Thus, the three Supreme Court members appointed by Thomas Jefferson were confirmed anti-Federalists from South Carolina, New York and the new state of Kentucky. Reagan's favorite president—Abraham Lincoln—selected his nominees on the basis of their adherence to the relatively new Republican party or, if a Democrat, their support of the Union against the Confederacy. Personal friendship played a part with many presidents, including Lincoln, who appointed his close associate and campaign manager, David Davis, to the Supreme Court.

Best known for his proposed "court packing" plan was another of Reagan's heroes, Franklin D. Roosevelt. FDR's approach to the selection of Supreme Court justices was no different from that of his predecessors. However, his frustration at seeing the court declare much of his reform legislation unconstitutional led him to propose adding a new member to the court for every justice over 70 who refused to resign, a scheme that many Democrats in Congress refused to support.[44]

Reagan's view of the judiciary as an instrument for advancing a particular socio-political philosophy was on a par with Roosevelt's, though aimed in the opposite direction. Yet he faced little opposition to his appointments to the federal courts, especially in the early years. Getting off to a rousing start with the nomination of Sandra Day O'Connor as associate justice of the Supreme Court, Reagan not only gained the support of all but the most conservative Republicans, he also broke the pattern he had established as governor of California when, despite urging by his advisors to appoint a woman to the state supreme court, he filled three vacancies with solidly conservative Republican males.[45]

His choice of O'Connor to replace the retiring Potter Stewart raised no hackles among Democrats, and the only question from reporters at the announcement of her nomination was her right-to-life position. Refusing to discuss the matter in any detail, Reagan said he was "completely satisfied" with her stand on that issue.[46] At a fund-raiser for Illinois Governor James R. Thompson later in the day, Reagan was more expansive, but no more specific, saying that O'Connor's appointment was "consistent with the principles enunciated in our party platform this past year."[47] His reference was to a section that demanded of judicial appointees "the highest regard for protecting the rights of law-abiding citizens," support for "efforts to return decision-making power to state and local officials," and respect for "the sanctity of innocent human life."[48]

Clearly, the emphasis was on the candidates' approach to law enforcement and the protection of values as defined by Reagan and Meese. Thus, regard for the rights of "law-abiding citizens" fit readily into the Meese view that nobody accused of a crime can be considered law-abiding because innocent people are not accused of crimes. The demand that federal judges adhere to the line that most decision-making power is best left to state and local officials would appear to be only one aspect of Reagan's concept of "the new federalism," but it encouraged those who would bow to local prejudice in the drafting and enforcement of discriminatory laws relating to education, housing, employment and elections. Similarly, "the sanctity of innocent human life" was a warning that an anti-abortion stance was one of the standards for judicial appointment. If professional training and expertise were taken for granted, so, too, must have been other standards that experts in the field of law insist on, such as "personal and professional integrity," and the "ability to think and write logically and lucidly."[49]

Reagan's adoption of the standards expressed in the 1980 Republican platform did not mean that he would personally examine each candidate on those points. More than any other president in this century, he relied upon his attorney general to select and examine the qualifications of candidates for even the highest federal judicial posts. And, having accepted the attorney general's recommendations, he never once withdrew a nomination or failed to urge confirmation—up to the time a nominee voluntarily withdrew—regardless of opposition, or evidence of incompetence or lack of professional integrity.

The Senate Judiciary Committee's confirmation hearings clearly illustrate the kinds of serious questions that should have made the president think twice about a nominee, but didn't. One candidate, Alex Kozinski, had worked as an attorney under fundamentalist Herbert E. Ellingwood in the federal Merit Systems Protection Board (MSPB). When Ellingwood's protege appeared before the Senate Judiciary Committee as nominee for appointment to the Ninth Circuit Court of Appeals—one step below the Supreme Court— he and others were questioned closely about his work as special counsel to the MSPB. Testimony revealed that Kozinski had debased MSPB's "responsibility for hearing and adjudicating appeals by federal employees of adverse personnel actions" by conducting seminars for federal management personnel "to teach federal managers how to beat the system and rid themselves of disfavorite employees without being charged with prohibited personnel practices." Legal Director Thomas Devine, of the independent Government Accountability Project (GAP), also found Kozinski somewhat less than truthful when the candidate denied any knowledge of a case that Devine had discussed with him only two days before the hearing.[50]

As to an evaluation of candidate Kozinski by his peers, Senator Paul Simon summed up as follows:

> Of the four qualifications by the bar association: exceptionally well qualified, well qualified, qualified, and not qualified, the majority gave you qualified, but a minority rated you not qualified. You are one of 7 out of 43 nominees [submitted from January to June 1985] who have received a not qualified.[51]

This lowest possible qualified rating did not prevent Kozinski from winning confirmation from the Republican-controlled Senate, where the administration argued that any qualified vote by a majority of the bar association panel was sufficient grounds for confirmation, regardless of the level of excellence (or lack thereof) indicated by the vote, or the size of the minority opposing approval.

Resistance to judicial nominees of questionable quality increased in 1986, even before the election that gave the Democrats a majority in the Senate and, as a result, in the Judiciary Committee. Occasionally, advance publicity was sufficient to stave off a nomination, as in the case of Texas law professor Lino A. Graglia who, in his classroom, referred to blacks as "pickininnies," and in his writings had expressed doubt that the Constitution had been a positive force in the development of "our national well-being."[52]

While even marginally qualified candidates were eventually confirmed, the nomination of Jefferson B. Sessions, III for appointment as a district court judge met a different fate. Sessions came under bitter attack from civil rights groups and Democratic senators who cited comments like these as evidence of Sessions' inability to meet even minimal standards for appointment to the federal judiciary:

> The National Council of Churches, the NAACP (National Association for the Advancement of Colored People), SCLC (Southern Christian Leadership Conference), and PUSH (People United to Save Humanity) are un-American organizations with anti-traditional American values. I thought those guys [members of the Ku Klux Klan] were OK until I learned they smoked pot.

> You know the NAACP hates white people; they are out to get them. That is why they bring these lawsuits, and they are a commie group and a pinko organization as well.

> The Voting Rights Act is an intrusive piece of legislation.[53]

Session's explanation of these comments was either that he had no recollection of having made such remarks, or that he didn't mean them the way they sounded, or, in the case of the Klan, that it was a joke. Unconvinced, the committee refused to submit the nomination to the Senate.

A month before the Judiciary Committee voted on Sessions, an even more bitter contest arose over Reagan's nomination of Daniel A. Manion to be a Circuit Court of Appeals judge in the seventh district, which is centered in Chicago. Following a routine hearing, the Judiciary Committee received a number of protests in which Manion's suitability for the second highest court in the land was questioned, both on the basis of his ideological orientation and his legal competence. Called to a second hearing, Manion was questioned closely on the views he had expressed on "The Manion Forum," a television program that features Clarence Manion, his father, who was fed questions on key constitutional problems by Daniel, acting as a kind of interlocutor. Following his father's lead, Manion criticized the U.S. Supreme Court's decisions on prayer in public schools, legislative redistricting, pornography and obscenity. In one broadcast, a father-and-son colloquy asserted that the Supreme Court's decision that the Fourteenth Amendment made the First Amendment applicable to the states was "invented" by Justice Hugo Black, who "just spun it out of his head" with no constitutional ground.[54] Insisting that as an appellate court judge he would be bound by those decisions, Daniel Manion acknowledged that as an Indiana legislator he had cosponsored a bill authorizing the posting of the Ten Commandments in public schoolrooms two months after the Supreme Court had found this practice to be a state-sponsored intrusion into religious matters in neighboring Kentucky. On that score, Manion said, he continued to think such action was desirable, as it represented the opinion expressed by Justice Rehnquist in his dissent in the Kentucky case. It was not revealed until later that in exercising the privilege of editing the hearing transcript to eliminate typographical or grammatical errors, Manion had revised his testimony on the bill he cosponsored. He altered his original admission that "it would have to be declared unconstitutional" and "it would have been overturned" so that the official hearing record now quotes him as saying that "it would have been ostensibly unconstitutional and it probably would have been repealed."[55]

Some questions were directed to his characterization of a book denying the Supreme Court's power to make binding decisions as "one of the finest summaries of the history of our country that I have ever read." He was also asked to explain a letter he wrote to the John Birch Society's bookstore urging it to "keep up your work," and promising "to help you in whatever causes you may have before the State legislature." Reminded by Senator Paul Simon that the letter had been written in response to the John Birch Society's message of condolence on the death of Manion's father, he said it was just an effort to "say something nice." But although his father had lauded the society's members as "people who are on the front line of the fight for constitutional freedom," he told Senator Simon, "I could not tell you what the policies of the John Birch Society are."[56]

Throughout the hearing, Manion was strongly supported by committee chairman Strom Thurmond and by Alabama's Republican Senator Jeremiah Denton, who found Manion's father "one of the most admired men in my life" and who believed the son had "inherited from his distinguished father [the] high degree of integrity, conscientiousness, fairness and legal ability" that made him "uniquely qualified" to serve as an appellate judge.[57]

A very different assessment came from other sources. The Chicago Council of Lawyers advised the Senate committee that although Manion had "a high reputation for integrity, conscientiousness, and fairness [and] would struggle to be fair in ruling on cases which present issues on which he has strong political views," he had little or no experience in dealing with federal law and constitutional issues. Even in the state courts to which Manion brought principally personal injury, commercial and small claims cases, he did not demonstrate "the high-level of expertise which the Council feels should be possessed by judges of the Seventh Circuit." By way of illustration, the council submitted evaluations of five legal briefs that Manion had identified as among his best. They included these observations:

> The brief is poorly written. It is riddled with spelling errors, typographical errors and grammatical errors. The brief is neither clear nor forceful. It repeatedly speculates on what a witness "possibly" would have said had testimony been allowed. The argument is unnecessarily hard to follow. A C-minus job, at best. In one instance . . . his sentence structure becomes so tangled that he states the exact opposite of what he intends. Mr. Manion's

writing is less than persuasive partly because his brief is not very well organized and the confusing syntax often makes his arguments difficult to follow.[58]

Even more unusual was the action of a group of some 30 deans of the country's most prestigious law schools, led by those at Harvard and Yale, who protested that Manion simply did not measure up to the criteria essential for a federal appellate court judge.[59]

Despite the seriousness of the criticisms of Manion's legal philosophy, both by Senate committee members and outside experts, and clear evidence of his lack of experience and ability, President Reagan refused to retreat. His Saturday radio talk of June 21 climaxed the administration campaign in support of the appointment. Combining his praise of Manion with an announcement of the nomination of William H. Rehnquist to replace retiring Supreme Court Chief Justice Warren Burger, Reagan asserted—incorrectly—that the American Bar Association had "declared him fully qualified to be a federal judge." Stretching the truth further by suggesting personal familiarity with Manion, the president said, "I know him to be a person who has the ability and determination to become the kind of judge the American people want in the federal courts."[60] In a later interview with a *New York Daily News* reporter, Reagan characterized the opposition as "liberals who couldn't swallow his philosophy as a conservative," and whose arguments were "based on a number of outright falsehoods." He was not asked either to identify the falsehoods or to explain why those same Senate liberals had not shown a similarly vigorous opposition to the 280 previous judicial appointments that had been almost routinely approved.[61]

Manion's ultimate confirmation was achieved by majority leader Bob Dole's parliamentary maneuvering to prevent a vote when the opposition was at full strength, and by an extraordinary presidential campaign that included overtly buying the threatened opposition votes of Republican Senators Slade Gorton and David Durenberger by promising to accept their nominees for vacancies in their states of Washington and Minnesota. The final result saw five other Republican senators joining 44 Democrats in opposition to the nomination, and Democratic Senator Howell Heflin of Alabama retreating from the declaration of principle he made in the Sessions case by voting with Democratic Senator Russell B. Long of Louisiana and the remaining Republicans to save the nomination by a single vote.[62]

For Reagan and his supporters this was a Pyrrhic victory, for it stimulated Democratic members of the Senate to more vigorous investigation of subsequent judicial nominees, a course they were able to pursue more effectively after they had won a majority in the Senate in the fall 1986 elections. Slade Gorton paid for his Manion vote by seeing his candidate for judicial appointment stricken from the list—even though his choice was a liberal Democrat.

Although the candidate was reconsidered and confirmed more than a year later, Gorton had by that time lost his Senate seat to Democrat Brock Adams. The Republicans' only solace in this sequence of events came when the ABA dropped from its evaluation committee a member who had irritated conservatives in the legal profession by voting against a number of Reagan candidates for judicial appointments.[63]

The shoddy character of the Manion appointment served to focus public attention on the administration's effort to use the courts to ensure support of its policies in many areas where it could not prevail through the democratic process of elections. Justice Department Terry Eastland's assertion that the qualified-unqualified rating given Manion by the ABA was "normal" for judicial nominees acknowledged more than he intended. An ABA study showed that this ranking was normal for appellate court nominees only for the first year after Meese took over the selection process. In that period more than one-third of those proposed for the circuit courts of appeal were rated qualified-unqualified. Exactly half received that rating or the lowest qualified rating. This was an increase from 36 percent during Reagan's first term and from 25 percent during the Carter administration.[64] An update of this study reported that in the Carter, Ford and Nixon administrations less than 6 percent of the appellate court candidates had received the mixed qualified-unqualified rating.[65]

Notwithstanding the increasingly poor quality of judicial candidates submitted for the Senate's approval, until 1986 Senate Democrats did little to challenge the suitability of Reagan's nominees. And except for the hoopla that accompanied the appointment of Sandra Day O'Connor to the Supreme Court, the media paid almost no attention to judicial appointments until the revolt against Sessions and Manion erupted. Subsequently, when President Reagan claimed during the 1986 congressional election campaign that "over and over again, the Democratic leadership has tried in the Senate to torpedo our choices for judges," the New York Times devoted only three paragraphs to a rebuttal which pointed out that the Senate had virtually rubber-stamped Reagan's nominations, approving 299 out of 304 submitted from January 1981 through October 1986.[66]

As for President Reagan's and Attorney General Meese's frequent diatribes against the "ideologues" in the opposition camp, the Justice Department's public relations officer revealed the other side of that coin when he observed that "a new appointment or two" at the Supreme Court level would bring that body around to the administration position on affirmative action and other aspects of civil rights in which the court's opinions of the previous year had not been in accord with the administration's concept of the protections that should or should not be afforded by the first and fourteenth amendments.[67]

President Reagan's opportunity to achieve his goal of an ideologically conservative Supreme Court came with the successive retirements of Chief Justice Warren Burger and Associate Justice Potter Stewart. Nominating Associate Justice William H. Rehnquist for the post of chief justice, and circuit court judge Antonin Scalia as Stewart's replacement, he experienced little difficulty in obtaining approval for these candidates, as dozens of judges, lawyers and law professors attested to their substantial experience, intelligence, and ability to present their views forcefully and effectively. The ABA accorded both men its "highest evaluation of the nominees to the Supreme Court—Well Qualified."[68]

In the face of such widespread support, the opposition had little chance of blocking these appointments. Only at Rehnquist's hearing was the question of legal ethics raised, and that was in connection with a case which also indicated the general trend of the Burger court. As an associate justice of the Supreme Court, Rehnquist had taken part in a case in which, when it first arose in the lower courts, he had acted as counsel for the defendant—the Department of Defense. Notwithstanding his subsequent submission of a long memorandum justifying sitting in judgment on a matter he had taken sides on earlier, his refusal to disqualify himself as a judge brought wide-spread criticism, including a letter from the Senate's leading constitutional lawyer, Sam Ervin. In his commentary, Senator Ervin also pointed out that the 3 to 4 opinion in which Rehnquist joined—upholding the army's right to spy on civilians—was based on evidence offered by the government which "had no relevancy whatever to the point being considered by the Supreme Court," which was whether the plaintiff was entitled to an injunction to prevent further surveillance of his activities by the army.[69]

If the opposition to Rehnquist and Scalia posed no threat to their con-firmation, it increased in both volume and intensity when Robert H. Bork, the favorite candidate of the extreme right wing, was nominated to replace retiring Supreme Court Justice Lewis F. Powell, Jr. Touted as "a friend of the Constitution" in Richard Viguerie's *Conservative Digest,* Bork came under immediate attack by members of the Congress as well as outside organiza-tions.[70]

The Senate Judiciary Committee had spent more than a week taking testimony from Bork and others, but had not yet finished when Democratic Senator Bill Bradley of New Jersey addressed the Senate on this subject. In doing so, he focused on what was to be the heart of the opposition to Bork's appointment. Reminding his colleagues of the century of struggle required just to eliminate racial segregation, and of "the foot-dragging that persisted throughout the 1970s in implementing the school desegregation which was ordered 20 years before," he pointed to certain aspects of Bork's record that made him question the nominee's fitness to serve on a court that would have the power to shape, or destroy, the nation's progress in achieving equality of treatment for all Americans:

> He has opposed decisions that upheld the constitutionality of the Federal Voting Rights Act. He has opposed a decision prohibiting State courts from enforcing racially restrictive covenants requiring home owners not to sell their property to non-whites. He has opposed a decision declaring the poll tax unconstitutional.

> His opposition to providing remedies for discrimination [under the Fourteenth Amendment] prevents him from upholding the laws that actually give minorities full equality.

Bradley acknowledged that "Judge Bork is erudite . . . has a quick mind and ready wit [and] the ability to provoke, to challenge assumptions, to argue fiercely," all "attractive qualities in a great college professor." But he argued that "his iconoclasm, while stimulating in a professor, can be disastrous in a judge. What is important . . . is not how nimble his argument will be but how his decisions will affect millions of Americans who will have to live by them." Bork's nimbleness of mind the senator found evident in the judge's responses to Judiciary Committee members' questions about his attitude toward previous court decisions. On the central issue of civil rights, Bradley said, "he chose ambiguity." Bradley's conclusion was that he would vote against Bork's confirmation, "not because I question his integrity, competence, or qualifications, but because I doubt that he has the commitment to civil rights and individual liberties on which the decency and well-being of our American community depends."[71]

Later the same day Republican Senator Larry Pressler of South Dakota opened the pro-Bork debate by stressing the very qualities Bradley had not challenged. "The confirmation process," Pressler said, "is designed to ensure that nominees are highly qualified and have neither ethical nor character problems." Implying partisan politics by the opposition, he confirmed the nature of the division with the statement that, "Robert Bork believes that excessively liberal interpretations of procedural rights do not serve the goal of protecting justice for all."[72]

As the lengthy hearings came to a close, but before the nomination went to the floor of the Senate for formal action, members of that body who had made up their minds at an early stage alternated with one another in speeches for or against the nomination. For the most part these exchanges offered details from Bork's background as evidence of his fitness, or unfitness, for a seat on the Supreme Court. Those in favor stressed Bork's considerable experience as Justice Department solicitor general, a federal appellate court judge, a law professor and a writer, whose credentials had been given the highest qualified rating by the ABA and whose opinions had won the praise of many of his peers as well as civic, religious and law-enforcement organizations. Many quoted such well-known Bork supporters as Chief Justice Warren Burger and former Attorney General William French Smith, who combined their praise of the nominee with charges that the opposition had lied, or had attempted to make the nomination an issue to be settled by public opinion polls.[73]

Senators wishing to go on record as opposing the nomination took a different tack. Using Bork's own words, they insisted that no one was fit to sit on the Supreme Court who had characterized as "unconstitutional" the court's earlier decisions on religion, abortion, and "one man, one vote," and had castigated as "unprincipled" and "intellectually empty" the court's denial of a state's right to make the use of contraceptives a crime or to require the sterilization of individuals with two theft convictions.[74]

President Reagan had ranked the Bork appointment "at the top of our nation's domestic agenda," and throughout the summer and early fall of 1987 he introduced that topic into his announcements, speeches and radio addresses no fewer than 20 times. In a strenuous effort to combat the campaign against Bork's appointment, he accused his opponents of "highly charged rhetoric" that was "irrational and totally unjustified." As the trend in Senate debates indicated the strength of the opposition, the president joined his supporters in their charges of lying and distortion by "special interests" that he said were intent on keeping Bork off the Supreme Court. His anger led him to the foolish suggestion that his power of appointment might be taken over by others, saying, "Now the special interests are determined to pack the Supreme Court and to distort the reputation of anyone who disagrees."[75]

The charge that "liberal special interest groups seek to politicize the court system" was given special emphasis in presidential messages calling upon the public to "tell your senators to resist the politicalization of our court system. Tell them you support the appointment of Judge Robert Bork to the Supreme Court."[76] When a reporter pointed out that "a number of Republicans have also come out against Mr. Bork," Reagan's response was, "I'm not going to take any more questions."[77] A week later the decision was all but sealed when a majority of the Judiciary Committee, now controlled by Democrats as a result of their victory in the 1986 congressional elections, voted 9 to 5 to recommend that the Bork nomination be rejected.[78]

The formal Senate debate, following receipt of the Judiciary Committee's recommendation, came on October 23. Little was new in either the arguments or the lineup of supporters and opponents, and the ultimate decision on the nomination was about as predicted, 42 in favor and 58 against.[79]

President Reagan's reaction to this defeat was not merely disappointment. In announcing that "my next nominee for the Court will share Judge Bork's belief in judicial restraint," he was confirming his furious comment made when the Bork nomination seemed headed for defeat: "If I have to appoint another one, I'll try to find one that they'll object to just as much as they did for this one."[80] Nothing could have done more to raise Senate hackles than this deliberately confrontational attitude. Thus, when Reagan announced that his next candidate was circuit court judge Douglas Ginsberg, to whom he attributed many of the same qualities he found in Judge Bork, his call to the Senate to "resolve that the process of confirming a Supreme Court nominee will never again be distorted" was received as a gauntlet slapped across a dueler's face. And his added comment that "I've gone the extra mile to ensure a speedy confirmation" could only be taken as an attempt to pressure the Senate into action before opposition could be organized.[81]

Republican senators took the hint and, instead of waiting for the opposition to make its move—as they had done when Bork was nominated—led off with a round of warmly supportive speeches immediately following Reagan's announcement. The opening speaker, Phil Gramm of Texas, echoed the administration's claim that the "presidential elections set a road map in terms of political philosophy, and we ought to expect the President to appoint someone who agrees with his philosophy." Senators Bob Dole, James A. McClure and Orrin G. Hatch followed, all attesting to Ginsberg's outstanding credentials and making a point of mentioning that he had clerked for the Supreme Court's most liberal member, Thurgood Marshall.[82]

The president's prodding for prompt committee hearings, repeated in his radio address to the nation on October 31, was to no avail. Five days later Minority Leader Dole read to the Senate a statement in which Ginsberg acknowledged that both in college and afterward he had used marijuana "on a few occasions." When Reagan was asked by a reporter if he should have "just said no" to the nominee, the president showed a tolerance not previously indicated in his vigorous anti-drug campaign, saying, "I'm old enough to have seen that era in which his generation and the generations earlier than that—how it was taken and all." Later in the day he addressed a group of ethnic minority and Republican leaders in the White House, praising Ginsberg for his admission of a youthful indiscretion and comparing him with other great justices who had been appointed to the Supreme Court in their early forties.[83]

The following day the question of Ginsberg's judicial ethics arose when it became known that he had participated as a circuit court judge in a case in which he had previously represented the Office of Budget and Management, and had disqualified himself only after attorneys opposing the government had demanded it.[84] Before the day was out, President Reagan had issued a one-paragraph statement announcing that he had received Ginsberg's request to have his name withdrawn from further consideration.[85]

Reagan's third choice for the Powell vacancy had been on Attorney General Meese's list of candidates from the beginning, but Anthony M. Kennedy had appeared far less aggressive than Bork or Ginsberg in his approach to the president's favorite theories of original intent and judicial restraint. Although Kennedy's credentials as a conservative were impeccable, neither his style nor his 12-year record as a circuit court judge suggested the kind of attitude that had aroused the critics of Judge Bork. In less than three months, the background check, committee hearings, and full Senate consideration were completed, all with scarcely a ripple of opposition. Confirmation by a vote of 97 to 0 followed a single hour of laudatory remarks—by liberals and conservatives from both parties—in which there was literally no debate.[86]

If the speed and unanimity of Judge Kennedy's confirmation signaled the relief which the Senate felt at the relatively moderate stance of Reagan's third choice, it also attested to the accuracy of the judgment offered by critics of his original selection of Judge Bork. Massachusetts Democrat John F. Kerry gave part of the explanation in this statement on the floor of the Senate:

What is clear is that when the President sent the Attorney General and Howard Baker to the Hill to consult on potential nominees a bunch of names were put in front of the leadership of the U.S. Senate. And I believe that those who knew the record of Judge Bork at that time said that his nomination would have difficulty, but there were other names on the list that would pass easily. . . . Judge Bork was selected precisely because of his ideology not his judicial record.[87]

Making a plea for a return to a more normal level of judicial politics, Illinois Senator Alan J. Dixon spoke for the majority of his Democratic colleagues:

I do not object to the nomination of a judicial conservative to the Supreme Court bench. I think the President is entitled to nominees that share his philosophy. I have voted for the nominations of judicial conservatives to the bench in the past, and I expect to support the nomination of judicial conservatives to judicial posts in the future. I have supported the nomination of Justice Rehnquist to be Chief Justice, and the nominations of Sandra O'Connor and Antonin Scalia to be Associate Justices. If the Senate rejects the nomination of Judge Bork, I fully expect President Reagan to send the Senate a conservative nominee, and fully expect the Senate will confirm a conservative nominee.

What President Reagan never seemed to realize was that this view had prevailed throughout his entire presidency, as evidenced by the routine approval given more than 95 percent of his proposed appointments to the federal courts. And with the help of his successor the goal of Reaganizing the

American system of justice will be realized, at least for some decades to come. For President George Bush, while carefully avoiding controversial candidates, has moved quietly to complete this aspect of the Reagan Revolution by appointing jurists who, in the words of his own White House counsel, will continue to "shift the courts in a more conservative direction."[88]

CHAPTER 7

Educator

" 'Train up a child in the way he should go,'
Solomon wrote, 'and when he is old he will not
depart from it'."[1]

THE EARLIEST REFERENCE TO RONALD REAGAN'S EDUCATION, MADE IN HIS
1965 autobiography, suggests a quality of comprehension as yet unknown to
experts in the learning process. Long before they were of school age, Ronnie
and his brother, Neil, sat each evening with their mother and listened to the
stories she read to them from children's books. The boys watched over her
shoulder, Reagan recalled, as she followed each word with her finger. Some
time before the age of five this extraordinary event occurred:

> One evening all the funny black marks on paper clicked into place. I was lying
> on the floor with the evening paper and Jack asked what I was doing—so I told
> him. "Reading." He said, "Well, read me something," and I did. Nelle was
> proud enough to canvass the neighbors and get them to come in while I
> proudly recited such events as the aftermath of a bomb that had exploded in
> San Francisco during a parade and the exciting details of the $40,000,000
> two-dead Black Tom explosion in New Jersey.[2]

With no further explanation, one is left with the impression that this
preschool child suddenly began reading the daily newspaper (not a child's
book) with the same facility as his parents, Jack and Nelle. This was reported
so casually, along with a disclaimer of special talent, that it evoked no
comment from any biographer. Professionals in the field of reading, however,
assert that such things do not happen. Dr. Horst G. Taschow, author of *The
Cultivation of Reading,* states flatly that "no one begins to read 'suddenly'," in
the fashion described by Reagan. Even with the experience of having been
read to regularly, Dr. Taschow says, "child Reagan will have recognized only
those words that, through such daily practices, he has learned to recognize."
The reason, he explains, is that if you are not familiar with a particular word,

"you can neither pronounce it nor understand it or 'read it' no matter how much you may try." As Professor Taschow pointed out, Reagan himself gave the show away by writing that when his mother called in the neighbors to witness an exhibition of Ronnie's new-found skill, he had "proudly *recited*"— not read—the events reported in the newspaper.

Descriptions of the reading process by other experts clearly indicate that words are symbols whose form and meaning must be learned, and are not divined in a sudden flash that brings immediate comprehension of everything on a printed page.[3] Like so many of Reagan's recollections, this account of his introduction to the world of literature has heretofore gone unchallenged.

By the age of ten Reagan had developed a normal boy's appetite for adventure stories like those of Tarzan and Frank Merriwell.[4] How effective his reading ability was in helping with his school work, Reagan does not say, but others attest to his ability to score well on examinations due to his "photographic memory."[5] One fifth-grade classmate recalls that in American history "Dutch was an 'A' student because he had such a good memory for dates."[6] This, as Reagan's contemporaries will recall, was an age in which rote recall of the date 1776 seemed more important to many teachers than the exciting details of that critical time in American history.

Reagan's talent for memorizing textbook material undoubtedly kept his high school average up to a low B, even though by that time his love of football had become what he later characterized as "a matter of life and death." To make the high school football team, he told one biographer, was "your goal and aim in life. Everything else was a game except football."[7]

The infatuation with football not only continued to dominate his educational experience beyond high school, it brought him an athletic scholarship—not nearly as common in the 1920s as it is today—that helped pay for his education at Eureka College. In a rare departure from his normal boast of having earned an education "all by myself," he once acknowledged that "in those days not very many got to college, and if you did it was because you could play football or something, which is how I got there."[8]

In college, too, his ability to memorize textbook material earned him passing grades, though he seemed less concerned than ever with the school's academic activities. The only references in his autobiography to this aspect of his college experience were an acknowledgment that he "only just" completed his freshman year, and a lengthy tale of his leadership of a student strike against the president's decision to reduce institutional expenditures by eliminating some courses from the curriculum.[9]

Long after leaving the Eureka campus he explained his indifference to academic achievement in different ways on different occasions. The commonly accepted reason is his statement that

I was so busy with these other things that I apportioned only a certain amount of time to study. A "C" average was required for eligibility for outside activities. I set my goals at maintaining eligibility. I know that wasn't right, but it also made room and time for other things that I think were valuable. [10]

On another occasion he made the point that wisdom is as important a product of higher education as knowledge, and wisdom, he said, was what he gained at Eureka. [11]

An explanation as unflattering as the first was this one, given an interviewer in 1939:

I was afraid if my grades were good I might end up an athletic teacher at some small school . . . raising other little football heroes. I was awfully afraid about what was going to happen after college. To get a coach's job you naturally had to have a certain scholastic standing, so I was careful not to get it. I even dropped some courses so that I'd be behind in the educational credits. I didn't want to take the chance of weakening when the time came. [12]

This extraordinary confession, of little significance to the outside world in 1939, did not resurface until it was published in Anne Edwards' *Early Reagan* in 1987. If it reflects accurately Reagan's attitude toward his studies while he was in college, it may account for the jocular introduction to an address he gave to a Eureka audience almost 30 years later. "Ten years ago," he said, "I stood in this place to receive an honorary degree—a happening which only compounded an already heavy guilt. I had always figured the first degree you gave me was honorary." On the other hand, this may have been yet another example of his penchant for opening almost any speech with a line calculated to make his listeners laugh. He must have appreciated the response because he repeated the joke when he returned to Eureka as commencement speaker in 1982, and again when he announced completion of a 1983 federal study of American education entitled *A Nation At Risk*. On these last two occasions the official transcripts of his talks, printed in the *Public Papers of the President*, included the parenthetical note "(laughter)" at the conclusion of the gag. [13]

*   *   *   *   *

Notwithstanding the humorous approach Reagan frequently took in references to his own schooling, once he entered the political arena the tone of his messages on education was not one to invite laughter. He made his position clear even before issuing the ringing appeal for Barry Goldwater that brought him into national prominence. In 1961 Reagan warned that one of the signs of ever-expanding government control was "the $900 million National Education Act of 1958." Declaring that "federal aid is the foot in the door to federal control," he pictured the awful prospects of government intrusion by attributing to unnamed educators such comments as, "We might have to have temporary federal control to bring about integration in the South" and, "We must have a national school system to compete on equal terms with Russia."[14]

About to assume the governorshp of California during the turbulent sixties, Reagan lectured the chancellors of the University of California in this fashion:

> If scholars are to be recognized as having a right to press their particular value judgments, perhaps the time has come also for institutions of higher learning to assert themselves as positive forces in the battles for men's minds.
>
> This could mean they would insist upon mature, responsible conduct and respect for the individual from their faculty members and might even call on them to be proponents of those ethical and moral standards demanded by the great majority of our society.[15]

A combination of scorn and distrust was expressed in subsequent remarks about college and university teachers. Often the criticism dealt with questions of ethics, but the undertone was political. This became more evident as time went on and Reagan made it clear that he associated professors with the liberalism that he believed was encouraging the irresponsibility and declining morality of college students. In his first inaugural address as governor he made the point that "taxpaying citizens who support the college and university systems" are entitled to ask of their faculties that, "in addition to teaching, they build character on accepted moral and ethical standards."[16]

Enlarging on this theme a few years later, he used a typical Reagan tactic of characterizing the opposition in extreme terms that would apply to only a few. Speaking on the subject of academic freedom, he said:

> [T]hat educator is wrong who denies there are any absolutes—who sees no black and white or right and wrong, but just shades of gray in a world where discipline of any kind is an intolerable interference with the right of the individual . . . he cannot escape a responsibility for the students' development of character and maturity. Strangely and illogically, this is very often the same educator who interprets his academic freedom as the right to indoctrinate students with his view of things.

Then, in an apparent contradiction of his insistence on the university's obligation to inculcate in its students what he deemed to be acceptable moral and ethical standards, Reagan added, "One thing we should all be agreed on is the university's obligation to teach, not indoctrinate."[17]

In another, bitter attack on "those who claim that private enterprise, including labor and management, is engaged in some kind of consortium with government to perpetuate war, poverty, injustice and prejudice," he blamed educators for "the accusations of our sons and daughters who pride themselves on 'telling it like it is'." Describing how the country's youth had been misled, he said:

[I]n a thousand social science courses they have been taught "the way it is *not*." They are not informed, they are *mis*informed, and they know a great many things that are not true. The overwhelming majority of them are fine young people who will turn out just great if we make sure they hear both sides of the story.[18]

As governor, Reagan's solution to the "one-sided ideological viewpoint" of some professors was to make their political orientation "a consideration [in] hiring of faculty" and, further, to take away from faculty the right to determine what courses were to be included in the curriculum. Although the latter suggestion was rejected by the University of California Board of Regents, the governor's influence on the university hierarchy made itself felt in the recruitment and granting of tenure to professors.[19]

The suspicion that higher education, like government, was dominated by "fashionable intellectuals and academics who in recent years would have us believe ours is a sick society" persisted through Reagan's governorship and became part of his 1976 campaign for the presidency.[20]

As for students, the word was discipline. Outraged by California student demands for participation in academic decision-making, Governor Reagan denounced their demonstrations at the University of California. In doing so he conveniently forgot his part in the student strike at Eureka College that led to the resignation of that institution's president. Student anger had been generated at Eureka in 1928 when the college president and board of trustees had decided on curriculum changes that Reagan charged were made "without any thought of consulting students or faculty." That was an era in which revolt against the ruling authorities of a college by students—or even faculty members—was almost unheard of, principally because it was almost certain to result in the dismissal of the offenders. Only two years before becoming governor Reagan had taken delight in recounting in his memoirs the leading role he had played in the 1928 student uprising. But as governor he deplored both student and faculty challenges to constituted authority. Forgotten also was his 1928 discovery of "the rights of man to universal education," as from the governor's office he pressed for elimination of the traditional free tuition at state colleges and asserted that taxpayers should not be asked to "subsidize intellectual curiosity" at the university level. This last remark led a professor at U.C.L.A. to exclaim, "What the hell does he think a university is all about?"[21]

Reagan's notion of what a university is all about evolved along with his conversion to conservative politics. Prior to that time—if his autobiography is any guide—he gave the matter no serious thought whatever. Student activism on California campuses, which reached riotous proportions during his campaign for governor, prompted him to make this an election issue. Promising to "clean up the mess at Berkeley," where student free-speech and anti-Vietnam War campaigns had coalesced with more radical antiestablishment movements, "Reagan and higher education saw each other as the enemy" from the day he won the office of governor.[22] His outspoken criticism of student protestors, along with his insistence on both tuition or fee increases and budget cuts for the state university system, increased antagonism in an already volatile situation. Unlike government and university officers in many other jurisdictions, Reagan did not encourage educational administrators to sit down with the protestors and try to work out solutions to their differences. Rather, he adopted the slogan, "Observe the rules or get out."[23] His confrontational approach was no doubt welcomed by campus radicals who responded with increasing violence. "Those who want to get an education, those who want to teach, should be protected in that at the point of bayonet if necessary," Reagan declared. And if this meant actually using bayonets as in war, he avowed on another occasion that he would not seek to avoid such a confrontation: "If there's going to be a bloodbath, let's get it over with."[24]

* * * *

At the national level, Reagan's antagonism toward any government activity which smacked of intrusion into areas "best left to the states or local communities" led him to conclude that education generally—from kindergarten to postgraduate university study—was none of Washington's business. The 1980 Republican platform committee had no difficulty designing an education plank that would reflect this point of view. Beginning with the statement that the importance of education comes after (1) religious training, and (2) the home, the committee expressed its sympathy for the dedicated and often underpaid teachers of America, but concluded that high educational standards could be assured by federal "deregulation" and the elimination of the Department of Education. This general statement of policy was followed by a list of more specific goals, including tax credits for parents who send their children to private schools, revival of prayer in public schools, and elimination of "forced busing" and bargaining power in teachers' unions.[25]

Implementation of this program was to start with the dismantling of the Department of Education. To oversee this task Reagan selected Terrel H. Bell, a professional educator who had been President Nixon's U.S. Commissioner of Education. The appointment did not go down well with administrative conservatives, who knew that Bell had supported President Carter's establishment of the Education Department only a year before the 1980 election. However, Reagan had acknowledged that the department performed "legitimate functions" which should be retained, and which might be assigned to "an independent federal agency of lesser status than a cabinet department."[26] How reduced this status was to be Bell learned when he found he was the only cabinet member not invited to attend the president's televised delivery of his first State of the Union address.[27] Within a month, Bell wrote after leaving federal service, he was "being nudged" by administration "keepers of the conservative dogma" to shut down his department "and get out of town." It was typical of the uncouthness of these millionaire Reaganites that the less-affluent Bell, who had rented a U-Haul truck to bring his belongings to Washington, would be asked whether he would "need some help on moving expenses" to return to his home in Utah.[28]

Beyond the snubs and snide remarks ("Oh, are you still here?"), Bell found himself repeatedly frustrated in his attempts to get White House approval for the top-level administrators he sought to appoint. Opposition came from what he subsequently referred to as the administration's "movement conservatives," led by Reagan's number one aide, Edwin Meese. Most of the candidates he selected, not only for their professional ability but also for their willingness to keep education on the federal agenda, were rejected in favor of others whose obvious goal was to eliminate every vestige of the educational function from federal jurisdiction. For each person of his own choice whom Bell eventually succeeded in placing, he was forced by movement conservatives to accept someone he knew would try to sabotage his operation. One of the latter was Edward Curran, forced upon Bell as director of the National Institute of Education. In his attempt to scuttle the very unit he headed, Curran sent his recommendations directly to President Reagan, without even the courtesy of a copy to the head of his department. Transferred (to the Peace Corps!) at Bell's either-he-goes-or-I-go demand, Curran's later nomination to be chairman of the National Endowment for the Humanities was rejected by the Senate Labor and Resources Committee, whose review of his record in education led its members to challenge not only his credentials but also his credibility.[29]

The ultimate frustration experienced by the education secretary was to see his reorganization proposal cut and trimmed until it became no more than a scheme for reducing the department to a financial-aid foundation. When the revised plan was put to Howard Baker, then number two in Reagan's White House team, Baker told Bell bluntly that he would not support the proposal, principally because he knew that Congress would not permit it.[30] Meese's contribution to the reorganization effort was to propose transferring the Education Department's civil rights office to the Justice Department and to spread other functions among the traditional cabinet officers. Bell felt that Meese's main purpose was "to make it more difficult for education lobbyists to influence decisions made in the federal bureaucracy."[31] This may have been true of most of the Meese transfer suggestions, but his subsequent record of non-enforcement of civil rights in the attorney general's office is clear evidence of his intent to take that critical responsibility out of the hands of untrustworthy liberals like Terrel Bell.

Bell's only real victory came with a survey of education by a commission of his own choosing, published as the widely acclaimed *A Nation At Risk*. One of three major studies issued in 1983, the commission report received by far the greatest publicity, including a nationwide televised blurb by President Reagan.[32]

Bell's pleasure in the enthusiasm with which the findings were received was dampened by the president's insistence on going beyond the commission's recommendations to include his standard pitch for "tuition tax credits . . . voluntary school prayer, and abolishing the Department of Education," none of which were mentioned in the report. On the contrary, while the commission acknowledged the *"primary responsibility* of state and local governments for financing and governing the schools," it stated specifically that the federal government "should help meet the needs of key groups of students such as the gifted and talented, the socioeconomically disadvantaged, minority and language minority students, and the handicapped." Misrepresenting the commission's view as calling for "an end to federal intrusion," Reagan avoided any of the report's references to federal funding or to the following recommendation, made under the heading of "Leadership and Fiscal Support":

> In addition, we believe the Federal Government's role includes several functions of national consequence that States and localities alone are unlikely to be able to meet: protecting constitutional and civil rights for students and school personnel; collecting data, statistics, and information about education generally; supporting curriculum improvement and research on teaching, learning, and the management of schools; supporting teacher training in areas of critical shortage or key national needs; and providing student financial assistance and research and graduate training.

All of this, the commission said, could be accomplished "with a minimum of administration burden and intrusiveness." President Reagan picked out that last term to report, quite inaccurately, that the Commission believed the federal government should end all "intrusion" into the field of education.[33]

Satisfied that the report documented, as it did most effectively, the declining quality of American education and the potential loss of American leadership in science, technology, and commercial enterprise, the president made "excellence in education" a campaign issue in the 1984 election. According to Bell, OMB director David Stockman went so far as to acknowledge that in cutting expenditures to meet budget targets, "the sensitive issue of education is an exception." The president appeared to confirm this when he told a group of black administration employees that he had put education "at the top of the national agenda."[34]

Warned by friends that he was being used by a president interested only in the political value of the commission's report, Bell persisted in taking the optimistic view that Reagan and Stockman meant what they said. Heartened also by the Republican platform committee's decision to drop its previous declaration that the Department of Education must be eliminated, Bell dismissed the warning of one of Meese's assistants that the abolitionists would be back in force after the 1984 election.

Reagan made the most of the commission report in speeches during the remaining months of 1983 and in his 1984 drive for reelection. Six of his Saturday radio talks to the nation were dedicated, in whole or in part, to the problem of education. From the time the commission report was issued until the November 1984 election, the topic was included in 62 of Reagan's public discussions, many of which were held at colleges, high schools, meetings of teachers and school administrators, and at periodic gatherings of the administration-sponsored National Forum on Excellence in Education.[35] Beginning with the message that he intended to oust the "Washington knows best" attitude by putting "basics back in the schools and parents back in charge," Reagan opened his September 1984 tour with the boast that under his leadership there had been a "national renewal in education" in which scholastic aptitude test scores had begun to improve.[36]

A Nation At Risk was the source of many Reagan quotes, but there were times when both this document and the opposition to Reagan's program were misrepresented. At one of the forum meetings Reagan said he approved the commission report "in its entirety." But when asked what he would do to assist states in meeting the cost of the commission's recommended salary increases, merit pay, and incentives for "master teachers," he rambled on for several minutes about the relative costs of education and defense and never did answer the question. On another occasion he blasted opponents of his scheme for advocating what, in fact, no one had proposed: "a nationalized school system," and "the abandonment of compulsory courses."[37]

Meanwhile, Secretary Bell joined in campaigning on behalf of the president, as well as for Republicans running for Congress. Often he was dismayed to find himself backing candidates who continued to advocate "slashing funds for the poor, for student aid, and for health care for the aged." What was worse, even before election day he learned that he had been double-crossed, not only on the budget but on the promise to make support for education reform a high priority. Even as the reelection campaign was in progress, the president was being cited by the comptroller general for having illegally withheld funds appropriated by Congress for the education of immigrant children—whose parents were not likely to be voters in the 1984 election.[38]

Once Reagan's reelection had been assured, Bell saw both pledges go down the drain. When his angry demand for fulfillment of pre-election promises was rejected, he decided to quit. His resignation, dated November 8, 1984, was received in complete silence: "I never heard a word," he wrote. "No one telephoned. Three days later the president announced to the press that I had resigned for personal reasons."[39]

The widespread suspicion that omission of the platform pledge to dismantle the Education Department was a plot to mask the administration's real intent was confirmed three days after Bell's unheralded farewell reception. In a December 21 interview with *Human Events* reporters, President Reagan said he was delaying appointment of a new secretary of education "because we've never given up our belief that the department should be eliminated."[40]

* * * *

The delay in choosing a new secretary of education was relatively brief. On January 10, 1985, Reagan announced his intention to nominate William J. Bennett to succeed Terrel H. Bell.[41] Unlike his predecessor, whose appointment had been bitterly opposed by movement conservatives, Bennett had been approved by a special-interest group of conservatives that the White House had permitted to interview prospective candidates for the top post in education. With that kind of backing, prospects for the more moderate Albert Quie, who had been a member of Bell's National Commission on Excellence in Education, were practically nil. Bennett not only satisfied the unofficial screening committee, he provided advance proof of his dedication to the Reagan philosophy of education by blasting the nation's colleges and universities for their "unwavering decline" in studies in the humanities, and by giving his blessing to the president's proposal for tuition tax credits.[42] Previously appointed by Reagan to the position of chairman of the National Endowment for the Humanities, Harvard Law School graduate Bennett was known to offer no threat of Bell-like fussing over budget commitments or challenges to far-right recommendations for high-level positions in the Education Department.

Bennett's choice of assistants gave early promise of what might be expected from his reorganized department. Three months after he had taken office, two of his appointees so outraged the educational community by their remarks that the reaction forced their resignations. One was Lawrence A. Uzzell, Bennett's choice to head the drive for tuition tax credits. Uzzell's contribution to the new departmental philosophy was to explain that all federal aid for elementary and secondary education should be eliminated, including programs for handicapped students.

A religious twist to this approach was provided by Eileen Marie Gardner, also a Harvard graduate, who was chosen by Bennett to be his special assistant for "educational philosophy and practice." Examining her credentials, Republican Senator Lowell P. Weicker's appropriations subcommittee discovered that her views regarding handicapped students were based on the religious concept that "nothing comes to an individual that he has not, at some point in his development, summoned," and that any handicap suffered by an individual "fits his level of internal spiritual development." Thus, as Gardner had written in a paper prepared for the Heritage Foundation, programs that would assist the handicapped were "misguided" because they used resources that should be devoted to the "normal school population."[43] This was the same Eileen Gardner who had been cited by President Reagan as "a widely respected educator," and whom he took delight in quoting when she echoed his own view in this statement:

> The record shows that when control of education is placed in federal hands it is not control by the people, but by small, yet powerful lobbies motivated by self-interest or dogma. When centralized in this way, it is beyond the control of the parents and local communities it is designed to serve. It becomes impervious to feedback.[44]

The public outcry provoked by Gardner's and Uzzell's sentiments was reported in both the *New York Times* and *Washington Post* on April 17, 1985, along with Secretary Bennett's defense of his two aides. Two days later the *Post* noted that after "an emotional clash" between Gardner and Senator Weicker, Gardner and Lawrence Uzzell both resigned. Bennett's own public statements, which he issued frequently and with great authority, were sufficiently provocative to keep him in the news. More polished than the president at depicting the benefits of returning to "the golden age" of higher education, Bennett won the applause of no less a luminary than Professor Jaques Barzun. But as former Stanford University president Richard W. Lyman pointed out, both Bennett and Barzun were perpetuating an old myth when they pictured the university student body of the early twentieth century as serious searchers after truth and academic proficiency. Lyman recalled Princeton president Woodrow Wilson's assessment that what later became known as extracurricular activities were, in his day, the "absorbing realities of nine out of every ten men who go to college." Wilson might well have been describing the experience of Ronald Reagan a generation later.[45]

Prohibited by Congress from eliminating his own department or emasculating the education budget, Bennett nevertheless was successful in curbing departmental activities in a number of ways. When a study by the American Council on Education showed that youngsters from families with less than $15,000 in annual income had to pay at least half the cost of their college attendance, Bennett's comment was that as some colleges were already "overpriced," federal aid to students might lead institutions to raise their prices even further.[46] At the same time he urged state superintendents of public schools to continue assisting private schools in every way possible. Accusing the Supreme Court of joining in the "disdain for religious beliefs," he promised the Knights of Columbus that his department would bend every effort "to nullify the damage done" by the court's decision that New York City's practice of using federal funds to pay the salaries of public employees who teach in parochial schools "violates the Establishment Clause of the First Amendment." The department's goals would be accomplished, he told another audience, by "legislation . . . judicial reconsideration and constitutional amendment."[47] These 1985 pronouncements were part of an administration campaign led by newly appointed Attorney General Edwin Meese who, in a series of speeches described in an earlier chapter, attacked the Supreme Court's use of the Fourteenth Amendment to provide Bill of Rights protections against the unconstitutional acts of state and local authorities.

President Reagan's acknowledgment that he had abandoned his plan to reduce the federal education function to something less than cabinet status because it had "received very little support from Congress" did not alter either his or Secretary Bennett's determination to reduce Washington's participation in solving educational problems.[48] Adopting the president's tactic of arranging a "photo opportunity" to insure media coverage, Bennett visited New Hampshire's Concord High School, taking over for one period the class of Christa McAuliffe, the teacher who was then in training for a flight on the space shuttle. His classroom lecture was, of course, followed by a news conference. Responding to questions about New Hampshire's dual problem of low salaries and teacher shortages, Bennett said that these matters were not the concern of the federal government. In "good, proud schools," he said, "you will find people lined up for teaching jobs." There is no record of Christa McAuliffe's reaction to the suggestion that if her school had difficulty in attracting teachers, it must be because it was not one of the "good, proud" schools. But her principal joined in the state-wide renunciation of the way Bennett's "smart-aleck" remarks evaded the question of how public schools were to achieve the level of excellence targeted by Bell's commission.[49]

The secretary found an atmosphere more conducive to "a place of learning" at the Eastside High School in Paterson, New Jersey, where principal Bullhorn Clark kept both students and parents under a tight rein. Anticipating Bennett's arrival, Clark personally turned out of the school parking lot a student's parents, whom he castigated as welfare cases and followers of Libyan strong man Muammar Qaddafi. Reporters on the scene were told they would be refused entry to the school if they dared speak to the "anti-American" couple that had been ejected, but they were invited to interview parents whom the principal had asked to attend.[50]

Taking the Americanism cue from his boss, Under Secretary of Education Gary L. Bauer told a meeting of textbook publishers that the instructional materials they were selling the country's public schools were "hypercritical of American institutions" and indifferent to the evils of communist regimes. Denying that he was advocating indoctrination that would support administration philosophy, Bauer charged publishers with misleading students when, for example, they included in a world history text statements about women being treated equally with men under Soviet law, neglecting to explain that legal protections were meaningless in the Soviet Union. Put on the defensive, one publisher pointed to his company's text, *America: The Glorious Republic,* as demonstrating their attachment to "the new patriotism." Neither the speaker nor Mr. Bauer appeared to notice that a title of this sort, with "U.S.S.R." substituted for "America," would fit perfectly into a list of Soviet textbooks.[51]

The president had announced in August 1985 Secretary Bennett's planned tour of the country's elementary, middle and senior high schools, telling his radio audience that in addition to paying tribute to the nation's teachers, his education secretary "should be having something of a learning experience himself."[52] Bennett's subsequent pronouncements gave little evidence of his having learned anything from his parade of one-day stands in American classrooms. The sop he offered to parents in low income brackets was what Reagan referred to as "our compensatory education program." This, the president said, would put the poor on a par with the rich by giving them "the right to choose the school that gives their children the best education."[53] When Secretary Bennett explained the plan a month later, it turned out to be a legislative proposal that would substitute a voucher system for the existing federal aid program for disadvantaged children. Low-income families would receive vouchers averaging $600 a year for each child of school age, "so they would choose from a variety of public and private schools." As the *New York Times* pointed out, this was substantially less than the average per-student federal expenditure under the old law, and only a fraction of the cost of education at either a private school or a public school away from home.[54]

Until his resignation in September 1988, Bennett continued to charge public school officials with maintaining "inadequate and incoherent" curricula, while giving them scant credit for the gains that had been made since the challenge issued in *A Nation At Risk.* His 1988 summary of the situation many educators found essentially negative, with little recognition of the time, effort and expense involved in achieving the kind of reforms proposed by the Bell commission.[55]

Colleges and universities drew Benentt's fire for what he regarded as pure greed and pandering to popular demands for credit courses in such uplifting studies as surfing and bachelor living. When Stanford University decided to alter its "Western Culture" program to one with a broader view of the world, which it called "Cultures, Ideas and Values," Bennett was scathing in his criticism. His attack focused on the proposed modification of a freshman reading list of "classics," previously made up entirely of European writings from the ancient Greeks down to later works of Dante, Darwin and Marx. Although the new list continued to feature Plato, the Bible and St. Augustine, the elimination of Dante and Homer to make room for treatises by women and writers from the world's non-white majority Bennett saw as "a political decision" that would lower the quality of higher education— presumably in the belief that classics were produced only by white European male philosophers.[56]

During this same period, President Reagan's speeches often included reminders of the goals he had set for reform of the educational system. And as he had done since the Bell Commission report was issued, he almost invariably embellished the commission's recommendations by incorporating into his reform proposals tuition tax credits and classroom prayer, occasionally substituting his voucher plan for tax credits.[57] Challenged by a Virginia high school student on the matter of prayer in public schools, Reagan said, "I have never asked for a doctrinaire prayer or a school to dictate a prayer," forgetting that on a previous occasion he had stated that he thought the prayer mandated by New York State—which the Supreme Court declared unconstitutional—was entirely acceptable.[58]

When speaking to students, which he did frequently, Reagan never failed to encourage them to "hit the books" and "strive for excellence." He also urged them to develop a "respect for hard work," seriously suggesting that if teachers didn't give homework the students should "ask them why." In between pleas for morality and hard work he could lightheartedly toss off the laugh-provoking confession, "I majored in extracurricular activities." As documented in many other chapters of this work, Reagan's recurrent urging of "respect for hard work" was hardly a reflection of his own experience in any field except collegiate extracurricular activities. Asked on one occasion to compare education today with education when he went to school, the president recalled only that in his day high schools required four years of English, three of math, two of science and two of a foreign language. He said nothing about the need for hard work or demands for excellence.[59]

Toward the latter part of his second term, Reagan concocted a new label for the villains in his morality play: teachers of what he called "value-neutral education." Speaking at a high school commencement in Chattanooga, Tennessee, he said this was "one of the worst fads" to come out of the sixties and seventies, "when some adults seemed to lose sight of the importance in education of moral and academic standards." Composing a new myth that school officials were often heard "saying that teaching right and wrong was none of their business," he cited an unidentified newspaper story of a guidance counselor who "wouldn't force his values" of right and wrong on the students in his class, even when they decided that returning a lost-and-found purse containing $1,000 "would be neither right nor wrong; it would be just dumb."[60]

The following day the president commended Education Secretary William Bennett for his department's report on schools for disadvantaged children, disposing of racial and poverty problems with the statement that "they know there are no such things as black values and white values or poor values and rich values. No, they know there are only basic American values." Typically he also associated his value system with patriotism, asserting that at well-run institutions

> they use what's tried and true: clear standards of behavior, long hours, hard work, and measurable goals. They teach the basics—reading, mathematics, science, and writing. And they teach about America—our history, literature, our great heroes, and our democratic principles. In fact, Secretary Bennett tells me that one of the most striking things that he's learned in his many visits to our nation's classrooms is that those schools which instill a sense of patriotism in their students by saying the Pledge of Allegiance or singing "The Star Spangled Banner" invariably are the most successful.[61]

In effect, he was offering proof—nowhere to be found in the Education Department report—of the accuracy of his statement of three years earlier that the function of education includes

> passing on to each new generation the values that serve as the foundation and cornerstone of our free democratic society—patriotism, loyalty, faithfulness, courage, the ability to make the crucial moral distinctions between right and wrong, the maturity to understand that all that we have and achieve in this world comes first from a beneficent and loving God.[62]

The point was made more forcefully when he told school officials:

> When I read the writings of our Founding Fathers, who designed our system, I always note how openly they gave praise to God and sought His guidance. And I just can't believe that it was ever their intention to expel Him from our schools.[63]

In this connection it is interesting to note that with all his talk of morality and concepts of right and wrong, Reagan rarely used the terms "ethics" or "ethical." This may well have been due to a desire—conscious or unconscious—to avoid language repeatedly used by critics who hailed the actions of one after another of the president's aides as unethical, if not illegal.[64] Yet, in an extension of the remarks cited previously, Reagan could quote Thomas Jefferson advising his nephew to "give up money, give up fame, give up science, give the earth itself and all it contains rather than do an immoral act. And never suppose that in any circumstances it is best for you to do a dishonorable thing, however slightly so it may appear to you."[65]

The religious theme persisted, for he told a new group of presidential scholars in 1987 that "the key to a good education is not in the pocketbook . . . but in the heart," and that in addition to mastering the three Rs students must absorb "what you might call the 3-Fs, and those are faith, family and freedom."

Reagan's suggestion that he was an avid reader of the literary output of America's revolutionary leaders was part of the facade of knowledge that he constructed out of the many quotations that were solely the product of his staff's research. He himself was, as Education Secretary Bennett so aptly described, "the world champion memorizer."[66] Had Reagan, for example, read in full Jefferson's letters to his nephew Peter Carr, he might have realized how far his hero went beyond his own concept of intellectual honesty, and how very different from his own were Jefferson's views on education, religion, and the connection between the two.[67]

*   *   *   *   *

Three aspects of the American education system bore the brunt of Reagan's strongest criticism: lack of classroom discipline, curricular innovations that seemed to give insufficient attention to the three Rs, and what he saw as federal usurpation of the authority of parents and state and local officials. The record of his own experience contains no evidence of resistance to anything his teachers ladled out. He has referred obliquely to having been sent to his public school principal's office for disciplinary action, but in the absence of corroborating evidence from his biographers, this would appear to be part of his keep-em-laughing speech-making. His one documented challenge to educational authority occurred in college, and had nothing to do with either classroom behavior or the general character of the curriculum, only the fact that the college proposed to drop some courses to reduce expenses.[68] In all his later diatribes on the disastrous state of education there was no hint of concern that students were not learning to think for themselves—even to challenge their instructors on the logic of their ideas or presentations. On the contrary, he was explicit in his arguments that teachers he considered leftists or proponents of value-free education should be replaced by those whose economic, social and political philosophy agreed with his own. Moreover, his stand on "returning God to the classroom," as the Supreme Court pointed out, only offered students the option of not participating at the expense of their classmates' opinion of them as unChristian and therefore not part of acceptable society.

Reagan's first presidential term was only three months old when the *New York Times* featured an article headlined "Classes in How to Think Spring Up Around Nation." Reporter Gene I. Maeroff had discovered that eighth-graders in one of New York City's most prestigious private schools were being taught the techniques of analyzing and testing ideas, whether they were the teacher's concepts or those of a historian, politician, or scientist, Two years later the *Times* gave this subject page one coverage in a special Sunday supplement on education. The lead article, again by Gene Maeroff, made much of the discovery that colleges had taken up this "new" approach to education, having found that high schools were not doing an adequate job in developing "reasoning and problem-solving skills." Citing Marymount Manhattan College as one of the pioneers of this movement, Maeroff apparently was unaware of the fact that some 30 years earlier the political science department at The City College of New York had introduced into the required reading for students in its basic course in American government a book entitled *How to Think Straight*. That supplement to the course textbook became the subject of classroom discussion—and at least one quiz—before there was any talk of government as such.[69]

If this aspect of education ever penetrated Reagan's consciousness, it was lost in the maze of his concern for the kind of excellence that is reflected in standard test scores. Nor did the Bell commission report include among its objectives the development of independent, analytical thinking, though its other goals could be assumed to lead in that direction.

As to progress in the areas discussed in *A Nation At Risk,* there was a measurable improvement in scores on both achievement tests (tests of knowledge in specific subjects such as English, geometry, etc.) and scholastic aptitude tests, the latter aimed at measuring a student's probable success in meeting the demands of college study. In other areas, improvement was less noticeable; in some there was regression. Two 1988 analyses by the country's leading educational agencies indicated where serious problems remained. The Carnegie Foundation for the Advancement of Teaching found that more than two-thirds of the country's public school teachers gave the reform movement initiated by the Bell Commission a grade of C or lower. Acknowledging that accomplishments included a clearer definition of educational objectives, a more demanding attitude toward student performance, and improvement in that performance as measured by rising test scores, 70 percent of the 13,500 teachers questioned in a nationwide survey felt that their own position had deteriorated in terms of teaching conditions and morale.[70]

One of the factors cited as contributing to the woes of instructional staff—one that would have shocked President Reagan if he had been made aware of it—was the increase in bureaucratic regulations and paper work. Other depressing influences came from inattention to the problems of teaching load, class size and non-teaching duties, some of which had increased rather than lessened. A further complaint was that there had been no financial support, as suggested in the Bell report, for superior performance and improved teaching techniques.

On the financial side, the Carnegie report provided a very different picture of the future than that painted by President Reagan. Asked in 1983 about the potential effect of local school boards cutting budget allocations for education, Reagan had said: "Many of the things the Commission on Excellence in Education is recommending are things that are not going to be affected by budgets or money." But an examination of the practical effects of budgeting showed that the state in which teachers rated school reform highest was South Carolina, which, unlike most, had sharply increased its expenditures for public education.[71]

A second 1988 study, undertaken jointly by the American Council on Education and the Education Commission of the States, focused on the problems of minorities. In a report purposely titled to recall FDR's famous "one-third of a nation" speech, the study group supported by ex-Presidents Gerald R. Ford and Jimmy Carter found that in education as well as employment, income and other areas, "gaps persist—and in some cases are widening—between members of minority groups and the majority population." Its conclusion was that "America is moving backward" in the matter of equal treatment of blacks, Hispanics and native Americans.[72]

The ultimate test of Reagan's willingness to offer federal support for improved education with something more than advice and slogans came when he was faced with the task of preparing his budget request. The influence of an upcoming election was as much a factor in his case as with any other president. In his 1984 fiscal year budget he boosted the previous year's request by 37 percent for elementary and secondary education, and by 30 percent for higher education. Having by then given up any hope of dismantling the Department of Education—after repeated rebuffs by a Congress that annually appropriated more funds than he requested—Reagan came to base his education budgets on what he believed would be the minimum allocation that Congress would accept. In 1988, when a far less popular Republican candidate was running for the presidency, and when 468 contests for all of the House and one-third of the Senate seats were at stake, he had more than his own reputation to consider. Moreover, having made excellence in education a major issue throughout his second administration, he had to temper his rhetoric about the enormous improvements that could be made without substantial infusions of federal funds. Hence, his executive budget for fiscal years 1989 showed a 4.5 percent increase above the level actually approved by Congress the previous year.[73] When the first appropriation bill came to him from the Senate, which had approved $8.3 billion for elementary and secondary education on a voice vote after the House had passed the measure by a vote of 397 to 1, the president held a signing ceremony in which he bemoaned only the fear that the Supreme Court might not uphold that portion of the law which banned transmission of pornographic messages over telephone lines by so-called dial-a-porn services.[74] He was equally compliant toward congressional recommendations for higher education, proposing in his final budget submission an allocation of $5.8 billion for that purpose.[75]

Reagan's approval of the 1989 education budget was, for all practical purposes, his last meaningful act in that area. And his submission of an overall budget calling for total 1989 expenditures of slightly less than $1.1 trillion was one of the final acts of a president who entered office as an avowed proponent of efficient government management.

CHAPTER 8

Chairman of the Board

"The cabinet would be my inner circle of advisers . . . almost like the board of directors."[1]

REAGAN BECAME ENAMORED OF THE CABINET-AS-BOARD-OF-DIRECTORS mode of operation when he was governor of California. His ostensible purpose was to make government function as efficiently as private business, and since the typical corporate form of organization was headed by a board of directors, he believed that basic structure would serve government equally well. In fact, he was forced to adopt a system in which his advisers would analyze the problems of office and feed him alternative solutions, because when he first entered the governor's office his own knowledge of conditions demanding the governor's attention was almost nil. Prior to his election as governor he had depended on what later became known as his kitchen cabinet—those millionaire backers of his campaign who also provided him with carefully chosen experts in finance, management and public relations. Once in office, Reagan naturally turned to his cabinet members for enlightenment on state problems and ideas for solving them. As reporter-biographer Lou Cannon discovered from his coverage of the governor's career,

> The minutes [of Reagan's cabinet meetings] confirm what reporters were learning in the weekly press conferences, which was that Reagan was heavily dependent upon a few top aides for his policy decisions. For information the governor usually relied on the stylized one-page "mini-memos" devised by his cabinet secretary William P. Clark. Issues, even those of great complexity, were reduced to four paragraphs—one of the statement of the problem, another for the facts, a third for discussion and a fourth for a recommended course of action.[2]

This system served Reagan so well that he determined to continue it when he reached the White House. With some pride he told representatives of several news agencies, "It's the first time that there has really been in operation what I call Cabinet government." He offered this description:

My idea of Cabinet government was that you recognize that there are very few problems that don't really overlap in a lot of areas, and I'm the fellow who has to make the decision. So we meet. We've met 29 times so far [as of 23 December 1981] as a full Cabinet, and the issues that come up and are put out on the table—there is debate entered into by everyone present, like a board of directors would debate something. The only difference between that and a board of directors meeting is, we don't take a vote. When I've heard enough to make a decision, I know that I have to make the decision.[3]

This explanation of the vital matter of executive decision-making apparently satisfied the assembled moguls of newspaper chains like Hearst, Knight-Ridder and Scripps-Howard, for none of their representatives raised a single question as to how the system worked in practice. Yet, three months later, the closest independent observer of Reagan's political career coauthored an article which made the particular point that Reagan never explained the process by which he made a decision. Comparing Reagan with former Presidents Carter, Ford and Johnson, all of whom freely discussed the way in which they had arrived at specific decisions, the article characterized Reagan's decision-making process as "a mystery" even to his own advisers.[4] Another analyst with extensive government experience, after interviews with Reagan and many of his aides, could offer no explanation of how the president arrived at his conclusions other than by "instincts and intuition."[5]

Much has been written about First Lady Nancy Reagan's influence on presidential decisions, but both Ronald and Nancy Reagan stated repeatedly that her part involved no more than the exchange of views which occur in private conversations between every president and his wife. If Michael Deaver's gossipy reminiscences can be relied on, the pair went over many substantive matters together, and Nancy prevailed "most of the time." Deaver attributed this to the first lady's method of waging "a quiet campaign, planting a thought, recruiting others of us to push it along, making a case: Foreign policy will be hurt . . . our allies will be let down." However, as Mrs. Reagan acknowledged in her memoirs, her husband ignored her suggestions that David Stockman be fired immediately after publication of the *Atlantic Monthly* article, that Raymond Donovan be released to end the attacks which limited his effectiveness, and that the president's visit to Bitburg be cancelled.[6]

What appears to be well documented is that, quite apart from policy decisions, the scheduling of Reagan's activities was in many cases dictated by the forecasts of California astrologer Joan Quigley, whom Mrs. Reagan called "my friend," and with whom she kept in constant touch. As first revealed by Donald Regan, Mrs. Reagan later confirmed that she had relayed to Mike Deaver, and subsequently, to Regan, the advice she received from the astrologer. Referring to the attempted assassination of her husband, Nancy confessed that "astrology was simply one of the ways I coped with the fear I felt after my husband almost died." However, she stressed that the use of Quigley's advice, for which she paid a substantial monthly fee, was "confined to timing—to Ronnie's schedule, and to what days were good or bad, especially with regard to his out-of-town trips." Never, she said, did the forecasts relate to policy or politics. Although Chief-of-Staff Regan found it necessary to develop "a color-coded calendar . . . (numerals highlighted in green ink for 'good' days, red for 'bad' days, yellow for 'iffy' days)," he did not suggest that matters of policy were affected.[7]

It is not clear when the president became aware of Nancy's use of an astrological warning system to regulate his schedule. She reports that she told him of it when he came into the room as she was talking to Quigley on the telephone, "quite a few months" after that association began. Presumably this occurred sometime in 1982. After Regan's book was published in 1988, a reporter asked the president, "Will you continue to allow astrology to play a part in the makeup of your daily schedule?" Reagan replied, "You asked for it. I can't because I never did." This question and answer were reported in the *Weekly Compilation of Presidential Documents*. What the official record did not include was Marlin Fitzwater's explanation to reporters immediately after the president's departure, that Reagan thought the question was whether astrology played a part in his policy decisions—a "misunderstanding" difficult to accept in view of the precise wording used by the reporter.[8]

* * * * *

The significance of the so-called cabinet government became less mysterious as time went on and Reagan aides admitted that many a policy was determined in an unheralded meeting with a very few of Reagan's closest confidants—often before the matter was ever taken up in a cabinet meeting—and then triumphantly announced as an on-the-spot decision by the president.[9] In these circumstances, tracing the origin and evolution of any decision attributed to Reagan's distillation of the give-and-take in a meeting depends not on empty presidential explanations, but on an analysis and comparison of statements made anonymously by his lieutenants and in the post-employment memoirs they published.

On the other hand, the ideas used by Reagan are readily discernible as recommendations originating in special committees or commissions. And the number of such groups would easily match the special-team appointments of previous presidents. In the area of management alone, Reagan established these advisory groups in the first fifteen months of his presidency:

1. Presidential Task Force on Regulatory Relief
2. Presidential Council on Integrity and Efficiency, to coordinate "an attack on waste and fraud"

3. White House Policy Team, to provide "guidance on implementing the President's decision to dismantle the Department of Energy"
4. Steering Group, to provide "coordination and direction to the activities of a series of working groups which will address in detail organizational, resource, legislative, and external relations issues"
5. President's Private Sector Survey on Cost Control, known informally as the Grace Commission
6. Property Review Board, "to improve the management of federal real property."[10]

To implement the recommendations of the Council on Integrity and Efficiency, Reagan in 1984 established a President's Council on Management Improvement. This group was directed to report through a previously unmentioned Cabinet Council on Management and Administration. And in the final year of his second term, Reagan issued Executive Order 12625 to establish another President's Council on Integrity and Efficiency, whose title and purposes were almost identical to those of the management group he had formed seven years earlier. An inquiry as to the activities and demise of the 1981 council brought no response from the White House Office of Public Liaison.[11]

Most of these advisory groups were composed largely of senior officers in the executive departments of the federal government. The Grace Commission, on the other hand, was made up of "experts from the private sector" whose presumably independent and disinterested judgments would be incorporated into recommendations that would go directly to the president. An effort to tie private and public officials together was undertaken by still another group, the Presidential Task Force on Private Sector Initiatives, whose objectives were to find "methods of developing, supporting and promoting private sector leadership and responsibility for meeting public needs," and to make "recommendations for appropriate action by the president to foster greater public-private partnerships and to decrease dependence on government."[12] But Reagan did not stop there. Because it appeared that in some areas American business was no longer a match for its foreign competitors, he formed a National Productivity Advisory Committee "aimed at keeping American business and the American worker ahead of the competition."[13]

Of all the management panels established by President Reagan, the Grace Commission is best known, largely because of the wide publicity given its mammoth report and the extravagant claims of its chairman, J. Peter Grace, as to the savings his recommendations would produce. Grace issued the commission's findings piecemeal in 1983, creating such headlines as "Commission Predicts $48 Billion Savings" in April, "Panel Offers Government a

Plan on Saving $137 Billion in Outlays" in July, and "PPSSCC + 161 + 1350 = $340,000,000,000" in August. When the director of the PPSSCC executive committee—also an employee of W. R. Grace and Co.—discussed the commission's work with a congressional committee, he rounded the savings estimate off to $300 billion, using a chart to explain that the $340 billion figure included some duplications.[14]

The following January, when Reagan acknowledged receipt of the commission's final eleven-volume report, which comprised 36 different task force analyses and 2,478 recommendations, he blithely accepted Grace's claim that the findings of his private-industry specialists "substantiate three-year ongoing savings of $424.4 billion, plus cash accelerations of $66 billion"![15]

Apart from the Peter Grace crew and White House staff, few analysts were as satisfied as President Reagan was with the commission's recommendations. Examining the proposed revenue-raising reforms, the Senate Finance Committee was able to confirm savings of only $3 billion of the $100 billion claimed by the commission. The Congressional Budget Office and General Accounting Office, in separate evaluations, could find no more than $98 billion in total savings over three years, a conclusion Grace said he was "very pleased" about. When Reagan announced publicly that savings of $12.5 billion had already been realized in debt collection alone, Budget Director David Stockman advised the White House that this figure—which had been supplied by his own assistant—was greatly exaggerated.[16]

Because the commission was advisory only, its recommendations had no force of law, but the administration reaped the benefit of this "nonpartisan" evidence of waste in government even before it had an opportunity to make good on its promise to study the proposals carefully. No subsequent headlines resulted from the administration's promised study. Nor did the White House give any publicity to one of the panel's chief findings: that greater savings could be made in the Department of Defense than anywhere else. When Defense Secretary Caspar Weinberger was asked about this, he promised to have the report examined "with care." But prior to that examination he was able to assure reporters that more than 80 percent of the $92 billion in savings recommended by reform of military procurement procedures would depend on action by Congress to change the laws.[17]

The same excuse was offered by Reagan in several of his many laudatory references to the commission's work.[18] On March 20, 1984, Reagan told reporters that "the bulk of them [the recommendations] will take legislation [to implement them]." Two years later he acknowledged indirectly that most of the proposals could be effected without enabling legislation. This was clear from the cover letter he sent to Congress with his 1987 budget request and a report entitled "Management of the United States Government, Fiscal Year 1987." In his letter the president summarized a number of the report's undocumented savings, concluding with this statement: "We have accepted or are in the process of implementing some 1,741, or over 80 percent, of the 2,160 unduplicated recommendations the Commission has produced." Only the proposals incorporated into the executive budget, he said, would require congressional approval. [19]

*   *   *   *   *

If Reagan's cabinet government was largely a myth, his concept of delegated authority was very real. The September 15, 1986 cover of *Fortune* magazine featured a picture of the president, together with the title of its lead article, "What Managers Can Learn From Manager Reagan" and his managerial code: "Surround yourself with the best people you can find, delegate authority, and don't interfere."

This principle of organization and operation Reagan had adopted when he was governor of California, and he referred to it repeatedly in later years. Rarely did he discuss the way in which the theory worked out in practice, but occasionally he would indicate in general terms what he expected of his administrators. To begin with, he told officials of the International Monetary Fund and World Bank, a department head would have to evaluate the situation he or she found when taking office. "Making an assessment and setting goals are, of course, nothing more than good management," he reminded his audience. [20]

It was understood that a department head's initial evaluation, and all policy decisions born of that assessment, were to be bound by Reagan's oft-repeated goal of "getting government off the people's backs." In general terms, this meant reducing regulatory controls to a bare minimum. In two cases—education and energy—the aim was to eliminate the departments altogether. For several agencies—The Bonneville Power Administration, Naval Petroleum Reserve, and Federal Housing Administration—the object was to sell them off to private entrepreneurs. [21]

These goals reflected Reagan's conviction that in most areas of human endeavor, "the best thing government can do is get out of the way." In other words, leave all the problems bearing on national well-being to private enterprise because, as he had said when he first sought the presidency, "every problem that besets us today—from dropouts to disease, from job training to student loans—is being solved somewhere in the country right now by a group of citizens who didn't wait for government." [22]

In line with his enduring confidence that private enterprise would take care of all the country's problems if left to its own devices, Reagan's explanation for widespread poverty, illiteracy, ill health, and recurring periods of substantial unemployment was that these conditions were brought on by government interference or mismanagement. Moreover, his notion that management of public affairs would be made more efficient by putting businessmen in charge hardly squared with his expressed opinion that "if there were men in government who were capable of running the nation's business, the nation's business would have long since hired them away from government."[23] To accept this as a basic principle of the American system would be to assert that personal enrichment is a stronger force than brotherhood, patriotism—even voluntarism—the values so frequently invoked by Reagan. The fact is that Reagan's strongest supporters—like Edwin Meese, Michael Deaver and Republican leaders in the Senate—enjoyed the power and recognition that public office brings more than the much higher income they could have gained from private employment.

Heralded as the mark of an efficient executive, Reagan's policy of delegation without monitoring by the chief executive eased his own job in more ways than one. First, it enabled him to keep a comfortable 9 to 5 work schedule, a routine common to clerical employees but one that most business executives running much smaller and less complex enterprises than the U. S. government would find impossible to follow. Reagan justified his easygoing approach to high public office with this gem from his endless store of aphorisms: "Show me an executive who works long, hard hours, and I'll show you a bad executive," prompting biographer Lou Cannon to observe, "Ronald Reagan was not the boardroom candidate among Republicans in the 1980 campaign."[24]

Within the civil-service type work schedule he chose for himself, President Reagan kept free an hour in the morning and another hour in the afternoon "to look at his paperwork, to read whatever he wants, or to catch up on his correspondence." Nor did he have any difficulty arranging frequent trips away from Washington, most of which were vacations that, measured in days, totalled more than those of any modern president except Richard Nixon.[25]

Larry Speakes recalled that the president often took a bundle of reports with him when he left the Oval Office in the evening. But his subsequent description of Reagan's average evening suggests that little time was available for serious work. "In the evenings," Speakes wrote of the president, "he spends an hour working out with weights in the mini-gym they had set up in his private quarters, and then (after a shower) he and Mrs. Reagan slip into their pajamas and robes and eat, watch television and read." The Reagan's closest friend, Mike Deaver, confirmed that "most nights after 6:00 P.M. . . . he would be wearing nightclothes."[26]

By all accounts, Reagan's fiercely protective wife, who made no secret of her primary concern that her husband have adequate rest and relaxation, saw to it that he did not overburden himself. And if Reagan spent no more time examining office material than he did the morning newspapers—which Speakes says the president "glanced at" after first reading the comics—his evening chores could not have been too taxing.[27]

When Donald Regan dared—as no other White House aide had ever done—to press the president to resume his normal work load a month after prostate surgery, Nancy Reagan's previous irritation with the chief of staff rose to fury. One week later Regan was an ex-White House employee. As devoted an admirer of the president as Larry Speakes acknowledged that "the Reagans didn't even do Regan the courtesy of informing him of his ouster before [television network] CNN reported it."[28]

In one sense, Regan brought misfortune on himself. Had he paid attention to the signals sent up by people around the president's wife, he might have profited from the warning expressed by one of that lady's speech writers, that Mrs. Reagan was to be "treated with the kind of gingerly respect due a lioness: one admires its beauty, anticipates its desires and never, never gets it angry."[29]

Reagan's system of delegation also passed to his subordinates responsibility for coming up with ideas, not only for improving government efficiency but for ways and means of solving the nation's domestic and foreign policy problems. Reagan himself contributed little to this effort, according to many of those who worked with him or observed his work. As his first presidential campaign manager, John Sears, acknowledged, "his decisions rarely originate with him. He is an endorser. It is fair to say that on some occasions he is presented with options and selects one, but it is also true that in other instances he simply looks to someone to tell him what to do."[30]

Finally, Reagan gained an extraordinarily protective cover from the way in which he managed to evade responsibility for actions taken to implement his policies. It was this aspect of Reagan's managerial system that gave rise to Representative Patricia Schroeder's characterization of his administration as "the Teflon-coated presidency." In a derisive tribute to Reagan's "great break-through in political technology," she charged: "He sees to it that nothing sticks to him. He is responsible for nothing—civil rights, Central America, the Middle East, the economy, the environment—he is just the master of ceremonies at someone else's dinner."[31]

In a fashion unprecedented in American history, the dangerous side effects of Reagan's hands-off style of delegation were for six years ignored by the public—and to a large extent by the media—even though cracks in the system appeared long before the entire foundation collapsed in the Iran-Contra scandal. Although Schroeder did not bother to document specific examples of Reagan's evasions, the list is a long one and includes situations in which he absolved himself of responsibility for questionable decisions or actions by pleading ignorance, leaving explanations to others, or flatly denying the truth of what had occurred.

All three variables of Teflon coating were revealed in the president's news conferences. When first challenged on his administration's attitude toward the Voting Rights Act, Reagan said he had not yet received a report on that subject.[32] Questioned about Secretary of State Haig's reference to the use of a "nuclear warning shot" as part of NATO's contingency plans, he said, "there seems to be some confusion as to whether that is still part of NATO strategy or not, and so far I've had no answer to that."[33] Asked why he had misled Chicago high school students by misrepresenting the facts relating to his policy of tax exemption for private schools guilty of racial discrimination, he pretended that he had been talking about an entirely different situation, which was as false as his original misstatement to the students.[34] He juggled the facts in similar fashion when he defended his "user fee" gasoline tax and denied having said earlier what was a matter of White House record, that he would not approve that tax, or any other, "unless there's a palace coup and I'm overthrown."[35]

There were times, of course, when administrative officers came out with such ridiculous pronouncements that Reagan, if he was aware of these idiocies, chose to ignore them. One outstanding example was Deputy Under Secretary of Defense Thomas K. Jones's assurance to the American public that everyone could be protected against a nuclear attack simply by digging a hole in the ground, covering it with a couple of doors, and piling three feet of dirt on top.[36] Another wild offering from this administration of efficiency experts came from Interior Secretary Donald Hodel, whose answer to the worldwide danger of ozone depletion was to campaign for public wearing of hats, sunglasses and tanning lotion.[37]

In areas of more immediate concern to President Reagan, his "unawareness" became increasingly evident as time went on. On November 1, 1985 he signed National Security Decision Directive 196, which included authorization for almost unlimited use of polygraph tests in federal agencies. After Secretary of State Shultz threatened to resign if he were asked to take a lie-detector test, Reagan told his aides he had not been aware of how widely his order applied to government employees.[38] When an American plane was shot down while flying supplies to the Contras inside Nicaragua, he professed not to know "the exact particulars" of such operations, despite having encouraged every form of private aid to Contra military forces.[39] By 1987 his cabinet members and chief supporters in Congress were showing concern over Reagan's inability to respond to policy proposals made in their private meetings, other than to wander off into personal reminiscences or anecdotes that had no relevance to the subject at hand.[40]

The awful significance of Reagan's unawareness, which had so long been glossed over or waved off as inconsequential, finally penetrated the public consciousness in November 1986 when the Iran-Contra story broke and, after three weeks of denials followed by half admissions, the president finally admitted, "I was not fully informed on the nature of one of the activities undertaken in connection with this initiative."[41] The extent and significance of this uniformed state in this extraordinary series of maneuvers will be considered in a later chapter. Here it is sufficient to indicate the seriousness of a system of delegated power that permitted subordinate officers to assume presidential authority in a fashion that thwarted the very purpose of American constitutional government and threatened the country's standing and credibility among the nations of the world.

* * * *

Only rarely are management skills a major requirement for elective office. Nevertheless, in elections for the presidency of the United States, a candidate who has held the position of governor of one of the fifty states is presumed to have accumulated the kind of experience that is needed to understand the complexities of public administration.

With Reagan's background in the governor's office in California, he was in a position to know the qualities required of a good department head. After winning the 1980 presidential election he told reporters that he preferred to hire successful businessmen who really "don't want a job in government" because it would be "a step down." Also, he wanted people "who will be the first to tell me if their jobs are unnecessary."[42]

Despite his expressed preference for business executives who were not interested in working for the government, many of Reagan's appointees to White House or cabinet-level posts had little or no business experience. Conservative Democratic Senator Sam Nunn of Georgia, for one, recognized that Reagan's criteria for his administrators were "more related to ideology than . . . to management experience."

Doctrinaire politics and limited business experience were especially evident at the top. Meese's only contact with business enterprise came in the one year he spent helping to defend Rohr Industries against a suit by the San Francisco Bay Area Rapid Transit Authority and four years in private law practice which he combined with teaching criminal law at the University of San Diego.[43]

As his employment record indicates, Meese had almost no management experience in private business. Moreover, long before assuming the position of attorney general of the United States, Meese had demonstrated his ineptness as an administrator. Associates and critics as diverse as Larry Speakes, Michael Deaver, one-time Reagan campaign manager John Sears, biographer

Lou Cannon, and Ralph Nader staffers Ronald Brownstein and Nina Easton agreed that in management terms Meese was a complete incompetent. Lacking organizational skills, Meese was the opposite of his boss in that he seemed incapable of delegating, insisting instead on knowing and directing everything. Among his co-workers, the standing joke that followed him from California to Washington was that once a document got into Meese's briefcase, it was lost forever.[44]

An equally poor example of an individual who would prefer private to public employment was Reagan's director of the Office of Management and Budget. David Stockman's entire postuniversity career had been in public service, which led him from Harvard directly to Washington as a staff member of the Republican Conference of the House of Representatives, then to the House itself as an elected representative from a relatively safe Republican district in Michigan. Secure in this position, to which he was twice reelected, Stockman actively campaigned for the job of federal budget director.[45]

In departments outside the executive office of the president, business experience assumed greater importance, but it was by no means a common denominator for all cabinet appointments. Six of Reagan's first cabinet members had been government employees for most of their adult lives. Defense Secretary Caspar Weinberger's principle business experience was as a vice-president of Bechtel Corporation, where he spent six years inbetween much longer periods of public service in the California state legislature, as Governor Reagan's finance director, President Nixon's budget director and, later, secretary of the Department of Health, Education and Welfare. Education Secretary Terrel Bell spent many years in the Utah public school system and was U.S. commissioner of education under Presidents Nixon and Ford. Energy Secretary James Edwards began his professional career as a dentist, but entered South Carolina politics via election to the state senate, graduating to the governorship in 1974. Health and Human Services Secretary Richard Schweiker grew up in Pennsylvania politics, spending 20 years in Congress, first in the House, then the Senate. State Department Secretary Alexander Haig was a West Point graduate who spent his whole life in the military, much of it in Washington where he served as President Nixon's chief of staff during the Watergate investigation. Housing and Urban Development Secretary Samuel Pierce was a lawyer whose previous experience included stints as assistant district attorney in New York, judge in that state, U.S. attorney, and member of President Eisenhower's Labor Department.

Attorney General William French Smith was a highly successful corporation lawyer, but had little acquaintance with criminal law or with those aspects of civil law that so frequently reach the Supreme Court in cases involving civil rights and constitutional freedoms. Interior Secretary James

Watt had long been a spokesman for large western landowners, ranchers, mining and oil companies, representing those special interests first as a lobbyist for the Chamber of Commerce and later as president of the Mountain States Legal Foundation.

Cabinet members who could truly qualify as successful business executives were Secretary of Agriculture John Block, Secretary of Commerce Malcolm Baldridge, Secretary of Labor Raymond Donovan, Secretary of Transportation Andrew Lewis, and Secretary of the Treasury Donald Regan. As a farmer, Block was in the top 5 percent of the country's growers, who accounted for approximately half of all agricultural output and more than two-thirds of the total income from agricultural products. His success story was matched by that of Baldridge, who rose from mill hand in a Connecticut iron foundry to president of that company in less than 15 years. From there Baldridge went on to demonstrate his administrative talent in bigger business, building Scovill, Inc. into a growing conglomerate. Lewis had also performed successfully as chief executive officer in several industrial firms. In addition, he had served as a trustee for the Reading Railroad during bankruptcy proceedings that ended with the takeover of Reading property by Conrail. Regan easily qualified as an expert in financial problems having spent 36 years with the Wall Streeet brokerage firm of Merrill Lynch, rising from trainee to president and chairman of the board of directors.[46]

Raymond Donovan was in another category altogether. Whatever understanding of labor problems Reagan may have gained from his experience as president of the Screen Actors Guild, it was not in evidence when he appointed Donovan as secretary of labor. The post does not automatically go to a labor leader, Republican presidents shying away from so direct an association more than Democrats. But seldom has a person been chosen whose experience with labor problems raised as many questions as that of Donovan. As head of a New Jersey construction firm, Donovan thrived in an industry that had deservedly earned a reputation of collaboration with both labor racketeers and dishonest government officials in such practices as rigged bidding, acceptance of substandard work, and "protection" arrangements with labor leaders on one side and government inspectors on the other. Disenchantment with Donovan's appointment persisted, even among Republicans, despite the finding of a special prosecutor that there was "insufficient evidence upon which to base a prosecution."[47] Donovan's voluntary retirement from public service was received by the president "with deep personal regret."[48]

*　　*　　*　　*　　*

Regardless of whether or not Reagan's agency heads met the criteria he had set for the administrators who were to lead the Reagan Revolution, their "integrity and efficiency"—the explicit goals of the first and last of his management councils—can be judged only by the record of their agencies' accomplishments. The evaluation of that record depends, of course, on the observer's concept of the purposes of government. President Reagan's view, for example, was that, in most circumstances, "the best thing government can do is nothing." This was the basis for his efforts to "cut and trim" every government activity except those associated with criminal-law enforcement and national defense. All other problems, he insisted, are best handled by individuals, and organizations or businesses acting in their private capacities. "Government does not really solve problems"; Reagan once explained, "it subsidizes them. And it does not produce a dime of revenue."[49]

That final comment illustrates Reagan's disdain for government as a nonproductive enterprise. Not that he wanted government to make money on its operations. Wherever that was possible—as in the sale or leasing of coal and oil reserves—he favored turning development over to private business. All that government should be concerned with, he said, are the relatively few functions that individuals and private enterprise cannot handle.

How these responsibilities would be carried out in practice he did not explain. Reagan never wondered about whether his theory was validated by his practices; but he was so certain that it was that he would assert as facts things that have been demonstrated here to be false. Moreover, his view of an efficient government was one that succeeded in eliminating all laws and regulations that would provide the protections called for by his theory.

As a practical politician, Reagan would abandon a position if it threatened his chances of being elected—as he abandoned his early diatribes against Social Security—but he never asked himself questions that would test his basic concepts. Questions such as, does one person's liberty to dispose of toxic chemicals in any way he chooses impinge on the liberty of his neighbors to breathe air, drink water, or raise crops without fear of being poisoned by the chemicals? Is the constitutional right of a low-income individual "to have the assistance of counsel for his defense" supported by efforts to eliminate legal aid for the poor? Are Americans adequately protected from aggressors when the only totalitarian threat recognized is that posed by left-wing governments? Is equal opportunity to obtain employment, desirable housing, the best education really the goal of an administration which insists that discrimination in these areas by private individuals or organizations is a permissible expression of their private opinions? Does government show compassion for people who are unable to care for themselves by cutting social programs first and most deeply in each annual budget? If questions like these did not occur to President Reagan, they did arise in the minds of many Americans as they observed the operation of his executive officers and administrators.

*   *   *   *

A department-by-department analysis of management successes and failures would fill many volumes. Here, too, what constitutes success or failure is partly in the eye of the beholder. James Watt consistently held to the position that his Interior Department's management of public lands was a great improvement over that of previous administrations. Organizations like the National Wildlife Federation and the Sierra Club disagreed, publicly and vigorously. Their protests against the despoiling of public lands were brushed aside as representing only the interests of nature lovers who could not appreciate the need for commercial development of natural resources by private enterprise. More difficult to rebut was the 1984 finding of a federal commission that Watt's coal leasing program was "deficient in all its functions." And Hodel's management of the enormous national timberlands was described by the president of a private land-investment firm as having permitted—even subsidized—the over-harvesting of federal forests by private lumber companies at a loss of millions of dollars in federal funds.[50]

Problems in the Department of Agriculture did not cease with the appointment of a highly competent farmer as secretary. Never known for its efficiency in any administration, it was expected to streamline and simplify its operating procedures under John Block. In many of its divisions, the opposite occurred. Intent on eliminating from the school lunch program every child who could not qualify for free or reduced-price meals, the department imposed new regulations that forced schools all over the country to hire additional personnel and to fill out lengthier reports on the use of funds than they had ever been asked for previously. Another branch of the department, the Farmers Home Administration, carried this kind of reform to an extreme. Responsible for providing "credit for those in rural America who are unable to get credit from other sources at reasonable rates and terms," the agency implemented Reagan's pledge to cut paperwork by discarding the existing four-page application farmers had been using to request government loans and substituting a form 26 pages in length. Meanwhile, the administration's drive on waste was marked by establishment of what Agriculture Department employees referred to as "the bone yard," where high-level civil service employees inherited from the Carter years were assigned to no-work jobs at salaries as high as $58,000 a year.[51]

A similar approach to savings was introduced by the Justice Department when it eliminated an Identical Bids Unit that, at a cost of $150,000 a year, had operated since 1961 to prevent the government from being subjected to price gouging by suppliers who collaborated to fix bids for materials and services, potentially leading to overspending by hundreds of millions of dollars annually.[52]

In the State Department, Secretary Shultz's choice for the post of under secretary for management was career foreign officer Ronald I. Spiers. His rise from foreign affairs officer to ambassadorships in the Bahamas, Turkey and Pakistan was impressive, but in all those posts his principal responsibility was with political affairs. Yet as ambassador he was sufficiently concerned about the sorry state of departmental management under corporation-trained Jerome W. Van Gorkom to complain to Secretary Shultz. This earned him a transfer—and promotion—from the embassy in Pakistan to the under secretary's office in Foggy Bottom. Two years later he may have understood why his predecessor had quit in disgust at his inability to overcome either the inertia of the establishment or the indifference of political appointees toward businesslike management methods. When a minor scandal over the mishandling of department travel funds erupted in 1988, he acknowledged that he was unaware of the disappearance or embezzlement of hundreds of dollars, and a record-keeping system so slovenly that no documentation could be found for a $695 advance to Oliver L. North four years after the money had been drawn. Spiers' only explanation for his condition was that because the department's major preoccupation was with foreign policy, "management issues do not get the attention they deserve."[53]

If a high level of efficiency was expected anywhere, it was in the Treasury Department, especially when that office was headed by as obviously competent a secretary as Donald Regan. For the most part Regan ran an effective operation, despite the fact that his boss had "laid down no rules and articulated no missions" for the department. Regan did not expect the president to suggest how he should run his shop, but the organization and direction of any agency depends in part on the priorities assigned to it. At the conclusion of his federal service, Regan wrote:

> In the four years that I served as Secretary of the Treasury I never saw President Reagan alone and never discussed economic philosophy or fiscal and monetary policy with him one-on-one. From first day to last at Treasury, I was flying by the seat of my pants. The President never told me what he believed or what he wanted to accomplish in the field of economics. I had to figure these things out like any other American, by studying his speeches and reading the newspapers. . . . I found this disembodied relationship bizarre.[54]

The one area in which serious operational problems arose was in the Internal Revenue Service. The 1981 changes in income tax laws required modification of forms and regulations and brought forth revisions so poorly designed that businessmen as well as the general public protested vehemently at the confusion, extra time, effort and frustration created by new W-4 (Employee Withholding Certificate) and 1040 individual tax return report forms. President Reagan's only comment was to remark that "it's good to remember that Albert Einstein said *he* didn't understand it [Form 1040]."

That the president's brush-off of poor performance was not acceptable in other government quarters Deputy Secretary of the Treasury Richard G. Darman learned some time later. Responding to contractors' complaints of government red tape, Darman blasted big corporations as "bloated, risk-averse, inefficient and unimaginative." When the next year's *Government Manual* came out, the second highest officer of the department was no longer listed as a federal employee.[55]

Substantial monetary savings in these and other departments were realized by reductions in staff and budgetary allowances for other operational needs, but little could be identified as the product of improved management. Agencies like the Veterans Administration, TVA and NASA were repeatedly cited for waste resulting from mismanagement, much of which was not unique to the Reagan presidency, but which reflected poorly on an administration that had pledged to "eliminate fraud and waste" by putting government in the hands of management experts.[56]

President Reagan's special targets for the elimination of waste and fraud were the social agencies. In his inimical anecdotal fashion, he found no lack of horrible examples of fraudulent claims for public assistance, Social Security benefits, and medical services. Some were taken from verifiable case files, but many were pure fiction.[57] However, the department that was responsible for the most documented fraud, waste and mismanagement was the one that Reagan supported fully in every one of its budget requests, no matter how extravagant were Secretary Weinberger's demands for his Department of Defense.

The first report of the comptroller general observed that although the Defense Department "generally followed through on its pledge to emphasize readiness . . . and quality of life for military personnel," it showed deficiencies in the use of the greatly expanded budget. These included limited success in eliminating marginal weapons systems, and less than desirable prudence in the use of the increased funding for ill-defined programs.[58]

Subsequent reports were far less flattering. Periodically the press learned of incidents in which the military had paid ridiculous prices for tools and replacement parts. Even more ominous were revelations of the failure of major weapons to perform as expected. After four years of almost unlimited spending under the leadership of a famous budget-cutter, "Mac the Knife" Caspar Weinberger, the Defense Policy Panel of the House Armed Services Committee offered an answer to its own question: "What have we got for $1 trillion?" The panel's report indicates that "after discounting for inflation . . . the current buildup is not merely large in peacetime terms but has already exceeded the wartime peaks of the Korean and Vietnam wars." Pointing out that "President Reagan himself has made inventory numbers a key element in his own judgments," the report found that a 91 percent increase in money for weapons had led to a less than 10 percent growth in weapons inventory; an 81 percent increase in allocations for "readiness" had brought a drop in flying hours per crew and less than a 5 percent rise in mission-capable rates; and basic technology improvements over the Soviets were nil despite a 56 percent increase in research and development funds. Only in personnel recruitment did a 10 percent increase in funding produce more than twice that ratio of re-enlistments and more than a fivefold increase in number of army enlistees with high school diplomas.[59]

Even before the commission report came out, 18 months of publicity about $7,622 coffee pots, $400 socket wrenches and $659 ash trays convinced the president of the need for a commission to look into military procurement. Named after its chairman, Nixon's deputy defense secretary David Packard, the Blue Ribbon Commission on Defense Management was authorized June 17, 1985, without fanfare and with no formal announcement in the *Weekly Compilation of Presidential Documents* until a month later when the remaining members of the panel were named.[60]

The commission's report went to the president February 28, 1986. Through an earlier leak, the *Washington Post* discovered that the first draft of this document had been discarded when some members of the panel complained that it was too critical of Secretary Weinberger who had, from the outset, opposed establishing the commission. Nevertheless, the published findings were sharply critical of Defense Department's system of military procurement, as well as of the by-product that the public now believed that defense contractors "put profits above legal and ethical responsibilities." Pointing in particular to the Pentagon's "inefficient procedures" and the absence of any channel through which the needs and views of various combatant commanders could be assembled and synthesized, the commission recommended establishing the post of under secretary of defense for acquisitions, and the designation of officers having the same responsibility in each of the three military services: army, navy, and air force. A further proposal was that DOD purchase standard, commercial nuts-and-bolts items, instead of designing "gold-plated" models that increased the cost as much as 1,000 percent.[61]

Having acknowledged the need for an investigation of military management, the president could not very well challenge his own commission's findings. But in typical fashion, he ignored the report's most important criticisms and congratulated chairman Packard on producing a "bipartisan and unanimous" set of recommendations which he said—not at all in jest— "follow the pattern of things that have already been started."[62]

Subsequent White House statements followed a similar line, adding that Congress would have to legislate those reforms which the DOD had not carried out under its own authority. Two years later, after commission chairman Packard had announced the development of a contractors' code of ethics, news stories revealed that the FBI—not DOD watchdogs—had discovered evidence of widespread fraud and corruption in the handling of military contracts.[63]

Ex-Secretary Weinberger, who had resigned in November 1987, continued to defend Defense Department practices, though he admitted that "if there are some procedures that permitted this to happen . . . then obviously the procedures need tightening." By midsummer of 1988, FBI pursuit of illicit dealing had led agents to search the offices of six Pentagon officials and fifteen private consultants, the latter category including assistant secretary of the navy Melvyn R. Paisley, retired navy admiral James A. Lyons, a former navy contracting officer who had been fired for insider trading, and two associates of senior members of Congress.[64]

In multiple attempts to sidetrack, block or obfuscate the investigation, officials in the Pentagon destroyed documents and attempted to convince Weinberger's replacement, Defense Secretary Frank C. Carlucci, that his deputy secretary and under secretary in charge of acquisitions be empowered to refuse permission to search Pentagon files. Actually, Deputy Secretary William H. Taft, IV had already sabotaged the effort to put a single officer in charge of the acquisitions program by having the principle function of that newly appointed assistant secretary transferred to himself. This occurred only five months after the Defense Department had implemented one of the few significant recommendations of the Packard commission. Weinberger had boasted that the appointment of James P. Wade, Jr. as assistant secretary of defense for acquisition and logistics would resolve all the problems cited in the Packard commission. But no sooner had Wade submitted a report proposing reform of a procurement process that he described as "ponderous, inflexible and so layered as to make it virtually impossible to maintain accountability," than he was relieved of his authority in that area by Taft, a move that was approved by Weinberger.[65]

Representative John D. Dingell (D. Mich.) said he had warned Weinberger about the problem of leaked information, but had been ignored. What angered Dingell even more was the White House contribution to the drive to sabotage military procurement reform. An op-ed piece in the *Washington Post* revealed that this bit of maneuvering had come to Dingell's attention by way of a secret National Security Defense Directive, apparently concocted by John Poindexter, then presidential assistant for national security affairs, because "the government let it be known that it expected the [defense] industry to police itself and voluntarily admit fraudulent activity to the government." That objective was openly expressed by the inspector general of the Defense Department who, only months before the 1988 scandal broke, "embraced self-policing by telling the *Cleveland Plain Dealer* . . . that she 'would like to try to increase the comfort level between contractors and the inspector general and the Department of Defense'."[66] The level of comfort already achieved became clear when news of the FBI investigation hit the headlines.

* * * *

Standards of conduct aside, Defense Department managers were responsible for a number of serious miscalculations in the production of military weapons. This was no novelty in American military history as ever since World War I, the armed forces had overestimated their needs and underestimated their problems. However, an administration dedicated to economy and efficiency might have been expected to reject the gold-plated approach to weaponry. A perfect example of its failure to do so is seen in the history of the Sergeant York antiaircraft gun, first conceived in 1977. In November 1981 the army awarded Ford a $1.5 billion contract for the production of 276 guns—$5,435,000 for each weapon. The army's first report of test results was described by the department's inspector general as "oversimplified" and "misleading." Notwithstanding continued questioning of the gun's effectiveness through 1983 and 1984, the army persisted in ordering more, aiming at a total of 614, at an estimated cost in excess of $6 billion. Only after it was discovered that tests of the weapon had been deliberately falsified by blowing up targets a few seconds after a gun had fired at it and missed, did Defense Secretary Weinberger acknowledge that "the Sergeant York was not operationally effective" and that the contract was being terminated. By this time the army had spent $1.8 billion on weapons fit only for the scrap heap.[67]

The Bradley Fighting Vehicle was another fiasco. Essentially an armored personnel carrier, it was intended to replace the old unplated vehicle, but at a ninefold increase in price. Reagan's own budget director protested that, as a combat transport, the Bradley "was too expensive to ride in and too vulnerable to fight in." After a series of disappointing tests, newspaper publicity, and complaints from OMB and Congress, this multi-billion dollar project was also abandoned.[68]

Attempting to replace the drones—called "remotely piloted vehicles"—used so effectively as reconnaissance planes in the Vietnam War but discarded by the Pentagon in 1981, the Defense Department sought designs for a newer, gold-plated model. Initially priced at $100,000, the cost ballooned to $1.8 billion in 1987. Like the Sergeant York gun and Bradley personnel carrier, the Aquila (meaning eagle) was declared a turkey and was abandoned after tests demonstrated that it could find its target only 7 times in 105 attempts.[69]

These and other failures were matched by projects that were completed, but at enormous cost, principally because of President Reagan's insistence that "defense is not a budget issue. You spend what you need."[70] Given this philosophy and Reagan's complete indifference to the problem of monitoring expenditures, the outcome was predictable. Weinberger and his military chiefs pushed relentlessly for production of more ships, more planes, more tanks, under contracts that one writer estimated were let without competitive bidding 94 percent of the time.[71]

Equally devastating was the dampening effect on reform of the military procurement process. To the very end of Weinberger's tour as defense secretary, the only changes made were in structure rather than in policy, as David Packard acknowledged shortly before the secretary's resignation.[72] Weinberger's replacement, Frank C. Carlucci, attacked the budget problem with vigor, but he opposed stricter control of procurement for fear that the proposed reforms would "impede weapons modernization." Nevertheless, he ultimately agreed to subject to top-level scrutiny private contractors' revised bids, called "best and final offers," which had been revealed as one method of utilizing illegally obtained information about competitors' bids.[73]

Even the efforts of whistleblowers, which Reagan had praised as a useful means of identifying waste and fraud, fared no better under his administration than in any other. The military, in particular, resisted every effort to curb overspending resulting from payroll padding and price gouging by contractors and tolerated under the cozy relations between contractors and Defense Department officials. Instead of welcoming suggestions for tightening controls over pricing and performance, the Pentagon continued its long practice of making life miserable for whistleblowers. George R. Spanton, the Pentagon's resident auditor at the Pratt & Whitney aircraft engine plant in West Palm Beach learned this when he submitted reports of "fraud, waste, and abuse of tax dollars" to his superiors in Washington. His reward was a "threat of unwanted transfer to Los Angeles" only 28 months before his scheduled retirement, pressure to retire earlier than planned, poor performance ratings, loss of annual leave, and a criminal investigation of allegations concerning his performance at Pratt & Whitney.[74]

From testimony at the hearing, it seems clear that one aspect of Spanton's report which raised official ire was the reflection it cast on Pentagon brass with the charge that Pratt & Whitney had included in its overhead costs expenditures for "lavishly entertaining high-ranking air force and navy officials." His most heinous crime, however, was leaking his charges of payroll-padding and phoney expense items to the press after his reports failed to produce any action by his own audit agency.[75]

The Pentagon's view of the matter was provided by Deputy Assistant Secretary of Defense for Administration David O. Cooke. He did not explain, and committee members had not done sufficient homework to ask, why the Pentagon had not sent the deputy assistant secretary for contract audit and control to testify. From Cooke the committee elicited no substantive information whatever. That administrator's initial statement merely outlined departmental procedures for handling reports of fraud or mismanagement. His responses to questions about Spanton's reports consisted almost entirely of promises to furnish answers in writing after the hearing was over. Not one of those answers, which were made part of the record, referred to any aspect of the Spanton case. In support of his position that meritorious work was rewarded, not punished, by the Defense Department, Cooke submitted a nine-page list of "monetary awards granted to DOD military and civilian personnel for achieving cost reduction in defense operations." Not a single award in that list was for exposing or recapturing excess charges by contractors. Only two were related to contract procedures. The remaining awards were for such contributions as: "repair of the truion assembly on semi-trailer straddle carriers," "modification of the T-Pins" on security locks, and "a tethering system for the maintenance of chronically catheterized monkeys."[76]

Almost a year later, President Reagan attempted to demonstrate that his 1980 campaign pledge to "root out waste and fraud in the federal government" was being carried out most effectively in the Department of Defense. Using a Rose Garden ceremony to pay tribute to the accomplishments of 12 "outspoken and creative Defense Department employees"—he did not use the term whistleblowers—he cited these two examples of their contributions to improved efficiency:

> One challenged the price of an aircraft lighting kit [which] resulted in the drop in price from $50 to $8 for every kit we buy. Another is an alert auditor who found some suspicious labor charges and . . . gathered enough evidence to convict a dishonest contractor and obtain $450,000 in fines and recoveries.[77]

With their customary deference to the commander-in-chief, the reporters present raised no questions about the absence of those celebrated auditors whose challenges affected contracts worth billions of dollars. As two op-ed contributors to the New York Times remarked later, the savings for which Reagan's 12 "unsung heroes" were responsible represented "only the tip of the iceberg," the underwater monster having been revealed by people like air force systems expert A. Ernest Fitzgerald and Spanton, whose absence from the Reagan party was more meaningful than the presence of 12 minor award winners.[78]

Military officers were not immune from retaliation, as four veteran army and navy officers discovered after they unearthed evidence of waste and fraud involving everything from lost military equipment to falsified pay records and illegal recruiting methods. Their reward was reminiscent of the Soviet

Union's reaction to its dissidents, all four being sent to military hospitals for psychiatric examination before being given unsatisfactory performance ratings.[79]

Equally severe was the punishment accorded whistleblowers in private corporations operating under government contract. Few of their experiences made the kind of headlines that announced the death of Karen Silkwood, whose charges of unsafe working conditions at a Kerr-McGee nuclear plant were settled by a posthumous payment of over $1 million to Silkwood's estate. But many personal tragedies resulted from the firing and blacklisting of employees who had been bold enough to expose waste and fraud in their own companies. Even a company owner discovered that the price of pointing out the wasteful practices of a government agency was a fine for refusing a $16,000 contract awarded for work at a Marine Corps base that the contractor found could be done for $200.[80]

Perhaps the most devastating evaluation of seven years' effort by the Reagan administration to upgrade the military service came from the last of its procurement chiefs, Robert B. Costello, who observed that the armament industry still was not ready for a wartime emergency. Remarkably, he was not referring to a nuclear war. Merely to reach a production level adequate to support a "police action" like the one undertaken in the Korean War, he said, would take America's military suppliers three more years.[81]

CHAPTER 9

Diplomat:
Crusader for Democracy

*"We have a moral responsibility to support any-
one who aspires to live in a true democracy, free
from communist interference."*[1]

WHENEVER REAGAN SPOKE OF AMERICA'S PLACE IN THE WORLD, HE AT-
tempted to arouse his audience with a two-pronged appeal to patriotism: this
nation's destiny to lead all others in the "crusade for freedom" and, in that
connection, the struggle to frustrate what he saw as communist Russia's
unrelenting drive to dominate the earth. Only after his reelection to a second
term in the White House did he temper the colorful rhetoric with which he
delivered these basic principles of the Reagan Doctrine. Even then, he
resisted all efforts to alter his approach to the settlement of U.S. differences
with those parts of the world he considered to be Soviet controlled. Nevertheless, having by 1984 gone as far as he could with his program of domestic
reform, he recognized that his place in history would depend in large
measure on his record of accomplishment in the conduct of foreign affairs. In
that area he had made little progress, despite the popular response to his
January 27, 1981 welcoming home of the hostages who had been held in
Teheran for more than two years, his October 1983 invasion of Grenada, and
his military sortie against the dictator of Libya's 3,876,000 people in April
1986.

* * * * *

As the earlier chapter of Reagan's knowledge of history demonstrated, his
view of the world evolved from partly digested and poorly coordinated ideas
put together in the same simplistic fashion as his domestic policies. On the
one hand he insisted—à la Milton Friedman—that economics is the basis of a
free society, and he warned that both free enterprise and democracy were

threatened by the "creeping socialism" of government regulation and exces-
sive taxation. That is to say, economic policy is the foundation for guiding or
restricting individual freedom.[2] But when evaluating countries in less fortunate circumstances than the U.S., he held that political structure determines
the free or non-free character of a nation. There are two reasons, he said, why
backward nations are backward and underdeveloped nations are underdeveloped:

> First, because of their political systems. Either they are too unstable, as in
> many of today's so-called emerging nations, or else these systems are in the
> grip of modern-day feudalism, as in Russia or China. Second, because they
> lack both the know-how and the political structure necessary to build busi-
> ness, industry and commerce.[3]

Morally, Reagan's approach to all matters of foreign policy was based on
the premise that the U.S. represents all that is good for the human race, and
the rest of the world should try to emulate this country in developing
political, economic and social structures. Any nation which challenged that
dogma was, ipso facto, an enemy of the U.S. and a threat to freedom
everywhere.

Reagan established the good-versus-evil theme with his first major political address on behalf of Barry Goldwater's presidential candidacy in 1964.
"We are faced," he said, "with the most evil enemy mankind has known in
his long climb from the swamp to the stars."[4] The theme did not change
with his ascension to the White House. In his first presidential news
conference he demonstrated his continuing inability to distinguish between
revolutionary communism and the non-revolutionary goals of many left-of-
center parties, some of which called themselves socialist. The danger, he
insisted, came from the Soviet aim of "a one-world socialist or communist
state—whichever word you want to use."[5] Four months later he combined a
blast at previous administrations for engaging in "more and more social
experimentation" with a warning against "an evil force that would extinguish
the light we've been tending for 6,000 years."[6] The identity of the freedom
fighters who had tended the light from the brutal days of 4,000 B.C. to 1776
was never revealed. However, this principle of good versus evil was to form
the basis of the Reagan Doctrine, with which the president declared his
intention to defend his concept of freedom against any and all challenges
from what he considered communist-inspired governments or revolts.

A secondary theme that evolved from the good-versus-evil principle led
people in many of Reagan's "so-called emerging nations" to conclude that
their freedom was less important to the U.S. than their support of the Reagan
Doctrine. Consider the implications of his assertion that "the Soviet Union

underlies all the unrest that is going on," and "if they weren't engaged in this game of dominoes, there wouldn't be any hot spots in the world."[7] Whether the opinion reflected willful blindness or unparalleled ignorance, it demonstrated Reagan's inability to grasp the significance of the many post-World War II revolts of Asian and African peoples against the colonialism of western European nations, as well as the revolutions of landless peasants against military dictators in Latin America and the uprisings of religious groups in Asia and the Middle East against governments dominated by leaders of other religious sects. Nor did his tunnel vision take in the ethnic, religious, nationalist, and poverty-based antagonisms that lit innumerable fires from Bangladesh through the Middle East to Africa and the Americas. These factors—if he recognized them at all—Reagan considered secondary to the simple question of who stood with the U.S. in its battle against the evil empire, and who did not.

Even as crude and undiscriminating an outlook as Reagan's required the backing of expert opinion. As president, he received this support from his secretary of state and White House advisers, who, if they did not parrot all his pet phrases, provided him with the statistics and arguments needed to back up his assertions. As Nancy Reagan put it, "People tell the president only what they think he wants to hear."[8]

For support on a more philosophical plane Reagan relied on his first ambassador to the United Nations, political science professor Jeane J. Kirkpatrick. Nominally a conservative Democrat, Kirkpatrick laid the foundation for Reagan's with-us-or-against-us policy in a scathing attack on the Carter administration, written in 1979.[9] The substance of her charge was that Carter and his policy advisers had applied double standards in their treatment of revolutionary (meaning communist or communist-oriented) regimes and "traditional" governments friendly to the U.S. She used Iran and Nicaragua as her principal examples of this policy at work. Before the revolutions that brought Ruhollah Khomeini and Daniel Ortega Saavedra to power, she said, both countries were led by traditional rulers, both were overtly anti-communist, and both were in full agreement with U.S. foreign policy. From these uncontested facts she went on to assert that opponents of those rulers were determined to alter the established social and political framework by revolutionary means. The repressive force used by Iran's shah Mohammed Reza Pahlavi and Nicaragua's dictator Anastasio Somoza Debayle to protect themselves Kirkpatrick felt was only natural. Excesses such as torture and police brutality, documented by journalists and observers from organizations like Amnesty International, she referred to as "alleged." Carter's crime was in failing to support these "moderate autocrats" against revolutionary elements that, predictably, Kirkpatrick said, replaced the moderate autocracies with more repressive dictatorships.

In establishing this convenient distinction between friendly autocracies and unfriendly dictatorships, Kirkpatrick arrived at some odd—if not contradictory—conclusions. Right-wing autocracies, she said, can and do evolve into democracies, although this may require anywhere from a few decades to a few centuries. She found no proof of this in the Middle East or Central America but cited experience on "the Iberian peninsula" (although Spain shed its dictatorship only after Francisco Franco's death in 1975), and in Brazil (where what Kirkpatrick termed "the first steps" toward democracy had in fact made precious little difference in the framework of political power). She conceded that the longer an autocrat remains in power the more he solidifies both his position and the nation's dependence on him. And the deeper the entrenchment (and dependence) the more disastrous will be the disruption of society if he falls from power. It follows—though Kirkpatrick didn't say so—that the more ironclad a dictatorship becomes, the less desirable it is to witness the overthrow of the dictator and the collapse of the society he rules.

Kirkpatrick acknowledged that traditional living patterns under autocracies commonly include widespread poverty, illiteracy and disease among most of the population, and untold corruption and self-aggrandizement among the relatively few who control the country's political institutions and economic resources. But people get accustomed to misery, she wrote, and if their rulers do not interfere with their religious practices and other "normal" living habits, this is better than revolution.

The same theme runs through the speeches that Kirkpatrick made during her tenure as Reagan's ambassador to the United Nations. A two volume collection of those addresses, published in 1988, reveals the extent to which Kirkpatrick's position on international relations deteriorated from the premise that "liberals tolerate communist dictatorships but not right-wing autocracies" to Reagan's unannounced but clearly demonstrated policy that in defending free enterprise and democracy, the end justifies the means. Summing up this philosophical discussion of the Reagan Doctrine, Kirkpatrick wrote in 1988:

> A government which takes power by force, and retains power by force has no *legitimate* grounds for complaint against those who would wreak power from it by force.
>
> And a government whose power depends on *external* support has no legitimate grounds for complaining that externally supported force is used against it.
>
> *Obviously it is legitimate for the U.S. to support an insurgency against a dictatorial government that depends on external support.* [10]

The most interesting aspect of this concept of international relations is the inconsistency with which it was applied. Nowhere did Kirkpatrick apply the above principles to the illegitimacy of the power-by-force Somoza government or the legitimacy of the pre-Somoza revolt led by non-communist Augusto Cesar Sandino against a succession of repressive dictatorships that were kept in power only through the "external support" of the U.S. Marines. Nor did she ever allude to the fact that the most powerful of Reagan's Nicaraguan "freedom fighters" was Colonel Enrique Bermudez, a Somoza National Guard commander who was the recipient of most of the military aid supplied by the CIA. The 1988 election of Bermudez by Contra officers to head their political directorate brought the resignation of seven non-Somozista commanders. Even Nicaraguan exiles in the U.S. saw this replacement of civilian leadership by the Somozista colonel as a "serious setback" to the Contra cause. [11]

From the philosophical base provided by Kirkpatrick, which confirmed Reagan's belief in the reasonableness of his approach to international politics, the president was emboldened to broaden his goal of combatting communism directly and declare that U.S. "support for freedom fighters is self defense."[12]

Behind this generalization was a host of misconceptions, many of which ignored plain facts. In his attacks on domestic opponents of his foreign policy, Reagan (and Kirkpatrick) tarred all with the same brush. No distinction was made between those relatively few liberals who were in fact blinded by their abhorrence of what they considered fascist dictatorships, and the majority of Reagan's critics who simply insisted that repression be given the same diplomatic treatment regardless of whether it came from the left or the right. If Ortega was to be castigated as a tyrant—as he was very effectively in most of the 250 pages Kirkpatrick's book devoted to *The Americas*—it should have been acknowledged that the most powerful Contral leader, Colonel Bermudez, hadn't the slightest interest in democratic government. But his name never appeared in any of the disquisitions on Central America by Reagan or his aides.

Other exceptions to the criteria of legitimacy were also ignored. Both Reagan and Kirkpatrick studiously avoided any analysis of the military revolt against the constitutionally elected government of Salvador Allende in Chile. There had been no dismantling of the democratic process by Allende, an admitted Marxist who neither sought nor received aid from the Soviet Union. Yet Kirkpatrick's only reference to Chile in her 1979 thesis was a suggestion that the country was more likely to evolve into a democracy under Augusto Pinochet than it would have done if Allende had not been murdered and replaced by this brutally repressive dictator. [13]

As for the startling breakdown of communist influence among the people of eastern Europe, the events of 1989 must have given Kirkpatrick second thoughts about the unyielding character of communist governments. Reagan, of course, gave primary credit to the democratizing influence of the U.S. and its NATO allies for the popular revolts in Warsaw Pact nations and among many non-Russian nationalities in the Soviet Union. This undoubtedly was a factor. But none of the reforms adopted within the Soviet sphere would have been possible had not confirmed Marxist Mikhail Gorbachev opened the door with his dual policies of *glasnost,* or openness, and *perestroika,* or economic restructuring. And the Kirkpatrick theory was completely confounded by the scheduling of free elections by every communist government in eastern Europe. Heralded in the American press all through the year 1989, these events overshadowed the "reforms" initiated by traditional autocrats in Chile and Paraguay, reforms that had permitted a yes-or-no referendum to confirm the appointment of Pinochet's successor to the Chilean presidency, and a controlled multi-party election which substituted another general for Paraguay's deposed dictator, Alfred Stroessner.

President Reagan's portrait of a freedom fighter was as flawed as his notion of legitimacy. He saw in every anti-communist a friend of the U.S. and therefore a devotee of democratic principles and the welfare of ordinary people. Nothing could blur that picture. Documentary evidence supplied by Amnesty International, Americas Watch and other independent organizations, if it was ever brought to his attention, could not convince him that Contra armies committed more atrocities against unarmed civilians, their hospitals, schools and food supplies, than Ortega's Nicaraguan forces.[14]

In other countries whose governments refused to support U.S. foreign policy, Reagan could discover no freedom fighters. Even the bitterly anti-communist followers of Khomeini could not qualify for that title; understandably, as their goal certainly was not a democratic society. But neither was democracy the aim of those annointed as freedom fighters in Afghanistan. Anti-communist they certainly were, and their struggle against a repressive government backed by Soviet military forces was surely justified. Nevertheless, Afghan resistance leaders made no bones about their dedication to the establishment of a theocratic Muslim state that, like the one in Iran, would function under the iron laws of the Koran.

Even when widespread condemnation of totalitarian rule did force the State Department to issue comments critical of apartheid in South Africa, or the murder, torture and confinement of opposition leaders in Paraguay and Chile, the oppressed in those countries were not considered "the moral descendants of men at Morristown and Valley Forge," a title bestowed by President Reagan on the Contras of Nicaragua.[15] Nor were the opponents of Philippine dictator Ferdinand E. Marcos and Haiti's "Baby Doc" Duvalier called freedom fighters, although Reagan jumped on both revolutionary bandwagons after it became clear that the tyrants, who had either been supported or tolerated by the U.S. for decades, would be evicted.

* * * * *

The effectiveness of President Reagan's foreign policy can be judged in terms of its success in achieving two of its primary objectives: to strengthen American leadership in the battle against Soviet influence, and to advance the cause of democracy throughout the world. Reagan's summary of his accomplishments came in his address to the 1988 Republican national convention. Urging the faithful to continue the Reagan Revolution with George Bush, he took credit for "these changes":

> We rebuilt our armed forces. We liberated Grenada from the communists and helped return that island to democracy. We struck a firm blow against Libyan terrorism. We've seen the growth of democracy in 90 percent of Latin America. The Soviets have begun to pull out of Afghanistan. The bloody Iran-Iraq war is coming to an end. For the first time in eight years we have the prospects of peace in Southwest Africa and the removal of Cuban and other foreign forces from the region. And in the 2,765 days of our Administration, not one inch of ground has fallen to the communists. Today we have the first treaty in world history to eliminate an entire class of U.S. and Soviet nuclear missiles. We are working on the Strategic Defense Initiative to defend ourselves and our allies against nuclear terror, and American-Soviet relations are the best they've been since World War II. [16]

Reagan's leadership was expressed principally in the massive outpouring of funds for military purposes and confrontation with the Soviets in every quarter of the globe. The quality of the military structure he achieved was discussed earlier, and the usefulness of his military ventures will require another chapter. The effectiveness of his diplomatic engagements varied from place to place and from year to year.

In the area closest to home, the growth of democracy "in 90 percent of Latin America" had little to do with Reagan's policies. As President Ford's Assistant Secretary of State for Inter-American Affairs William D. Rogers put it, Reagan's claim to leadership in advancing democracy in Latin America came as "a big surprise" to leaders in many countries that were struggling to work out the major problem of civilian versus military rule without asking for or receiving any aid from the U.S. [17]

As for the economic underpinning of democratic society, most Latin leaders saw the U.S. as at least partly responsible for the rise in interest rates that drained their economies through burgeoning debt payments. Countries seeking help from the International Monetary Fund—an institution dominated by the U.S.—were faced with Reaganesque demands for budget cuts that would eliminate the social programs directly aimed at easing the awful poverty that is always a threat to democratic growth. United States counter-complaints of corruption and mismanagement were in many cases valid. But neither the Reagan administration nor this country's financial giants—which had so eagerly entered the foreign loan market in Latin America—were swayed from pure self-interest in their approach to economic problems south of the border. [18]

It was precisely this insistence on traditional economics that led more than a few members of Latin America's Catholic clergy to call for greater attention to the problem of poverty and less to the goals of power and profit. The "liberation theology" advanced by priests serving the most downtrodden people in South and Central America was regarded as such a serious challenge to Catholic orthodoxy that the Vatican sent a warning message regarding the use of concepts borrowed from various currents of Marxist thought. [19]

On this point Rome and President Reagan were in complete agreement. But Pope John Paul II's concern for people caught in the trap of grinding poverty or the chaos of war far exceeded that of Ronald Reagan. Two weeks after the instruction was issued, the pontiff went on television to denounce the "imperialist monopoly" exercised by the world's rich nations, which he felt were indifferent to the widespread poverty in less fortunate countries. This brought no comment from Reagan. However, his favorite columnist, more-Catholic-than-the-pope William F. Buckley, Jr., used his syndicated newspaper column to advise John Paul to stop talking like a third-world UN delegate and take his cue from Reagan for "the correct Christian decision" in matters of international economics. [20]

One of the most interesting aspects of Reagan's concept of acceptable and unacceptable revolts is the language he used to differentiate between the two. The term "revolution" was applied only to revolts against governments friendly to the U.S., no matter how oppressive in character. Uprisings against Marxist regimes were described as the efforts of freedom fighters to achieve a democratic society. It was as if the word "revolution" had become anathema to a nation that owed its independent existence to a revolt against a government far less oppressive than some of those supported by the Reagan administration.

Applying this concept to what Reagan characterized as the "backyard" of the U.S., the immediate threat to Central America, Mexico and the U.S. was seen to be the revolutionary government of Daniel Ortega Saavedra in Nicaragua; therefore the Ortega regime had to be eliminated. Reagan's repeated explanation that he was interested only in cutting off Nicaraguan aid to communist rebels in El Salvador, Honduras and Guatemala suggested a return to the "containment" policy of previous administrations. However, mere containment—or interdiction, as it was called—was never acceptable to Reagan. His goal was revealed, perhaps inadvertently, in 1985. When a reporter asked if the president's constant urging of greater military support for the Contras didn't indicate that he was "advocating the overthrow of the present government," Reagan replied that would not be the case "if they'd say 'Uncle'." Prodded in a subsequent interview to explain how saying Uncle could mean anything except to surrender, Reagan said, "Well, maybe that was an unfortunate choice of words." Continuing with a lengthy answer that purported to review the history of the revolt against Somoza, he claimed his phrasing was, in fact, "a refutation of saying that we want the overthrow of the government as such." Repeating his own concocted myth that Somoza had voluntarily stepped down "to stop the bloodshed," Reagan closed the interview with the remark, "And that's all I meant by 'Uncle'," a comment that drew derisive laughter from the attending reporters.[21]

The full extent of Reagan's commitment to a military, rather than a diplomatic solution in Central America will be seen in an examination of his role as commander-in-chief. The record of Central American diplomacy clearly shows that every effort made by Latin American nations to reach a negotiated peace was rejected—if not sabotaged—by Reagan. Whether or not the plan contrived by Mexico, Venezuela, Colombia and Panama, meeting on Contadora Island in January 1983, would have succeeded if allowed to run its course, is anyone's guess. What is not a matter of conjecture is Reagan's opposition to this attempt by Latin American countries to solve their own problems.[22]

A later peace plan suggested by Costa Rican President Oscar Arias Sanchez received similar treatment. In August 1987 President Arias called for an immediate cease-fire between all contending forces in Central America, negotiations aimed at ending all outside military aid, and free elections in all five Central American countries. President Reagan's reaction was to summon Arias to Washington to tell him bluntly that the plan was unacceptable because it was "too lenient on the Sandinista government of Nicaragua." Reagan followed this relatively unpublicized blast with his own initiative, which called for an immediate cease-fire between Nicaraguan and Contra forces and gave Nicaragua two months to accept his demands for democratic reform. Under the Reagan plan the U.S. would be a party to all negotiations for peaceful settlements to disputes in the five Central American countries.[23]

Reagan's seven-year economic boycott and proxy war against the Sandinista government did succeed in smashing the Nicaraguan economy and bringing the majority of the population to a level of near-starvation never before achieved against any wartime enemy of the U.S. The final test of Reagan's callous indifference to the effects of his policy was seen in his reactions to two 1988 events. When Samozista Colonel Enrique Bermudas was "elected" to head the Contra's political directorate, the president had no comment. When an October hurricane killed scores of Nicaraguans, left 300,000 homeless, and devastated the country's farmlands, Reagan refused to permit any humanitarian aid to the afflicted people, although after the same storm caused less damage to the island of Jamaica he had immediately sent American technicians to assist that country and had authorized the expenditure of $125 million for food and medical supplies.[24]

The unrelenting U.S. diplomatic pressure to gain continent-wide support for its economic boycott of Nicaragua resurrected some of the old bitterness toward the Colossus of the North. Evidence of the growing resistance to U.S. attempts to dictate policy for all of the Americas is seen in the position taken by the presidents of Argentina, Brazil, Colombia, Mexico, Panama, Peru, Uruguay and Venezuela at a November 1987 summit meeting to which President Reagan was not invited. Defying the U.S. call for diplomatic isolation of Cuba, the eight presidents of countries that, with one exception, Reagan had declared to be democracies, decided that Cuba should be brought back into the Latin-American States (OAS), from which it had been expelled twenty years earlier at U.S. insistence.[25]

*   *   *   *

On the southern hemisphere's other major battleground, U.S. diplomacy faced at least as severe a test as in Latin America. Western-style democracy had limited influence on the people of Africa, and no appeal whatever to those in power. On the contrary, most of the former colonies of Great Britain, France, Belgium, Spain, Portugal and Germany tended to ignore the example set by democratic European governments in the design of governmental institutions and, instead, retained the worst elements of the colonial system, using against Europeans and local dissidents the very laws their former masters had enacted to keep the African natives in subjection. Decades after most African nations had achieved their independence, only two could meet Freedom House standards to qualify as "free" countries, rather than "partly free" or "not free." And these two—Botswana and Mauritius—were of little consequence in the grand strategy of Reagan's State Department. By comparison, the two major players—Egypt in the north and South Africa at the other end of the continent—were judged only "partly free" as late as 1987.[26]

The post-World War II struggles of African people seeking freedom from their colonial over-lords offered greater opportunities for Marxist influence than for nations of western democracy. For with the most notable exception of Portugal, democratic ideals were being pressed upon Africans by the very countries that had kept them in colonial servitude for centuries. Understandably, the most serious contests were in the southern half of the continent where the people of Angola and Mozambique had suffered brutal suppression under Portuguese dictator Antonio de Olivera Salazar and his successor, Marcello Caetano. Belgian, British and French governments had exploited their colonies with, at best, an occasional superficial show of concern for native welfare. But in the Portuguese colonies, the slightest sign of unrest brought reprisals by a military force that did not hesitate to lay waste an entire village of men, women and children.[27]

Caetano's overthrow and exile in 1974 opened the way for representative government in Portugal and soon thereafter, freedom for that country's African colonies. By November 1975, both Angola and Mozambique had won their independence, and both began with governments committed to socialist principles.

U.S. policy in Angola contrasted sharply with Washington's attitude toward Mozambique, notwithstanding the common ideology shared by the two former Portuguese colonies. In Angola, Moscow and Beijing backed contending forces in a three-way war with the U.S. for control of the new government. In the end, the Soviet-sponsored MPLA (Popular Movement for the Liberation of Angola) gained the upper hand when Cuba sent troops to join the battle.

Even before the Soviet arms buildup and infusion of Cuban troops brought MPLA control of the Angolan government, Nixon's CIA lent its support to FNLA (National Front for the Liberation of Angola), led by Holden Roberto, who had accepted aid from China prior to the revolt that brought an end to Portuguese rule. Later, when UNITA (National Union for the Total Independence of Angola), under the leadership of Jonas Savimbi, took the lead in resistance to MPLA and Cuban forces, the U.S. openly shifted its support to UNITA.[28]

Mozambique's independent government received more attention from China than from the USSR. But, like Angola, the country was subjected to both direct attack and internal subversion fostered by South Africa. Denying any enmity toward the U.S., Mozambique was torn by a revolt initiated by the government of Ian Smith in Southern Rhodesia, whose intelligence agents organized a group known by the acronym RENAMO (Mozambican National Resistance). When in 1979 the native population of Rhodesia won a majority of seats in parliament, South Africa took over sponsorship of RENAMO. Although South Africa signed a nonaggression treaty with Mozambique in 1984, promising to end its support of the organization, it did not keep that promise.[29] The result was a continuation of the civil war in which RENAMO was described by one observer as "pursuing a devastating policy of destroying economic targets without concern for the long term impact of such actions for the country." The same observer commented of RENAMO as late as 1988:

It attacks economic targets large and small—from the electrical lines from the Cahora Bassa Dam to peasant crops. It destroys schools and health posts. It enters villages, kills some people, kidnaps others, burns huts and then vanishes, apparently unconcerned that its tactics may antagonize rather than win support from the population.

The writer concluded that "RENAMO is more successful at destroying Mozambique than it is at destroying the party in power."[30]

The accuracy of private studies and press reports of RENAMO massacres of civilians—even those in hospitals—was confirmed by the State Department after extensive on-site interviews, conducted in 1988 with 200 of the estimated 872,000 refugees who had fled from RENAMO terror to countries bordering Mozambique. The State Department report concluded that RENAMO may have slaughtered as many as 100,000 civilians in its war against the Mozambique government.[31] Given these conditions, and acknowledging that the overtly socialistic government of Mozambique had accepted some western suggestions for economic reform, the U.S. government joined with a number of other western nations in extending modest amounts of aid to that beleaguered country.

In both Mozambique and Angola the U.S. discovered the reality of South Africa's determination to dominate that part of the continent and to wipe out, by military force or economic pressure, all black nationalist opposition to its doctrine of apartheid. Its economic power was as intimidating as its armies, for the five landlocked countries of that region depended on South Africa for their fuel supplies and access to world markets. However, the rest of the world was alerted by reports of attacks by South African troops against government forces inside the territory of Angola. Much as the Reagan administration wished to see the communist government of Angola fall, it was a constant embarrassment to side against it with a country whose classification as "partly free" reflected the bald fact that freedom was enjoyed by its obedient white minority only. This, as much as any other factor, pushed the State Department to unrelenting efforts to achieve a peaceful settlement of the undeclared war between South Africa and Angola, and to convince South Africa that withdrawal from Namibia was in its own interest.[32]

The final year of Reagan's presidency produced the first signs of progress in the seemingly endless rounds of negotiations seeking the withdrawal of Cuban troops from Angola and South African troops from Angola and Namibia, and independence for Namibia in accordance with 1978 Resolution 435 of the United Nations Security Council. An agreement setting forth these objectives was signed by representatives of Angola, Cuba and South Africa July 13, 1988. This was followed in October by a South African pledge to withdraw its troops and grant Namibia independence within a year, and a promise by Cuba and Angola that Cuban troops would be repatriated over a 24-month period.[33]

In all of these talks the U.S. assumed the role of honest broker, with Assistant Secretary of State for African Affairs Chester A. Crocker heading the American delegation. President Reagan, in his address to the 1988 Republican convention, was unreserved in claiming credit for any progress in bringing the parties to agreement on the means for peaceful settlement of the problems of southwest Africa.[34] In full agreement with South Africa's demand that Cuban troops be removed from Angola, he nevertheless supported the UN decision that Namibia—the name given by the UN General Assembly to the South African territory of South West Africa—should be free and independent.[35] However, Reagan's term of office ended with the parties still wrangling over the details of implementation. Meanwhile, rebel leader Jonas Savimbi, favored by Reagan to overthrow the Marxist Angolan government, startled most of black Africa by traveling to Johannesburg to praise President Botha and to criticize black leaders in the country who refused to negotiate a peaceful settlement of their grievances. Like Reagan, Savimbi stressed the changes that Botha had made purportedly to ease the impact of apartheid. Little wonder that on his next visit to Washington, he took special pains to convince members of Congress that he was not "a puppet of South Africa."[36]

South Africa itself presented a problem that bedeviled the Reagan administration through its entire eight years. Resisting all efforts to apply the kind of political and economic pressure the U.S. had used against leftist dictatorships, Reagan argued that more could be gained through "quiet diplomacy" and what he called "constructive engagement" than by actions that would antagonize "a friendly nation like South Africa." From the outset he insisted that there had been "a failure, maybe for political reasons in this country, to recognize how many people, black and white, in South Africa are trying to remove apartheid and the steps that they've taken and the gains that they've made."[37] He persisted in this fantasy of progress and good intentions on the part of the South African government to the very end of his term in office.

Addressing the UN in 1984, Reagan cited as evidence of South Africa's retreat from military ventures against its neighbors the "historic accord on nonaggression and cooperation" between South Africa and Mozambique and an agreement with Angola "on a disengagement of forces." He also asserted that "the groundwork had been laid for the independence of Namibia, with virtually all aspects of Security Council Resolution 435 agreed upon." The only accurate statement in this review of South Africa's foreign policy was the reference to the treaty with Mozambique, although South Africa had already shown, in the months between its signing and the UN meeting attended by Reagan, that it had no intention of abiding by the terms of that pact. As to the South African government's treatment of 80 percent of its population made up of blacks and people of mixed race, Reagan could say only that "the

United States considers it a moral imperative that South Africa's racial policies evolve peacefully but decisively toward a system compatible with basic norms of justice, liberty and human dignity."[38]

A month after Reagan's appearance at the UN, black Anglican Bishop Desmond Tutu was awarded the Nobel Peace Prize for his efforts to resolve the racial conflict in South Africa by nonviolent means. Reagan wrote to congratulate Tutu on that achievement, assuring him that "we continue to urge the South African government to engage in a meaningful dialogue with all its citizens aimed at accomplishing a peaceful transition away from apartheid."[39] But when Tutu visited the White House in December of that year, he gained little satisfaction from his meeting with the president. Contesting the bishop's assertion that the situation in his country had worsened despite U.S. constructive engagement, Reagan said flatly, "It has not." Acknowledging to reporters that "there has been a surge of violence here and there," he asserted that this had been brought about by "violence from the other side." In other words, any repressive action by government forces was simply a response to violence initiated by protesters. When pressed to explain how the U.S. could justify "dealing with a nation that does not recognize something so basic as the concept of racial equality," Reagan retreated behind the curtain of confidentiality, saying, "if you're practicing quiet diplomacy, you can't talk about it or it won't be quiet anymore." Ignoring his own repeated public demands that Soviet and Nicaraguan governments permit free elections and freedom for all people to express their opposition to official policies, Reagan took a 180-degree turn with this defense of his approach to South Africa:

> I have always believed that it is counterproductive for one country to splash itself all over the headlines, demanding that another government do something, because that other government then is put in an almost impossible political position. It can't appear to be rolling over at the demands of outsiders.[40]

Shortly after this exchange with reporters the president learned that out of the tens of thousands of imprisoned protesters, the government of South Africa had released eleven black labor leaders. He offered this as evidence of the effectiveness of U.S. influence, a claim promptly rejected by South African President P. W. Botha, who retorted that "neither quiet diplomacy nor hard shouting" would keep his government from making "these decisions for ourselves."[41] Eight months after Botha's disclaimer of American influence, Reagan asked reporters to

> look at the gains that have been made so far by our so-called constructive engagement—the increase in complete biracial education; the fact that Amer-

ican businesses there have over the last several years contributed more than $100 million to black education and housing; the fact that the ban on mixed marriages no longer exists; that some, I think, 40-odd business districts have been opened to black-owned businesses; labor union participation by blacks has come into being; and there's been a great desegregation of hotels and restaurants and parks and sport activities and sports centers and so forth.[42]

The picture these gains conjured up was largely fantasy. Botha's 1982 asserted goal of equal education for all was never intended as a plan for biracial instruction. Even the notion of separate-but-equal education—a fraud discarded in the U.S. after a century of experience—was neither contemplated nor accomplished. The contributions of American business in that area affected their own employees only, and consisted largely of on-the-job training pursued entirely outside the formal system of public education. The ban on mixed marriages had, indeed, been dropped, but that legal change made precious little difference to couples who, contrary to Reagan's belief, could not live in areas reserved for whites only, or send their children to white schools, or claim the privilege of voting in white-only elections. Nor could they open a business in a white district without special government permission. And the great desegregation of public facilities was pure Reagan mythology.

Unions were indeed permitted, but they had virtually no bargaining power. When 60,000 black miners struck for wages that were seldom more than half those paid to whites, they were threatened with loss of jobs, eviction from the compounds in which they were forced to live without their families, and closing of the food kitchens on which they depended. In the face of such odds, which included an employer's legal right to fire strikers at will, the strike was broken in two days. This occurred only four weeks after Reagan's boast of the great gains in working conditions that his influence had brought. A few months later 20,000 workers were fired for striking three of South Africa's largest platinum mines.[43]

In Reagan's second term South Africa experienced a rising tide of violence. As Bishop Tutu had warned, his nonviolent pleas for reform would not satisfy the disenfranchised black population indefinitely. P. W. Botha, in a speech described by the *New York Times* as "defiant and sometimes belligerent," refused to consider any of the concessions being demanded by South African blacks and leaders of other nations. He scorned the proposals of those he called "our enemies, both within and without South Africa," for offering "ready panaceas such as one man, one vote [and] freedom and justice for all."[44] Lacking arms and military organization, black radicals reacted to repression with stone-throwing, bombing, and the murder of blacks who, covertly or openly as members of government security forces, supported their oppressors. Reagan made much of this riotous activity but accepted in silence news of massive government raids on black communities, homes and churches, the shooting of hundreds and arrest and detention of thousands, often without charges or trials.

Badgered repeatedly by reporters seeking justification for continuation of the policy of constructive engagement, Reagan held grimly to the belief that President Botha shared his view that apartheid was "repugnant," going so far as to make the absurd statement that the South African government "has even expressed its desire to rid the country of apartheid."[45] His only complete exposition of his South Africa policy was so defensive of that country's government that it elated South African officials while igniting new fires of opposition among both Democratic and Republican senators, driving administration stalwarts Robert Dole and Richard Lugar into a pro-sanction coalition with Edward Kennedy![46]

A serious threat to Reagan's policy took shape when Democratic representatives and senators pressed for a sanctions bill in the summer of 1985. Reagan attempted to preempt that action by issuing an executive order prohibiting certain bank loans to the South African government, banning the export of nuclear technology and computers for use by security forces or "any apartheid enforcing agency," and the importation of arms, ammunition, or military vehicles manufactured in South Africa.[47]

The fact that the restrictions in the executive order were limited principally to those aiding enforcement agencies left the measure far short of what Congress had in mind. Speaking to reporters, Reagan said the difference was that his order would not hurt the South African economy, as congressional proposals would do.[48]

In any case, the widespread antagonism generated by South Africa's increasingly severe treatment of its domestic opponents of apartheid was not diminished by Reagan's executive order. Gallup pollsters, who had given little attention to South Africa in 1985, learned early in 1986 that approximately 75 percent of Americans who had followed the situation in that country were more sympathetic toward South African blacks than to Botha's government. In September, when the issue of sanctions was at the boiling point, 55 percent of those polled believed the U.S. should bring more pressure to end apartheid, while only 14 percent voted for less pressure and 24 percent for no change in policy.[49]

Push came to shove in September 1986 when Congress forced President Reagan to depart from his policy of polite persuasion by passing the Comprehensive Anti-Apartheid Act, with 79 percent of the members in each house—far more than the required two-thirds—voting to override Reagan's veto of the measure.[50]

In 1987 President Reagan sent Congress a report, required annually by the Comprehensive Anti-Apartheid Act, on the progress made "toward ending the system of apartheid and establishing a non-racial democracy in South

Africa." That report, for the first time, concluded that "there has not been signficant progress toward ending apartheid since October 1986," and that "none of the goals outlined in Title I of the Act . . . have been fulfilled." Moreover, the president said, "the South African government's response to the act over the past year gives little ground for hope that this trend will soon be reversed." Denying that South Africa had been materially affected by economic sanctions, Reagan nevertheless abandoned the term constructive engagement and wrote that what the U.S. needed now was a period of "creative diplomacy to bring the peoples of South Africa together in a democratic society."[51]

Presidential references to South Africa were few and far between in the final year of the Reagan administration. Meanwhile, sporadic rioting continued in that country and was met with ever-increasing repression. *Index on Censorship* had reported in August 1982 that there were then 106 laws limiting freedom of the press. Subsequent to the 1986 declaration of emergency, the *Index* reported that "the emergency clearly obliterated what was left of the independent role of the newspaper observer in South Africa." Two years later it quoted satirist-actor Pieter-Dirk Uys as saying, "One can't tell the truth as truth [in South Africa]. One has to tell it as a Disneyland horror story. Then one can get through to an audience. . . . Apartheid is so grotesque and obscene that it has created a lobotomized society beyond satire."[52]

Making a mockery of its earlier revocation of the infamous Pass Law, the South African government in 1986 had enacted new legislation declaring any form of opposition to government action to be subversive and subject to heavy fines and imprisonment. Some of the covered offenses were printed on the front page of a Johannesburg newspaper, which gave a list of the government agencies to be contacted for permission to even discuss such subjects as a consumer boycott, actions of the police or other security forces, release or treatment of detainees, formation of street committees or "people's courts."[53] Other regulations made it a crime even to report the actions of security forces or the arrest and detention of demonstrators, no matter how peaceful their protest might have been. This effectively curtailed the dissemination of news stories, pictures and videotapes of either demonstrations or police actions, like the arrest of the newly appointed Archbishop Desmond Tutu and twenty-odd church leaders for marching in protest against the banning of 17 anti-apartheid organizations.[54] This was the state of affairs in South Africa when President Reagan turned the White House over to George Bush.

* * * * *

If President Reagan could take partial credit for his State Department's efforts to keep alive negotiations for a peaceful settlement of the problems in the southern half of Africa, his Middle East policy brought satisfaction only to the extent that U.S. military aid to the Afghan rebels helped convince the Soviets that their continued occupation of that country was likely to strain their resources and arouse the same domestic and foreign antagonisms as the war in Vietnam did for the U.S.

Military intervention replaced quiet diplomacy in the Persian Gulf as well as in Afghanistan. And although Reagan cited the Iran-Iraq war as one reason for extending in 1981 the declaration of emergency that President Carter had issued with respect to Iran, his primary concern was the possible spread of Soviet influence.[55] Reagan's reliance on military force in this area, as well as in Lebanon and the eastern Mediterranean, will be discussed later. Peaceful diplomatic measures, which Reagan professed to prefer, he reserved for the 40-year war between Israel and its Arab neighbors, and there the record was one of complete failure.

Like every president from Truman to Carter, Reagan acknowledged the fact that Israel was the only truly democratic nation in the entire Middle East and, for that reason alone, deserved American support.[56] However, many other factors influenced U.S. policy makers in the State Department as well as in the White House. The basic premise of the Reagan Doctrine was that the Soviets must not only be confronted wherever they intervened in other lands, they must be prevented from even attempting to widen their sphere of influence. In the Middle East, it was no secret that Soviet aid was going alternately to Syria and Iraq, two countries dedicated to the destruction of Israel. Further, the Syrian government was known to be one of the sources of Mideast terrorism.

On the other hand, there was always the matter of oil, the one resource which Arab states held in abundance and used very effectively to balance the appeal of Israel's democratic institutions and the political clout of her supporters in the U.S. The availability of this source of energy, on which our NATO allies and Japan depended far more than ourselves, had long accounted for U.S. willingness to accommodate Arab rulers despite their unwavering attachment to anti-democratic traditions. Faced with bitter Israeli and congressional opposition to his proposal to send arms to Saudi Arabia and Jordan, Reagan argued that he was only trying to be "fair and evenhanded in dealing with moderate Arab states."[57] His ignorance of the nature and outlook of governments he termed moderate was revealed early in his first administration when he told reporters that he thought Saudi Arabia could lead the way in recognition of Israel's right to exist, and that the absolute monarchies of Saudi Arabia and Kuwait "want to be a part of the west [because] they associate more with our views and our philosophy."[58] Three years later he defined the task in this fashion: "We must find more Egypts."[59] Where he hoped to find even one more Egypt among the other

Arab states was difficult to imagine, as not one of those countries had given the slightest indication that it regarded the war with Israel as finished.

Most active in keeping the war alive was the Palestine Liberation Organization (PLO) which, even after being driven from Jordan by King Hussein and harassed by the troops of Syria's President Assad, continued its raids on Israeli towns from shifting bases in Lebanon. Undeterred by this guerilla warfare, or by the increasingly riotous resistance to Israeli control in the West Bank and Gaza, Reagan sanctioned a kind of shuttle diplomacy, using the secretary of state, an assortment of assistant secretaries, and his special roving ambassador, Philip C. Habib, in an eight-year effort to bring the opposing parties together. His failure to accomplish this was due in large part to conditions that, whether he knew it or not, were beyond his control. One was the undisguised death-to-Israel attitude of Syrian, Iraqi, Iranian, Libyan and PLO leaders. Another was the intransigence of the Israeli religious right, which stirred the anger of Arabs and non-Arabs alike—including many Israelis—by its persistent demand for the eviction of all Arabs from the West Bank and the outright annexation of all lands under Israeli control.

PLO chairman Yasir Arafat's November 15, 1988 declaration of an independent state of Palestine opened a new chapter in Middle East affairs. Although press reports interpreted the PLO statement that it accepted the UN's 1967 call for peace in its Resolution 242 as "implicit" recognition of Israel's right to exist, reporters could not get Arafat to confirm this. On the contrary, Arafat's leader of PLO's militant Popular Front for the Liberation of Palestine flatly rejected any such gloss of the declaration. State Department spokesmen could do no more than say that while the reference to Resolution 242 represented "an advance" in PLO thinking, its announcement would have to be clarified by recognition of Israel in "clear and unambiguous" language before it could be taken seriously.[60]

Barely a month before President Reagan left office, Arafat modified his language to make it acceptable to the State Department, renouncing terrorism and recognizing Israel by including it among the nations that should participate in a settlement of the Palestinian problem. However, this did not end clashes between Palestinian Arabs and Israelis. Moreover, the fall 1988 election that led Prime Minister Yitzhak Shamir to form a new Israeli government with the support of the hard right religious parties offered little hope of compromise from that establishment.

* * * * *

Direct diplomacy, in which President Reagan attempted to use the force of his personality and his talent as a performer to win friends and influence other heads of state, was, for the most part, reserved for allies or prospective allies in the global contest with the Soviet Union. This was evident in his travel plans. For example, presidents and prime ministers from almost all of the African nations were welcomed to the White House, but that continent was never visited by President Reagan.[61] Nor was any part of eastern Europe so favored until the rising fear of nuclear war brought a substitution of conferences for fiery speeches.

Asia was accorded much more favorable treatment. In that area Vice-President Bush acted as advance man for Reagan who, during the first two years of struggle with domestic problems, limited his foreign travel to economic conferences in Canada and Mexico in 1981, and a European tour combining an economic conference at Versailles with speaking engagements in NATO capitals of London, Rome and Bonn in 1982.[62] Bush set the tone with his first Far East tour, in which he paid tribute to Philippine president-dictator Ferdinand Marcos with the memorable phrase, "We love your adherence to democratic principles."[63] Similar sentiments were more appropriately expressed on his visit the following year to Australia, greater restraint being shown as he moved to China.

President Reagan's three tours of the Far East began with visits to Japan and Korea in 1983. Diplomatically ignoring the first two thousand years of Japanese history, the president toasted the country as a democracy which, like the U.S., was "founded on the sacredness of the individual." In a later speech at Emperor Hirohito's banquet he reiterated the theme that "the ties between our people are based on common ideals and values." The emperor did not deign to respond to this misguided attempt at flattery. Prime Minister Yasuhiro Nakasone, with regard for the sensitivities of his guest, made no reference to either nation's history or institutions, but joined the president in asserting the firmness of their friendship.[64]

All of these events were fully covered by American reporters and their ever-present camera crews. In Japan the scene was one of pomp and ceremony, with lavish expressions of brotherhood and unity in the face of Soviet aggression. Cameras played an even more important part in the trip to Korea. As chief image-maker and travel agent Michael Deaver wrote about the ceremonies he orchestrated in Normandy, and on the Korean border:

> The trip to the Demilitarized Zone on the border between North and South Korea was a symbolic high point of the Reagan years. Standing there, staring across that buffer zone, drawing the contrast between freedom and oppression, this was what Ronald Reagan did best.[65]

A second presidential journey to the Far East took Reagan to China the following spring. The president set the tone in his opening toast to China's President Li when he expressed a wish that their two countries might become "dear and trusted friends," a phrase that must have sent shudders through his far-right supporters in the U.S. as well as his erstwhile allies in Taiwan.[66]

The purpose of this visit was not simply to conclude a few commercial and cultural agreements. Establishing a friendly relationship was also part of the U.S. strategy of building barriers against the extension of Soviet influence. For this, Reagan's State Department advisers and speech writers had prepared him well. Avoiding the direct references to the Soviet Union and its allies that had marked his speeches in Japan and Korea, Reagan nevertheless interspersed his remarks about progress in U.S.-Chinese relations with comments on "the brutal and illegal occupation of Kampuchea," and "the evil and unlawful invasion of Afghanistan."

From that point on, the volume of traffic between Washington and Beijing increased rapidly. Relations continued to improve as trade between the two countries increased and to President Reagan's delight, the doctrinaire Marxist economy was relaxed sufficiently to permit an element of private enterprise. The following year the State Department reported that in the field of science and technology the two countries had concluded formal protocols covering exchanges in 29 fields, from agricultural and biomedical sciences to nuclear physics and space technology. And in June of that final year of the Reagan administration, Under Secretary Michael H. Armacost assured members of the National Council for United States-China Trade that relations between the U.S. and China had "become thoroughly normal."[67] Exaggerated as this description was, Reagan had managed to build upon the foundation laid by President Nixon, who achieved his greatest foreign-policy triumph by breaking through the icy wall that had separated the U.S. from China. At that point, no one could foresee that the Chinese government would not, like the governments of eastern Europe, give way to demands for democratic reform, but would revert to a policy of brutal repression.

A stopover in the Philippines had been on the president's November 1983 schedule, but a month before his departure for the Far East Reagan dispatched his deputy, Mike Deaver, to express his regrets in personal messages to President Marcos and the heads of government in Thailand and Indonesia, explaining that the press of legislative business at home had shortened his trip.[68] In fact, the uproar over the August 21 assassination of Marcos's leading opponent, Senator Benigno S. Aquino, Jr., was a more significant factor in the president's change of plans than the burden of domestic duties.

Like Vice-President Bush, Reagan had been unstinting in his praise of Marcos, pointing in a 1982 tribute to the Philippine dictator's "record of solid economic growth . . . hospitable attitude toward free enterprise and private initiative . . . dedication to improving the standard of living of your people." Six weeks after Aquino's murder under the eyes of a Philippine military escort ordered by Marcos, Reagan wrote in the letter carried by Deaver to Manila, "Our friendship for you remains as warm and firm as ever."[69]

After an 18-month investigation, a commission appointed by Marcos concluded that Aquino's assassination was the result of "a criminal plot" carried out by "one of the military group" sent to guard the senator. Nevertheless, a Marcos-appointed court cleared all those accused of participation in the plot, giving the dictator the ammunition he needed to "prove" the innocence of his military aides.[70]

As conditions in the Phillipines continued to boil, Reagan reaffirmed the "close relationshp and alliance" between the U.S. and Marcos governments. Responding to a reporter's question, he repeated his assumption that the Marcos regime was democratic when he said, "We realize there is an opposition party that, we believe, is *also* pledged to democracy," and he promised to do "everything we can as a longtime friend to see that the Philippines *remain* a democracy" (emphasis added). At the same time, he warned that the only threat of totalitarian government came from "the communist element."[71]

Throughout the ensuing struggle by Aquino supporters to oust Marcos, Reagan refused to acknowledge that his longtime friend was in fact a corrupt and unregenerate dictator. When in 1985 Marcos called for elections to demonstrate that the Philippine people were still with him, it was at the suggestion of CIA director William Casey, according to Senator Paul Laxalt who, as Reagan's personal representative, that he advised Marcos to dramatize the election decision by announcing it on ABC's "This Week" television program. President Reagan was made aware of this on October 22 when Laxalt reported to him on the results of his meeting with Marcos.[72]

The challenge by Senator Aquino's widow, Corazon, who declared herself a candidate to oppose Marcos for the presidency, drew no comment from Reagan until a few days before the February 1986 election. His statement said that Marcos had invited the U.S. to provide observers of the election process, and that the president planned to send an official delegation "composed of members of Congress from both parties and of distinguished Americans from the private sector."[73] Reagan also made a point of noting that the Philippine National Citizen's Movement for Free Elections (NAMFREL) would have "hundreds of thousands of citizen election observers on February 7." How freely opposition candidates were permitted to campaign did not concern him. A reporter, recalling the importance of Reagan's television appearances in his 1980 election, wondered how the president felt about Mrs. Aquino's lack of access to Philippine television facilities, all of which were owned or controlled by Marcos and his friends. Reagan's response was, "I don't think it's right for me to criticize their method of conducting an election."[74]

Almost as quickly as balloting began, fraud, intimidation and murder by Marcos supporters were reported by NAMFREL as well as by President Reagan's observers and an international group led by a member of the British

Parliament.[75] Questioned about this by *Washington Post* reporters Lou Cannon and David Hoffman, Reagan said he didn't know if there was enough evidence to justify "pointing the finger," and suggested that the fraud may not have been "all one-sided." After his official observers had returned, Reagan said the team had told him "there was an appearance of fraud and yet . . . they didn't have any hard evidence beyond that general appearance." His opinion that fraud and violence "was occurring on both sides," he told reporters, was based on "just an interim few remarks" from his observation team, who would not file a final report until the counting of votes had been completed. Meanwhile, he said, "We're neutral."[76]

Reagan's declaration of neutrality elated Marcos and horrified Aquino supporters, both interpreting that statement as evidence of support for the dictatorship. However, four days later the president issued a statement through his press secretary acknowledging "sadly, that the elections were marred by widespread fraud and violence perpetrated largely by the ruling party," and that "it was so extreme that the election's credibility had been called into question both within the Philippines and in the United States."[77] That he had gained this knowledge earlier from the "interim few remarks" of his observers was attested to by Senator Lugar, who told a congressional committee of his report to the president, which included the observation that "an audit trail was there through the NAMFREL for a Mrs. Aquino win, probably a better one than through the government COMELEC count that had come under question after 30 young people left, testifying that they were being asked to cook the figures in the count."[78] Lugar joined Republican Senator Bob Dole and Democrat Sam Nunn in publicly protesting Reagan's request that Congress defer final judgment on the election pending receipt of a report from special emissary Philip C. Habib, whose post-election assignment to check on the Philippine situation could only be taken as a slap at the president's own team of observers.[79]

In any event it was the heroic action of thousands of unarmed Filipinos, who refused to give way to the army's tanks and guns, that led both military and government leaders to abandon Marcos and install Aquino as president. Yet, incredibly, Reagan was congratulated by the chairman of the Anti-Defamation League of B'nai B'rith for having "so skillfully managed the transition in the government of the Philippines." Later, Reagan would adopt this same posture, taking credit for helping to bring about the Aquino victory.[80]

Official recognition of the new government was extended February 25, 1986, and in September of that year President Aquino was welcomed to a meeting with President Reagan in Washington.[81] However, Reagan never returned that visit, although a few months earlier, on the way to an economic summit in Tokyo, he had taken time to make good on his previous promise to visit Indonesia, a land as securely under the dictatorial control of President Soeharto—another "longtime friend" of President Reagan—as the Philippines had been under President Marcos. The character of Soeharto's rule did not prevent Reagan from including that nation in his sweeping generalization about "the winds of freedom" blowing in Southeast Asia, an expression one observer characterized as sounding "magnificent and downright silly" at the same time.[82]

Reagan's stubborn support of Marcos almost to the point of his ouster came home to roost during the 1988 negotiations to revise the agreement permitting U.S. military bases in the Philippines. The 26 weeks of talks (compared to 7 weeks for the 1983 renewal) and the important concessions required of the U.S. before Manila would sign the revision undoubtedly reflected the vexation of the Aquino government over Reagan's unwillingness to support what most Filipinos regarded as their freedom fighters in the struggle to overthrow the Marcos dictatorship. Reagan's letter to Aquino expressed pleasure in promising military and economic assistance totaling $962 million beginning October 1, 1989, more than double the level of aid provided in the first two years of the post-Marcos period. Reagan promised additional assistance in the form of loans, guarantees, and insurance from the Export-Import Bank and the Overseas Private Investment Corporation. But his letter made no mention of the consultation required of his government in matters of labor regulations on U.S. bases and "the storage or installation of nuclear or non-conventional [chemical and biological] weapons" in Philippine territory. This agreement clearly signaled that the days of cozy companionship, based on easy acceptance of American priorities along with its gratuities, were at an end.[83]

*   *   *   *   *

In no area did President Reagan feel more at ease than among America's NATO allies. Not that he could count on solid support for all his policies. Periodically he was vexed by criticism of his activity in other parts of the world. Before his first year was out, four NATO nations had joined Mexico in pushing a UN resolution calling upon the U.S.-backed government of El Salvador to try negotiating with its rebels before holding elections.[84]

Socialist governments showed more uneasiness than conservative regimes at taking sides in the new cold war between the U.S. and U.S.S.R. that marked Reagan's first term. This was one factor bearing on Spanish and Greek criticisms of U.S. policy. In Germany, Social Democratic Chancellor Helmut Schmidt, while firmly committed to NATO, was far less enthusiastic about Reagan's plan to deploy nuclear missiles in western Europe than conservative Helmut Kohl, who replaced Schmidt after Germany's 1983 elections.[85] France, regardless of the political cast of its government, was outspoken in expressing its independence in matters of policy and jurisdiction, refusing to place any of its military forces under a NATO commander. And when Britain and West Germany applied sanctions against Syria for its involvement in a plot to blow up an Israeli airliner at London's Heathrow airport, a move that the U.S. approved, France not only refused to join in this punitive effort, but made clear that it intended to negotiate with Syria in an effort to curb terrorism—at least that element of terrorism which had been directed against its own territory and citizens. Greece also rejected the proposal for sanctions.[86]

Quite apart from the problem of military preparedness—which will be discussed in a later chapter—the countries of western Europe did not always see eye-to-eye with the Reagan administration on relations with the Soviet Union and its European satellites. All were critical of the Polish government's 1982 crackdown on Solidarity, but when Washington called for broad trade sanctions against both Poland and Russia, Common Market nations were, at best, lukewarm in their response. Only England matched the punitive measures taken by the U.S.[87] President Reagan's attempt to block Soviet construction of a gas pipeline from Siberia by withholding needed material was thwarted by France and West Germany, who declared themselves ready to supply equipment and credit for the project.[88] After three years of Reaganesque perorations on the Evil Empire, NATO foreign ministers approved a Belgian suggestion that East-West relations be reviewed to determine how western nations might reach "a more constructive dialogue" with Warsaw Pact countries. This formal statement acknowledged that "military strength alone cannot guarantee a peaceful future."[89]

Within the Reagan administration there was no unanimity as to the best approach to international problems. Hard-liners like Assistant Secretary of Defense Richard Perle opposed almost every effort to achieve a peaceful resolution of East-West differences, contending that no communist government could be counted on to live up to any agreement.[90]

The one government that Reagan could depend on for support in almost every instance was that of Britain's Prime Minister Margaret Thatcher. Her views on almost every subject relating to government responsibility and domestic economy were in perfect tune with Reagan's. And if Thatcher refrained from using Reagan's colorful rhetoric in her references to the Soviet Union, she was his most consistent supporter in matters of foreign policy, both before and after his 1984 switch from long-range salvos at Moscow to face-to-face discussions with Kremlin leaders. Only when Reagan ordered U.S. troops into British territory in Grenada did Thatcher show momentary irritation with her American friend. However, her disappointment was mild and unpublished, the prime minister no doubt having in mind Reagan's aid in the Falkland Islands dispute, when the U.S. joined Great Britain in vetoing a UN Security Council resolution calling for an immediate cease-fire in the battle with Argentina that England was sure to win.[91] That veto added fuel to the smoldering fires of the long-standing Latin-American resentment against the Colossus of the North. It also reflected Reagan's willingness to risk adverse public reaction to the use of force whenever the odds were strongly in favor of a military success.

CHAPTER 10

Diplomat:
Slayer of Dragons

*"I urge you to beware the temptation . . . to
ignore the facts of history and the aggressive
impulses of an evil empire."*[1]

THE DIPLOMATIC ENERGY DEVOTED TO CENTRAL AMERICAN AFFAIRS, EVI-
dent from day one of the Reagan presidency, seemed to put that area at the
head of the administration's list of foreign policy problems. Yet, despite the
low level of diplomatic activity between the White House and the Kremlin,
there was no doubt whatever that Reagan considered the Soviet Union to be
the source of most of this country's worries about world affairs.

For most of his first term, Reagan substituted rhetoric for diplomacy. One-
third of the 74-page Republican platform of 1980 was devoted to a section
labeled "Peace and Freedom," which began with the warning that "at the
start of the 1980s the United States faces the most serious challenge to its
survival in the two centuries of its existence." For 24 closely printed pages
the narrative alternated between attacks on the Carter administration's "ne-
glect" of defense needs and terrifying pictures of the Soviet drive for military
supremacy and the worldwide network of surrogate communist governments.

Notwithstanding the heavy emphasis on the Soviet threat, Reagan left
Soviet affairs to the State Department during his first year in office, con-
centrating instead on his domestic targets of tax reform and the elimination
of as many government regulations and regulatory agencies as possible.
However, when questions of foreign policy were raised by journalists or
special interest groups, the president's responses reflected the same outlook as
he had expressed in successive political campaigns from 1964 to 1980.
Calling detente "a one-way street" that the Soviet Union had used to promote
world revolution and "a one-world socialist or communist state," in his first
news conference he maintained his pre-election stand that in dealing with the

Soviets it was necessary to remember that "they reserve unto themselves the right to commit any crime, to lie, to cheat" in order to attain their objectives. Asserting later that he was willing to negotiate if the aim was to achieve "verifiable reductions" in arms, especially in strategic nuclear weapons, he adopted the "linkage" concept by adding, "you can't just deal with just one facet of the international relationship; you've got to deal with all of the problems that are dividing us."[2]

As early as March 1981 Reagan indicated what his agenda would be if and when talks were undertaken with the Russians. In an interview with Walter Cronkite of CBS News he stressed these objectives: reduction in strategic nuclear weapons, evacuation of Afghanistan, and more attention to human rights in the Soviet Union.[3] Writing to Leonid Brezhnev in April, he ignored the Soviet leader's suggestion of a summit meeting. While the letter was not made public, Reagan told members of the National Press Club that in addition to urging greater regard for all peoples' aspirations for peace and freedom, it contained these four specific proposals for discussion by U.S. and Soviet representatives when they would meet in Geneva, Switzerland beginning November 30: reduction of intermediate range missiles by both sides; negotiations for Strategic Arms Reduction Talks (START) to begin in 1982; reduction of conventional forces in Europe; and reduction of the risk of surprise attack "and the chance of war arising out of uncertainty or miscalculation."[4]

Overshadowing the few references to possible peace talks were Reagan's more widely publicized attacks on Soviet policies, both domestic and foreign. His January 29 news conference blast at the lying, cheating methods of Soviet diplomats was followed by repeated citations of Soviet evil intent, especially in military buildup, but also in the manipulation of governments and/or revolutions in Afghanistan, Central America, Cuba, and Poland.[5] Fulfillment of his campaign pledge to American farmers to lift the embargo on grain to the U.S.S.R. was delayed for several months, until he felt it could not be misinterpreted as "a weakening of our position" vis-a-vis the Soviet Union.[6]

Over the next two years the anti-Soviet rhetoric grew more heated, even though Reagan assured reporters early in 1982 that "we've always had in mind a meeting with Brezhnev."[7] As the Russians replied in kind, fear that the rising anger and booming arms race would explode into nuclear war provoked popular demands for an immediate halt to the massive accumulation of nuclear weapons and for discussions in place of saber-rattling by the two major contestants.

Reagan derided the freeze movement as a scheme devised by the Soviets to head off his effort to close what he called America's window of vulnerability. Europeans, who coupled their demands for a freeze with demonstrations against U.S. plans to install nuclear weapons in West Germany, Reagan accused of "carrying the propaganda ball for the Soviet Union." In the U.S., as well as abroad, he insisted that "the propaganda that has led to this, the ability to turn it on, can be traced back to the Soviet Union." Asked for evidence to support this charge, Reagan said he couldn't go beyond what had appeared in the press "because I don't discuss intelligence matters."[8]

In fact, there was nothing new about the concept of a freeze on arms production as a means of lessening the threat of war. Tsarist Russia took the lead in suggesting the outlawing of projectiles with "inflammable substances" in the 1868 Declaration of St. Petersburg, of poisoned weapons in the 1874 Declaration of Brussels, and of rapid-fire artillery at the first Hague Peace Conference in 1899.[9]

With the discovery of the awesome power of the atomic bomb, a new element entered the picture. At a time when popular democracies had replaced autocratic governments in many of the world's most advanced nations, the demand for military restraint came not only from governments afraid of being out-gunned, but from people who saw the contest for nuclear supremacy as a staging ground for a war that might well mean the end of civilized society. This fear made best sellers out of books like Jonathan Schell's *The Fate of the Earth*.

The danger of a nuclear holocaust had been recognized almost as quickly as nuclear weaponry came into existence. Yet, except in Japan, which felt the full force of the only atomic bombs ever used in combat, popular understanding of the significance of the explosions at Hiroshima and Nagasaki was lost in the wild enthusiasm which greeted the end of the war.

One U.S. official, who might be considered the first American to suggest a freeze on the production of nuclear weapons, wrote to President Truman scarcely a month after atomic bombs had totally destroyed two Japanese cities and killed 100,000 men, women and children. Secretary of War Henry L. Stimson assumed first, that the atomic bomb was "too revolutionary and dangerous" to be treated as just another weapon and, second, that Russia was "the crux of the problem." He urged an immediate approach to that nation to reach agreement on controls, and ultimately "the proposal that we would stop work on the further improvement in, or manufacture of, the bomb as a military weapon, provided the Russians and the British would agree to do likewise."[10]

President Truman chose instead to act through the United Nations. The first definitive statement of policy, proposed in a secret State Department memorandum, included among its goals "the elimination from national armaments of atomic weapons and of all other major weapons adaptable to mass destruction, and . . . effective safeguards by way of inspection and other means to protect complying states against the hazards of violations and evasions."[11] A subsequent confidential memorandum from General Leslie Groves, commander of the supersecret Manhattan Engineer District (popularly known as the Manhattan Project), warned that "if the agreement were broken, the world would head directly into an atomic weapons armament race."[12] In the absence of such an agreement, this is precisely what happened.

The Soviet-American military buildup met its first crisis in the 1962 showdown over Russian missiles in Cuba. Although President Kennedy's stand forced a Soviet retreat from that base, the Kremlin's reaction was to increase the pace of its arms production and its fortifications in the satellite countries on its perimeter. A temporary lull in Soviet-American antagonism came in 1963 with the signing of a Nuclear Test Ban Treaty and establishment of a "hot line" for emergency communication between Washington and Moscow. [13]

From 1963 to 1980 presidents of the U.S. and general secretaries of the Soviet Union signed ten treaties or executive agreements between their two countries. Three of the treaties, including SALT II, were never approved by the Senate and were denounced by Reagan—both before and after his election to the presidency—as either inadequate or contrary to American national interest. During this same period the U.S. and U.S.S.R. also joined a host of other nations in approving eight multilateral treaties, including those banning nuclear weapons in outer space and on the seabed, biological weapons, and the "deliberate manipulation" of the natural environment as a means of conducting warfare. [14]

In the White House, President Reagan rejected any moratorium on nuclear arms production, insisting that "the first man who proposed the nuclear freeze was, on February 21, 1981, in Moscow—Leonid Brezhnev." A month earlier he had told reporters there was "plenty of evidence" to prove that Soviet agents "were sent to help instigate and help create and keep such a movement going."[15] A White House spokesman followed this last remark with the prediction that a forthcoming report by the House Select Committee on Intelligence would provide documentation to support the president's statement. That report was issued the very day Reagan announced that Brezhnev had been the originator of the freeze movement. Contrary to White House expectations, however, the report cited testimony by both CIA and FBI officials in concluding that although the Soviets commonly made every effort to manipulate public opinion in the United States and around the world, they had "no significant influence on the nuclear freeze movement."[16]

Early in 1982 former President Carter said he had suggested a freeze in 1979 but had been turned down by Brezhnev. And a reporter covering a meeting at which scientists from 40 countries urged a freeze on nuclear weapons recalled that Canadian Prime Minister Pierre Trudeau had made a similar proposal in 1978.[17]

Among the earliest grass roots appeals in the U.S. were those received by Senator Patrick Leahy in March 1981 from 15 Vermont towns and cities asking their senators and representatives to urge President Reagan to negotiate an immediate halt to the nuclear arms race. Alternately using the terms freeze and moratorium, most of these resolutions said that the U.S. and U.S.S.R. should "agree to halt immediately the testing, production and deployment of nuclear warheads, missiles and delivery systems with verification safeguards satisfactory to both countries."[18]

The question was picked up by Gallup pollsters, who in May 1981 found that 72 percent of people in a national survey favored "an agreement between the U.S. and the Soviet Union not to build any more nuclear weapons in the future." The high level of approval was particularly striking in view of the fact that only 33 percent thought it likely that the Soviets would abide by such an agreement. Equally remarkable were responses to questions asked in November 1982 regarding an "immediate, verifiable freeze." Nationwide, 71 percent were in favor. Moreover, 65 percent of those polled favored such an agreement even if verification was not possible, and 68 percent approved regardless of whether the U.S. or the Soviet Union was stronger in nuclear arms at that moment.[19]

The freeze movement reached its peak in 1982. By June 30, representatives in the U.S. Congress had submitted 21 arms control resolutions and senators had added 13 more.[20] By year's end, "voters in 10 states, 15 counties, and 23 cities approved resolutions for an immediate, mutual, and verifiable freeze in the nuclear arms race." They were supported by a variety of civic and religious organizations, including more than half of all evangelical Christians queried in a 1983 Gallup poll.[21]

On the president's side were most fundamentalist Protestants, many leading Catholic churchmen, star television evangelists led by Jerry Falwell, the Mormon hierarchy, and lay organizations led by the Coalition of Peace Through Strength and the American Security Council. Campaigning on behalf of Republican congressional candidates, President Reagan suggested that the freeze movement was "inspired by, not the sincere, honest people who want peace, but by some who want the weakening of America and who are manipulating many honest and sincere people."[22] A widely circulated pamphlet from the State Department put the case more politely, saying that "a freeze at existing nuclear levels would have adverse implications for international security and stability [because] it would lock in existing nuclear inequalities while making further progress in arms control difficult, if not impossible."[23]

Notwithstanding the determined campaign conducted by the administration and its supporters, public approval of a freeze remained at 70 percent or more through 1983 and down to election time in 1984.[24] However, for practical purposes the freeze movement died with Reagan's landslide reelection in November 1984. Congressional sponsors of freeze resolutions who had been unable to muster majority support in either the Senate or House—though they lost one House contest by only a single vote—could see no possibility of improving their chances for success. Moreover, President Reagan was soon to cut the ground from under the movement by a radical change in his approach to U.S.-Soviet relations.

*   *   *   *   *

In July 1983 President Reagan marked the annual observance of Captive Nations Week by offering his religious "vision" of a world divided by two opposing beliefs:

> The first believes all men are created equal by a loving God who has blessed us with freedom. . . . The second vision believes that religion is opium for the masses. It believes that eternal principles like truth, liberty and democracy have no meaning beyond the whim of the state.[25]

As election year 1984 opened, a new tone was evident in Reagan's public pronouncements on Soviet-American relations. His State of the Union message, though strong on the need for action against "state sponsored terrorism" and the need to preserve the U.S. as "this last best hope of man on earth," included a plea to the Russian people to join with Americans in the search for peace. Reiterating the view both he and Brezhnev had stated previously, that "a nuclear war cannot be won and must never be fought," he avoided any charges of evil intent by the Soviet Union.[26] In a less formal setting he acknowledged that he would no longer describe the Soviet Union as the "focus of evil," although he rejected a reporter's suggestion that using terms like Evil Empire might have contributed to the difficulty of negotiating with the Soviets.[27]

The first month of his second term saw Reagan adopting this restrained approach to U.S.-Soviet relations in a half-hour television address to the nation. A month later he devoted one of his Saturday radio talks to the same subject. On each occasion he stressed the need for "peaceful solutions to problems through negotiations." In an exchange with reporters that was not published in presidential documents he said he was optimistic about the prospect of improved relations because the whole tone of a meeting between Vice-President Bush and the new Soviet general secretary, Konstantin Chernenko, "indicated that he [Chernenko] believed that there was an area for us to come to agreement." However, he would not commit himself either to a summit meeting with Chernenko or to a get-acquainted meeting. A summit, he said, requires careful planning and an agreed agenda, while a meeting just to get acquainted would serve no useful purpose and might even be counterproductive.[28]

Lower-level discussions on the subject of arms control had produced little in the way of concrete results, despite a marked reduction in the stridency of the 1980 call to arms and a 1984 platform promise to seek "substantial reductions in nuclear weapons rather than freezing nuclear weapons at their present level."[29] Whatever appeal the notion of reduced weaponry might have had in the U.S., it had none for the Soviets, who saw a major threat to their country in Reagan's plan to add U.S. medium-range nuclear missiles to those already sited in western Europe by England and France. The off-and-on talks about control of such weapons, which had proved fruitless during the years of heated rhetoric and mutual name-calling, broke down when the Soviets refused to continue while the U.S. was deploying missiles in Europe.

In January 1984, ABC newsman David Hartman assessed the cumulative effect of Reagan's first four years as a period of rising tension and fear. Without disputing the need for a strong American defense establishment, Hartman put the problem to the president this way:

[T]ensions are at their greatest with the Soviet Union since the early sixties. The Soviets have left the negotiating table, and quite frankly, people across this country are more afraid than they have been in many, many years that we might be going to war. How long do the people of our country, right now, have to wait for your philosophy of negotiate from strength to pay off, because right now they're frightened, Mr. President.

Reagan responded that he hoped to prove in the upcoming election campaign that "we are safer and more secure than we were several years ago [when] the United States had allowed its own defensive strength to decline to the point that you could look and say we weren't too far from a point of weakness in which the enemy could be tempted because we didn't have the strength."[30] When the election brought Reagan a resounding victory, he took it as a vote of approval for all his foreign and domestic programs, including his Strategic Defense Initiative (SDI), which was quickly labelled "Star Wars" by headline-conscious journalists. Nevertheless, by November 1984 it was clear that however adamant he remained about pursuing both a weapons reduction plan and SDI, he was prepared to re-enter negotiations with the Soviets in an atmosphere devoid of recriminations and ideological rhetoric.

Political trends in NATO countries encouraged—may even have instigated—Reagan's new approach. Top officials in NATO capitals remained firm in their alliance, despite significant popular protests against U.S. nuclear policy. But along the southern tier, from Greece to Italy, Spain, Portugal and France, socialist party leaders had won elections that put the reins of government in their hands. In such a situation, Reagan was well advised to curb his habit of treating socialists and communists as though they were one and the same. At home, he was pressed by a 77 to 22 Senate vote to re-submit the un-ratified Threshold Test Ban Treaty negotiated by President Nixon, and the Peaceful Nuclear Explosions Treaty signed by President Ford and Leonid Brezhnev.[31]

Reagan continued to resist any resurrection of earlier treaties, but he did agree to reopen the economic talks with the Soviet Union which had been broken off by President Carter immediately after the Soviet invasion of Afghanistan. He also responded to prodding by some Republican members of Congress by telling reporters, "I am willing to meet and talk anytime." After initially rejecting a Soviet offer to discuss means for preventing the mili-tarization of outer space, he was reported by Larry Speakes to have "softened" his attitude on this subject.[32]

No softening was noticeable in subsequent public exchanges with the Soviets regarding meetings on space weapons. On the contrary, the matter was taken up only in press releases, where it became another war of words.[33] Emotions on both sides rose higher when Reagan, addressing what he thought was a dead microphone, broadcast to the nation the quip, "My fellow Americans, I'm pleased to tell you today that I've signed legislation that will outlaw Russia forever. We begin bombing in five minutes." Reactions to this remark, and to the uproar it created, were typical of both the Kremlin and the White House. In the press, Moscow raged at what it characterized as "hypocrisy" by a longtime foe who had only recently tried to give the impression of peaceful intentions. President Reagan explained his remark as "a kind of satirical blast against those who were trying to paint me as a warmonger," and charged the media with "broadcasting it worldwide in such a way that it could create an incident."[34]

The first sign that both sides were seriously considering meaningful negotiations came in January 1985 when Secretary of State George Shultz met Soviet Foreign Minister Andrei Gromyko to get the movement started. Even this cautious beginning was not achieved easily. What difficulties Chernenko had to overcome may never be known. But the sources of opposition in the U.S. were easily identified. Within the Reagan administra-tion, Assistant Secretary of Defense Richard Perle never ceased his effort to block any attempt at negotiations with the Soviets, arguing that there was no possibility of reaching a treaty the U.S. could rely on "to produce a safer world."[35]

A similar campaign was conducted by Perle's admirers in the private sector. Norman Podhoretz, editor of *Commentary*, saw the proposed U.S.-Soviet negotiations on arms control as "a screen for unilateral cuts by the democratic side." Following the theme of President Reagan's favorite treaty analyst, Laurence Beilenson, Podhoretz warned that any arms control agreement with the Soviet Union would be as disastrous to the U.S. as the treaties of the 1920s and 1930s, which he said left the democracies helpless before the war-minded totalitarian nations.[36] He did not identify the treaties that so weakened the west; which is understandable, as the only multilateral compact between democratic and totalitarian countries in that period was the 1922 naval treaty which maintained the supremacy of U.S. and British fleets over those of Japan and Italy—with Germany excluded altogether. A British-German naval treaty signed in 1935 kept England at a three-to-one advantage in ships of war.[37]

Given the strength of the oppostion to any discussions that might lead to U.S. concessions in the matter of arms control, the president's January 9, 1985 news conference statement that "there was no infighting among our group" and that the U.S. delegation to the arms conference was "in complete unanimity" on its objectives, was certainly misleading, even if it was intended to describe only Shultz's handpicked team of negotiators.[38]

Nevertheless, Secretary Schultz did win a substantial victory over hardline oppositionists in his own department as well as in Congress and the Department of Defense. Meeting in Geneva, Switzerland, Shultz and Gromyko agreed to open formal negotiations in the spring of 1985. Their joint communique, released to the media January 8, declared that the purpose of the negotiations was "to work out effective agreements aimed at preventing an arms race in space and terminating it on earth, at limiting and reducing nuclear arms and at strengthening strategic stability." In separate statements both Shultz and Gromyko acknowledged the difficulty and complexity of the issues they had to face, but both told television audiences—Gromyko in Moscow, Shultz on NBC's "Meet the Press"—that they hoped a new dialogue would lessen the threat of war.[39]

The negotiations that began in March proved as difficult as Washington and Moscow had expected. Months of talks produced no tangible results. Shortly after the death of Chernenko and his replacement by Mikhail Gorbachev, President Reagan decided that "some of those [issues] could probably be advanced" if he and the Soviet general secretary met. He therefore wrote to the new Soviet leader, inviting him to a summit meeting in the U.S. "whenever he found it convenient." Gorbachev's unpublished response was said to be positive but dependent upon further discussion of an appropriate time and place for the meeting. Ultimately, the summit was scheduled for November 19–20 in Geneva.[40]

Gorbachev's first public statement on foreign policy included a call for a freeze on development of space arms and strategic weapons, an announcement of a seven-month unilateral moratorium on the deployment of Soviet intermediate-range missiles, and an acknowledgment that "a serious impulse should be given to Soviet-American relations at a high political level." He followed that with a July statement that the Soviet Union would cease all nuclear test explosions from August 1985 to January 1, 1986. All of these suggestions the White House dismissed as propaganda ploys, meanwhile releasing a series of reports to the press and Congress on the need for continued testing and arming to offset Soviet noncompliance with earlier agreements.[41]

Although the tone of President Reagan's public references to U.S.-Soviet relations was relatively moderate, the reiteration of charges from both Moscow and Washington of treaty evasion and disregard for proposals from the other side did little to lessen the strain between the two capitals.[42] When the dates and location of the summit meeting were finally decided, the announcement came without fanfare at a non-public press briefing, not from President Reagan, but from Secretary of State Shultz. The secretary's subsequent report of a preliminary meeting that he had attended in Moscow was described as "bleak" by UPI correspondent Helen Thomas.[43] Asked in September whether U.S. anti-satellite weapons tests might better be held after the summit meeting, so as not to provoke needless controversy, Reagan said, "No, I don't think so, because, as I said, we're playing catchup." He disputed the views of his own analysts on the relative military strengths of the U.S. and U.S.S.R., insisting that "the United States is still well behind the Soviet Union in literally every kind of offensive weapon." This provoked Senator Sam Nunn—a Democrat, but no dove by any means—to remark that if the president would occasionally check with his joint chiefs he would learn of the advantage the U.S. held in submarines, aircraft carriers, cruise missiles and bombers.[44]

Given this kind of build-down, it came as no surprise that the joint statement of accomplishments issued by Reagan and Gorbachev after their meetings on November 19 and 20 could boast of agreement only on such generalities as that "a nuclear war cannot be won and must never be fought," and the need to "accelerate the work" of their negotiators on nuclear and space arms, as well as "the idea of an interim INF agreement." Other agreements simply reaffirmed the mutual commitment to non-proliferation of nuclear weapons and the desire to achieve "a complete prohibition of chemical weapons and the destruction of existing stockpiles of such weapons." Putting the best possible face on the personal relationship gained from this meeting with the Soviet chief executive, Reagan included in his report to Congress an aside that "out in the parking lot" he had invited Gorbachev to

Washington and had accepted the Soviet leader's invitation to visit Moscow.[45]

Gorbachev's post-summit account delivered in a November 21 press conference in Geneva, acknowledged that it was a "significant event," principally because it brought the two leaders face to face. However, he compared his side's "concrete and radical proposals" on arms control with what he called the "indeterminate and largely inequitable" suggestions from the U.S. He complained of American stubbornness in pursuing its SDI program, which he denied was purely defensive, and declared, "We will find a response" [to that system].[46] A month later the Soviets offered to open their nuclear test range to inspection if the U.S. would join in an underground test moratorium. This offer was immediately rejected by the White House, which instead proposed on-site inspection of nuclear tests in both countries.[47]

The year 1986 opened with televised messages from President Reagan to the Soviet people and General Secretary Gorbachev to the American people, broadcast simultaneously on New Year's Day. Both spoke only of peace, with neither overt nor implied criticism of the other's government.[48] On January 15, President Reagan announced the next day's opening of the fourth round of nuclear and space arms talks in Geneva. He said the U.S. would propose cutting in half the nuclear arsenals of both sides, adding that this was negotiable, "not a take-it-or-leave-it proposition."[49] His statement made no reference to another summit, but all through that spring it was widely assumed that the negotiating teams were testing the ground on whether another Reagan-Gorbachev meeting would be useful. At the same time, mutual sniping continued in public speeches and such incidents as the enforced reduction of the Soviet UN mission staff and Soviet retaliation against American diplomats. Reagan also let it be known—through a breakfast chat with reporters that was not published in *Presidential Documents*—that if Gorbachev did not come to the U.S. in 1986, "There won't be an '87 summit in Moscow."[50] Subsequently, he denied a reporter's suggestion that a new chill had entered U.S.-Soviet relations. But even as he asked Gorbachev "to join us without delay in bilateral discussions on finding ways to reach agreement on essential verification improvements of the Threshold Test Ban (TTBT) and Peaceful Nuclear Explosions Treaty (PNET)," he sent Congress a lengthy message detailing Soviet depredations in various parts of the world. Gorbachev countered with a televised speech blasting Reagan for refusing to negotiate a true test ban treaty.[51]

Congressional elections were coming up in the fall of 1986, and Reagan did not want to schedule a meeting with Gorbachev during the peak campaign period from Labor Day to Election Day. His repeated calls for a summer summit went unanswered from Moscow. Early in August, Reagan answered a German journalist's question about summit prospects in this fashion:

> While no dates have been set, Secretary Shultz and Soviet Foreign Minister Shevardnadze will meet September 19 and 20 here in Washington to discuss details, and we are working on the assumption that there will be a summit this year as agreed.[52]

The atmosphere did not improve in September when the FBI arrested as a spy Gennadi Zacharov, a member of the Soviet UN delegation and, in obvious retaliation, Russian police seized and charged American journalist Nicholas Daniloff with spying in the Soviet Union. Reagan's September 22 speech to the UN General Assembly included a reference to the justified arrest of Zacharov and the "trumped-up charges" on which Daniloff was jailed. Nevertheless, he was "pleased to say that the Soviet Union has now embraced our ideas of radical reductions in offensive weapons systems. . . . So there has been movement."[53] He was much more effusive in an unpublished exchange with reporters in early October, when he characterized as "amazing" the change in Soviet attitude that had come about under Gorbachev.[54]

Reagan's warming toward the Gorbachev regime was undoubtedly influenced by the fact that by September 30 it had been agreed that the two leaders would meet in Reykjavik, Iceland on October 11 and 12. The president announced this at a special press briefing, which was introduced by Secretary Shultz with a report of the exchange of Zakharov for Soviet dissident Yuriy Orlov. In the question period that followed, Reagan denied that the simultaneous release of Daniloff had anything to do with the Zakharov-Orlov swap. He also asserted that the Reykjavik meeting was "not a summit," and that though he had accepted it at Gorbachev's suggestion, he was holding to the earlier agreement that the next real summit would be in the U.S.[55]

As it turned out, Reykjavik produced only bitter frustration. The published accounts of both participants indicated that on the major topic of discussion each, in President Reagan's words, "seemed willing to find a way to reduce, even to zero, the strategic ballistic missiles we have aimed at each other." However, agreement foundered on the shoals of the SDI program. The sense of failure was evident from the very demeanor of the participants as they made their final exit from the meeting place. It was confirmed by their separate and contrasting reports of the event. Reagan put his case for SDI to the American people this way:

> I offered a proposal that we continue our present research. And if and when we reached the stage of testing, we would sign, now, a treaty that would permit

Soviet observation of such tests. And if the program was practical, we would both eliminate our offensive missiles, and then we would share the benefits of advanced defenses. . . .

In an effort to see how we could satisfy their concerns . . . we proposed a 10-year period in which we began with the reduction of all strategic nuclear arms. . . .

The General Secretary wanted wording that, in effect, would have kept us from developing the SDI for the entire 10 years. In effect, he was killing SDI. And unless I agreed, all that work toward eliminating nuclear weapons would go down the drain—cancelled.[56]

Gorbachev's explanation of the breakdown was expressed rather differently. Citing Soviet concessions in agreeing to set aside "the nuclear potential of France and Britain," to reduce Soviet missiles in Asia, and to accept a "toughened" system of verification, he explained the ultimate breakdown in this fashion:

Our proposal came down to the following. We will strengthen the unlimited-duration ABM Treaty through identical commitments by both sides that they will not use their right to withdraw from the treaty during those 10 years . . . during which the reduction of nuclear potential will be taking place. . . . In our proposal, we emphasized that throughout the 10 years all requirements of the ABM Treaty would be strictly observed, that only research and testing in a laboratory framework would be permitted. . . . The President insisted to the end that America must have the right to study and test everything related to SDI not only in laboratories but also outside them, including space. . . . All this could have been signed in Washington during my visit. The American side wrecked this decision.[57]

*   *   *   *   *

In a December 7, 1987 summary of superpower summit meetings going back to the 1955 discussions between President Eisenhower and Nikita Khrushchev, the *New York Times* rated the Nixon-Brezhnev signing of the ABM (Anti-Ballistic Missile) and SALT I treaties as the only meeting to have produced concrete results. Reagan's Geneva conferences with Gorbachev it found "useful" as an opportunity for the two to get to know one another. But Reykjavik it could characterize only as "undisciplined and disruptive."[58] A Gallup survey taken a few months later reported that only 37 percent of Americans believed in the possibility that all nuclear weapons would ever be eliminated. The same canvass indicated that 69 percent saw no advantage to the U.S.S.R. from the further building or refining of nuclear weapons.[59]

Post-Reykjavik gloom offered little hope of accommodation between the two superpowers. Yet the intensity of the desire of both Reagan and Gorbachev to dispel the fear of war and to show solid achievement in the control of nuclear weapons brought a surprisingly quick break in the deadlock. The U.S. campaign for a renewed effort was marked by a flood of State Department informational and policy publications, as well as public appearances by State, Defense and White House officials. The gist of their message was that despite the disastrous ending at Reykjavik—which presidential adviser Paul Nitze attributed to "an extensive propaganda campaign" conducted by the Soviets in advance of the conference "to exploit the anticipated failure of the meeting"—the basis for agreement was there.[60]

President Reagan avoided such remarks, opening the movement for greater harmony by renewing a request he had made prior to Reykjavik, that the Senate reconsider and give its consent to ratification of the Threshold Test Ban and Peaceful Nuclear Explosion treaties which had been signed by U.S. and Soviet leaders more than a decade earlier.[61] In April, negotiations on an Intermediate-Range Nuclear Forces (INF) treaty opened in Geneva. A program for U.S.-Soviet cooperation in space exploration, which had been cancelled by Reagan in 1982, was renewed. And in the same month Secretary of State Shultz was given an opportunity to talk directly to the Russian people on a Soviet television program.[62]

In May the Soviets discontinued their jamming of Voice of America radio programs for the first time since Reagan assumed the presidency.[63] May also brought agreement to establish in Washington and Moscow the Nuclear Risk Reduction Centers that had been suggested by Senators Sam Nunn and John Warner. Using direct satellite links, this special communications system was in addition to the hot line and was intended solely and specifically "to reduce the risk of a U.S.-U.S.S.R. conflict—particularly nuclear conflict—that might result from accident, misinterpretation or miscalculation."[64]

The summer and early fall were marked by a succession of speeches by the president and State Department officers who, along with their standard cautions about the difference in U.S. and Soviet philosophies and objectives, spoke favorably of evidence of a new attitude among Soviet leaders and new opportunities for a more friendly relationship. Assistant Secretary of State John D. Negroponte briefed a House committee on the renewal of scientific exchanges between the U.S. and U.S.S.R. Under Secretary Michael H. Armacost announced that while the U.S. continued to oppose an increased Soviet military presence in the Persian Gulf, "there is a constructive role the Soviets can play in relation to the gulf war." More startling was Armacost's acknowledgment that "the United States has worked closely with the Soviets in fashioning a cease-fire resolution." President Reagan struck a similar chord in an August speech in which he alternated his reminders of Soviet malfeasance with observations about their "parallel interest" in ending the Iran-Iraq war and the Soviet "movement toward openness, possibly even progress toward respect for human rights and economic reform." Even Reagan's

September speech to the UN General Assembly included a brief reference to "new prospects for improvement in U.S.-Soviet relations."[65]

The "restraint" in the cross-talk between Washington and Moscow, noted by the media here and abroad, relaxed Soviet and American officials sufficiently to make possible reconsideration of Reagan's dream of holding the next summit in Washington and a final one in Moscow, thus fulfilling his parking-lot agreement with Gorbachev. The first indication that this might be arranged came with the announcement that Secretary Shultz and Foreign Minister Shevardnadze had agreed "in principle . . . to conclude an INF treaty." When Reagan and Shultz met reporters to release this information, the president was asked repeatedly why, after opposing the Evil Empire for so many years, he was "ready to make a deal with them." After ignoring the first three Evil Empire questions, Reagan finally turned the matter aside with the remark, "I don't think it's still lily white." After almost daily badgering by reporters, Reagan held an October 30 briefing session in the White House to reveal that Gorbachev had accepted his invitation to come to Washington for a summit meeting "beginning on December 7."[66]

The subsequent buildup to this historic event was marked by many expressions of good will from both sides. At the same time, both Reagan and Gorbachev took steps to assure their respective party conservatives that they were not abandoning their basic principles. Reagan's November 30 speech at the Heritage Foundation contained not the slightest hint of compromise. Touching only briefly on arms control, which one political analyst called a "nightmare for conservatives," the president spoke at length of Soviet violations of the ABM treaty, its Red Shield program, which he said "dwarfs SDI," and Moscow's continued attempts to impose communist rule in other countries. He even suggested that the Soviets were partly responsible for the famine in Ethiopia by sending in weapons instead of food and medicine.[67]

Gorbachev's method of reassurance was to remind the Supreme Soviet and the Central Committee of the Communist Party of the glorious history of the revolution and his unshakable allegiance to its principles. His rousing speech concluded with these words:

> Today the fate of the great cause of the Revolution, of Lenin's great cause, is in our hands. Once again we are blazing a new trail. . . .
>   In October 1917 we left the old world behind, rejecting it once and for all. We are moving toward a new world—the world of communism. We will never turn off this path! (Stormy, prolonged applause).[68]

A very different face was presented to the people of the U.S. and U.S.S.R. Through the fall of 1987 Soviet spokesmen referred to the concept of "reasonable sufficiency" in arms production, suggesting a purely defensive posture in Moscow's military planning. In a November 28 interview with Tom Brokaw of "NBC News," Gorbachev offered his "sincere greetings to all the television viewers who are watching, listening to us, and to all the American people." He spoke feelingly of the 80,000 letters he had received from Americans, and of his dedication to peaceful resolution of the problems facing their country and his. On the relation of arms reduction to Star Wars, he said, "We are prepared to accept a 50 percent reduction in the first stage, with strict observance of the ABM Treaty. In the degree that SDI does not run counter to the ABM Treaty, let America act, let America indulge in research."[69]

Reagan was equally accommodating, responding in mild terms to written questions from *Izvestia,* the official journal of the Communist party in the Soviet Union. Although he defended his SDI program and his criticism of Soviet military policies, the tone of his reply—which was not published in *Weekly Compilation of Presidential Documents* (WCPD) or in any White House press release—was moderate. Including a plea for cooperation between the U.S. and U.S.S.R. "as partners and friends," his message was sufficiently appealing to Soviet authorities to permit its being published without the kind of forceful rebuttal that *Izvestia* and *Pravda* normally printed side-by-side with any statement from Washington.[70]

*   *   *   *   *

The December 1987 summit meeting in Washington was the high point of President Reagan's diplomatic career. As he quite accurately remarked at the arrival ceremony for General Secretary Gorbachev, "I've welcomed a good number of foreign leaders to the White House in these last seven years. And today marks a visit that is perhaps more momentous than many which preceded it, because it represents a coming together not of allies but of adversaries."[71]

Gorbachev spent three days in Washington, but it required only a few hours of the first day to arrange the props for efficient camera coverage of the two superpower leaders signing the INF Treaty. The introductory remarks were brief, even lighthearted, as Reagan and Gorbachev congratulated one another on making "this impossible vision a reality," Reagan recalling a story by the Russian writer Ivan Krylov, and Gorbachev quoting Ralph Waldo Emerson.[72] In post-conference statements, both sides cited as their major achievements agreement on the complete elimination of nuclear weapons with a range of 300 to 3,400 miles, and a verification system that would permit inspectors from both nations to visit the other's missile sites and missile assembly facilities, to observe the "numbers, locations, and technical characteristics of all INF missiles and launchers . . . and to help verify that INF activity had ceased."[73]

Hailed by the White House as a triumph of American firmness and persistence, and supported by most Democrats, the INF Treaty was not greeted with universal acclaim. Mutterings from right-wing Republicans indicated that the pact would face a serious challenge in the Senate. California Democratic Senator Alan Cranston warned of a repetition of the 1920 campaign in which Republican opponents of the League of Nations defeated President Wilson's effort to bring the U.S. into that peace organization by amending the treaty to death. The attack he anticipated was not long in coming.[74]

Hearings on the INF Treaty began January 25, 1988 before the Senate Committee on Foreign Relations. Brief opening statements by committee chairman Claiborne Pell and senior minority member Jesse Helms set the stage for the two months it would take the committee to complete its hearings. Pell expressed the sympathies of most Democrats and moderate Republicans when he stressed the importance of the treaty as "the necessary first step in reversing the nuclear arms race." Helms called for "intense scrutiny" of every clause, clearly indicating the course he planned to take in attacking the treaty. "The administration," he said "has given the American people the impression that this treaty reduces nuclear weapons. The President has said so. The Vice-President has said so. The Secretary of State has said so. But the truth is that not one nuclear weapon will be destroyed."[75] The thrust of his argument, which he pursued throughout the hearings, was that if, as the treaty provided, the nuclear material and the guidance system were removed from each warhead and not destroyed along with the reentry vehicle, there really would be no reduction in the quantity of nuclear arms. This logic ignored several facts. First, as Secretary of Defense Frank Carlucci later explained, no one had found a way of destroying fissionable material. As to the undestroyed guidance systems, it was known, but seldom discussed in political circles, that American military brass were as reluctant as their Soviet counterparts to reveal the secrets of these control devices to inspectors from the other side. Finally, the removed material could hardly be remounted on other missiles, as Helms suggested, since all missiles of the class for which this equipment were specifically designed were to be destroyed.

As the Senate hearings progressed, administration officials did their best to sell the treaty to the general public. They were aided in this by signs that the "new thinking" in the Kremlin indicated, as Secretary Shultz put it, "an effort to come to grips with the reality of a world being shaped not by the Soviet Union and its allies but by the community of free nations and the forces of freedom."[76] An important element in that effort was the Soviet decision to withdraw its troops from Afghanistan. The series of written agreements that confirmed Moscow's intent and restored normal relations between Afghanistan and Pakistan were concluded in April, shortly before the Senate began debating its Foreign Relations Committee recommendation to approve the INF Treaty.[77]

Given the substantial treaty support indicated by public opinion polls and discussions in Congress, Senate consent to ratification would have been a simple matter had it not been for two sources of suspicion. One was the distrust of any deal with the Soviets expressed by Senators Jesse Helms, Malcolm Wallop and Steven D. Symms, three of only five senators who voted against treaty approval. The other was the irritation shown by many Democrats over Reagan's refusal to acknowledge that the reasons given by an earlier Republican administration for requesting approval of the ABM Treaty should have barred him from reinterpreting that pact to allow his Star Wars program.

Secretary of State Shultz's testimony on the latter point did not satisfy Democratic Senator Joseph Biden, who wrote to the secretary requesting answers to specific questions regarding the completeness of the record made available to the Senate. Shultz's guarded response was that he believed the documents already submitted would provide an accurate account of the treaty, and that the Senate could rely on them and on the testimony of State Department officers in determining U.S. obligations under the treaty. Denying Biden's charge that his department's reinterpretation of Nixon's ABM treaty was unconstitutional, Shultz stated, "The Reagan Administration will in no way depart from the INF Treaty as we are presenting it to the Senate."[78]

Not satisfied that this reassurance would protect against attempts by future presidents to disavow the 1988 understanding, a group of senators led by Joseph Biden and Sam Nunn insisted on attaching to the ratification resolution a series of conditions and declarations. This method avoided having to amend the treaty, which would have meant sending the entire document back for renegotiation with the Soviets. The very first conditions listed were these:

1(a) The United States shall interpret the Treaty in accordance with the common understanding of the Treaty shared by the President and the Senate at the time the Senate gave its advice and consent to ratification;

  (b) such common understanding is based on:

  (i) first, the text of the Treaty and the provisions of this resolution of ratification; and

  (ii) second, the authoritative representations which were provided by the President and his representatives to the Senate and its Committees, in seeking Senate consent to ratification, insofar as such representations were directed to the meaning and legal effect of the text of the Treaty; and

  (c) the United States shall not agree to or adopt an interpretation different from that common understanding except pursuant to Senate advice and consent to a subsequent treaty or protocol, or the enactment of a statute.[79]

Delighted as he was to carry a ratified copy of the treaty to the Moscow summit, Reagan was not about to accept the conditions the Senate had attached as a guard against any possible bait-and-switch maneuver in its interpretation. After a two-week delay to permit his legal advisers to design a response, Reagan addressed a message to the Senate in which he accused that body of attempting "to alter the law of treaty interpretation," saying he would not accept the proposition "that a condition in a resolution of ratification can alter the allocation of rights and duties under the Constitution." Insisting that he had "no intention of changing the interpretation of the INF Treaty which was presented to the Senate," he nevertheless held that "the principles of treaty interpretation" are, under the Constitution, applied by the President, and he would not "accept any diminution" of his constitutional powers "claimed to be effected" by conditions such as those the Senate had attached to its ratification resolution.[80]

There is, of course, no such thing as a law of treaty interpretation. However, experts in constitutional and international law must tingle at the excitement that would be generated among their colleagues by a Supreme Court contest on this issue between the president and the Senate of the United States.

* * * * *

President Reagan's visit to Moscow for the second half of the parking-lot arrangement was planned to begin May 29, 1988, on the assumption that this would allow ample time for Senate consideration of the INF Treaty. As debate dragged on through the latter half of May, a nervous White House pondered the effect of the president's going to the Soviet Union without a ratified treaty in hand. Russian poet Yevgeny Yevtushenko, as fully aware of the politics of accommodation as any political analyst, observed that "conservatives and reactionaries" in both the U.S.S.R. and the U.S. wanted the ratification effort to fail, staking their hope of reelection on bad relations between the two countries. Relief came little more than 24 hours before Reagan's scheduled departure, when he received news of the Senate's 93 to 5 vote of approval.[81]

It was Reagan's hope that his success in reaching agreement on elimination of Soviet and American intermediate-range nuclear forces would be repeated during his Moscow visit by a pact to reduce by 50 percent long-range nuclear missiles, characterized by the State Department as "systems that are most destabilizing—ballistic missiles, especially heavy intercontinental ballistic missiles (ICBMs) with multiple warheads." Unlike the shorter range missiles that eastern and western European nations aimed at each other, the ICBMs deployed in the U.S. and U.S.S.R. had only Soviet and American targets. Strategic Arms Reduction Talks (START) had begun in 1982 but had been broken off by the Soviets when the U.S. indicated it would neither postpone nor abandon its planned deployment of intermediate-range missiles in NATO countries. Resumed in 1985, the talks made little progress for as long as the Soviets insisted on tying agreement in this area to termination of the American Star Wars (SDI) system.[82]

When these two subjects were treated separately—in Geneva, Reykjavik and Washington—considerable progress was made. President Reagan sought to encourage optimism both in the American public and in Soviet circles, coining a new phrase, "realistic engagement," to describe the state of Soviet-American relations. In the months prior to his departure for Moscow he made a point of praising Soviet authorities for improving the civil rights of their citizens, while also acknowledging the legitimacy of Soviet charges of "social and economic shortcomings" in the U.S.[83]

Despite the general atmosphere of good will, Reagan's hope of a second diplomatic triumph was not to be realized. Opening formalities, which the *New York Times* described as "filled with mutual praise and good cheer," were followed by private discussions in which Reagan irritated his hosts by plunging immediately into the matter of Soviet human rights policies. Gorbachev had more than hinted in his ceremonial toast at the first state dinner that building good relations "should be done without interfering in domestic affairs, without sermonizing or imposing one's views and ways, without turning family or personal problems into a pretext for confrontation between states." Reagan's disregard of this warning was not the only thing that raised Gorbachev's hackles. American journalists reported the general secretary as remarking testily on the lack of progress in arms discussions. Nor could he have been pleased at Reagan's obvious success in attracting the attention of Russian students, intellectuals, church people, and would-be emigres in his peregrinations about Moscow.[84]

When all was done, the joint statement issued at the close of the conference acknowledged that "serious differences remain on important issues." The further statement that the two sides had "achieved a better understanding of each other's positions" was found to mean only that "a joint draft text of a treaty on reduction and limitation of strategic offensive arms has been elaborated," and that "the sides have continued negotiations to achieve a separate agreement concerning the ABM Treaty."[85] Thus, despite a measure of agreement on specific items such as on-site inspections to verify the elimination of strategic weapons (as in the INF Treaty), it was clear that the conference had not come close to completing a pact that Reagan and Gorbachev could offer their people—and the world—as evidence of their extraordinary accomplishment in the name of peace. As always, however, Reagan sought to portray the conference results in the best possible light, remarking in the closing ceremony that he thought "our efforts during these past few days have slayed a few dragons."[86]

Of the two, Reagan felt the need for some striking achievement far more than Gorbachev, having only seven months before he would be obliged to leave office. In the final months of his second term he did his best to encourage his negotiators to continue working in Geneva on the terms of a strategic arms treaty. He also strove to impart his optimism to western audiences. On his return trip from Moscow he stopped in London to share with his NATO partners the belief that if, as he hoped, the world was entering a new era of freedom, "it's because of the steadfastness of the allies, the democracies."[87] Back home he devoted his first Saturday radio broadcast to a description of the great strides that had been made at the Moscow summit. And in subsequent speeches, meetings and press releases he offered equally glowing accounts of his trip and optimistic forecasts of progress in the renewed negotiations on strategic arms and space weapons.[88]

In October Reagan settled a dispute between State and Defense officials as to the verification system the U.S. would propose for strategic weapons, opting for the same inspection procedures as were specified in the INF Treaty, rather than the more extensive inspections pushed by the Pentagon. The president also called for an international conference "to reaffirm worldwide political commitment to the [1925] Geneva Protocol," which prohibits the use of chemical and bacteriological agents in warfare.[89]

Meanwhile, verification procedures under the INF Treaty became a reality as U.S. inspectors took up their station at the Soviet Union's major nuclear testing ground, and Soviet inspectors were observers at an underground nuclear explosion in Nevada. These first contacts were marred only by an American team member's attempt to ship back to the U.S. "militarily sensitive materials," whose export from either the U.S. or U.S.S.R. was prohibited by the treaty.[90] This isolated event seemed to have no effect on Gorbachev's "new thinking," which continued to evoke such startling reactions as a suggestion from the Kremlin's chief ideologist for experiments in western-style market economics, a Soviet journalist's characterization of Russia's 1968 invasion of Czechoslovakia as "a mistake," Soviet military officers permitting NATO observers to attend the maneuvers of Warsaw Pact armies in East Germany, and a handful of votes opposing government-sponsored legislation in a Supreme Soviet that, since the days of Joseph Stalin, had never known support to be anything but unanimous.[91]

The one ironic note in post-INF U.S.-Soviet relations was introduced by Reagan's suggestion that the Soviet Union agree to compulsory jurisdiction by the International Court of Justice for particular categories of disputes, including those involving treaty obligations. Prompted by Gorbachev's earlier call for action by the UN Security Council to strengthen the World Court's compulsory jurisdiction, the U.S. proposal was offered with none of the embarrassment that might have been expected in light of this country's refusal to accept World Court jurisdiction in the case brought by Nicaragua after the mining of its harbors.[92]

CHAPTER 11

Commander in Chief

"America is the 'A-Team' among nations, bursting with energy, courage and determination."[1]

REAGAN'S DESCRIPTION OF THE U.S. AS THE MORAL EQUIVALENT OF THE cinematic quartet that overcomes all evildoers with its ingenuity, wit and machine guns, although addressed to a group of high school students, paired perfectly with his lordly assertion to reporters that "anything we do is in our national interest."[2] These two remarks, made within five months of one another, combined Reagan's Hollywood concept of the hero as a tough, gun-toting defender of right with his fundamentalist belief in both the rightness and righteousness of his cause.

For all his militant sermonizing on the need to demonstrate America's determination to arm to the hilt in order to preserve the U.S. as "the last best hope of man on earth," Reagan was most circumspect in his use of force. When asked how he felt about more effective action than indirect military support of favored groups in Central America, he replied, "We know better than to engage in armed intervention; gunboat diplomacy could turn off a lot of friends."[3] Thus, notwithstanding his abhorrence of all communist regimes, he only resorted to direct intervention as an instrument of foreign policy in situations where the U.S. had overwhelming military superiority and could anticipate no danger of defeat, or battlefield confrontation with the Soviet Union. In all other situations he relied, as the Soviets did, on surrogate governments or rebel forces to fight their own wars, supplying them with money, weapons and intelligence to do so.

This policy can be traced to Reagan's bitter memory of the Korean and Vietnamese wars. He accused past administrations of "preventing us from allowing General MacArthur to lead us to victory in Korea," and of debasing the "noble cause" in Vietnam by engaging in a war in which "no one [in the U.S. government] had any intention of allowing victory." As Reagan recalled in 1984, he had long before argued that "we should have asked for a declaration of war [against North Vietnam] and called it a war." He did not remind his listeners that, as governor of California, one of the reasons he gave for urging a declaration of war was to make peaceful demonstrations against government policy punishable as acts of treason. "If we are officially at war," he said then, "the anti-Vietnam demonstrations and the act of burning draft cards would be treasonable."[4]

Despite that earlier belligerent posture, as president, Reagan ignored the recommendation of his favorite journalist, William F. Buckley, Jr., who on separate occasions called for declarations of war against Nicaragua and Cuba. He was equally careful to avoid any suggestion of war status even when taking direct military action against another country, as he did in Grenada and Libya. Moreover, in justifying each military action, whether it was a support mission, a bombing run, or a display of military might thinly disguised as a naval training maneuver, he very deliberately avoided any reference to the War Powers Act, always citing a variety of other legislative or constitutional provisions.[5]

*   *   *   *   *

Many years will pass before documentation is available to reveal the occasions, if any, on which Reagan, like every post-World War II president before him, must have considered the possibility of using nuclear weapons against another country. What we do know is that once he felt the U.S. had achieved military parity with the Soviet Union, he was ready to acknowledge the futility of a nuclear war between the two nations. Even at that point, however, he refused to disavow "first strike" as one of the options in a threatening situation. On the contrary, a basic element of his philosophy of deterrence was expressed in a remark first made at the height of the Vietnam War: "I don't think anyone would cheerfully want to use atomic weapons. But the last person in the world that should know we wouldn't use them is the enemy. He should go to bed every night being afraid that we might."[6] His later White House reference to this seemingly clever tactic revealed a dangerous lack of perception: that an enemy convinced of his intention to order a first strike might not go to bed thinking about it, but might instead decide on a preemptive first strike of his own, and thus initiate a nuclear holocaust that would destroy both nations.

Because superpower military might had come to be measured principally in terms of nuclear weapons, much of the debate over the arms buildup was directed at the danger of nuclear war. Even proposals for expanding the bomber force or the submarine fleet were based on the advantage to be derived from the additional nuclear missiles each plane and submarine would be able to direct at the U.S.S.R. Reagan's defense of these military plans was extended to every aspect of nuclear development, including the proliferation of nuclear power plants. In his radio addresses of 1977 and 1978, he labeled critics of the lax safety standards applied to nuclear power plants as "the unwitting victims of Soviet designs." President Carter he accused of "bowing to Kremlin propaganda" by delaying deployment of the neutron bomb. Subsequently, as he campaigned for the presidency in 1980, Reagan charged the Carter administration with blocking the MX missile and B1 bomber programs and exhibiting "hypocrisy at its worst in cozying up to the Soviets."[7] He did not level similar charges against Republican stalwart Barry Goldwater who, a few years later, not only recommended abandonment of the MX missile, but called for a freeze on military spending at the 1983/84 level.[8]

Differences of opinion as to the effectiveness of particular weapon systems were less significant than debate over Reagan's Strategic Defense Initiative. According to Gregg Herken, senior research associate at the University of California, the 1980 Republican platform's call for "overall military and technological superiority over the Soviet Union," and for "vigorous research and development of an effective anti-ballistic missile system" were taken from a 1979 memorandum to Reagan by campaign aide Martin Anderson.[9]

As Herken pointed out, this was not the first space-based defense system considered by American scientists, but it was the first to offer the shield concept using space-based x-ray lasers. Pressed upon Reagan by physicist Edward Teller in a January 1982 meeting at the White House, Project Excalibur became the focus of attention in meetings which Teller held with members of Congress and both civilian and military brass in the Pentagon. Final acceptance of the plan, and the timing of a public announcement of the new approach to nuclear war, apparently was made by Reagan after he had consulted with National Security Council advisers Robert McFarlane and John Poindexter, but without notification to anyone in the Pentagon. Coming only two weeks after his Evil Empire speech, Reagan's disclosure that he was "launching an effort which holds the promise of changing the course of human history" climaxed a series of dire warnings of the threat posed by the Soviet Union's growing military might.[10]

Following the issuance of a National Security Decision Directive confirming the plan, editorial comment in the press complained of the lack of detail as to the nature of the program and its prospective cost. These remarks Reagan characterized as "irresponsible." However, he offered no further information at his next White House discussion with reporters.[11]

For almost two years after his initial announcement of the proposed defense system, President Reagan's references to it were couched in general terms. When questioned by reporters, his responses usually were limited to three points: it would be better to save lives than to avenge them; the proposed space weapons would be strictly defensive; and the Soviets were far ahead of the U.S. in this type of research.

On January 3, 1985, the White House had the Government Printing Office produce a formal report entitled "The President's Strategic Defense Initiative." Written in December 1984, only the foreword was made public in the *Weekly Compilation of Presidential Documents* of January 7, 1985. The *Washington Post* reported that its request for a copy of the complete document went unanswered. When finally released, the easily-read text pictured the proposed "layered defense" as capable of intercepting some missiles shortly after launch, others during the "post-booster phase," still more during their "relatively long (tens of minutes) mid-course phase of flight," and the remainder "during the terminal phase as they approach the end of their ballistic flight."

Although this description gave an impression of complete protection for the entire country, the following statement suggested that the system might not be invulnerable:

> The combined effectiveness of the defense provided by the multiple layers need not provide 100% protection in order to enhance deterrence significantly. It need only create sufficient uncertainty in the mind of a potential aggressor concerning his ability to succeed in the purposes of his attack. The concept of a layered defense certainly will help do this.[12]

In a question-and-answer section, most criticisms of the plan were ascribed to Soviet propaganda, with no acknowledgment of the many flaws pointed out by American analysts who lacked any possible motive for advancing Soviet interests.

On one point, anti-SDI arguments by Soviet and American critics coincided: if a nation with a space-defense system believed that system would enable it to win a nuclear war, it might institute a first strike on the assumption that it could successfully ward off any retaliatory action by the stricken enemy. Other Soviet objections were obvious reflections of that country's fear of losing the technological race for new and more effective weapons either for defense or offense, or of being bankrupted by the cost of such a race.

Opposition within the U.S. also cited the enormous cost of SDI, but challenged the need for annual multi-billion dollar expenditures on three grounds: SDI's conflict with the terms of the ABM Treaty that the U.S. had ratified in 1972; the effect on non-military programs which, lacking the same national security status, would be funded inadequately or not at all; and the inability of SDI to provide the kind of defense claimed for it.

On the legal side, the 1972 treaty between the U.S. and U.S.S.R. limiting anti-ballistic missile systems states in article 5: "Each party undertakes not to develop, test, or deploy ABM systems or components which are sea-based, air-based, space-based or mobile land-based."[13] Only fixed land-based systems were omitted from this restriction, as President Nixon's treaty negotiators had assured the Senate in 1972. The Reagan administration's reinterpretation of the ABM Treaty denied that the SDI program constituted a breach of the earlier agreement, the president repeatedly asserting that SDI was merely "a research program, and it is within the provisions of the ABM Treaty which proscribed development, testing and deployment but did not mention research."[14]

The State Department's legal adviser, Abraham D. Sofaer, was called upon to certify the accuracy of the new interpretation. He disposed of the testimony of Nixon's negotiators as "unilateral assertions," and proceeded with a lengthy elaboration of the point that the treaty was ambiguous about its "applicability to future systems," as a result of which SDI was permissible. His conclusion, he said, was based on details in the negotiating record that he could not reveal because they were classified, but which showed that the "Soviets stubbornly resisted U.S. attempts to adopt in the body of the treaty any limits on such systems or components based on future technology." Two years later Sofaer acknowledged that his analysis had been based on research that turned out not to be entirely accurate. However, he refused to identify those portions of the research—or his conclusions—that were flawed.[15]

A member of the State Department who resigned over Sofaer's original interpretation later testified that department experts had not been permitted to take part in the analysis, which he said was rushed to completion in a "flawed decision memorandum" to the president. That memorandum was probably the basis for President Reagan's still-classified National Security Decision Directive 119 of January 6, 1984, which gave formal approval for SDI research and development.[16]

To scientists, the legal justification for the SDI program was far less important than its usefulness. And here there were sharp differences of opinion, even among researchers at the Los Alamos and Lawrence Livermore laboratories where Project Excalibur was in full swing. Roy D. Woodruff and Ray Kidder, both veteran employees of Livermore Laboratory, were among those who challenged the conclusions and predictions of Teller and his Livermore protege, Lowell L. Wood, Jr. Teller, who had convinced President Reagan of the feasibility of constructing a laser-based defense in 1982, wrote enthusiastically the following year of the speed with which the laboratories were approaching that goal. Only portions of Teller's letters have been declassified, but those limited passages are sufficient to explain the outrage of Woodruff and Kidder at the extravagant claim made by Teller in December 1983 that because an x-ray laser had actually been tested in the laboratory, it was ready for the "engineering phase" of development. When Woodruff demanded that a letter of clarification be sent to Reagan's science adviser,

George A. Keyworth, who had received Teller's secret memorandum, Livermore Laboratory director Roger Batzel refused to forward Woodruff's explanation that the work was nowhere near the engineering phase. Woodruff's second attempt to correct Teller's inaccuracies was rebuffed a year later, after Teller had sent this Buck Rogers description of laser capability to U.S. arms negotiator Paul Nitze:

> A single x-ray laser module the size of an executive desk which applied this [strategic defense] technology could potentially shoot down the entire Soviet land-based missile force, if it were launched into the module's field-of-view. . . . A handful of such modules could similarly suppress or shoot down the entire Soviet submarine-based missile force, if it were to be salvo-launched. [17]

When Congress finally decided to ask the General Accounting Office to review the claims and counterclaims made for Project Excalibur, the best conclusion the GAO could come up with was that "there was no general agreement among these scientists [at Livermore Laboratory] regarding the accuracy of the statements" made by Teller and Woodruff. Although the GAO record included testimony from Dr. Kidder that Woodruff's clarification letters "provided a frank, objective and balanced description of the program as it existed at the time [and] the Teller letters did not," the GAO report omitted that testimony. Instead it published such statements by the laboratory director as, "there was nothing in Dr. Teller's letters that violated any laws of physics," and "there were no data refuting Dr. Teller's concept." [18]

A few months after President Reagan's January 1985 defense of SDI as a program permitted by the ABM Treaty, the House Armed Services Committee met in executive session to hear an administration spokesman describe SDI and how it was expected to work. The spokesman was John Gardner, director of the systems division of the Defense Department's newly formed Strategic Defense Initiative Organization. [19] No other witnesses were invited, and no scientists who opposed the administration view were permitted to attend. Gardner's description of the four-layer defense system suggested that all attacking missiles would be intercepted, a proposition no other administration expert ever claimed. Assuming an attack by 1,000 missiles, Gardner said, 70 percent would be destroyed in the first (boost) phase of flight. Of the remaining 300, 200 would be destroyed in the second (post-boost) phase in which each undestroyed missile would spew out ten "reentry vehicles" (warheads) that would have separate targets. Only the reentry vehicles of 100 missiles would escape and of those, 70 percent would be destroyed during their phase-three flight through upper space. As the last of the reentry vehicles approached the atmosphere in their descent to their targets, "the fourth layer of defense would be activated and it would intercept the few hundred remaining reentry vehicles."[20]

Questioning by committee members was deferential to the point of timidity, each of the few who spoke prefacing his questions with the assurance that he was only trying to understand this complicated scientific problem. When Representative Charles E. Bennett was bold enough to ask whether the logical thing for the enemy to do "would be to put a lot more missiles in the air to counteract that defense," he was told by Gardner that "from the Soviet Union's viewpoint, faced with these kind [sic] of comprehensive defenses . . . they could easily convince themselves that proliferation of their offensive forces would not work."[21] He followed this contradiction of every public statement by Soviet officials with so bewildering a flow of "simple calculations" that at one point Bennett had the impression that the Soviets had only 1,200 ICBMs (intercontinental ballistic missiles), rather than the 8,500 previously mentioned.

To rebut "the clear consensus of the scientific community" that SDI would not work as claimed, Gardner derided that as the opinion of "people that are not technically knowledgeable about the program at all." Presumably he included in that category Hans Bethe, former director of the Los Alamos Theoretical Division; Norris Bradbury, former director of the Los Alamos National Laboratories; Wolfgang Panofsky, former director of the Stanford Linear Accelerator; and George Rathjens, former deputy director of the Defense Advanced Research Projects Agency; as well as Livermore Laboratory rebels Woodruff and Kidder.[22]

Given Gardner's assurance of 100 percent protection of the population and facilities of the U.S., no committee member inquired as to whether people or facilities would be given preference in case of doubt. The answer appeared in a detailed analysis of SDI by the Union of Concerned Scientists, which pointed to Assistant Secretary of Defense Richard Perle's unequivocal statement that the purpose of SDI was "not the defense of the nation as a whole, not of every city and person in it, but the defense of America's capacity to retaliate."[23]

A year and four months after Perle's admission, President Reagan abandoned the myth of SDI as being merely a research program, announcing to the applause of supporters at the White House: "We will research it. We will develop it. And when it's ready we'll deploy it." Finally, less than two months before the end of Reagan's term in office, his repeated description of SDI as a purely defensive system was demolished when the Pentagon acknowledged the appropriateness of the term Star Wars by revealing that the plan included weapons capable of destroying satellites—not missiles—orbiting in space.[24] Further, a decision to modify Ski Lite, the Pentagon's most powerful Miracl (Mid-Infrared Advanced Chemical Laser) laser to turn it into a weapon of offense against satellites was revealed in the *New York Times* January 1, 1989.

The cost-effectiveness of SDI was as hotly debated as its practicality. Paul Nitze established the administration standard, saying, "It must be cheaper to add additional defensive capability than it is for the other side to add the offensive capability necessary to overcome the defense." Otherwise, he explained, "the defensive systems could encourage a proliferation of countermeasures" instead of a redirection of effort from offense to defense.[25]

Nitze did not provide an estimate of the program's ultimate cost. Nor did the president's two annual reports on national security contain any dollar signs.[26] But critics of the program challenged it on the very grounds that Nitze had set forth as a litmus test of effectiveness. As the Center for Defense Information put it, "simple and relatively cheap countermeasures" would include weapons designed to destroy U.S. laser stations in space, releasing thousands of decoys to divert laser attacks from enemy missiles, acceleration of missile production to increase the chance that more warheads would penetrate the defense, and use of weapons other than missiles in an attack.[27]

The cost question was raised on several occasions in congressional committee hearings. John Gardner told the House Armed Services Committee in 1985 that the original plan for SDI anticipated a "cost of $15 to $18 billion over the 1985 to 1989 time-frame." By the end of 1985, this had been reestimated at $23 to $26 billion.[28] Three years later another committee put the question in terms of management control, noting that by early 1988 over 3,000 contracts had been awarded. At this hearing, committee chairman Jack Brooks estimated that "the costs of the earliest part of the deployed strategic defense system could be as much as $150 billion.[29]

Other interested parties went beyond Brooks' consideration of only "the earliest part" of system costs. The Council on Economic Priorities believed that "once the program moves into production and deployment it could cost anywhere from $400 billion to $1 trillion depending on the type of system that will be deployed." The CEP report quoted a study by members of the Foreign Policy Institute at Johns Hopkins University that calculated the costs of producing and deploying four different types of SDI systems as ranging "from $160 billion to $770 billion each."[30] Retired Rear Admiral Gene R. La Rocque's Center for Defense Information summarized the cost factor in this fashion: "No one knows precisely how much a system to shoot down ballistic missiles would cost, but according to experts it could exceed $1 trillion. One system being explored could cost over $250 billion just to lift into space."[31] These estimates were not challenged in official documents published by the White House or in budget hearings, all of which offered estimates of annual expenditures only through fiscal year 1989 or 1990.[32]

* * * * *

The major objectives of Reagan's military buildup, for which SDI provided
the icing on the cake, were to keep the U.S. as number one among world
powers and to counter the might and influence of the U.S.S.R. The former
aim was a product of his patriotic fervor; the latter stemmed from his firm
belief in Milton Friedman's concept of freedom, and an equally firm conviction that America is the "promised land" and that Americans "were chosen by
God to create a better world."[33]

For as long as he openly presented his vision of the world as a battleground
engaging the forces of good and evil, Reagan's evangelistic and militarist
foreign policy only exacerbated anti-American feeling already existing in
every quarter of the globe. Whether or not he recognized this, he was careful
to limit his overt use of military force to targets that had little power to
retaliate. Even his proxy wars in Afghanistan, Angola and Central America
were tailored to avoid any direct involvement of U.S. troops.

The earliest of Reagan's overt military ventures was directed at Libya—
more specifically, at that country's head of state, the bitterly anti-American
Muammar al-Qaddafi. Barely seven months after Reagan entered the White
House, the first of a long series of Mediterranean naval maneuvers took U.S.
warplanes into the air over the Gulf of Sidra, a deep indentation along the
shores of Libya.

Relations between the U.S. and Libya had been strained since the early
1970s, due largely to Qaddafi's tough treatment of American oil companies,
his bitter enmity toward Israel, his threats against Egypt for having made
peace with Israel, and his support of international terrorism.[34] When a mob
emulating the rioters in Teheran invaded and set fire to the American
embassy in Tripoli in December 1979, President Carter's response had been
to withdraw all embassy personnel from the Libyan cappital. In the spring of
1981 the Reagan administration closed the embassy in Libya after rumors
that Qaddafi's death squads were seeking out Libyan exiles in the U.S.

Washington knew, and the U.S. Navy knew, that Qaddafi had always
claimed the Gulf of Sidra to be Libyan territory and had designated the limits
of Libyan jurisdiction by a line drawn 12 miles north of both ends of the gulf.
The U.S. considered the Gulf of Sidra to be international waters and permitted its ships and planes to penetrate that area at will, knowing full well that
such movements would be regarded as a threat by Libyans. Moreover, as Navy
Secretary John F. Lehman, Jr. acknowledged, Libyan planes had been intercepted and turned back without incident on a number of occasions when they
had entered the U.S. fleet's maneuvering zone far outside the gulf. However,
on August 19 American fighters did not wait for a Libyan patrol to exit the

gulf, much less approach U.S. ships. After picking up two Libyan jets on their radar, the Americans entered the gulf to meet the planes and, when one of the Libyans fired a missile, shot down both of them.

Explanations by Pentagon officials and President Reagan stressed these administration views: the maneuvers were routine, all Mediterranean nations had been notified when and where they would take place, the Navy fliers were over what the U.S. considered international waters, and their pilots had acted in self-defense. Answering reporters' questions, both Secretary of Defense Caspar Weinberger and President Reagan insisted that no provocation was intended. But the joint chiefs' director of operations, Lt. General Philip J. Gast, suggested the tone that led to the encounter when he referred to the Libyan planes as "enemy aircraft"; and when a reporter asked the president whether he "wouldn't be sorry to see Qaddafi fall,"[35] Reagan acknowledged that "diplomacy would have me not answer."

The matter was treated so routinely by the White House that Reagan's chief of staff, Edwin Meese, didn't consider it necessary to awaken his vacationing president until 7:24 A.M., six hours after Meese had been alerted to the incident. Reagan seemed equally unconcerned, going back to sleep after receiving the information. Asked later in the day what he thought the message of the previous day's events should be, the president showed that he viewed it in the context of his battle with the Evil Empire by saying, "We're determined that we are going to close that window of vulnerability that has existed for some time with regard to our defensive capability."[36] What bearing Libya's puny offensive power had on America's window of vulnerability he did not explain.

The circumstances of this aerial dogfight indicated the path Reagan intended to follow in dealing with Libya. As legal counsel Abraham D. Sofaer was to testify five years later, by March 1986 U.S. warships had been "in the Gulf of Sidra area 16 times since 1981, and . . . had crossed Qaddafi's so-called line of death seven times."[37] That is to say, units of the Mediterranean fleet cruised off Libyan shores an average of three times a year, and once or twice each year deliberately baited the Libyans by sailing into the Gulf of Sidra.

Relations with the U.S. continued to deteriorate, exacerbated by the charges and countercharges, and by near-incidents like the one sparked by the rumored threat of a Libyan coup in Sudan, which prompted the U.S. to send four AWACS (Airborne, Warning and Control System surveillance planes) to the area. Secretary of State George Shultz made a point of going on television to describe how U.S. action had put Qaddafi "back in his box where he belongs." Yet Shultz later opposed the CIA and NSC "madmen in the White House," who urged a joint U.S.-Egyptian invasion of Libya following the 1985 hijacking of TWA Flight 847.[38]

Overt military action was not long delayed, but was prefaced by Reagan's Executive Order 12543 of January 7, 1986, which declared a national emergency to deal with "the policies and actions of the Government of Libya [which] constitute an unusual and extraordinary threat to the national security and foreign policy of the United States." The order cut off trade and transportation between the U.S. and Libya and directed American oil companies to wind down their Libyan operations.[39] Discussing the matter with independent network bureau chiefs, Reagan refused to expand upon the wording of his executive order, saying, "I don't add anything to what might be on our minds for the future. Let him [Qaddafi] wonder what's on our mind." The same day, the State Department issued a statement charging Qaddafi with terrorist acts in the U.S., Egypt and five European countries.[40]

The boiling point was reached three months later. On March 24, U.S. ships and planes operating inside the Gulf of Sidra were fired upon from missile sites on the Libyan coast. In response, U.S. ships launched two high-speed radiation missiles at the SA-5 site at Sirte. When Libyan patrol boats approached the fleet they were attacked. Three were sunk and one damaged, with no American casualties and no damage to U.S. ships or aircraft. Asked by a reporter attending a Defense Department briefing, "Is this war?", Secretary Weinberger rejected that suggestion and characterized the U.S. action as "a peaceful navigational exercise in international waters."[41]

Unable to cope with American forces in direct combat, Libya struck back in a different fashion. On April 5 a bomb exploded in a West German nightclub, killing American Sergeant Kenneth Ford and a Turkish woman and wounding 230 others, including 50 American military personnel. Information released subsequently indicated that by monitoring radio traffic between the Libyan embassy in East Berlin and the Libyan capital of Tripoli, U.S. intelligence had learned that Tripoli had ordered "a terrorist attack against Americans," that its People's Bureau in East Berlin had radioed Tripoli April 4 of its plan to carry out an attack, and on April 5 had reported "the great success of their mission." Based on this information, the U.S. planned and executed a series of strikes by long-range bombers against selected targets in Libya.[42]

Although denied by the administration, one purpose of the attack was to kill Qaddafi. Destruction of his home was alleged to have been a mistake, but that mistake took the life of his 15-month-old adopted daughter and put his wife and eight other children in the hospital. The purported target of the raid—the command post in el-Azziziya barracks in Tripoli—was not hit by any of the bombs dropped by U.S. planes. On the other hand, a miscalculation by one F-111 crew caused bombs to fall in a residential area, killing more than 100 civilians.[43]

Thanks to the effectiveness of the publicity campaign linking Qaddafi with the Berlin bombing, 68 percent of the American public agreed that the U.S. was right in bombing Libya. A solid 80 percent believed military action would again be warranted if Libya were to carry out or instigate new terrorist acts against the U.S. Abroad, reactions varied more widely. In France, whose government had refused permission for U.S. bombers to fly over its territory en route to their target, the popular approval rate was 61 percent. But in England, where the government had allowed its airfields to be used to launch the attack, only 30 percent of those polled favored it. And in West Germany, whose government refused to accept U.S. intelligence reports as conclusive evidence of Libya's involvement in the nightclub explosion, only 25 percent of the general population approved the U.S. retaliatory action.[44]

A canvass of the foreign press indicated a largely negative reaction. British and Israeli papers supported the U.S. raid, while in France, West Germany, India and most Arab countries, the raid was severely criticized. Most critics expressed a view that, interestingly enough, coincided with that of 40 percent of Americans polled by Gallup, namely, that the U.S. raid would very likely bring an increase in terrorism, rather than a decrease.[45]

The U.S. Senate and House of Representatives largely supported the raid on Libya, but many members showed serious concern about a warlike decision of this kind being made without consultation with Congress. Beginning with a defense of the initial decision to conduct naval maneuvers off the Libyan coast, State Department legal adviser Sofaer argued that the War Powers Resolution "was not intended to require consultation before conducting routine maneuvers in international waters or airspace." He insisted that "the threat of a possible hostile response is not sufficient, in our judgment, to trigger the consultation requirement in section 3 [of the War Powers Resolution] which refers only to actual hostilities and to situations in which imminent involvement in hostilities is clearly indicated by the circumstances." Implicitly, this was a denial of what many observers believed, and officers inside the Pentagon acknowledged off the record, that the U.S. maneuvers were intended to bait Qaddafi into aggressive action.[46]

As to consultation prior to an overt attack, Sofaer maintained that congressional leaders "were advised of the President's intention after the operational deployments had commenced, but hours before military action actually occurred." This flimflam was exposed by Representative Dante Fascell who was one of those briefed on the action after the attacking planes were halfway to their target. "We went down there at 4 P.M." he recalled, "and we were told: Gentlemen, you will be happy to know a decision has been made. Planes are in the air. And then . . . we were given all the details. About halfway through, somebody said, well, do you have any objection. Well, of course, nobody objected." What Congress was offered in the case of the attack on Libya, he correctly insisted, was not consultation, but "mere notification."[47]

The 1986 raid did not conclude Reagan's effort to put Qaddafi back in his box. Interviewed by ABC's David Brinkley on December 21, 1988, Reagan said he was "reasonably sure" that a new plant that Qaddafi had said was to manufacture pharmaceuticals was really designed to produce poison gas. Brinkley reminded the president that he had once bombed Libya for terrorist activity and asked if he would bomb the poison gas facility, and "if not, why not." The president refused to answer, saying only that such a decision had not yet been made, leaving Brinkley to conclude, "I guess when you decide, we will hear about it."[48]

Those comments aroused the fears of countries other than Libya. Two weeks after the interview the State Department acknowledged that Saudi Arabia—no friend of Libya—had offered to mediate the U.S.-Libya dispute over chemical weapons and had been turned down.[49] This admission came after the Sixth Fleet had renewed its "routine training operations" in the eastern Mediterranean, this time with its planes scouting the area between Crete and Libya's Bumbah Bay. During the maneuvers, two navy jets flying in the direction of the Libyan coast detected the takeoff of two Libyan fighters from al-Bumbah. According to the Pentagon, the American pilots then "maneuvered to avoid the closing aircraft" by changing speed, altitude and direction. But their change of direction never took them away from the Libyan coast. When the Libyan planes got to within 14 miles, the leading U.S. pilot decided their intent was hostile and both U.S. planes fired missiles that destroyed the Libyan jets. Only after reporting two "good kills" did the tape of this incident record the lead pilot's instruction to "head north," away from Libya and back to the U.S. fleet.[50]

Libya's protest to the UN Security Council, and its demand for condemnation of the U.S. action, produced only a resolution that "deplored" the shooting down of the Libyan planes. Even that watered-down statement failed to pass because it was vetoed by the U.S. and two of its NATO allies, Britain and France.[51]

President Reagan left office without giving the order to destroy the factory believed to have been planned to produce poison gas, and without relieving Qaddafi of the need to "wonder about what we'll do."

*   *   *   *   *

Lebanon became a combat zone for American forces, not out of any desire on Reagan's part to settle that country's civil war by force, but because of his conviction that the overwhelming power of an American presence would calm the contending factions and help bring about a peaceful settlement of their differences. His effort to resolve that situation, which was complicated by the Israeli conflict with PLO forces based in Lebanon, was later summed up by his onetime official spokesman Larry Speakes in a single paragraph. Reagan and his advisers, Speakes wrote, "had stumbled through mine fields and booby traps, meandering from Sadat to his successor, Hosni Mubarak, to King Hussein of Jordan, to President Hafez al-Assad of Syria." By the end of 1983, he said, "Reagan was forced to admit that our attempts to keep the peace in Lebanon were a failure."[52]

Speakes' emphasis was on the diplomatic aspect of Reagan's Middle East initiative, but the failure of the military effort was even more devastating. Initially authorized by a congressional resolution approving U.S. participation in a multinational force to monitor implementation of the peace treaty between Egypt and Israel, the first use of military units in the area met little resistance.[53] However, when in the summer of 1982 U.S. Marines were ordered to join French and Italian contingents to bring peace to Lebanon, "the obvious concerns of inserting some portion of the 32d MAU [Marine Amphibious Unit] between 30,000 Israelis and 15,000 PLO and Syrian fighters were well recognized."[54]

The first task—to evacuate some 6,400 Palestinians, including PLO fighters and their families—was concluded without bloodshed. But when president-elect Bashir Gemayel was assassinated and the Marines, who had been withdrawn to stations in Italy, were ordered back to Beirut, the situation deteriorated seriously.

In March, 1983 sniping at the peacekeeping forces began. When an American sentry was fired on, Marines returned fire for the first time. The very next day, April 18, a van carrying 2,000 pounds of explosives was driven to the entrance of the U.S. embassy where it exploded, collapsing the front portion of the building and killing 63 of the occupants.[55]

The degeneration of the "relatively benign environment" that according to a later report had been assumed would protect the multinational force, brought a change in the rules. At the American ambassador's temporary quarters in the British embassy, Marine guards were told to disregard earlier instructions about carrying unloaded weapons. On a printed card, each Marine was directed to fire on any individual or vehicle committing "a hostile act."[56] For some inexplicable reason the same instructions were not distributed at the main Marine base at the Beirut airport, even though, during the months that followed, that area suffered a series of attacks by artillery, rocket and machine-gun fire from both Druse and Shiite forces. Only after fighting between Lebanese troops and Druse and Amal soldiers brought an increasing number of shells and rockets into the Marine camp were American gunners told to return any fire directed at them. U.S. warships were also ordered into action, and they rained high explosives on Syrian positions in the hills surrounding Beirut. Later in the year, salvos from the Sixth Fleet were accompanied by raids by U.S. planes.

Increased naval and air action, which had little effect, was partly an angry response to the most devastating attack of all, which destroyed the U.S. Marines' headquarters building at the airport and killed 241 Marines and sailors. When that blow came in October, guards at the American compound were still carrying unloaded rifles, no concrete barriers had been installed (as they had at the British embassy), and no alert was sounded when the dynamite-laden truck cruised slowly around the parking lot outside the camp's simple wire fence. An hour later it returned, circling again twice before dashing by sentries and through an open gate to blow the main building and its occupants sky-high with a head-on crash.

Putting the blame largely on inadequate support from U.S. intelligence, a Defense Department investigative team nevertheless acknowledged that "the security measures in effect at the MAU compound were neither commensurate with the increasing level of threat confronting the U.S.M.N.F. nor sufficient to preclude catastrophic losses such as those that were suffered on the morning of 23 October 1983."[57]

The first public hint that the usefulness of American forces in Lebanon was at an end was Reagan's February 7, 1984 announcement that the Marines would be redeployed to warships offshore. A brief statement implying the failure of the initiative was buried in a narrative containing his February 7 order to the navy to "provide naval gunfire and air support against any units firing into greater Beirut from parts of Lebanon controlled by Syria."[58]

Not until April did the president acknowledge that in fact the U.S. had withdrawn—not just redeployed—its forces from Lebanon. Asked subsequently by foreign journalists why the effort had failed, his answer was a direct rebuttal: "The idea that we 'failed' in Lebanon is simply wrong . . . even though things had not worked out as we had hoped."[59]

America's troubles did not end with the Marines' departure. The second building selected by the State Department to house the embassy was, like the first, destroyed by a car bomb, on September 20, 1984. Outrage at this repeat performance was directed more at the administration than at its perpetrators. Bitter criticism came from administration friends and foes alike. Columnist George Will reminded his friend President Reagan that the commander in chief had a responsibility to see that his subordinates moved with dispatch to provide the kind of security that the previous year's experience had shown to be essential. Castigating Reagan's "laconic, complacent comparison" of the problems involved in constructing suitable embassy barriers with those entailed in renovating a kitchen in an American home, he reminded the president that, unlike the inconvenience resulting from the lackadaisical performance by a kitchen contractor, "if the commander in chief's employees are dilatory, people die."[60]

Reagan had, in fact, offered two explanations for the inadequate security at the embassy. Will's appropriately caustic reference was to the characteristic remark that "anyone that's ever had their kitchen done over knows that it never gets done as soon as you wish it would."

To a student at Bowling Green State University, he put it differently. "For real protection," Reagan said, it was necessary "to rebuild our intelligence to where you'll find out and know in advance what the target might be and be prepared for it." Implying that President Carter had adopted the naive approach of President Hoover's secretary of state, Henry L. Stimson ("gentlemen do not read one another's mail"), he made the flatly false statement that his predecessor had taken the view that "spying is somehow dishonest, and let's get rid of our intelligence agents."[61]

Faced with repeated retorts that U.S. intelligence had, in fact, warned of probable attacks on embassy personnel, Reagan ultimately responded to an irate call from Jimmy Carter, returning the call to explain—without apology—that he had not meant to lay the blame for the bombing at Carter's door.[62]

For the balance of his term in office Reagan tried to keep his Middle East peace initiative alive, but with little success. His original exposition of that policy, set forth in a 1982 address to the United Nations, dwelt at length on fulfillment of the Camp David agreement between Egypt and Israel, and UN Resolution 242 calling for peaceful settlement of the Palestine issue. As to his repeated claim to realism, his ability to substitute fantasy for fact was revealed in an earlier presidential evaluation of Saudi Arabia, a country devoted to the two anti-democratic principles of absolute monarchy and Islam. The Saudis, he said, "want to be part of the West. They associate more with our views and our philosophy."[63]

From 1985 through 1988, the prospects for settlement of the conflict over the West Bank and Gaza strip dimmed as Israeli conservatives, with the aid of religious extremists, came to dominate that country's government at the same time as Yasir Arafat's star rose with the PLO declaration of the establishment of an independent state of Palestine. The latter move, coming just two months before the end of Reagan's term of office, put the White House and State Department in a quandary. Because the PLO statement only "hinted" at recognizing Israel's right to exist, the U.S. refused to accept PLO assurances on that point. Secretary Shultz also denied Arafat's request for a visa to enter the U.S. to address the UN, citing the law against admission of terrorists. Widely condemned at home and abroad as contrary to American principles of free speech, this act merely prodded most UN members to approve holding a special session in Geneva just to hear Arafat.[64]

Ultimately, Arafat put his message in words acceptable to Washington, renouncing terrorism "in all its forms" and urging a settlement "among the parties . . . including the state of Palestine, Israel and other neighbors." That statement was accepted by President Reagan as meeting U.S. conditions, and on December 14 he formally announced that he had "authorized the State Department to enter into a substantive dialogue with PLO representatives." Israel, however, let it be known that it did not "recognize the PLO as a viable partner for negotiations."[65]

The broader, area-wide conflict, which in December 1988 Reagan acknowledged as evidence that "the Middle East . . . is still technically in a state of war," remained unresolved. Nevertheless, there were a few bright spots for the departing president. Iran and Iraq had finally acceded to UN Secretary General de Cuellar's plea for a halt in their nine-year war, Libya had called off its war with Chad, and the Soviet evacuation of Afghanistan was proceeding according to schedule. If Reagan could not take full credit for these events, he could at least assume that U.S. military intervention in each area had contributed to the ultimate exhaustion of the participants.

*   *   *   *   *

Even as the American public was reeling from the shock of the October 1983 bombing that killed U.S. Marines and sailors at the Beirut airport, the tiny Caribbean island of Grenada, population 87,000, was in the throes of a power struggle that had seen one prime minister assassinated. Washington had been aware of the character of the Grenada government ever since the communist New Jewel Movement took power in 1979 in a bloodless coup. Officials of the Reagan administration had been in touch with Grenada's neighbors and were fully prepared to act if and when an opportunity arose. The murder of Prime Minister Maurice Bishop and the subsequent crackdown by his successor, Bernard Coard, led Reagan to divert a ten-ship naval task force from its Lebanon destination to patrol the waters around Grenada. Two days of negotiations with Grenada's island neighbors produced a formal request from the Organization of Eastern Caribbean States (OECS) for assistance from the U.S. in "restoring order and democracy in Grenada."

The fact that Reagan did not seriously consider any alternative to military action is suggested by his 1982 reference to Grenada as a Cuban-Soviet base aimed at spreading the Marxist "virus" among its neighbors, and his March 1983 charge that Cuba's effort to make Grenada a "naval base [and] a superior air base" endangered U.S. national security.[66] Captured documents later revealed that Grenada's Marxist government had indeed signed agreements with the U.S.S.R., Czechoslovakia and North Korea to obtain free supplies of arms and ammunition. But in those documents—which included records of many government meetings, most of the discussions turned about ways and means of ingratiating the New Jewel Movement with other communist regimes, particularly the Soviet hierarchy. The few references to Grenada's military force had to do with organizing "the defense of the revolution in the face of qualitatively stepped up aggression from [U.S.] imperialism." At a central committee meeting of the NJM, held only a month before the American invasion, one member of the committee warned: "The small Caribbean islands are being driven into an alliance against Grenada and all the left organizations in the region."[67]

When the murder of Grenadian Prime Minister Maurice Bishop created a crisis, Reagan's most obvious first step was to consult with his British friends, as Grenada was a member of the British Commonwealth of Nations and Queen Elizabeth II, its official head of state. Reagan called the British prime minister, who not only refused to join in a military takeover, but argued strongly against any such action by the U.S. How seriously England regarded the proposed military assault is suggested by the queen's polite but succinct post-invasion public statement in which she pointed out that if Cuban influence was the real danger, although Cuba is much closer to the U.S. than Grenada, "you don't go into Cuba because you don't like Cuban attitudes. But you go into Grenada because Cuba is there."[68]

Undeterred, Reagan never considered the full implications of his decision to authorize military action, unlike his idol, Abraham Lincoln. Being ignorant of all but the most historic of that president's pronouncements, Reagan could never have read the advice Lincoln gave in response to his law partner's assertion that the president must be the sole judge of when to protect the U.S. by invading the territory of another country:

> Allow the president to invade a neighboring nation whenever *he* shall deem it necessary to repel an invasion, and you allow him to do so *whenever he may choose to say* he deems it necessary for such purpose—and you allow him to make war at pleasure. . . . If, today, he should choose to say he thinks it necessary to invade Canada, to prevent the British from invading us, how can you stop him? You may say to him, "I see no probability of the British invading us" but he will say to you "be silent; I see it, if you don't."[69]

Lincoln went on to remind his friend, William Herndon, that his view "places our President where kings have always stood."

In the case of Lebanon, Congress noted that the navy and Marines had acted in self-defense, which justified their engaging in acts of war. No such excuse applied to the Grenada invasion, which was first explained as America's response to "an urgent, formal request from five member nations of the Organization of Eastern Caribbean States to assist in a joint effort to restore order and democracy on the island of Grenada." Likening the assault to the Sinai and Lebanese situations by calling it "a multinational effort with contingents from Antigua, Barbados, Dominica, Jamaica, St. Lucia, St. Vincent and the United States," Reagan further misled his television audience by his reference to restoring democracy to Grenada.[70] His listening public was never informed—if, indeed, Reagan himself knew—that for 23 of the first 28 years after England agreed to the transition of Grenada from colonial status to an independent member of the Commonwealth, it was governed by Sir Eric Gairy, who, in the words of one observer, "headed a ruthless dictatorship in the mold of 'Papa Doc' Duvalier's in Haiti."[71]

Continuing his televised address to the nation, Reagan enlarged on the purposes of the invasion, saying that "American lives are at stake" and that his action was intended "to protect our own citizens, to facilitate the evacuation of those {medical students} who want to leave," as well as to restore Grenada's "democratic institutions." As to the threat posed by the island's Marxist regime, he said the government there was building an airport which "it claimed was for tourist trade, but which looked suspiciously suitable for military aircraft, including Soviet-built long-range bombers." Also, 600 Cubans posing as construction workers were really "a military force." Finally, he said, the 100 American citizens on Grenada were not able to get out and might have been harmed or held hostage.[72]

All of these statements proved false. Dr. Charles Modica, chancellor of the island's medical school, immediately challenged one of Reagan's assertions and testified that the Grenadian government had not only permitted the departure of 30 American students who decided to leave, but also promised protection for those who stayed and delivered water to the campus when the college reported that its supply was running low. By comparison, he said, when he telephoned the State Department for information about the announced invasion, he could not get any information that he could pass on to students and faculty.[73]

More inaccuracies in government reports came out day by day. Admiral Wesley L. McDonald's statement that there were 1,100 Cubans, "well-trained professional soldiers," on Grenada was corrected by the State Department's announcement that Cubans numbered only 784, as claimed by Cuba. Of these, the Pentagon confessed that "only about 100" could be classified as combatants.[74] The White House also acknowledged that the Grenada airport had not been closed to prevent people from leaving, as previously reported. President Reagan's claim that the invasion produced no civilian casualties proved erroneous when it was revealed that U.S. planes had bombed a mental hospital by mistake, killing at least 17 civilians. The three warehouses that Reagan said were stacked to the ceiling with enough weapons to supply thousands of terrorists, on examination were found to be only half full, and "many weapons were antiquated." These, and other examples of "official misinformation" were catalogued in a full-page report in the New York Times on November 6. Four months later, White House Spokesman Larry Speakes issued a written statement (no questions, please) that tourism would indeed be encouraged by the previously planned airport construction, and Washington would donate $19 million toward the cost of that project.[75]

The errors and inconsistencies in reports issued by the president and his military aides made little impression on American readers, the majority of whom were stirred by their leader's boldness in carrying the battle to a readily identifiable enemy and crushing the foe with a decisiveness never experienced since World War II. They accepted without question Reagan's assertion that his action "to protect innocent lives" was forced upon him "by events that have no precedent in the eastern Caribbean and no place in any civilized society."[76]

The press was irked at having been kept in the dark until after the landings had been completed, even though a report of the pending invasion appeared in British newspapers two days before the event. Larry Speakes much later acknowledged that when an American reporter, having read the British story, asked whether the U.S. was planning to invade Grenada. Speakes checked with NSC director Admiral Poindexter and then repeated to the reporter Poindexter's response: "Preposterous." Twenty-four hours later the landings began, unaccompanied by any reporters, who were refused a privilege never denied in any previous war. When Reagan chided the media for using the word invasion, insisting that this was a "rescue mission," the public sided with him again, showing little sympathy with media carping at the secrecy of the operation. And when NBC's John Chancellor aired reporters' complaints against the government's information blackout, he admitted later that letters to the network "ran 5 to 1 against his commentary."[77]

Few members of Congress were disturbed by anything except the news blackout, which kept them in the same state of ignorance as the general public. A court suit challenging the constitutionality of the president's action in ordering the invasion was supported by only 11 congressmen and was ultimately dismissed as moot because the action had ended. Otherwise, the Grenada conquest received the plaudits of Republicans and Democrats alike, and even House Speaker Tip O'Neill retracted his initial charge of "gunboat diplomacy."[78] The Senate paid its tribute in this declaration:

> It is the sense of the Senate that the United States Armed Forces engaged in military operations at Grenada are to be commended for their rescue of United States citizens of that island, and for their valor, success, and exemplary conduct in battle, which has been in the highest traditions of the military service.[79]

The army contributed to the cause by awarding 8,612 medals to the 7,000 officers and men who actually reached Grenada, as well as to support troops in bases within the U.S. or in the Pentagon.[80]

On one point Congress would not give way. Its view of presidential war power was expressed in a House resolution of October 26 which stated that "the requirement of section 4(a)(1) of the War Powers Resolution became operative on October 25, 1983, when United States Armed Forces were introduced into Grenada." President Reagan's messages to the speaker of the House and president of the Senate, if they mentioned the War Powers Act at all, invariably used the expression "consistent with the War Powers Resolution," rather than "in accordance with" that law, and just as invariably cited his constitutional power as commander in chief of the armed forces.[81] Ultimately, the administration endorsed William Herndon's 1848 view, restated by Assistant Secretary of State J. Edward Fox in this response to an inquiry from Congressman Fascell: "The determination as to whether those conditions [stipulated in the War Powers Resolution] exist is a matter for the President to decide, based on all the facts and circumstances as they would relate to the threat to U.S. forces at that time."[82] This despite a National War College study which acknowledged that the War Powers Resolution "states that the President's constitutional power to commit U.S. troops to actual or imminent hostilities is limited to a declared war, a specific statutory authorization, or a national emergency created by attack on the United States, its territories or possessions, or its armed forces."[83]

Abroad, the U.S. action found little support except from the OECS nations that had contributed 300 men to the invasion forces. A State Department release citing the OECS treaty, OAS and UN charter provisions for collective self-defense in justification was challenged not only by countries normally critical of American foreign policy but by NATO allies and key members of OAS, including Argentina, Bolivia, Colombia, Costa Rica, Peru and Venezuela.[84]

When the matter came before the UN Security Council, the U.S. was the only member to vote against a resolution which "called for the immediate withdrawal of the foreign troops," and "deplored the intervention as a violation of international law."[85] Of America's allies, only Great Britain abstained, while France, the Netherlands and Pakistan joined eight other council members in voting for the resolution. The United States' veto prevented the resolution from being adopted, but the state of world opinion had clearly been expressed, not only in the U.N. but also in the international press.[86]

Secure in the comfort of public approval at home, Reagan brushed off foreign criticism with the remark that "100 nations in the United Nations have not agreed with us on just about everything that's come before them where we're involved. And, you know, it didn't upset my breakfast at all."[87]

A year and eight months after their arrival, the last of the American invasion force departed Grenada, leaving behind a 30-man team to conduct a three-month training course for Caribbean security units. No subsequent evaluation of the new democracy was made by the Reagan administration, but some visitors were struck by the difficulty experienced by the island's newly elected officials in adjusting to democratic government.

One of two American reporters who had produced a highly praised documentary on the assassination of Prime Minister Bishop and the subsequent U.S. invasion returned to Grenada in April 1984 to cover the trial of Bernard Coard and his accomplices and to gather information for a documentary on the new Grenada. When he undertook to investigate the police shooting of a 17-year-old boy, he was expelled from the country on grounds of "national security"—a decision made by the island's police commissioner.[88] Another American observer reported that the court in which Coard was tried was "self-confessedly unconstitutional," and that the prisoners had been subjected to "savage beatings" and denied their constitutional right to legal consultation and to appeal to the island's Privy Court.[89] In 1987 Grenada's prime minister, in what *Newsweek* described as "a burst of censorship reminiscent of Grenada's previous left-wing rulers," decided that "politically sensitive" songs would not be permitted to be broadcast from the country's one and only (government-owned) radio station.[90]

Admittedly, six years is too brief a period in which to judge the ability of a country unaccustomed to democratic ways to adapt to so different a concept of government. However, Washington's apparent indifference to Grenada's progress, or lack thereof, is disturbingly reminiscent of its attitude toward Guatemala after the CIA had deposed a far less radical government than that of Bernard Coard. As one CIA agent of that earlier period commented, instead of exerting diplomatic pressure to assure that the new regime performed as expected, "Washington breathed a collective sigh of relief and turned to other international problems."[91]

CHAPTER 12

Commander in Chief, but Not in Charge

"I'm trying to find out, too, what happened {in the Iran-Contra affair}."[1]

IF THE HUMBLING OF LIBYA AND CONQUEST OF GRENADA REPRESENT Reagan's greatest domestic victories as a commander in chief, his dealings with Iran and Nicaragua all but destroyed his credibility as a latter-day crusader. His loathing for the Nicaraguan Ortega government stemmed from the revulsion he felt for communism generally. Khomeini's regime in Iran he regarded as the instrument of unprincipled and barbaric terrorists. He was happy to be the beneficiary of the Iranian chief's decision to release the American hostages who had been imprisoned in the U.S. embassy in Teheran for the last 14 months of President Carter's administration, but his approach was one of action. When it came his turn to deal with a hostage situation, his chief of staff wrote, "he would say why can't we just get somebody to lead a group in there and storm their installation and take them?"[2]

* * * * *

In Central America, the Reagan program began as a system of aid to anti-communist Nicaraguan rebels and the governments of El Salvador and Honduras. However, the direct participation of U.S. diplomatic, military and paramilitary personnel in resupply, training, and overt hostilities like the mining of Nicaraguan harbors, ultimately marked this as an undeclared war against a country with which the U.S. continued to maintain diplomatic relations. This, together with U.S. involvement in El Salvador's civil war, revived fears of another Vietnam, a fear the Reagan administration hoped to allay by adopting an approach which four lieutenant colonels in the U.S. Army have described this way:

The essence of that approach has been to provide a besieged ally with weapons, ammunition, and other equipment, economic aid, intelligence support, strategic counsel, and tactical training—while preserving the principle that the war remains ultimately *theirs* to win or lose.[3]

While the focus of attention in the U.S. was always on the war against Nicaragua, these military observers of the El Salvador conflict pointed out that American intervention in Honduras and El Salvador was likely to exacerbate the age-old antagonism between those two Central American countries.[4] If they were critical of U.S. policy in "small wars," it was because they believed that "great powers will likely find that overall they have more to lose than to gain from the outcome of the struggle." Nevertheless, they agreed with President Reagan that there is no substitute for victory. "Once having decided to use force to gain its ends, the United States needs to abandon 'business as usual' and to *commit* itself to winning."[5]

For most Americans the implications of other Central American rivalries were lost in the continuous, often heated debate over U.S. policy toward Nicaragua. In that context, two issues stand out: the contest between the president and Congress, and the U.S. position in international law.

Congressional attitudes toward administration policy in Central America wavered back and forth, influenced by events in that area as well as by the information—and disinformation—supplied to Congress and the general public by the White House, the NSC and CIA. Much of the opposition to Reagan's policies arose out of an inherent dislike of covert military operations and political intrigue as tools of democratic government. The reluctance to approve such operations did not extend to undercover activity in the gathering of information about other governments' aims and plans, or in efforts to intercept and break coded diplomatic and military messages that might reveal the objectives and tactics of other governments. The most anti-administration member of Congress never challenged the president's right—even obligation—to authorize these means of discovering potential threats to the welfare of the U.S. However, Reagan's obvious preference for the use of military and intelligence forces in lieu of the diplomatic service in dealing with "unfriendly" countries aroused a great deal of opposition in the legislature. As the earlier discussion of Grenada and the ABM Treaty interpretation demonstrated, it also raised the question of how far the commander in chief could go in using military forces abroad without crossing the line established by federal law in 1973, when Congress overrode President Nixon's veto of its War Powers Resolution.[6]

To demonstrate that the intent of Congress was to prevent *any* executive effort to overthrow a government with which the U.S. was at peace, in June 1987 Democratic Representative Bill Alexander asked the Library of Congress to assemble from the records of Congress all except closed-door debate on the Boland amendments (named after Edward P. Boland, chairman of the House Permanent Select Committee on Intelligence, who authored amendments to bills authorizing defense and intelligence activities). Unable to include discussions held in secret, Alexander nevertheless pointed out that, prior to the first secret session held to hear administration arguments against the Boland amendment, "the assertion that the law enacted in the Boland amendment did not apply to the President or the National Security Council [was] conspicuously absent." On the contrary, he said, the Republican floor manager of the debate declared that the administration strongly opposed the Boland amendment "because it severely restricts the President's ability to conduct an effective foreign policy in Central America."[7]

The earliest efforts to head off a leftward turn in Nicaragua were conducted by Assistant Secretary of State Thomas O. Enders. The diplomatic correspondence of the 1980s will not be published until the year 2000, at the earliest,[8] but reporters occasionally were successful in ferreting out information about the State Department's confidential negotiations with Nicaraguan officials. By December 1981, it was known that these negotiations could not bridge the gap between U.S. fear of a Marxist-oriented government infiltrating neighboring Central American countries, and Nicaraguan fear of U.S. proposals, which Ortega described as opening a door "so small that in order to pass through it we would have to do it on our knees."[9]

What the news stories did not reveal in 1981 was that a covert operation to build an anti-Sandinista force had been put into place by the CIA even before Reagan took office. This was expanded enthusiastically by Reagan's CIA director, William Casey, whose objective was to build the FDN (Nicaraguan Democratic Forces), which in July 1982 the U.S. Defense Intelligence Agency estimated to consist of only "800 activists," into an army capable of overthrowing the Sandinista government.[10] Casey reinforced his agency's organizing activity with a propaganda campaign whereby reporters were paid to write anti-Sandinista stories for Central American newspapers.[11] Within the U.S., a Casey protege, Walter Raymond, Jr., was assigned to the National Security Council to develop a "public diplomacy" program to sell administration policy to the American people.[12] Meanwhile, Washington turned a blind eye to news reports that "Nicaraguan and Cuban exiles were openly (and in clear violation of international law) training in paramilitary camps in Florida and elsewhere, with the objective of 'liberating' their homelands."[13]

By early 1982, journalistic suspicions had been aroused sufficiently to prompt questions at the president's press conferences. Asked in February whether he had approved "covert activity to destabilize the present government of Nicaragua," Reagan replied, "This is something upon which the national security interest—I will not comment." When the question was rephrased to inquire about his policy on covert operations to destabilize any government anywhere, his answer again was, "No comment."[14] Later that month he introduced what was to be the theme of his Nicaraguan policy for the remainder of his presidency. Addressing the Organization of American States (OAS), he declared: "Nicaragua has served as a platform for covert military action. Through Nicaragua, arms are being smuggled to guerrillas in El Salvador and Guatemala." Citing the Rio Treaty of 1947 as authority for U.S. intervention under what he called "reciprocal defense responsibilities," he nevertheless promised, "We will not, however, follow Cuba's lead in attempting to resolve human problems by brute force."[15]

The public record of congressional action on the administration's Central American policy—which contains "no excerpts from any relevant classified reports or non-public debate"—was outlined in the *Congressional Record* as follows:

> Congress began in 1982 to restrict intelligence support for the insurgents or contras, in a series of provisions known as the Boland Amendments. The first legislative restriction . . . which barred support for the purpose of overthrowing the Sandinistas or of provoking a confrontation between Nicaragua and Honduras, later was enacted as statutory language in the FY 83 Defense Appropriation Act. The FY 83 restriction was followed by a $24 million cap for FY 84 on all intelligence agency support of military or paramilitary operations in Nicaragua. . . . Congress initially barred use of any intelligence agency funds during FY 85 for assisting the contras, subject to authority to expend funds upon issuance of certain presidential findings and subsequent congressional approval. Toward the end of FY 85, however, Congress appropriated $27 million for humanitarian assistance. . . . Meanwhile, the general restriction against intelligence agency expenditures in support of the contras' military or paramilitary efforts was extended through FY 86 by the intelligence authorization for that year. In early FY 87 Congress made a significant amount of money [$100 million] available to support the contras. At the same time, Congress has continued a requirement that all intelligence agency support of the contras be specifically authorized by law or made in accordance with specified spending provisions.[16]

The absolute ban on the use of FY 1983 defense appropriations for furnishing military equipment, military training or advice to the Contras[17] did not stifle Reagan's campaign to bring down the Sandinista government. In February 1983 the U.S. and Honduras joined forces to conduct military maneuvers close to Nicaragua's northern border. This led 75 members of the House of Representatives to send President Reagan a letter of protest against what they saw as "a pattern of escalating U.S. military involvement in the area."[18] Unfazed by this criticism, Reagan approved repeated military and naval exercises near or off the coast of Nicaragua, always insisting that the practice was "routine" and "traditional." Periodic charges of massive aid to Nicaragua from Cuba and the Soviet Union, some documented, some not, were used by Reagan to coax Congress into relaxing the ban on military assistance to the Contras. By 1988, however, congressional acceptance of the repeated charge that Nicaragua was supplying arms to Marxist rebels in El Salvador had reached its limit, and the president was denied funds for anything but food, clothing and medical supplies.[19]

Meanwhile, at the insistence of Costa Rica's Nobel Peace Prize winner, President Oscar Arias, Contra and Sandinista leaders agreed in March 1988 to a cease-fire and peace negotiations. Initially, concessions by both sides gave hope of a final agreement. However, after CIA-backed Colonel Enrique Bermudez, of Somoza's National Guard, assumed control of the Contras' political arm (he was already in charge of the largest Contra military force), he introduced new demands that were unacceptable to the Nicaraguan government.[20] Washington's attempt to obtain from all Central American countries except Nicaragua agreement on a communique that one U.S. official characterized as "a virtual declaration of war" was rebuffed by both Costa Rica and Guatemala. Nevertheless, the administration renewed its overt propaganda and covert aid to the Contras in a deliberate effort "to provoke Sandinistas" into overreacting.[21] The effort failed, but so did the attempt to reach a permanent solution to the conflict, and the year ended with both sides marking time, awaiting a signal from the incoming administration of President George Bush.

Throughout his campaign against Nicaragua, Reagan argued that his actions were in accordance with international law and the concept of collective self-defense under the Rio Treaty.[22] This position was suspect from the start, but three specific actions by agents of the CIA laid the foundation for a Nicaraguan appeal to the International Court of Justice to rule on Managua's charges that "in recruiting, training, arming, equipping, financing, supplying and otherwise encouraging, supporting, aiding and directing military and paramilitary actions in and against Nicaragua" the U.S. was violating the UN charter's injunction against the threat or use of force against any state, and that it had broken other international agreements, including its 1956 Treaty of Friendship, Commerce and Navigation with Nicaragua.[23]

In 1983 the CIA planned, directed, and supplied equipment for a Contra raid on oil terminals in several Nicaraguan cities. That same year the CIA supplied the Contras with a manual titled *Operationes Sicologicas en Guerra de Guerrillas* (Psychological Operations in Guerrilla Warfare) which included a section on "Selective Use of Violence for Propagandistic Effects." That section instructed the Contras on the "extreme precautions" needed to neutralize carefully selected and planned targets, such as court judges, *mesta* judges, police and state security officials, CDS chiefs, etc." In January 1984, the CIA planned and directed the mining of Nicaraguan harbors, resulting in damage to Dutch, Panamanian and Soviet vessels as well as two Nicaraguan fishing boats.[24]

Extensive hearings by the World Court confirmed what American journalists and members of Congress were learning bit by bit: that the CIA was the controlling agency behind all three of the operations mentioned previously.[25] Subsequent investigations by the Tower Commission and the Iran-Contra Committee revealed the extent to which President Reagan had supported every phase of the war against Nicaragua, except the use of money from arms sales to Iran.

The U.S. participated in the World Court action only long enough to contest the court's right to take jurisdiction in the matter. When that challenge was rejected by the court—in a unanimous decision that included the vote of U.S. judge Stephen M. Schwebel—the U.S. withdrew from the proceedings and President Reagan declared that he was terminating this country's 1946 agreement to accept the court's compulsory jurisdiction in such cases.[26]

Legal justification for abandoning a system which the U.S. had been happy to use in successfully pressing its earlier charge of hostage-taking against Iran came from State Department advisor Abraham D. Sofaer.[27] "The chief factor motivating the administration's review of our [1946] acceptance of the Court's jurisdiction," Sofaer told a House committee, "was indeed our experience with the Nicaragua case." And the reason for terminating that agreement, he said, was "what the court did with [the] arguments presented to it."[28] Having withdrawn from the case, U.S. attorneys were not present when the court examined evidence which led it to reject their plea of "collective self-defense," and to conclude that U.S. actions were "in breach of its obligation under customary international law not to intervene in the affairs of another state."[29]

A critical element in the court's consideration of the merits of the case was the testimony of a disillusioned former political leader of the Nicaraguan Democratic Force (FDN) and a former CIA employee. Edgar Chamorro, until 1984 a stalwart supporter of the Contras, submitted an affidavit from which the court drew the following conclusions:

> The FDN came into being as a coalition of political opposition groups and an armed force called the 15th of September Legion "through mergers arranged by the CIA." In 1982, former Somozista National Guardsmen in exile (most of them in the U.S.) were offered regular salaries from the CIA, and from then on arms, ammunition, equipment and food were supplied by the CIA. When he

worked full time for the FDN, he himself received a salary from the CIA, as did other FDN directors.

The court's report went on to describe the specific attacks made by Contras "acting on the direct instructions of U.S. military or intelligence personnel." After the mine-laying incident, in which Chamorro said the FDN played no role, "he was instructed by a CIA official to issue a press release over the clandestine radio on 5 January 1984 claiming that the FDN had mined several Nicaraguan harbors."[30]

As for the manual on psychological warfare, the CIA later admitted this "error in judgment." However, it failed to mention that 2,000 of the 5,000 pamphlets distributed to members of the FDN were modified to delete two pages containing these paragraphs:

> If possible, professional criminals will be hired to carry out specific selective "jobs."
>
> Specific tasks will be assigned to others, in order to create a "martyr" for the cause, taking the demonstrators to a confrontation with the authorities, in order to bring about uprising or shootings, which will cause the death of one or more persons, who would become martyrs, a situation that should be made use of immediately against the regime, in order to create greater conflicts.[31]

The testimony of former CIA employee David MacMichael was directed principally to the U.S. charge that ever since the Sandinistas had come to power, Nicaragua had funnelled arms to Marxist rebels in El Salvador. Acknowledging that there was evidence of such traffic from late 1980 to early 1981, when he worked "for the most part on inter-American affairs" for the CIA, he said that the agency detected no traffic in arms from Nicaragua to El Salvador.[32]

Based on all the evidence available to it, the court in June 1986 found the U.S. guilty of violating international law and its treaty with Nicaragua, of encouraging "acts contrary to the general principles of humanitarian law," and obligated to pay reparations for its breach of treaties. On most counts, the vote was 12 to 3, British and Japanese judges joining U.S. judge Schwebel in the minority, and the Soviet judge being absent. The decision calling for reparations for breach of the Treaty of Friendship, Commerce and Navigation between the U.S. and Nicaragua was opposed only by Schwebel.[33]

Having lost the 1984 contest over the court's jurisdiction, President Reagan gave notice on May 1, 1985, that the treaty with Nicaragua would be terminated effective May 1, 1986.[34] Thereafter, U.S. participation in the Nicaraguan civil war took a turn which ultimately involved the presidential office in a pattern of skullduggery that came closer to undermining the American constitutional system than Watergate had done a decade earlier.

* * * * *

As in Nicaragua, the impact of an American presence in Iran was felt long before Reagan entered the White House. Post-World War II turmoil in Iran centered about a contest between Shah Mohammed Reza Pahlavi and a nationalist coalition intent on eliminating foreign control over Iranian resources and institutions.[35] When the Iranian parliament (*majlis*) voted to nationalize the British-owned Anglo-Iranian Oil Company, the shah fought that decision, then fled to avoid retribution. Certain that this meant a Soviet takeover, President Eisenhower's secretary of state, John Foster Dulles, and his brother, CIA director Allen Dulles, devised a scheme for putting the shah back on the throne. In August 1953 "Kermit Roosevelt, with a handful of aides and a suitcase full of money" bought enough support from Iranian army officers, politicians, and street mobs to topple the nationalist government and restore the shah to the throne.[36]

The CIA mission was completely successful. But for all Roosevelt's vaunted expertise in Iranian affairs, he badly misjudged the strength of the shah's religious opponents. Writing about his Iranian adventure in 1979, when the revolt that put Ayatollah Ruhollah Khomeini into power was already under way, Roosevelt made no mention of that fact or of Khomeini.[37]

The November 3, 1979 capture of the American embassy in Teheran, and the inability of the Carter administration to free the resulting hostages, brought bitter criticism from presidential candidate Ronald Reagan. All Carter had to do, he said, was to "stand up and stand beside the shah's government and there wouldn't have been a successful revolution."[38]

After assuming the presidency, Reagan refused to commit himself to any specific stand on Iran, limiting his early remarks to a 1981 warning that "when the rules of international behavior are violated, our policy will be one of swift and effective retribution." Yet when a reporter reminded him that there were three non-embassy Americans still being held hostage in Iran, Reagan's only comment was that he knew about them and had "told our people about them." Pressed about retribution, he requested "forbearance . . . until we've finished our study of this whole situation." No study results were ever announced, but as late as 1983 the president was still referring to the 1978–79 Teheran hostage crisis as "the most degrading symbol" of America's pre-Reagan deterioration as a world power.[39]

As the 1987 Tower Commission report indicated, U.S. relations with Iran during the Reagan administration were complicated by several factors. One was the bitter aftermath of the embassy hostage-taking, during which diplomatic relations were severed and economic sanctions were adopted to cut off practically all trade with Iran. In the same 1979–80 period, the Soviet Union invaded Iran's neighbor Afghanistan, and Iraq attacked Iran, opening a war that was to last through the entire Reagan presidency. When an international claims commission was established to arbitrate monetary disputes between the U.S. and Iran, some economic sanctions were lifted; but an absolute embargo on arms shipment to Iran remained in effect.[40]

It was the arms embargo that proved to be the stumbling block that tripped the president and brought into the open the nature of his attitude toward the presidency, the Congress, and his responsibilities to the American people. For, long before the notion of diverting Iranian money to the Contras became a reality, Reagan's representatives were arranging—with his approval—arms shipments to Iran that were in direct violation of the embargo and the law which explicitly forbade supplying arms to any country found to be a source of international terrorism. This occurred in the face of evidence that "Iran had played a role in hijackings and bombings, notably the bombings of the American Embassy and of the Marine barracks in Beirut on October 23, 1983," actions which led to the formal designation of Iran as a sponsor of international terrorism.[41]

In 1984, studies conducted by the National Security Council and CIA stressed the strength of Soviet influence in Iran and the danger that this posed to U.S. interests.[42] There is little doubt that this was a major factor in President Reagan's decision to reject the advice of Secretary of State Shultz and Defense Secretary Weinberger and adopt a proposal from NSC which was described by its drafters as "a vigorous policy designed to block Soviet advances in the short-term while building our leverage in Iran and trying to restore the U.S. position which existed under the Shah over the longer-term." Put into the form of a National Security Decision Directive (NSDD), the first draft, sent to State and Defense departments for comment, drew caustic criticism from both Shultz and Weinberger.

Shultz flatly opposed the suggested policy. His criticism focused on two points: the exaggerated estimate of Soviet influence in Iran, and the disastrous effect of encouraging arms deliveries to that country. He reminded Robert C. McFarlane—then head of NSC—that under the shah "Iranian-Soviet relations were closer and more cooperative than they are now."

Weinberger's comments were even more blunt. Testifying before the Review Board, he said his initial reaction to the proposed NSDD was to write "absurd" in the margin. "I also added that this is roughly like inviting Qaddafi over for a cozy lunch." In his formal reply to McFarlane, Weinberger had written: "Under no circumstances . . . should we now ease our restriction on arms sales to Iran. [Such a] policy reversal would be seen as inexplicably inconsistent by those nations whom we have urged to refrain from such sales."[43]

These protests, registered in June and July of 1985, failed to convince the president, although they delayed the redrafting of the NSDD for some six months. Meanwhile, he may have drawn encouragement from an Israeli inquiry asking "if the United States would approve an arms shipment to Iran" from that country, and from a CIA officer's suggestion that arms from "friendly states" might convince Iran "that it had alternatives to the Soviet Union."[44]

More significant to the president was the possibility of using arms as an incentive to Iran to order the release of American hostages held in Lebanon. When the president gave the green light to a further investigation of that idea, Shultz agreed to opening a dialogue if it did not include the offer of arms.[45] The president later acknowledged that "sometime in August [1985], he approved the shipment of arms by Israel to Iran . . . also the replenishment [by the U.S.] of any arms transferred by Israel to Iran."[46] Subsequently, when asked whether he assented to the Israeli shipments before or after they were made, Reagan offered one of his nonexplanations, saying, "I don't remember." After Israel had delivered more than 500 TOWs (Tube-launched, Optically-tracked, Wire-guided missiles), a single hostage—the Reverend Benjamin Weir—was released.

Disappointed that the remaining five American hostages had not been set free, McFarlane next approved a plan devised by Lieutenant Colonel Oliver North calling for Israel to deliver 80 HAWK missiles to Iran, with another 40 scheduled for later delivery. Again, the president's memory of this event was hazy. First he told the Review Board that "he objected to the shipment, and that, as a result . . . the shipment was returned to Israel." A month later, he testified that he could not remember "any meeting or conversation in general about a HAWK shipment [or] anything about a callback of HAWKS."[47] In fact, an initial shipment of 18 HAWKS had been made without the president's approval, had been found by Iran not to meet its requirements, and had been returned for that reason.

North continued to press his arms-for-hostages plan, making greater headway after McFarlane resigned and was replaced as National Security Adviser by Vice Admiral John M. Poindexter in December 1985. A meeting with the president on December 7 opened the door to the direct sale of weapons by the U.S. to Iran. Attended by Shultz, Weinberger, Regan, McFarlane and Poindexter, the conference was conducted without a formal agenda, with no preparatory paper, no minutes, and in such secrecy that Poindexter asked Shultz—a known opponent of North's plan—not to show the appointment on his calendar.[48] Although the only agreement reached was to send McFarlane to London to convey to Iranian businessman Manuchehr Ghorbanifar the United States' interest in getting the hostages freed without offering arms in exchange, North was suspected of having followed his own course in talking privately with Ghorbanifar.

Meanwhile, CIA Deputy Director John McMahon had learned of his agency's part in the November shipment of HAWKS and requested a presidential finding to justify the action. He pointed out that whenever the CIA became involved in such covert operations, the law required a finding that the operations were "important to the national security of the U.S." The initial finding was drafted by CIA counsel Stanley Sporkin and was forwarded to Poindexter by director William Casey. Rewritten by North, it was submitted to the president for his signature January 6, 1986 and again, after minor modification, on January 17.[49] Incredibly, President Reagan told his Review Board the following January that he did not recall signing the January 6 finding. He did, however, remember putting his name to a slightly revised version on January 17, having received it with a three-page explanatory memorandum from Poindexter, which Reagan told the board "he was briefed on . . . but did not read"![50]

The terms of the finding were striking, not only in their content but in the naivete of their underlying assumptions. The document's declared purpose was to "establish relationships with Iranian elements, groups, and individuals sympathetic to U.S. government interests and which do not conduct or support terrorist actions against U.S. persons, property or interests." In a second paragraph these groups and individuals were referred to as "moderate elements within and outside the Government of Iran." From these people the U.S. expected three things: establishment of a "more moderate government," intelligence regarding the Khomeini government's intentions with respect to its neighbors and acts of terrorism, and release of the American hostages held in Beirut. These objectives were to be attained, not through direct action or negotiation by U.S. officials, but through "friendly foreign liaison services, third countries and third parties." Translated, this meant allied intelligence organizations, Israel, and such trusted friends of democracy as Ghorbanifar and retired general Richard V. Secord.[51]

Exercising his extraordinary power of self-delusion, Reagan clung, to the bitter end, to the notion that all of the finding's goals could be reached by working with Iranian "moderates." The cold fact, as CIA Deputy Director McMahon advised the president and others at the December 7, 1985 White House meeting, was that "we had no knowledge of any moderates in Iran, that most of the moderates had been slaughtered when Khomeini took over."[52] Further, the most simple-minded observer had to realize that only the Khomeini government could be the controlling party in negotiations to receive arms and to force the release of hostages.

When Admiral Poindexter took over from McFarlane as national security advisor, North's involvement in the Iranian affair increased. The first suggestion that the U.S. would ship arms directly to Iran instead of through Israel came in a December 9, 1985 memorandum from North to Poindexter.[53] Also, under Poindexter, North continued to use Ghorbanifar in negotiations with Teheran, notwithstanding the latter's reputation as a self-serving manipulator, and despite his having failed a lie-detector test administered by the CIA.[54]

With the signing of the January 17, 1986 finding, the U.S. became a direct supplier of arms to what it had officially designated as a terrorist government. As if this were not a sufficient breach of statutory law and moral commitment to America's allies, the availability of funds from the sale of weapons to Iran led Colonel North to consider bypassing the U.S. Treasury and using that money to support the Contras in Central America.

Through the spring and early summer of 1986, North attempted to carry out what he called Operation Rescue, a pure arms-for-hostages deal with Iran, in which he was the man in charge and Poindexter was his source of authority and unquestioning supporter. The character of North's operation is best described by his February 18 memorandum to Poindexter, in which he reported the delivery of 500 TOWs with 3,000 more to follow if the hostages were released. In his suggested negotiating team, he himself would represent the "office of the president," Richard Secord would pretend to be U.S. "director of current intelligence," and Secord's business associate Albert Hakim would pose as Secord's assistant and would translate for the group. In a subsequent note, North identified Hakim as "an AMCIT [American citizen] who runs the European operation for our Nicaraguan support activity."[55]

Despite North's failure to secure the release of any additional hostages, McFarlane, now the president's special envoy to the Middle East, was so impressed with North's efforts that he wrote "Ollie," saying, "If the world only knew how many times you have kept a semblance of integrity and gumption to U.S. policy, they would make you Secretary of State. But they can't know and would complain if they did—such is the state of democracy in the late 20th century."[56] President Reagan felt the same way about the place of secrecy in a democracy, for when McFarlane was called upon in May to join the negotiating team, "the president directed that the press not be told about the trip."

Like North before him, McFarlane told the Iranians that he represented the president. Claiming the status of "a Minister," he demanded to speak to an Iranian official of equal rank. Otherwise, he said, "you can work with my staff." Like North, he went home empty-handed.[57]

*   *   *   *   *

On November 3, 1986, the day that the Iran-Contra scheme was blown wide open by a report in the Lebanese magazine *Al Shiraa* that the U.S. had been supplying arms to Iran, Americans were rejoicing at the news that hostage David Jacobson had been released by the Islamic Jihad. Although the release made headlines across the nation, the small print explained that while Jacobson was the third hostage to be freed, in the 13 months since the first hostage was released three others had been taken, leaving six Americans in terrorist hands: the same number as when bargaining with Iran had begun.[58] A few days later, a reporter managed to slip into a bill-signing ceremony the question, "Do we have a deal going with Iran?" The president's answer was, "No comment." But he added, "The speculation, the commenting and all, on a story that came out of the Middle East . . . has no foundation."[59]

This denial, and those of his staff over the weeks that followed, could not stem the avalanche of conjecture that had been started by *Al Shiraa*. As reporters scrambled about looking for the story behind the Beirut report, the head of Iran's parliament announced that McFarlane and four other Americans had been in Iran "on a secret diplomatic mission." This, the *Washington Post* said, was acknowledged to be true by "U.S. intelligence sources." Day by day, as these intelligence sources continued to leak information, the story of the secret negotiations was pieced together—including the protests registered by Shultz and Weinberger.[60]

By November 11, with Congress clamoring for a response from the administration, Admiral Poindexter was ready to admit to a few members of the Senate and House that the planning group in the White House had made "a miscalculation on who it could trust in Iran." The White House refused to reveal any details of the operation, but reporters had a field day gathering statements made previously by U.S. officials who had assured the public that a license to export aircraft or spare parts to Iran would not be granted "as long as the Iranian regime continues in its present hostile policies"; the U.S. was "making substantial efforts to diminish the flow of arms to Iran from free world sources as a means to induce Iran to end the fighting" with Iraq; and, "as long as Iran advocates the use of terrorism, the U.S. arms embargo will continue."[61]

By November 13, the volume of information unearthed by the media, here and abroad, impelled President Reagan to address the subject publicly. On that date, reading from a prepared script, he told a nationwide radio and television audience that in place of the stories "attributed to Danish sailors, unnamed observers in Italian ports and Spanish harbors, and especially unnamed government officials in my administration," the country was "going to hear the facts from a White House source, and you know my name." His exposition of the facts opened with this paragraph:

For 18 months now we have had underway a secret diplomatic initiative to Iran. That initiative was undertaken for the simplest and best of reasons: to renew a relationship with the nation of Iran, to bring an honorable end to the bloody 6-year war between Iran and Iraq, to eliminate state-sponsored terrorism and subversion, and to effect the safe return of all hostages.[62]

As an expression of administrative intent, that statement could not be challenged. However, what followed was this succession of half-truths, distortions and outright lies:

The charge has been made that the United States has shipped weapons to Iran as ransom payment for the release of American hostages in Lebanon, that the United States undercut its allies and secretly violated American policy against trafficking with terrorists. Those charges are utterly false. Other reports have surfaced . . . of the U.S. sending spare parts and weapons for combat aircraft . . . not one of them is true.

I authorized the transfer of small amounts of defensive weapons and spare parts for defensive systems to Iran. . . . These modest deliveries, taken together, could easily fit into a single cargo plane.

Some progress has already been made. . . . Hostages have come home, and we welcome the efforts that the Government of Iran has taken in the past and is currently undertaking. Although the efforts we undertook were highly sensitive, and involvement of government officials was limited to those with a strict need to know, all appropriate Cabinet officers were fully consulted. The actions I authorized were, and continue to be, in full compliance with Federal law. And the relevant committees of Congress are being, and will be, fully informed. Our government has a firm policy not to capitulate to terrorist demands. . . . We did not—repeat—did not trade weapons or anything else for hostages nor will we.

In the week that followed this explanation of the Iranian initiative, reporters learned of the coincidence of arms shipments and the release of hostages, which occurred in this sequence:

September 14, 1985, first plane-load of arms delivered from Israel; September 15, Reverend Benjamin Weir set free. July 4, 1986, second delivery; July 26, Father Lawrence Jenco freed. October 29, 1986, third shipment; November 2, David Jacobson released.[63]

Also revealed was the fact that President Reagan had authorized arms shipments in the secret memorandum (finding) dated January 17, 1986, and had instructed the CIA not to inform congressional oversight committees of these shipments.[64]

These revelations occupied most reporters at the president's news conference on November 19. Responding to a question about his credibility "in light of the prolonged deception of Congress and the public in terms of your secret dealings with Iran," Reagan said "there was no deception intended." Claiming the legal right to defer informing Congress of covert activities until he believed it could be done safely, Reagan ignored the obvious fact that he would not have disclosed the Iranian deal, even after 18 months, if it had not been made public in Lebanon. Instead he asserted—as though he had arrived at a decision independently of the publicity—"That's why I have ordered in this coming week the proper committees will be briefed on this."[65] Every other question produced a denial of error or culpability, including the overtly false statement that "we did not condone and do not condone the shipment of arms from other countries." On that last point, a hurried correction was issued shortly after the press conference to explain that there had been a "misunderstanding" about the assurance that no other countries had participated in the delivery of arms, as "there was a third country involved in our secret project with Iran."[66]

It took almost three weeks for President Reagan to be convinced that only a formal inquiry into the handling of the Iranian initiative would satisfy both the media and the general public. His first move in that direction was to announce that he had instructed Attorney General Meese to look into the matter. In his briefing of reporters Reagan took occasion to let them know that Meese's four-day preliminary inquiry led him to conclude that "I was not fully informed on the nature of one of the activities undertaken in connection with the initiative." Reagan made it clear that only the implementation of the plan was flawed, but he refused to explain the nature of the flaw, or that the plan itself had been a mistake. Yet his simultaneous announcement that both Admiral Poindexter and Colonel North had been relieved—not fired ("No one was let go. They chose to go.")—attested to the seriousness of the flaw.[67]

An explanation of the one subject on which the president had not been fully informed was left to Attorney General Meese, who revealed on November 19 that some of the millions of dollars paid by Iran for American weapons had been diverted to support the Contras in Central America.[68]

For a thorough investigation, Reagan appointed a special board "to review past implementation of administration policies and to conduct a comprehensive study of the future role and procedures of the National Security Council's staff in foreign and national security policy." He assured the three-man board—Senator John Tower, former Secretary of State Edmund Muskie, and General Brent Scowcroft—that he wanted "all the facts to come out." He promised the board that it would have "the full cooperation of all agencies of the executive branch and the White House staff." In that announcement Reagan also opened the door to the possibility that an independent counsel might be appointed to deal with any serious transgressions found by the board. The very next day he advised the American people in a brief televised message that, at the suggestion of Attorney General Meese, he had authorized the appointment of an independent counsel "to look into allegations of illegality in the sale of arms to Iran and the use of funds from these sales to assist the forces opposing the Sandinista Government in Nicaragua."

Although the phrasing of the directive to the independent counsel appeared to acknowledge as facts the sale of arms to Iran and the diversion of Iranian funds to the Contras, Reagan's only specific instruction was to determine whether or not those transactions were illegal. Yet a year after leaving the White House, when forced to testify in the trial of Admiral Poindexter, he made this statement in a formal deposition given orally before federal judge Harold H. Greene:

> I had no knowledge then or now that there had been a diversion, and I never used the term. And all I knew was that there was some money that came from some place in another [Swiss bank] account, and that the appearance was that it might have been part of the negotiated sale [of arms to Iran].

In his 1990 deposition Reagan repeated much of what he had told his Review Board, insisting as he had earlier that he could not remember some of the key meetings and discussions he had conducted with his national security adviser, secretary of state, secretary of defense and other senior aides. Asked about specific meetings with Poindexter to discuss the Iranian initiative, his response on so many occasions was "I can't remember," or "I don't recall," that at one point he felt obliged to explain his poor memory in terms of the great number of people he had to meet and talk with, day after day. However, when questioned about statements that McFarlane had made to congressional investigating committees and had later admitted were false, Reagan not only denied authorizing any deception but stated flatly, "I don't think any false statements were made." Faced with documentary evidence that McFarlane had falsely claimed that no support for military activity in Nicaragua had been provided by the NSC staff, and that the president had been given proof of the falsity of McFarlane's claim, Reagan three times evaded admitting that he recognized that McFarland had lied—even when the question was put to him by Judge Greene. Such was President Reagan's contribution to the search for truth in the Iran-Contra affair. [69]

*　*　*　*　*

Diversion of funds paid by Iran for American weapons was only one of Oliver North's ideas for supporting the Contras, but it was clearly the most illegal of his various schemes for overthrowing the Sandinista government. He also arranged for a secret bank account to be opened in Geneva, Switzerland, to receive donations to the Contra cause from other countries. However, the president's Review Board had to learn about these maneuvers from such dissembling members of the Reagan administration as Assistant Secretary of State for Inter-American Affairs Elliot Abrams. Both North and Poindexter declined the board's invitation to testify as to their part in the Iran-Contra affair. Having been given no authority to subpoena witnesses, the board was powerless to compel their attendance. And President Reagan, who had announced publicly that the board would have "full and complete access to the NSC staff," refused to direct North and Poindexter to answer its questions. Rejecting board chairman John Tower's request that, in his capacity as commander in chief, the president order North and Poindexter to cooperate, Reagan left his legal staff to reply. Counsel Peter J. Wallison did so, informing Tower that while the president wanted North and Poindexter to "cooperate fully with all on-going inquiries," he recognized that their "constitutional right not to testify . . . must be respected even when its assertion unduly hampers the disclosure process the President himself has set in motion."[70]

The board spent three months attempting to follow the president's injunction that "all the facts come out." After reviewing the entire history of the NSC and, in the process, interviewing over 50 high officials directly concerned with national security in the Reagan and previous administrations, the board offered a number of recommendations for improving NSC operations and controls. Only two of these suggestions were aimed at the president. Assuming from the outset that "the primary responsibility for the formulation and implementation of national security policy falls on the president," the board recommended that "each administration formulate precise procedures for restricted consideration of covert action and that, once formulated, those procedures be strictly adhered to." On the negative side was a recommendation "against having implementation and policy oversight dominated by intermediaries," a clear reference to the many private individuals used by North and others in the Iran-Contra affair.[71]

The most obvious omission from the board's report was any reference to the proper function of the NSC. Its conclusion that "in the case of the Iran initiative, the NSC process did not fail, it simply was largely ignored," sidestepped the problem of whether or not the normal process should permit the NSC to engage in covert operations. The implication was that if NSC and CIA officials had kept the president informed of what they were doing, their activities would have been legally and ethically acceptable.[72]

Congress did not wait for the board to conclude its work before taking matters into its own hands. The two intelligence committees, of the Senate and House, opened separate investigations with briefings by the board, as promised by President Reagan. Then, convinced that a presidential commission without enforcement powers would be incapable of ferreting out all the facts, the legislature determined early in January 1987 that it would combine its investigative efforts. In a remarkable show of unity, the overwhelming majority of Republicans and Democrats agreed to hold hearings before joint meetings of the House Select Committee to Investigate Covert Arms Transactions with Iran, and the Senate Select Committee on Secret Military Assistance to Iran and the Nicaraguan Opposition.[73]

Most of the witnesses called to the televised public hearings of the Iran-Contra committee had been interrogated in closed session prior to their public appearance. Oliver North was the principal exception, refusing to be questioned behind closed doors.[74] Some of the information elicited during the private questioning remains classified. And most of the documents later published in the committee's hearing reports have large sections blacked out by administration intelligence watchdogs. Thus, the public record is far from complete, and probably never will be made available in full. Nevertheless, the testimony of 32 key participants in the Iran-Contra affair revealed the extent to which the process of democratic government was subverted by an administration purportedly committed to "letting the people know."[75]

Most illuminating were the testimonies of Lieutenant Colonel Oliver North and Admiral John M. Poindexter, the two people most deeply involved in the Iran-Contra story who declined to appear before the president's Review Board. But other witnesses shed light on the corners of activity that President Reagan, as well as North and Poindexter, skirted so dexterously. For example, the very first witness to appear before the television cameras that brought the Iran-Contra hearings to the general public destroyed the myth that U.S. negotiators were attempting to deal with "moderates" in and out of the Iranian government. Former Major General Richard V. Secord, who accompanied McFarlane on his trip to meet Iranian representatives in Frankfurt, told the Iran-Contra committee: "It was high on the agenda of the American side to achieve a high-level government-to-government meeting with Iranian officials."[76] Wherever Reagan's aides expected to find Iranian moderates, it certainly could not have been in the higher levels of the Teheran government.

The extent of Reagan's self-delusion was illustrated by the testimony of McFarlane, who recalled a meeting in which the president explained that "if these people in Iran" were interested in changing Iranian policy and were against terrorism, "to provide them with arms would not be at variance with his policy since he wasn't providing arms to Khomeini, but to people opposed to Khomeini's policies."[77]

The curtain went up on the Iran-Contra television series May 5, 1987, but the two star performers did not come on stage until July 7 and July 15, respectively. In Oliver North's case, two volumes of testimony, taken over a period of seven days, were highlighted by admissions of lying, deception, destruction of government documents, and an assumption of authority by a lieutenant colonel that, in Representative Fascell's words, entitled North's exploits to be included "in the *Guiness Book of World Records*."[78] North's admitted duplicity included denying any government connection with the

Contra supply plane piloted by Eugene Hasenfus, putting out a false story about the Israeli sale of HAWK missiles to Iran, doctoring of the chronology of events in the Iranian negotiations, and covering up a "full service covert operation" in support of the Contras.[79]

Deception by methods short of outright falsehood was equally important to North's plan of operation. Adopting the concept of "plausible deniability," North attempted to protect the president from the effects of overt operations by destroying any evidence of participation or approval by the commander in chief. He even went to the ridiculous extreme of suggesting that a presidential finding authorizing a covert action need not be presented in writing. While this would avoid even a secret record of possible skullduggery, it would also leave the administration without evidence that the president had complied with the law in authorizing a covert action.

To keep his activities forever secret, not only from the American people but from the attorney general and any other potential investigative agency, North attempted to shred all documents relating to the Iran-Contra affair. His failure to accomplish this is evidenced by the 1,646 pages of documents that make up the collected appendixes to North's 542 pages of testimony.[80]

The most chilling aspect of North's performance in the NSC was his almost casual assumption of authority as the commander in chief's alter ego. Asked by committee counsel John Nields what legal authority he had for conducting a full-service covert operation to support the Contras, North said it was "the authority I sought from my superiors in setting up the activity to begin with and then conduct it." Given the go-ahead, he assumed that the planning and running of the operation were his to command.[81]

When restrictions on U.S. funding of the Contras was put into effect by the Boland amendment, North took it upon himself to seek support elsewhere. Assuming the role of diplomat as confidently as he had those of intelligence officer, military strategist and public relations director, he contacted—or requested other members of the administration to contact—foreign officials about the possibility of donating funds to keep the Contra campaign alive. Acknowledging that he had personally discussed such matters with representatives of some foreign countries, he eventually testified that at least ten nations were approached by him or his allies in and out of government. In the public record, these countries were identified only by number.[82]

Incredulous members of the Iran-Contra committee had difficulty believing that "a colonel in the White House" was "largely instrumental in implementing the president's policy."[83] Queried by counsel Nields as to who, if anyone, knew of the decisions that North was making, the colonel's response was enough to shock all but his most staunch supporters. Of the chief executive, he said, "I have absolutely no idea of what the President's knowledge [was] specifically about what I was doing." Speaking of Central America, he told the committee, "I made every effort to keep my superiors fully apprised as to what I was doing and the effect that it was having in the region," a statement that was later contradicted by his onetime boss Robert McFarlane.[84]

Asked if the vice-president's office knew of his resupply efforts in Nicaragua, North recalled talking to one member of that staff, but without "going into any detail." In the State Department, he said, Assistant Secretary Elliott Abrams "knew enough to turn to me" for information about the Central American operation. The Assistant Secretary for East Asia and Pacific Affairs, Gaston J. Sigur, North used to set up meetings for North to talk to representatives of other countries. Referring to Sigur, North's parenthetical remark was, "I believe at the time I probably told him why." On the military side, North said he briefed CIA director Casey "frequently in detail," and had many conversations with Major General Paul Gorman, who headed the army's Southern Command in Central America.[85]

Unlike North's militant, flag-waving presentation, Vice Admiral John M. Poindexter offered his testimony in a restrained, seemingly unemotional style. Recalling his five-and-one-half years of service to President Reagan, from military assistant in the NSC to the top post in that agency, he felt that he knew the president's wishes well enough to make decisions without bringing them to the White House for approval. "More importantly," he said, "I thought I had the authority to do that." When he cited a memorandum he had written to alert his staff to the president's desire to aid the Contras without congressional approval, committee counsel Nields pointed out that Poindexter was talking about "special powers of the president. . . . Not powers of the national security adviser who had never been elected by anybody." Poindexter agreed that was true, but reverted to his conviction that he knew the president's mind as his reason for assuming that Reagan wanted him to exercise those special powers.[86]

Even on the subject of diversion of Iranian funds to the Contras, Poindexter challenged the White House statement that the president would not have permitted this if he had been asked. Reagan had indicated as much in a March news conference when he told reporters that although he had forgotten a lot of conversations about Iran and Central America, it was inconceivable that he would forget being told about the diversion of funds. "You would have heard me without opening the door to the office if I had been told that at any time," he said.[87] Nevertheless, Poindexter continued to insist that Reagan would have approved the diversion if it had been put to him.

Like North, Poindexter readily admitted that the concept of deniability was an integral part of his procedure. "In the continuing plan that I had always had of providing deniability to the president," he told the committee,

"I did not want to provide that detailed information at that time, because I wanted the president and his staff to be able to say they didn't know anything about it."[88]

On many other points Poindexter refused to reply directly. Repeatedly he used the phrase, "I don't recall." Another favorite rejoinder was, "It never crossed my mind." But on other occasions he professed to feel "comfortable" with a decision he had made independently of the president.[89]

One of the conversations he could not recall occurred only a short time before his public testimony, when he was questioned by the committee in executive session. On that occasion he had said, "I told Colonel North repeatedly not to put anything in writing on the transfer of funds to the Contras and not to talk to anybody about it." His attorney's lengthy objection to persistent questioning on that point could not obscure these facts: that before Attorney General Meese ordered a Justice Department team to check North's files, Meese warned Poindexter that "he was going to send some people over" to go through North's collection of documents; that Poindexter passed Meese's warning on to North; that North proceeded to shred what he thought were all the documents relating to the Iran-Contra affair; and that Meese's men did not stop or question the shredding, which continued even as they were conducting their inspection.[90]

Although he left the task of destroying evidence largely in North's capable hands, Poindexter was not above such tactics himself. He acknowledged that he had received a draft finding from CIA director Casey which was "essentially a straight arms-for-hostages" proposal. This earlier document was read and signed by President Reagan December 5, 1985, *a year before* the finding that was eventually used to justify supplying Iran with weapons. Never acted upon, the 1985 finding was put in Poindexter's safe and forgotten until November 21, 1986, the day Poindexter received the call warning him that Meese intended to review documents going back to 1985. When an aide brought the 1985 finding to Poindexter's attention with the remark, "They'll have a field day with this," the admiral immediately tore it up.[91]

*   *   *   *   *

The North and Poindexter testimonies were received with emotions ranging from horror to vague misgivings to enthusiastic applause. Those elements of the general public that had happily joined President Reagan in his flag-waving ceremonies and foreign adventures accepted his designation of Colonel North as a hero, and cheered "Ollie" mightily at his post-hearing fund-raising appearances around the country. Within the Iran-Contra committee, North and Poindexter were championed first and foremost by Representative Henry J. Hyde (R, Ill.), who referred scornfully to those who persisted in "sermonizing" that "the end doesn't justify the means." In both the North and Poindexter hearings, Hyde used one example after another in an attempt to demonstrate that circumstances determine when extreme means are justified. In every case—beginning with President Truman's use of the atomic bomb—he presented the "facts" as though there were only two options, which of course was not true in any of the instances he cited.[92]

Despite what administration supporters regarded as outstanding service by Colonel North and NSA chief Poindexter, the performance of these two military officers revealed an awesome authoritarian approach to decision-making. Many people in and out of Congress deplored the dangerous trend they saw in acceptance of the two concepts that any means are justifiable in defense of American democracy, and that non-elected officers of the government may, with impunity, assume powers granted by the Constitution solely to the president and/or Congress.

At one point in the hearings, Representative Jack Brooks (D, Texas) raised a question regarding North's participation in "a contingency plan in the event of emergency that would suspend the American Constitution." This is only one of the many questions to which the public may never hear an answer, as Chairman Inouye cut Brooks off for touching upon "a highly sensitive and classified area" that should only be taken up—if at all—in executive session.[93] Other unexplored areas were cited in this paragraph of the introduction to the Iran-Contra committee's final report:

> The conclusions in this Report are based on a record marred by inconsistent testimony and failure on the part of several witnesses to recall key matters and events. Moreover, a key witness—Director of Central Intelligence William J. Casey—died, and members of the NSC staff shredded relevant contemporaneous documents in the fall of 1986. Consequently, objective evidence that could have resolved the inconsistencies and overcome the failures of memory was denied to the committees—and to history.[94]

That report also summed up the majority view of the seriousness of conditions uncovered by the committee's investigation. Summarizing the testimony which revealed the cover-up, confusion, dishonesty and secrecy that characterized the administration's handling of the Iran-Contra affair, the committee pointed to the several ways in which the president and his aides had simultaneously pursued two contradictory foreign policies, one public and one secret:

> The public policy was not to make any concessions for the release of hostages lest such concessions encourage more hostage-taking. At the same time, the United States was secretly trading weapons to get the hostages back.
> The public policy was to ban arms shipments to Iran and to exhort other governments to observe this embargo. At the same time, the United States was secretly selling sophisticated missiles to Iran and promising more.

The public policy was to improve relations with Iraq. At the same time, the United States secretly shared military intelligence on Iraq with Iran, and North told the Iranians, in contradiction to United States policy, that the United States would help promote the overthrow of the Iraqi head of government.

The policy was to urge all governments to punish terrorism and to support, indeed encourage, the refusal of Kuwait to free the Da'wa prisoners who were convicted of terrorist acts. At the same time, senior officials secretly endorsed a Secord-Hakim plan to permit Iran to obtain the release of the Da'wa prisoners.

The public policy was to observe the "letter and spirit" of the Boland Amendment's proscriptions against military or paramilitary assistance to the Contras. At the same time, the NSC staff was secretly assuming direction and funding of the Contras' military effort.

The public policy, embodied in agreements signed by Director Casey, was for the Administration to consult with the Congressional oversight committees about covert activities in a "new spirit of frankness and cooperation." At the same time, the CIA and the White House were secretly withholding from those committees all information concerning the Iran initiative and the Contra support network.

The public policy, embodied in Executive Order 12333, was to conduct covert operations solely through the CIA or other organs of the intelligence community specifically authorized by the President. At the same time, although the NSC was not so authorized, the NSC staff secretly became operational and used private, non-accountable agents to engage in covert activities.[95]

A minority report, signed by all but two of the Republican members of the joint committee, contested every conclusion of the majority but one: that "President Reagan and his staff made mistakes in the Iran-Contra Affair." Opening with that admission, the minority proceeded to assert, incorrectly, that "the president himself has already taken the hard step of acknowledging his mistakes." In fact, Reagan had merely acknowledged that mistakes had been made by others, not by himself. Nevertheless, the minority's "bottom line" was that "the mistakes of the Iran-Contra Affair were just that— mistakes in judgment and nothing more." Their denial of misdeeds swept away majority criticisms in this capsule statement, carefully crafted to rephrase majority conclusions to make them far broader than was ever intended:

There was no constitutional crisis, no systematic disrespect for "the rule of Law," no grand conspiracy, and no Administration-wide dishonesty or cover-up. In fact, the evidence will not support any of the more hysterical conclusions the Committee's Report tries to reach.[96]

No one claimed that a constitutional crisis existed, only that the methods used by Reagan and his aides threatened to undermine constitutional government, had they not been discovered. The terms "systematic" disrespect for the law, "grand conspiracy," and "administration-wide" dishonesty, falsely suggested that the majority had attributed these qualities to all of the hundreds of thousands of employees in the executive branch and in the Pentagon.

Point by point, the Republican members of the joint committee—with the exception of Senators William S. Cohen of Maine and Paul S. Trible, Jr. of Virginia—echoed President Reagan's view of the whole affair. In the process, the minority repeatedly stressed the reasonableness of legal interpretations opposed to those accepted by the majority. Questions of ethics and accountability were not faced directly, but were touched upon in comments such as that it would have been better if President Reagan had simply vetoed the Boland amendment.[97]

Despite the strenuous efforts of the minority to interpret every administration act as reasonable "in the context" in which it was performed—a favorite phrase of Colonel North, Admiral Poindexter, and their attorneys—the evidence clearly warranted the majority's closing comment that the importance of the Iran-Contra affair could best be expressed in an observation made 50 years earlier by Supreme Court Justice Louis Brandeis, who warned:

> Our government is the potent, the omnipresent teacher. For good or for ill, it teaches the whole people by its example. Crime is contagious. If the government becomes a lawbreaker, it breeds contempt for law, it invites every man to become a law unto himself, it invites anarchy.[98]

CHAPTER 13

The Great Communicator

"As the Scriptures say, 'Know the truth and the truth will make you free'."[1]

LONG BEFORE REAGAN ENTERED THE NATIONAL ARENA AS A POTENTIAL candidate for public office, he was a strong advocate of an open society. That concept had an important place in his 1964 speech in support of Barry Goldwater for president. His slashing attack on the incumbent Democratic administration, which endeared him to the Republicans whose party he had joined only two years earlier, included the charge that government in the U.S. "to an ever increasing degree interferes with the people's right to know." He continued to pontificate on his attachment to the principle of open government through all the years that followed. At his first inauguration as governor of California he asserted that "government is the people's business." Two years later he lectured a group of UPI editors on the same subject, warning that "agencies of government at every level are seeking to perform their services more and more with less attention to the right of the people to know." Both public officials and the media, he said, have a responsibility to inform the public of the facts about their government's operations, "whether pleasant or unpleasant, and to make sure they *are* facts."[2] The message did not change with Reagan's election to the presidency. After three years in the White House he marked the honoring of the unknown serviceman of the Vietnam War with the statement that "government owes the people an explanation and needs their support for its actions at home and abroad."[3]

Comparing Reagan's promise with his performance is a dismal experience. The entire record of the Reagan administration was characterized by bitter resistance to the release of information to the public, not only in so-called security matters but in domestic affairs of direct concern to millions of Americans and having not the remotest connection with national security. His ability to retain his personal popularity in the face of such a record can be attributed largely to his style as a communicator and to the media's ineffectiveness in "letting the people know" the extent of his mistakes, evasions, distortions and fabrications.

Reagan's approach to the problem of communication was that of an actor. He threw himself into the part of president as he had done his Hollywood roles. Describing the latter, he wrote in his autobiography, "So much of our profession is taken up with pretending, with the interpretation of never-never roles, that an actor must spend at least half his waking hours in fantasy, in rehearsal or shooting."[4] More than half way through his first term in the White House, he was still more adept at box-office analysis of a politically oriented film than at interpreting the impact of the picture on government policy. Asked for his reaction to the horrors of nuclear war depicted in the film *The Day After,* Reagan had no comment on the substance of the picture. All he said was, "Well, any motion picture or any drama or play is based on one thing: It isn't successful unless it has or evokes an emotional response. If the audience does not have an emotional experience, whether it's one of hating something or crying or having a lot of laughter, then you've got a failure out there."[5]

Reagan's acting ability allowed him to adapt to radical changes in occupation, from lifeguard to sports announcer to actor to traveling public relations man for General Electric to governor to president. In each job, he sought to "evoke an emotional response" that would indicate approval of his performance. And in every case the "M.O." (method of operation) was the same: a description of the scene, subject or problem that would give the audience a feeling of personal involvement, sympathy and support. That he so often achieved a positive public response was a tribute to his engaging personality as well as his way of casting himself as an ordinary man with the same interest in sports, the same taste in books, food, entertainment and everyday living as the average individual. "Nothing about me to make me stand out on the midway," was the expression he used in 1942.[6]

Despite his pretensions to ordinariness, however, Reagan's lifelong adoration of hero figures may have been the stimulus behind his casual attempts to convey an impression of superiority in many areas. "Lauded as a star in sports," "a motion picture star," and participant in "one of the better-kept secrets of the war [World War II], ranking up with the atom bomb project," were a few of the honors he conferred upon himself, with no supporting evidence in two of the three cases, and only nominal justification for the claim of stardom in Hollywood.[7]

* * * * *

In his political career Reagan was anything but ordinary. His ability to judge what the public wanted to hear was superior to that of his professional advisers. And his knack of getting his message across with the greatest possible impact put him on a par with Franklin D. Roosevelt and John F. Kennedy. He was especially effective on television broadcasts in which he was undisturbed by inquiring reporters or other distractions. Knowing every trick in the cameraman's book, he never failed to make use of the medium that most closely resembled the controlled setting of a Hollywood studio. Even the 10- or 15-second "photo opportunities" offered by meeting with foreign dignitaries, or signing an important piece of legislation, or simply waving a smiling good-bye from a helicopter on the White House lawn, were carefully planned to allow for television coverage.

Particular care was taken with the staging of press conferences, each of which was preceded by two days of rehearsals in which answers were supplied for all the questions that the White House staff could anticipate. Even the president's entry into the press room and his position in front of the open doors, Mike Deaver later explained, was part of the effort to present the best possible picture for a television audience. Reagan's chief press spokesman for six years put the case in a single sentence: "Underlying our whole theory of disseminating information in the White House was our knowledge that the American people get their news and form their judgments based largely on what they see on television."[8]

Reagan not only gave television credit for bringing public officials into the homes of voters in a more effective way than radio could do, he praised it for qualities that it did not have. "Television," he said, "even more than radio, is actually a return to our old-time tradition of taking to the stump [and] has made it possible for more people than ever before to judge a man on his merits."[9] This, of course, was nonsense. Stump speeches of old were made in front of live audiences who could—and often did—heckle, challenge and contradict the speaker. Under those conditions, "the merits" of a candidate's opinions could be put to the test by direct confrontation, a situation Reagan did not relish. Rather, except for his infrequent news conferences, and the few so-called debates he reluctantly agreed to in his presidential campaigns, he used television to air—without interruption and with the benefit of cue cards and mirrors—speeches carefully crafted by the largest and most professional group of writers and researchers ever assembled in the White House. One of the few members of the White House press office who had worked under four previous presidents compared the Kennedy public relations "catch-as-catch-can operation of nine persons" with the Reagan crew of "almost 40 persons," whose function was "to control events rather than be controlled by them." Reagan himself remarked after his fourth meeting with Soviet leader Mikhail Gorbachev that the event reminded him of one of movie producer Cecil B. deMille's "great historical spectacles."[10]

As president, Reagan portrayed himself as a dedicated defender of the Constitution in the tradition of Washington, Madison and other founding fathers. In fact, he was quite unlike those political pioneers, in personality, in intellect and, to a large extent, in political philosophy. Our early politicians appealed to the voting public through serious, often scholarly, writings and speeches. They may have chosen with care the locations and publications used to present their views, but they did not rely on teams of writers and researchers for their facts or their scripts. Nor indeed, did they require prepared scripts, cue cards, or teleprompters that display, on a hidden screen, not only the words of a speech but appropriate gestures and facial expressions for the speaker to use. Most of them had a thorough knowledge of the world's political systems and the writings of a philosophers from Plato to Adam Smith—knowledge they had gained from reading the histories and commentaries of earlier times, not from brief quotations dredged up by library aides. True, they had the advantage of dealing with a voting public made up largely of educated—or at least literate—male landowners, who constituted a very small percentage of the total population. Their stump speeches and orations in the legislatures of that era may have produced some theatrics, but never the pure theater that characterized Reagan's public appearances.

One of the features of Reagan's speechmaking was the planned humor he introduced into the program. Jokes and anecdotes peppered not only his speeches, but his informal conversations as well. At each of his meetings with Gorbachev, he attempted to entertain him, as well as inquiring reporters, with Russian-oriented jokes or proverbs.[11]

At home, according to Chief of Staff Donald Regan, the president, "started nearly every meeting with a story, no matter whether the participants were people he saw every day or the hereditary ruler of a remote kingdom who had never before laid eyes on an American president." Reagan's store of quips was kept up-to-date by Mike Deaver, who "had a new joke or bit of amusing gossip for him every morning *as the first order of business* [emphasis added]." After Deaver left the White House, Regan said that he and Vice-President Bush continued the practice of supplying the president with additions to his collection of humor.[12]

*   *   *   *

For all his pretense at realism, Reagan was never concerned with any facts except those that supported his preconceived notions of good and evil, truth and falsehood, the real and the make-believe. Those that did provide such support, he came to accept as true and representing reality. Having memorized them—a feat he performed as an expert—he would repeat them over and over. This became apparent to observers early in Reagan's political career. Lou Cannon put it this way:

What unnerved reporters who spent considerable time with Reagan . . . was not his misstatements but his proclivity for repeating the same memorized answers over and over again in the manner of a man who is saying them for the first time. It was as if someone had hit the "play" button on a tape cassette recorder.[13]

During his governorship, the play button would produce stock answers to questions about his administrative inexperience and the support he was getting from the John Birch Society. By the time he reached the White House, the memorized messages had turned to descriptions of the Evil Empire and America's "window of vulnerability."

It may be true that Reagan regarded every memorized opinion and explanation as a fact, even though this was not always the case. His long-time friend Mike Deaver wrote about Reagan's "inability to deceive" in his 1987 memoirs: "When Reagan believes his truthfulness is being doubted, as in the case of the Iranian arms flap . . . his anger tends to rattle him . . . he finds it inconceivable that anyone would accuse him of lying."[14] The book in which this opinion was offered was still a display item in bookstores when the Iran-Contra hearings revealed some of the deliberate falsehoods that Reagan had perpetrated. These examples came as no surprise to those who had followed his earlier career and could remember occasions during his governorship when Reagan had knowingly lied about homosexuals in his administration and about his understanding of the abortion legislation that he had reluctantly signed.[15]

Beyond the flat falsehoods were the misrepresentations which, had they been brought to the public's attention more forcefully, and as frequently as they occurred, might have returned Mr. Reagan to what he liked to call "the ash heap of history." One astute observer, Professor James David Barber, has written at some length about the misleading picture of Reagan's governorship that, as presidential candidate, Reagan foisted upon the public—with few challenges from either reporters or opposing candidates. Barber pointed out that Reagan's partly false and largely misleading boast of having reduced welfare rolls, increased employment, tightened abortion laws, and cut taxes and expenditures was disproved by "recorded information presented by six leading Republican legislators who had supported Reagan in his California campaigns."[16]

Reagan's method of handling facts did not change after he reached the White House. Following his successful drive for tax reduction, which was accompanied by sharp cuts in non-defense spending, he claimed that his tax policies were "more beneficial [to] people at the lower end of the earning scale . . . than to anyone else." Two weeks later, in a relatively obscure part of its national weekly edition, the *Washington Post* pointed out that the numbers cited by Reagan were "demonstrably wrong," that a slight increase in the share of total income taxes collected from people having over $50,000 annual income reflected the enormous gains they had realized, in contrast to the increasing poverty of the lowest income earners.[17]

Much of the misinformation dispensed by President Reagan was a product of his ignorance. Calling a special meeting of reporters to update them on plans for MX missile production, which he had discussed that very morning with Republican and Democratic members of the Senate, the president's description of a compromise agreement reached with the legislators only served to confuse his listeners. Asked what effect the agreement would have on basing modes, he went into a second lengthy explanation that led one bewildered reporter to ask, "Where is the compromise, and who was involved?" Reagan's answer was, "Well, the compromise is going to involve— would you like to explain what the compromise is, John Tower?" Senator Tower, who had been at the morning meeting, explained in one paragraph what the president had failed to explain in eight.[18]

The most memorable of Reagan's blunders—also on his favorite subject of the military buildup—was one he later denied having made. However, the taped record of his May 14, 1982 statement contained the following bit of "reasoning" on his approach to arms reduction:

> [N]othing is excluded. But one of the reasons for going at the ballistic missile—that is the one that is the most destabilizing. . . . That is the one that people know that once that button is pushed, there is no defense; there is no recall. . . . Those that are carried in bombers, those that are carried in ships of one kind or another, or submersibles, you are dealing there with a conventional type of weapon or instrument, and those instruments can be intercepted. *They can be recalled* if there has been a miscalculation (emphasis added).[19]

Two years later, *Washington Post* writer Philip Geyelin remembered that Reagan had made the same assertion—that missiles from submarines and airplanes "could be called back"—at a February 1982 breakfast news conference which was not reported in the *Public Papers of the Presidents*. At neither 1982 meeting was the recall statement challenged, but two months after Geyelin's article appeared, and one day after Reagan's presidential debate with Walter Mondale, reporters raised the question at the Kansas City airport. At that point Reagan said he had been talking about "submarines and airplanes, that *they* could be called back," which would have made sense, but was not what he had said on either of the two earlier occasions.[20]

Often it is difficult to determine whether a Reagan anecdote was the product of his own imagination or if it had been told to him by a well-wisher or given him by his own staff. An example of a clearly fabricated item was included in a 1982 speech that he made in support of Texas Governor Clements. On that occasion, Reagan quoted Supreme Court Justice Oliver Wendell Holmes as saying, "Keep government poor and remain free." This quote was taken from a longer statement in Reagan's autobiography, which also credited Holmes with saying, "Strike for the jugular. Reduce taxes and spending." Holmes never said any of those things, as researcher Walter Scott pointed out just before the 1982 election. But having said it once, Reagan had the line engraved in his memory and could call it up at will.[21]

Now and then Reagan would concoct a story on the spur of the moment. While in Reykjavik for a summit meeting with Gorbachev, he attempted to impress a group of U.S. servicemen by comparing his attitude toward their heroic defense of the nation with that of Congress. "Sometimes they get strange ideas about reducing pay rates for the military," he said. "But don't worry; I'll never let them."[22] Never in his administration—or in any other after World War II—had Congress proposed a reduction in pay rates for members of the armed forces.

Anecdotes about the misuse of welfare funds were among Reagan's favorites. In that area he simply accepted—and passed on—any story that would illustrate the evils of welfare. Many incidents of welfare fraud were carefully documented by employees of the Health and Human Services Department, but Reagan did not stop with those. He preferred juicier items than the routine cases of multiple claims that eventually were caught by the responsible government agency. One of the many examples was his tale of an individual purchasing one orange with food stamps and using the change to buy a bottle of vodka. Apart from the fact that food stamps could not be used to buy liquor of any kind, change from a food stamp purchase may not exceed 99 cents, which would not be enough to buy even the cheapest brand of vodka. When queried about such stories, the only defense his aides could offer was that "the president was misinformed."[23]

Another favorite target, especially during Reagan's first administration, was the Soviet Union. Few people were inclined to challenge any accusation leveled at the Evil Empire, but experts in Soviet history were quick to declare that there was never any such thing as "the Ten Commandments of Nikolai (sic) Lenin," to which Reagan referred in a White House exchange with reporters on the second anniversary of his inauguration.[24]

The half-truth, or kernel-of-truth, story was another Reagan specialty. He was aware of the existence of films taken by U.S. Army photographers that showed the ghastly conditions at the Nazi death camps when they were liberated. Although he had nothing whatever to do with the filming of those scenes, he told visiting Israeli Prime Minister Yitzhak Shamir and famed Nazi-hunter Simon Wiesenthal, in separate interviews, that he had been part of the signal corps "taking pictures of the camps." When Shamir and

Weisenthal repeated his story, Reagan denied it, insisting that he had told them "he never left the country." Reagan's most knowledgeable biographer tried to track down the story, but could find no reference to it in any of the source materials, including Reagan's autobiography. Nor was there any clue as to why, if Reagan had a copy of the death camp film as he said he did, he never showed it or made its existence known until his Israeli guests arrived.[25]

Reagan's research and speech-writing staff supplied him with statistics and most of the attention-getting phrases that in his public appearances he tossed off as smoothly as though he had originated them himself. Although his aides cannot be held responsible for the president's muddling of statistical data, they seem rarely to have corrected him or to have apprised him of the origins or implications of the material fed to him. Whoever found Ben Franklin's suggestion that the Constitutional Convention begin each day with a prayer neglected to inform Reagan that the convention rejected this proposal. The researcher who gave him the "ash heap of history" as the ultimate fate of Soviet communism surely did not explain that this phrase originated with Leon Trotsky, who used it to dispose rhetorically of the opponents of the Bolsheviks in the Russian Revolution of 1917. The most talented of his speech writers, Peggy Noonan, may not have known that the strong man of the Nicaraguan "freedom fighters" was a Somozista National Guard commander when she wrote the line with which President Reagan described the Contras as "the moral equal of our Founding Fathers."[26]

More than any previous president, Reagan relied on his speech writers to provide not only the detailed information he refused to grapple with in his everyday administration of the nation's affairs, but the theatrics more commonly associated with Hollywood scripts. As one journalist has pointed out, the "hired word-processors" in the White House receive little of the credit that the public readily grants to movie script writers. Put pithily by Ellen Goodman:

> In politics . . . we reverse the theatrical rules. The audience assigns authorship to the person who delivers the lines, rather than to the person who writes them. We know what the president "said" today, when in fact he may only have read it today.[27]

With presidential handling of facts as careless as Reagan's, it was not unexpected that administrators in his executive departments showed the same inclination. Especially talented in the art of deception were the Department of Defense and the Environmental Protection Agency, both of which went far beyond the normal tendency—found in any administration—to present their positions in the most favorable light possible. Evidence of persistent falsification of records and doctoring of reports by military and

EPA officers was cited in an earlier chapter. If other departments were less flagrant in their programs of disinformation, all were extremely active in advertising their achievements—real or imagined. The dollars spent on publicity cannot be determined from the most careful scrutiny of the executive budget, but the proliferation of personnel in White House and departmental public relations offices is evident from an examination of successive issues of the *United States Government Manual*.

*   *   *   *   *

Far more ominous than figure-fiddling and anecdotal nonsense was Reagan's carefully disguised policy of restricting the amount of information on government operations that would be made available to the public. Both before and after his election to the presidency his most emphatic pronouncements on the basic character of the American political system stressed the importance of maintaining an open society, with full information to allow the public to participate intelligently in the democratic process of shaping policy decisions. Supporting Nixon in 1968, he castigated "advocates of big government and more government controls [who] don't think you and I have any real right to know what is going on." He insisted that "government is best when kept closest to and most responsive to the people."[28]

Notwithstanding these early tirades against government secrecy, one of the most important actions taken by Reagan in the first year of his presidency was to order a revision of President Carter's Executive Order 12063 governing "United States Intelligence Activities." Simultaneously, he had his staff work up a new set of regulations relating to security classification for government documents and information. Rumors of these efforts led a few journalists to inquire as to their purpose. While the two executive orders were still in draft stage, President Reagan and his chief counsel, Edwin Meese, held a working luncheon with editors from around the country. One of the group recalled Reagan's campaign promise and commented: "There's talk about a change in the executive order governing the CIA to enlarge the CIA's area of activity in domestic matters. . . . Does this seem to you a contradiction to this pledge to get the government off the backs of the people?" Reagan, who had introduced the question-and-answer session with the remark that "etiquette does not prevail, and speaking with your mouth full will be considered a military necessity," responded, "I'm sorry, I'm eating."

Then to Meese, he said, "Go ahead." Meese's method of answering was to cite the reduction in the number of pages of regulations published in the *Federal Register,* and the enormous cost of supplying information under the Freedom of Information Act to people like Philip Agee, "the renegade ex-CIA person" who had written extensively about that agency's covert activities. He spoke of legislative "reforms" that would make it easier for the news media to obtain information, but gave no hint as to what those might be.

Getting around finally to the editor's question about the CIA, Meese said:

> There is absolutely nothing in the proposed intelligence order which will expand the ability of the CIA to engage in domestic spying. That is totally false, and it's propaganda being put out by some staffers on the Hill who are part of Frank Church's infamous intelligence committee that was so destructive of our intelligence authorities some years ago. [29]

Meese's description of the Church Committee report, which in 1976 had brought into the open the "unsavory and vicious tactics" employed by federal investigative agencies against American citizens, revealed the true purpose of Reagan's "reforms," which was to restore to those agencies the very power that had been used to subvert the democratic principles so fervently expressed in his public speeches. [30]

When Executive Order 12333, the first of Reagan's intelligence orders, was issued on December 4, 1981, the section dealing with the CIA gave the lie to Meese's assertion that no extension of the agency's authority in domestic affairs was intended. To begin with, the order omitted any reference to that portion of the basic National Security Act of 1947 which states unequivocally that "the Agency [CIA] shall have no police, subpoena, law-enforcement powers or internal-security function." Instead, it conferred on the CIA authority to "conduct counterintelligence activities within the United States in coordination with the FBI as required in procedures agreed upon by the Director of Central Intelligence and Attorney General." In addition, the CIA was given undefined power to "conduct special activities approved by the President," as well as "services of common concern for the Intelligence Community as directed by the National Security Council." The phrase "special activities" had long been used by intelligence officers to refer to undercover operations that might or might not be legal. [31] Remarkably, not a single reporter raised a question about any aspect of Executive Order 12333 at the president's next news conference, held on December 17.

Step two in the Reagan plan was accomplished with publication of a new classification system. Billed as an instrument for defining "a uniform system for classifying, declassifying, and safeguarding national security information," Executive Order 12356 wound up its list of categories with these two loopholes, both of which allow a classifier unlimited authority to hide from the public any information that he or she decides could "reasonably be expected to cause damage to the national security" if disclosed:

(9) a confidential source; or
(10) other categories of information that are related to the national security and

that require protection against unauthorized disclosure as determined by the President or by agency heads *or other officials who have been delegated original classification authority* by the President [emphasis added][32]

Although this statement made it appear that classification authority had to come personally from the President, section 5.3 of the order authorized each agency to "designate a senior agency official to direct and administer its information security program." As a practical matter, this meant that the person so designated would not only oversee the application of the order but would recommend to the agency head—or department secretary—the people who would be given classification authority. Steven Garfinkel, appointed by Reagan to be director of the Information Security Oversight Office, assured Congress that this would not result in any increase in the 7,119 people given original classification authority under the Carter administration—a number that had been reduced from 17,626 under Nixon.[33]

The list of departments and agencies covered by Executive Order 12356, which was not published until a month after the order had been released, indicated how widely the rules of secrecy would be applied. Not limited to the Departments of Defense and State, the FBI, CIA and NSC, the list included the Departments of Commerce, Energy, Justice, Treasury and the Offices of Management and Budget, Science and Technology, General Services, Emergency Management, International Development, and International Communications. The Environmental Protection Agency, whose cozy relationship with companies found to be polluting the countryside had reached scandalous proportions, was given authority to classify as confidential whatever documents its officers deemed "related to national security."[34]

Examining the details of the president's order, members of the House Committee on Government Operations expressed serious concern over a number of its provisions. For one, the order allowed reclassification of information that had been declassified, which meant that if an agency received a request for unclassified or declassified material under the Freedom of Information Act, it was free to classify or reclassify the requested documents on the spot, to prevent their being made public. And once a document was classified, this catch-22 applied: "an agency shall [not "may"] refuse to confirm or deny the existence or nonexistence of requested information whenever the fact of its existence or nonexistence is itself classifiable."

Under the Carter administration, if there was a reasonable doubt about which classification level was appropriate (Top Secret, Secret, or Confidential), or whether information should be classified at all, the less restrictive level was to be used, or the information was not to be classified at all. Reagan took the reverse approach: if there was a reasonable doubt about the need to classify information, that doubt should be resolved in favor of classification "pending a determination within 30 days by an original classification authority." If there was a doubt about the appropriate level of classification, the higher level was to apply pending a review—which might never occur.[35]

On the specific question of determining what information might be classified as confidential, the Carter order had stipulated that this category be used only if its unauthorized disclosure "reasonably could be expected to cause identifiable damage to the national security." Reagan deleted the word "identifiable" from his order, thus opening the door to what the Government Operations Committee described as "the tendency of bureaucrats to classify too much information." This was a polite reference to the extent to which Reagan administrators surpassed their predecessors in concealing information merely because it might cause embarrassment.[36]

A further Reagan innovation was to add "confidential sources" to the Carter list of classifiable information. That term was defined to mean:

> Any individual or organization that has provided, *or that may reasonably* be expected to provide information to the United States on matters *pertaining to* the national security with the expectation, express *or implied,* that the information or relationship, or both, be held in confidence [emphasis added].[37]

The italicized phrases indicate the sweeping compass of this section. Based on the unchallengeable judgment of a William Casey, John Poindexter or Oliver North, almost any individual or organization in the country could be "reasonably expected to provide" information which the cloak-and-dagger experts would find "pertaining to national security," and which they could assume the prospective informant would want to be kept confidential.

When the president signed Executive Order 12356, he said it reflected "a coordinated effort involving officials of the executive branch, members of Congress, and representatives of concerned private organizations." This may have been what he was told by his advisers, but the statement was grossly misleading. The facts were these:

—Revision of President Carter's Executive Order 12065 began in February 1981, a month after President Reagan assumed office.
—An intelligence community task force, under the direction of the CIA, was assembled to write a new executive order. Successive drafts prepared by this group never circulated outside White House security offices. And unlike the Carter order, proposed revisions were never announced to the public.
—When a near-final draft was sent to a few congressional committee chairmen on February 4, 1982, it was accompanied by a routing slip that read: "The materials are being provided with the understanding that access to them will be limited to committee members and necessary staff personnel."
—Congressional hearings were scheduled for March 10 and 11, and National

Security Adviser William Clark and Attorney General William French Smith were invited to appear or send representatives to explain the new directive. Both declined the invitation, Clark's assistant writing that the revised order had been provided to selected congressional committees "on the explicit understanding that Administration witnesses would not appear at hearings while the internal deliberative process was underway." Not only was this false—no such message ever having been sent to the committees— administration witnesses never did appear even after the order was put into final form.

—On March 11, a letter was sent to President Reagan requesting that he designate a spokesman to appear before the committee prior to the issuance of the final order. A month later—and two weeks *after the president had signed Executive Order 12356*—an assistant to the president wrote the committee chairman, assuring him that his letter had been "brought to the president's immediate attention" and that the national security staff would provide the committee with "a full response." In its report on this subject, the committee noted that "no response from the national security staff was ever received."[38]

To guard against public awareness of what was being done behind the protective curtain of the first two executive orders, Reagan's security experts drew up a National Security Decision Directive that expanded the controls established in the classification order by forbidding any employee or ex-employee of any federal agency from ever revealing anything he or she learned while in government service if the information was "related to the national security . . . as determined by the President or by agency heads" to whom he had delegated authority to classify material. The nature of this protection was spelled out in a requirement that "all persons with authorized access to classified information shall be required to sign a nondisclosure agreement" and to submit to a polygraph examination as a check on unauthorized disclosure.[39]

The directive was distributed to all "heads of Offices, Boards, Divisions and Bureaus" under a March 11, 1983 memorandum in which Attorney General William French Smith advised those officers that "many of the specific requirements of the directive involve no change from current Department of Justice policy." This was followed by an acknowledgment that the entire federal civil service would undergo policy changes to conform established rules to the new regulations.

Publication of NSDD 84 raised a storm of protest from members of Congress, civil rights groups, scientists, librarians and, most vocal of all, newspaper editors and writers. Former Nixon speechwriter William Safire— no card-carrying ACLU member—labeled the new directive "infamous," and called the lie detector provision "a civil-liberties abomination." Constitutional lawyer Floyd Abrams pointed out that the nondisclosure agreement would require a writer or speaker to submit to government censors references not just to classified documents, but to unclassified material as well, since the government claimed the right to determine what was classifed—or classifiable—and what was not. Witnesses at House committee hearings testified to the encouragement that the new directive would give to agencies that were already interfering with the public's right to receive or disseminate information, citing such examples as the Department of Commerce blocking the reading of a scholarly paper that contained only unclassified information; U.S. Customs agents preventing the importation of goods "sold freely on the streets of Teheran;" and the CIA's policy of charging exorbitant fees for documents requested under the Freedom of Information Act. (One applicant was charged $1,250 to research and copy a single two-page memorandum.)

The first Senate committee hearing elicited from government witnesses estimates that "over 100,000 people" in the Defense Department alone would be covered by the lifetime nondisclosure agreement. In 1988 a House committee learned that "approximately 3 million secrecy pledges" had been signed by the end of 1987, which led committee chairman Jack Brooks to exclaim that if there were that many employees with access to the country's most sensitive secrets, "they aren't sensitive secrets anymore."[40]

To many observers the new directive was further evidence of the administration's intention to curtail public inquiries previously permitted under the Freedom of Information Act (FOIA). Responding to the public uproar over this extraordinary grant of authority to agency heads to conceal any and all information by defining it as "related to national security," the White House gulled the media into believing that implementation was being suspended, pending review. Administration stalwart James J. Kilpatrick was one of the journalists who swallowed this rumor, regurgitating it on the December 22 "Agronsky and Company" television program. The usually alert William Safire was also taken in, reporting to his readers in a March 9, 1984 column that the directive had been "temporarily withdrawn." That fraud was still circulating at the close of 1984, when the provost of the University of Pennsylvania Law School made reference to the purported withdrawal in a letter published in the *New York Times* December 28. In fact, as the *Columbia Journalism Review* had reported in the summer of 1984, the NSC had made sure that no administration executive had been led astray by sending letters to some fifty agency heads reminding them that all but two sections of the directive were still in effect. Except for the legally challengeable lie-detector provision, all other provisions—including the lifelong censorship of all employee and ex-employee books, articles, or analyses of government policy—remain in effect in mid-1991.[41]

Friends of President Reagan were not without influence in the attempt to defend against public criticism of administration policies. One of Reagan's ever-helpful supporters at the American Enterprise Institute took on this task in an op-ed piece in the *New York Times*. Deriding what he called the "compulsion" felt by ordinary Americans to voice their opinions on a variety of public problems, senior fellow Stephen Miller recommended that they limit their discussion of political affairs to an admission of their ignorance of such matters. If asked for an opinion by a poll-taker—a profession Miller also detested—his advice was, "Tell him you have none."[42]

Members of Congress were concerned about the administration's overt censorship policy for more reasons than its effect on the individual's constitutional right of free expression. To a great extent that policy severely curtailed the inclination of employees to expose government fraud and inefficiency. A reluctant administration supporter, Senator Goldwater acknowledged this when he said, "the most-used rubberstamp in this town is that red one that says 'Top Secret'."[43]

President Reagan attempted to explain NSDD 84 to federal employees in a letter of August 30, 1983, which was not published in *Presidential Papers*. Stressing the danger of unauthorized disclosure of government information, he reminded his several million helpers that there were "mechanisms for presenting alternate views and opinions within our government," and that "workable procedures for reporting wrongdoing or illegalities" were also available. These assurances did nothing to ease the fear of the retaliation that every would-be whistleblower knew awaited him if he should embarrass his superiors by revealing their incompetence, negligence or dishonesty. Nor could they fail to grasp the message in Reagan's further advice that dissatisfied employees were always free to leave government service in order to exercise their right to disagree with his policies. In that paragraph though, Reagan neglected to remind his readers that if they had signed nondisclosure statements, they were forbidden for all time to comment, without prior clearance from their former bosses, on the operations of those officials.[44]

Precisely because whistleblowers had, in case after case, been subjected to punishment, ranging from official rebuke to dismissal, Congress persisted in its efforts to pass a whistleblower protection bill. Defeated by a Republican majority in the Senate during Reagan's first term, a Democratic majority was able to incorporate such a provision into the 1988 defense authorization bill, only to have it vetoed by President Reagan. Senator William Proxmire's summary comment was that administration barriers to attempts by whistleblowers to enlist congressional support for an examination of their criticisms had made a mockery of the 75-year-old Lloyd-LaFollette Act, which states:

The right of persons employed in the Civil Service of the United States, either individually or collectively, to petition Congress or any Member thereof, or to furnish information to any House of Congress or to any committee or Member thereof, shall not be denied or interfered with.[45]

*   *   *   *   *

Much of Reagan's irritation over criticism leveled at the questionable activities that his secrecy policy failed to conceal, or at his errors and misstatements, he attributed to the news media. His resistance to public display, however, was evident only when cameras and questioners touched those aspects of his private life, his opinions, his knowledge—or ignorance—that he was unwilling to expose. In the halcyon days of his GE employment Reagan faced friendly, approving audiences whose enthusiastic response to his philosophical platitudes led him to confess that "I enjoyed every whizzing minute of it."[46] "My speeches," he said of his GE experience, "underwent a kind of evolution, reflecting not only my changing philosophy but also the swiftly rising tide of collectivism that threatens to inundate what remains of our free economy."[47]

This change of heart notwithstanding, Reagan continued to feel that he had much in common with Roosevelt, Truman and Kennedy. Actually, there was little basis for such an assumption, either in terms of political philosophy or press relations. Roosevelt and Kennedy established a rapport with the press never achieved by Reagan, and both held frequent news conferences in which their knowledge and intellect permitted them to stand firm in the give-and-take with reporters. Truman was more openly combative, even contemptuous of some reporters—in particular, those in the Hearst newspaper chain. But he was also more candid than Reagan in his response to journalists' questions. A 1982 rating on a scale of 1 to 10 by experienced White House correspondents of presidents from Eisenhower to Reagan, gave Reagan high marks for humor (second only to Kennedy) but a score of only 4 for the "informative value" of his conferences.[48]

Neither Reagan nor Truman was the first president to hold an unflattering opinion of the news media. Woodrow Wilson held journalists in very low esteem. Nevertheless, despite his austere, impersonal attitude toward reporters, he initiated the press conference in 1913 as a method of keeping the public apprised of his views on policy matters and held such meetings regularly, twice a week for almost two years, then once a week until he abandoned the arrangement as the country prepared for war with Germany.

Wilson's successors were more cautious, insisting that all questions be submitted in advance and in writing. Not until Franklin D. Roosevelt entered the White House was there a return to frequent, unrehearsed meetings with reporters. Roosevelt had his own ground rules, which he explained to the White House press corps at his first meeting: no direct quotations except by special permission; indirect quotation permitted unless he indicated otherwise; background information to be expressed in "such euphemisms as 'the president is known to think that . . .' "; and off-the-record comments and information not be attributed to him, even indirectly.[49] Given these circumstances, and the fact that Roosevelt's average of 80 press conferences a year helped him to dominate the news, it is understandable that author and columnist Chalmers Roberts rated FDR "the best presidential communicator . . . in modern times."[50]

If Roosevelt lost nothing by lacking television during his White House tenure, Reagan gained much of his reputation as "the Great Communicator" through use of that medium. Running for the presidency in 1980, he directed his speeches to the television cameras rather than to reporters who might question his facts and opinions. Recognizing the candidate's talent in that direction, one expert observer remarked during the 1980 campaign: "Ronald Reagan is a professional performer, and it is the single most important fact about him. He is a consumate performer who trained to be governor of the nation's most populous state and trained for the presidency by perfecting his skills as an actor and communicator."[51]

Knowing this did not prevent the media from being lulled into accepting, and giving largely uncritical coverage to, the image of the president rather than the substance of his acts. This may have been understandable during the first-year honeymoon, when every new president is normally accorded an opportunity to put into practice the policies he pledged to introduce. However, by the end of that year, Reagan's misstatements had accumulated to a level that reduced him to McCarthy-like references to documents—which he refused to release—to "prove" that of six statements challenged in a single week, he had been "right" in five of them. This created minor headlines, partly because of his rejection of requests to see his proof, but also because in the same news conference, his recitation of events in Vietnam contained three significant errors of fact.[52]

Convinced that reporters in general were "out to get him" and would use any opportunity to lead him into an embarrassing exchange, Reagan avoided open press conferences in favor of off-the-record sessions with a few favored journalists. This practice was characterized by William Safire—one invitee who refused to participate in such closed meetings—as "a pernicious conspiracy to protect candidates for high office that entices reporters to become insiders and leaves the public outside." Maneuvers of that kind were coupled with maximum use of pictorial coverage of mass meetings at which the Secret Service sometimes joined with local police to establish barricades against the public and checkpoints where anti-Reagan signs were confiscated as efficiently as in a police state. Even such flagrantly anti-democratic methods—in cities from Cincinnati, Ohio to San Jose, California—received minimal media coverage.[53] But they gave evidence of the administration's inordinate desire for a controlled press.

Notwithstanding Reagan's retreat from public news conferences to the safety of White House press releases, televised appeals for public support on key policy issues, and weekly radio broadcasts conducted without question-and-answer sessions, the presidential image continued to be accepted, and in large part perpetuated, by journalists. In one of the few in-depth discussions of this phenomenon to appear in the news section of the country's most prestigious daily, a reporter found policy-making television executive Paul Greenberg of NBC "Nightly News" summing up his 1984 evaluation of Reagan by saying, "This man seems presidential." What that meant, Greenberg did not explain, but the article's comparison of Reagan's television presence with that of Carter and Ford made it clear that "presidential" to television newsmakers refers to a speaker's effective use of the camera. By that standard the dour George Washington, acerbic John Adams, and diminutive soft-spoken James Madison would merit scarcely a passing glance from today's television networks. Yet these were the revolutionary giants who molded a nation and a constitution by force of intellect rather than by contrived, camera-conscious creation of an "image" of leadership.

In short, the media were more than fair to President Reagan. And in the process, they were less than fair in carrying out their most important responsibility, which is to the public, not to candidates or officeholders.

* * * * *

To assert that "the Great Communicator" was not an appropriate title for Ronald Reagan is not to deny his very considerable ability to convince the public that he was the man to raise the country out of despair and on to new heights of glory. Two sweeping election victories demonstrated the effectiveness of his appeal.

Reagan's own interpretation of the 1980 election results was expressed in these terms:

> The people have made it plain. . . . They want an end to excessive government intervention in their lives and the economy, an end to burdensome and unnecessary regulations and a punitive tax policy that does take "from the mouth of labor the bread it has earned." They want a government that cannot only continue to send men across the vast reaches of space and bring them safely home, but that can guarantee that you and I can walk the park of our neighborhood after dark and get safely home. And finally, they want to know that this nation has the ability to defend itself against those who would seek to pull it down.[54]

Two of the leaders of Reagan's 1980 campaign attributed his victory in part to his personal qualities. The outcome, they said, resulted from a combination of Reagan's "resourcefulness, his knowledge, and above all, his great ability to win people over to his views on important issues." However, they assigned equal importance to "the broad acceptance of conservative principles by the American people."[55]

A rather different evaluation was offered by a group of journalists on the staff of the *Washington Post* who focused on the public perceptions gained—or conveyed—through media coverage. In that context, they considered the most important factor in the election to be the candidates' appearance, personality and style in dealing with the public. Here they found Reagan to have a decided advantage, partly because of his talent as "a superb television performer," but to an even greater extent his ability to convey his "unremitting vision of America" which brought an "emotional popular reaction to every speech in which he expressed the dream of 'family, work, neighborhood, freedom, peace'."[56]

The effect of Reagan's success in reducing taxes, inflation and nonmilitary spending might have been offset by his continued government-bashing and his pretense that he was not part of the system he persisted in castigating with his slogan, "Government is the problem." A hint of this is seen in the public's response to the question: "From which level of government do you feel you get the most for your money—federal, state or local?" In 1984, the 24 percent who named the federal government was the lowest level ever recorded since the question was first asked twelve years earlier—even lower than in 1974, following the Watergate debacle.[57] Meanwhile the president went merrily on, happy to live in the cocoon that James Reston characterized as "no-fault politics," pretending that "mistakes never happen."[58] As his most enthusiastic director of communications, Patrick Buchanan, recalled after leaving that post, "For Ronald Reagan the world of legend and myth is a real world."[59]

The most remarkable aspect of Reagan's presidency was that so much of the public accepted him on his own terms. When Bob Woodward of the *Washington Post* got hold of a three-page memorandum written by John Poindexter detailing a program of disinformation about Qaddafi that was to be circulated through the U.S. press, the president was quick to "challenge the veracity of that whole story."[60] As far as he was concerned, it had never happened. And as far as his loving public was concerned, the *Post* learned which side they were on when its telephones "rang off the wall" with calls from readers who "raged against disclosure of things they didn't want to hear about that nice man in the White House."[61]

What kept Reagan immune from the virus of public criticism was his extraordinary ability to convince people that he was not really part of the evil thing called government, that he was in the White House not as a politician, but as a crusader intent on cleaning up the mess left by previous administrations. Representative Patricia Schroeder had named him "the Teflon president," and his most knowledgeable biographer made a similar observation when he devoted an entire newspaper column to a demonstration of how "bad news just won't stick to him."[62] Even overseas, the power of the Reagan personality was evident, especially when he addressed non-political audiences. The *New York Times* headline on a news story about his talk to students at Moscow University said it all: "President Charms Students, But Not by Dint of His Ideas."[63]

James Reston once remarked that the American people didn't "elect" Ronald Reagan, they "fell in love with him."[64] The extraordinary nature of his appeal is revealed in speech-writer Peggy Noonan's book *What I Saw at the Revolution,* which glows with the love for Reagan that she freely admits, even as she characterizes his mind as "barren terrain."[65] Public opinion polls certainly support Reston's view. From 1981 to 1988 Gallup pollsters asked not only whether people approved or disapproved Reagan's policies, but whether they approved of him as a person. Only once, during the 1982 recession, when approval of his performance as president fell to a low of 37 percent, did the personal rating drop slightly below 70 percent. In the darkest days of the Iran-Contra affair, when 75 percent of the polled population believed Reagan had not told everything he knew, his personal approval rate held within a range of 71 to 74 percent.

When Reagan was compared with the two leading Democratic candidates in the 1984 race, he was ranked lower in intelligence than either Mondale or Glenn, but higher than both as a "colorful" personality and for offering "a well-defined program." Asked, "Can you believe him?", only one-third of respondents answered yes. Only 23 percent believed Reagan sided with the average citizen, and fewer still—21 percent—found him sympathetic to the poor. Despite shockingly low marks in these three areas, Reagan's personal popularity brought him as sweeping a victory in 1984 as it had in 1980. His overall approval rate, which had peaked at 68 percent in May 1981, dropped into the 40s through all of 1982 and early 1983, recovering to 53 percent after the Grenada invasion and soaring back into the 60s when his turnabout on the Soviet Union bore fruit in greatly improved relations with that country.

In the aftermath of the Iran-Contra scandal, public approval again fell below the 50 percent level. This loss of confidence occurred even without the later, more extensive evidence of Reagan's playing with the truth, either by self-delusion or through ignorance. The most remarkable example of his self-delusion came in a 1990 deposition, when he swore under oath that he had told the American people that in selling arms to Iran "we were not doing business with Khomeini. Quite the contrary. We were keeping it very secret from him what we were doing."[66]

* * * * *

Readers concerned only with the accuracy or reliability of Reagan's statements might well wonder what earned an individual so indifferent to the facts a title like "the Great Communicator." Reagan may have expressed it best himself when, in his farewell address, he acknowledged having "won" that nickname: "I wasn't a great communicator, but I communicate great things."[67] His explanation fell flat only when he identified the great things as the concepts that made up the Reagan Revolution. That was merely an attempt to establish as a matter of record that all his policies reflected the will of the people and the "rediscovery of our values and our common sense." If he won the title for anything, it was for frequently broadcasting—with throat-catching emotion—what the people of any nation love to hear: that they are the earth's bravest, noblest, most resourceful and generous men and women, that they are God's chosen people, living in a country designed by the Deity to preserve all that is good and to save the world from all that is evil.

This was the essence of Reagan's appeal—wholly personal, highly emotional and, as election results so forcefully demonstrated, eminently more compelling than indications of administrative competence, intellect, or erudition. Indeed, had it not been for the Twenty-Second Amendment, which limits a president to two terms in office, Reagan might well have been given an opportunity to extend the myth of the Great Communicator from eight to twelve years.

CHAPTER 14

President

"The way I see it, there were two great tri-umphs, two things that I'm proudest of. One is the economic recovery. . . . The other is the recovery of our morale. America is respected again in the world and looked to for lead-ership." [1]

AS A RULE HISTORIANS DEFER EVALUATION OF A PRESIDENT UNTIL SUFFI-cient time has elapsed to permit an independent review of his work based on the accumulated evidence of a decade or two of research and analysis con-ducted in an atmosphere removed from the passions of the period under consideration. But there is also place for an appraisal that takes into account the emotions engendered by a president's performance—even emotions expe-rienced by the evaluator.

Certainly, judgments based on observations by a president's contempo-raries are as justified as those the president makes of his own administration, the latter invariably being strongly tainted by self-interest. In the case of President Reagan, not even the accounts he prepares during his retirement can be expected to shed much new light on his administration, as he was given ample evidence of an unwillingness to retract, alter, or even vary the words he once used to explain and justify an action or policy. If any documentation of Reagan errors, either in the handling of facts or the setting of policy, finds its way into his memoirs, it will be a mark of the skill and integrity of his autobiographical ghost.

* * * * *

There are many ways of assessing the quality of a president's performance. One is to measure his achievements against the goals he established at the outset of his administration. The weakness of grading a president on this basis is that it assumes the acceptability of his concept of what is good for the country. Most presidents would deny that there is any conflict between the two. In President Reagan's words, "Anything we do is in our national security interest." However, to take but one example from the Reagan record: are reduced income tax rates desirable if the effect is to destroy the traditional system of apportioning the tax load on the basis of ability to pay? As the previous discussion of Reagan's economic policies indicated, my answer to that question is a resounding "no."

A more reasonable basis for evaluation would be to consider his performance in terms of the various qualities that mark a president as outstanding, good, average or below average. That is the method used in the following review of Reagan's presidency.

Public Image and Popularity

Rarely can a president boast of the personal appeal that Ronald Reagan enjoyed during his eight years in the White House. His detractors point to Reagan's relatively low "job approval" rating compared with that of Eisenhower, Kennedy, Nixon and Carter, not only during the "honeymoon" period of his first term, but even after two years in office. Acknowledging the difference between personal popularity and job approval, it is nevertheless true that his success in gaining approval for many of his programs was due in large part to public adulation.

On many of the specific foreign and domestic issues discussed in earlier chapters, Reagan had only minority support. Yet after four years and a disastrous loss of seats in Congress, his popular majority in the 1984 election was more commanding than in 1980.[2] Moreover, that popularity index persisted through good times and bad, recovering from a very respectable low of 71 percent during the humiliating Iran-Contra hearings, to an almost standard 75 percent a few months later.[3]

Reagan's job performance rating also recovered from the battering it took during the Iran-Contra investigation. To a large extent this resulted from the successful conclusion of an arms reduction treaty with the Soviet Union. Postponement of Oliver North's trial until after the 1988 election also helped, simply by keeping the subject out of the news. With economic indicators showing no sign of a new recession, and with the help of a Republican victory in the November presidential election, public approval of Reagan's job performance closed the year 1988 at the acceptable level of 60 percent.[4]

Misleading as popularity polls may be, they provide a major source of support, particularly for a president whose talents in other areas leave much to be desired. Members of Congress are more reluctant to criticize a popular figure than one whose public standing is low. This, in turn, may affect the entire legislative program and the resulting policies under which the country will be governed. The same boost is supplied by media portrayals of a chief executive they consider to be "presidential" in appearance, bearing or character, for such treatment of him in the news will reflect that feeling of deference. It will also enhance the president's stature as a strong leader and great innovator, an image that Reagan's public relations staff attempted to project on every possible occasion.

One achievement that Reagan certainly did not anticipate was improvement in the public attitude toward government. Considering his unremitting criticism of government as "the problem, not the solution," and private enterprise as the answer to all problems, studies of public confidence show a startling trend during the period 1983–1986. They indicate, ironically, that President Reagan "had revived faith in government but not in the private sector" of business and labor.[5]

Courage and Integrity

In physical terms, Reagan's courage shone brightly, both in his reaction to the attempted assassination and to the threats of illness that arose periodically. His relatively slow return to a normal work schedule after each illness was more the result of his wife's protectiveness than his own inclination.

He seemed to enjoy his battles with Congress over questions of domestic and foreign policy, especially when he could take his case to the people, either on television or in public gatherings. Unencumbered by doubts of any kind, he could defend his position with vigor.

A different side of the Reagan character is seen in his unwillingness—or inability—to accept any fact or opinion that clashed with his own concept of reality. Nor would he recognize, much less take responsibility for, the malfeasance or misfeasance of his administrators. As to errors and evidence of bad judgment, his inability to face these kinds of facts may have been a product of his dream-world mentality rather than cowardice. In either case, his approach to the problem of responsibility was justly characterized by one commentator as "no-fault politics."[6]

More important was the wide discrepancy between Reagan's professed approach to truth and the record of his performance. Claiming to have done his own research to reach the truth about conditions in the 1930s, he came up with a description of New Deal objectives that would have been given a failing grade by any high school civics teacher. Incredibly, he persisted in classifying Franklin Roosevelt's aides as either fascist- or communist-oriented, even after several additional decades of research and experience had elevated him to the highest office in the land. When reaching for that exalted position, he stressed the public's need to know all the facts about their government's operations, "pleasant and unplesant." But once in the White House he adopted a policy of secrecy that would be difficult to justify in wartime, protecting himself and his assistants from public scrutiny of their acts even where no reasonable connection with national security could be established.

This misuse of historical evidence and zealous guarding against public knowledge of his administration's operations indicates a serious lack of intellectual integrity. It is often said that Reagan had the courage of his convictions. What is equally apparent is that he did not have the courage to subject his convictions to the test of the whole truth and nothing but the truth.

Dedication

The depth of a president's devotion to the country may well be expressed in how hard he works at his job. But devotion to one's country and dedication to the job at hand are two different things. If the latter meant long hours in the Oval Office, Reagan did not see that as the characteristic of a good president. "Show me an executive who works long hard hours," he once remarked, "and I'll show you a bad executive." Yet he chose to replace Edwin Meese as his chief of staff with a powerful Wall Street operator who had earned a reputation for rarely limiting the hours he felt were necessary to accomplish whatever job he took on. In Washington, Donald Regan showed the same dedication to his public post as he had to work in private business. In fact, it was because Regan urged the president to resume a "normal" work schedule a month after prostate surgery that Mrs. Reagan's intense dislike of the man reached a boiling point early in 1987 and led shortly to his resignation.

As has been shown, President Reagan's normal work day could hardly be called taxing.[7] An unofficial biographer recalls the president remarking, "It's true hard work never killed anybody, but I figure, why take the chance?" This was taken as a joke, although it may well have been the kind of humor that tells more than the speaker would have his listeners believe. What other president would engage in such banter with reporters, or would open a briefing session with the remark that he "didn't have anything better to do."[8]

Equally revealing is this further description of Reagan's work habits by political analyst Lou Cannon:

"Hard work" means different things to different people, and Reagan works very hard, if physical energy is the principal measurement. . . . What Reagan lacks is a willingness to expend intellectual energy unless it is an absolute requisite of his job. He will work hard enough when presented with a speech draft on deadline, usually in reaction to the ideas of others. He has an almost total lack of curiosity and no interest at all in solving a problem for its own sake. Aides cannot remember the last time he read a book.[9]

If Reagan's aides were quoted correctly, their report contradicts the president's frequent assertion that he was an "avid reader." Certainly his avidity did not extend to the mounds of reports and background papers that were prepared for his information and guidance. He may, as his former press secretary writes, have taken home an armful of these documents when he left the office at the end of his work day, but there is no evidence that he read anything but the one- or two-page summaries that his assistants knew were all that he was interested in receiving, even on major policy questions.

Bad news, or information that might bring embarrassment, Reagan preferred not to hear. This was an old trait that had been observed during his California governorship when his aides suddenly shocked him with the results of a lengthy investigation of a purported homosexual clique within his administration. Reagan had known nothing of either the rumors or the investigation. Although quiet resignations avoided public scandal, Reagan's closest associates failed to realize what a more knowledgeable observer saw as the central problem: "A governor's unwillingness or inability to make himself informed."[10] A similar and far more critical situation arose—and could not be kept from the public—when, as president, Reagan confessed that he had no notion that Iranian money was being diverted to aid the Nicaraguan Contras.

Another political analyst pointed up Reagan's failings by comparing him to the candidates in the 1988 presidential election. Either Bush or Dukakis would be better, he said, because:

They work. They even read. They are not ideologues. They don't bait the Congress. They don't think Ollie North was a "hero" or that Ed Meese was a "great Attorney General." And they respect brains and recruit good people.

They're not "great communicators" but they're not great pretenders either. They're not very good at disarming voters. They lack Reagan's easy optimism, his amiable incompetence, his tolerance of dubs and sleaze, his cronyism, his preoccupation with stars, his indifference to facts and convenient forgetfulness. In short, they lack many qualities America could very well do without.[11]

Creativity, Brilliance

In light of the foregoing chapters, there is little left to say about President Reagan's creativity or brilliance. It does not take a detractor like actor James

Garner, who was vice-president of the Screen Actors Guild when Reagan was its president, to explain that others "used to tell him what to say," and that Reagan "never had an original thought."[12] Correspondent Robert Lindsey recalls a similar view being expressed by John P. Sears, Reagan's campaign manager in 1976 and briefly in 1980. "As governor, Sears asserted, Reagan seldom came up with an original idea, and often, like a performer waiting for a writer to feed him his lines and for a director to show him how to say them, he waited for others to advise him what to do."[13] In the White House, reporters had little difficulty identifying the speech-writers who coined the fine phrases and snappy slogans that spiced the president's addresses.

Reagan himself made no claim to brilliance. On the contrary, his self-portrait was always that of "Mr. Average." However, he often took credit for originating "initiatives" conceived by others. His own originality was likely to take the form of off-the-cuff remarks that he thought might provoke laughter from his audience. Such witticisms often were harmless one-liners, but on occasion they reflected a thoughtless insensitivity to the force of any comment from the president of the United States. A case in point was his microphone-testing announcement that the bombing of the Soviet Union would start five minutes later. At times, his tendency to shoot from the lip, without giving a thought to the accuracy or aptness of his remarks, led him to charge others with faults more appropriately laid at his own door. A prime example was this quip in his reputation-making Goldwater speech: "It isn't so much that liberals are ignorant. It's just that they know so much that isn't so."[14]

This mental blindness was matched by a similar inability—or unwillingness—to witness some of the more depressing conditions in the Land of the Free. Asked if he ever noticed from his White House windows the Lafayette Park soup kitchens that were set up daily for the homeless of Washington, Reagan said he had "very little occasion" to look out of the windows on that side of the house, although he was over there every day when he used the exercise room at about the time the line of hungry people would be forming.[15] As president or private citizen, the incurious and intellectually sterile Ronald Reagan saw only what he wanted to see, heard only what he wanted to hear, and remembered only what it pleased him to recall.

Political Leadership

President Reagan's political leadership was most clearly demonstrated at the party level. Once he had secured the Republican nomination in 1980, he reigned unchallenged through the next seven-and-one-half years. Not that he satisfied all elements of the party all of the time. But on most issues his position had the firm support of an overwhelming majority of Republicans in and out of Congress. And thanks to his impressive election victory over Jimmy Carter, he faced minimal opposition from Democratic members of Congress in pushing through his initial package of tax cuts, military increases and reductions in non-defense spending.

One major disadvantage that was unique to the Reagan administration was the minority position of his party in the House of Representatives through the entire eight years from 1981 to 1989. If this wasn't enough to demonstrate public disapproval of some of his key domestic programs and foreign policies, that attitude came through loud and clear in 1986, when Republicans lost control of the Senate as well, leaving a Republican president in the rare and unenviable position of facing a Democratic majority in both houses of Congress.

The embarrassment of a Democratic majority in the House was to some extent offset by Reagan's personal popularity and by the support he received from those conservative southern senators who had not defected to Republican ranks. The movement of white Southerners from Democratic to Republican rolls, long delayed by bitter memories of the Civil War, got its start during the civil rights challenges that erupted during the Eisenhower administration. Reagan's repeated claim to leadership in the protection of minorities against discrimination made little impression on either the country's minorities or on those voters who recognized and approved of him as a prophet in the tradition of Puritan preacher John Winthrop.

The 1980 election victory that gave Reagan a mandate to set in motion a program of fiscal reform also encouraged him to believe that he could return to state and local authorities responsibility for many of the services that the federal establishment had taken on during the decades from Roosevelt's New Deal to Johnson's Great Society. A first step in what Reagan later termed the "new federalism" was the initiation of block grants that gave states greater authority in the use and administration of federal funds than they had had under the more closely controlled categorical grants that had previously formed the heart of federal revenue-sharing programs. Although Congress accepted his first block grant plan, when he subsequently proposed "mega-blocks" that would cut grant allocations in half, Congress balked.[16] Had his scheme not involved such drastic cuts, it might have been better received and would have greatly simplified the revenue-sharing program.

The effectiveness of a president's leadership is inevitably affected by his choice of advisers. This is particularly true of a chief executive whose managerial philosophy is to "surround yourself with the best people you can find, delegate authority, and don't interfere." Reagan's choice of Ed Meese as his principal adviser was hardly a means of ensuring that he would receive "a full range of reactions" on major political issues. Nor could he expect to learn all the facts relating to such critical problems as military preparedness from a secretary of defense who used statistics—including falsified evidence—in whatever way would support his burgeoning budget requests.

Administrative Talent

A comment by the special Review Board which Reagan appointed to look into the Iran-Contra affair goes to the heart of his failure as an administrator. Aimed only at the National Security Council, this observation can be applied administration-wide:

> The NSC system will not work unless the President makes it work. After all, this system was created to serve the President of the United States in ways of his choosing. By his actions, by his leadership, the President therefore determines the quality of its performance.

Signs of the fundamental weakness of Reagan's delegate-and-don't-interfere policy appeared in his first term, when EPA officials were left free to act as if they were consultants to the private corporations they were mandated by law to monitor. It also permitted two of the three highest White House officials to feel free to use their influence on behalf of friends doing business with the federal government. Moreover, these and other examples of illegal or unethical practices by Reagan appointees were encouraged by his persistent denial of any wrongdoing by members of his administration, no matter how convincing the evidence against them.[17] Little wonder, then, that when McFarlane, North, Poindexter and company undertook to make good the president's pledge to support the Contras in spite of congressional and public resistance, they did not expect any interference or recrimination from the Oval Office. Reagan himself justified their confidence in an explanation of how his management style applied to the Iran-Contra situation. Repeating the formula that "you get the best people you can to do a job" and then "you don't hang over their shoulder criticizing everything they do," he concluded that "the only time you move is if the evidence is incontrovertible that they are not following policy or they have gone down a road in which they're not achieving what we want." Yet his move to set up a board of inquiry was not based on such incontrovertible evidence. Rather, it was forced by public outcry at the first suggestion of devious, and possibly illegal, maneuvering in support of Reagan's objectives. To be sure, that evidence began to surface as soon as the Tower Commission opened its investigation, but Reagan continued to complain that he was ignorant of "what was going on," even after receiving the commission's report.[18]

World Leadership

Ronald Reagan's introduction to international politics was not unlike that of the millions of Americans caught up in the fervor of World War II and the enthusiasm which that conflict aroused for a United Nations organization that could prevent any repetition of the devastation the world had suffered from 1939 to 1945. Claiming in his autobiography to have been "busily joining every organization I could find that would guarantee to save the world" in 1945 and 1946, Reagan offered nothing to suggest his support for the United Nations. His contempt for that organization began to show the year he enrolled in the Republican party. Soon after, as governor of California, he refused to join the president and other state governors in their annual proclamation of United Nations Day. President Nixon's initiative in reopening relations with communist China did not alter Reagan's opinion that the UN members' decision to enroll China in place of Taiwan "confirms the moral bankruptcy of that international organization."[19]

As president, Reagan took every opportunity to address the UN General Assembly and to lecture its delegates on the superior morality of the U.S. and the purity of its objectives compared with those of the Soviet Union. The tone of those annual speeches altered significantly only after he had concluded the INF agreement with Gorbachev and could speak of "the prospect of a new age of world peace."[20] When the General Assembly or the Security Council passed a resolution criticizing a particular action by the U.S.—such as the invasion of Grenada or the mining of Nicaraguan harbors—Reagan brushed off the reproof as the standard response of governments that were forever finding fault with U.S. policies. If a resolution of this kind came before the Security Council, his representative did not hesitate to veto it, confidently using a power uniformly disparaged by the administration when applied by the Soviet Union.

In the context of Soviet-American relations, Reagan scorned entente as naive acceptance of a standoff that could benefit only the Soviet Union. He insisted that a tough attitude and a massive military buildup of U.S. arms were needed to bring the Kremlin to terms. When, after much heated rhetoric and six years of enormous military expenditures, he successfully negotiated the INF Treaty, he saw that sequence as proof of the logic of his position. What he ignored was the fact that every public blast at the Evil Empire had brought a reply in kind, and every boost in the military budget was offset by a corresponding increase in Soviet military output. This was anticipated by an independent study of previous experience which showed that the "coercive bargaining" favored by Reagan had been less effective in bringing the Soviets around than "a reciprocity strategy" which combined "a demonstration of resolve with cooperative initiatives."[21] From this 1983 analysis it followed that the less abrasive approach adopted by Reagan in his second term should be more productive, as indeed it was. However, that did not alter Reagan's interpretation of history.

The new, second-term approach which Reagan took to relations with the U.S.S.R brought considerable relief to countries around the world, especially those in western Europe that had lived in fear of being caught in the middle of a superpower conflict. However, the road to a weapons reduction treaty was a pioneer trail, not easily traveled. The first Soviet-American summit at Reykjavik ended in bitter recriminations over who was responsible for the last-minute blocking of an agreement that would have fulfilled the brightest hopes of all concerned. Then, on the heels of Reykjavik, the Iran-Contra scandal broke, and reactions abroad ranged from polite questions in England as to Reagan's "detached style of leadership," to concern in Thailand that Reagan might "lose his ability to negotiate arms control." A poll of world news organizations to identify the ten top stories of 1986 showed that only the physical disasters experienced by the U.S. spacecraft *Challenger* and the Soviet nuclear power plant at Chernobyl outranked the diplomatic disasters of Reykjavik and Irangate.[22]

Prodded by the realization that failure to reach an accord on arms control could have a devastating effect on the prospects for relieving not only East-West tensions but also the economic strains imposed by mounting military budgets, both Reagan and Gorbachev undertook to put the derailed negotiations back on track. The eventual conclusion of an INF Treaty was Reagan's greatest triumph, one which brought almost universal praise from governments on both sides of the ideological fence, and from many unaligned nations as well.

From a global point of view, resolving the East-West conflict overshadowed all other problems associated with the United States. NATO governments, believing that their safety depended on the strength of American arms, were consistently supportive of Reagan's policy of maintaining a strong western alliance. Except for Britain's Margaret Thatcher, their leaders were less enthusiastic about Reagan's handling of problems elsewhere, most notably in Central America, South Africa and Iran. Latin American nations accepted U.S. aid but resented Reagan's attempts to impose his concepts of democracy and freedom on governments in the western hemisphere. Third World countries reacted similarly, content to receive the blessings of economic assistance—usually in return for expressions of anti-communist sentiment—but insistent on their right to follow their own domestic and foreign policies.

Regard for Law

Like most occupants of the White House, President Reagan applied the law as he saw fit, and when the law did not reflect his view of right and wrong, he sought to have it changed. Also like many of his predecessors, he was not above evading or disregarding a law that did not suit his purposes. But few, if any, of the former presidents could match his extra-legal use of executive authority which, in Reagan's case, stemmed from his messianic conviction that "anything we do is in the national interest." Even the warranted wartime illegalities of Lincoln and Franklin Roosevelt could not compare with Reagan's peacetime abuse of his authority.

The first step in the administration's attack on disfavored legislation came with Reagan's appointments to cabinet and other senior positions. Many of these officials used—or failed to use—their regulatory powers to achieve what Congress refused: the freeing of business and industry from government controls. Except for posts in defense and national security offices, administrators were expected to curtail the activities of their departments as much as possible.

In the litany of misfeasance, malfeasance and nonfeasance cited in earlier chapters, nonfeasance was the outstanding characteristic of Reagan's appointees to critically important posts, not only in Interior, Agriculture and EPA, but in the White House and the Department of Justice. Failure to enforce the law as Congress intended was often as significant to the welfare of large segments of the population as either evasion or direct flouting of the law. Reagan's two attorneys general, William French Smith and Edwin Meese, were under constant fire for their reluctance to enforce civil rights legislation and the many laws intended to protect the environment, public health, and safety in the workplace.

In one respect the approach taken by departments and agencies concerned with national security was the reverse of the cut-and-slash program followed elsewhere. In the Defense Department, CIA, NSC and, to some extent, the State Department, Reagan's appointees tackled their jobs with enthusiasm and the will to expand, rather than contract, their operations. In those quarters, disregard for the law took the form of maneuvers like those involved in defense contract irregularities, and in arming Iran and supporting the Contras.

Misuse of authority is remediable to the extent that a pattern of illegal, unethical or biased administration can be reversed by a change in leadership attitude or a change in personnel. What cannot be reversed, except over a long period of time, is the effect Reagan achieved through his appointments to the federal judiciary. In his eight-year tour of duty, President Reagan appointed almost half of the 761 federal judges who will for years to come decide how the Constitution and laws of Congress will be applied to more than 300,000 cases brought before the district courts, the circuit courts of appeal, and the Supreme Court of the United States every year.

Because of its prestige and the finality of its judgments, the Supreme Court is most frequently cited as Reagan's chief weapon in effecting a reversal of the liberal interpretation of the Constitution reflected in decisions handed down over the previous 25 years. His appointment of three justices to that august body, plus his promotion of its principal conservative member from associate justice to chief justice, has already, by 1991, made a significant difference in the court's handling of some—by no means all—social issues. What is less widely appreciated is the impact that his 300-odd appointments to district and appellate courts will have, not only in the majority of decisions that are never carried to a higher level, but in the promotions that inevitably carry many district judges to the courts of appeal and, in a few cases, to the Supreme Court.

The problem is not just that on one occasion Reagan selected for the Chicago Circuit Court of Appeals a John Birch Society supporter whose "lack of judicial experience at any level and demonstrated incompetence in the preparation of legal documents" brought protests from two Republican members of the Senate Judiciary Committee, the Chicago Council of Lawyers, and 40 law school deans. Rather, it is that the foremost—and most conservative—legal society in the country gave Reagan nominees increasingly lower ratings: "Of 28 persons considered in the early part of Reagan's second administration for appointment to the appellate level (one step below the U.S. Supreme Court), 14 were assigned the ABA's minimum qualification rating, and most of these were classified at the questionable level of 'qualified/unqualified'."[23]

Ethical Standards

Students of history who undertake to evaluate past presidents generally think of Grant and Harding as least qualified for the office of chief executive, largely because of their inability (in Grant's case) or unwillingness (in Harding's) to deal with the pervasive corruption that characterized their administrations. Had Reagan bothered to study the real-life experiences of Grant and Harding—as the founding fathers had done with governments of the previous 2,000 years—he might have recognized and understood the significance of the extraordinary number of cases of legal and ethical violations committed by high officials in virtually every branch of his administration.

To the very last day of his presidency, Reagan denied any wrongdoing by his aides. Interviewed by Mike Wallace of CBS less than a week before vacating the White House, Reagan engaged in this exchange on the subject of ethics:

> Wallace: More than 100 political appointees, men and women that you and your staff selected, have left office amid charges of ethical misconduct. I know some have been cleared of those charges. Many were not. Why did your administration seem to attract more than its share, perhaps, of people who tried to convert their public office into personal gain?
>
> Pres. Reagan: Well, Mike, I think that has been greatly overemphasized. But the other thing that I wonder is, Mike, those who were guilty of—they—we didn't cover up.
>
> Wallace: It must have been a matter of great sorrow that your old friend Mike Deaver and your old friend Lyn Nofziger went wrong, in effect.
>
> Pres. Reagan: I don't think they went wrong.
>
> Wallace [voice over]: But two juries did. Mike Deaver was convicted of perjury, lying to Congress. Lyn Nofziger was convicted of illegally lobbying White House aides.
>
> Pres. Reagan: Neither one of them ever—and we've known each other for years—ever raised a finger to ask me to do anything for them. And I don't think that they asked anyone else. And that's why both of those men have declared to others they would not accept a pardon if I offered one, because they feel they are innocent.[24]

A similar tolerance was shown executives and employees in private industry. One of the earliest recommendations of Attorney General William French Smith was to ease the terms of the law prohibiting bribery of foreign officials by American businessmen seeking contracts abroad. Smith was disarmingly frank in explaining to a group of international lawyers that the administration's goal was "to eliminate the more offensive provisions of our law that both harm our companies' ability to compete abroad and offend the business sensibilities of other countries."[25]

Recognition of the low state of business ethics was not a new discovery. As the Scythian philosopher Anacharsis remarked some 2,500 years ago, "The market is the place set apart where men may deceive each other." With that introduction, U.S. Senator Warren Magnuson wrote in 1968 that while he had always had "some realization of how poorly the American consumer is protected and how he is exploited by the unscrupulous and irresponsible few of the business community," after studying the matter he realized that he had "not fully felt the depth of the problem: its serious social consequences, its detrimental effect on ethical business, its viciousness among the poor, its threat to human life; in short, its true cancerous qualities in the fiber of American life."[26] A decade later a professor of law and business at the University of Connecticut told members of the national honor society for business school students that "American business has increasingly lost the trust of substantial sectors of the American public" because business management clearly was not, as it claimed, operating in the public interest, or even in the interest of its stockholders.[27]

Against this background, one would not expect a drastic change in the level of government or corporate ethics, were it not for Reagan's claim to leadership in the drive to restore "the virtues and values" of early America, values that he found "rooted in the source of all strength, a belief in a Supreme Being, and a law higher than our own." This was his introduction to the presidency. Six years and an endless string of ethical lapses later, he was asked what he hoped his legacy would be in terms of the values being taught to young Americans. His answer was, "Well, I hope that the imprint would be left on [as?] one of high morality."[28]

The very different imprint that was left might have been anticipated by E. Pendleton James, Reagan's first assistant for presidential personnel, who regarded the government ethics law as the "chief obstacle to businessmen who might want to enter government."[29] While this may have discouraged many potential candidates for appointment by President Reagan, it did not appear to inhibit those who did join his administration. The result was a record of ethical malpractice which, if it lacked the wholesale plundering of the public treasury experienced during the Grant and Harding administrations, surpassed even those years in the frequency with which Reagan appointees were obliged to resign (they were never fired) for illegal or unethical practices.

Equally depressing was the legacy of corporate corruption and a general business atmosphere in which the ambition to get rich reduced all other goals to secondary importance. Corporate raiders, interested only in economic power and prestige, became the new heroes; business buyouts and hostile takeovers, arranged with enormous profits to the negotiators, their lawyers and bankers, but with no product improvement or other benefit to the general public, became all the rage.[30] Meanwhile, the stock market alternatively plunged and rose in seesaw fashion as Wall Street was rocked by one insider-trading scandal after another from October 1987 well into 1989. And as the country's major defense contractors came under criminal investigation for "bribery, kickbacks, false claims, gratuities, bid rigging, cost mischarging and product substitution," the most prestigious law firm in New York boasted to its clients of its influence in government circles by its "direct access" to members of Congress and to officials in the Treasury Department and Internal Revenue Service, where five of the firm's partners had once held senior positions.[31] By 1988, the sorry state of business ethics had given rise to a new profession, that of "ethics consultants." These experts conducted seminars for business executives, wrote pamphlets and designed instructional programs for government contractors and their employees. Business schools added new courses on ethics, and the University of Virginia's business branch offered "a four-day seminar that promises to 'demystify' ethics for the unacquainted."[32] That was in the school year 1987–88, which began only a few months after Reagan had expressed the hope that he would leave a legacy of high morality for the young of America.

Accomplishments—Domestic

President Reagan capsuled what he regarded as his chief accomplishments under two headings: economic recovery and recovery of morale. Each of these incorporated a number of specifics, which he cited on many occasions and which he repeated in the first of his several farewell addresses. Under economic recovery, he included reduction of income taxes, interest rates and unemployment, the creation of 19 million new jobs, "real family income up, the poverty rate down, entrepreneurship booming, and an explosion in research and technology."[33] He also noted that U.S. exports were on the rise, indicating an improvement in American competitiveness in world markets.

On the tax side, there is no question that Reagan achieved most of his promise to abandon the progressive income tax in favor of a system in which assessments would be made at very nearly equal rates for all taxpayers.

The practical effect was to eliminate families at the poverty level from the tax rolls and leave high-income families with what Reagan referred to as "72 cents of every dollar earned," a conservative figure that did not take into consideration the many deductions and evasions available only to the rich. By comparison, a family of three with a single breadwinner earning $18,000 a year would have its income reduced to less than $17,000, a far more serious sacrifice for the millions of such people than the suffering that the 1 percent in the highest group would experience by the loss of 28 percent of six- and seven-figure incomes. When federal excise taxes and the increasingly popular state and local sales taxes are taken into account, the unfairness of "equal treatment" for rich, middle-income and poor is even more obvious. The end product of Reagan's tax reform was a system in which, except for people whose income was so low that they were relieved of tax payments, little was left of the long-established concept that the burden of supporting the government should be shared in proportion to the benefits each individual realizes from the American economy.

While some regard Reagan's tax reform as a retreat from the fairer progressive system based on ability to pay, no one would debate the benefits accruing from the substantial decline in inflation and interest rates that occurred from 1981 to 1987. As Reagan left office, both were moving back up, but for most of his administration their downward trend had greatly eased the economic burdens of many people.

The employment situation took longer to bring under control and never did reach the idyllic state pictured by Reagan. One important aspect of this problem was the national shift from a predominantly goods-producing economy to a predominantly service-oriented one, a trend that began long before Reagan appeared on the scene and which continued, unaffected by his policies. Jobs in manufacturing and other goods-producing industries, which had experienced little growth since the 1960s, actually declined from 1980 to 1988. During the same period, jobs in service industries, which in 1980 employed almost twice as many people as goods producers, increased by more than 30 percent. As a 1988 report of the Economic Policy Institute pointed out, "Since 1979, some 85 percent of the new jobs have been in the lowest paying industries—retail trade and personnel, business and health services."[34]

By the close of 1988, unemployment had reached a low of 5 percent, a level long considered by classical economists as the minimum desired in a competitive economy. Interestingly enough, Reagan helped reduce unemployment by ignoring his pledge to "cut and slash" the Washington bureaucracy, instead increasing the number of federal employees from 2,898,000 in 1980 to 3,112,000 by the close of 1988. More than two-thirds of the increase were civilian personnel. Of course, the official unemployment rate, which translated to 6.6 million unemployed, did not include an additional 5.4 million people who were not considered part of the labor force because, although they wanted jobs, they had given up looking for them. And among the 116.7 million people on the job in 1988, 20.7 million— almost 18 percent—were employed only part-time.[35]

Although the percentage of the population living in poverty decreased from 15.2 percent in 1983 to 13.5 percent in 1987 (the last year for which data were available at the time of writing), the number of individuals in that condition fell less sharply as the total population increased. In 1987, there were 32.5 million Americans who could not afford to live even at the poverty level, defined by the federal government as having an income sufficient that one-third would buy "the lowest-cost nutritionally adequate diet."[36]

The impact of Reaganomics on the disparity between the highest and lowest income groups was highlighted in the report cited previously. Measuring average cash incomes of all families in 1987 dollars, from the top 20 percent to the bottom 20 percent, the study found that in the Reagan years the income of the latter group actually fell by 6.1 percent, while that of the most affluent 20 percent rose 11.1 percent.

Another worrysome factor was the billowing burden of public debt. The first four Reagan budgets brought unprecedented deficits of $110.6 billion, $195.4 billion, $212.3 billion and $221.1 billion, respectively. With Congress refusing to go beyond the first two years' cuts in social programs, and Reagan's rejection of all suggestions for reducing military spending, the prospect of continued deficits on so grand a scale gave rise to the Gramm-Rudman-Hollings bill, ultimately enacted as the Balanced Budget and Emergency Deficit Control Act of 1985.[37] Sharp reductions began in fiscal year 1987, but by the close of the Reagan administration the public debt had ballooned from the $997.9 billion inherited from President Carter to more than $2.4 trillion. By Reagan's own standards, broadcast over a number of years in bitter tirades against a government that refused to limit its spending to the amount of revenue it collected, eight years of record deficit spending documented his most dismal domestic failure.

Reagan's second major category of achievement—recovery of morale—was meant to include public confidence that the country's future was bright with opportunity and that America was standing tall in the eyes of the world, acknowledged as the defender of democracy everywhere. That confidence began on a high note in 1981 when Reagan won the tax-reduction battle. It surged briefly after the conquest of Grenada, the boxing of Qaddafi and, with greater relief, on the signing of the INF Treaty. But there were many low spots.

As indicated earlier, Reagan's personal popularity did not necessarily extend to his policies. The administration's drive to deregulate business undoubtedly made many executives happy, but it opened the door to the excesses that invariably occur when government turns a blind eye to sleaze in private industry. The most outstanding example of the failure of deregulation is seen in its effect on the nation's banks.

Included in the collapse of hundreds of financial institutions were commercial banks, savings and loan banks, farm credit cooperatives and the first federal land bank ever to go out of business. Relatively few were important enough to be identified in news stories, but the failure of even the smallest bank meant serious trouble for the community in which it operated. Rural areas, which had known only one credit association bankruptcy in the 50 years from 1933 to 1983, suddenly saw 11 cooperatives fail within a period of 18 months.[38]

Especially hard hit were savings and loan institutions, which fell in clusters all though the 1980s. In the early warning stage, President Reagan signed the Garn-St. Germain bill (October 15, 1982), which he hailed as "the most important legislation for financial institutions in the last 50 years." Calling it "proconsumer," he said, "It means help for housing, more jobs, and new growth for the economy." Before his second term ended, his bank regulators had closed dozens of failing banks, from Ohio to Texas to California. A last-minute bailout of 34 savings and loan institutions, which were sold to investors at a cost of $23.8 billion to the government, occurred in December 1988, just before time ran out on the special tax breaks that the buyers would realize.[39]

Even then, the worst was yet to come. In the first year of President Bush's administration, facing potential losses of $200 to $300 billion, Congress was induced to pass a bill committing the federal government to a ten-year program that would spend up to $176 billion in taxpayer money, as against $63 billion supplied by the Home Loan Bank Board and the savings and loan industry.[40] Should a sum like this be added to a national debt that by 1988 was costing taxpayers over $200 billion annually in interest payments alone, future generations will have little reason to exult over the economic revolution wrought by Reaganomics.

Accomplishments—International

Reagan's farewell recitation of his achievements in world affairs opened with a reference to his welcoming the 1989 New Year by toasting "the new peacefulness around the globe." Taking credit for cessation of the "regional conflicts that rack the globe" in the Persian Gulf, Afghanistan, Cambodia and Angola, he told viewers, "We meant to change a nation, and instead we changed a world."

Judging the quality of a president's accomplishments in world affairs is far more difficult than rating his performance at home, especially in the short term. For one thing, documentation from foreign sources is limited to what government officials are willing, in their own interests, to reveal. Rarely do such revelations include expositions of motive, or of inner-council discussions that led to particular policies or actions. On the origins of U.S. policy, more information is generally available, thanks in part to the country's democratic tradition of openness and, more specifically, to the Freedom of Information Act. Under the Reagan administration, however, much of what the country learned was revealed in spite of, rather than because of, Reagan's method of "letting the people know." In an administration obsessed with secrecy, this slogan turned out to mean informing the public of only as much as the White House thought advisable, which was precious little, especially in the realm of foreign affairs, where the Reagan concept of national security encouraged maximum use of the "Top Secret" rubber stamp.

Available evidence indicates that on the international scene Reagan's success was mixed. His one outstanding achievement was the breakthrough on arms control, which occurred only after he abandoned his Evil Empire attacks on the Soviet Union. The fact that he was unable to sustain the momentum until agreement was reached on reduction of strategic weapons and conventional arms does not detract from the effect that the INF Treaty had in relaxing the dangerous U.S.-Soviet tension that had kept the world on edge since the collapse of detente.

The importance of Reagan's contribution to peaceful settlement of conflicts in the Persian Gulf, Afghanistan, Cambodia and Angola is difficult to determine. His tilt toward Iraq, whose government had initiated the war against Iran, and his use of naval forces to protect shipping only against Iranian—not Iraqi—attacks, certainly hastened the collapse of Iran's military capability as well as its oil-based economy. It may also have encouraged Iraq to reject the first Iranian offer of an armistice and, a few years later, to invade Kuwait. In any case, the Iran-Iraq war was ended by the mutual exhaustion of the warring nations and the personal intervention of UN Secretary General Javier Perez de Cuellar. And Iraq's invasion of Kuwait was halted only after more than 300,000 American troops had, at President Bush's direction, joined small detachments of other UN members to evict the Iraqi army from Kuwait and destroy its war-making capacity.

American influence in ending Soviet participation in the struggle for control of Afghanistan may have been greater than in the Iran-Iraq contest, principally because the supply of U.S. Stinger missiles and other military equipment enabled anti-government, anti-Soviet guerrillas to fight more effectively. There is no doubt that U.S. aid increased the casualty rate among Russian and government forces, but the fervor of the rebels, and their effective use of Afghanistan's mountainous terrain showed their intention to carry on the war against Kabul indefinitely, with or without outside help, and regardless of whether Russian troops stayed or left. Given that attitude, it is clear the U.S. intervention did not bring peace to the land, although it may have contributed to reducing the conflict to a purely civil war.

In a very real sense, Afghanistan was Russia's Vietnam. Although the Soviets faced no such domestic protest as Presidents Johnson and Nixon did, Kremlin leaders came to recognize the futility of continuing a campaign that would drain their resources and create a public mood that might threaten their program of domestic reform. In any event, it is unlikely that outsiders will ever learn just how Moscow's decision to withdraw from Afghanistan was taken, or how great a factor U.S. policy played in reaching that decision.

Cambodia is hardly in the same class with Afghanistan as an example of U.S. influence in the peacemaking process. Washington was torn between supporting any group opposing the Vietnam-sponsored government in Phnom Penh and repugnance at the thought of aiding the Khmer Rouge which, although mounting the only effective opposition, had been responsible for the massacre of over a million Cambodians during its brief period of rule. Published reports of U.S. activity in that region were based largely on hearsay, and three months after Reagan left office the White House was reported still to be trying to determine whether there were any non-communist rebel factions worthy of U.S. aid.[41]

From Washington's point of view, the situation in Angola presented a problem similar to that in Afghanistan: a communist government supported by the Soviet Union, in this case both directly and through its surrogate, Cuba. Two complicating factors were South Africa's military intervention on the side of Angola's rebel leader, Jonas Savimbi, and the simmering but less militarily active revolt against South African rule in Angola's southern neighbor, Namibia. Embarrassed as he was by South Africa's repeated incursions from Namibia into Angola, U.S. Ambassador Chester Crocker was successful in bringing the parties back together time after time until agreement on a cease-fire was reached in the waning days of the Reagan administration. This represented the administration's most clear-cut, positive contribution to regional peace, notwithstanding the fact that the armistice affected only the forces of South Africa, Cuba, the Angolan government, and the Namibian rebels fighting for freedom from South Africa. As in Afghanistan, withdrawal of foreign troops from Angola still left that country in a state of civil war and left a new American president the task of deciding how to approach that problem.

In his final catalog of achievements Reagan mentioned "knocking down protectionist walls" only in passing, omitting specific reference to the free-trade agreement with Canada, a truly striking accomplishment. In the unlikely event that other major trading nations could be convinced of the benefits of similar tariff-destroying treaties, this would indeed revolutionize not only the conduct of international trade but patterns of production the world over.

Other notable omissions in Reagan's recitation of his experience in world affairs were the problems and policies associated with Central America, South Africa, and the Iran-Contra affair. Each of these marked a failure, not only in terms of domestic opinion but in the eyes of a large part of the world in which Reagan longed to stand tall. In the case of South Africa, the failure of the administration's policy of "constructive engagement" was reflected in reactions both at home and abroad. Margaret Thatcher's government in Great Britain was unique in its steadfast support of Reagan's policies, in South Africa as well as Central America. Israel, whose stand on most international issues was solidly behind the U.S., remained aloof from the debate over South Africa, though she continued her lucrative trade with that country. Most of the rest of the world agreed that South Africa's domestic policy of apartheid and purposeful intimidation of her African neighbors made her a pariah among nations. Reagan remained unpersuaded, and the wrist-slap he ultimately decided upon was designed simply to preempt the stronger measures which Congress finally forced upon a reluctant president.

The blackest mark against Reagan's conduct of foreign matters was earned by his handling of the Iran-Contra affair. The president's own commission of inquiry turned up enough evidence to reveal him as an inept overseer of his national security staff; congressional hearings brought to light the duplicity and disregard for the rule of law that characterized the actions of those working to carry out his policies; and the testimony and documents offered in the trial of Oliver North strongly suggested that the president knew more of what was being done in his name than he ever admitted. Presentation of more damaging evidence was blocked by Attorney General Dick Thornburgh's refusal to release secret documents relating to the diversion of Iranian funds to the Contras. This forced special prosecutor Lawrence E. Walsh to drop all charges bearing on the diversion. Thornburgh's move also effectively removed from North's trial the question of President Reagan's culpability, as the remaining charges had to do only with whether North had, or had not, lied to Congress, obstructed its investigations, destroyed or falsified government documents, and used government funds for personal purposes. On these questions, federal judge Gerhard A. Gessell ruled that "there has been no showing that President Reagan's appearance is necessary to assure Lieutenant Colonel North a fair trial."[42] That decision effectively closed the book on Reagan's part in the Iran-Contra scandal. No information that would mar the image of the Great Communicator can be expected from his memoirs. Only from the documented memoirs of other participants, or from such official papers as are published in *Foreign Relations of the United States* after Reagan's death, can historians hope to learn more about this ignoble chapter of American history.

* * * *

Thanks to the heavy veil of secrecy that the Reagan administration drew across many of its activities, firm judgments about a multitude of Reagan's decisions may be long delayed. In this observer's judgment, one aspect of that evaluation is that Ronald Reagan was the greatest fraud who ever occupied the White House. There are many evidences of this, but several stand out. From the earliest days of his political activity he castigated his enemies for three things: hiding their actions behind a curtain of secrecy, pretending that their elitist administrators knew better than the people what was good for them, and setting a trend toward godless, immoral living. Yet, no previous president erected so many peacetime barriers to public access to information on government activities; no administration charged by Reagan as elitist professed more superior, unchallengeable knowledge and ability than his own; and only Grant and Harding could match him in his blind acceptance of the most pervasive pattern of unethical—often illegal—behavior ever tolerated by the White House.

On the positive side, Reagan's most important contribution may have been the lift that he gave to the general spirit of the country early in his first administration. If this was accompanied by a growing fear that his militarist drumbeating might bring the country to the brink of a third world war, that fear was allayed by his second-term success in negotiating the first of what was intended to be a succession of arms-reduction treaties with the Soviet Union.

On other fronts he left a far less promising legacy. His economic philosophy fostered attitudes that led the nation into what economist Robert J. Samuelson—no radical of any kind—called "a vast spoils system." As Samuelson pointed out, this was not the goal of Reagan's eighteenth-century hero, Adam Smith, who saw the competitive society as one that would "generate new wealth." Reagonomics, on the other hand, encouraged an excess of greed that, by stock manipulation, corporate raiding, or outright fraud, snatched assets from others and added nothing to the wealth or productive capacity of the country.

While the more affluent members of society were enjoying the fruits of Reagan's tax reforms and business deregulation, the less affluent found life increasingly difficult, their incomes keeping pace with moderate market-basket inflation but not with the extraordinary increases in the cost of housing, education and health care. As to the millions of jobless workers and tens of thousands of homeless people, President Reagan's opinion echoed that of Edwin Meese. Many choose to be unemployed, he told one interviewer, or prefer living on the streets. Ignorant of the living conditions of a segment of society he never visited, he probably did not know that the working poor who could afford shelter of some kind were forced to use up to 70 percent of their income for housing, rather than the 30 percent considered by his own Department of Housing and Urban Development to be "affordable" for the lowest income groups.[43]

Imbued with a philosophy that idealized personal ambition, the uninhibited accumulation of wealth and the influence that wealth brings, President Reagan and his associates in and out of government seemed immune to the by-products of that philosophy: the downgrading of civil rights as compared to economic freedom; indifference to, or manipulation of, laws that did not fit the president's concepts of right and wrong; an almost total blackout in the matter of ethics. When questioned about this, Reagan's defense was that the accusations were the product of a "lynch mob atmosphere" in which "no attention is paid to the fact of how many of them [the accused], when it actually came to a trial, was [sic] found to be totally innocent." To support that generalization he offered the names of just two people, Ray Donovan and Jim Beggs, whose transgressions did not include demonstrably criminal acts and who were therefore never brought to trial.[44] Like President Grant, Reagan simply would not believe the charges leveled at his friends and associates.

By adopting for himself the role of innocent bystander, Reagan earned the title of Teflon president. If mistakes were made, they were someone else's; if plans went awry, it was a subordinate's doing. Research for this study turned up only one instance on which Reagan said, "I was wrong." That admission came in a Saturday radio address that dealt briefly with the Iranian arms sale after it became known that Caspar Weinberger and George Shultz had opposed any such deal.[45] His acknowledgment of error was not repeated in his subsequent discussions of the Iran-Contra affair.

* * * * *

The annual meeting of the American Political Science Association, held in September 1988, produced what was termed as informal assessment of Ronald Reagan as "an above average president." Contributors to that evaluation included not only political scientists but "consultants, lobbyists and political reporters." One of those who judged Reagan to be above average because he "was in tune with the mood of the country" was lobbyist Jim Jones, former chief of staff for President Johnson.[46]

The reported consensus of the convention had some support from members of the public who in the fall of 1988 were asked, "How do you think Ronald Reagan will go down in history—as an outstanding president, above average, average, below average, or poor?" The largest number of those polled—40 percent—rated Reagan above average. Some 12 percent thought him outstanding, while 24 percent ranked him as average, and 20 percent put him down as below average or poor. An unusually low 4 percent expressed no opinion. Given the fact that in the previous poll a majority of those questioned disapproved of his handling of economic conditions, the budget deficit, and his treatment of both Nicaragua and Panama, it seems clear that personality, rather than performance, was the major influence in the public's rating of presidential quality.[47]

A more realistic appraisal of Ronald Reagan as president than the informal assessment of the 1988 political science convention would require weighing all of the positive qualities and accomplishments discussed in the preceding chapters against these negative factors:

—His intellectual shallowness and sophomoric interpretations of history.
—His adoption of a religious mantle as a means of leading the country back to the precepts of Puritan John Winthrop and the "higher law" that he

presumed to be his guide in the conduct of the presidency.

—His inability to recognize or act upon the breaches of legal and ethical standards by his friends and associates in public office.

—His encouragement of a grasping, money-hungry trend in society that put personal ambition above the general welfare and economic aggrandizement above all other human rights.

—His blatant emotional appeal for support in the name of what he called the New Patriotism.

—His unthinking, almost unconscious rejection of his election pledge to openness with the public.

—His lighthearted approach to the demands of office and lack of control over subordinates to whom he delegated almost unlimited authority to carry out his policies.

When these qualities and practices are put on the scale, Reagan's presidential rating will place him no higher than the bottom of the average category.

"Reagan's book reminded me of his presidency...It makes you feel good, you don't remember a thing he said, and when it's over it hits you that you still owe the twenty bucks on your credit card."

Jim Borgman
The Cincinnati Enquirer
King Features Syndicate

EPILOGUE

Ex-President Reagan's 1990 autobiography, *An American Life,* was published after this book was finished but before it went to press. The jacket of *An American Life* describes it as "a work of major historical importance," written "with absolute authority" and "full of new insights." However, as I predicted in my concluding chapter, Reagan's memoirs reveal little that had not been known earlier, and his insights are largely a rehash of the same selected facts, the same fantasies and fabrications that he offered the public throughout his political career. If the quality of his self-evaluation can be reduced to a single sentence, perhaps the caption on Jim Borgman's cartoon in the *Cincinnati Enquirer* says it best (see cartoon on facing page).

The pity of it is that the talented Robert Lindsey, who helped to prepare the autobiography, and who had observed and written clear-headed news reports and penetrating analyses of Reagan's activities before and during his presidency, was given so little to work with and therefore had so little influence on the substance of the book. This may explain why the title page does not include the standard line, "with Robert Lindsey," following Ronald Reagan's name. Which may be just as well, as the book is so obviously intended to sustain and justify the image Reagan worked so hard to create during his years in public office.

The liberties taken with facts in this new Reagan narrative begin with his reminiscences about his early life. In his 1965 autobiography, *Where's the Rest of Me?* (written "with Richard G. Hubler"), Reagan quoted his father's first comment about baby Ron as, "For such a little bit of a fat Dutchman, he makes a hell of a lot of noise, doesn't he?" By 1990 Reagan senior had acquired an extraordinary prescience, his remark now reported as, "He looks like a fat little Dutchman. But who knows, he might grow up to be president some day."[1]

Ronald Reagan's 1965 recollection of his first experience with reading underwent a similar transformation. In that earlier book he wrote that the ability to read came instantaneously—like a flash of lightning. One minute the printed words meant nothing; then suddenly "all the funny black marks on paper clicked into place." In his current work Reagan says, "I don't have any recollection of ever learning how to read." But he still remembers that his father discovered him reading a newspaper "one day before I entered school."[2]

As to his college experience, Reagan's initial version of being content with the "C" average required to remain eligible for sports is larded in 1990 with the unsupported claim that "my grades were higher than average."[3]

Reagan's Hollywood experience included a long and bitter battle with left-wingers in the entertainment field, many of whom were subsequently identified as communists. His first memoir reported a visit from "three men from a well-known government agency" with whom he "exchanged information" about communism in Hollywood, presumably on a onetime basis. In retirement he identifies his visitors as FBI agents and acknowledges that he agreed to meet with them "periodically to discuss some of the things that were going on in Hollywood." This is a veiled reference to something that Reagan has never acknowledged, but which was discovered by the San Jose *Mercury News* from FBI records, namely, that Reagan was a secret FBI informant for all the years during which he so gallantly refused to "point a finger" when testifying publicly on the subject of communism in the film industry.[4]

By far the greatest portion of the new autobiography is devoted to Reagan's political career. For almost 600 pages he continues the pattern set in the earlier chapters. One bit of new material is an explanation of his conversion from liberal Democrat to conservative Republican, a subject curiously missing from his 1965 memoirs, which concluded with the statement that he had found his true place ("the rest of me") in politics. His 1990 account of that transformation is entirely believable although, like other parts of the narrative, it leaves many questions unanswered. And it gains little strength from quotations of questionable relevance dished up short-order style by his ten researchers from the writings of Thomas Jefferson, Abraham Lincoln, Woodrow Wilson, Franklin D. Roosevelt, and Douglas MacArthur. Nevertheless, his explanation that he was won over to Nixon's side in the 1960 election by his former employer, president of General Electric Ralph Cordiner, is understandable, given Reagan's high regard for Cordiner. Also in character is the comment he made to his wife, Nancy, that same year: "All these things I've been criticizing about government getting too big, well, it just dawned on me that every four years when an election comes along, I go out and support the people who are responsible for the things I'm criticizing."[5]

Subsequent chapters deal extensively with Reagan's presidency. What is new here is the interpretation given some of the events of those years. A few examples will serve to illustrate the character of Reagan's reporting.

On his first day in the White House, Reagan writes, he announced that "President Carter's efforts to free the fifty-two Americans held hostage for 444 days in Iran had been successful, and that the plane carrying the hostages had just crossed the border and was no longer in Iranian airspace." To state that he had given Carter credit for obtaining the release of the hostages gives the appearance of a generous heart, but it is blatantly false. His announcement of the release, printed verbatim in the *Public Papers of the President,* contains no reference to President Carter.[6] This is only one of many instances in which Reagan substitutes his dreamlike image of himself for the documentary record available to anyone who can read.

The history of Reaganomics also appears in a new light. Denying that he had embraced supply-side economics, Reagan now credits the ancient Egyptian philosopher ibn-Khaldoon with the theory of taxation more recently propounded by supply-sider Arthur Laffer, one of Reagan's campaign advisers, who in 1980 delighted the candidate with his explanation of the Laffer Curve.[7] To justify the economic package that was based upon the proposals of Laffer and others not even mentioned in the index of *An American Life,* Reagan cites unidentified public opinion polls which he says "showed ninety-five percent of the American people were behind the proposed spending cuts and almost as many supported the thirty-percent, three-year tax cut." The polls actually show that of the 87 percent who knew of the recommended tax cuts, 59 percent favored them, 30 percent were opposed, and 11 percent had no opinion. Weaker still was public support for his suggested spending cuts, which 34 percent thought were too great, 12 percent thought too small, and 44 percent thought "about right."[8] Another false claim is that "despite continuing population growth, the size of the federal civilian work force declined about five percent during the eight years we were in Washington." In fact, the government's own statistics reveal that after a first-year drop, federal employment increased from the 2.866 million inherited from the Carter administration to almost 3 million in December of 1988.[9]

In some cases it is difficult to determine whether Reagan has chosen to forget some of the critical aspects of a problem or has never believed any view of a situation contrary to his own and therefore cannot call up from his memory bank this information, since it was never entered there. His recollection of his friend Ferdinand Marcos, for example, is not of a ruthless dictator who bled his country for personal gain, but of a firm ally of the United States and "our best counterforce to the communist rebels" in the Philippines. He mentions only briefly the 1986 election contest between Ferdinand Marcos and Corazon Aquino, omitting any citations from his diary or from the published record of reports from his own observers indicating widespread fraud and violence by Marcos forces. Nor does he recall his own insistence that "both sides" were guilty of gross illegalities, or his final acknowledgment, days after being briefed by Senator Lugar, that this was not the case. Instead he writes with apparent sadness of his offer of a safe haven in Hawaii for Marcos and his wife, adding that he and Nancy "couldn't help but remember how well they [Ferdinand and Imelda] had lived in Malacanang Palace when we first met them when I was governor—and note how different their lives are now."[10]

Reagan's defense of his foreign policy decisions remains much as it was during his presidency. Occasionally he strikes a new note that raises more questions than he would have wanted to while he was in office. One is the admission that he deliberately ordered the U.S. Navy to conduct maneuvers inside the Gulf of Sidra "to let him [Qaddafi] know that America wasn't going to tolerate [his support of] terrorist groups around the world." He also recalls the glee with which a navy admiral received his instruction that if a U.S. plane was fired upon, its pilot should not only fire back but should apply the doctrine of hot pursuit to follow the enemy plane "all the way into the hangar."[11]

In another contested area, Reagan finally admits what had already become common knowledge, that the Contras were not only financed and supplied by the CIA, but were originally organized into a fighting force by that agency. From that point his description of the long sequence of events involving both the Contras and Iran follows the well-trodden path he laid out while he was in the White House. Here again, "with absolute authority," he replays the tape explaining that "everything I had done was within the law," and that in the case of Iran he was not dealing with terrorists or a terrorist government, but was "trying to help some people [Iranian "moderates"] who are looking forward to becoming the next government of Iran." Nevertheless, he finally acknowledges that it would have been better if he had brought John Poindexter and Oliver North into his office and instructed them, "Tell me what really happened and what it is that you have been hiding from me. Tell me everything."[12]

A characteristic monologue on arms control provides a fitting final act. Whatever color is injected into the script at this point is understandable, as negotiation of the INF Treaty with Gorbachev was, indeed, Reagan's outstanding accomplishment in the realm of foreign affairs. Professionals in that field will appreciate his inclusion of some of the letters he exchanged with Soviet leaders, even though these add little to what is known of both American and Soviet views of arms reduction and SDI. However, a diary entry made sometime in February 1984 does help explain Reagan's sudden abandonment of his Evil Empire rhetoric in favor of a softer tone. At that time the joint chiefs of staff advised the president that American technology was substantially superior to the Soviets', and improvements in the training and readiness of American troops was "inspiring." Reagan's very next letter to Soviet General Secretary Konstantin Chernenko was noticeably milder, almost friendly, in comparison with his previous communications.[13] And although there were many less polite messages in the years that followed, the end result was a major triumph.

Not unexpectedly, the story ends with a typically misty-eyed epilogue, which demonstrates only that Reagan is still Reagan.

NOTES

Sources

Because supporting evidence is vitally important in any historical work, particular care has been taken to document all references to the words and actions of the individuals and organizations mentioned in this study.

Most of the sources used can be found in any large public or university library. Coded references to the most frequently used documents are indicated below. For other sources, the author and title are given in full in the first citation, and in abbreviated form thereafter. All reference materials are included in the bibliography that follows immediately after the notes.

AAL—Ronald Reagan, *An American Life.*

ATFC—Alfred Balitzer, ed., *A Time for Choosing: The Speeches of Ronald Reagan, 1961–1982.*

BUSG—*Budget of the United States Government.*

CR—*Congressional Record.* Daily issues, published before bound volumes were available, are cited as: CR (daily).

FRUS—*Foreign Relations of the United States.*

ICI—Hearings of the House-Senate Committees on the Iran-Contra Investigation.

NYT—*New York Times.*

PPP—*Public Papers of the Presidents of the United States: Ronald Reagan.*

RRTTA—Ronald Reagan, *Ronald Reagan Talks to America.*

WP—*Washington Post.*

WCPD—*Weekly Compilation of Presidential Documents.*

WTROM—Ronald Reagan, with Richard G. Hubler, *Where's the Rest of Me?*

USGM—United States Government Manual.

Chapter 1—Preacher

1. News conference, 21 February 1985.
2. "The Peril of Ever-Expanding Government," 30 March 1961, ATFC, pp. 21–38.
3. ATFC, pp. 53, 57.
4. Lou Cannon, *Reagan,* p. 108.
5. WTROM, pp. 6, 301.
6. Inaugural address, 5 January 1967, ATFC, p. 62.

7. January 1967 speech to Merchants and Manufacturers Association, RRTTA, pp. 43–44.
8. Speech to national convention of industrialists, 8 February 1967, RRTTA, p. 50.
9. Speech at dedication of Eureka College Library, 28 September 1967, ATFC, p. 75.
10. Speech in Sacramento, California, 4 September 1970, ATFC, pp. 91–92.
11. Speech to Southern GOP in Atlanta, Georgia, 7 December 1973, ATFC, p. 148.
12. Campaign speech, 6 July 1976, ATFC, pp. 165–79.
13. Speech in Washington, D.C., 6 February 1977, ATFC, p. 201.
14. The successive charters granted by British monarchs for settlements in New England are reproduced in Ben Perley Poore, *The Federal and State Constitutions, Colonial Charters, and other Organic Laws of the United States*, 1:922–56.
15. Jeoffrey Barraclough, ed., *The Christian World: A Social and Cultural History*, p. 210.
16. PPP, 1982, p. 1182.
17. PPP, 1983, p. 880.
18. Speech to the National Association of Evangelicals, PPP, 1983, p. 364.
19. Quotation from a 1969 speech to the Women's National Press Club, RRTTA, p. 113.
20. A. James Reichley, *Religion in American Public Life*, p. 319.
21. MacNeil-Lehrer Report, 6 May 1982, Transcript no. 1724, p. 4.
22. Lipset and Raab, "The Election and the Evangelicals," *Commentary*, March 1981, pp. 25–31.
23. Acceptance address at Republican National Convention, 17 July, 1980.
24. PPP, 1983,. pp. 3–4.
25. Ibid., pp. 77–78.
26. Ibid., p. 269.
27. PPP, 1982, pp. 157–60; 1983, pp. 151–54. WCPD, 1984, pp. 121–23; 1985, pp. 129–31.
28. See Reagan speeches in PPP, 1981, pp. 815–17, 881–87; 1982, p. 1135; 1983, pp. 659–65.
29. WCPD, 1985, pp. 1315, 1371.
30. PPP, 1982, pp. 157, 946, 1010–14; 1983, pp. 151, 510, 1449–53, 1760.
31. Michael Deaver, *Behind the Scenes*, p. 26.
32. PPP, 1981, pp. 396–97.
33. Ibid., p. 890.
34. Ibid., pp. 173, 523, 560, 847, 1237, 1650.
35. Ibid., p. 173.
36. Ibid., p. 847, remarks to Anti-Defamation League of B'nai B'rith, 10 June 1983; celebration of Hanukkah, 4 December 1983, pp. 1650–51.
37. WCPD, vol. 20,. pp. 350, 358, 371, 1367, 1658–60.
38. NYT, 15 February 1984. President's news conference, 21 March 1985, WCPD, vol. 21, pp. 346–47.
39. NYT, 12 April 1985.

40. WCPD, vol. 21, p. 475.

41. Ibid., pp. 478–79.

42. PPP, 1982, p. 465.

43. PPP, 1981: message to Pope John II, 13 May, p. 423; address at Notre Dame, 17 May, p. 432; telephone conversation with the pope, 14 December, p. 1154; PPP, 1982: news conference, 19 January, p. 37; remarks in Vatican City, 7 June, pp. 736–39; 1983: White House meeting with reporters, 14 January, p. 51.

44. PPP, 1981, pp. 434, 781, 1093, 1247; 1982, pp. 401, 698, 719, 730, 770, 771, 789, 1010; 1983, pp. 51, 488, 904, 975, 981.

45. U.S. House of Representatives, Conference Report no. 98–563 on HR 2915, pp. 13–14.

46. Fascell to author, 9 April 1987. As used here, "recede" is a legislative corruption of the word to indicate agreement with something previously proposed.

47. For text of the original bill, see House Committee on Foreign Affairs, Report no. 98–130, 98th Congress, 1st session. House Foreign Relations chairman Zablocki submitted H. J. Res. 316 "providing for the establishment of U.S. diplomatic relations with the Vatican," 30 June 1983, CR, p. H4895, which had no effect on the appropriations bill that the House had passed and sent to the Senate weeks earlier. Senator Lugar's amendment to the House bill originated 3 August 1983 as S. 1757, "A bill to provide for the establishment of United States diplomatic relations with the Vatican," CR, p. S11444. It was subsequently incorporated into the appropriations bill which, as finally approved, became PL 98-164, 22 November 1983.

48. CR (daily) 7 March 1984, p. S 2384.

49. See fall 1983 articles reproduced in U.S. Senate, Committee on Foreign Relations, Hearing: Nomination of William A. Wilson, 98th Congress, 2d session, 2 February 1984, pp. 66–71.

50. Ibid., pp. 41–163. Charles H. Whittier, "Diplomatic Relations Between the United States and the Holy See: A Pro-Con Analysis," unnumbered Congressional Research Service report, 8 November 1983. Whittier, "Religion and Public Policy: Background and Issues in the 80s," CRS Report No. 84-104 GOV, 13 October 1984, pp. 37–38.

51. Kennedy speech to the Greater Houston Ministerial Association, 12 September 1960, cited at the Senate Hearing, Nomination of William A. Wilson, p. 30.

52. See testimony, letters and articles, Ibid.

53. CR (daily), 7 March 1984, p. S 2390. One of the original sponsors of the Lugar amendment, Helms voted against Wilson's appointment. His decision to remove his name as an original sponsor of the amendment was reported by the Christian Science Monitor, 6 February 1984, as a reaction to strong pressure from his Southern Baptist constituents.

54. Christian Science Monitor, 12 January 1984.

55. David G. Bromley and Anson Shupe, New Christian Politics, pp. 53–57. A. J. Reichley, "Religion and the Future of American Politics," Political Science Quarterly, 1986, pp. 26–27.

56. Quoted in Flo Conway and Jim Siegelman, *Holy Terror,* p. 358.
57. Ibid., p. 359.
58. PPP, 1981, pp. 276–77.
59. Ibid., pp. 278–79.
60. Speech to National Religious Broadcasters, 30 January 1984, PPP, 1984, p. 118.
61. Speech to National Association of Evangelicals, 6 March 1984, Ibid., pp. 304–10.
62. For views of Julie Belaga and Marilyn Thayer see MacNeil-Lehrer News Hour, 21 August 1984, Transcript no. 2322.
63. NYT, 17 August 1984.
64. NYT, 2 August 1984.
65. WCPD, vol. 20, p. 1161.
66. Five-minute exchange with reporters on South Lawn of White House, Ibid., 2 September 1984, p. 1212.
67. Speech to fundamentalist Christian educators, WP, 3 November 1984.
68. *The Gallup Poll: Public Opinion,* 1984, p. 259.
69. WCPD, 1985, p. 129.
70. *Gallup Poll,* 1984, pp. 270–71.
71. WCPD, 1985, p. 108.
72. Stephen E. Ambrose, *Eisenhower: The President,* vol. 2, p. 38. *The Eisenhower Diaries* contains only two index references to Frank Carlson, neither of which suggests a close personal relationship between the senator and Eisenhower. Carlson does not appear anywhere in the index to the Ambrose biography.
73. Deaver, *Behind the Scenes,* p. 192.
74. WCPD, 1985, pp. 107–108.
75. Author to President Reagan, 19 August 1987.
76. WCPD, 1985, p. 109.
77. See Eusebius, *History of the Church from Christ to Constantine,* and Barraclough, *The Christian World,* pp. 50–51.
78. WCPD, 1986, pp. 153–54.
79. PPP, 1983, p. 361.
80. WCPD, 1984, p. 1747; 1985, pp. 8, 73, 85, 144, 1229; 1986, pp. 80, 138, 171, 782, 862, 1048; 1987, pp. 42, 75, 177, 437, 879.
81. PPP, 1981, p. 212.
82. PPP, 1983, p. 876.
83. WCPD, 1986, p. 171.
84. Message to Congress, 17 May 1982, PPP, 1982, p. 647. Proposal for a constitutional amendment on prayer in public schools, PPP, 8 March 1983, p. 365. Remarks to women leaders of Christian organizations, PPP, 12 October 1983, p. 1450.
85. WCPD, 7 October 1984, p. 1449.
86. Ibid., 1984, pp. 1449, 1467, 1536; 1985, pp. 144, 753, 1001, 1117; 1986, pp. 171, 188, 861; 1987, pp. 63, 77, 177.
87. Address to National Association of Evangelicals, PPP, 8 March 1983, p. 360.

88. NYT, 4 April 1987; WP, 25 April, 12 May, 22 August 1987; *Newsweek*, 13 July 1987.
89. Sarah Overstreet, "The Limits of Prayer," *Lewisburg Daily Journal*, 24 April 1987.
90. George R. Plagenz, "A Minister's Lifestyles," *Lewisburg Daily Journal*, 27 March 1987. Reprinted by permission of NEA, Inc.

Chapter 2—Philosopher

1. WTROM, p. 297.
2. Ibid., pp. 168–69.
3. Speech to the Phoenix, Arizona Chamber of Commerce, 30 March 1961, ATFC, pp. 21–38.
4. Quoted in Lou Cannon, *Reagan*, p. 91.
5. Quoted in Ambrose, *Eisenhower*, vol. 1, p. 517.
6. Statement in 22 January 1951 issue of *Fortnight*, quoted in Cannon, *Reagan*, p. 87.
7. Ibid., p. 86.
8. WTROM, pp. 297–98.
9. Ibid., p. 298.
10. These objectives were repeated in Reagan speeches from 1961 on. See ATFC, pp. 32, 192, 193.
11. Ibid., pp. 187–88.
12. Ibid., p. 191. The next 2 pages of this speech consist of quotations from the 1976 Republican platform. See Donald Bruce Johnson, *National Party Platforms*, vol. 2, p. 966.
13. 1967 speech to Southern Republicans, RRTTA, p. 49.
14. Nationally televised address, 6 July 1976, ATFC, p. 176.
15. PPP, 1981, p. 1.
16. News conference, PPP, 13 August 1981, p. 710.
17. News conference, PPP, 20 April 1982, p. 499.
18. Campaign speech, 6 July 1976, ATFC, p. 175; acceptance address at Republican nominating convention, 17 July 1980, Ibid., p. 221.
19. Ibid., p. 80. The collection of speeches put together by Reagan backer Richard M. Scaife included this address but did not include the section quoted here; see RRTTA, pp. 174–75.
20. RRTTA, p. 5; first inaugural address as governor of California, p. 27.
21. Speech to Southern Republicans in Atlanta, 7 December 1973, ATFC, pp. 137–38.
22. Ibid., pp. 138–39.
23. Ronnie Duggan, *On Reagan: The Man and His Presidency*, p. 245.
24. Copyright, 1981, *U.S. News & World Report*, interview with the president, 28 December 1981, p. 26.
25. "Morality Among the Supply-Siders," *Time*, 25 May 1981, pp. 18–20.
26. NYT, 23 November 1981, 14 November 1983; WP, 28 March 1985.

27. NYT, 26 July, 14 November 1983.
28. WP, 27 March 1985.
29. WP, 8 August 1987.
30. WP, 3 December 1981.
31. WP, 7 January, 9 April 1982.
32. WP, 3 December 1981.
33. *Time,* 25 May 1987.
34. WP, 23 December 1983.
35. WP, 5 March 1985, 26 June 1987.
36. WP, 13 August 1985; NYT, 20 August 1985.
37. WP, 18 March 1985.
38. NYT, 19 November 1985.
39. NYT, 24 August 1982.
40. WP, 10, 21 April 1982; NYT, 28 September 1982.
41. U.S. House of Representatives, Committee on Energy and Commerce, Subcommittee on Oversight and Investigations, *EPA Withholding of Superfund Files,* p. 32
42. Ibid., pp. 44, 83, 246.
43. For reports of mismanagement and illegal conniving with the companies EPA purported to regulate, see articles cited earlier, plus NYT, 15 March and 28 December 1982; WP, 27 December 1982, 16 March 1983. Reagan's appointment of Ruckelhaus was announced 21 March 1983, PPP, p. 426.
44. U.S. House of Representatives, Committee on Energy and Commerce, Subcommittee on Oversight and Investigations, *Investigation of the Environmental Protection Agency,* p. iii.
45. See previously cited articles plus overall review in WP, 30 March 1984.
46. WP, 26 June 1987.
47. NYT, 23 May; 10, 18, 24, 25 June; 25 July; 31 August; 5 September; 28 October 1989. Marianne Lavelle, "Ethics, HUD and the Law," *National Law Journal,* 28 August 1989.
48. WP, 19 August 1981.
49. Jack Anderson, "Secretary Watt and His Promise," WP, 4 May 1981.
50. NYT, 18 May, 11 October 1983. WP, 29 September 1983.
51. NYT, 21 January 1983.
52. WP, 12 April 1983.
53. CR (daily), 5 October 1983, p. S13608.
54. NYT, 16 May 1980.
55. NYT, 23 September 1983.
56. PPP, 9 October 1983, p. 1438.
57. WP, 4 December 1985.
58. NYT, 25 May 1985.
59. NYT, 12 March, 19 June 1986. WP, 17 April 1986.
60. NYT, 26 June 1987.
61. WP, 26 September, 11 December 1986.
62. NYT, 16 August 1981.
63. NYT, 28, 31 December 1983; 4, 7 January 1984.

64. WP, 28 June 1987.
65. NYT, 25 November 1986.
66. WP, 9 July 1987.
67. The term "sleaze" was used by presidential candidate Walter Mondale in the campaign of 1984.
68. *USGM,* 1983/1984, p. 80. Meese's title at that time was Counsellor to the President.
69. U.S. Senate, Committee on the Judiciary, *Nomination of Edwin Meese, III.*
70. The report of the independent counsel was excerpted in NYT, 21 September 1984.
71. *Wall Street Journal,* 28 January 1985.
72. A selection of editorial comments criticizing the Meese appointment was published in a full-page advertisement in the *Washington Post,* 28 January 1985, by Common Cause.
73. WCPD, 1985, p. 16.
74. WP, 7 July 1987.
75. NYT, 3 July 1987.
76. *National Law Journal,* 3 August 1987.
77. WP, 1 January 1987.
78. NYT, 16, 24 June 1987.
79. WP, 17 December 1982; 12, 17 December 1985; 1 January 1986. NYT, 18 December 1982; 31 August 1984.
80. NYT, 29 May; 10, 17, 18 July 1987; 12 February 1988.
81. NYT, 25 May 1987, 9 April 1988, 28 June 1989.
82. *Wall Street Journal,* 28 October 1980. NYT, 30, 31 October 1980.
83. WP, 23 November 1981. PPP, 4 January 1982, p. 3.
84. Peter Hannaford, *The Reagans: A Political Portrait,* p. 57.
85. Ibid., p. 161; Dugger, *On Reagan,* p. 371.
86. WCPD, 1985, p. 265.
87. "Mike Deaver's Rise and Fall," *Newsweek,* 23 March 1987, pp. 22–23.
88. MacNeil-Lehrer News Hour, 28 April 1986.
89. News conference, WCPD, 9 April 1986, p. 461.
90. WP, 13 August 1986.
91. WCPD, 21 May 1986, p. 670.
92. NYT, 13 May 1986, 18 March, 16 June, 10 July 1987. WP, 13 August 1986, 26 February 1987.
93. NYT, 18 March, 16 June 1987.
94. Iran-Contra Hearings, 30 July 1987.
95. *USGM,* 1985–86, p. 601.
96. WP, 13 August 1982.
97. WP, 30 September 1986.
98. WP, 1 July 1987.
99. NYT, 21 May 1981.
100. Ibid., 8 June 1986.
101. A copy of the *National Review* ad, received by mail 26 March 1987, is in the author's files.

102. Irving Kristol, "Post-Watergate Morality: Too Good for Our Good?", *New York Times Magazine,* 14 November 1976.
103. News conference, PPP, 28 June 1982, pp. 931–32.
104. Ibid., 29 July 1981, p. 676.
105. News conference, WCPD, 24 July 1984, p. 1067.
106. WCPD, 20 September 1984, p. 1330.
107. News conference, WCPD, 9 April 1986, p. 461.
108. PPP, 3 January 1983, p. 4.
109. Ibid., 28 April 1983, p. 607.
110. Informal exchange with reporters, WCPD, 17 April 1986, p. 501. The first edition of David Stockman's book, *The Triumph of Politics,* was published in the spring of 1986. The second edition, containing a postscript that focused more directly on Reagan's personal responsibility for "the debt-spending spree of the 1980s," appeared in 1987.
111. NYT, 24 November 1988. A defense of the ethical integrity of his aides was offered by President Reagan in an interview with reporters, published in *U.S. News and World Report,* 25 May 1987, p. 25.

Chapter 3—Economist

1. 1979 speech to Women's National Press Club, RRTTA, p. 110.
2. WCPD, 1984, pp. 798, 985.
3. Cannon, *Reagan,* p. 39.
4. ATFC, p. 56.
5. Milton and Rose Friedman, *Free to Choose,* pp. xv–xvi. The Friedman "bible" is Adam Smith's *An Inquiry into the Nature and Causes of the Wealth of Nations,* originally published in England in 1776. Quotations from *The Wealth of Nations* are taken from the Harvard Classics edition, vol. 10.
6. Smith, *The Wealth of Nations,* p. 70.
7. Ibid., pp. 219–20.
8. Ibid., p. 220.
9. Friedman, *Free to Choose,* pp. 25–26.
10. Nigel Cameron, *Hong Kong, The Cultured Pearl,* p. 176.
11. Ibid., p. 208.
12. WP, 12 March 1987.
13. Leonard Silk, "On the Supply Side," in Hedrick Smith, et. al., *Reagan, The Man, The President,* p. 54.
14. Christopher Lehmann-Haupt in a review of *Dangerous Currents: the State of Economics* by Lester C. Thurlow, NYT, 15 June 1983.
15. Out of a total voting-age population of 160.5 million, only 86.5 million, or 54 percent, went to the polls in 1980. Reagan received 43,901,812 votes. This was 8.4 million more than Carter received, but John Anderson and other candidates polled 7.1 million votes. Reagan's plurality in 1984, when no significant third-party choice was available, was much greater—16.8 million—but his total vote came from only 32 percent of the electorate.

16. *Gallup Poll,* 1980, pp. 198–99, 233, 235, 249–51. Harris Poll, WP, 12 June 1980. NYT, 3 February 1981.
17. PPP, 1981, p. 221.
18. David A. Stockman, *The Triumph of Politics,* p. 93.
19. Ibid., pp. 10–11.
20. Compare Reagan's 1961 speech to the Chamber of Commerce, ATFC, pp. 21–31 with the 1980 Republican platform, pp. 18, 33–35.
21. News conference, PPP, 10 October 1981, p. 871.
22. Loc. cit.
23. William Greider, "The Education of David Stockman," *Atlantic Monthly,* December 1981, pp. 27–54.
24. PPP, 12 November 1981, p. 1039; 21 January 1982, p. 60. The vehemence of the attack on Stockman made in private by members of the White House staff is described in Stockman's *The Triumph of Politics,* pp. 4–5.
25. Ibid., pp. 323–24.
26. RRTTA, p. 48.
27. Ibid., p. 67.
28. 1980 Republican party platform, p. 48. News conference, PPP, 28 July 1982, pp. 981–82; NYT, 3 February 1981.
29. Message to Congress, PPP, 10 March 1981, pp. 221–22. NYT, 11 March 1981.
30. News conference, PPP, 17 December 1981, pp. 1165, 1170.
31. PPP, 26 January 1982, pp. 72–79.
32. BUSG, FY 1984, sec. 9, p. 55.
33. *Congressional Research Service Review,* January 1987, p. 3.
34. BUSG, FY 1988, sec. 5, p. 29; FY 1990, sec. 1, p. 3, sec. 10, p. 11.
35. NYT, 19 July 1985.
36. NYT, 11 July 1985. Stockman, *Triumph of Politics* p. 289.
37. Michael Moffitt, "Economic Decline, Reagan-Style: Dollars, Debt, and Deflation," *World Policy Journal,* vol. 2, p. 390.
38. Stockman, *Triumph of Politics,* p. 122. However, as the *Washington Post* reported 15 July 1986, in the first draft of his book Stockman stated flatly that the succession of annual deficits was the result of *Reagan's* deficit spending.
39. BUSG, FY 1983, sec. 9, p. 11; FY 1988, sec. 5, p. 29, deficits for the fiscal years 1987–1989 estimated.
40. Interest rates on U.S. securities, reported in the government's monthly *Economic Indicators,* show percentage rates ranging from 14.029 to 5.40 on 3-month bills, from 14.44 to 6.39 on 3-year notes, and from 13.91 to 7.14 on 10-year bonds for the period 1981 through 1986.
41. For an analysis of the relative benefits accruing to different tax brackets from Reagan's original 30 percent tax cut proposal, see Taxation with Representation *Newsletter,* April 1981. As finally passed, the total reduction was 25 percent: 5 percent the first year and 10 percent in each of the next two years.
42. Because the Social Security tax in 1988 was applied only to the first $37,800 of earnings, all who earn up to that amount suffer the full 7.51 percent reduction

in income. But a person earning $75,000 has only 3.8 percent of his income withheld. At $100,000, the rate falls to 2.8 percent.

43. Stockman, *Triumph of Politics*, p. 385.

44. PPP, 1983, p. 304.

45. BUSG, FY 1984, sec. 4, p. 4.

46. WCPD, 1984, p. 993.

47. *Social Security Bulletin*, "Your Social Security Rights and Responsibilities: Retirement and Survivors Benefits," January 1987.

48. NYT, 25 August 1983.

49. Ibid., 25 October 1983.

50. The AMC letter was reproduced in Taxation with Representation *Newsletter*, July 1981.

51. The 1986 study was reported in WP, 18 July 1986; the Treasury and CBO analyses in NYT, 6 March 1990.

52. *Economic Report of the President,* 1987.

53. WCPD, 1987, pp. 776, 786, 839, 884, 909, 925, 932, 937.

54. PPP, 20 January 1981, p. 2.

55. News conference, PPP, 1 October 1981, p. 867.

56. News conference, PPP, 19 January 1983, p. 37. The number of employed did increase in 1981, but fell back in the recession of 1982.

57. U.S. Department of Labor, Bureau of Labor Statistics, *Employment and Earnings,* January 1989.

58. Many of the "nuances of the unemployment figures" are discussed in *Employment in America,* published by Congressional Quarterly in 1983, and in a report of the House Committee on Government Operations, *Counting All the Jobless: Problems with the Official Unemployment Rate,* H. Rpt. 99-661, 1986.

59. NYT, 9 August 1987.

60. Barry Bluestone and Bennett Harrison, "The Grim Truth About the Job 'Miracle'," NYT, 1 February 1987.

61. *Economic Report of the President,* 1983, p. 46. The phrase "safety net" was concocted by the Republican platform committee in 1980 and appears in the 1980 platform on p. 28.

62. NYT, 16 August 1983.

63. WCPD, 1986, p. 1401. Office of Technology Assessment, *Technology and Structural Unemployment: Re-employing Displaced Adults,* p. 7.

64. Quoted in Arthur M. Schlesinger, Jr., *The Crisis of the Old Order,* p. 89.

65. Precise figures on car ownership are not available for the years prior to 1947, but data on population and automotive registrations permit a reasonable estimate. See *Historical Statistics of the United States,* 1975 ed., pp. 41, 717.

66. Ibid., p. 383.

67. For Reagan's own story of his family's condition during his youth, see WTROM, chaps. 2–4.

68. Speech in Sacramento, California, 4 September 1970, ATFC, p. 89.

69. WTROM, p. 45. *Historical Statistics,* p. 164.

70. NYT, 3 August 1983.

71. For President Reagan on hunger, see NYT and WP 3 August 1983; for Edwin

Meese, NYT, 10, 15 December. George Graham's opinion was aired on a CBS television newscast December 28. Task force report, NYT, 8 January 1984 and WP, 11 January 1984.

72. NYT, 16, 17 October 1987.
73. Bureau of Labor Statistics, *Employment and Earnings,* December 1980 and August 1987, table B-2. The total number of employees, shown in table A-1, rose from 100,907,000 to 114,447,000.
74. *National Law Journal,* 28 September 1987.
75. *Employment and Earnings,* November 1987, p. 95.
76. Joseph Grunwald and Kenneth Flamm, *The Global Factory: Foreign Assembly in International Trade,* p. 3.
77. Ibid., p. 13.
78. Ibid., pp. 138, 140.
79. Friedman, *Free to Choose,* pp. 37–38.
80. *Congressional Research Service Review,* May 1987, p. 13. WP, 31 October 1983, 29 January 1987. *Washington Spectator,* 15 May 1985. NYT, 12 February 1986.
81. PPP, 9 December 1982, p. 1581.
82. ATFC, p. 30.
83. NYT, 10 November 1987.
84. BUSG, FY 1987, p. 6d-46; FY 1988, appendix, pp. I–E 32–34.
85. "Doctors Find Hunger is Epidemic," NYT, 27 February 1985. "New Poor Swell AFDC Rolls," WP, 20 April 1985. "Study Finds Poverty Among Children Is Increasing," NYT, 23 May 1985. "From Poor to Poorer," NYT, 1 February 1986. "Demand for Emergency Food, Shelter Up About 25% in '86," WP, 19 December 1986. "8,900 Line Up for 200 Jobs in West Virginia," NYT, 4 April 1987.
86. PPP, 5 October 1981, p. 886.
87. PPP, 1981, pp. 885, 894, 926. Executive Order 12329, 14 October 1981, p. 928.
88. PPP, 1982, pp. 28, 58, 76, 158, 371, 455, 517, 590, 596, 597, 604, 961, 1021, 1132, 1373, 1460, 1463, 1578, 1655.
89. Executive Order 12427, PPP, 27 June 1983, p. 921.
90. WCPD, 14 June 1985, pp. 789–91.
91. PPP, 27 January 1981, pp. 30–31.
92. NYT, 12 August 1983.
93. Ibid., 4 April 1982.
94. WP, 2 April 1983.
95. Compare the White House report in WCPD, 1984, pp. 1006–1008 with the account in WP, 11 July 1984.
96. NYT, 3 November 1983.
97. WP, 18 March 1985.
98. NYT, 2 July 1984.
99. See Reagan's statement on signing the Superfund bill, WCPD, 1986, p. 1412, and "Pipeline Firm Probed After Dumping PCBs," WP, 21 February 1987.
100. NYT, 10 August 1984.
101. NYT, 10 July 1984. WP, 17 January 1987. WCPD, 1986, pp. 237–38.

102. WP, 3 August 1987.
103. WCPD, 1987, p. 815.
104. BUSG, FY 1988, sec. 2, p. 2.
105. Ibid., sec. 2.
106. Ibid., FY 1989, sec. 6g, p. 7.
107. The term "safety net" was used in the 1980 Republican platform (p. 28) only in connection with unemployment due to foreign competition. Reagan later broadened it to include all government assistance programs.
108. 1980 Republican platform, p. 18.
109. Ibid., p. 18 for pledge; 25 January 1983 State of the Union message for tax proposal.
110. 1980 Republican platform, pp. 27–28.
111. Television address to the nation, PPP, 16 August 1982, p. 1050. Reagan's commissioner of internal revenue estimated that from $3 to $4 billion was lost annually by non-reporting of dividend and interest income. See *U.S. News and World Report*, 11 April 1983, p. 17.
112. WP, 6 August 1983.
113. Interview with IRS Commissioner Roscoe L. Egger, *U.S. News and World Report*, 11 April 1983, p. 17.
114. BUSG, FY 1984, sec. 4, pp. 8–10.
115. News conferences, PPP, 28 September, p. 1229; 11 November 1982, p. 1451.
116. Department of the Treasury, Internal Revenue Service, *Explanation of the Tax Reform Act of 1986 for Individuals*, Pub. No. 920, August 1987, pp. iv, 2
117. NYT, 29 November; 1, 6 December 1983. For Feldstein's letter of resignation, see PPP, 8 May 1984, p. 653.

Chapter 4—Historian

1. Speech to American Truckers Association, 16 October 1974, ATFC, p. 155.
2. Cannon, *Reagan*, pp. 19–20.
3. *New Yorker*, 23 November 1987, p. 33.
4. PPP, 8 June 1982, p. 744. WCPD, 18 March 1985, p. 323.
5. This reference to the founding fathers was a central point in Reagan's address at Notre Dame University, PPP, 17 May 1981, p. 433.
6. Reagan's frequently repeated states-rights message was introduced in his inaugural address as president, PPP, 20 January, 1981, p. 2.
7. Opposition to the Constitution came largely from those known as anti-Federalists. See Jackson Turner Main, *The Anti-Federalists: Critics of the Constitution, 1781–1788*.
8. An excellent one-volume documentary history of the Constitutional Convention, edited by Charles C. Tansill for the Library of Congress, is *Documents Illustrative of the Formation of the American States*. For a discussion of the founding fathers' attitudes toward popularly elected conventions for ratifying the Constitution, see Wilbur Edel, *A Constitutional Convention: Threat or Challenge?*, chap. 2.
9. *Thomas Jefferson: Writings*, pp. 902–903.

10. Philip S. Foner, ed., *The Complete Writings of Thomas Paine*. See especially "The Age of Reason," "The Rights of Man," and "Agrarian Justice."

11. PPP, 3 March 1983, p. 364.

12. Remarks at the U.S. Institute of Peace, WCPD, 26 February 1986, p. 284.

13. All these events are discussed and documented in Richard Hosftadter's *Great Issues in American History. National Party Platforms*, vol. 1, pp. 3–4.

14. WTROM, pp. 142, 266.

15. Ibid., chap. 4.

16. News conference, PPP, 28 September 1982, p. 1225.

17. WTROM, pp. 52–54.

18. U.S. Department of Commerce, Bureau of the Census, *Historical Statistics of the United States*, 1975 ed., vol. 1, p. 383.

19. WTROM, p. 74.

20. Speech to Phoenix, Arizona Chamber of Commerce, 30 March 1961, ATFC, p. 31.

21. Interview with Robert Ajemian, *Time*, 17 May 1976, p. 17.

22. John P. Diggins, *Mussolini and Fascism: The View from America*, pp. 146–47.

23. Ibid., pp. 20–22.

24. "Ben Wattenburg at Large," interview with President Reagan, broadcast 25 December 1981 by PBS station WETA-TV 26.

25. For comments about communism by Ickes see *The Secret Diaries of Harold L. Ickes*, vol. 2, pp. 349, 428, 492–93, 683–85.

26. Diggins, *Mussolini and Fascism*, p. 279.

27. WTROM, p. 75.

28. Interview with Walter Cronkite, PPP, 3 March 1981, p. 194. The text of Roosevelt's quarantine speech can be found in *The Public Papers and Addresses of Franklin D. Roosevelt*, vol. 6, pp. 406–411.

29. WCPD, 26 October 1984, p. 1652.

30. *The Gallup Poll*, vol. 1, 1935–1948, pp. 49, 92, 132.

31. WTROM, p. 6.

32. Ibid., especially chaps. 9–14.

33. Ibid., p. 114.

34. Ibid., pp. 117–20.

35. Ibid., pp. 117–18.

36. B. H. Liddell Hart, *History of the Second World War*, p. 601. Winston Churchill, *The Second World War*, vol. 5, pp. 226–35.

37. Dwight D. Eisenhower, *Crusade in Europe*, pp. 293–94.

38. Interview with Walter Cronkite, PPP, 6 June 1984, p. 821.

39. Address to joint session of Congress, PPP, 27 April 1983, p. 601.

40. Hart, *Second World War*, p. 384. For further detail see ibid., chap. 24 and Churchill, *Second World War*, vol. 3, chap. 8.

41. Cannon, *Reagan*, p. 20.

42. One of the many occasions on which Reagan expressed his opinion of the Vietnam War was at the Memorial Day services for an unknown serviceman of that war, PPP, 28 May 1984, p. 750.

43. WCPD, 18 March 1985, p. 323.

44. Dugger, *On Reagan*, p. 514. Dugger's work is based, in part, on the most extensive collection available of Reagan's pre-presidential radio addresses.
45. PPP, 18 February 1982, p. 185 and 4 April 1984, p. 467.
46. Ronald H. Spector, *United States Army in Vietnam: The Early Years, 1941–1960*, p. 4.
47. Mark Green & Gail MacColl, *There He Goes Again: Ronald Reagan's Reign of Error*, p. 32.
48. PPP, 18 February 1982, pp. 184–85.
49. Library of Congress, Congressional Research Service, *The U.S. Government and the Vietnam War: Executive and Legislative Roles and Relationships, Part 1, 1945–1961*, prepared for the Senate Committee on Foreign Relations, 98th Cong., 2d Sess., p. 2.
50. Cordell Hull, *The Memoirs of Cordell Hull*, vol. 2, p. 1597.
51. *The U.S. Government and the Vietnam War*, pp. 20–22.
52. Robert F. Futrell, *The United States Air Force in Southeast Asia: The Advisory Years to 1965*, p. 4.
53. Loc. cit.
54. *Pentagon Papers*, Gravel edition, vol. 1, pp. 64, 66.
55. FRUS, 1952–1954, vol. 16: The Geneva Conference, pp. 1505–10, 1540–42. Although the U.S. refused to associate itself with the decisions of the conference, it was an active participant in the proceedings, ibid., pp. 403–13.
56. Ibid., p. 1503.
57. Ibid., pp. 419, 421.
58. FRUS, 1955–1957, vol. 1, *Vietnam*, p. 492.
59. *The U.S. Government and the Vietnam War*, p. 300.
60. News conference, PPP, 18 February 1982, p. 185. For a similar statement made by Reagan in 1978, see Green & MacColl, *There He Goes Again*, p. 33.
61. News conference, PPP, 4 April 1984, pp. 465, 467.
62. News conference, PPP, 18 February 1982, p. 185.
63. *Pentagon Papers*, vol. 2, pp. 354–56.
64. NYT, 16 October 1971.
65. One of the best accounts of the last four years of the war is Frank Snepp's *Decent Interval*. A military view of that period, written by the then chairman of the South Vietnam Joint General Staff, is Cao Van Vien, *The Final Collapse*.
66. Remarks at White House luncheon with editors and broadcasters, WCPD, 18 April 1985, p. 472.
67. PPP, 24 February 1982, p. 210.
68. WCPD, 10 May 1985, p. 619.
69. The president's remarks were recorded in PPP, 4 December 1982, p. 1565. The State Department's clarification was reported in WP, 7 December 1982.
70. Green & McColl, *There He Goes Again*, p. 12.
71. The "treaty table" incident was reported by Senator Moynihan in his newsletter of 27 December 1987.
72. NYT, 13, 16 April 1958.
73. Quoted by James Reston, NYT, 5 May 1985.

Chapter 5—Champion of Civil Rights

1. News conference, PPP, 17 May 1983, p. 729.
2. 1980 Republican platform, p. 12.
3. The Republican party first proposed an equal rights amendment in 1940. The Democratic party followed suit in 1944. *National Party Platforms*, vol. 1, pp. 393, 403; vol. 2, p. 976.
4. 1980 Republican platform, p. 10.
5. WP, 10 July 1980.
6. 1980 Republican platform, p. 13.
7. Cannon, *Reagan,* pp. 144, 390.
8. PPP, 7 July 1983, p. 596.
9. Cannon, *Reagan,* p. 313.
10. PPP, 1981, 9 March, p. 214, 30 July, p. 683, 7 October, p. 901, 21 December, p. 1174; 1982, 10 February, p. 166.
11. Ibid, 1981, p. 214.
12. Ibid, 1981, p. 901.
13. Ibid, 1981, p. 1174.
14. Ibid., 1982, p. 988.
15. NYT, 10 July 1983.
16. WP, 4 August 1983.
17. PPP, 24 August 1983, p. 1196.
18. NYT, 10 August 1983.
19. Grove City College v. Bell, Slip Opinion No. 82-792, 28 February 1984.
20. News conference, PPP, 22 May 1984, pp. 729–30.
21. Inter-party maneuvering on this issue was described by Republican Senator Orrin Hatch and Democratic Senator Howard Metzenbaum on the MacNeil-Lehrer News Hour, 3 October 1984, Transcript no. 2353, pp. 2–6.
22. See CR (daily) 5 September 1984, p. S10748 for the quoted statement from the 1984 Republican platform. The first national political organizations to propose women suffrage were the Prohibition and Greenback parties in the election of 1884. In 1912 the Progressive party advocated "equal suffrage to men and women alike." The Republican and Democratic parties did not support voting rights for women until 1916. See *National Party Platforms,* vol. 1, pp. 176, 199, 207.
23. WP, 15 November 1984.
24. Ibid., 17 November 1984.
25. WP, 14 May 1986.
26. Ibid., 8 September 1986.
27. Ibid., 18 November 1985.
28. NYT, 21 November 1985.
29. News conference, 17 December 1981, PPP, 1163. Official documents compiled from 1981 through 1988 report the president's statements of his views on civil rights with the following frequency: 1981, 17; 1982, 14; 1983, 18; 1984, 17; 1985, 13; 1986, 10; 1987, 8; 1988, 15.

30. PPP, 28 July 1983, p. 1099.
31. Morton Mintz, *Quotations from President Ron,* p. 31.
32. PPP, 29 June 1981, p. 573; 14 June 1984, p. 858.
33. James Nathan Miller, "Ronald Reagan and the Techniques of Deception," *Atlantic Monthly,* February 1984, pp. 62–68.
34. Dugger, *On Reagan,* pp. 314–15.
35. NYT, 14 April 1987.
36. PPP, 1 August 1983, p. 1113. Miller, "Ronald Reagan and the Techniques of Deception," p. 66.
37. PPP, 25 February 1983, p. 307.
38. WP, 2 August 1985.
39. WP, 10 July 1984.
40. H.R., Committee on Government Operations, *Civil Rights Enforcement by the Department of Education,* 100th Cong., 1st sess., 23 April 1987, p. 1. Evidence of backdating was found in the Education Department's Office of Inspector General and was published in the hearings report, pp. 103–72.
41. *National Journal,* 27 March 1982, p. 540.
42. Green v. Kennedy, 309 F. Supp. 1127 (D.C.), Cannon v. Green, 398 U.S. 956. The IRS' amended construction of the tax code was upheld by the Supreme Court in Coit v. Green, 404 U.S. 997.
43. All references to this issue are taken from Bob Jones University v. United States, Slip Opinion no. 81–3, 24 May 1983.
44. 1980 Republican party platform, p. 15. U.S. Senate, Committee on the Judiciary, *Hearings: Nomination of Edwin Meese, III,* March 1984, pp. 85–86.
45. PPP, 12 January 1982, p. 17.
46. NYT, 26 August 1982.
47. PPP, 10 May 1982, p. 604; 13 May 1982, pp. 624–25.
48. Michael Wines, "Administration Says It Merely Seeks A 'Better Way' to Enforce Civil Rights," *National Journal,* 27 March 1982, pp. 536–41.
49. NYT, 9 July 1984.
50. WP, 19 July 1985. The Justice Department memorandum was dated 13 November 1981.
51. WP, 27 February 1985.
52. NYT, 16 May 1987. Johnson v. Transportation Agency, Santa Clara County, Slip Opinion no. 85-1129, 25 March 1987.
53. Speech at Dickinson College, reported in NYT, 18 September 1985.
54. NYT, 3 December 1983; 10, 29 November 1985; 6 November 1986; 21 January; 1 April 1987. WP, 16 August 1985; 1 May 1986.
55. Cannon, *Reagan,* p. 131, from governor's press conference of 13 June 1967.
56. News conference, PPP, 19 January 1982, p. 40.
57. Cannon, *Reagan,* p. 131.
58. Televised address, 6 July 1976, ATFC, p. 170.
59. News conference, PPP, 6 March 1981, p. 212.
60. PPP, 19 January 1982, p. 40; 3 August 1982, p. 1012.
61. Roe v. Wade, 409 U.S. 817.

62. Some of the 38 public references that Reagan made to abortion from 1982 to 1987 were brief, others were significant elements of his presentation. The more important pronouncements were reported in his public papers. In PPP: 14 September 1982, pp. 1150–51; 21 January 1983, p. 95; 16 June 1983, p. 876; 2 March 1984, pp. 292–93; 6 March 1984, p. 308. In WCPD: 7 October 1984, pp. 1452–53; 22 January 1985, pp. 73–75; 6 February 1985, p. 144; 22 January 1986, p. 81; 4 February 1986, p. 138; 6 February 1986, p. 171; 22 January 1987, pp. 42–45; 27 January 1987, p. 75; 20 February 1987, p. 177.

63. PPP, 14 September 1982, p. 1151. WP, 17 September 1982, Quoted in Mintz, *Quotations*, p. 39. A major point in support of the Supreme Court decision in Roe v. Wade was the "established medical fact [that] until the end of the first trimester mortality in abortion is less than mortality in normal childbirth."

64. Speech to Conservative PAC, WCPD, 27 April 1987, p. 177.

65. Statement at Reagan-Bush rally, WCPD, 2 November 1984, p. 1747.

66. WCPD, 22 January 1985, p. 74. NYT, 11 March 1985.

67. See Judiciary Committee Report No. 97-465, *Human Life Federalism Amendment*, 97th Cong., 2d sess., 1982. CR (daily), 28 June 1983, p. S 9310.

68. PPP, 8 March 1983, p. 361 to National Association of Evangelicals.

69. Remarks to National Religious Broadcasters, PPP, 30 January 1984, p. 119; to Conservative PAC, ibid., 2 March 1984, p. 293.

70. United States v. University Hospital, 729 F. 2d (CA 2, 1984). Bowen v. American Hospital Association, Slip Opinion no. 84-1529, 9 June 1986.

71. Bowen v. American Hospital Association, p. 35.

72. Address to Chamber of Commerce, 30 March 1961, ATFC, pp. 31, 36.

73. Ibid., p. 43.

74. Nationally televised address, 6 July 1976, ATFC, p. 170.

75. 1980 Republican platform, p. 10.

76. PPP, 8 March 1983, pp. 360–61.

77. Radio address to nation, PPP, 16 June 1984, p. 860.

78. Speech to Knights of Columbus, WCPD, 5 August 1986, pp. 1043–50; at March for Life rally, ibid., 22 January 1987, pp. 42–44.

79. The new case was Akron v. Akron Center for Reproductive Health, 462 U.S. 416, decided 15 June 1983. The president's statement was published in PPP, 16 June 1983, p. 867.

80. Representative Mary Rose Oakar to Nat Hentoff, 20 November 1985.

81. WCPD, 3 January 1985, p. 8.

82. WCPD, 22 January 1987, p. 43.

83. H. R. Committee on the Judiciary, Subcommittee on Civil and Constitutional Rights, *Hearings: Abortion Clinic Violence*, 99th Cong., 1st and 2d sess., 1985–86.

84. *Hearings: Abortion Clinic Violence*, pp. 90–121. WP, 11 June 1986.

85. WP, 25 June 1986.

86. PPP, 15 January 1983, p. 60.

87. Court cases dealing with these forms of discrimination, beginning with Ex parte Yarbrough in 1884, were cited by Chief Justice Warren in Reynolds v. Sims, 377 U.S. 533 (1964).
88. Baker v. Carr, 369 U.S. 186 (1962).
89. Wesberry v. Sanders, 376 U.S. 1 (1964).
90. Reynolds v. Sims, 377 U.S. 533 (1964).
91. P.L. 89–110, 79 Stat. 437, especially sections 2 and 5.
92. Mahan v. Howell, 410 U.S. 315 (1973). White v. Regester, 412 U.S. 755 (1973). Mobile v. Bolden, 446 U.S. 55 (1980).
93. PPP, 15 January 1981, p. 513.
94. Ibid., 1 October 1981, p. 869.
95. Ibid., 17 October 1981, p. 959.
96. Ibid., 6 November 1981, pp. 1018, 1020.
97. Public Law 97-205, 96 Stat. 134.
98. PPP, 29 June 1982, pp. 822–23.
99. See Reynolds' remarks on MacNeil-Lehrer News Hour, 3 February 1982, Transcript no. 1658, p. 2.
100. WP, 31 August 1985. The case, Thornburg v. Gingles, No. 83-1968, was decided by the Supreme Court 30 June 1986.
101. *Federal Register,* 6 May 1985, pp. 19122–32.
102. H. R. Committee on the Judiciary, Subcommittee on Civil and Constitutional Rights, *Voting Rights Act: Proposed Section 5 Regulations,* 99th Cong., 2d sess., July 1986, pp. 2, 5, 8, 11.
103. U.S. Senate, Committee on the Judiciary, *Hearings: Nomination of William Bradford Reynolds to be Associate Attorney General of the United States,* 99th Cong., 1st sess., June 1985.
104. WCPD, 15 June 1985, pp. 800–801.
105. Ibid., p. 841.

Chapter 6—Apostle of Justice, Law and Order

1. Law Day Address, 1968, RRTTA, p. 85.
2. Dugger, *On Reagan,* pp. 11–12.
3. WTROM, pp. 20, 133.
4. Inaugural address, 5 January 1967, ATFC, p. 66. Proposal to California legislature, 6 April 1967, RRTTA, p. 81.
5. Speech of 4 September 1970, ATFC, p. 87.
6. ATFC, pp. 183–201. Republican party platform, 1976, in *National Party Platforms,* vol. 2, pp. 965–94, especially p. 978.
7. *Common Cause Magazine,* June 1981, p. 15.
8. 1980 Republican party platform, pp. 26–30.
9. WP, 11 January 1983.
10. NYT, 16 May 1983, 2 October 1984, 26 May 1987. Donovan's resignation was reported in WCPD, 15 March 1985, pp. 310–11.
11. WP, 7 February 1984.

12. WTROM, p. 138.

13. Dugger, *On Reagan*, p. 328.

14. The billion-dollar program was announced at a news conference, PPP, 5 January 1983, p. 17. The Job Training Partnership Act was explained in the *Economic Report of the President*, February 1983, p. 46. The court order to release funds was reported in NYT, 16 August 1983.

15. Brock's nomination as secretary of labor, announced in WCPD, 20 March 1985, was confirmed with little opposition. McLaughlin was not opposed at all.

16. RRTTA, p. 43.

17. Ibid., pp. 92–93, 100.

18. Ibid., pp. 187–89.

19. Speech to American Bar Association, PPP, 1 August 1983, p. 1114.

20. RRTTA, p. 110.

21. Reagan's praise of King was repeated daily from January 14 to 16, 1986, and concluded with his January 18 proclamation of January 20 as Martin Luther King Day. See WCPD, 1986, pp. 54, 57, 65–66, 73–74.

22. Cannon, *Reagan*, p. 162.

23. Dugger, *On Reagan*, pp. 27–28.

24. Brownstein and Easton, *Reagan's Ruling Class*, p. 355.

25. The writer was dean of administration at Lehman College in the City University of New York when the wave of student revolt reached New York. As the officer in charge of campus security, he never once called for police intervention. President Leonard Lief's response to sit-ins and building takeovers was to invite student leaders to meet with him and his aides to discuss their grievances. Those discussions ultimately led to the introduction of courses in black and Puerto Rican studies and the inclusion of elected student representatives in what had traditionally been an exclusively faculty council. Changes of this kind, which were adopted by many of the country's major universities, did not affect either entrance or graduation requirements and were accomplished without the introduction of either police or national guard troops (unlike in California under Governor Reagan), and with no "battle casualties" except to the feelings of some conservative faculty members who resented student participation—even on the limited scale agreed to—in decisions regarding curriculum and other academic matters.

26. Dugger, *On Reagan*, p. 242.

27. Ibid., p. 295.

28. Brownstein and Easton, *Reagan's Ruling Class*, p. 644.

29. *U.S. News and World Report*, "The Man They Call 'President Meese'," 2 March 1981, p. 7; "Reagan's Big Three," 2 November 1981, p. 28.

30. *Hearings: Nomination of Edwin Meese*, p. 21.

31. Ibid., pp. 100, 179–84, 202, 203, 281–98.

32. Quotations are from Meese's 9 July 1985 speech to the American Bar Association, the text of which was obtained from the Department of Justice.

33. Court decisions cited by Meese as contrary to the founders' intent were Aquilor

v. Felton, no. 84-237; Wallace v. Jaffree, no. 83-812; City of Grand Rapids v. Ball, no. 83-990; and Thornton v. Caldor, no. 83-1158.

34. The first 13 state constitutions can be found in Poore, *Federal and State Constitutions*.

35. Main, *Anti-Federalists*, p. 159.

36. Julian P. Boyd, ed., *The Papers of Thomas Jefferson*, vol. 2, p. 546.

37. *Congressional Globe*, 39th Cong., 2d sess., pp. 1088, 2766.

38. Hibben v. Smith, 191 U.S. 310, 325.

39. Gitlow v. New York, 268 U.S. 652 (1925). Cantwell v. Connecticut, 310 U.S. 296 (1940).

40. Everson v. Board of Education, 330 U.S. 1 (1947).

41. Permoli v. New Orleans, 3 Howard 589 (1845).

42. Other cases illustrating federal and state court refusal to apply either the First or Fourteenth amendments to protect religious groups against discrimination by state and local authorities include Donahoe v. Richards, 38 Me. 376 (1854); Spiller v. Woburn, 12 Allen 127 (1866); Ferrite v. Tyler, 48 Vt. 444 (1876); Hamilton v. Regents, 293 U.S. 245 (1934); Minersville v. Gobitis. Minersville was reversed in West Virginia v. Barnette, 319 U.S. 624 (1943).

43. The first associate justices were John Blair of Virginia, William Cushing of Massachusetts, James Iredell of North Carolina, John Rutledge of South Carolina and James Wilson of Pennsylvania.

44. A detailed review of Supreme Court members from 1789 to 1975 is provided in Henry J. Abraham's *Justices and Presidents: A Political History of Appointments to the Supreme Court*.

45. Cannon, *Reagan*, pp. 256, 313.

46. PPP, 1981, p. 597.

47. Ibid., p. 601.

48. 1980 Republican platform, p. 48.

49. Abraham, *Justices and Presidents*, p. 4.

50. U.S. Senate, Committee on the Judiciary, *Confirmation Hearings on Federal Appointments*, 99th Cong., 1st sess., Part 2.

51. Ibid., p. 98.

52. *Student Lawyer*, February 1986.

53. U.S. Senate, Committee on the Judiciary, *Nomination of Jefferson B. Sessions, III to be U.S. District Judge for the Southern District of Alabama*, 13 March 1986, 99th Cong., 2d sess., pp. 28–30.

54. This exchange was printed in the Judiciary Committee's report on the *Nomination of Daniel A. Manion*, 99th Cong., 2d sess., Exec. Rpt. 99-16, 19 June 1986, p. 26.

55. Ibid., p. 26; *Confirmation Hearings on Federal Appointments*, Part 3, 99th Cong., 2d sess., p. 223.

56. Ibid., pp. 208–209.

57. Ibid., p. 186.

58. Report on the *Nomination of Daniel A. Manion*, pp. 29–34.

59. NYT, 24 June 1986.

60. WCPD, 1986, p. 851.
61. Ibid., 9 July 1986, p. 924.
62. For the parliamentary maneuvering that avoided Manion's rejection, see CR (daily), 26 June 1986, S8573 and 23 July 1986, S9539.
63. WP, 18 July 1986.
64. NYT, 25 May 1986.
65. Ibid., 16 September 1986.
66. Reagan statement at Alabama election rally for Senator Jeremiah A. Denton, whose views of the courts and the U.S. Constitution approximated those of the John Birch Society's leaders, WCPD, 28 October 1986, p. 1471. NYT, 1 November 1986.
67. NYT, 28 March 1987.
68. U.S. Senate, Committee on the Judiciary, *Nomination of Justice William Hubbs Rehnquist,* 99th Cong., 2d sess., July 29–August 1, 1986, pp. 101–104. *Nomination of Judge Antonin Scalia,* August 5–7, 1986, pp. 113–117.
69. See Rehnquist nomination, pp. 181–86 for testimony and Senator Ervin's letter. The case in question was Laird v. Tatum, 408 U.S. 1 (1972).
70. Bork's nomination was submitted to the Senate 7 July 1987, WCPD, 1987, p. 798. Patrick B. McGuigan's article, "Judge Robert Bork Is A Friend of the Constitution," appeared in the *Conservative Digest,* October 1985, pp. 91–102.
71. CR (daily), 29 September 1987, pp. S 12983–84.
72. Ibid., p. S 13075.
73. See especially the remarks of Senators Jesse Helms, Gordon J. Humphrey, and Alan K. Simpson, CR (daily), 1–6 October, 1987, pp. S13343–45, 13412, 13588–90, 13671–73.
74. Ibid., 30 September–7 October, 1987, pp. S13199, 13120, 13746.
75. WCPD, 15 August 1987, pp. 947; 11 September 1987, p. 1010; 2 October 1987, p. 1119.
76. Radio addresses, 3, 10, 14 October 1987, WCPD, pp. 1126, 1158, 1171–73.
77. WCPD, 5 October 1987, pp. 1130–31.
78. Exec. Rpt. no. 100–7. Pennsylvania Republican Arlen Specter joined eight Democrats in voting against Bork.
79. CR (daily), 23 October 1987, pp. S14913–15011.
80. WCPD, 14, 23 October 1987, pp. 1169, 1223.
81. Ibid., 29 October 1987, pp. 1246–48.
82. CR (daily), 1987, pp. S15412, 15416–19.
83. WCPD, 6 November 1987, pp. 1288–92.
84. NYT, 8 November 1987.
85. WCPD, 7 November 1987, p. 1298.
86. CR (daily), 3 February 1988, pp. S483–516.
87. Ibid., 23 October 1987, p. S14923. For reasons unknown to this writer, the Senate Judiciary Committee hearings on the Bork and Kennedy nominations were not published until May 1989.
88. NYT, 10 April 1990.

Chapter 7—Educator

1. Quoted from Proverbs 22:6 in speech to National Religious Broadcasters, PPP, 30 January 1984, p. 120.
2. WTROM, p. 12.
3. Letter, Taschow to Edel, 23 May 1987. See also Stanley Krippner, "The Boy Who Read at Eighteen Months," *Exceptional Children,* November 1963, pp. 105–109; Bruno Bettelheim & Karen Zelan, *On Learning to Read;* Bonnie Lass, "Portrait of My Son as an Early Reader," *The Reading Teacher,* October 1982, pp. 20–28, and February 1983, pp. 508–15. In this connection, biographer Anne Edwards reports (p. 40) that Reagan's mother was still reading to the boys when Ronnie was seven.
4. Anne Edwards, *Early Reagan,* p. 53.
5. Boyarski, *Ronald Reagan,* p. 40, Cannon, *Reagan,* p. 39, Edwards, *Early Reagan,* p. 39.
6. Edwards, *Early Reagan,* p. 41.
7. Boyarski, *Ronald Reagan,* p. 29. Edwards' search of school records (p. 82) provides the basis for the estimated "low B" high school average.
8. PPP, 1981, p. 1099.
9. WTROM, pp. 28–30.
10. Boyarski, *Ronald Reagan,* p. 40.
11. Ibid., p. 42. Speech at dedication of Eureka College Library, 28 September 1967, ATFC, pp. 75–86.
12. Edwards, *Early Reagan,* p. 95.
13. ATFC, p. 75. PPP, 9 May 1982, pp. 580–86; 26 April 1983, pp. 584–86.
14. To Phoenix, Arizona Chamber of Commerce, 30 March 1961, ATFC, pp. 28–30.
15. RRTTA, p. 173.
16. ATFC, p. 66.
17. RRTTA, p. 186.
18. ATFC, pp. 87–88.
19. Dugger, *On Reagan,* pp. 241–43.
20. ATFC, p. 167.
21. WTROM, pp. 26–30. Dugger, *On Reagan,* p. 318. Cannon, *Reagan,* pp. 151–53.
22. Cannon, *Reagan,* p. 148.
23. Loc. cit. Reagan would never acknowledge that rules change with the times. The "open admissions" policy adopted by the New York City Board of Higher Education eased admission regulations for the City University and provided substantial remedial assistance for students with inadequate language and mathematics skills, but it never lowered the requirements for graduation.
24. Cannon, *Reagan,* p. 151. Dugger, *On Reagan,* pp. 241–43.
25. 1980 Republican platform, pp. 14–15.
26. News conference, 6 November 1980; Terrel H. Bell, *The Thirteenth Man: A Reagan Cabinet Memoir,* p. 5.

27. Bell, *Thirteenth Man*, p. 24.
28. Ibid., p. 26.
29. Ibid., pp. 56–58. NYT, 20 October 1985.
30. Bell, *Thirteenth Man*, p. 94.
31. Ibid., p. 91.
32. National Commission on Excellence in Education, *A Nation At Risk: The Imperative for Educational Reform*. C. Emily Feistritzer, *The Condition of Teaching: A State by State Analysis*. Joseph Froomkin, ed., *The Crisis in Higher Education*. The president's remarks at the announcement of the commission report were published in PPP, 26 April 1983, pp. 584–86.
33. PPP, 1983, p. 586. *A Nation At Risk*, pp. 32–33.
34. Bell, *Thirteenth Man*, p. 131. WCPD, p. 903.
35. See PPP and WCPD index references under Education and Department of Education.
36. PPP, 30 April 1983, pp. 621–23. WCPD, 8 September 1984, pp. 1247–48.
37. PPP, 6 June 1983, p. 836; 14 June 1983, pp. 859–60.
38. Comptroller general to the president of the Senate and Speaker of the House of Representatives, 23 March 1984. This letter pointed out that the president had no authority to withhold appropriated funds unless he first submitted a recision proposal for congressional approval, an action he had not taken.
39. Bell, *Thirteenth Man*, pp. 157–61. WCPD, 1984, pp. 1811–12. The announcement Bell refers to in his memoirs did not appear in WCPD.
40. WCPD, 1984, p. 1911. No mention of the reception, or Reagan's remarks on that occasion, appear in WCPD.
41. WCPD, 1985, p. 39.
42. NYT, 22 November 1984.
43. Ibid., 17 April 1985. WP, 19 April 1985.
44. Address to National Association of Independent Schools, WCPD, 28 February 1985, p. 236.
45. Richard W. Lyman, "Demythologizing Those Golden Academic Days of Yore," NYT, 20 March 1985.
46. WP, 29 July 1985.
47. NYT, 8 August, 15 September, 12 November 1985. Aguilar v. Felton, No. 84-237, 1 July 1985.
48. WP, 30 January 1985, excerpted a letter from President Reagan to Senator Orrin Hatch.
49. WP, 17 September 1985.
50. NYT, 8 June 1986.
51. WP, 16 January 1986.
52. WCPD, 24 August 1985, p. 1001.
53. Ibid., 1 October 1985, p. 1177.
54. NYT, 14 November 1985.
55. William J. Bennett, "American Education: Making it Work," Report to the president, April 1988. For reports of reactions, see NYT, 26 April 1988.
56. For the substance of Bennett's attack, see *The Stanford Review*, 18 April 1988.

Opposing points of view appear in NYT, 20 April, 2 May 1988.

57. WCPD, 10 October 1985, p. 1229; 4, 6, 7 February 1986, pp. 37–38, 167–68, 188.

58. Ibid., 7 February 1986, p. 188. PPP, 10 May 1982, p. 591.

59. Talks with students at Farragut, Tennessee, High School, PPP, 14 June 1983, p. 865; and St. Agatha High School, Reford, Michigan, WCPD, 10 October 1984, p. 1482. See also WCPD, 1984, p. 1187; 1986, pp. 305, 620–22, 664–65, 852–54; 1987, pp. 1399–1403.

60. Rarely do guidance counselors perform their function in the classroom. Nevertheless, this is the way Reagan told the story, which was reported in WCPD, 19 May 1987, p. 553.

61. WCPD, 20 May 1987, p. 565. This conclusion was not included in Bennett's report.

62. Remarks to presidential scholars, PPP, 19 June 1984, p. 878.

63. WCPD, 17 June, 5 October 1987, pp. 692, 1128.

64. See Chapter 2.

65. PPP, 1984, p. 879. The quotation is from Jefferson's letter to Peter Carr, dated 19 August 1785.

66. WCPD, 1986, p. 306. The occasion was one on which Reagan and Bennett went through an obviously rehearsed stage routine—made to appear spontaneous—with the two reciting alternate lines of a humorous poem.

67. See Jefferson's letter to Peter Carr in *Thomas Jefferson: Writings,* pp. 814–18, 900–906, 1346–52.

68. WTROM, pp. 28–30. The basic facts of this confrontation have been confirmed by Reagan biographers Cannon, Boyarsky and Edwards.

69. NYT, 21 April 1981, 9 January 1983. The City College approach to political science was already in place when this writer began teaching the elementary government course there in 1948. That innovation would not have been noticed by anyone at the *New York Times* because that journal rarely paid any attention to the city's public colleges until the campus revolts of the late 1960s made news of upheaval wherever it occurred.

70. Carnegie Foundation for the Advancement of Teaching, *A Report Card on School Reform: The Teachers Speak,* pp. 2–5, 7–9.

71. Ibid., tables 14–17, 19, 23, 31, 36, 38.

72. Commission on Minority Participation, *One-Third of a Nation,* p. vii. The title of this report was taken from a phrase in President Franklin Roosevelt's second inaugural address in which he described "one-third of a nation ill-housed, ill-clad, ill-nourished."

73. BUSG, FY 1989, p. 5–92.

74. H. R. 5, "Elementary and Secondary School Amendments of 1988," was signed into law 28 April 1988. Reagan's remarks at the signing were reported in WCPD, 1988, pp. 540–41.

75. BUSG, FY 1990, p. I-III.

Chapter 8—Chairman of the Board

1. 1980 campaign speech, cited in Dugger, *On Reagan,* p. 25.
2. Cannon, *Reagan,* p. 125.
3. PPP, 23 December 1981, p. 1193.
4. Lou Cannon and Lee Lescaze, "Reagan's Decision-Making Process Still A Mystery," WP, 22 March 1982.
5. Leslie H. Gelb, "The Mind of the President," *New York Times Magazine,* 6 October 1985.
6. Deaver, *Behind the Scenes,* p. 39. Nancy Reagan, *My Turn,* pp. 60–63.
7. Nancy Reagan, *My Turn,* pp. 44, 49, Regan, *For the Record,* p. 4.
8. Nancy Reagan, *My Turn,* p. 51. WP, 9 May, 1988. WCPD, 9 May 1988, p. 591. MacNeil-Lehrer News Hour, 9 May 1988.
9. Lou Cannon and David Hoffman, "The Inner Circle Decides and the Outer Circle Ratifies," WP, 19 July 1982.
10. 1: PPP, 22 January 1981, p. 30. 2: Executive Order 12301, PPP, 26 March 1981, pp. 287–90. 3, 4: PPP, 12 January 1982, p. 18. 5: News conferences, PPP, 18 February 1982, p. 180 and 1 March 1982, p. 262. 6: Executive Order 12348, PPP, 25 February 1982, p. 220.
11. Executive Order 12479, PPP, 24 May 1984, pp. 743–44. Executive Order 12625, WCPD, 27 January 1988, p. 133. For a brief analysis of the use and value of presidential advisory groups see Robert Beneson, "Presidential Advisory Commissions," *Congressional Quarterly,* 6 January 1984.
12. Executive Order 12329, PPP, 14 October 1981, p. 928.
13. PPP, 1981, p. 751.
14. *Public Administration Times,* 15 April 1983. NYT, 1 July, 4 August 1983. H. R., Task Force on Entitlements, Uncontrollables and Indexing, *Hearing: Report of President's Private Sector Survey on Cost Control,* 98th Cong., 1st sess., 2 November 1983, pp. 3, 19. Only administration witnesses were invited to this hearing, and only Representatives Brian Connelly of Massachusetts and Geraldine Farraro of New York questioned them.
15. PPP, 16 January 1944, pp. 44–46. For Peter Grace's letter to the president, see J. Peter Grace's privately published *War on Waste,* pp. v–x.
16. NYT, 29 February 1984. WP, 21 May, 1 June 1984.
17. The Grace Commission projected 3-year savings of $44.5 billion in the Defense Department and said that only 7 percent of its recommendations would require congressional approval.
18. See index listings under Private Sector Survey on Cost Control in PPP, 1983 and 1984.
19. PPP, 1984, p. 386. WCPD, 5 February 1986, pp. 146–49.
20. WCPD, 29 September 1987, p. 1083.
21. News conference, PPP, 29 January 1981, p. 60. NYT, 14, 23 December 1985. WP, 24 December 1985.
22. For two other analyses of Reagan's management style, see chapters 3 and 9 in Hedrick Smith et al., *Reagan the Man.* Reagan's quoted remarks appear in WCPD, 1987, pp. 1083–84 and RRTTA, p. 43.

23. January 1967 speech, RRTTA, p. 41.
24. Lou Cannon, "The GOP's Corporate Tradition," WP, 14 March 1988.
25. Larry Speakes, *Speaking Out: Inside the Reagan White House*, pp. 111–114. WP, 28 December 1982. According to *Parade Magazine* of 2 June 1985, tabulations by the *Santa Barbara News Press* indicate that President Reagan spent 15.5 percent of his first administration at his California ranch or with friends in that state.
26. Speakes, *Speaking Out*, pp. 114, 285. Deaver, *Behind the Scenes*, p. 26.
27. Speakes, *Speaking Out*, p. 111. President Reagan confirmed part of Speakes' analysis, saying "I begin with the comics." WCPD, 13 April 1988, p. 468.
28. NYT, 21 February 1987. WP, 10 May 1988. Speakes, *Speaking Out*, p. 298.
29. Mona Charen, "What the White House Women Think of the White House Men," *The Washingtonian*, September 1986, p. 139.
30. Dugger, *On Reagan*, p. 437.
31. CR (daily), 2 August 1983, p. H6216.
32. PPP, 1 October 1981, p. 869.
33. Ibid., 10 November 1981, p. 1033.
34. Ibid., 10, 13 May 1982, pp. 604, 624–25.
35. Ibid., 28 September, 11 November 1982, pp. 1229, 1451.
36. Robert Scheer, *With Enough Shovels: Reagan, Bush and Nuclear War,* p. 18.
37. WP, 30 May 1987.
38. WP, 24 December 1985.
39. NYT, 9 October 1986. WCPD, 8 October 1986, pp. 1348–49.
40. Martin Tolchin, "An Inattention to Detail is Getting More Attention," NYT, 14 January 1987.
41. WCPD, 25 November 1986, p. 1604.
42. Views expressed in post-election interviews with reporters of *Time* and *New York Times,* 12 November 1980.
43. U.S. Senate, Committee on the Judiciary, *Hearings: Nomination of Edwin Meese, III.*
44. Speakes, *Speaking Out*, pp. 68, 70–71. Deaver, *Behind the Scenes,* p. 196. Cannon, *Reagan,* pp. 306–7. Brownstein and Easton, *Reagan's Ruling Class,* pp. 645–46.
45. See Marjorie Hunter's analysis in NYT, 12 December 1980.
46. For sketches of these appointees, see NYT, 18 April 1983 and 12 December 1980; Brownstein and Easton, *Reagan's Ruling Class,* pp. 168–70, 229–31, 289–91; Donald T. Regan, *For the Record: From Wall Street to Washington,* chap. 7.
47. NYT, 29 June 1982.
48. WCPD, 15 March 1985, p. 310.
49. ATFC, p. 113,
50. NYT, 9 February 1984; 29 February, 30 April, 11 May 1988. WP, 25 May 1988.
51. USGM, 1987/88, p. 106. WP, 29 December 1983, 13 February, 25 May 1984. *Common Cause Magazine,* March/April 1988, pp. 18–20.
52. WP, 29 December 1983.

53. PPP, 1983, p. 1124. NYT, 25 March 1985. WP, 28 April 1988.

54. Regan, *For the Record,* pp. 142–43.

55. NYT, 8 November 1986, 13 February 1987; *Common Cause Magazine,* 8 November/December 1987, p. 37. WCPD, 1984, pp. 1312, 1316, 1381. Richard Darman's remarks were delivered in a 7 November 1986 speech.

56. GAO investigations of 23 federal agencies were summarized in NYT, 27 December 1985. See also NYT, 23 April, 8 May 1986; WP, 27 May 1986.

57. For samples of Reagan's fictional anecdotes, see Green and MacColl, *There He Goes Again,* pp. 84–97.

58. Comptroller General of the U.S., *Defense Budget Increases: How Well Are They Planned And Spent?* 13 April 1982, pp. i–1.

59. H. R. Committee on Armed Services, "Report of the staff to accompany H.A.S.C. no. 99-66," 99th Cong., 1st sess., October 1985, pp. 2–4, 16–17.

60. PPP, 20 August 1983, p. 1186. NYT, 28 February 1984, 18 June 1985. WCPD, 15 July 1985, p. 904.

61. WP, 19 February 1986. NYT, 1 March, 18 April 1986.

62. WCPD, 28 February 1986, pp. 291–92.

63. Ibid., 2, 5, 24 April, 12 June 1986, pp. 439, 443, 540–41, 788. GAO reports: "More Controls Needed Over Army's Obligations of Funds," May 1987; "DOD Inventory Management, Revised Policies Needed," January 1988; "Ethics Enforcement, Results of Conflict of Interest Investigations," February 1988; "Navy Inventory Management, Accuracy Problems," March 1988.

64. NYT, 16 June, 7 July 1988.

65. Ibid., 7 December 1985.

66. Dina Rasor, "Sidetracking Reform at the Pentagon," WP, 1 July 1988. For reports of Dingell's warning to Weinberger, see WP, 18 and 27 June 1988.

67. NYT, 7, 28 August 1985. Weinberger's formal statement was issued 17 August and published the following day.

68. Stockman, *Triumph of Politics,* p. 304. NYT, 27 January 1985.

69. NYT, 28 March 1988.

70. Stockman, *Triumph of Politics,* p. 307.

71. Ibid., pp. 300–309. Winston Williams, "Bungling the Military Buildup," NYT, 27 January 1985. Molly Moore, "Travails of the Centerpiece Weapon," WP, 10 August 1987. NYT, 1 January, 20 May 1985.

72. NYT, 15 July 1987.

73. NYT, 5 December 1987, 27 July 1988. WP, 13 July 1988.

74. U.S. Senate, Committee on the Judiciary, Subcommittee on Administrative Practice and Procedure, *Hearing: Role of Whistle-blowers in Administrative Proceedings,* 98th Cong., 1st sess., 14 November 1983, pp. 4–5.

75. Ibid., pp. 10–15.

76. Ibid., pp. 16–19, 84–97.

77. WCPD, 5 October 1984, p. 1434.

78. Dina Rasor and Donna Martin, "Protecting Pentagon Whistlers," NYT, 23 October 1984.

79. NYT, 11 December 1984, 18 March 1985, 9 November 1986. WP, 5 March

1985, 20 July 1988. *Parade Magazine,* 10 July 1988, pp. 16–19.
80. WP, 9 November, 16 December 1986.
81. NYT, 19 October 1987.

Chapter 9—Diplomat: Crusader for Democracy

1. Remarks to conference of Caribbean heads of state, WCPD, 19 July 1984, p. 1044.
2. The theme of government interference with private activity, which formed the core of Reagan's 1964 speech for Goldwater, was repeated in almost every major address down to and including his 1984 State of the Union characterization of America as "this last best hope of man on earth." PPP, 1984, p. 93.
3. February 1967 speech, RRTTA, p. 51.
4. Ibid., pp. 17, 46, 123. For Reagan's first reference to the Soviet Union as "an evil empire" and "the focus of evil in the modern world," see PPP, 8 March 1983, pp. 363–64.
5. PPP, 29 January 1981, p. 57.
6. Ibid., 27 May 1981, p. 464.
7. Hedrick Smith, et al., *Reagan the Man,* p. 100.
8. Nancy Reagan, *My Turn,* p. 65.
9. Jeane Kirkpatrick, "Dictatorships and Double Standards," *Commentary,* November 1979, pp. 34–35.
10. Jeane Kirkpatrick, *Legitimacy and Force,* vol. 1, p. 437.
11. NYT, 17, 20, 21 July 1988. The election which elevated Bermudez to political leadership and ousted civilian leader Pedro Joaquin Chamorro was held in the Dominican Republic.
12. State of the Union message, WCPD, 6 February 1985, p. 146. In *Legitimacy and Force,* vol. 1, p. 427, Kirkpatrick cites Reagan's 1984 State of the Union message as the source.
13. Pinochet was not on the ballot in the 1989 election, but he remains head of the army and the National Security Council.
14. Amnesty International, *Nicaragua: The Human Rights Record.* Americas Watch Committee, *Human Rights in Nicaragua, 1985–86.* Lawyers Committee for Human Rights, "Human Rights in Nicaragua," 1987. The annual reports of Amnesty International and monthly issues of *Index on Censorship* are invaluable for up-to-date information on repression in all countries.
15. WCPD, 5 March 1986, p. 312.
16. Ibid., 15 August 1988, pp. 1064–65.
17. William D. Rogers, "Reagan Spurred Latin Democracy? Nonsense," NYT, 5 August 1988.
18. For articles on the difficulties faced by democratic elements in South American countries, see *Current History,* February 1984, January 1987, and January 1988.
19. Vatican press release, 3 September 1984. A new instruction, dated 5 April, dwelt at much greater length on the theme that "the priority of work over

capital places an obligation in justice upon employers to consider the welfare of the workers before the increase of profits."

20. Pope John Paul II's speech was televised from Edmonton, Canada, 17 September 1984. William Buckley's column, "The Pope and the Poor Nations," appeared in WP, 22 September 1984.
21. News conference, WCPD, 21 February 1985, p. 213, and *Newsweek* interview, WCPD, 11 March 1985, pp. 281–82.
22. For references to the Contadora proposals by President Reagan, see PPP, 1983, pp. 1719, 1736; 1984, pp. 222, 384, 504, 660, 671, 700.
23. NYT, 21 June; 6, 10 August; 7 November 1987. WP, 6 August 1987. WCPD, 5 August 1987, p. 902. No record of the Reagan-Arias meeting appeared in WCPD. A revised version of the Arias peace plan was signed 5 August 1987 by the presidents of Costa Rica, El Salvador, Guatemala, Honduras and Nicaragua. For an English translation, see *Current History,* December 1987, p. 430.
24. NYT, 25 October 1988.
25. Ibid., 29 November 1987. Cuba's readmission to OAS had not been effected as this book went to press.
26. Raymond D. Gaston, *Freedom in the World,* pp. 29–36, 54–65. For a country-by-country analysis, see pp. 267–415. This volume is updated annually and is often cited by the State Department in its annual *Country Reports on Human Rights Practices.*
27. Fred Bridgland, *Jonas Savimbi, A Key to Africa.*
28. John Stockwell, *In Search of Enemies,* pp. 235–45. Bridgland, *Jonas Savimbi,* chap. 33.
29. Acknowledgement of treaty violations by South Africa's foreign minister was reported in NYT, 20 September 1985.
30. Marina Ottoway, "Economic Reform and War in Mozambique," *Current History,* May 1988, pp. 201, 202, 223.
31. WP, 24 July 1987. NYT, 21 April 1988.
32. WP, 3 February 1986. NYT, 24 July 1988.
33. NYT, 21 July and 10 October 1988.
34. WCPD, 15 August 1988, p. 1065.
35. For a review of UN action on South West Africa, see *United Nations Yearbook,* 1966, pp. 598–607; 1967, pp. 690–97; 1968, pp. 778–87.
36. NYT, 7 June 1987, 1 July 1988.
37. Interview with CBS correspondent Walter Cronkite, PPP, 3 March 1981, pp. 196–97.
38. WCPD, 24 September 1984, p. 1355.
39. Ibid. 19 October 1984, p. 1574.
40. Ibid., 7 December 1984, p. 1881.
41. Ibid., pp. 1884–85. The White House report of the release of black South African labor leaders did not include the president's comments. Reagan's claim of U.S. influence and President Botha's rejoinder appeared in NYT, 8, 14 December 1984.

42. WCPD, 5 August 1985, p. 963.
43. NYT, 2, 4 September 1985. *Los Angeles Times,* 7 January 1986.
44. NYT, 16 August 1985.
45. WCPD, 9 April, 23 June, 9 July 1986, pp. 465, 860, 922.
46. WCPD, 22 July 1986, pp. 975–80. This speech to the Foreign Policy Association was followed by a question-and-answer session, of which no record was kept.
47. Executive Order 12532 and message to Congress, WCPD, 9 September 1985, pp. 1051–55
48. Ibid., p. 1051.
49. *Gallup Poll,* 1986, pp. 74, 200.
50. Reagan's veto was overriden by a vote of 313 to 83 in the House, and 78 to 21 in the Senate. For debate and votes on overriding the veto, see CR (daily), 29 September 1986, pp. H8648-72 and 2 October 1986, pp. S14629-61.
51. WCPD, 1 October 1987, pp. 1110–16.
52. *Index on Censorship,* August 1982, p. 46; August 1986, p. 7; quotation from March 1988 issue, p. 22.
53. *Weekly Mail* announcement, reproduced in NYT, 13 December 1986.
54. NYT, 12 December 1986.
55. PPP, 12 November 1981, pp. 1039–40; 8 November 1982, p. 1438.
56. Ibid., 13 March 1984, p. 345.
57. Ibid., 5 August 1981, p. 694; 20 March 1984, p. 389.
58. Ibid., 17 October 1981, p. 949.
59. Ibid., 20 May 1984, p. 755.
60. NYT, 15, 17 November 1988.
61. Visits by African chiefs of state were reported in PPP.
62. PPP, 1981, for report of the Ottawa Economic Summit, pp. 635–49, and Cancun International Meeting, pp. 978–84.
63. WP, 4 July 1981.
64. PPP, 10 November 1983, pp. 1565–69, 1573.
65. Deaver, *Behind the Scenes,* pp. 147, 175.
66. PPP, 26–30 April 1984, pp. 577–609.
67. Department of State, Current Policy no. 948, 22 April 1987; Gist, Feb. 1988; Current Policy no. 1079, 1 June 1988.
68. PPP, 3 October 1983, p. 1401. Tour was planned in June.
69. PPP, 16 September 1982, p. 1167. Reagan's letter to Marcos was not published in PPP but was reported in NYT, 5 October 1982.
70. NYT, 24 October 1984; 24 January, 3 May, 3 December 1985.
71. WCPD, 12 February 1985, p. 170.
72. NYT, 18 July 1986. WCPD, 22 October 1985, p. 1299. A private discussion of the Philippine situation between the president and Laxalt was noted but not reproduced in WCPD, 3 December, p. 1468.
73. WCPD, 30 January 1986, pp. 110–11.
74. Ibid., 6 February 1986, p. 157.
75. NYT, 20 January 1986. WP, 10, 11 February 1986. AP radio network news, 13 February 1986.

76. WCPD, 10, 11 February 1986, pp. 206, 211–12.
77. NYT, 12, 13 February 1986. WCPD, 15 February 1986, p. 229.
78. H.R., Committee on Foreign Affairs, Subcommittee on Asian and Pacific Affairs, *Hearings and Markup: The Philippine Election and the Implications for U.S. Policy,* 19 February 1986, p. 7.
79. NYT, 14 February 1986.
80. WCPD, 5 March 1986, p. 312.
81. Ibid., 25 February, 17 September 1986, pp. 265, 1201.
82. Radio address to the nation, WCPD, 26 April 1986, pp. 551–52. Speech in Bali, Indonesia, ibid., 1 May 1986, pp. 566–67. Lou Cannon, "Making Unsupportable Claims," WP, 5 May 1986.
83. Department of State, "Selected Documents no. 33: U.S.-Philippines Military Bases Agreement Review 1988."
84. NYT, 25 November 1981, 22 June 1983.
85. NYT, 7 March 1983.
86. NYT, 25, 30 October 1986. WP, 28 October, 28 November 1986.
87. PPP, 29 December 1981, p. 1209. NYT, 30 December 1981, 6 February 1982.
88. NYT, 9, 12 March 1982.
89. Ibid., 1 June 1984. The foreign ministers meeting was held in December 1983.
90. WP, 16 December 1986. NYT, 17 December 1986, 2 February 1987.
91. NYT, 5 June 1982.

Chapter 10—Diplomat: Slayer of Dragons

1. PPP, 8 March 1983, p. 364.
2. Ibid., 1981: 29 January, p. 57; 24 February, pp. 152–53.
3. Ibid., 3 March 1981, pp. 191–97.
4. Ibid., 18 November 1981, pp. 1063–66.
5. Ibid., 1981: 29 January, p. 57; 18 February, p. 112; 24 February, p. 153; 3 March, pp. 192–97; 6 March, p. 207; 26 March, p. 294; 30 March, p. 309; 22 May, pp. 453–55; 16 June, pp. 525–26; 13 August, pp. 707–11; 18 September, p. 812; 23 September, pp. 826–27; 24 September, pp. 832–33; 1 October, p. 871; 2 October, p. 896; 17 October, pp. 956–57; 17 December, pp. 1161–72; 23 December, pp. 1185–88; 27 December, pp. 1199–1200; 29 December, pp. 1202, 1209.
6. PPP, 24 April 1981, p. 382.
7. Ibid., 8 January 1982, p. 10.
8. Ibid., 13 August 1981, p. 710; 17 October 1981, p. 951; 11 November 1982, p. 1455. From 2 September 1981 through the following year Reagan referred to the state of U.S. military unpreparedness as this country's "window of vulnerability." See PPP, 1981, pp. 746, 871, 950 and chapter 10 citations.
9. Carnegie Endowment for International Peace, *Documents Relating to the Programs of the First Hague Peace Conference,* pp. 30–32, and Quincy Wright, *A Study of War,* vol. 1, p. 798.

10. Henry L. Stimson, *On Active Service in Peace and War,* pp. 642–66.
11. FRUS, 1946, vol. 1, pp. 712–13.
12. Ibid., pp. 1197–98.
13. These and all subsequent Soviet-American treaties and agreements can be found in *Arms Control and Disarmament Agreements,* which is periodically updated.
14. Ibid., 1982 ed.
15. PPP, 10 December 1982, p. 1595; 11 November 1982, p. 1455.
16. NYT, 10 December 1982.
17. NYT, 7 May 1982, 4 September 1981.
18. CR (daily), 23 June 1981, pp. S6703–6706.
19. *Gallup Poll,* 1981, pp. 134–35, 1982, pp. 280–81.
20. H.R., Committee on Foreign Affairs, Report No. 97-640, 19 July 1982. Senate Committee on Foreign Relations, Report No. 97-493, 12 July 1982.
21. Wilbur Edel, *Defenders of the Faith: Religion and Politics from the Pilgrim Fathers to Ronald Reagan,* p. 173.
22. PPP, 5 October 1982, p. 1263.
23. Department of State, "The Nuclear Freeze," April 1982, pp. 1, 8. This pamphlet contained no suggestion of Soviet influence in the freeze movement.
24. *Gallup Poll,* 1983, p. 72; 1984, p. 245.
25. PPP, 19 July 1983, p. 1053.
26. Ibid., 25 January 1984, p. 93. Leonid Brezhnev told a *Pravda* reporter on 21 October 1981 that "to try to prevail over the other side in the arms race or to count on victory in a nuclear war is dangerous madness. . . . Only he who has decided to commit suicide can start a nuclear war in the hope of emerging from it as a victor." *Current Digest of the Soviet Press,* 18 November 1981, p. 13.
27. Interview with WP reporters, PPP, 16 January 1984, p. 63.
28. PPP, 16 January, 11, 13 February 1984, pp. 40–42, 191–92, 199–200. NYT, 16 February 1984.
29. The 1984 Republican platform was printed in CR (daily) 5 September 1984, pp. S10739–56.
30. PPP, 30 January 1984, p. 123.
31. NYT, 21 June 1984. For treaty texts see *Arms Control and Disarmament Agreements,* 1982 ed., pp. 167–189.
32. NYT, 16 May 1984. News conferences, PPP, 14 May, 22 May, 14 June 1984, pp. 693–94, 726–29, 852.
33. NYT, 28, 30 July, 3 August 1984.
34. NYT, 15 August 1984. In the absence of a full-fledged news conference during the fall election campaign, Reagan offered no explanation of his remarks until a reporter questioned him two days before Election Day. WCPD, 4 November, p. 1772.
35. Richard Perle's influence, with quoted opinions, was reviewed in NYT, 2 January 1985.
36. Norman Podhoretz, "Arms Control Illusions," NYT, 24 January 1985.
37. History professor David E. Kaiser pointed out these and other flaws in the Podhoretz piece in NYT, 6 February 1985.
38. WCPD, 9 January 1985, pp. 35–36.

39. NYT, 9 January, WP, 10, 14 January 1985.
40. WCPD, 21 March 1985, p. 343. WP, 8 April 1985.
41. NYT, 8 April, 11, 12 September, 16 November 1985. *Defense Monitor,* vol. 4, no. 8, 1985, p. 7. Department of State, Special Reports nos. 129 and 131, June 1985 and Current Policy no. 751, 15 October 1985. WCPD, 20 August 1985, pp. 991–92. WP, 4 September, 23 October 1985. *Time,* "An Interview with Gorbachev," 9 September 1985, p. 22, and "The Great War of Words," ibid., pp. 32–33.
42. See speeches of Secretary of State George Shultz, Secretary of Defense Caspar Weinberger, Soviet Foreign Minister Eduard Schevardnadze and Marshal Sergei Khromeyev in NYT, 25 September, 10, 15, 18 October 1985.
43. WCPD, 3 July 1985, p. 873, 6 November 1985, p. 1358.
44. News conferences, WCPD, 17 September 1985, pp. 1103, 1107. James Reston, "Stumbling to Geneva," NYT, 25 September 1985.
45. WCPD, 21 November 1985, pp. 1422–23, 1426.
46. NYT, 28 November 1985, excerpted Gorbachev remarks; complete statement in *Current Digest of the Soviet Press,* 26 November 1985, pp. 10–17.
47. NYT, 20, 25 December. WP, 24 December 1985.
48. WCPD, 1 January 1986, pp. 4–6.
49. Ibid., p. 56.
50. WP, 6 March 1986.
51. WCPD, 13, 14 March, 9 April 1986, pp. 346, 356–64, 464.
52. Ibid., p. 1068.
53. Ibid., p. 1235.
54. James Reston, "Reagan Backs His Hunch," NYT, 8 October 1986.
55. WCPD, 30 September 1986, pp. 1297–99.
56. Radio-television address to the nation, WCPD, 13 October 1986, p. 1376.
57. Translation copyright by *Current Digest of the Soviet Press,* published weekly at Columbus, OH, 12 November 1986, pp. 2–8, quotes from p. 4.
58. NYT, 7 December 1987.
59. *Gallup Poll,* 1987, pp. 63–64.
60. Department of State, press releases entitled "Gist," "Current Policy" and "Special Reports" issued throughout 1987. For Paul Nitze's analysis, see Current Policy no. 910, 14 January 1987, p. 2
61. Department of State, Special Report no. 161, January 1987.
62. NYT, 16 April 1987. Department of State, Current Policy no. 955, 27 April 1987.
63. NYT, 26 May 1987.
64. Department of State, Gist, June 1987.
65. Department of State, Current Policy no. 997, 25 June 1987; no. 985, 1 July 1987; no. 995, 26 August 1987. WCPD, 21 September 1987, pp. 1051–56.
66. WCPD, 18 September 1987, pp. 1038–39; 30 October 1987, p. 1251. Questions directed to Secretary Shultz were omitted from WCPD but were reported in NYT, 19 September 1987.
67. WCPD, pp. 1391–96.
68. Translation copyright by *Current Digest of the Soviet Press,* published weekly at Columbus, OH, 9 December 1987, p. 16.

69. The Brokaw-Gorbachev interview was taped 28 November in Moscow and televised in the U.S. 30 November 1987.

70. Reagan's exchange with *Izvestia* rated just six inches of type midway in section 1 of NYT, 5 December 1987.

71. WCPD, 8 December 1987, pp. 1454–55.

72. Ibid., pp. 1457–58.

73. Department of State, Gist, December 1987. For text of treaty and leaders' remarks see WCPD, 8 December 1987, pp. 1459–87; 10 December 1987, pp. 1502–1506, and NYT, 11 December 1987.

74. Alan Cranston, "A Debacle Like the League of Nations?" NYT, 21 December 1987.

75. U.S. Senate, Committee on Foreign Relations, *Hearings: The INF Treaty,* 100th Cong., 2d sess., part 1, pp. 2–3, 103; part 2, pp. 7–8.

76. Department of State, Current Policy no. 1043, 5 February 1988.

77. See NYT, 8 April 1988 for text of joint Soviet-Afghan statement on troop withdrawals, and 15 April for key sections of the Afghan-Pakistani agreement.

78. *Hearings: INF Treaty,* part 1, p. 446.

79. Formal debate on the INF Treaty filled many pages of the *Congressional Record* from 20 April to 27 May 1988. The final vote, together with the Senate's conditions and declarations appear in CR (daily) 27 May 1988, p. S6937. For Senator Nunn's earlier attack on President Reagan's reinterpretation of the ABM Treaty, see CR (daily), 20 May 1987, pp. S6809–31.

80. WCPD, 10 June 1988, pp. 779–81.

81. Yevtushenko was a guest on the MacNeil-Lehrer News Hour, televised 27 May 1988.

82. Department of State, Gist, April 1988.

83. WCPD, 21 April 1988, p. 504; 4 May 1988, pp. 570–74.

84. NYT, 30 May, 1 June 1988. WCPD, 30 May 1988, p. 699.

85. WCPD, 1 June 1988, p. 718–19.

86. Ibid., 2 June 1988, p. 734.

87. Ibid., 3 June 1988, pp. 735–38.

88. Ibid., 1988, pp. 748–52, 766–69, 921–22, 1097. See also speeches by State Department officers in Department of State, Current Policy nos. 1080, 1088, 1089, 1090.

89. NYT, 26 October 1988. Department of State, Gist, October 1988.

90. NYT, 12, 18 August 1988.

91. Ibid., 25 August, 6, 25, 29 October 1988.

92. NYT, 6 October 1988. For the World Court's decisions on charges brought by Nicaragua, see International Court of Justice, *Military and Paramilitary Activities in and Against Nicaragua* (Nicaragua v. United States of America), 27 June 1986.

Chapter 11—Commander in Chief

1. WCPD, 7 February 1986, p. 184.

2. Ibid., 16 July 1986, p. 951.

3. Copyright, 1981, *U.S. News & World Report,* interview with the president, 28 December 1981, p. 27. The phrase, "the last best hope of man on earth," first used in Reagan's 1964 Goldwater speech, was repeated many times.

4. PPP, 4 April 1984, pp. 465, 467. WCPD, 18 April 1985, p. 472. Dugger, *On Reagan,* p. 240.

5. Most frequently cited were article 1, section 2 of the Constitution; the National Emergencies Act; and the International Emergency Economic Powers Act.

6. Dugger, *On Reagan,* p. 346.

7. Ibid., pp. 274–76.

8. WP, 6 December 1984.

9. Gregg Herken, "The Earthly Origins of Star Wars," *Bulletin of the Atomic Scientists,* October 1987, p. 20. 1980 Republican platform, pp. 54, 56.

10. Televised address to the nation, PPP, 23 March 1983, pp. 437–43.

11. PPP, 25, 29 March 1983, pp. 458, 463–67.

12. Office of the President, "The President's Strategic Defense Initiative," January 1985, p. 2.

13. *Arms Control and Disarmament Agreements,* 1982 ed., p. 140.

14. WCPD, 9 January 1985, pp. 31, 34.

15. Department of State, Current Policy no. 755, "The ABM Treaty and the SDI Program," 22 October 1985. WP, 27 March 1987.

16. WP, 30 April 1987, 26 January 1984.

17. The unclassified portions of Teller's letters of 22 December 1983 and 28 December 1984 were published in *Bulletin of the Atomic Scientists,* November 1988, p. 5. The efforts of Roy Woodruff and Ray Kidder to counter the extravagant claims made by Teller and Wood were detailed in William J. Broad's article, "Beyond the Bomb: Turmoil in the Labs," *New York Times Magazine,* 9 October 1988.

18. General Accounting Office, *Strategic Defense Initiative Program: Accuracy of Statements Concerning DOE's X-Ray Laser Research Program,* June 1988, pp. 3, 6, 8, 11, 13. Excerpts from Dr. Kidder's letter were published in *Bulletin of the Atomic Scientists,* cited above.

19. From 1984, when it was first established, to 1988, the Strategic Defense Initiative Organization expanded from a Defense Department unit of 9 divisions to one with 25 divisions and, so far as can be ascertained from the Executive Budget, an indeterminate number of employees. See USGM, 1985–86, p. 238, and 1987–88, pp. 252–53.

20. H.R., Committee on Armed Services, *Hearing: Strategic Defense Initiative Program,* 99th Cong., 1st sess., 6 June 1985, p. 45.

21. Ibid., pp. 18–19.

22. Ibid., p. 42. Letters from Bethe, Bradbury, Panofsky and Rathjens and from Batzel and Kerr were published in *Bulletin of the Atomic Scientists,* November 1985, pp. 11–13.

23. Union of Concerned Scientists, *Star Wars: Myth and Reality,* January 1987, p. 2.

24. WCPD, 23 November 1987, p. 1375. NYT, 27 November 1988.

25. DS, Current Policy no. 677, 28 March 1985.
26. Office of the President, *National Security of the United States,* January 1987, January 1988.
27. Center for Defense Information, *Defense Monitor,* vol. 17, no. 1, 1988. Union of Concerned Scientists, *Star Wars: Myth and Reality,* January 1987. Bruce Parrott, "The Soviet Debate on Missile Defense," *Bulletin of the Atomic Scientists,* April 1987, pp. 9–12. Statements by five former defense secretaries were published in *Common Cause Magazine,* "Campaign to Stop Star Wars," January 1987.
28. See *Hearing,* note 20, p. 23.
29. H.R., Committee on Government Operations, *Hearing: Management of the Strategic Defense Initiative,* 100th Cong., 2d sess., 29 March 1988, pp. 1, 3, 21.
30. Council on Economic Priorities, *Newsletter,* June 1987.
31. Center for Defense Information, *Defense Monitor,* vol. 17, no. 1, 1988.
32. Department of Defense, *Report to the Congress on the Strategic Defense Initiative,* April 1987, pp. 11–16. BUSG, FY 1989, p. 2b2. H.R. Committee on Appropriations, *Department of Defense Appropriations for 1989,* part 1, p. 27.
33. PPP, 2 March 1984, p. 289.
34. John K. Cooley, "The Libyan Menace," *Foreign Policy,* Spring 1981, pp. 74–93.
35. NYT, 20 August 1981, printed a transcript of the news conference held by Secretary Weinberger and General Gast. PPP, 20 August 1981, pp. 722–23, reported President Reagan's remarks.
36. NYT, 20 August 1981. PPP, 20 August 1981, p. 722.
37. H.R., Committee on Foreign Affairs, Subcommittee on Arms Control, International Security and Science, *Hearing: War Powers, Libya and State-Controlled Terrorism,* 99th Cong., 2d sess., 29 April 1986, p. 9.
38. WP, 21 February 1983, 20 February 1987.
39. WCPD, 7 January 1986, pp. 19–22.
40. Ibid., p. 31. NYT, 9 January 1986.
41. WCPD, 24 March 1986, pp. 412–23. NYT, 25 March 1986.
42. Reagan's address to the nation: WCPD, 14 April 1986, pp. 491–93; NYT, 15 April 1986.
43. Seymour Hersh, "Target Qaddafi," *New York Times Magazine,* 22 February 1987, p. 17.
44. *Gallup Poll,* 1986, pp. 84–87.
45. "Gaddafi and Terrorism," *World Press Review,* June 1986, pp. 21–26. *Gallup Poll,* 1986, pp. 85–86.
46. See *Hearings,* note 37, pp. 8–9.
47. Ibid., pp. 10, 36–37.
48. WCPD, 21 December 1988, p. 1647.
49. NYT, 7 January 1989.
50. NYT, 5 January 1989, reported the initial Pentagon briefing. Excerpts from tapes which recorded the pilots' conversations in the American F-14 fighter planes were published 6 January.
51. NYT, 12 January 1989.

52. Speakes, *Speaking Out,* p. 166.
53. S.J. Res. 100 was approved 20 December 1981 as Public Law 97-132, 95 Stat. 1693.
54. Benis M. Frank, *U.S. Marines in Lebanon 1982–1984,* p. 10.
55. Ibid., pp. 59–60.
56. Ibid., p. 64.
57. NYT, 29 December 1983, published excerpts of the "Report of the D.O.D. Commission on Beirut International Airport Terrorist Act, Oct. 23, 1983."
58. PPP, 7 February 1984, pp. 185–86.
59. Ibid., 4 April 1984, pp. 463–64; 1 June 1984, p. 785.
60. George W. Will, "The Beirut Bombing: Someone Should Resign," WP, 26 September 1984.
61. WCPD, 26 September 1984, pp. 1373–74.
62. NYT, 28 September, 20 October 1984. WP, 29 September, 18, 19 October 1984.
63. PPP, 17 October 1981, p. 949.
64. NYT, 15–17, 27 November 1988. WCPD, 14 November, p. 1492; 27 November, p. 1570; 8 December 1988, p. 1608.
65. NYT, 14–16 December 1988. WCPD, 14 December 1988, pp. 1625–26.
66. NYT, 9 April 1982. PPP, 10 March 1983, p. 373.
67. Paul Seabury and Walter A. McDougall, eds., *The Grenada Papers,* pp. 23–53, 282.
68. NYT, 8 November 1983.
69. Lincoln letter to William Herndon, 15 February 1848, Roy P. Basler, ed. *The Collected Works of Abraham Lincoln,* vol. 1, p. 451.
70. PPP, 25 October 1983, p. 1505.
71. Michael Massing, "Grenada Before and After," *Atlantic Monthly,* February 1984, p. 80.
72. PPP, 25 October 1983, pp. 1506, 1520–21.
73. MacNeil-Lehrer News Hour, 25 October 1983, Transcript no. 2107, pp. 9–10.
74. NYT, 6 November 1983.
75. WP, 3 March 1984.
76. *Gallup Poll,* 1983, p. 262. PPP, 25 October 1983, p. 1506.
77. "The Presidency, the Press & the People," a co-production of KPBS-TV and the University of California, San Diego, televised nationally over the Public Broadcasting Network 2 April 1990, transcript p. 22. PPP 3 November 1983, p. 1534. NYT, 15 Nov. 1983.
78. NYT, 1, 9 November 1983. WP, 29 June 1985.
79. Public Law 98-181, Stat. 1153, Sec. 2004.
80. NYT, 30 March 1984.
81. H.R. Committee on Foreign Affairs, Subcommittee on Arms Control, International Security and Science, *The War Powers Resolution: Relevant Documents, Correspondence, Reports,* 100th Cong., 2d sess., May 1988, pp. 85–87.
82. Ibid., p. 97.
83. Robert D. Clark et al., *The War Powers Resolution,* p. 5.

84. Department of State release, 26 October 1983. NYT, 26, 27 October 1983.
85. *Yearbook of the United Nations,* 1983, p. 211.
86. "The World Looks at Grenada," *World Press Review,* December 1983, pp. 17, 42–44. WP, 27 October 1983. NYT, 29 October, 3 November 1983.
87. PPP, 3 November 1983, p. 1534.
88. *Columbia Journalism Review,* July/August 1984, pp. 9–10.
89. Letter to the editor, NYT, 30 June 1988.
90. *Newsweek,* 27 July 1987, p. 37.
91. David Atlee Phillips, *The Night Watch,* p. 53.

Chapter 12—Commander in Chief, but Not in Charge

1. WCPD, 23 December 1986, p. 1668.
2. Regan, *For the Record,* p. 24.
3. A. J. Bacevich et al., *American Military Policy In Small Wars: The Case of El Salvador,* p. v. Original emphasis.
4. Ibid., p. 48.
5. Ibid., p. 50.
6. Public Law 93-148, 87 Stat 555.
7. CR (daily), 15 June 1987, p. H4584.
8. The standard lapse of 20 years before publication of official documents in *Foreign Relations of the United States* (FRUS) gradually lengthened after World War II. Most of the volumes issued during the Reagan administration were released 30 years after the fact. For a discussion of the quality of these reports, see Wilbur Edel, "Diplomatic History State Department Style," *Political Science Quarterly,* Winter 1991.
9. NYT, 3 December 1981. WP, 10 December 1981.
10. Joy Hackel and Daniel Siegel, *In Contempt of Congress: The Reagan Record on Central America,* 2nd ed., p. 16.
11. "The Secret War for Nicaragua," *Newsweek,* 8 November 1982, p. 42. Martha Honey, "Contra Coverage—Paid for by the CIA," *Columbia Journalism Review,* March/April 1987, p. 31. NYT, 4 December 1982. Michael Massing, "Nicaragua's Free-Fire Journalism," *Columbia Journalism Review,* July/August 1988, pp. 29–35.
12. Robert Parry and Peter Kornbluh, "Iran-Contra's Untold Story," *Foreign Policy,* Fall 1988, pp. 3–30.
13. Thomas W. Walker, ed., *Nicaragua: The First Five Years,* p. 108.
14. PPP, 18 February 1982, p. 182.
15. Ibid., p. 214.
16. CR (daily), 15 June 1987, p. H4585.
17. Public Law 97-377, 96 Stat. 1865.
18. NYT, 2 February 1983.
19. CR (daily), 3 February 1988, p. 217. NYT, 11 August 1988.
20. NYT, 25 March, 29, 30 May, 11 June 1988. WP, 4 May, 10 June 1988.
21. NYT, 25 September 1988.

22. The text of the Inter-American Treaty of Reciprocal Assistance is printed in CR (daily), 15 June 1987, pp. H4864–65.

23. International Court of Justice, "Case Concerning Military and Paramilitary activities in and against Nicaragua (Nicaragua v. United States of America), Order of 10 May 1984," p. 5.

24. Findings of fact in connection with these incidents are detailed in International Court of Justice, "Military and Paramilitary Activities in and Against Nicaragua (Nicaragua v. United States of America): Merits," 17 June 1986, pp. 34–39, 54–57.

25. NYT, 16 April 1984. WP, 18 April 1984.

26. International Court of Justice, "Order of 10 May 1984," p. 21. H.R., Committee on Foreign Affairs, Subcommittee on Human Rights and International Organization, Hearing: U.S. Decision to Withdraw from the International Court of Justice, 99th Cong., 1st sess., 30 October 1985, pp. 10–11.

27. For details of the Iranian case, see International Court of Justice, Case Concerning United States Diplomatic and Consular Staff in Tehran (United States of America v. Iran), 1982.

28. See Hearing cited in note 26, pp. 12–17.

29. International Court of Justice, Nicaragua v. U.S.: Merits, pp. 137–41.

30. Ibid., pp. 36–39.

31. Ibid., pp. 55–57. See also Jaqueline Sharkey, "Back in Control," Common Cause Magazine, September/October 1986, pp. 26–40.

32. Nicaragua v. United States of America: Merits, pp. 62–63.

33. Ibid., pp. 137–41.

34. Department of State, Treaties in Force, 1 January 1976, p. 131.

35. Yonah Alexander and Allan Nanes, The United States and Iran: A Documentary History, pp. 116–17, 213–15.

36. Thomas Powers, The Man Who Kept the Secrets, p. 85.

37. Kermit Roosevelt, Counter Coup. H.R., Permanent Select Committee on Intelligence, Iran: Evaluation of U.S. Intelligence Performance Prior to November 1978. See also, Gary Sick, All Fall Down, chaps. 5, 6.

38. Hedrick Smith et al., Reagan the Man, p. 101.

39. Remarks to hostages on their return from Teheran, PPP, 27 January 1981, p. 42. Address to American Legion, PPP, 22 February 1983, p. 265.

40. Report of the President's Special Review Board, 26 February 1987, pp. B-1, B-2.

41. Ibid., p. B-2.

42. Ibid., pp. B-2 to B-9.

43. Ibid., pp. B-9, B-10.

44. Ibid., pp. B-6, B-7.

45. Ibid., p. III-6.

46. Ibid., p. III-7.

47. Ibid., p. III-9.

48. Ibid., p. III-10.

49. Review Board, pp. B-38–39.

50. Ibid., p. III-12.

51. Photocopies of the findings of December 5, 1985, January 6 and January 17, 1986, and Poindexter's accompanying memoranda appear in ICI, vol. 7, pp. 266–310.
52. *Review Board,* p. B-45.
53. Ibid., p. III-11.
54. Ibid., pp. III-5, B-3.
55. Ibid., pp. B-75, 76.
56. Ibid., p. B-78.
57. Ibid., pp. B-103, 121.
58. NYT and WP, 3 November 1986.
59. WCPD, 2, 6 November 1986, pp. 1517, 1534.
60. WP and NYT 4, 5, 6, 7 November 1986.
61. "Administration Statements on Iran," WP, 12 November 1986.
62. WCPD, 13 November 1986, pp. 1559–61.
63. Some of the dates reported in NYT and WP 13–15 November 1986 were inaccurate. Precise dates were given in the *Review Board* sequence of events, pp. B-27, B-139, B-162.
64. WP and NYT, 15, 16 November 1986.
65. WCPD, 19 November 1986, p. 1584.
66. Ibid., p. 1591.
67. Ibid., 25 November 1986, pp. 1604–5.
68. NYT, 30 November 1986. Additional hostages taken in 1987 raised to eight the number of Americans held at the close of the Reagan administration.
69. United States v. Poindexter, DC no. CR 88-0080 HHG, Deposition of Ronald W. Reagan, 16 February 1990, pp. 44, 156, 158, 211–21, courtesy of Balmar Printing and Graphics. For quotations from the president's announcements regarding the appointment of a Special Review Board and an independent counsel see WCPD, 1, 2 December 1986, pp. 1610–11, 1613–14.
70. *Review Board,* pp. G-5, G-6, G-7.
71. Ibid., pp. V-1 to V-7.
72. Ibid., p. IV-10.
73. H. Res. 12, 7 January 1987, was adopted by a roll-call vote of 416 to 2. S. Res. 23, 6 January, was passed 88 to 4. For the organization and conduct of the investigating committees, see the final *Report of the Congressional Committees Investigating the Iran-Contra Affair,* November 1987, pp. 783–90.
74. NYT, 18 June 1987.
75. Unclassified portions of the depositions taken in closed session were published in 27 volumes of Appendix B to the final report cited in note 73.
76. ICI, vol. 1, p. 103.
77. Ibid., vol. 2, p. 47.
78. Ibid., vol. 7, part II, p. 58.
79. Ibid., vol. 3, part I, pp. 9, 25, 29, 36, 47–48, 169; part II, pp. 207–209.
80. Ibid., vol. 3, parts I, II and III.
81. Ibid., part I, pp. 75, 164.
82. Ibid., part I, pp. 75–85.
83. Ibid., part II, p. 57.

84. Ibid., part I, p. 163; Part II, p. 207.
85. Ibid., part I, pp. 85, 160–61.
86. Ibid., vol. 8, pp. 161–63, 183.
87. WCPD, 19 March 1987, p. 277.
88. ICI, vol. 8, p. 119.
89. Ibid., pp. 89, 197.
90. Ibid., p. 116.
91. Ibid., pp. 17–20, 462–63.
92. Ibid., vol. 7, part II, pp. 99–100; vol. 8, pp. 219–23.
93. Ibid., vol. 7, part II, p. 122.
94. *Report of the Congressional Committees Investigating the Iran-Contra Affair,* p. xvi. To avoid the lengthy names of the two investigating committees, I have used the singular "Iran-Contra Committee," or the "joint committee."
95. Ibid., p. 12.
96. Ibid., p. 437.
97. Ibid., pp. 437–53, introduction to the minority report.
98. Ibid., p. 22.

Chapter 13—The Great Communicator

1. Quoted by President Reagan from the Bible, John 8:32. WCPD, 17 August 1984, p. 1133.
2. RRTTA, pp. 5, 19, 160–61. Reagan's emphasis.
3. PPP, 28 May 1984, p. 749.
4. WTROM, p. 6.
5. PPP, 19 December 1983, pp. 1713–14.
6. Cannon, *Reagan,* p. 59.
7. WTROM, pp. 4, 7, 118.
8. Speakes, *Speaking Out,* p. 220.
9. RRTTA, pp. 163–64.
10. Barbara Gamarekian, "Connie Gerrard: For 25 Years the Guiding Hand Behind White House News Flow," NYT, 3 November 1988. WCPD, 8 June 1988, p. 766. Lou Cannon and Don Oberdorfer, "The Scripting of the Summit," WP, 9 June 1988. Dudley Clendinen, "Actor as President: Half-Hour Commercial Wraps Him in Advertising's Best," NYT, 14 September 1984.
11. WCPD, 12 October 1986, p. 1374; 11 December 1987, pp. 1491, 1507; 3 June 1988, p. 740.
12. Regan, *For the Record,* pp. 249–50.
13. Cannon, *Reagan,* p. 115.
14. Deaver, *Behind the Scenes,* p. 77.
15. Cannon, *Reagan,* pp. 130–31, 136–37.
16. James David Barber, "Candidate Reagan and the Sucker Generation," *Columbia Journalism Review,* November/December 1987, pp. 33–36.
17. News conference, PPP, 14 June 1984, pp. 858–59. WP, National Weekly Edition, 2 July 1984.

18. PPP, 14 December 1982, pp. 1603–4.
19. Ibid., 13 May 1982, p. 623.
20. Philip Geyelin, "What He Doesn't Know," WP, 17 August 1984. WCPD, 22 October 1984, p. 1611: Reagan's emphasis.
21. PPP, 15 June 1982, p. 782. WTROM, p. 297. Parade Magazine, 3 October 1982, p. 2.
22. WCPD, 12 October 1986, p. 1374.
23. NYT, 25 March 1982.
24. PPP, 20 January 1983, p. 76. WP, 22 January 1983. Vladimir Ilyich Ulyanov began writing his propaganda tracts under the pseudonym "N. Lenin," later using his true initials as "V. I. Lenin." He never used the name Nikolai.
25. WP, National Weekly Edition, 19 March 1984, p. 23.
26. Among the many articles written about President Reagan's speech writers are: Francis X. Clines, "The Voices That Blend Into Reagan's Speeches," NYT, 8 October 1982 and "Meanwhile Back At the Ranch," NYT, 12 November 1984; Ellen Goodman, "The Ghosts Now Walk By Day." WP, 11 February 1986; Howard Fineman, "The Wordsmith Behind the Speech," Newsweek, 22 August, 1988, p. 16. The origin of the "ash heap of history" was brought to public attention by a letter from Harrison E. Salisbury to the New York Times, 30 June 1985.
27. Ellen Goodman, "The Ghosts Now Walk By Day," WP, 11 February 1986, © 1986, The Boston Globe Newspaper Co./Washington Post Writers Group. Reprinted with permission.
28. RRTTA, pp. 52–55.
29. PPP, 17 October 1981, pp. 947–48, 955–56. George Lardner Jr., "CIA Doublespeak Cloaks Proposals for Homespy and Datahide," WP, 13 November 1981.
30. The Church Committee's "Summary of the Main Problems," detailed in the 6-volume Final Report of the Senate Select Committee to Study Governmental Operations, appears in Book II, p. 5.
31. Executive order 12333, PPP, 4 December 1981, p. 1132. The text of the National Security Act appears in H.R., Permanent Select Committee on Intelligence, Compilation of Intelligence Laws and Related Laws and Executive Orders of Interest to the National Intelligence Community, March 1987, pp. 3–23. For the quoted section, see p. 8.
32. PPP, 2 April 1982, pp. 411–20, contains the text of Executive Order 12356.
33. H.R., Committee on Government Operations, Security Classification Policy and Executive Order 12356, 97th Cong., 2d sess., 12 August 1982, pp. 20–21.
34. Federal Register, 11 May 1982, p. 20105.
35. See note 33, p. 14.
36. Loc. cit.
37. Executive Order 12356, sec. 6.1(f).
38. See note 33, pp. 28–30. This list of events first appeared in Edel, "Diplomatic History State Department Style," published in Political Science Quarterly, Winter 1991–92.
39. U.S. Senate, Committee on Governmental Affairs, National Security Decision

Directive 84, 98th Cong., 1st sess., 13 September 1983, pp. 85, 86.

40. Ibid., p. 22. William Safire, "His Own Petard," NYT, 24 November 1983. MacNeil-Lehrer Report, 29 April 1983. WP, 22 April 1983. H.R., Committee on Government Operations, *Hearing: Congress and the Administration's Secrecy Pledges,* 100th Cong., 2d sess., 10 August 1988, p. 93.
41. "The Secret Life of NSDD 84," *Columbia Journalism Review,* July/August 1984, p. 22.
42. Stephen Miller, "Maybe You're Not Entitled to Your Opinion," NYT, 20 May 1982.
43. CR (daily), 20 October 1983, p. S14285.
44. WP, 1 September 1983.
45. *Congress and the Administration's Secrecy Pledges,* (note 40), pp. 1, 5, 13–14.
46. WTROM, p. 261.
47. Ibid., p. 266.
48. Kenneth W. Thompson, ed., *Ten Presidents and the Press,* p. 69.
49. Ibid., pp. 23–24.
50. Ibid., p. 22. For a more detailed analysis, see Graham H. White, *FDR and the Press.*
51. Robert Lindsey, "Creating the Role," in Hedrick Smith, et al., *Reagan the Man,* pp. 21–22.
52. PPP, 18 February 1982, pp. 184–85. NYT, 19 February 1982.
53. WP, 23 August 1984. NYT, 3 October 1984.
54. PPP, 17 May 1981, p. 434.
55. F. Clifton White and William J. Gill, *Why Reagan Won: A Narrative History of the Conservative Movement, 1964–1981,* pp. 16–19, 38.
56. Richard Harwood, ed., *The Pursuit of the Presidency, 1980,* pp. 254–55.
57. WP, National Weekly Edition, 23 July 1984.
58. James Reston, "How to Fool the People," NYT, 5 October 1986.
59. NYT, 9 March 1988.
60. Bob Woodward, "Gadhafi Target of Secret U.S. Deception Plan," WP, 20 October 1986. WCPD, 2 October 1986, pp. 1322–23.
61. WP, 7 October 1986.
62. Lou Cannon, "They Don't Call Reagan the 'Teflon President' for Nothing," WP, National Weekly Edition, 30 April 1984.
63. NYT, 1 June 1988.
64. James Reston, "America Takes the Fifth," NYT, 8 March 1987.
65. Peggy Noonan, *What I Saw at the Revolution,* p. 268.
66. United States v. Poindexter, DC no. CR 88-0080 HHG, Deposition of Ronald W. Reagan, 16 February 1990, p. 29.
67. WCPD, 11 January 1989, p. 54.

Chapter 14—President

1. Farewell address, WCPD, 11 January 1989, pp. 53–54.
2. In 1980, Reagan topped the combined total of 41.2 million votes for Carter

and Anderson by 2.7 million. In 1984, with Anderson out of the running, Reagan's vote surpassed that of Mondale by 6.8 million.

3. See data cited in chapter 13.

4. NYT, 18 January 1989.

5. Seymour Martin Lipset and William Schneider, "The Confidence Gap During the Reagan Years, 1981–1987," *Political Science Quarterly,* Spring 1987, pp. 1–23.

6. James Reston, "How to Fool the People," NYT, 5 October 1986.

7. For details and documentation, see chapter 7.

8. WCPD, 11 September 1984, p. 1262.

9. Lou Cannon, "A Critical Shortcoming," WP, 24 August 1987, © 1987 Washington Post Writers Group. Reprinted with permission.

10. Cannon, *Reagan,* p. 135.

11. James Reston, "They'll Be Better Than Reagan," NYT, 1 August 1988, copyright 1983/88 by the New York Times Company. Reprinted by permission.

12. *Parade Magazine,* 29 September 1985, p. 28, quoted from Raymond Strait, *James Garner.*

13. Robert Lindsey, "California Rehearsal," in Hedrick Smith, et al., *Reagan the Man,* p. 48.

14. ATFC, p. 47.

15. Report of interview cited in Morton Mintz, *Quotations,* p. 54.

16. Reagan's proposed 10-year plan was outlined in his 1982 State of the Union message, PPP, 26 January 1982, pp. 75–77. For an analysis of this plan see George E. Peterson, "Federalism and the States," in John L. Palmer and Isabel V. Sawhill, eds., *The Reagan Record,* chap. 7.

17. For details, see chapters 2 and 8.

18. News conference, WCPD, 19 March 1987, p. 280.

19. WTROM, p. 141. Dugger, *On Reagan,* pp. 430–31.

20. Compare the president's 1983 address with that of 1988: PPP, 26 September 1983, pp. 1350–54 and WCPD, 26 September 1988, pp. 1205–1212.

21. Russell J. Leng, "Reagan and the Russians: Crisis Bargaining Beliefs and the Historical Record," *American Political Science Review,* vol. 78, pp. 338–55.

22. *World Press Review,* January 1987, pp. 11–15; February 1987, pp. 8–10.

23. Wilbur Edel, *Defenders of the Faith,* pp. 215–16.

24. CBS "60 Minutes," televised 15 January 1989, transcript pp. 4–5.

25. WP, 1 September 1981.

26. Warren G. Magnuson and Jean Carper, *The Dark Side of the Marketplace,* pp. v, ix.

27. Phillip T. Blumberg, "Corporate Morality and the Crisis of Confidence in American Business," *Beta Gamma Sigma,* January 1977.

28. PPP, 17 May 1981, p. 434. WCPD, 28 April 1987, p. 442.

29. WP, 19 July 1983.

30. For a picture of the takeover process, see U.S. General Accounting Office, *Hostile Corporate Takeovers: Synopses of Thirty-Two Attempts,* March 1988.

31. NYT, 20 June 1985. WP, 27 May 1988. H.R., Committee on the Judiciary,

Subcommittee on Monopolies and Commercial Law, *Oversight Hearing: Corporate Takeovers*, 97th Cong., 2d sess., 10 June 1982. See also *New York Times Index* under these headings: Stocks and bonds (items in bold type); Insiders, Stocks; Fraud and Swindling, Stocks.

32. "The Path of Sleaze Resistance," *Common Cause Magazine*, May/June 1988, p. 8.
33. WCPD, 11 January 1989, p. 54.
34. Lawrence Mishel and Jacqueline Simon, *The State of Working America*, p. iii.
35. U.S. Department of Labor, Bureau of Labor Statistics, *Employment and Earnings*, January 1989, pp. 13, 24, 59, 83.
36. H.R., Committee on Ways and Means, *Background Material and Data on Programs Within the Jurisdiction of the Committee on Ways and Means*, 1989 ed., 101st Cong., 1st sess., pp. 939–45.
37. Figures on the deficit and federal debt are from summary tables in annual issues of BUSG.
38. NYT, 22 April 1985, 11 December 1987.
39. PPP, 15 October 1982, pp. 1331–32.
40. For the text of H.R. 1278 and for House and Senate debate on this bill, see CR, 14, 15, 16 June and 4 August 1989, pp. H2553–2580, H2602–2704, S10180–10214.
41. NYT, 20 April 1989.
42. Day-by-day reports of North's trial appeared in all major newspapers from 19 February to 21 April 1989. Reports cited here are from NYT, 17 March 1988; 6, 7 January 1989; 1, 7, 14 April 1989.
43. President Reagan's comments on the homeless and unemployed were made in an interview with David Brinkley of "ABC News." His remarks were reported in NYT, 22 December 1988 but were edited out of the account published in WCPD, 21 December 1988, p. 1647.
44. News conference, WCPD, 24 February 1988, p. 258.
45. WCPD, 14 March 1987, p. 261.
46. NYT, 5 September 1988.
47. *Gallup Poll*, 1988, pp. 183, 114–15.

Epilogue

1. WTROM, p. 3. AAL, p. 21.
2. WTROM, p. 12. AAL, pp. 24–25.
3. "Unsupported" characterizes most of *An American Life*. Quotations from private correspondence and an otherwise inaccessible diary appear here and there, but the book contains none of the notes that are normally used to provide the reader with information as to the nature and location of material that will support assertions or interpretations in the text. Reagan's habit of confusing fact and fancy does not inspire confidence in the accuracy of his reporting, nor the reliability of his "absolute authority." For a closer look at his scholastic record, see Anne Edwards, *Early Reagan*, 88, 95, 107, 109.
4. AAL, p. 111. The report in the August 25, 1985 issue of the San Jose

(California) *Mercury News* was based on official FBI documents obtained under the Freedom of Information Act. The story was repeated in 1987 in Anne Edwards' book, *Early Reagan,* pp. 306–7, but was given no prominence in the media which was then preoccupied with the Iran-Contra hearings.

5. AAL, pp. 132–34.
6. AAL, p. 227. PPP, 20 January 1981, p. 16.
7. AAL, pp. 231–32. Stockman, *Triumph of Politics,* p. 10.
8. AAL, pp. 284–85. *Gallup Poll,* 1981, pp. 123–24, 202.
9. AAL, p. 339. U.S. Department of Labor, Bureau of Labor Statistics, *Employment and Earnings,* January 1989, p. 83.
10. AAL, pp. 362, 366. WCPD, 11 February 1986, pp. 209–10, 211–12; 18 February 1986, pp. 228–29.
11. AAL, pp. 281, 289.
12. AAL, pp. 512, 532, 543.
13. AAL, pp. 594–97.

Bibliography

U.S. Government Documents and Publications (Unless otherwise indicated, all federal documents are published in Washington by the Government Printing Office.)

"Arms Control after the Moscow Summit." *Congressional Research Service Review*, July/August 1988.

"Arms Control and Disarmament Agency." *Arms Control and Disarmament Agreements*, 1982 edition.

"The Budget Dilemma." *Congressional Research Service Review*, May 1988.

"Central American Peace Prospects." *Congressional Research Service Review*, April 1988.

Clark, Robert D., Andrew M. Egeland, Jr., and David B. Sanford. *The War Powers Resolution*. Washington: National Defense University Press, 1985.

Congress. *Congressional Globe*, as cited.

———. *Congressional Record*, as cited.

"Contra Aid and the Reagan Doctrine." *Congressional Research Service Review*, March 1987.

Department of Commerce, Bureau of the Census. *Historical Statistics of the United States*. 1975 edition. 2 vols.

———. *Measuring the Effect of Benefits and Taxes on Income and Poverty: 1986*. Consumer Income Series no. P-60, no. 164-RD-1.

Department of Defense. *Annual Report to Congress*, FY 1984, 1988.

———. Strategic Defense Initiative Organization. *Report to the Congress on the Strategic Defense Initiative*, April 1987.

Department of Justice, Office of Professional Responsibility. Memorandum from Counsel Michael E. Shaheen, Jr. to Attorney General Dick Thornburgh: Results of our review of the Independent Counsel's inquiry into certain activities of Attorney General Edwin Meese, III.

———. "Presidential Directive on Safeguarding National Security Information." 11 March 1983.

Department of Labor, Bureau of Labor Statistics. *Employment and Earnings*. Monthly reports, January 1981–January 1989.

Department of State. *A Plan for Fully Funding the Recommendations of the National Bipartisan Commission on Central America*. Special Report no. 162, March 1987.

———. *The Camp David Summit*. September 1978.

———. "CSCE, Vienna Follow-Up Meeting: A Framework for Europe's Future." Selected Documents no. 35, January 1989.

———. *Foreign Relations of the United States*. Annual volumes, as cited.

———. *Fundamentals of U.S. Foreign Policy*. 1988.

———. *The Nuclear Freeze*. 1982.

————. *Revolution Beyond Our Borders: Sandinista Intervention in Central America.* 1985.

————. *The Strategic Arms Limitation Talks.* Special Report 46 (revised), May 1979.

————. "U.S. Policy Regarding Limitations on Nuclear Testing." Special Report no. 150, August 1986.

————. *U.S. and Central America: Implementing the National Bipartisan Commission Report.* 1986.

Department of the Treasury, Internal Revenue Service. *Explanation of the Tax Reform Act of 1986 for Individuals.* Pub. no. 920, August 1987.

"The Farm Crisis and Prairie Populism." *Congressional Research Service Review,* May 1987.

"Farm Problems." *Congressional Research Service Review,* May 1987.

Federal Register, as cited.

Federal Reserve Bulletin, as cited.

Frank, Benis M. *U.S. Marines in Lebanon, 1982–1984.* Washington: U.S. Marine Corps, 1987.

General Accounting Office. *Air Force Can Improve Controls Over Contractor Access to DOD Supply System.* GAO/NSIAD-88-99, March 1988.

————. *Army Training: Need to Strengthen Internal Controls Over Troop Schools.* GAO/NSIAD-88-208, August 1988.

————. *Budget Deficit, The.* Transition Series. GAO/OCG-89-1TR, November 1988.

————. *Central America: U.S. National Guard Activities.* GAO/NSIAD-88-195, July 1988.

————. *Defense Issues.* GAO/OCG-89-9TR, November 1988.

————. *Ethics Enforcement: Filing and Review of the Attorney General's Financial Disclosure Report.* GAO/GGD-87-108, August 1987.

————. *Laws Cited Imposing Sanctions on Nations Supporting Terrorism.* GAO/NSIAD-87-133FS, April 1987.

————. *More Controls Needed Over Army's Obligation of Funds.* GAO/AFMD-87-18, May 1987.

————. *Navy Inventory Management: Inventory Accuracy Problems.* GAO/NSIAD-88-69, March 1988.

————. *Quality Assurance: Concerns About Four Navy Missile Systems.* GAO-NSIAD-88-104, March 1988.

————. *Shuttle and Satellite Computer Systems Do Not Meet Performance Objectives.* GAO/MTEC-88-7, August 1988.

————. *Strategic Bombers: B-1B Parts Problems Continue to Impede Operations.* GAO/NSIAD-88-190, July 1988.

————. *Strategic Defense Initiative Program: Accuracy of Statements Concerning DOE's X-Ray Laser Research Program.* GAO/NSIAD-88-181BR, June 1988.

————. *Weapons Testing: Quality of DOD Operational Testing and Reporting.* GAO/PEMD-88-32BR, July 1988.

House of Representatives:

Committee on Agriculture, Subcommittee on Forests, Family Farms, and Energy. *Hearing: Status of the Family Farm and Prospects for the Future.* 100th Cong., 2d sess., 18 March 1988.

Committee on Agriculture and Select Committee on Hunger. *Joint Hearing: Hunger Emergency in America.* 100th Cong., 2d sess., 24 February 1988.

Committee on Armed Services. *Hearing: Strategic Defense Initiative (SDI) Program.* 99th Cong., 1st sess., 6 June 1985.

Committee on Armed Services, Acquisition Policy panel. *Hearing: Whistleblower Protection in the Military.* 100th Cong., 1st and 2d sess., 19 November 1987, 16 March 1988.

Committee on Armed Services, Military Installations and Facilities Subcommittee. *Over-*

sight Hearing into the Current Political, Economic, and Civil Unrest in the Philippines. 99th Cong., 1st sess., 5 December 1985.

Committee on Armed Services, Special Operations Panel. *Hearings: Special Operations Forces.* 100th Cong., 2d sess., February–March 1988.

Committee on the Budget, Task Force on Defense and International Affairs. *Hearing: National Security Policy/Budget Issues.* 100th Cong., 1st sess., 19 October 1987.

Committee on Energy and Commerce, Subcommittee on Oversight and Investigations. *Additional Documents Related to the Subcommittee Investigation of the Activities of Michael K. Deaver and Associates.* 100th Cong., 1st sess., July 1987.

Committee on Foreign Affairs. *Hearing: Narcotics Review in Central America.* 100th Cong., 2d sess., 10 March 1988.

———. *Hearing: Nicaraguan Government Involvement in Narcotics Trafficking.* 99th Cong., 2d sess., 11 March 1986.

———. *Hearing: Review of U.S. Foreign and National Security Policy.* 100th Cong., 2d sess., February–March 1988.

———. *Hearing: Update on the Central American Peace Process.* 100th Cong., 1st sess., 13 October 1987.

———. *Hearing and Markup: Investigation of United States Assistance to the Nicaraguan Contras.* vols. 1, 2. 99th Cong., 2d sess., March–June 1986.

———. *Markup: Concerning U.S. Military and Paramilitary Operations in Nicaragua.* 98th Cong., 1st sess., May–June 1983.

———. *Report: Authorizing appropriations for fiscal years 1984 and 1985 for the Department of State* [etc]. 99th Cong., 1st sess., 16 May 1983.

———. *Report: Calling for a mutual and verifiable freeze on and reductions in nuclear weapons and for approval of the SALT II agreement.* 97th Cong., 2d sess., 19 July 1982.

———. *Report: Providing that the President shall continue to adhere to the numerical sublimits of the SALT agreements as long as the Soviet Union does.* 99th Cong., 2d sess., 17 June 1986.

———, Subcommittee on Africa. *Hearing: Possible Violation or Circumvention of the Clark Amendment.* 100th Cong., 1st sess., 1 July 1987.

———, Subcommittee on Arms Control, International Security and Science. *Hearing: ABM Treaty Interpretation Dispute.* 99th Cong., 1st sess., 22 October 1985.

———. *Hearing: Biological Warfare Testing.* 100th Cong., 2d sess., 3 May 1988.

———. *Hearing: The President's Certification on Anti-Satellite (ASAT) Weapons Testing.* 99th Cong., 1st sess., 11 Sept. 1985.

———. *Hearings: War Powers, Libya, and State-Sponsored Terrorism.* 99th Cong., 2d sess., April–May 1986.

———. *Hearings: War Powers: Origins, Purposes, and Applications.* 100th Cong., 2d sess., August–September 1988.

———. *The War Powers Resolution: Relevant Documents, Correspondence, Reports.* 100th Cong., 2d sess., May 1988.

———, Subcommittee on Asian and Pacific Affairs. *Hearing and Markup: The Philippine Election and the Implications for U.S. Policy.* 99th Cong., 2d sess., February 1986.

———, Subcommittee on Europe and the Middle East. *Hearing: Developments in Lebanon and the Middle East, January 1984.* 98th Cong., 2d sess., 26 January 1984.

———. *Documents and Statements on Middle East Peace, 1979–82.* 97th Cong., 2d sess., June 1982.

———. *Hearings: Islamic Fundamentalism and Islamic Radicalism.* 99th Cong., 1st sess., June, September 1985.

———, Subcommittee on Human Rights and International Organizations. *Hearings: Recent Developments in U.S. Human Rights Policy.* 100th Cong., 2d sess., February 1988.

———. *Hearing: Status of U.S. Participation in the United Nations System, 1988*. 100th Cong., 2d sess., 23 September 1988.

———. *Hearing: U.S. Decision to Withdraw from the International Court of Justice*. 99th Cong., 1st sess., 30 October 1985.

———, Subcommittees on International Economic Policy and Trade, and on Western Hemisphere Affairs. *Hearing: Review of the United States Economic Embargo Against Nicaragua and Humanitarian Exports*. 100th Cong., 1st sess., 15 December 1987.

———, Subcommittee on International Operations. *Hearings: Oversight of the National Endowment for Democracy*. 99th Cong., 2d sess., May–June 1986.

———, Subcommittee on Western Hemisphere Affairs. *Hearing: Central America: The Ends and Means of U.S. Policy*. 98th Cong., 2d sess., 2 May 1984.

———. *Hearings: The Status of Democratic Transitions in Central America*. 100th Cong., 2d sess., June 1988.

———. *Hearing: U.S. Policy in Honduras and Nicaragua*. 98th Cong., 1st sess., 15 March 1983.

———. *Hearing: United States Policy Toward Guatemala*. 98th Cong., 1st sess., 9 March 1983.

———. *Hearing: United States Volunteers in Nicaragua and the Death of Benjamin Linder*. 100th Cong., 1st sess. 13 May 1987.

Committee on Government Operations. *Hearing: Civil Rights Enforcement by the Department of Education*. 100th Cong., 1st sess., 23 April 1987.

———. *Hearing: Limits on the Dissemination of Information by the Department of Education*. 98th Cong., 1st sess., 13 Nov. 1985.

———. *Hearing: Management of the Strategic Defense Initiative*. 100th Cong., 2d sess., 29 March 1988.

———. *Twenty-Ninth Report: Security Classification Policy and Executive Order 12356*. 97th Cong., 2d sess., 12 August 1982.

Committee on the Judiciary, Subcommittee on Administrative Law and Governmental Regulations. *Hearings: Post-Employment Conflicts of Interest*. 99th Cong., 2d sess., May, July 1986.

———, Subcommittee on Civil and Constitutional Rights. *Hearing: Civil Rights Implications of Federal Voting Fraud Prosecutions*. 99th Cong., 1st sess., 26 September 1985.

———. *Oversight Hearings: Executive Order on Intelligence Activities*. 97th Cong., 2d sess., October 1981–January 1982.

———. *Oversight Hearings: FBI Undercover Activities*. 98th Cong., 1st sess., February–November 1983.

———. *Report: Voting Rights Act: Proposed Section 5 Regulations*. 99th Cong., 2d sess., July 1986.

Committee on Merchant Marine and Fisheries. *Hearings: Kuwaiti Tankers*. 100th Cong. 1st sess., 18 June, 6 August 1987.

Committee on Post Office and Civil Service. *Hearings: Whistleblower Protection Act of 1986*. 99th Cong., 2d sess., February 1986.

Committee on Rules. *Item Veto: State Experience and Its Application to the Federal Situation*. 99th Cong., 2d sess., December 1986.

Committee on Ways and Means. *East Asia: Challenges for U.S. Economic and Security Interests in the 1990's*. 100th Cong., 2d sess., 26 September 1988.

Permanent Select Committee on Intelligence. *Compilation of Intelligence Laws and Related Laws and Executive Orders of Interest to the National Intelligence Community*. 98th Cong., 1st sess., April 1983.

Select Committee on Children, Youth, and Families. *Hearing: Children and Families in Poverty: The Struggle to Survive*. 100th Cong., 2d sess., 25 February 1988.

Select Committee on Hunger. *Hunger Among the Homeless: A Survey of 140 Shelters, Food Stamp Participation and Recommendations.* 100th Cong., 1st sess., March 1987.

House-Senate Committee of Conference. *Report, Authorizing appropriations for fiscal years 1984 and 1985 for the Department of State* [etc.]. 98th Cong.; 1st sess., 17 November 1983.

House-Senate Committees on the Iran-Contra Investigation: House Select Committee to Investigate Covert Arms Transactions with Iran; Senate Select Committee on Secret Military Assistance to Iran and the Nicaraguan Opposition. *Joint Hearings:* vol. 1. *Testimony of Richard V. Secord;* vol. 2. *Testimony of Robert C. McFarlane, Gaston J. Sigur Jr. and Robert W. Owen;* vol. 3. *Testimony of Adolfo P. Calero, John K. Singlaub, Ellen C. Garwood, William B. O'Boyle, Joseph Coors, Robert C. Dutton, Felix Rodriguez, and Lewis Am Tambs;* vol. 4. *Testimony of Tomas Castillo;* vol. 5. *Testimony of Elliott Abrams, Albert Hakim, David M. Lewis, Bretton G. Sciaroni, and Fawn Hall;* vol. 6. *Testimony of Glenn A. Robinette, Noel C. Koch, Henry H. Gaffney, Jr., Stanley Sporkin, Charles J. Cooper, and W. Neil Eggleston;* vol. 7. *Testimony of Oliver C. North and Robert C. McFarlane;* vol. 8. *Testimony of John M. Poindexter;* vol. 9. *Testimony of George P. Shultz and Edwin Meese, III;* vol. 10. *Testimony of Donald T. Regan and Caspar Weinberger;* vol. 11. *Testimony of Dewey R. Clarridge, C/CATF {Chief, CIA Central American Task Force}, and Clair George.* 100th Cong., 1st sess., 1987.

———. *Report of the Congressional Committees Investigating the Iran-Contra Affair.* November 1987.

———. Appendix B to *Final Report: Depositions.* 27 vols. March 1988.

Joint Economic Committee. *Hearings: The U.S. International Imbalances.* 100th Cong., 1st sess., 1987.

Joint House-Senate Committee on Foreign Affairs and Committee on Foreign Relations. *Legislation on Foreign Relations through 1983.* March 1984.

Library of Congress. *Letters of Delegates to Congress 1774–1789.* Edited by Paul H. Smith. Vols. 1–15. August 1774–August 1780.

———. "U.S.-Holy See Diplomatic Relations?" *Congressional Research Service Review,* April 1984, pp. 14–16.

———, Congressional Research Service. "Diplomatic Relations Between the United States and the Holy See: a Pro-Con Analysis," by Charles H. Whittier. Mimeo. 8 November 1983.

———. "Religion and Public Policy: Background and the Issues in the 80's," by Charles H. Whittier. Mimeo. 17 October 1984.

McDonald, John W. Jr, and Diane B. Bendahmane, eds. *Conflict Resolution: Track Two Diplomacy.* Washington: Foreign Service Institute, 1987.

National Commission on Excellence in Education. *A Nation At Risk: The Imperative for Educational Reform.* Report to the president, 1983.

Office of the Federal Register. *Codification of Presidential Proclamations and Executive Orders, 20 January 1961–20 January 1985.*

———. *Public Papers of the Presidents of the United States: Ronald Reagan.* 6 vols, 1981–1984.

———. *United States Government Manual.* Annual editions from 1980–81 to 1988–89.

———. *Weekly Compilation of Presidential Documents.* 1 July 1984–20 January 1989.

Office of Technology Assessment. *Technology and Structural Unemployment: Reemploying Displaced Adults.* 1986.

Office of the President. *Budget of the U.S. Government.* Annual reports from fiscal year 1980 to 1990.

———. *Economic Report of the President.* Annual reports from 1982 to 1988.

————. "National Security Strategy of the United States." Reports to Congress, January 1987, January 1988.

Poore, Ben Perley, comp. *The Federal and State Constitutions, Colonial Charters, and other Organic Laws of the United States*. 2d edition, 1878.

Report of Independent Counsel In Re Edwin Meese, III. 2 vols. 1988.

Reule, Fred J., et al. *Dynamic Stability: A New Concept for Defense*. Maxwell Air Force Base, Ala.: Air University Press, 1987.

Senate:

Committee on Foreign Relations. *Hearing: Angola: Options for American Foreign Policy*. 99th Cong., 2d sess., 18 February 1986.

————. *Hearings: Authorization for U.S. Marines in Lebanon*. 98th Cong., 1st sess., November 1983.

————. *Hearings: Caribbean Basin Initiative*. 97th Cong., 2d sess., March 1982.

————. *Hearing: Central American Policy*. 98th Cong., 1st sess., 4 August 1983.

————. *Hearings: Nuclear Testing Issues*. 99th Cong., 2d sess., May-June 1986.

————. *Hearings: The INF Treaty*. 5 vols. 100th Cong., 2d sess., 1988.

————. *Hearing: Nomination of William A. Wilson*. 98th Cong., 2d sess., 2 February 1984.

————. *Hearing: The Philippine Presidential Election*. 99th Cong., 2d sess., 23 January 1986.

————. *Insurgency and Counterinsurgency in the Philippines*. 99th Cong., 1st session, November 1985.

————. *Meeting of the International Commission for Central American Recovery and Development*. 100th Cong., 2d sess., September 1988.

————. *Nuclear Arms Reductions*. 97th Cong., 2d sess., 12 July 1982.

————. *The U.S. Government and the Vietnam War: Executive and Legislative Roles and Relationships*. Part I, 1945–1961; Part II, 1961–1964. 98th Cong., 2d sess., April, December 1984.

————. *Visit to the Philippines August 2–15, 1985*. 99th Cong., 2d sess., April 1986.

————. *The War Power after 200 Years: Congress and the President at a Constitutional Impasse*. 100th Cong., 2d sess., July–September 1988.

————, Permanent Subcommittee on Investigations. *Hearing: Drugs and Money Laundering in Panama*. 100th Cong., 2d sess., 28 January 1988.

Committee on Governmental Affairs. *Hearing: Cost and Management of Nuclear Safety and Cleanup and Compliance at Department of Energy Defense Sites*. 100th Cong., 2d sess., 13 July 1988.

————, Subcommittee on Federal Spending, Budget, and Accounting. *Hearing: Oversight of the Government in the Sunshine Act*. 100th Cong., 2d sess., 19 April 1988.

————, Permanent Subcommittee on Investigations. *Hearings: Federal Government's Handling of Soviet and Communist Bloc Defectors*. 100th Cong., 1st sess., October 1987.

————, Subcommittee on Oversight of Government Management. *Hearing: Office of Government Ethics' Review of the Attorney General's Financial Disclosure*. 100th Cong., 1st sess., 9 July 1987.

Committee on the Judiciary. *Hearings: Confirmation Hearings on Federal Appointments. Part 2*. 99th Cong., 1st sess., 1985.

————. *Hearings: Confirmation Hearings on Federal Appointments*. 99th Cong., 2d sess., 1986.

————. *Report: Nomination of Daniel A. Manion*. 99th Cong., 2d sess., 1986.

————. *Hearings: Nomination of Edwin Meese, III*. 98th Cong., 2d sess., 1984.

————. *Hearings: Nomination of Jefferson B. Sessions, III to be U.S. District Judge for the Southern District of Alabama*. 99th Cong., 2d sess., 1986.

———. *Hearings: Nomination of Judge Antonin Scalia.* 99th Cong., 2d sess., 1986.

———. *Hearings: Nomination of Justice William Hubbs Rehnquist.* 99th Cong., 2d sess., 1986.

———. *Hearings: Nomination of William Bradford Reynolds to be Associate Attorney General of the United States.* 99th Cong., 1st sess., 1985.

Committee on Labor and Human Resources. *Hearings: Civil Rights Restoration Act of 1987.* 100th Cong., 1st sess., March 1987.

———. *Hearings: Poverty in the 1980's.* 100th Cong., 1st sess., 7 October 1987.

———. *Hearing: Strategies to Reduce Hunger in America.* 99th Cong., 2d sess., 21 May 1986.

Select Committee on Intelligence. *Hearings: Oversight Legislation.* 100th Cong., 2d sess., November, December 1987.

Supreme Court of the United States. *United States Reports,* as cited. (See also the individual court cases listed following.)

Tower, John, Edmund Muskie, and Brent Scowcroft. *Report of the President's Special Review Board.* 26 February 1987.

"Treaty of Friendship, Commerce and Navigation Between the United States of America and the Republic of Nicaragua." *U.S. Treaties and Other International Agreements.* Vol. 9, 1957.

United States Code, as cited.

United States Observer Delegation. *Report to the President of the United States of America on the February 7, 1986 Presidential Election in the Philippines.* Senate print no. 99-166, June 1986.

"War Powers and the Persian Gulf." *Congressional Research Service Review,* November/December 1987.

"Welfare and Poverty Among Children." *Congressional Research Service Review,* July 1987.

Court Cases (cited in text and notes)

Aguilar v. Felton, 473 U.S. 402 (1985).

Akron v. Akron Center for Reproductive Health, 462 U.S. 416 (1983).

Baker v. Carr, 369 U.S. 186 (1962).

Bob Jones University v. United States, 461 U.S. 574 (1983).

Bowen v. American Hospital Association, No. 84-1529, 9 June 1986.

Cannon v. Green, 398 U.S. 956 (1970).

Cantwell v. Connecticut, 310 U.S. 296 (1940).

Coit v. Green, 404 U.S. 997 (1971).

Donahoe v. Richards, 38 Me. 376 (1854).

Everson v. Board of Education, 330 U.S. 1 (1947).

Ferrite v. Tyler, 48 Vt. 444 (1876).

Gitlow v. New York, 268 U.S. 652 (1925).

Green v. Connally, 330 F. Supp. 1155 (D.C. 1971).

Grove City College v. Bell, No. 82-792, 28 February 1984.

Hamilton v. Regents, 293 U.S. 245 (1934).

Hibben v. Smith, 191 U.S. 310 (1903).

Johnson v. Transportation Agency, Santa Clara County, No. 85-1129, 25 March 1987.

Mahan v. Howell, 410 U.S. 315 (1973).

Minersville School District v. Gobitis, 310 U.S. 586 (1940).

Mobile v. Bolden, 446 U.S. 55 (1980).

Permoli v. New Orleans, 3 Howard 589 (1845).

Reynolds v. Sims, 377 U.S. 533 (1964).

Roe v. Wade, 410 U.S. 113 (1973).

Spiller v. Woburn, 12 Allen 127 (1866).

Thornburg v. Gingles, No. 83-1968 (1986).

Thornton v. Caldor, 472 U.S. 703 (1985).

United States v. University Hospital, 729 F. 2d (CA2, 1984).

Wallace v. Jaffree, 472 U.S. 38 (1985).

Wesberry v. Sanders, 376 U.S. 1 (1964).

West Virginia State Board of Education v. Barnette, 319 U.S. 624 (1943).

White v. Register, 412 U.S. 755 (1973).

General

Abraham, Henry J. *Justices and Presidents: A Political History of Appointments to the Supreme Court.* New York: Oxford University Press, 1985.

Adler, David Gray. "The Constitution and Presidential Warmaking: The Enduring Debate." *Political Science Quarterly,* Spring 1988, pp. 1–36.

Alexander, Yonah, and Nanes, Allan, eds. *The United States and Iran: A Documentary History.* Frederick, Md.: Aletheia Books, 1980.

"Alexander Haig." *Time,* 2, 9 April 1984.

Ambrose, Stephen E. *Eisenhower.* 2 vols. New York: Simon and Schuster, 1984.

Americas Watch Committee. *Human Rights in Nicaragua 1985–1986.* New York: Americas Watch Committee, 1986.

Amnesty International. *Nicaragua: The Human Rights Record.* London: Amnesty International, 1986.

———. *Torture in the Eighties.* London: Amnesty International, 1984.

Amnesty International Report. London: Amnesty International, 1985, 1986, 1987, 1988.

Anderson, Jack. "Secretary Watt and His Promise." *Washington Post,* 4 May 1981.

Anderson, Martin. *Revolution.* New York: Harcourt Brace Jovanovich, 1988.

"Antitrust Enforcement at the Federal Trade Commission: The Reagan-Miller FTC, the Carter-Pertshuk FTC and the Last 20 Years." Congress Watch pamphlet, 20 January 1984.

Arbess, Daniel. "Star Wars and Outer Space Law." *Bulletin of the Atomic Scientists,* October 1985, pp. 19–22.

Aruri, Naseer; Moughrabi, Fouad; and Stork, Joe. *Reagan and the Middle East.* Belmont, Mass.: Association of Arab-American University Graduates, 1983.

Bacevish, A. J.; Hallums, James D.; White, Richard H.; and Young, Thomas F. *American Military Policy in Small Wars: The Case of El Salvador.* New York: Pergamon-Brasey, 1988.

Bagley, Bruce M.; Alvarez, Roberto; and Hagedorn, Katherine J., eds. *Contadora and the Central American Peace Process.* Boulder, Col.: Westview Press, 1985.

Bailey, Harry A., Jr., ed. *Classics of the American Presidency.* Oak Park, Ill.: Moore, 1980.

Bailey, Thomas A. *Presidential Greatness.* New York: Appleton-Century, 1966.

Baldwin, Deborah. "The Loneliness of the Government Whistle-blower." *Common Cause Magazine,* January/February 1985, pp. 32–34.

Bamford, James. "Carlucci and the N.S.C." *New York Times Magazine,* 18 January 1987, pp. 16–19+.

Barber, James David. "Candidate Reagan and the Sucker Generation." *Columbia Journalism Review,* November/December 1987, pp. 33–36.

———. *The Presidential Character.* 2nd edition. Englewood Cliffs, N.J.: Prentice-Hall, 1977.

Barraclough, Geoffrey. *The Christian World: A Social and Cultural History.* New York: Harry N. Abrams, 1981.

Barrett, Todd. "Business Ethics for Sale." *Newsweek,* 9 May 1988.

Bartlett, Bruce. *Reaganomics: Supply Side Economics in Action.* Westport, Conn.: Arlington House, 1981.

Beilenson, Laurence W. *The Treaty Trap.* Washington: Public Affairs Press, 1969.

Bell, Terrel H. *The Thirteenth Man: A Reagan Cabinet Memoir.* New York: Free Press, 1988.

Bettelheim, Bruno, and Zelan, Karen. *On Learning to Read.* New York: Knopf, 1982.

Bluestone, Barry, and Harrison, Bennett. "The Grim Truth About the Job 'Miracle'," *New York Times,* 1 February 1987.

Blum, Deborah. "Weird Science: Livermore's X-Ray Laser Flap." *Bulletin of the Atomic Scientists,* July/August 1988, pp. 7–13.

Blumberg, Phillip I. "Corporate Morality and the Crisis of Confidence in American Business." *Beta Gamma Sigma,* January 1977.

Boller, Paul F., Jr. *Presidential Campaigns.* New York: Oxford University Press, 1984.

Bollier, David. *Liberty and Justice for Some.* New York: Frederick Ungar, 1982.

Bonner, Raymond. "Our Man in Manila." *Common Cause Magazine,* July/August 1987, pp. 27–31.

———. *Waltzing With A Dictator: The Marcoses and the Making of American Policy.* New York: Times Books, 1987.

Booth, John A. "War and the Nicaraguan Revolution." *Current History,* December 1986, pp. 405–408.

Borden, Morton, ed. *America's Ten Greatest Presidents.* Chicago: Rand McNally, 1961.

Bosworth, Barry P. *Tax Incentives and Economic Growth.* Washington: Brookings Institution, 1984.

Braestrup, Petter, rapporteur. *Battle Lines: Report of the Twentieth Century Fund Task Force on the Military and the Media.* New York: Priority Press, 1985.

Boyarsky, Bill. *Ronald Reagan: His Life and Rise to the Presidency.* New York: Random House, 1981.

Brauer, Carl M. *Presidential Transitions: Eisenhower Through Reagan.* New York: Oxford University Press, 1986.

Breckinridge, Scott D. "A Presidential 'Finding' for the White House Iran Initiative." *Foreign Intelligence Literary Scene.* January/February 1988, pp. 1–2.

Brennan, William J., Jr. "The Quest to Develop a Jurisprudence of Civil Liberties in Times of Crisis." Jerusalem: Law School of Hebrew University, 22 December 1987.

Bridgland, Fred. *Jonas Savimbi: A Key to Africa.* New York: Paragon House, 1987.

Broad, William J. "Beyond the Bomb: Turmoil in the Labs." *New York Times Magazine,* 9 October 1988.

Bromley, David G., and Shupe, Anson. *New Christian Politics.* Macon, Ga.: Mercer University Press, 1964.

Brownstein, Ronald, and Easton, Nina. *Reagan's Ruling Class.* Washington: Presidential Accountability Group, 1982.

Buckley, William. "The Pope and the Poor Nations." *Washington Post,* 22 September 1984.

CBS. "60 Minutes," 15 January 1989, transcript.

Cameron, Nigel. *Hong Kong, the Cultured Pearl.* Hong Kong: Oxford University Press, 1978.

"Campaign to Stop Star Wars." *Common Cause Magazine,* January 1987.

Cannon, Lou. "A Critical Shortcoming." *Washington Post,* 24 August 1987.

———. "The GOP's Corporate Tradition." *Washington Post,* 14 March 1988.

———. *Reagan.* New York: G. P. Putnam's Sons, 1982.

———. "They Don't Call Reagan the 'Teflon President' for Nothing." *Washington Post,* National Weekly Edition, 30 April 1984.

Cannon, Lou, and Hoffman David. "The Inner Circle Decides and the Outer Circle Ratifies." *Washington Post,* 19 July 1982.

Cannon, Lou, and Lescaze, Lee. "Reagan's Decision-Making Process Still a Mystery." *Washington Post,* 22 March 1982.

Cannon, Lou, and Oberdorfer, Don. "The Scripting of the Summit." *Washington Post,* 9 June 1988.

Caraley, Demetrios. *The President's War Powers: From the Fededralists to Reagan.* New York: Academy of Political Science, 1984.

Carnegie Endowment for International Peace. *Documents Relating to Programs of the First Hague Peace Conference.* Oxford: Clarendon Press, 1921.

Center for Strategic and International Studies. *Making Defense Reform Work.* Washington: Johns Hopkins Foreign Policy Institute, 1988.

Chandler, Alfred D., Jr. *The Visible Hand: The Managerial Revolution in American Business.* Cambridge, Mass.: Belknap Press, 1977.

Charen, Mona. "What the White House Women Think of the White House Men." *Washingtonian,* September 1986, p. 139.

Churchill, Winston. *The Second World War.* 6 vols. Cambridge, Mass.: Houghton Mifflin, 1948–1953.

Clendinen, Dudley. "Actor as President: Half-Hour Commercial Wraps Him in Advertising's Best." *New York Times,* 14 September 1984.

Clines, Francis X. "The Voices That Blend Into Reagan's Speeches." *New York Times,* 8 October 1982.

Cockburn, Leslie. *Out of Control.* New York: Atlantic Monthly Press, 1987.

"Colby: Arms Control's Secret Weapon." *Common Cause Magazine,* July/August 1987, pp. 12–15.

Commission on Minority Participation. *One-Third of a Nation.* Washington: American Council on Education, 1988.

Committee for the Compilation of Materials on Damage Caused by the Atomic Bombs in Hiroshima and Nagasaki. *Hiroshima and Nagasaki: The Physical, Medical and Social Effects of the Atomic Bombings.* New York: Basic Books, 1981.

Conway, Flo, and Siegelman, Jim. *Holy Terror.* New York: Dell, 1984.

Cooley, John K. "The Libyan Menace." *Foreign Policy,* Spring 1981, pp. 74–93.

Cranston, Alan. "A Debacle Like the League of Nations?" *New York Times,* 21 December 1987.

Crittendon, Ann. "The Age of 'Me-First' Management." *New York Times,* 18 August 1984.

Dallek, Robert. *Ronald Reagan: The Politics of Symbolism.* Cambridge, Mass.: Harvard University Press, 1984.

Deaver, Michael K., with Herskowitz, Mickey. *Behind the Scenes.* New York: William Morrow, 1987.

Demac, Donna A. *Liberty Denied: The Current Rise of Censorship in America.* New York: PEN American Center, 1988.

Demause, Lloyd. *Reagan's America.* New York: Creative Roots, 1984.

Dewart, Janet, ed. *The State of Black America, 1988.* New York: National Urban League, 1988.

Dickey, Christopher. *With the Contras.* New York: Simon and Schuster, 1985.

Di Clerico, Robert E., and Uslaner, Eric M. *Few Are Chosen: Problems in Presidential Selection.* New York: McGraw-Hill, 1984.

Diggins, John P. *Mussolini and Fascism: The View from America.* Princeton, N.J.: Princeton University Press, 1972.

"Domestic Security Investigations and Individual Rights Under the Justice Department's New Guidelines." Committee report. Washington: American Bar Association, 14 January 1985.

"A Draconian Cure for Chile's Economic Ills." *Business Week,* 12 January 1976, pp. 70–73.

Dugger, Ronnie. *On Reagan: The Man and His Presidency.* New York: McGraw-Hill, 1983.

Durkin, Dolores. *Teaching Young Children To Read.* Boston: Allyn and Bacon, 1972.

Dye, Thomas. R. *Who's Running America?: The Reagan Years.* Englewood Cliffs, N.J.: Prentice-Hall, 1983.

Edel, Wilbur. *A Constitutional Convention: Threat or Challenge?* New York, Praeger, 1981.

————. *Defenders of the Faith: Religion and Politics from the Pilgrim Fathers to Ronald Reagan.* New York: Praeger, 1987.

————. *The State Department, the Public and the United Nations.* New York: Vantage Press, 1979.

Edwards, Anne. *Early Reagan.* New York: William Morrow, 1987.

Eisenhower, Dwight D. *Crusade in Europe.* Garden City, N.Y.: Permabooks, 1952.

————. *The Eisenhower Diaries.* Edited by Robert H. Ferrell. New York: W. W. Norton, 1981.

Emerson, Steven. *Secret Warriors: Inside the Covert Military Operations of the Reagan Era.* New York: G. P. Putnam's Sons, 1988.

Employment in America. Washington: Congressional Quarterly, 1983.

Erickson, Paul D. *Reagan Speaks: the Making of an American Myth.* New York: New York University Press, 1985.

Eusebius. *History of the Church from Christ to Constantine.* New York: Dorset Press, 1965.

Farrand, Max, ed. *The Records of the Federal Convention of 1787.* Revised edition. 4 vols. New Haven: Yale University Press, 1966.

Feistritzer, C. Emily. *The Condition of Teaching: A State by State Analysis.* Princeton, N.J.: Carnegie Foundation for the Advancement of Teaching, 1983.

Fineman, Howard. "The Wordsmith Behind the Speech." *Newsweek,* 22 August 1988, p. 16.

Fitzgerald, A. Ernest. *The Protagonists: An Insider's View of Waste, Mismanagement, and Fraud in Defense Spending.* Boston: Houghton Mifflin, 1989.

Foote, Joe S. "Reagan on Radio." Paper presented to International Communication Association, 25 May 1984.

Foxley, Alejandro. "The Neoconservative Economic Experiment in Chile." Chapter in J. Samuel Valenzuela, *Military Rule in Chile.* (See following.)

Friedman, Milton and Friedman, Rose. *Free to Choose.* New York: Aron, 1981.

Froomkin, Joseph, ed. *The Crisis in Higher Education.* New York: Academy of Political Science, 1983.

Frost, Elizabeth, ed. *The Bully Pulpit: Quotations from America's Presidents.* New York: Facts on File, 1988.

Futrell, Robert F. *The United States Air Force in Southeast Asia: The Advisory Years to 1961.* Washington: Office of Air Force History, 1981.

"Gaddafi and Terrorism." *World Press Review,* June 1986, pp. 21–26.

Gallup, George H. *The Gallup Poll.* 16 vols. New York: Random House, vols. 1–3, 1935–1971; Wilmington, Del.: Scholarly Resources, 1972–1988.

Gamarekian, Barbara. "Connie Gerrard: For 25 years the Guiding Hand Behind White House News Flow." *New York Times,* 3 November 1988.

Garcia, Jose Z. "El Salvador: A Glimmer of Hope." *Current History,* December 1986, pp. 409–12.

Garthoff, Raymond L. *Detente and Confrontation: American-Soviet Relations from Nixon to Reagan.* Washington: Brookings Institution, 1985.

Gaston, Raymond D. *Freedom in the World.* New York: Freedom House, 1988.

Gelb, Leslie H. "The Mind of the President." *New York Times Magazine,* 6 October 1985.

Geyelin, Philip. "What He Doesn't Know." *Washington Post,* 17 August 1984.

Gleijeses, Piero. "The Reagan Doctrine and Central America." *Current History,* December 1986, pp. 101–104.

Goldschmidt, Arthur, Jr. *A Concise History of the Middle East.* 2d ed., revised. Boulder, Col.: Westview Press, 1983.

Goodman, Ellen. "The Ghosts Now Walk by Day." *Washington Post,* 11 February 1986.

Grace, J. Peter. *War on Waste*. New York: Macmillan, 1984.

"Great War of Words." *Time*, 9 September 1985, pp. 32–33.

Green, Mark. "Reagan's Law." *New York Times*, 22 August 1983.

———. "To Error is Reagan." *Mother Jones*, 1987.

Green, Mark and McColl, Gail. *There He Goes Again: Ronald Reagan's Reign of Error*. New York: Pantheon, 1983.

Greenstein, Fred I., ed. *The Reagan Presidency: An Early Assessment*. Baltimore: Johns Hopkins University Press.

Greider, William. "The Education of David Stockman." *Atlantic Monthly*, December 1981, pp. 27–54.

Grossman, Michael Baruch, and Kumar, Martha Joynt. *Portraying the President: The White House and the News Media*. Baltimore: Johns Hopkins University Press, 1981.

Grunwald, Joseph and Flamm, Kenneth. *The Global Factory: Foreign Assembly in International Trade*. Washington: Brookings Institution, 1985.

Guide to the U.S. Supreme Court. Washington: Congressional Quarterly, 1979.

Hackel, Joy and Siegel, Daniel. *In Contempt of Congress: The Reagan Record on Central America*. Washington: Institute for Policy Studies, 1987.

Halliday, Fred. *The Making of the Second Cold War*. London: Verso, 1983.

Hanneford, Peter. *The Reagans: A Political Portrait*. New York: Coward-McCann, 1983.

Hanson, C. T. "Gunsmoke and sleeping dogs: the prez's press at midterm." *Columbia Journalism Review*, May/June 1983, pp. 27–34.

Hart, B. H. Liddell. *History of the Second World War*. New York: Paragon Books, 1979.

Harwood, Richard, ed. *The Pursuit of the Presidency, 1980*. New York: Berkley Books, 1980.

Hankin, Louis. "Foreign Affairs and the Constitution." *Foreign Affairs*, Winter 1987/88, p. 305.

Herken, Gregg. "The Earthly Origin of Star Wars." *Bulletin of the Atomic Scientists*, October 1987, p. 20.

Hersh, Seymour M. "Target Qaddafi." *New York Times Magazine*, 22 February 1987, p. 17.

Hess, Stephen. *The Government/Press Connection*. Washington: Brookings Institution, 1984.

Hofstadter, Richard, ed. *Great Issues in American History*. 2 vols. New York: Vintage Books, 1958.

Honey, Martha. "Contra Coverage—Paid for by the CIA." *Columbia Journalism Review*. March/April 1987, p. 31.

Howard, Michael. "A European Perspective on the Reagan Years." *Foreign Affairs*, vol. 66, no. 3, pp. 478–93.

Hoxie, R. Gordon, et al. *The Presidency and National Security Policy*. New York: Center for the Study of the Presidency, 1984.

Hull, Cordell. *The Memoirs of Cordell Hull*. 2 vols. New York: Macmillan, 1948.

Ickes, Harold L. *The Secret Diaries of Harold L. Ickes*. 2 vols. New York: Simon and Schuster, 1953–54.

International Court of Justice. *Case Concerning Military and Paramilitary Activities in and Against Nicaragua (Nicaragua v. United States of America): Merits*. The Hague, 27 June 1986.

———. Order of 12 May 1981.

———. Order of 10 May 1984.

———. *Case Concerning United States Diplomatic and Consular Staff in Tehran (United States of America v. Iran)*. The Hague, 1982.

"Interview with Gorbachev." *Time*, 9 September 1985, p. 22.

Jacoby, Tamar. "The Reagan Turnaround on Human Rights." *Foreign Affairs*, Summer 1986, pp. 1066–86.

Jefferson, Thomas. *Thomas Jefferson: Writings.* Edited by Merrill D. Peterson. New York: Library of America, 1984.

————. *The Papers of Thomas Jefferson.* Edited by Julian P. Boyd. 21 vols. Princeton, N.J.: Princeton University Press, 1950–83.

Joe, Tom, and Rogers, Cheryl. *By the Few, for the Few: The Reagan Welfare Legacy.* Lexington, Mass.: Lexington Books, 1985.

Johnson, Donald Bruce, comp. *National Party Platforms.* 2 vols. Revised edition. Urbana, Ill.: University of Illinois Press, 1978.

Jordan, Amos A., and Taylor, William J., Jr. *American National Security.* Revised edition. Baltimore: Johns Hopkins University Press, 1985.

Karp, Walter. "Liberty Under Siege." *Harper's,* November 1985, pp. 53–67.

King, Elliot, and Schudson, Michael. "The Myth of the Great Communicator." *Columbia Journalism Review,* November/December 1987, p. 37.

Kirkpatrick, Jeane J. "Dictatorships and Double Standards." *Commentary,* November 1979.

————. *Legitimacy and Force.* 2 vols. New Brunswick, N.J.: Transaction Books, 1988.

Kissinger, Henry A. "A New Era for NATO." *Newsweek,* 12 October 1987.

Klare, Michael T. and Arnson, Cynthia. *Supplying Repression: U.S. Support for Authoritarian Regimes Abroad.* Washington: Institute for Policy Studies, 1981.

Kosterlitz, Julie. "The Case Against Ed Meese." *Common Cause Magazine,* January/February 1985, pp. 12–19.

Krippner, Stanley. "The Boy Who Read at Eighteen Months." *Exceptional Children,* November 1963, pp. 105–109.

Kristol, Irving. "Post-Watergate Morality: Too Good for Our Good?" *New York Times Magazine,* 14 November 1976.

Kwitney, Jonathan. *Endless Enemies: The Making of an Unfriendly World.* New York: Penguin Books, 1986.

Lardner, George, Jr. "CIA Doublespeak Cloaks Proposals for Homespy and Datahide." *Washington Post,* 13 November 1981.

Lass, Bonnie. "Portrait of My Son as an Early Reader." *The Reading Teacher,* October 1982, pp. 20–28; February 1983, pp. 508–15.

Lawyers Committee for Human Rights. *Human Rights in Nicaragua: 1987.* New York: Lawyers Committee for Human Rights, 1987.

Lehmann-Haupt, Christopher. Book review of *Dangerous Currents* by Lester C. Thurlow. *New York Times,* 25 June 1983.

Leng, Russell J. "Reagan and the Russians: Crisis Bargaining Beliefs and The Historical Record." *American Political Science Review,* vol. 78, pp. 338–55.

LeoGrande, William M. "The Revolution in Nicaragua: Another Cuba?" *Foreign Affairs,* Fall 1979, pp. 28–50.

————. "Through the Looking Glass: The Kissinger Report on Central America." *World Policy Journal,* Winter 1984, pp. 251–84.

Levy, Leonard W. *Original Intent and the Framers' Constitution.* New York: Macmillan, 1988.

Lienesch, Michael. "Right-Wing Religion: Christian Conservatism as a Political Movement." *Political Science Quarterly,* Fall 1982, pp. 403–25.

Lincoln, Abraham. *The Collected Works of Abraham Lincoln.* Edited by Roy P. Basler. New Brunswick, N.J.: Rutgers University Press, 1953.

Linsky, Martin, ed. *Television and the Presidential Elections.* Lexington, Mass.: Lexington Books, 1983.

Lipset, Seymour Martin, and Raab, Earl. "The Election and the Evangelicals." *Commentary,* March 1981, pp. 25–31.

Lipset, Seymour Martin, and Schneider, William. "The Confidence Gap during the Reagan Years, 1981–1987." *Political Science Quarterly,* Spring 1987, pp. 1–24.

Lyman, Richard W. "Demythologizing Those Golden Academic Days of Yore." *New York Times,* 20 March 1985.

Maas, Peter. "Oliver North's Strange Recruits." *New York Times Magazine,* 18 January 1987, pp. 20–22.

MacNeil-Lehrer Reports, as cited.

Madison, James. *The Papers of James Madison.* Edited by William T. Hutchinson and William M. E. Rachal. 17 vols. Chicago: Chicago University Press, 1962–83.

Magnuson, Warren G., and Carper, Jean. *The Dark Side of the Marketplace.* Englewood Cliffs, N.J.: Prentice-Hall, 1968.

McGuigan, Patrick B. "Judge Robert Bork is a Friend of the Constitution." *Conservative Digest,* October 1985, pp. 91–102.

Main, Jackson Turner. *The Anti-Federalists: Critics of the Constitution.* New York: W. W. Norton, 1974.

"The Man They Call 'President Meese'." *U.S. News & World Report,* 2 March 1981, p. 7.

Marro, Anthony. "When the Government Tells Lies." *Columbia Journalism Review,* March/April 1985, pp. 29–41.

Massing, Michael. "Grenada Before and After." *Atlantic Monthly,* February 1984, p. 80.

———, "Nicaragua's Free-Fire Journalism." *Columbia Journalism Review,* July–August 1988, pp. 29–35.

"The Media and the Presidency." *Presidential Studies Quarterly,* Winter 1986.

"Mike Deaver's Rise and Fall." *Newsweek,* 23 March 1987, pp. 22–23.

Miller, James Nathan. "Ronald Reagan and the Techniques of Deception." *Atlantic Monthly,* February 1984, pp. 62–68.

Miller, Merle. *Lyndon.* New York: Putnams' Sons, 1980.

Miller, Stephen. "Maybe You're Not Entitled to Your Opinion." *New York Times,* 20 May 1982.

Millet, Richard. "Guatemala's Painful Progress." *Current History,* December 1986, pp. 413–16.

Mintz, Morton. *Quotations from President Ron.* New York: St. Martin's Press, 1986.

Moffitt, Michael. "Economic Decline, Reagan-Style: Dollars, Debt, and Deflation." *World Policy Journal,* vol. 2, p. 390.

Moore, Molly. "Travails of the Centerpiece Weapon." *Washington Post,* 10 August 1987.

"Morality Among the Supply-Siders." *Time,* 25 May 1987, pp. 18–20.

Moyers, Bill. *The Secret Government: The Constitution in Crisis.* Washington: Seven Locks Press, 1988.

National Security Archive. *The Chronology: The Documented Day-by-Day Account of the Secret Military Assistance to Iran and the Contras.* Edited by Malcolm Byrne. New York: Warner Books, 1987.

NATO Basic Documents. Brussels: NATO Information Service, n.d.

Ottoway, Marina. "Economic Reform and War in Mozambique." *Current History,* May 1988.

Overstreet, Sarah. "The Limits of Prayer." *Lewisburg Daily Journal,* 24 April 1987.

Paine, Thomas. *The Complete Writings of Thomas Paine.* Edited by Philip S. Foner. New York: Citadel Press, 1969.

Palmer, John L., ed. *Perspectives on the Reagan Years.* Washington: Urban Institute Press, 1986.

Palmer, John L., and Sawhill, Isabel V., eds. *The Reagan Experiment.* Washington: Urban Institute Press, 1982.

———. *The Reagan Record.* Cambridge, Mass.: Balinger, 1984.

Parrott, Bruce. "The Soviet Debate on Missile Defense." *Bulletin of the Atomic Scientists,* April 1987, pp. 9–12.

Parry, Robert, and Kornbluh, Peter. "Iran-Contra's Untold Story." *Foreign Policy,* Fall 1988, pp. 3–30.

Patel, Dinker, policy analyst, and Bullock, Joyce, ed. *Campaign Finance, Ethics & Lobby Law Blue Book 1988–1989*. Lexington, Ky.: Council of State Governments, 1988.

"The Path of Sleaze Resistance." *Common Cause Magazine*, May/June 1988, p. 8.

Pederson, William, and Laurin, Ann M., eds. *The Rating Game in American Politics*. New York: Irvington Publishers, 1987.

Pentagon Papers. 4 vols. Senator Gravel edition. Boston: Beacon Press, 1971.

Phillips, David Atlee. *The Night Watch*. New York: Atheneum, 1977.

Plagenz, George R. "A Minister's Lifestyle." *Lewisburg Daily Journal*, 27 March 1987.

Preston, Larry M. "Freedom, Markets, and Voluntary Exchange." *American Political Science Review*. December 1984, pp. 959–70.

Powers, Thomas. *The Man Who Kept the Secrets*. New York: Knopf, 1979.

Rasor, Dina. "Protecting Pentagon Whistleblowers." *New York Times*, 23 October 1984.

———. "Sidetracking Reform at the Pentagon." *Washington Post*, 1 July 1988.

Reagan, Nancy, with William Novak. *My Turn*. New York: Random House, 1989.

Reagan, Ronald. *A Time for Choosing: The Speeches of Ronald Reagan 1961–1982*. Chicago: Regnery Gateway, 1983.

———. *An American Life*. New York: Simon and Schuster, 1990.

———. *Ronald Reagan Talks to America*. Old Greenwich, Conn.: Adair, 1981.

Reagan, Ronald, with Richard G. Huber. *Where's the Rest of Me?* Reprint. New York: Korz, 1981.

Reagan Administration's Record on Human Rights in 1985. Washington: Lawyers Committee for Human Rights, 1986.

"Reagan's Big Three." *U.S. News & World Report*, 2 November 1981, p. 28.

Regan, Donald T. *For the Record: From Wall Street to Washington*. New York: Harcourt Brace Jovanovich, 1988.

Reichley, A. J. "Religion and the Future of American Politics." *Political Science Quarterly*, 1986, pp. 26–27.

———. *Religion in American Public Life*. Washington: Brookings Institution, 1984.

Relyea, Harold C. *The Presidency and Information Policy*. New York: Center for the Study of the Presidency, 1981.

Report Card on School Reform: The Teachers Speak. New York: Carnegie Foundation for the Advancement of Teaching, 1988.

Reston, James. "America Takes the Fifth." *New York Times*, 8 March 1987.

———. "How to Fool the People." *New York Times*, 5 October 1986.

———. "Reagan Backs His Hunch." *New York Times*, 8 October 1986.

———. "Stumbling to Geneva." *New York Times*, 25 September 1985.

———. "They'll Be Better Than Reagan." *New York Times*, 1 August 1988.

———. "Tips for Presidents." *New York Times*, 30 July 1987.

Roberts, Paul Craig. *The Supply-Side Revolution*. Cambridge, Mass.: Harvard University Press, 1984.

Roelofs, H. Mark. "Liberation Theology: The Recovery of Biblical Radicalism." *American Political Science Review*, June 1988, pp. 549–66.

Rodgers, William D. "Reagan Spurred Latin Democracy? Nonsense." *New York Times*, 5 August 1988.

Rohatyn, Felix G. "Ethics in America's Money Culture." *New York Times*, 3 June 1987.

Roosevelt, Franklin D. *The Public Papers and Addresses of Franklin D. Roosevelt*. 12 vols. Edited by Samuel I. Rosenman. New York: Random House, 1938–1942.

Roosevelt, Kermit. *Countercoup: The Struggle for Control of Iran*. New York: McGraw-Hill, 1979.

Rosenberg, Mark B. "Honduras: The Reluctant Democracy." *Current History*, December 1986, pp. 417–20.

Rousseas, Stephen. *The Political Economy of Reaganomics*. Armonk, N.Y.: M. E. Sharpe, 1982.

Safire, William. "His Own Petard." *New York Times,* 24 November 1983.

Sandoz, Ellis, and Crabb, Cecil V., Jr., eds. *A Tide of Discontent: The 1980 Elections and Their Meaning.* Washington: Cambridge University Press, 1981.

Scheer, Robert. *With Enough Shovels: Reagan, Bush and Nuclear War.* New York: Vintage Books, 1982.

Schell, Jonathan. *The Fate of the Earth.* New York: Knopf, 1982.

Schlesinger, Arthur M., Jr. *The Crisis of the Old Order.* Boston: Houghton Mifflin, 1957.

Seabury, Paul, and McDougall, Walter A. The Grenada Papers. San Francisco: ICS Press, 1984.

"The Secret Life of NSDD 84." *Columbia Journalism Review,* July/August 1984, p. 22.

"The Secret War for Nicaragua." *Newsweek,* 8 November 1982, p. 42.

Sheehan, Neil; Smith, Hedrick; Kenworthy, E. W.; and Butterfield, Fox. *The Pentagon Papers. New York Times* edition. New York: Bantam Books, 1971.

Shepherd, David R. *Ronald Reagan: In God I Trust.* Wheaton, Ill.: Tyndale House, 1984.

Shulman, Marshall D. "The Superpowers: Dance of the Dinosaurs." *Foreign Affairs,* vol. 66, no. 3, pp. 494–515.

Sick, Gary. *All Fall Down: America's Tragic Encounter With Iran.* New York: Penguin Books, 1986.

Silk, Leonard. "On the Supply Side." Chapter 4 in Hedrick Smith, et al. *Reagan the Man, the President.* (see following.)

Smith, Abbot. "Who Declares War?" Chapter 3 in Demetrios Caraley, ed., *The President's War Powers.* (see previous.)

Smith, Adam. *An Inquiry into the Nature and Causes of the Wealth of Nations.* (1776). Harvard Classics, vol. 20. New York: P. F. Collier & Son, 1910.

Smith, Hedrick, et. al. *Reagan the Man, the President.* New York: Macmillan, 1980.

Snepp, Frank. *Decent Interval.* New York: Vintage Books, 1978.

Social Security Bulletin, as cited.

Speakes, Larry, with Robert Pack. *Speaking Out: The Reagan Presidency from Inside the White House.* New York: Scribner's, 1988.

Spector, Ronald H. *United States Army in Vietnam: The Early Years, 1931–1960.* Washington: Center of Military History, U.S. Army, 1983.

"Star Wars: Myth and Reality." Pamphlet. Washington: Union of Concerned Scientists, January 1987.

Stimson, Henry L. *On Active Service in Peace and War.* New York: Harper, 1948.

Stockman, David. *The Triumph of Politics: The Inside Story of the Reagan Revolution.* New York: Avon, 1987.

Stockwell, John. *In Search of Enemies: A CIA Story.* New York: W. W. Norton, 1978.

Stubblebine, Wm. Craig, and Willett, Thomas D., eds. *Reaganomics: A Midterm Report.* San Francisco: ICS Press, 1983.

Talbott, Strobe. *Deadly Gambits: The Reagan Administration and the Stalemate in Nuclear Arms Control.* New York: Knopf, 1984.

Taschow, Horst G. *The Cultivation of Reading.* New York: Teachers College Press, 1985.

Taylor, Porcher L., III. "Star Wars and Legal Realism." *National Law Journal,* 1 August 1988, p. 13.

Tebbel, John, and Watts, Sarah Miles. *The Press and the Presidency.* New York: Oxford University Press, 1985.

Thompson, Kenneth W., ed. *Ten Presidents and the Press.* Washington: University Press of America, 1983.

Tillman, Seth P. *The United States in the Middle East.* Bloomington, Ind.: Indiana University Press, 1982.

Tolchin, Martin. "An Inattention to Detail is Getting More Attention." *New York Times*, 14 January 1987.

Tolchin, Martin and Susan J. *Dismantling America: The Rush to Deregulate*. Boston: Houghton Mifflin, 1983.

Tribe, Laurence H. *Constitutional Choices*. Cambridge, Mass.: Harvard University Press, 1985.

Turner, Stansfield. *Secrecy and Democracy: The CIA in Transition*. New York: Harper & Row, 1986.

Tutu, Desmond M. "Blacks Will Suffer." Commencement address at Hunter College, New York, 29 May 1986.

Union of Concerned Scientists. *Star Wars: Myth and Reality*. January, 1987.

University of Miami. *Miami Report II: New Perspectives on Debt, Trade, and Investment—a Key to U.S.-Latin American Relations in the 1990s*. Coral Gables, Fla.: University of Miami, 1988.

Valenzuela, J. Samuel and Valenzuela, Arturo. *Military Rule in Chile*. Baltimore: Johns Hopkins University Press, 1986.

Vien, Cao Van. *The Final Collapse*. Washington: Center of Military History, U.S. Army, 1983.

Vig, Norman J., and Kraft, Michael E. *Environmental Policy in the 1980s: Reagan's New Agenda*. Washington: Cambridge University Press, 1984.

Walker, Thomas W., ed. *Nicaragua: The First Five Years*. New York: Praeger, 1985.

Waller, Douglas C. *Congress and the Nuclear Freeze*. Amherst, Mass.: University of Massachusetts Press, 1987.

White, F. Clifton, and Gill, William J. *Why Reagan Won: A Narrative History of the Conservative Movement, 1964–1981*. New York: Regnery Gateway, 1981.

White, Graham J. *FDR and the Press*. Chicago: University of Chicago Press, 1979.

Will, George W. "The Beirut Bombing: Someone Should Resign." *Washington Post*, 26 September 1984.

Williams, Winston. "Bungling the Military Buildup." *New York Times*, 27 January 1985.

Wines, Michael. "Administration Says It Merely Seeks a 'Better Way' to Enforce Civil Rights." *National Journal*, 27 March 1982, pp. 536–41.

Witt, Elder. *A Different Justice: Reagan and the Supreme Court*. Washington: Congressional Quarterly, 1986.

Wohlstetter, Albert. "The Delicate Balance of Terror." *Foreign Affairs*, January 1959, pp. 211–234.

Woodward, Bob. "Gadhafi Target of Secret U.S. Deception Plan." *Washington Post*, 20 October 1986.

"The World Looks at Grenada." *World Press Review*, December 1983.

Wright, Quincy. *A Study of War*. 2 vols. Chicago: University of Chicago Press, 1942.

Yankelovich, Daniel, and Smoke, Richard. "America's 'New Thinking'." *Foreign Affairs*, Fall 1988, pp. 1–17.

INDEX